W9-DAY-514

JOY STREET

Joy Street

FRANCES PARKINSON KEYES

JULIAN MESSNER INC.

NEW YORK

DRAWINGS FOR CHAPTER HEADINGS BY SUE STOREY SHAW
ENDPAPER BY THOMAS FRANSIOLI, JR.

TO

LEBARON BARKER

WHO KEPT INSISTING THAT THIS BOOK MUST BE WRITTEN

UNTIL I GAVE IN AND DID IT

AND TO THE MEMORY OF

ELIZABETH SOULE SWEETSER

WHO LONG BEFORE LEBARON BARKER WAS BORN

AND ALSO

LONG BEFORE HE OR ANYONE ELSE THOUGHT OF ME AS AN AUTHOR

WAS CONFIDENT THAT SOME DAY I WOULD WRITE BOOKS

WHICH WOULD BE A CREDIT TO THE BOSTON

OF WHICH SHE WAS THE FINE FLOWER

Foreword

IN THE course of a recent voyage to and from Venezuela, I wrote an article entitled *The Cost of a Best Seller*. The editor of *The Atlantic Monthly*, in discussing this article with me, had urged me not to attempt brevity, but to set forth, fully and freely, all that it cost me, in cash and in kind, to produce a best-selling novel. The result was an extended eruption of long pent-up feeling; and when the material was handed in, the editor, while admitting his earlier instructions, remarked that the script, though well suited for a book, was outsize for a periodical, and that it would have to be cut after all. My publisher seized upon this remark and took the indicated action; and, in the interval before the page proof came in, I thought up so many additional aspects of the subject under discussion that she was finally obliged to wire me saying the presses were closed! Despite this expansion of my original theme, the conclusion reached at the end of both article and book remained unchanged: the cost of being a writer was high, but the game was worth the candle.

If the presses had been closed a little later, the book might have had a different ending; for while it was being prepared for publication, I was working on the novel to which this forms the Foreword, amidst a series of disappointments so acute that they still appear impossible of compensation and under handicaps which seemed almost insurmountable. I had written in *The Cost of a Best Seller* about various restrictions and sacrifices incident to meeting a deadline; but I had not mentioned—or indeed visualized—a three months' sojourn in the city where I grew up which would not afford enough leisure to communicate with a single one of my former classmates, or a working schedule so tight that moments spent in bathing and hair-brushing had to be carefully counted, and meals—if such they may be called!—limited, day after day, to a cup of tea and a sandwich in the course of an eighteen-hour stretch. I had not mentioned—or indeed visualized—the necessity of working straight through virus pneumonia and an aftermath of weakness and pain so great that no physician can yet say when the end will be in sight, or the series of wheelchairs and ambulances without which I could not have gone on to the next assignment. When the final chapter of *Joy Street* was dispatched by airmail, special, at one o'clock on the morning it was due, I was too completely exhausted to feel the slightest elation or even to be conscious of relief from pressure. I could not believe the ordeal was over; it had become one of those nightmares which apparently has no end, but goes on and on, its violence slackening only to renew itself.

Since then, I have been able to find a certain satisfaction in quoting St. Paul to myself, I hope not too presumptuously, and saying, "I have fought the good fight, I have finished the course, I have kept the faith." But I do not wish to fight any more such battles against illness, I do not wish to run any more such races against time, and I hope my faith will not be so severely tried again. I also hope that *Joy Street* will seem worth while to enough other people, so that eventually the effort which went into it will seem worth while to me, after all.

Meantime, I wish to acknowledge, with infinite gratitude, the help which I received from various quarters and without which all my efforts could not have brought about the present achievement, because my own lack of knowledge, experience and skill would have rendered this impossible.

I am reasonably sure that maternal affection is not alone responsible for my feeling that my greatest indebtedness is to my eldest son, Henry Wilder Keyes. On many evenings and over most week ends during a long period he worked with me; and in addition to this, he worked alone or with fellow-lawyers, in order that he might add to my slender stock of legal lore, authenticate and clarify legal details and facilitate the presentation of cases and trials. While I was still hesitating about undertaking a novel with a Boston setting, a well-known Boston lawyer who was an old and valued friend, urged me to do so and made suggestions for the framework of the plot. Without the counsel, encouragement and information he gave me, I never could have formed a mental image of Roger Field, Pellegrino de Lucca, Brian Collins and David Salomont—indeed, I doubt if I could even have named them effectively and convincingly without his help. I certainly could never have started them on their careers, conceived their mingled destinies, or foreseen their logical development without his expert advice. But once the impetus for the story had been given by this distinguished contemporary of mine, it was my son Henry, who helped me to bear the burden of carrying on; and incidentally, it was his wife and his children who uncomplainingly accepted his frequent absences from home and the cancellation of all pleasant vacation plans, including a trip abroad. So, in connection with Henry, my thanks are also due to my daughter-in-law Betty, and my three small granddaughters, Margaretta, Frances Parkinson II and Sarah Louise.

The next acknowledgment of indebtedness should certainly go to my faithful, efficient and uncomplaining secretary, Geraldine Bullock, and to her friend and mine, Louise Bergin, without whose part-time but invaluable additional secretarial services, Deanie and I could certainly have never made the grade. Like myself, Deanie has worked seven days in the week and very often seven nights as well; Louise, while holding down a job in a bank, where she was obliged to report at eight-thirty in the morning, five days in the week, came to us after banking hours on those five days, began work with Deanie and me when we did on Saturdays and Sundays, and very seldom left us before eleven at night during the last months that we were working on *Joy Street*. No one who operates on a five-day, forty-hour week, can possibly estimate the strain, both mental and physical, which such a schedule involves. But I can, because that is the sort of schedule I follow myself. The cost of a best seller is high, not only to an author, but also to her secretarial staff. The staff should certainly share in the recognition which is given her and I hope it will share her rewards.

Again, my best editorial adviser has been Hermann B. Deutsch, Associate Editor of the *New Orleans Item*, who, at great personal inconvenience, was kind enough to come twice all the way to New England, besides helping me while I was in Louisiana, in order to give me the benefit of his wisdom and skill. If it is not apparent that I have profited by these, that is my fault and not his.

In fields other than those legal, secretarial and editorial, I have been equally fortunate in the caliber of the assistance given me, though the character of the story has not indicated it in such large quantities. Lieutenant-Colonel E. Pendleton Hogan, an old friend and a fellow-author, has been kind enough to check on certain military details; so has Mr. Randall T. Cox, a prominent Boston lawyer, who was formerly a Squadron Intelligence Officer, and to whom I was referred by my friend, Major Richard R. Baker of Keesler Air Force Base. Mr. Eberhard P. Deutsch, an outstanding attorney residing in New Orleans, who is another very good friend, and who served with great distinction of steadily mounting rank in both the First and Second World Wars, has given me the privilege of ascribing some of his achievements to my imaginary character, Pellegrino de Lucca; and Gertrude Storey Bancroft has been equally generous in permitting me to fictionize some of the experiences she had while serving in the WAC and to attribute these to my imaginary character, Priscilla Forbes. Mr. Frank Wallis, another prominent Boston lawyer, has been kind enough to permit the use of his name in the reference to the Nuremberg trials on page 437. Mr. Wallis did serve on the Tribunal there, though of course there was no one by the name of David Salomont on his staff. Mr. William B. Wheelwright, the public-minded citizen who was really the moving spirit which brought the Bay State Club into being, has shown the same degree of co-operation by consenting to let me credit the imaginary Homer Lathrop with this notable contribution to the war effort.

My research on Cape Cod, where I was hitherto almost a stranger, was greatly facilitated through the good offices of Mrs. LeBaron Barker, Sr., whose son, LeBaron Barker, to whom this book is dedicated, first insisted that it should be written; and through those of my niece by marriage, Gertrude Baker, many of whose ancestors, on her father's side, were Cape Codders. My niece's helpfulness, moreover, was by no means confined to the Cape; she is one of many Bostonians who showed such confidence in my ability to interpret the Boston scene that I was really appalled by the degree of their trust; and without their co-operation I could not have done any sort of justice to various phases of Boston life. These friendly assistants were so numerous that I cannot possibly mention them all by name—indeed, the kind of help given by one was so often intermingled with that given by another that I could not always differentiate between these. However, among the many who held out helping hands were Sister Mary Elizabeth of St. Margaret's Convent, Doctor Greene Fitz Hugh, Mr. Horace Morison, Dr. Jerome C. Hunsaker, Mr. and Mrs. St. John Smith, Mr. Philip Sullivan, Mr. Henry Marr, Mr. Henry Flory, Mr. Arthur Vitagliano and Sue Storey Shaw.

As far as the Vermont scene is concerned, I have always flattered myself that I did not need anyone to help me interpret it, but that was before I began to have lawyers for my leading characters! So, a further word of acknowledgment should go to my cousin, James Brock, a rising young attorney of Montpelier, with thanks for permission to incorporate some of his delightful stories in my text.

All the stories about Nazi atrocities which David Salomont tells to Priscilla Forbes are, alas!, not only based on fact, but true in every tragic detail. Most of them have been known to me for a long while; I have verified them afresh through consultation with my friends, Hugo and Hannah Schiff—the former now Assistant Rabbi of the Washington Hebrew Congregation—and Robert Spielmann, who was, himself, a child refugee, and who is now a promising student of journalism at a leading American university.

The character of Morris Brucker, as a character, is entirely imaginary. However, it would not have been possible to include in this novel, accounts of experiences, achievements, and possessions attributed to him, had it not been for the kindness and co-operation of those two famous connoisseurs and collectors, Armand and Victor Hammer. My acquaintance with them came about in a way that seems to me both significant and arresting; and on the chance that my readers may feel the same way about it, I should like to tell them how it happened:

Among the wedding presents given to my imaginary heroine, Emily Thayer, by her grandmother, Old Mrs. Forbes, I mentioned a silver-gilt tea set, of whose origin Emily, herself, is ignorant. Her first caller after her marriage is David Salomont, a junior in the same law office as her husband, Roger Field; and David casually remarks he is interested to notice that his hostess is in possession of the "missing" tea set from the Winter Palace in St. Petersburg. As the tea set then began to show signs of assuming an important position in my story, I became fearful that I had begun to draw too freely on my imagination, and, in the course of an editorial conference, asked my publisher, Kathryn Messner, if she knew whether any such tea set had ever been brought out of Russia. Her reply was immediate.

"I do not know myself, but I can tell you who would know—Mr. Victor Hammer of Hammer Galleries. I will get in touch with him immediately and let you know."

Within a few days I had my answer: not one such tea set, but five, had been brought out of Russia! They had now all been sold, but Mr. Hammer had a photograph of the handsomest one, which he would be pleased to show me; he would also be pleased to give me any other information which might be of help to me. Perhaps the next time I was in New York I would visit his Galleries and have lunch with him. . . .

I accepted this attractive invitation with alacrity, and spent an entertaining and illuminating day in Mr. Hammer's company. He not only proved to me that the tea set, instead of being a figment of my own imagination, really existed, but showed me numerous other rare examples of Russian art, among them a magnificent old Kovsh, the possession of which, in my story, is attributed to the fictitious David Salomont. As I was leaving, feeling that I had already taken up too much of Mr. Hammer's valuable time, he asked courteously, "Are you very sure there is nothing else I can do for you? Nothing else you described, believing it was only a figment of fancy, that I might authenticate for you?"

I hesitated, because I was still afraid of imposing on him, and then I decided to take further advantage of his generosity. "Well," I said, "I have described a Russian ring in my story."

"A ring? What kind of a ring?"

"It does not have to be any special kind, actually. I could change the description, easily enough, at this stage of my story."

"Yes, but how have you described it?"

"As a man's signet ring, set with a single huge emerald, which is carved with the double-headed eagle."

Mr. Hammer gave me a very strange look, and then he instructed a clerk to go to a certain safe, and take from it a box which he would find in a certain place. Five minutes later the ring which I had described lay before me!*

Mr. Hammer and I were both so struck by the singularity of this coincidence, that I offered to send for his inspection, the copy book containing

*Two months later I had an almost equally weird experience. I described a large rambling weatherbeaten house, surmounting a cliff on Cape Cod. When I wrote this, I had never been to Cape Cod, but the following week I spent there, for the purpose of authenticating my material. The morning I left, I was advised to drive around a certain bay, which I had hitherto failed to visit, and there, looming up before me, was an almost photographic likeness of my fictitious house and fictitious location.

that part of my rough draft in which the reference to the ring appeared, in order that he might see for himself exactly what I had written; it was one thing to have visualized a silver-gilt tea set, of which there were actually five; it was quite another to visualize a signet ring of which there was only one! Mr. Hammer accepted my offer and this led to another: I said that, if he cared to have it, Mr. Hammer should be in permanent possession of the entire original first draft of *Joy Street* and I have accordingly given it to him. I hope and believe that he sets some store by it. In like measure, I value as a souvenir of my delightful day with him, and also as valuable source material, the copy of his brother's book, *The Quest of the Romanoff Treasure*, which Dr. Armand Hammer was kind enough to send me. With his permission, I have drawn on it for reference, though I should again emphasize that in doing so I have adapted these references to fictitious requirements, and that none of these relates to the Hammer brothers personally. The wholesale murders in the Ural and the state funeral at Ekaterinburg, to which Dr. Hammer refers on page 155, are well-known historical facts with which I was acquainted before reading his book. If, however, one of the Romanoffs who was slaughtered there, actually bore the name of Feodor, like my fictitious character, this is simply another strange coincidence.

With such a variety of co-operation and documentation, I am hopeful that there are comparatively few errors in my text. However, before some reader, gentle or otherwise, writes in to tell me that, though there were slight flurries of snow early on Christmas Eve, 1936, no heavy fall of it mantled Beacon Hill, I hasten to say that I am aware of this fact. I checked as carefully with the Weather Bureau as with all other sources of available information. But, in this instance—and, as far as I know, only in this one—I have taken poetic license, by describing the Hill as I saw it on Christmas Eve, 1948, and as I have seen it on many previous years and hope to see it on many future ones. It is a lovely sight—one of Boston's best; and Joy Street is an integral part of it.

FRANCES PARKINSON KEYES

THE FIRST OUTLINE FOR JOY STREET WAS MADE AT THE RITZ-CARLTON HOTEL IN BOSTON DURING DECEMBER OF 1948. THE ACTUAL WRITING WAS BEGUN AT THE OXBOW, NEWBURY, VERMONT, DURING OCTOBER AND NOVEMBER, 1949. THIS WRITING WAS CONTINUED IN THE FOLLOWING PLACES AND AT THE FOLLOWING TIMES:

S.S. SANTA PAULA	DECEMBER, 1949
RITZ-CARLTON HOTEL,	JANUARY, 1950
BOSTON, MASS.	

BEAUREGARD HOUSE,
   NEW ORLEANS, LA.
      AND

COMPENSATION, CROWLEY, LA.	FEBRUARY, 1950– APRIL, 1950
RITZ-CARLTON HOTEL, BOSTON, MASS.	MAY AND JUNE, 1950
CAPT. HALLETT'S COTTAGE, CHATHAM, MASS.	JULY, 1950
RITZ-CARLTON HOTEL, BOSTON, MASS.	AUGUST, 1950

IT WAS FINISHED AT THE OXBOW, NEWBURY, VERMONT, SEPTEMBER, 1950.
THIS FOREWORD WAS ADDED ON R.M.S MAURETANIA OCTOBER, 1950.

CONTENTS

JOY STREET

Part One

CHRISTMAS EVE, 1936, TO JUNE, 1938

ROGER

Chapter 1

EMILY THAYER STOOD beside the Christmas tree in the drawing room of the old Forbes house on Louisburg Square, looking out at the candle-lighted windows across the park and listening to the carolers who came stamping through the snow. At least, this was what she appeared to be doing. As a matter of fact, she was hardly conscious of the illuminations or of the hearty songs; she was watching for Roger Field, who had promised to drop in at her grandmother's house sometime during the course of the evening, and who was later than she expected.

Momentarily, her notice was attracted by a unique group of bell ringers who stopped in front of the house and, according to their custom, proceeded to give their repertoire, beginning and ending with "St. Paul's Steeple." This group was led by an old family friend—a certain Mrs. Shurcliff—who had been interested in bell ringing from the time she was a young girl. She had been thwarted in her first efforts at practicing on local church bells, among them those of the Church of the Advent; so she had perfected her art in England and later she had experimented with special hand bells which could be used for playing familiar tunes requiring neither sharps nor flats. The experiment had been so successful that she and her children had formed a little band of their own, and had gone about regularly every Christmas Eve with a bell in each hand, giving their remarkable concert. Now the children had grown up and gone away, but five or six of Mrs. Shurcliff's faithful friends always accompanied her when she made her rounds and all her other faithful friends made a point of listening to her and telling outsiders about her great contribution to the lively arts. The bells had a fine, clear tone and the performance was note-worthy. Emily had always considered it one of the highlights of the Beacon Hill celebration and hitherto had watched eagerly for the arrival of Mrs. Shurcliff and her bell ringers. But on this occasion they had almost finished playing "St. Paul's Steeple" for the first time before she noticed them and waved to them; and even the merry air of "Jingle Bells" did not serve wholly to divert her thoughts from Roger.

He was very dependable; if he were late, something must have hap-

3

pened to detain him. She could not help visualizing all the different kinds of accidents which could occur when the streets were slippery and the traffic heavy between Cambridge and Boston; besides, there was a great deal of flu going around and sometimes it struck very suddenly. She thought the world of Roger, and the mere supposition that he might be injured or ill was painful to her. Moreover, she was almost sure that he meant to propose to her that night and she had made up her mind to accept him, though she knew that such a decision would be far from pleasing to her parents, her grandmother and Homer Lathrop, the old family friend who acted as trustee for the substantial fund her grandfather had left her. She had not only been looking forward to the proposal with pleasurable excitement for some time, she wanted to get behind her the inevitable arguments about the inadvisability of her engagement.

Not that her parents and Homer Lathrop disliked or disapproved of Roger Field; they could not very well help admitting that socially the Fields' standing was equal to that of the Forbes' and the Thayers', even though financially it was not; and they had already told her, separately and collectively, that they "had nothing against Roger." But this, Emily knew, was damning with faint praise. Her elders never mentioned anything that was actually in his favor; and, every now and then, they made some allusion to the fact that his father had never set the world on fire, implying that the ability to do this was more or less requisite in a suitor, and that there was a strong family resemblance between the late Mr. Field and his only son. Less casually—in fact, as emphatically as was consistent with good breeding—they expressed their very real dislike for Roger's sister Caroline, who was ten years his senior, still unmarried, and very pronounced in her views, with few of which Mr. and Mrs. Sumner Thayer, Old Mrs. Forbes and Mr. Homer Lathrop were in agreement.

Unconsciously, Emily shook her head and sighed. She was by nature a peace-loving girl and she dreaded arguments. Moreover, she could not argue about Caroline, with any degree of conviction, because she herself intensely disliked Roger's sister. She was determined not to admit, even to herself, that she was "in love" with Roger until after he had proposed; but she certainly was very fond of him, so fond that she was prepared to put up with the arguments, and even with Caroline, in order to become engaged to him. . . .

A band of carolers slackened their pace as they neared the old Forbes house; then they came to a stop and grouped themselves around the doorstep. They were carrying no horns or bells and the last faint notes of the song that heralded their approach had already trailed off into silence before they took the places designated by their leader. The light from a street lamp shone brightly upon him as he stationed himself directly in front of the house. He had on a heavy overcoat, but his head and hands were bare. A few snowflakes glistened on his thick curly hair, intensifying its blackness, and his black brows gave his handsome face a forceful look which it might otherwise have lacked. He had one arm around a girl who was wearing a shabby shawl draped over her forehead and around her shoulders, which she held closely in place under her chin with tightly clenched fingers. Her face, thus framed, was very beautiful. The other carolers had formed a semicircle with their backs to the steps, and Emily had only a general impression of dark figures—bareheaded men and girls with shawls or scarves over their hair. But the two persons facing her were unmistakably striking. For the first time since her attention had been arrested by the bell ringers, of whose departure she had hardly been aware, her thoughts focused on realities instead of hopes, fears and surmises.

The leader released the girl at his side and raised both hands. Instantly the carolers began to sing, the sound of their vigorous young voices ringing out through the frosty air:

"Adeste fideles,
Laeti triumphantes;
Venite, venite in Bethlehem,
Natum videte, Regem angelorum.
Venite adoremus,
Venite adoremus,
Venite adoremus Dominum."

"Those must be some of the worthless Italians from St. Leonard's, that Roman Catholic church down on Prince Street. I must admit they sing better than most of the young hoodlums who are out making a night of it. Don't you think so, my dear?"

Emily turned quickly. She had been so absorbed in the singers that she had not been aware of Homer Lathrop coming up behind her and she was startled when she felt his hand on her shoulder—startled and a little disappointed. For a moment she had thought that perhaps Roger. . . . Not that Roger had ever given her a casual caress like that, or indeed any caress at all. But she had been hoping that, tonight, if he did propose. . . . And instead of Roger, who was rather awkward and apologetic and did not wear his clothes particularly well, here stood Homer Lathrop, who was the personification of both assurance and polish. He had fresh ruddy skin, keen blue eyes and snowy hair and, at all times, managed to produce the effect of being freshly showered and newly clad. He wore a small pointed beard and, until Emily was past such childish pleasures, had delighted in playing Santa Claus for her benefit; he prided himself on knowing how to unbend. His linen was glazed and immaculate and he patronized the best tailor in town. To be sure, his fine clothes fitted him just a shade too snugly and his laundered look did not prevent him from suggesting the bon vivant; in another city, gossip would have had it that he might be a bachelor, but that nothing about him indicated the celibate. In Boston— that is, in Homer Lathrop's Boston—no such unkind comment was ever made or, at any rate, circulated. Privately, Emily thought his personality much more engaging than that of her handsome, defeated father, though she had never voiced such an opinion and did her best to suppress it, as disloyal. After all, though she had always called Homer Lathrop "Uncle Homer," he was not even distantly related to either the Forbes' or the Thayers.

"You must agree with me about the singing," Homer Lathrop went on, as she did not instantly answer his question about the carolers' talent. "You seemed completely spellbound when I came up to you. I'm sorry if I frightened you."

"You didn't frighten me, Uncle Homer—that is, not exactly. It was just. . . . Yes, I do think they sing wonderfully. And aren't they wonderful *looking* too—the man and the girl who are facing us, I mean?"

Homer Lathrop shrugged his shoulders slightly. "I suppose so, if you care for that type. Personally, I've always thought the Italians were just one notch below the Irish—and you know where that would place them, in my opinion. The Hill's fairly swarming with them too—the other side, of course. But the next thing we know, they'll be over the top of it—right on top of us. They'll be grabbing for power and getting it, just the way the Irish have done."

"They're not—well, quite so aggressive, are they?" Emily inquired, less because she was interested in the comparative qualities of the Irish and the Italians than because she realized she was expected to say something.

"They're just as violent—and they fight with knives instead of with their fists when they're aroused. They never should have been admitted to this country. I've asked Russell again and again why something wasn't done, years and years ago, to curb immigration."

"Something *has* been done now, hasn't it? I mean, since Uncle Russell was in the Senate."

"Oh, something! But nothing anywhere nearly drastic enough. I've told Russell so."

When Homer Lathrop announced that he had made a statement, he meant that this was conclusive and that it should be convincing. Russell Forbes, who had been Governor of Massachusetts and was now the junior United States Senator from that commonwealth, was generally regarded as the most distinguished living member of his clan; moreover, he was the only one who had actively and successfully opposed the control of those Irish politicians so misprized by the rest of his family. But when Emily's grandfather had established the trust fund for her, both Russell and Homer had felt entitled to manage it, Russell because he was really her uncle and Homer because his outstanding success as an investment broker qualified him, to an exceptional degree, for the task. Emily's father, Sumner Thayer, was not entitled to any such responsibility, in the opinion of old Mr. Forbes. Sumner had been very extravagant in his college days, and, since his allowance, though adequate for all reasonable needs, had not been elastic enough for superfluous expenditures, some quiet investigations had been made. These had led to the damaging disclosure that he had been supplementing the allowance with his winnings at bridge; and though he had committed no further financial follies, his father-in-law never trusted him again where money was concerned. Russell was already preoccupied with politics when the fund was established and old Mr. Forbes had finally agreed that Homer's position was the stronger of the two; there had been hard feeling between him and Russell ever since. It was this feeling which Homer was now obliquely voicing. . . .

The Italian carolers had finished their song and their leader was motioning to them to be on their way. He had slipped his arm around his companion's waist again and, as he did so, she looked up at him with loving eyes. He bent his head and kissed her. She raised her hand to stroke his cheek and, in doing so, inevitably released her shawl, which fell to the ground. Her parted hair, roped around her head, was heavy and black, like the leader's; but it was straight and smooth where his was wavy and unruly. The young man picked up the shawl, shook it free from snow and replaced it caressingly over her head and shoulders. Then, once more holding her embraced, he started down the Square, followed by his little band.

"That was what Caroline Field would have called 'disgusting' and for once I should have agreed with her," Homer Lathrop remarked, with visible repugnance. "I might have said, while I was on the subject of the Irish, that most of those with whom I have been forced to come in contact, however corrupt they may be in other ways, are fairly respectable in matters of—well, if you'll pardon the word, my dear, in matters of sex. But the Italians are completely shameless. You've just had an example of this sad fact. I believe them to be quite without any sort of moral standard."

"Did you really think that was disgusting, Uncle Homer?"

"Why, yes! Didn't you?"

"No-o-o. It seemed so natural. So—so instinctive. I thought it was rather sweet."

"You *did?*"

"Yes, I did. Truly, Uncle Homer."

Homer Lathrop gazed at Emily, his astonishment tinged with displeasure. He had always been greatly attached to her, and this attachment was largely based on the fact that she had never disappointed him, but had fitted perfectly into his most approved pattern: the Winsor School, the Petite Ecole Française, the Junior League, the Vincent Club; the traditional coming-out tea on Louisburg Square and the ultrasmart coming-out ball at the Ritz Carlton; no nonsense about going off to college for several years, but a few special courses in English literature at Radcliffe and in Romance languages at the Sorbonne; a transitory interest in nursing, which, fortunately, had not progressed beyond a Nurse's Aide course at Massachusetts General; a reasonable interest in sports and the ability to sit

7

a horse well and play a good game of tennis, but no tweedy, doggy tastes; charm and vivacity enough to hold her own at a Hasty Pudding Club dance or a Beck spread, but no predilection for parked cars, roadhouses or night clubs; the possession of sufficient emotional stability to cope pleasantly but conclusively with her numerous suitors, none of whom had apparently made much impression upon her, which was all to the good, since, so far, strangely enough, there had been no definite prospect of a really advantageous alliance. . . .

All in all, her standards, her intellect, her behavior and her appearance had consistently pleased him from the time she was a very little girl. Her manner was still deferential and he had never seen her look prettier. Usually she was rather pale, but tonight there was a little color in her cheeks, which was very becoming, and he liked the new way she was doing her hair—parted in the middle and drawn down over her ears into a large, smooth coil at the nape of her neck. In deference to his wishes, it had never been cut; it was abundant, but it was soft and fine and he knew she had difficulty with it; therefore, he appreciated all the more both her amenity in regard to its length and the pains she took with it. Really, it was beautiful hair, with lovely warm lights in it—so different from Caroline Field's, for instance, which had been much the same color brown when she was Emily's age, but which she had allowed to become drab, as well as definitely unkempt. Homer Lathrop quickly dismissed the distasteful vision of Caroline to dwell with added satisfaction on the pleasing picture of Emily. Her dress of golden-brown velvet suited her perfectly. So did the topaz earrings and necklace she wore with it. She never went in for extremes, but she had a certain style of her own and knew enough to adhere to it; and certainly she would have a faultless figure as soon as it had filled out a little more. When all that he could see was so eminently satisfactory, it seemed doubly unfortunate that some invisible element should prove unworthy of what met the eye. He could have sworn that Emily would always personify her inward and spiritual grace and he wondered what could have brought about the change in her. Then suddenly he was afraid he knew.

"Well, let's forget about the carolers," he said leniently. "I didn't come here to discuss street roisterers. I—"

"But, Uncle Homer, they aren't any more roisterous than Mrs. Shurcliff's bell ringers! You said yourself that they sang beautifully. I had almost the same feeling, while I was listening to them, that I have when I hear the nuns singing in the chapel of St. Margaret's Convent."

"I didn't know you were in the habit of going to the chapel in St. Margaret's Convent."

"It's not a habit exactly. But I do go there sometimes for 'meditation and prayer.' The nuns have always made me feel very welcome."

"I wish you wouldn't refer to those Episcopal nursing sisters as nuns," Homer Lathrop interposed irritably. "Besides—"

"Those Episcopal nursing sisters call themselves nuns, so I don't see why I shouldn't too," Emily remarked placidly. "Look, Uncle Homer! Some of them are at the windows of their Convent right now! Don't they look lovely, standing there like that?"

It would have been almost impossible to give a negative answer. The candles in the windows of the Convent were placed in a straight line, across each central sash, and above this band of light, the veiled heads and shoulders of the sisters took on a nameless quality of radiance. Even a cynic like Homer Lathrop found that he could not gaze at it unmoved and, annoyed by his unwelcome emotion, he turned away and made a comment which he strove, not altogether successfully, to keep slightly sarcastic.

"Look here, Emily, I hope you're not seriously interested in religion. If you are, let me tell you that it's just a phase—a phase that passes very quickly. Almost every girl, and not a few boys, briefly imagine, sooner or later, that—"

Her laugh interrupted him. "I'm not imagining I want to be a nun, if that's what you're worrying about," she said merrily. "Rather the contrary. Do you feel better now?"

"I'm not sure that I do. You don't sound like yourself tonight, Emily. But this discussion doesn't seem to be very productive and I don't think we ought to prolong it, in any case, because I came to fetch you. We've missed you. In fact, your grandmother's asked for you twice now. She and the rest of the family are sitting around the library fire, chatting and enjoying each other's company. There's no reason why you should stay here in the drawing room by yourself. If you're really interested in the Christmas illuminations, you can see those even better from upstairs. But I don't see why you should be. They're no novelty to you."

"No, but I think they're even more beautiful than usual. And it's such a perfect night! I was afraid, when it began to snow again, late this afternoon, that we were going to have another storm. But just look at those stars!" As she spoke, she thought inconsequentially of the snowflakes on the young Italian's black hair. He must have been outdoors for a long time. The little flurries of snow to which she referred had passed briefly over the city several hours earlier; obviously, he had been wandering through the streets ever since then, for otherwise the snowflakes would have melted; it was the cold which had kept them intact. It was very cold now, as well as very clear. Emily wondered if all the time the dark young man had been leading his carolers, he had kept his arm around that beautiful girl's waist, holding her warm. . . .

"You can see the stars from the library too, Emily. As for the lighted windows with the shades all up—don't you ever feel, on Christmas Eve, that we're permitting the public to share our privacy a little too freely, even if we don't actually open our doors to them indiscriminately, as so many persons do?"

9

"No—just that we're inviting them to share our privileges. Most of those people wandering around in the streets don't live in houses like ours, I'm afraid. I think it means something to them, merely to have glimpses. It must. There wouldn't be such crowds of them if it didn't."

Obviously, some alien influence was at work on Emily, Homer Lathrop thought, with increasing uneasiness. This time he decided to voice his vague anxiety. But before he could find words to frame it, Emily proceeded to upset him still further.

"Besides, I wasn't just listening to the carolers and looking at the lighted windows and the stars," she went on, courage coming to her as she spoke. "I was watching for Roger. I hope nothing's happened. I thought he'd be here long before this."

"Watching for Roger? Roger Field? But my dear Emily, why should you watch for him? Naturally he will ring the doorbell when he arrives and naturally Pearson will let him in, if your grandmother has invited him to come here this evening."

"She didn't. But she said I might. I asked her if I couldn't."

"I'm rather sorry you did that, Emily. I thought your grandmother was so wise in deciding that the Christmas gathering this year should be limited to a family group—a family group and a poor lonely bachelor like myself who happens to be a close friend. It's a relief to me that she's declined to keep open house or to go in for a big, rowdy party like Mrs. Putnam's."

Homer Lathrop glanced disapprovingly toward a large handsome house on the opposite side of the Square. This was more elaborately illuminated than any of its neighbors, even the dormers, which divided the snow-covered roof into glittering sections, revealing arches of candles. The drawing room displayed an elaborate Santa Claus scene, complete with chimneys, reindeer and laden sleigh and the entrance was literally ablaze with festooned lights. As Homer spoke, the front door swung open to admit a group of visitors, and blasts of syncopated music, mingled with boisterous laughter, streamed out of it.

"I've been to one or two of Mrs. Putnam's parties," Emily announced surprisingly.

"You have!"

"Yes. They're fun, sort of. I think you'd like her, Uncle Homer, really I do, if you got acquainted with her."

"I doubt if the occasion for me to find out will arise," Homer Lathrop said, rather coldly. "And now, my dear, as I've already reminded you, your grandmother—"

"I think Grandmamma will understand if you just tell her I'm waiting for Roger. We'll come up together, by-and-by."

She raised her eyes and met his steadily. Again, he realized that he had never seen her look as lovely as she did tonight. Like her hair, her eyes had warm lights in them. Homer Lathrop had sometimes regretted that

Emily's eyes did not add to the gentleness of her expression, as they might have if they had been a deep soft brown, the color of her velvet dress. On the contrary, something about their clear hazel occasionally detracted from her look of docility, as did the deep dimples in both her cheeks. They did so now. The gaze and the smile with which she regarded him were not only sparkling, they were definitely determined and definitely disarming.

"I think you're making a great mistake, Emily."

"I'm sorry, Uncle Homer, very sorry."

"Then, why not—"

"I meant I'm sorry you felt that way about what I'm doing. I didn't mean I was sorry I was doing it."

Obviously, there was no use in pursuing the argument any further. Homer knew that Emily hated arguments and he had counted on this aversion as an ally. Now he realized that she intended to remain in the drawing room, watching for Roger Field, no matter who tried to dissuade her. The situation must be much more serious than he or any member of the united families had realized.

"You haven't come to some sort of an understanding with Roger Field, without consulting any of us, have you, Emily?" he said, grasping at straws. "Because I think I should tell you—"

"I haven't yet, but I'm hoping to. And there isn't anything you could tell me, Uncle Homer, that would change my mind."

She turned away and went closer to the window, drawing the draperies more widely apart. Then she stood motionless, gazing out into the Square. She did not look at Homer Lathrop again, or move when he finally left the room.

Chapter 2

HOMER LATHROP HAD guessed right; Emily would have watched and waited all night for Roger Field. But the necessity did not arise; her trustee had hardly left the drawing room when she saw her suitor coming up the front steps.

The street light which had illumined the young Italian's strong head and vigorous form now shone on Roger Field's earnest face and thin figure. When he caught sight of Emily, he removed his hat, so he, too, was uncovered as he approached; but his well-cut hair was without luster and was brushed back in a way that made his fine forehead appear too high. His movements, without being exactly clumsy, lacked distinguishing grace and, as usual, his clothes did not seem to suit him, though there was nothing particularly wrong about them. The refinement and intelligence of his countenance redeemed it from mediocrity; and, as Emily threw open the door for him, the smile with which he greeted her gave his expression sudden animation and elusive charm.

"How nice of you to let me in yourself! How did you guess exactly when I'd get here?"

"I didn't. I've been watching for you."

"Why, that's nicer still! It's wonderful. Only I'm afraid you've had a long wait. I'd no idea I'd be so late. I'm awfully sorry."

"It didn't matter. That is, I enjoyed looking at the lights and listening to the carolers while I waited. But I began to be afraid there'd been an accident."

"No—I ought to have telephoned. Caroline was alone and I didn't like to leave her on Christmas Eve. I thought she'd go to her room right after dinner. Usually she does. But tonight she started talking and—well, there just didn't seem to be any good place to interrupt, for quite a while. You didn't think I wasn't coming, did you?"

"Oh, no! I knew you would, as soon as you could. You always keep your word. It's just that I was a little anxious."

While they were talking, Roger had taken off his overcoat, folded it carefully, and placed it on a chair in the hall with his hat and gloves neatly

12

laid on top of it. Then, smoothing down his unruffled hair, he followed Emily into the drawing room.

"Do we really have this all to ourselves? How did you manage?"

"The others are in the library. Uncle Homer was here until a moment ago, trying to get me up there too. He said Grandmamma sent him for me. But I don't feel so sure."

"I suppose he didn't want you to stay down here and wait for me. Or didn't you tell him that's what you were doing?"

"Yes, I told him."

Emily had walked back to the bay window. Now, instead of standing beside it, close to the Christmas tree, as she had before, she sat down on a love seat which she had previously moved from its traditional position by the fireplace.

"Uncle Homer says we can see the illuminations just as well from the library," she went on. "I don't agree with him. I think you can see them much better from here. Look at that crèche in the Dorrs' house! We couldn't see that at all if we were looking down, instead of being on the same level with it. And it's really exquisite! So are the Della Robbia plaques at the Drummonds' next door—one in almost every windowpane. You must have noticed those as you came by."

"I'm afraid I didn't."

"Well, look at them now!"

Obligingly, Roger turned in the direction of the Drummonds' house. The Della Robbia plaques were certainly very striking; but, in spite of the lavishness with which they had been used, they did not entirely obscure the scene inside, with which they seemed to have no logical connection, and which he found even more arresting. The drawing room had been cleared for dancing and from the central chandelier was suspended a large bunch of mistletoe. Young men were laughingly engaged in steering their partners in its direction and young girls, equally merry, were putting up a halfhearted show of resistance. Large punch bowls had been placed on either side of the festooned chimney piece and slightly older groups were patronizing these in a liberal and jocund manner.

"The Drummonds are certainly celebrating in a big way," Roger remarked, turning from the window. "Even though I missed the plaques, I don't see how I could have missed the mistletoe." He and Emily laughed together, as if he had really said something witty, and he went on, "The truth is, I was hurrying so fast, trying to make up for lost time, that I didn't see much of anything. I bumped right into one group of carolers."

"What sort of a looking group?"

"Why—I don't know. They looked just like any other group to me. The streets are simply swarming with carolers. What makes you ask?"

"Because some Italians stopped here that didn't look just like all the others. There was a young man who made me think of Michelangelo's David—except that this man was ever so much more striking because of

13

his coloring. And the girl with him made me think of a Botticelli Madonna."

"You did your sight-seeing thoroughly when you were in Florence didn't you, Emily?"

"Of course I did. But nobody made me. I wanted to."

"I was only teasing you—well, so this living art gallery stopped in front of the house and—"

"And sang divinely. Even Uncle Homer admitted that. And you know how he despises Italians. But after he had admired their singing, the leaders kissed each other, and you can imagine the effect that had on him."

"Yes, I can. I'm sure he denounced them unsparingly. But don't you think that was partly because he enjoys denunciation on general principles? He almost never praises anyone or anything—at least, I've never heard him. I can't believe he never felt like kissing anyone himself though. Or that he didn't do it, either."

"Not in the street!"

"No, I suppose not. But he must have had a sweetheart sometime somewhere, even if it was 'long ago and far away.'" Privately, Roger was of the opinion that Homer Lathrop had kissed a good many women in his day and even suspected that such embraces were not entirely delights of the past. But like everyone else who was not wholly silent on the subject he usually voiced his suspicions in a guarded way. Now an unwonted bitterness crept into his voice. "Probably Lathrop didn't marry because he discovered no one completely suitable."

"Who's critical now? You're not fair to Uncle Homer, Roger!"

"Perhaps I'm not. And I don't claim for a minute that two wrongs make a right. But do you think he's fair to me?"

He had seated himself beside her, and now, very quietly, he took her hand.

"He knows I'm in love with you, Emily, and he knows there isn't any real reason why I shouldn't tell you so. But he's done everything he could to convince you that you shouldn't listen to me when I did, hasn't he?"

"Yes, but—"

"He thinks I'm not good enough for you. Of course I'm not—no man could be. But when he says 'good enough,' he isn't thinking of character the way you and I would be. He's thinking of money and power and prestige. He knows I'm not rich, that Father left Caroline and me just enough to get by on. Money's very important in Homer Lathrop's book. Of course, it has to come from the right sources. A rich butter-and-egg man wouldn't be suitable for you, or a lumber king or the owner of a chain of scandal sheets; he's visualizing a husband who'll have as much wealth as a typical tycoon, but who hasn't had to fight his way to success the way such men have. He's all for inherited fortunes. And he hasn't any confidence in my future as a lawyer. He's asked me over and over again

14

whether I'd made the *Review* and he knows perfectly well I haven't. He's also asked me over and over again whether Fiske, Ford and Gibbons had approached me any time during the fall. He also knows perfectly well that no one from the firm has. And, if a senior at the Harvard Law School hasn't been approached by Fiske, Ford and Gibbons, or some firm just like it, he's bound to be a failure at the Massachusetts bar, as far as Homer Lathrop's concerned!"

"Yes, but—" Emily began again.

"And, of course, all your family agrees with him," Roger went on, speaking with a vehemence as unwonted as the bitterness a few moments earlier. "Your father and mother and your grandmother and Senator Forbes. I don't know about the others; I suppose most of them never heard of me. But I know about those four and it's a pretty powerful combination, added to Homer Lathrop. I know everything they'd say to keep you from marrying me. And lots of those things would be unfair. Not all of them. Of course, I know as well as they do that you could marry someone ever so much richer and ever so much brighter and ever so much more promising—at least, he'd probably not be more promising because he'd be established already. I'm sure that's what they'd really like—someone who's a junior partner at Fiske, Ford's, with a nice house on lower Marlborough Street or out in Dedham, or maybe both. And servants who'd been in the family for years and two cars, a Lincoln and a Cadillac. And the taste and the cash to buy you just the right diamond engagement ring and just the proper size string of pearls for a wedding present! Someone with a trust fund twice as big as yours, so that he could keep the wolf from the door, Depression or no Depression!"

This time, Emily did not try to break in; she waited for Roger to go on. In all the years she had known him, she had never before heard him make a long speech, much less two long speeches in succession; and still he had not said quite what she wanted to hear, and she thought he might if she let him alone, now that he seemed headed in the right direction.

"They don't think it matters that I've loved you all my life," Roger went on. "Ever since we first went to dancing school at the Somerset and riding on the swan boats in the Public Garden and I bought you balloons and pinwheels—remember? They must know I have, even if I couldn't do showy things to prove it to them or to you. But, thank God, I've had a break at last! I've finally had a chance to ask you to marry me!"

He jumped up, pulling her to her feet with him. Then he drew her toward him and looked searchingly down at her. To his amazement, he saw that she was gazing at him not only tenderly, but laughingly.

"I kept trying to tell you," she said, "that it didn't make any difference who tried to convince me I shouldn't listen to you. I meant to, right along. Only I thought you'd never say anything I *could* listen to. I mean anything that mattered. Of course, that's why I waited for you here tonight, Roger—because I thought that, perhaps, at last you would!"

15

They reluctantly agreed, half an hour later, that it might be better if they went to the library on their own initiative than if they remained downstairs until someone came to fetch them. It was improbable that they would have much more leeway; and a lone emissary would be much less hampered, when it came to making comments on their protracted absence and asking questions about it, than the assembled family. Not that it would be really necessary to ask many questions. Emily was sure that whether the emissary were her father or her uncle or Homer Lathrop, he would instantly suspect what had happened. But that would not prevent him from making inquiries just the same; and Roger and Emily had agreed that they would rather not "tell anyone" until after Christmas.

"We can't keep them from suspecting, especially if we stay down here much longer," Emily said. "But if we go up to the library, not holding hands or anything, they won't actually demand an explanation. That is, I don't believe they will. I think we ought to try the casual approach, because the result is bound to be at least the lesser of two evils. . . . I do hate to, though," she confessed. She was sitting with her head on Roger's shoulder, with his arm around her waist, and she never would have believed, beforehand, that she would feel so completely at ease on the stiff little love seat which she had dragged over from its position by the fireplace, even though she had so clearly visualized its proper purpose. It really was a love seat at last, not a museum piece of gilded woodwork and fine needle point; indeed, the entire drawing room had a new significance, now that it had provided her with such blessed seclusion and such fruitful opportunity. Hitherto, she had associated it only with large formal parties —her grandmother's stately dinners, the concerts given to select groups for well-chosen benefits, her own magnificent debut. Now, miraculously, in spite of its Louis Quinze furnishings, its innumerable paintings and *objets d'art* and its formidable proportions, it had become a secret bower. Its glittering chandeliers were dimmed and no long vistas were reflected in its great mirrors. Only the lights on the Christmas tree in the window cast their benignant glow on the love seat beneath; the rest of the room was engulfed in shadow and stretched vaguely away into the distance. Only the songs of the carolers outside penetrated its stillness; Emily knew that all the rest of her life she would associate the words, "I love you, my darling," with the words, "Silent Night, Holy Night". . . .

"So do I. Don't let's, just yet," Roger said, in a voice that did not sound quite natural. It was partly because of this unnatural quality and partly because it was so long since she herself had spoken that Emily did not immediately realize he was echoing her reluctance to go to the library. He himself had been deep in thought, but his reflections had been less joyous than his beloved's. He had been wondering whether he should talk to her a little about his prospects, since these were not quite as gloomy as she had hitherto been given to understand, both by himself and by others. He thought it might be fairer if he did, because of course he would have

16

to tell her father and her trustee about them very shortly, and he felt Emily was entitled to hear the encouraging news first. It did seem as if this one time, at least, he and she might have been spared the discussion of any intrusive subject. Yet, on the other hand. . . . As always, his conscience prevailed against his desire. "There's something else I want to tell you before we go upstairs," he added slowly.

"It can't be as important as what you've told me already."

"It isn't. But it might be pretty important at that. I have a prospect—just a slight one—of a job."

"You do! Oh, Roger, how marvelous! Why didn't you tell me so before?"

"Well, as you said yourself, the other was more important." He bent his head and brushed his lips over her hair and forehead, drawing her a little closer to him as he did so. Then, realizing that a more fervent embrace would automatically postpone the telling of his great news, he went on, "There's nothing definite about it yet, but I honestly think there may be, a little later. . . . You know Mr. Harold Swan, don't you? Marion Swan's father?"

"I know Marion, just slightly. She went to Miss May's."

"So she did. And of course she's an older girl too—about halfway between you and Caroline, I should think. But Caroline happens to know her quite well and I've been to the Swans' house a few times with her, when I knew you were tied up with something else, like last night."

"Was it just last night that—"

"That's right. Mr. Swan asked me if I'd made any special plans for next year. Only he didn't put the question the way Homer Lathrop always does, as if he were perfectly sure that I hadn't. He sounded as if he thought I might have. And he seemed quite pleased when I said no."

"Is Mr. Swan a lawyer?"

"Yes. I've never heard much about his firm either—Cutter, Mills and Swan. But it's in one of the best buildings on Devonshire Street."

"Well, of course, that counts for a lot. What did Mr. Swan say after you told him you didn't have any plans for next year?"

"He asked me to drop by and see him at his office someday soon. He said he'd like to talk to me about an experiment his firm was making."

"Did he give you any idea what kind of an experiment it was?"

"Yes. He said Mr. Cutter, the head of the firm, had very progressive ideas about its development. Mr. Mills doesn't always agree with him, but Mr. Swan thinks he's on the right track. At first, they always picked their juniors from Harvard, like Fiske, Ford. For instance, they took in Elliot Berkeley and Cyrus Fletcher. You know them, don't you?"

"Not very well. Of course they're both older. I have met Elliot Berkeley at one or two hunt balls and ridden in the same horse shows that he has. But I've never been to his house in Hamilton and I don't think Grandmamma ever asked him here. Isn't he—doesn't he—"

17

"Yes. He's a little on the thirsty side. But he is a wonderful horseman. And of course, very, very social register. More so than Fletcher. And I think he has more brains, of a sort. Fletcher really hasn't much between the ears and he's almost as much of a sissy as Berkeley is of a he-man. But then Fletcher's family owns most of the shipyards and practically all the granite quarries in Quincy. Not that those amount to as much as they used to, but I suppose they help to give him a semblance of intellect and masculinity."

"I suppose so," Emily said rather doubtfully. "Well, you were telling me—"

"I was saying that Cutter, Mills and Swan followed the standard practice of picking their juniors from Harvard at first. And, as far as I know, Berkeley and Fletcher have been perfectly satisfactory. It would look that way, because they're about to be taken into the firm. But Cutter isn't sticking entirely to Harvard any longer. He's picking graduates from other law schools—men with all sorts of different backgrounds."

"Why, you're at Harvard!"

"I know. But Mr. Swan thought there might be a place, next year, for one Harvard graduate, if he qualified in other ways. You see, Mr. Cutter has been carrying this experiment of his so far that Mr. Mills is getting pretty disagreeable about it. An Irishman who graduated from Holy Cross and an Italian who graduated from Boston College were taken in. Both Roman Catholics, of course. The Irishman, Brian Collins, is a South Boston product. Mr. Mills accepted him without too much fuss. It seems his father's a very successful contractor and he was sure to bring lots of new clients into the firm. He's brought in quite a few wealthy ones already and he's only been there two years. Law firms have to be practical about things like that."

"Yes, I suppose so."

"But Mr. Mills raised a row over the Italian," Roger went on rather hurriedly. He could tell from Emily's tone that the word "practical" in connection with the experiment troubled her a little. It troubled him too. "Mr. Swan didn't say where he lives and I can't remember his name. But I gather he wasn't as well fixed as Collins."

"You know how Uncle Homer feels about Italians, Roger."

"Yes, I certainly do. I've heard him enlarge on the subject often enough! He and Mr. Mills ought to get together. Well, to finish the story, Mr. Cutter added insult to injury by taking in a fellow named David Something-or-Other, who'd been an honor student at Columbia."

"But then he must be awfully bright!"

"He is. Phi Beta Kappa, *summa cum laude*, the whole works. He's also a Jew."

"Oh! And Mr. Mills—"

"That's right. Mr. Mills is even more allergic to Jews than he is to Roman Catholics. He threatened to leave the firm if Mr. Cutter went on

18

with his experiment. Mr. Mills said the next thing he knew, they'd have a Digger Indian in the firm. And Mr. Cutter said that might not be such a bad idea, either; he'd make a note of it. Well, I guess things got pretty hot around the office for a while. But finally, Mr. Cutter promised that the next man they took in would be—well, someone more like me. And he asked Mr. Swan to keep on the lookout."

"You like Mr. Swan, don't you, Roger?"

"Yes, very much. He reminds me of my father. He's got very high ideals."

"And this experiment the firm's making—you think that's based on high ideals?"

"I'm sure it is, as far as Mr. Swan's concerned. It was really very moving, the way he talked—about bringing together different racial groups that had never mixed very well in Boston before. He made me feel it would be a privilege to have a part in an undertaking like that. And, if I had you to help me—"

Again he drew her closer to him. There were other aspects of the case, which he had not mentioned, and which Mr. Swan had not stressed in talking with him; but Roger knew they existed and that sooner or later he must discuss those with Emily too. She deserved nothing less than complete candor from him, just as she deserved nothing less than complete devotion; he must give her the one in the same measure that he had already given her the other. But not tonight—not on Christmas Eve, when he had at last asked her to marry him and she had so joyously and quickly consented. If it had not been for the contemptuous attitude of her family, his only words that night could have been of love. He would always feel that the radiance of betrothal had been dimmed by the intrusion of material things, and that this intrusion might have been avoided if he had not needed to justify himself in his beloved's eyes. Well, he had told her now that his future was not altogether without some promise of those things by which her elders set such store; perhaps, in so doing, he had made things easier for her, since, reassured, she might find ways to reassure the others. But having told her, he had the right to be the lover again.

"You know I'll help you, dearest, in every way I can!" Emily was murmuring. But she could say no more, before he sealed her lips.

Chapter 3

WHEN EMILY AND ROGER entered the library, having discreetly unclasped hands before reaching the threshold, they were not immediately observed by the girl's parents and Homer Lathrop. These three greatly resented the amount of bell ringing and horn blowing which now resounded through the Square; it had become so loud and persistent that they decided its perpetrators—doubtless intoxicated!—were bent on disturbing the public peace and they wished to locate the center of the pandemonium before complaining to the police. The bay window offered a vantage point from which to identify the miscreants, and the indignant trio, while attempting to do this, stood with their backs to the room, exchanging vexed remarks.

"We should really be thankful that Major Higginson did not live to see such a perversion of his plan," Mrs. Thayer was saying. "Christmas Eve on Beacon Hill was truly beautiful, as he visualized it. But now, instead of an atmosphere of good will, there is all this frightful rowdyism."

"I agree with you, Eleanor. And I think the worst of that noise is coming from across the park, near Mrs. Putnam's house."

"I'm afraid you're right, and in that case her guests are probably making most of it. We can't very well complain to the police, under those circumstances."

"I don't see why not. It's regrettable that Mrs. Putnam was ever permitted to acquire property in Louisburg Square. Any action that makes her feel unwelcome here would have my complete approval."

"We're lucky," Emily whispered to Roger, "if they'd only been concentrating on the street hoodlums, they'd have turned around in a minute. But now that they've got started on Mrs. Putnam too, their righteous wrath will have no bounds. Come on, we'll say Merry Christmas to Grandmamma."

Old Mrs. Forbes, as she was invariably called, was enthroned in a great carved chair by the fireplace, under the splendid portrait of her which Sargent had painted when she was in her prime. Except for this one portrait, the high walls of the immense room were lined with books; and it had none of the drawing room's forbidding qualities. The draperies at the bay window were made of crimson velvet, and the deep chairs and huge, overstuffed sofas were upholstered in the same material. The Persian rug which covered the floor was patterned in rich, blending colors, and the pleasant lamplight and glowing coals gave added radiance to the whole interior. Moreover, it had the lived-in look which revealed it as the center of family life. Before this evening, it was the room that Emily had always loved best in the house; never had she entered it with reluctance or hesitation. But now she did so with a sensation amounting almost to dread.

Old Mrs. Forbes also appeared to be deep in conversation. But the animated discussion in which she was engaged with her son, Russell, had not prevented her from observing the approach of her granddaughter and Roger Field. Their discreet gesture had not been quite quick enough to escape her eagle eye or their hushed voices quite low enough to strain her excellent hearing. Emily was quick to sense this; she knew that her grandmother still had the use of all her faculties and that these were acute. Old Mrs. Forbes had put on a great deal of weight with advancing years and she moved about with difficulty, using a cane when she did so; but mentally she was even more nimble than when her sumptuous figure had been conspicuous for its perfection in exclusive ballrooms from Boston to Budapest.

"Good evening, Roger," she said agreeably if a little condescendingly. "I had been wondering what had become of you. I didn't hear you ring."

She extended a hand that was still comely in spite of its fleshiness and which set off its superb rings well. Old Mrs. Forbes had always been extremely fond of jewelry and she wore a great deal of it—much more than her daughter, Mrs. Thayer, approved. In addition to the rings, she was now wearing a diamond necklace, a diamond bar pin, a diamond wrist watch and diamond-studded combs in her iron-gray hair, which was sleek and abundant and elaborately dressed; and all these diamonds served as accessories to the magnificent black and silver brocade which was her latest Worth importation. "Mamma—just for a family party too!" Mrs. Thayer had said rebukingly, when she arrived that evening; and as she spoke, she glanced fleetingly but approvingly at the reflection in a near-by mirror of a trim, middle-aged woman who had kept her figure and who was appropriately turned out in dark crepe marocain and medium-sized pearls. But Old Mrs. Forbes did not care a whit what Eleanor Thayer thought of her taste, or anyone else either. She intended to go on wearing her diamonds and her brocades till the day of her death—in fact, she intended to be buried wearing large quantities of both. Diamonds and brocade had been her forte, even when she was seventeen and everyone said she was too young for them. Now that she was seventy, everyone said she was too old for them. She had known better in the first place and she still knew better. They suited her whether Eleanor and Eleanor's dull contemporaries had sense enough to realize it or not.

Roger kissed the extended hand, which was what he was expected to do. Old Mrs. Forbes had spent a great deal of time in foreign courts when her husband was alive, and there were some who said she had been the better diplomat of the two; there was no doubt that she had left the more lasting mark or that she still enjoyed being treated like an ambassadress. Roger knew that she also expected a reply to her indirect question; but while he was wondering how best to frame it, Emily answered for him.

"Roger couldn't very well leave Caroline alone on Christmas Eve. So he had dinner with her and stayed with her until she went to her room. We ought to have invited her tonight too, Grandmamma."

"What an exemplary brother! Of course, I should have been pleased to invite Caroline too, my dear, if you had suggested it, and any number of other young people, as far as that goes. But when you mentioned only Roger, I naturally concluded that, for some strange reason, you wished to see him alone."

"Oh—Uncle Russell, I'm so sorry! You remember my friend Roger Field, don't you? You should! He's always been one of your greatest admirers."

Old Mrs. Forbes looked at her granddaughter with a glint of pride in her shrewd old eyes as the Senator, with something of his mother's condescension and less of her grand manner, tardily permitted himself to be drawn into the conversation. So the girl had had the gumption to take the bit in her teeth after all! For some reason she wanted this inept, well-meaning Field boy and she intended to have him. She had succeeded in getting him to propose, in spite of his hesitancy in the face of her family's opposition; and now that she was definitely engaged to him, she would marry him, no matter what her family said or did. All of them might as well give in gracefully and let her have her Trinity Church wedding and wear the ancestral rose point veil and go around the world on her honeymoon; because, if they thwarted her in these matters, she would be very difficult to live with the next few months. She might even elope. Old Mrs. Forbes looked at Emily still more closely, recognizing the girl's new radiance, and knew exactly what had happened during that hour in the drawing room, before the newly engaged pair had come up to the library. It took a very special kind of kissing to make a girl look like that. Involuntarily, Old Mrs. Forbes sighed. It was many, many years since she. . . . And no matter what anyone said, there was nothing to equal it, nothing in the whole world. . . .

"Besides, I have every reason to believe—" Mrs. Thayer said, turning from the window. Then she caught sight of Roger and Emily, standing by the fireplace. "Oh—how do you do, Roger?" she went on, as coolly as was consistent with her ideas of courtesy. "This is quite a surprise. I didn't expect to see you here this evening."

"I did," Old Mrs. Forbes said tersely. "I invited him. I suppose I don't have to tell you beforehand, Eleanor, every time I invite someone to my own house."

"Of course not, Mamma. But you did say this was just a family party, so I thought—"

"We agreed a long time ago that Homer was one of the family, that he should always be included—that is, if he cares to be—he's showing very little sign of it tonight." Old Mrs. Forbes glanced in the direction of the window, where Sumner and Homer were still standing and, as if galvanized into action by this piercing look, they both tardily turned and came forward, Sumner giving Roger a limp hand and Homer merely nodding in his direction. "I decided it was time to expand the circle again," Old Mrs. Forbes went on. "Unfortunately, it is not as large as most family groups in Boston and we were growing rather static. . . . Are you really going to telephone the police, Sumner? If you are, why don't you go and do it, now that you have finally said good evening to Roger? Well, of course, I knew you were only talking, as usual. If I hadn't, I'd have blocked the telephone call. I don't remember what Major Higginson's idea was, but mine is that the celebration of Christmas Eve on Beacon Hill is about as close as Boston ever gets to letting itself go—and at that, it's pretty far behind New Orleans on Mardi Gras or even New York on New Year's. . . . Eleanor, will you please ring for Pearson? I don't see what we are waiting for, now that we are all here. I wish to have the punch and cakes brought up at once. I have been growing steadily hungrier and thirstier for nearly two hours now—ever since Emily so mysteriously disappeared. Perhaps it is all this talk about tariff that has made me feel the need of more sustenance. Do you always talk about tariff, Russell? No wonder your wife left you!"

And no wonder everyone within the orbit of Old Mrs. Forbes was afraid of her, Roger said to himself, as he went down the front steps into Louisburg Square about two hours later; no one was safe from her eyes and her ears and her tongue, unless they escaped from her completely. Russell Forbes and Eleanor Thayer had never done so; and inevitably Eleanor's husband and daughter and their family friend had been drawn into the same sphere of dominating influence. Roger had already been made to feel the force of it; though Old Mrs. Forbes had spoken and acted in his defense, he knew she would expect—and exact—tribute in payment for her largess; and unless he were very careful, that payment might well take the form of a great loss in independent thought and action.

Of course, there were a few who had escaped from her, which explained why her family circle was smaller than that of most prominent Bostonians. Roger did not believe for a moment that Russell Forbes' wife, Letitia, had left him because he had talked too much about the tariff, though Roger was ready to concede that, run into the ground, this might be a very tiresome subject; when Old Mrs. Forbes made the remark, she was simply lashing out at her son to prove her power. But she had not been powerful enough to cow Letitia, though the girl had looked so frail and flowerlike

23

when she married Russell. Letitia had divorced Russell on grounds of cruelty—allegedly his, but undoubtedly really his mother's! She had not only given up her proud position as a senator's wife and a Boston Brahmin; she had further flown in the face of Providence by marrying an Austrian violinist who had refugeed to the Riviera—not to Menton or Cannes or to Antibes, but to some funny little town no one had ever heard of before! And she had told a representative of the Associated Press—who, of course, had wired the story far and wide—that even if she hadn't made a go of her second marriage the divorce would have been worth while, if for no other reason than that by getting it she had also got even with her mother-in-law!

When Roger had come in from Cambridge most of the streets not barred to traffic were already lined with closely parked cars; he had been obliged to leave his dilapidated Ford on Beacon, beyond the State House. Now, as he turned from Louisburg Square into Mount Vernon and began the climb that led steeply toward the Hill's summit, he scarcely noticed the carolers who were making a night of it or the candles which continued to burn brightly in the windows. He was still thinking about Letitia, living meagerly in an obscure little French town, and he wondered whether she did not sometimes long for the fleshpots she had abandoned and wish that she had learned to accept her yoke with at least a semblance of submission. As to the others who had eluded Old Mrs. Forbes, there was her younger son, Sherman, who lived on the Cape all the year round, and said he couldn't take time to come to Boston—though everyone knew that his manager, Jarvis Compton, was perfectly capable of looking after the cranberry bogs from which he derived the ample income that, added to his wife's fortune, made him entirely independent of his mother. Old Mrs. Forbes hated Sue, Sherman's wife, because she made no proper use of her fortune. Even as a debutante, Sue had looked better in a cardigan sweater and a tweed skirt than she did in sequins and tulle, and now she practically lived in shorts or slacks, according to the season. It was doubtful if she spent a hundred dollars a year on clothes; and she liked to do her own housework, so she spent almost nothing on servants either. And she let her children run wild. If she went on at this rate, she would be one of the richest women in the United States, with nothing to show for it. She did not care for the opera or the theater or even for symphony concerts; she disliked travel and every form of city life. She had always gone in for long walks, gardening, dogs, fresh air and that sort of thing and she had grown more and more set in her regrettable habits and tastes as she grew older. Sherman encouraged her to indulge in these tastes and habits and also to share in the sports which he enjoyed himself, such as hunting, fishing and sailing. Of course, it was sheer nonsense for him to pretend that he spent all his time in the cranberry bogs—far more often he was out in a marsh, shooting ducks, or out in a boat trolling for "blues" off the coast or salmon fishing in Long Pond. And Sue went with him; she prided herself on being the best woman shot on the Cape and she had learned how to handle any kind of a boat from a yawl to a sailing canoe.

In short, everything about Sue Forbes' tastes and her mother-in-law's was so antagonistic that they never voluntarily sat in the same room. Besides, Old Mrs. Forbes hated the Cape as much as she hated Sue. She owned a house at Manchester-by-the-Sea and another at Dublin, New Hampshire; but, except when the World War had interrupted her schedule, she had spent at least part of every year in Europe. She was at home in any place and in any tongue, except the cranberry country where her son, Sherman, had chosen to live and the clipped colloquialisms which he had adopted for his speech.

Her separation from Sherman automatically separated her from all her grandchildren except Emily, for Russell and Letitia had been childless and her younger daughter, Elizabeth, had never married. Undoubtedly, Old Mrs. Forbes would have enjoyed having Sherman's big brood about her, partly because children were more easily dominated than grown persons, and partly because she could not play the matriarch as effectively as she might have wished in a circle so regrettably small as that made up of Russell—who was in Washington most of the time—Sumner, Eleanor, Emily and Homer Lathrop. But in this instance, neither Mahomet nor the mountain yielded; Sherman remained stubbornly among his cranberries, and his mother, with equal stubbornness, on Louisburg Square. . . .

The crowds on Mount Vernon Street were not quite as dense as they had been on Louisburg Square, but they were even more hilarious. A solitary pedestrian who plodded along, neither singing nor blowing a horn nor jingling bells, looked strangely out of place among the merrymakers; more than once, Roger felt that he was the butt of some jeering comment as he forged past a boisterous group. Other carolers, more convivially inclined, caught hold of him and urged him to join them. One of these was so insistent and so obviously drunk that a burly policeman intervened.

"Come on, boys, break it up. If you don't, I'll have to run in the both of you, as sure as my name's Tim Tupperty."

"I'm sorry, officer. This gentleman seems to be under the impression that I know how to sing. I'm trying to convince him that I don't."

As he spoke, Roger made a quiet but determined effort to free himself. The drunk, who by this time had one arm around his victim's neck in a strangle hold, waved the bottle which he held in his free hand toward the policeman.

"Have a nip, ossifer. Jes' a li'l one. Then you'd better 'rest *this* gennel'-man. *He's* drunk."

The policeman obligingly took the bottle and the drunk, still clutching Roger, broke into song.

"Good Kin' Wen—Wen-chus—Wen-chus-lush—look here, you gotta help me out. Never could get that so-and-so's name straight. What's his name, Percy?"

"I think it's Wenceslaus."

"Course it is. Course you can sing it too. Come on now!

'Good King Wen-chus-lush—look'out
On the feast of Steven
When the snow lay round about
Deep an' crisp an' even—an' even an' even' "

"Say, tha's a lot like tonight, isn't it, Percy? Come on, le's sing the res' of this. Then we'll all have a li'l nip!"

"That's a nice enough song, but enough's enough. I said, break it up, boys!" Without visible effort, the policeman freed Roger and handed the bottle back to its rightful owner, administering a slight shove as he did so. "Get going," he said genially. "We don't want a lot of company down at the Joy Street Station Christmas morning. Beat it while your shoes are good."

Roger lost no time in taking advantage of his welcome release. When he was at a safe distance, however, feeling that he had been rude and abrupt, he called back a Merry Christmas, adding that he was sorry that he hadn't been able to join in the song. As a matter of fact, conviviality was far from his mood; he had succeeded in dismissing Sherman and Sue from his mind, only to find himself dwelling on the subject of Old Mrs. Forbes' younger daughter, Elizabeth, who had also eluded her.

Elizabeth taught chemistry at Bryn Mawr and spent her vacations in northern Vermont, where she lived in a brick farmhouse, which she had remodeled with intelligence and affection. If she had chosen to teach history or French, or even the theory of music and one of the dead languages, her mother might have managed to meet her on a common ground; but Old Mrs. Forbes, who had an excellent knowledge of the liberal arts herself, even though, of course, she had never gone to college, knew nothing of the sciences; on the rare occasions when she and Elizabeth still saw each other, she could have sworn—and so could several other persons—that the college professor went out of her way to make her conversation unintelligible. Old Mrs. Forbes was graciously willing to concede that there might be a few persons of background and culture in the Vermont village which Elizabeth used as a post-office address. But the remodeled farmhouse was two miles back in the hills; and though Emily and her friends greatly enjoyed using it for headquarters during the midwinter period when the special "snow trains" were running, the accommodations it offered were certainly not calculated to cater to the comfort or appeal to the taste of a lame and luxury-loving old lady. Moreover, there was a conspicuous lack of good hotels within a radius of miles. It was never feasible for Old Mrs. Forbes to visit Elizabeth and she suspected—as others did—that there was method in her daughter's choice of a home, just as there was method in her choice of a profession and of her conversational topics. . . .

As Roger trudged along through the snow, finding the going harder and harder all the time, he kept on thinking anxiously of those persons who had taken desperate measures to escape Old Mrs. Forbes, instead of thinking only of Emily, as he expected he would and as he still wanted to do. He also thought of the two other Forbes children who had eluded their mother even more irrevocably than Sherman and Elizabeth. He shivered a little when he did so and, telling himself that it was growing colder every minute, turned up the collar of his overcoat and buttoned it more closely around his throat. But it was not the cold which made him shiver and he knew this; it was the recollection that one of these children had died during a bitter winter in St. Petersburg and the other during a torrid summer in Rome and that, in both instances, Old Mrs. Forbes— who was then young and beautiful and the American Ambassadress—had been warned that the climatic conditions were unhealthful as far as her children were concerned—or so her enemies had said and, like most other women who were beautiful and rich and powerful, she had never lacked enemies. But even those who spoke of her most scathingly did not claim that the pitiful little victims of her worldliness had failed to receive the final tribute which was their due. They had not been buried in distant, foreign cemeteries; their small bodies had been brought home and interred, with all due ceremony, in the great family lot at Mount Auburn.

It began to appear certain to Roger that, short of dying, the only way to find escape from Old Mrs. Forbes was to move away from Boston—as far away as was humanly possible, even if that meant the Pacific Coast or the Deep South. But he feared he would not fit into either of these regions; he would not know how to get on with men who slapped him jovially on the back and called him by his Christian name the first time he met them or with men whose ideas of civilized drinking began and ended with bourbon and champagne and who spent their money on carnival balls and race tracks instead of underwriting symphonies and endowing museums. Besides, Emily would not get on with the wives of such men; she had left Boston very little, except for brief visits to Washington, made under the highest official auspices, and for the sojourns in Europe which her grandmother had supervised. Even in Boston, she had moved almost entirely in a small, circumscribed circle; why, she had said, "Marion Swan went to Miss May's," as if that explained why she did not know Marion well! He had heard other girls who went to Miss Winsor's say the same sort of thing and, for the first time, he wondered whether the girls who went to Miss May's made equally conclusive remarks. Probably they did. And if he took Emily to Seattle or San Francisco or Birmingham or New Orleans, she would meet many young women who had attended public high schools and had never been to Europe; she would be baffled in her attempts to talk with them because she would have nothing on which to base the conversation; they would not think about the same things or do the same things that she did.

27

Moreover, if he took the desperate step of moving away from Boston, he would lose the one possible opportunity for suitable employment which had presented itself to him so far. He knew that the firm of Cutter, Mills and Swan did not have the prestige of Fiske, Ford and Gibbons and other firms of long-established standing. But it must be sound financially, or it could not have had offices in a highly reputed Devonshire Street building; perhaps it might even pay its juniors better than the old firms, some of which were extremely niggardly when it came to money, on the principle that any young man fortunate enough to be connected with them, in any capacity, should be so sensible of his privileges as to be above considerations of filthy lucre. Roger wished that he himself might be above such considerations; but in view of his slender resources, he realized he could not afford to be.

He did not know how much it would cost to support a wife, but he had a vague idea that he had heard the sum of five thousand dollars mentioned as a minimum, with the qualifying remark that, of course, this meant a very small house and only one maid and that it was to be hoped there would be no children. Roger hoped nothing of the sort; he wanted very much to have children and—though of course he had never spoken to her on such a subject—he would have been bitterly disappointed to discover that Emily did not feel the same way. He and Caroline were managing on a good deal less than five thousand, because they had to; he had given up living in a dormitory, which he had greatly enjoyed, and they did not have a house at all, only a very small apartment in an unfashionable section of Cambridge and only a part-time maid. He could not expect Emily to live like that. Naturally, she would never have to; her family would have seen to it that she did not, even if it had not been for the trust fund, which Roger, like everyone else, knew about. But he shrank from the idea of having Emily accept more than was absolutely necessary from the Forbes' and the Thayers. It was the irony of fate that his own straitened circumstances made it doubly humiliating to accept bounty from others. If he had been wealthy enough to give Emily everything she really needed, he would not have minded letting her family supply her with luxuries; and he would have been actually glad to see her in possession of an allowance from a trust fund. He knew that girls liked the sense of independence which such allowances gave, and these carried with them no implication that the girls' husbands were unable to support their wives. But if Emily were putting more into the household budget than he was, *besides* paying for her own clothes and her own amusements and contributing to her own pet charities, he would feel that she was supporting him and this would be very hard to endure.

If he could only have taken her to the house in Brookline where he and Caroline had grown up, it would not have been so bad; that had really been very pleasant and comfortable and sunny, even if it were shabby and graceless and located in a neighborhood which was fast going downhill. But that house had been sold to settle his father's estate, and if it had not been, probably Caroline would have felt she had a right to live with him and Emily, which would never have worked out either. Poor Caroline, she would be terribly alone after he was married! And she would be no more pleased with the engagement than the Forbes' and the Thayers, though for different reasons. She did not hesitate to say that Old Mrs. Forbes was a termagant, Russell an opportunist, Eleanor a snob, Sumner a weakling and Homer—whom she bracketed with the others—a wolf in sheep's clothing. She had never said anything really derogatory about Emily; but she had not failed to imply that there was not much hope for a girl brought up under such unfortunate influences.

What was it, Roger wondered, still plodding patiently uphill through the snow, that happened to women as they grew older if they did not have the normal fulfillment of marriage and motherhood—and sometimes even when they did? He was sure that Old Mrs. Forbes, when she was young and beautiful, had not been so ruthless and so dominating; if she had, she would never have been the toast of two continents or twisted princes and potentates around her little finger. Something must have happened. . . . But as for poor Caroline, she had never been the toast of any region, or a belle, much less an enchantress, even in Boston; her debut had been a tragic farce and her brother had never known her to have a serious suitor. No matter what had changed the fabulous Evelina Forbes from a radiant charmer into a venomous old despot, she must still have her glowing memories, and she had kept her power and her riches in her old age; Caroline would have no memories and she would be poor and lonely and sad. It was all very tragic.

Concern for Caroline now added itself insistently to Roger's other worries. He tried to tell himself that if Cutter, Mills and Swan were really as liberal with their juniors as he was hopefully imagining, he might eventually earn enough to give Caroline a small allowance, besides doing his share to support himself and Emily and their children. But the endeavor was so unsuccessful that he dismissed it, dwelling instead on the new policies with which the firm was experimenting and deliberately avoiding consideration of its "practical" elements. Since Harold Swan, as Roger sincerely believed, was an idealist, and since he had been instructed to find a young lawyer who would share and fulfill his ideals, certainly no occasion would ever arise in which he would ask his protégé to compromise with high principles. . . .

As Roger finally turned from Mount Vernon into Joy and began to walk downhill, he was startled by a sharp, sudden noise which seemed out of harmony with the Christmas celebration and, stopping, looked around him, trying to locate and identify it. He did not succeed in doing so; but, as he glanced about, he was aware of a large, squarely built brick house, looming up across the street. It stood on a corner and it had the substantial, massive look of a place which had been built to endure. But only one window in it was lighted and this solitary illumination was electrical and as out of harmony with seasonal festivities as the sound which had puzzled him. It served only the better to display a large placard which read:

FOR SALE
To Settle Estate
Apply to Brooks, Brimmer and Shaw
20 State Street

For some moments, he stood still, gazing at the sign; then his eyes wandered away from the window where it was displayed and he surveyed the entire structure. It had none of the architectural beauty which distinguished so many houses on the Hill; apparently it belonged to a later period than the stately, porticoed mansions on Mount Vernon Street which he had just passed, almost unseeingly. But it bespoke solidity and spaciousness and cultured, orderly living. He could visualize double parlors, with an ample dining room leading out of them; an upstairs library, comparable in size and comfort to the one he had just left; a master's bedroom and dressing room, guest chambers, day and night nurseries. This was the sort of house to which he might bring Emily with pride, where they could live happily together and welcome their friends and bring up their children in a way which even her family would be bound to approve and actually to admire. Slowly he unbuttoned his overcoat and felt for the small pad, with an infinitesimal pencil attached to it, which he always carried in his waistcoat pocket. When he had extracted it, he jotted down the number of the house and the name and address of the real estate agents. Afterward he replaced the pad and, with one last look across Joy Street, started downhill again. He had forgotten about the noise, which had stopped. Again he was deep in thought. Probably that house cost more than he could earn in a lifetime. Still it did no harm to dream. . . .

"Hey! Look out where you're going! What you doing anyway? Sleep-walking?"

"Oh, I'm sorry—terribly sorry! I don't see how I could have. . . ."

For the second time that night he had collided with a band of carolers, this time with such force that one of them would have slipped and fallen if her companion had not quickly caught her up. Roger's confused and halting apology brought forth a sharp retort; but his distress was so obvious and his own inept attempts at helpfulness so kindly that the other man's anger died down as quickly as it had flared.

"Skip it. We ought to have yelled at you. But we thought you'd be bound to see us before you started knocking us over. . . . You're all right, aren't you, *carissima?*"

The bareheaded young man with the glistening black hair had turned from Roger to his companion. She smiled up at him tenderly.

"*Si, si!* I didn't fall—you wouldn't have let me." Then, looking toward

Roger, she said, reassuringly, "Don't feel bad, please, sir. It wasn't anything at all. Just gives us the chance to wish you Merry Christmas!"

She spoke slowly and with a decided accent, as if English were still an unfamiliar language to her. But her voice was very sweet, her manner lovely and disarming. Her companion smiled suddenly, revealing teeth that were startlingly white in his dark face.

"That's right! Merry Christmas to you, whoever you are! And we've got just the song for you. Haven't we, boys? Haven't we, girls? Come on, let's go! We haven't much time before Mass!"

With no further trace of ill-feeling and with no self-consciousness, the carolers grouped themselves around their leader. Roger could not very well continue abruptly on his lonely and troubled way in the face of such friendliness; it would have been too ungracious. Besides, something that Emily had said, earlier in the evening, began forcing itself to the forefront of his mind. "A young man that made me think of Michelangelo's David, except that this man was ever so much more striking because of his coloring—and a girl with him who looked like a Botticelli Madonna. . . ."

"These must be the same carolers," he said to himself. "I'll call Emily and tell her about this the first thing in the morning." He would have liked to shake hands with the leader, to say that he was Roger Field and learn the names of the young Italian and of the girl addressed only as *carissima*. But innate shyness prevented such a gesture. Besides, the group was already singing and presently, without any pause in the song, it broke ranks and went on up the hill. The song floated back to Roger:

> "God rest ye merry, gentlemen,
>   Let nothing ye dismay
> For Jesus Christ Our Saviour
>   Was born on Christmas Day."

Chapter 4

AFTER EMILY HAD bade Roger a lingering good night and returned to the library, she found, as she had expected, that her family was awaiting explanations; and now that the inevitable moment had arrived, she was able to face it with more courage and treat it more highhandedly than she would have believed a few hours earlier. Exhilarated by her first experience with declared and released love, she acted and spoke on the impetus this had given her.

"I'm sorry if you're annoyed because I didn't come upstairs right after you sent Uncle Homer to fetch me, Grandmamma," she said, almost casually. "You see, Roger was telling me about his new job and I got so interested that I didn't realize the flight of time."

"His new job! What job?" the family asked, almost in unison. Only Old Mrs. Forbes did not join in the chorus. She looked steadily at her granddaughter, and Emily knew this piercing gaze was meant to remind her that Homer Lathrop had been sent to fetch her some time before Roger Field's arrival, and that though the others might have forgotten this, Old Mrs. Forbes had not. The girl returned the look with one which accepted the challenge.

"He's just been offered one—that is, practically. By Mr. Harold Swan. You know his firm, of course—Cutter, Mills and Swan."

"Know his firm? Who doesn't?"

"Well, of course I realized it was a very important one, but—"

"*Important!* It's notorious! What your father meant, Emily, was that it's a firm headed by a bounder, a renegade and a dreamer."

"If you'll pardon me, Homer, I think I'm capable of explaining to Emily without your help."

"Very well, Sumner. If you know of any better way to describe Roscoe Cutter than to call him a bounder, I'd like to hear it."

"There are ladies present," Eleanor remarked sarcastically. "That puts Sumner at a disadvantage in this case."

"Sumner is quite welcome to call Roscoe Cutter anything he likes, as far as I am concerned," remarked Old Mrs. Forbes. "Evidently, you are already acquainted with the epithet he had in mind, Eleanor. And I suppose Emily will have to hear it, sooner or later. This might be as good a time as any. Except that I think she had started to tell us something when she was so rudely interrupted."

"Really, Mamma!"

"If you please, Eleanor! As you were saying, Emily—?"

"I was saying that this firm is trying a very interesting experiment. Two of the original juniors are going to be taken into partnership pretty soon and—"

"Are you referring to that horsy inebriate, Elliot Berkeley, and that inbred moron, Cyrus Fletcher?"

"If that's the way you want to characterize them. As I was saying, the firm's now taking in juniors from several different groups that haven't been represented in the leading law firms here in Boston before and—"

"Dagos! Shanty Irish! Sheenies!"

"Wops is the more modern term, I think, Lathrop. And the Shanty Irish are the ones who keep pigs in their parlors, not the ones who send their sons to law schools. Those are locally known as Castle Irish. And now that Mr. Brandeis is a respected member of the Supreme Court—"

"As if representatives of all our best families hadn't signed a petition protesting against that appointment!"

"And as if the Senate had taken any notice of such a ridiculous petition! Go on, Emily!"

It was Emily's turn to take the initiative in exchanging glances with her grandmother. Even her new-found daring had not emboldened her to look for any help from this all-powerful quarter and, amazingly, she was getting it. She continued her recital with increasing assurance.

"I think the Brian Collins Roger mentioned must be Castle Irish. His father's a very wealthy contractor. He's brought lots of clients to the firm already and he's only been there two years. Roger says Mr. Cutter is very practical about such things."

"Practical!"

"If you groan like that again, Sumner, I shall certainly have Pearson call a physician. As I said before, go on, Emily!"

"And the firm has another junior who was Phi Beta Kappa at Columbia and graduated from there *summa cum laude*."

"The Jew, no doubt," interposed Homer Lathrop.

"Yes. Roger couldn't remember his last name, but his Christian name's David."

"I suppose you mean his first name. Your Uncle Homer just reminded you that he isn't a Christian. And to hear you talk, Emily, anyone would think you were quite prepared to call him by his first name, in the course of a nice, friendly chat in your own house."

"Why, I am, Mamma! You see, Roger—"

33

"I do wish you'd stop quoting Roger Field as if he were the Law and the Prophets."

"I suppose you didn't mean to make a poor pun, Eleanor. But I think we may as well reconcile ourselves to the fact that Roger Field is the law, as far as Emily is concerned. Isn't that what you were gradually leading up to, Emily?"

Once again Emily met her grandmother's direct gaze. The look she saw there was all she needed.

"Yes," she said. "That is, I didn't mean to tell until after Christmas, but from the way you're all acting and talking, I think I might as well. Roger Field proposed to me tonight and I accepted him. That's really why I was downstairs so long. I mean, the proposal itself didn't take much time and neither did the acceptance. But I had to wait quite a long while for him to come and then afterward—well, of course, afterward, I wanted him to make love to me. And he did."

Sumner Thayer groaned again and Eleanor gave a small, shocked cry. But neither of them had time to interrupt their daughter before she went on.

"I know everything you're going to say. You're going to tell me, in a minute, if I give you the chance, that the only reason Mr. Harold Swan is offering Roger a job is because the firm can't get anyone better and the time's come when it's got to have a name like Field in it to offset Collins and whatever the names of the others are. Maybe that's so, but I don't care. You're going to tell me Roger can't support me and I know he can't. He knows it too. But if you'll give him a chance, he'll prove he can hold down a job and that he can get better and better at it all the time. You're going to tell me I don't know my own mind and I'd like to prove that I do. We're both willing to have a long engagement—we won't even call it an engagement if you'd rather we didn't, for the present. We'll just call it an 'understanding.' We won't even see each other. I'll join the Frontier Nursing Service. I asked Mrs. Breckinridge to let me two years ago and there wasn't any place for me then. But there is now. So I'll go to Kentucky. Of course I'll have to go as a courier, but at that, what I learned in my Nurse's Aide course might come in handy. And Roger will start working for Cutter, Mills and Swan as soon as he's graduated and save his money all next winter. But a year from next June I'll be twenty-two, and after that I can have half the income from my trust fund. When I'm twenty-five I can have the whole income and, in the mean-time, I can just run up bills if Uncle Homer won't be a good sport and let me have what I need—everyone knows I'm going to get the money sometime. I'm not going to wait around forever to marry a man I'm in love with and I'm not going to live in a tenement when I do marry him. I'm going to have a nice big house and invite all the people he knows to come to it—those Sheenies and Dagos you were talking about, Uncle Homer, and the *Castle Irish* too! You're going to tell me Roger'll never set the world on fire. Well, I don't want the world to be on fire. I want it to be peaceful and pleasant and safe. I want to share my place in it with Roger Field. And I'm going to!"

Emily walked over to Old Mrs. Forbes' chair and threw her arms around her grandmother's neck. Then, defiantly, she faced the others. Old Mrs. Forbes heaved her great weight from her thronelike chair and reached for her stick.

"Well," she said, "that all sounds pretty conclusive to me. I don't know that we'll gain anything by arguing about it at this hour. Why don't you spend the night here, Emily? I can send Doris over to get your things. I'd like to have a little talk with you, alone, in the morning. No, not an argument. I realize you don't like those and that it wouldn't do any more good to argue with you then than it would now. Besides, I think your Frontier Nursing idea is a very good one. Mary Breckinridge is a fine woman and it won't do you any harm to see something of confinement cases in one-room cabins. I'm not going to say anything against Kentucky or anything about the facts of life, either. I believe that's what's generally meant by 'a little talk,' when a young girl's concerned. But if you don't know about those already, you will very soon and you'll have a much better time learning about them from Roger than you would from me. I should say, by the look of you, that you'd had your first lesson already and that you'd found it very pleasant. What I meant was just a pleasant conference about trousseaux and things like that. I'm afraid diamonds and brocade wouldn't ever suit you, but I think possibly sapphires and satin— well, we'll settle all that later when we don't have so many antagonistic onlookers. Come along, I'm going to put you in the Chippendale guest room. Good night, the rest of you. Don't blame either Emily or me if you don't have a Merry Christmas."

Old Mrs. Forbes was right about the futility of further argument. Homer Lathrop and both Eleanor and Sumner Thayer attempted it, but vainly. According to Emily, who departed promptly for Kentucky, her mail reached her very irregularly there; and she had no time to answer letters even when she did get them. Her angry trustee and her distracted parents were thwarted by her tactics. Roger graduated creditably from the law school, passed his written examinations for the Massachusetts bar and immediately thereafter went to work for Cutter, Mills and Swan. It was understood from the beginning that, since he had no vacation that summer, but stayed on the job while all the other juniors were having theirs, he should take double time off the following year. He worked early and late at the office and saved every penny he could possibly spare, including his Christmas bonus. By spring of the following year, he had put by five hundred dollars. Insignificant though this sum appeared to Homer Lathrop, he could not deny that, in a rather plodding way, Roger was making good; and when he announced his first raise, Homer threw up his hands and wired Emily to come home. On her twenty-second birthday, she and Roger were married in Trinity Church and the wedding reception was held on Louisburg Square.

The ostensible reason for this arrangement was the spaciousness of Old Mrs. Forbes' house. The residence of Mr. and Mrs. Sumner Thayer on Gloucester Street belonged to a later period and had obviously been designed with an eye to keeping the width of a building lot within economical limits. It was the very narrow type, with only a stiff little reception room beside the front door, and an inadequate dining room, facing an alleyway, beyond a butler's pantry dominated by a dumb-waiter, an airless lavatory finished in mahogany, and a channel-like hall which was shrouded in almost perpetual gloom. The parlor and library, located respectively at the front and back of the second floor, were more sizable and cheerful in themselves; but the fact that the stairway leading to them was steep and small, and that they did not connect with each other, lessened their feasibility for entertaining. Moreover, there was no place for guests to leave their wraps until they had climbed still another flight of stairs to the third floor, where the bedrooms of Mr. and Mrs. Thayer were located and effectively separated by twin dressing rooms equipped with set basins and massive wardrobes, and by a slitlike, depressing bathroom with a zinc tub. Emily herself occupied the front room on the fourth floor, where a linen closet had eventually been converted into a more modern bath for her. The household staff—bathless and heatless until the irritating servant problem indicated unmistakably that something must be done to make domestics slightly more comfortable—was still crowded into tiny rear rooms.

The late Mr. Forbes was thought to have had the limitations of this house in mind when he gave it to his daughter, Eleanor, for a wedding present; the unprincipled and prodigal tendencies of her husband would inevitably be curbed, at least as far as lavish hospitality was concerned, in a residence of this sort. The Ambassador's wife had seen its advantages too; Eleanor, with so little space at her command, would constantly be obliged to turn to her parents for more; invitations would go out in their names and entertaining would take its tone from them. When the "fabulous Evelina Forbes" became a widow and her sobriquet changed to "Old Mrs. Forbes" the pattern remained the same. Sumner Thayer never once sought to change it until the details of Emily's wedding came up for discussion. Then, to the amazement of all concerned, he resisted his mother-in-law's will.

"Emily's my only daughter," he objected. "My only *child*. I think it would be much more fitting—"

"My dear Sumner, you talk as if someone had accused you of having numerous illegitimate offspring, hitherto successfully concealed. I'm sure I don't know why—no one's even intimated anything of the sort. At least, not in my hearing." Old Mrs. Forbes' piercing glance darted from one member of the assembled family to another, as if challenging them to make statements of importance except in her hearing. "If you will tell me how you expect to get several hundred guests into that Gloucester Street house of yours, I'd be very much interested in learning."

Old Mrs. Forbes always spoke of the Gloucester Street house with disparagement and with the intimation that Sumner alone had been responsible for the choice of such a cramped and tasteless habitation. He had borne patiently with this attitude for years and he ignored it now. But he persisted in his contention that, such as it was, the house must serve.

"I don't see any reason why we should have several hundred guests. And, as I started to say, I think it would be much more fitting for our only daughter to be married from her parents' home than—"

"Sumner, you can be almost as tedious and inaccurate as Russell once you get started. Emily isn't going to be married from anyone's home— and, incidentally, the way you mouth that word it sounds like a charitable institution. Emily's going to be married in Trinity Church. I thought that much was settled, at least."

"Yes, of course it is. But I still think it's more fitting that she should make her first appearance, as a married woman, in her home and leave from it on her wedding trip. If we had a breakfast, instead of a reception, and limited it to the immediate family—"

"I don't suppose even you would suggest excluding the bridesmaids and the ushers, would you, Sumner? Or, for that matter, the maid of honor and the best man? And perhaps you've forgotten that Sherman and Sue have four children. Emily's own cousins have got to be considered immediate family, haven't they?"

"I hadn't the least idea Sherman and Sue were coming to the wedding. I was sure there'd be some special reason why the cranberries couldn't be left in late June, just as there's always a special reason why they can't be left during the Christmas holidays."

If Sumner had not been stung almost past endurance, he never would have spoken in such a way. Fully realizing this, Old Mrs. Forbes proceeded to sting him still further.

"Of course they're coming to the wedding. Priscilla is going to be one of the bridesmaids, which means that, for once, I'll see her out of blue jeans. Incidentally, Roger also has several own cousins, not to mention uncles and aunts. So that brings us up to about forty for the wedding party and the family. How many can you seat comfortably in that horrible little dining room of yours in the Gloucester Street house? I thought it was ten."

"The breakfast could be a buffet—"

"And the guests could carry their plates of salmon and of salad and their glasses of champagne upstairs, I suppose, and then bring them down again when the wedding cake was cut and then go up again, all the time spilling things and knocking each other over and looking around hopelessly for a place to sit down."

"I see how you feel, Papa," Emily said gently, as her father made no immediate retort to this latest thrust. To her distress, she could see that her father's weak, handsome mouth was twitching and she longed to spare him further humiliation; but the moment seemed to have come when she, too, must make an unexpected and unwelcome announcement. "Perhaps, if there were just the family, we could work something out. But Roger told me last night he hoped we wouldn't mind if he enlarged his list a little. You see, since I've asked Marion Swan to be one of my bridesmaids—of course, I felt I ought to under all the circumstances—we naturally have to ask *her* family, her father and mother and brother and sister. Then we can't very well ask Mr. Swan and not ask the other members of his firm too. So that means Mr. and Mrs. Cutter and Mr. and Mrs. Mills and their children—ten more persons."

"I will never, never ask people like the Cutters to my house!" Eleanor exclaimed.

"I'm sorry you feel that way, Mamma. I think they should be invited. And not just the Cutters and the Swans and the Mills' either. The younger men who are Roger's associates."

"You're not referring to that flannelmouthed Mick and the rest of the disreputable gang Cutter's trying to force on his clients, are you?" Homer Lathrop broke in heatedly.

"I mean Brian Collins and Pellegrino de Lucca and David Salomont," Emily answered. Her voice was quiet, but it had a warning note in it. "I agree with Roger about asking them too. He likes them all very much."

"I shall never, never—" Eleanor Thayer began again. Her pale cheeks were flushed and she spoke loudly and angrily. Her mother interrupted her.

"Well, that seems to settle it. If you will never, never invite the Cutters and Mr. Cutter's partners and the juniors of the firm to your horrid little Gloucester Street house, of course Sumner will have to give in about the wedding reception. Because I agree with Roger and Emily; they have to be asked and I am perfectly willing to ask them here. I don't suppose you will ever learn, Eleanor, that there is such a thing as expediency. Or that people who are really important are not afraid to invite anyone they please to their houses. It's only people who are socially insecure themselves who worry about things like that. I don't know any reason why you should have become insecure, but it's like Sumner's illegitimate children. I never heard of those before either."

"You're terribly unjust, Mamma. You *know* I'm secure. You *know* Sumner hasn't any illegitimate children. It's just that you're determined to thwart us. And that Emily's going out of her way to make us unhappy. As if it weren't bad enough that she's going to marry this Field boy at all—"

Emily leaped up and, without looking at her mother, rushed from the room. Old Mrs. Forbes reached for the pad and pencil which she had temporarily laid aside.

"Don't be a bigger fool than you can help, Eleanor," she said casually. "Let's see, where were we, before Sumner advanced that senseless idea of his about the Gloucester Street house? Oh, yes—the wording of the invitations. 'Reception immediately after the ceremony, 24 Louisburg Square.' No name's necessary there, Sumner, so you're spared the public announcement that your only daughter isn't making her first appearance as a married woman in her own home. And of course, you and Eleanor will receive with me and the bride and groom. I'm glad Roger doesn't have any parents to consider in that connection. I've always thought a long receiving line was very provincial—the sort of thing midwestern women's clubs and southern memorial societies go in for. Where is that guest list? We must add those names Emily just gave us. Does anyone here know how to spell Pellegrino and Salomont?"

So the real reason that the wedding reception was held at Old Mrs. Forbes' house, whatever was generally circulated to the contrary, was because she was willing to invite Roger's new associates to it and her daughter was not. Though this reception was very large, Emily had known nearly all the guests from childhood; therefore, she had no difficulty in immediately identifying the few who were strangers and in giving them an especially gracious greeting, despite the relatives and close friends who came crowding in upon them as they went down the line. Roger did not fail to voice his appreciation of this when he and Emily were settled in their drawing room on the train for New York, with their handsome new baggage piled up all around them. The baggage was liberally labeled, for though Roger's commitment to Cutter, Mills and Swan did not give the bridal couple enough leeway for a trip around the world, they were going briefly to Europe, and were to sail that same night, going direct from the Grand Central Station to the pier. Roger counted the suitcases, hatboxes and overnight bags to be sure nothing was missing, and shifted the position of several pieces to make them more orderly, before he pulled down the shades and, seating himself beside Emily, clasped her in a fond embrace.

"You looked like an angel, darling," he told her after an interlude. "Really, I never saw such a beautiful bride! I'm not telling you that because I love you so much. I'm saying it because it's true. And you acted like an angel too—making everyone feel welcome and at home and giving them the idea you were really glad to see them." Of course, he did not add "and this meant all the more to me because the 'total strangers,' without your gracious greeting would not have been allowed to forget, for one moment, that they were outsiders." But she knew this was in his thoughts and answered all the more warmly on that account.

39

"But I was really glad to see them! I liked all your friends, Roger, ever and ever so much."

"Truly? Not just the ushers and the rest of my old crowd? Of course, you knew them already. But the juniors in the firm—could you get any idea what they were like, seeing them so hurriedly?"

"Of course I could. I'll describe them to you. Then you'll know I'm not pretending." She locked her fingers a little more firmly in his and went on, "David Salomont was almost the first person who came down the line. He didn't look a bit as I'd expected."

"What did you expect?"

"Oh—spectacles and a pasty complexion and rather oily hair. And I thought he'd be either undersized or a good deal too fat—sort of pudgy. And that his Phi Beta Kappa key would be in great evidence on a flashy waistcoat."

Roger laughed. "In other words, a thoroughly obnoxious-looking creature! What a relief it must have been to discover how mistaken you were!"

"It was. I thought he was very arresting. And very—very virile. There is such a word, isn't there?"

Roger laughed again. "There certainly is—also such a quality. Yes, David has it all right. And arresting describes him too. I can see how you'd remember him. He does stand out in a crowd, not just because of his size or his good looks or his wonderful clothes either."

"No. . . . And he's also got an exceptional voice. I noticed that right away too. I should think he could do almost anything he wanted with it."

"He can and does. He's a born spellbinder. It doesn't matter much what he says, because he says anything and everything so darned well. I'll never be able to argue cases the way he does, Emily."

A slight wistfulness had crept into his happy voice. Emily tightened the clasp of her fingers again and leaned over to kiss him.

"Of course you will. Or if you aren't, you'll do something else better than he does. He might make the mistake of being a little too forceful and insistent. That doesn't appeal to everyone. It doesn't especially appeal to me."

"Doesn't it really?"

"No. And I thought of it when he came back in the line a second time. He made me feel as if he were determined to talk with me. I was glad to, because I do think he's very attractive—very intriguing. But there were lots of other people I had to talk to and he didn't seem to be taking them into consideration at all. And somehow, I was glad I'd thanked him for his wedding present right away and that I'd remembered exactly what it was—you know, the punch set in the scroll design. I don't suppose he really would have asked me whether I was pleased with it if I hadn't mentioned it first, but still I had a queer feeling that he might."

"All right, that'll do for Dave. What about Brian?"

"Well, I didn't like him quite so much. He isn't forceful; he's almost impudent. Of course, he wasn't impudent to me. I don't mean that. But I felt he could be. I thought he was a little crude. He drank a good deal of champagne. Then he went over to the window and shouted to one of the policemen he caught sight of outside—evidently a crony of his, and afterward I overheard him making two or three jokes that were—well, they weren't nice at all. I'm not used to men that make jokes like that."

"But you said you liked all my new friends!"

"I did. I do. But I like them in different ways. I liked David instinctively and I liked Brian in spite of myself! And if it hadn't been that I fell in love with you before I ever met him, I'm sure I'd have fallen in love with Pellegrino de Lucca at first sight!"

It was her turn to laugh, joyously and spontaneously, as if she knew Roger would understand how silly it was to suppose for one moment that she could possibly have fallen in love with anyone but him. He smiled pleasantly and kissed her again, but he did not laugh with her, and after a little she went on again in the same light and lilting way that she had spoken a moment earlier.

"Besides, I had the funniest feeling this wasn't the first time I'd ever seen him. Do you think I could have possibly met him anywhere else?"

"No, I'm almost certain you couldn't have. Pell's really poor. I'm sure everything he had on was hired for the occasion and that even renting clothes cost more than he could afford. Brian isn't poor at all and I imagine David's better fixed than he'd admit. But Pell lives somewhere on the north side of the Hill and never talks about his family or asks anyone to come and see him. He doesn't go much of anywhere himself, either. I was surprised that he came today." And I'm afraid he was sorry he did, Roger added mentally. Pell can't forge ahead for himself the way Dave and Brian can. He was a lot more hurt than they were at being treated like an outsider.

"I'm glad he did come though, aren't you?" Emily said quickly, again divining his unspoken thought. "Because I think there's really something very fine about him. How did Mr. Cutter happen to run across him?"

"I haven't the slightest idea."

Emily gathered he had talked as much as he cared to about the juniors and tactfully changed the subject, telling him how remarkably well she thought Caroline had looked in her maid of honor's dress, that several other persons had commented on it. Roger answered her gratefully, but guardedly. He had been deeply touched because she asked Caroline to be her maid of honor, instead of some younger and more attractive girl, and he had tried to tell her so several times already, only to feel that he did so inadequately. Unless he frankly admitted his sister's lack of charm, he could not express his sense of his obligation and hers to his fiancée. Well, Emily was not his fiancée any longer; they were married at last, and he should be able to speak to her without reservation on the subject of Caroline or on any other. But suddenly he felt very tired and did not want

41

to talk at all. It had been hard work, keeping up with the endless requirements of the office during the same period that he was expected to attend
the innumerable parties given in Emily's honor. Very often he had been
obliged to sit up all night in order to do both, though he had never told
her so. And the night before, his bachelor dinner had seemed interminable
to him, and he had not been able to forget that, in order to give it, he had
been obliged to sell certain securities. And he had already sold others in
order to buy Emily the right ring. There had been absolutely no way to
manage the pearl necklace. She had been sweet about it, saying she would
much rather have the pendant that had belonged to his mother, which he
gave her instead; but he knew she should have had the pendant and the
pearls too. And he knew that the maid of honor and the bridesmaids
should have had much larger bouquets, and that those carried by the
flower girls would have had a much quainter touch if he had gone to a
better florist. He knew that Emily had told the truth when she said she
would really rather carry just a white prayer book, with flowered streamers
attached; she was not thinking of expense when she told him so. But if she
had wanted a great spray of white orchids instead, he would have had to
sell still another security.

Here it was again, this hideous question of money, raising itself to
torment him even on his wedding day. His starting salary with Cutter,
Mills and Swan had been fixed at fifteen hundred dollars a year and this
was more, he learned, than the other juniors, who had been taken on
earlier in the Depression, had been given to begin with; his first raise gave
him an extra three hundred and his Christmas bonus had come to one
hundred dollars more; meanwhile, his annual income from his father's
estate was a little less than two thousand. If a well-to-do uncle, who had
hitherto shown himself very stingy, had not unexpectedly come forward
with the startling suggestion that he wanted to give the young couple their
trip abroad for a wedding present, they would have been almost forced to
accept Elizabeth Forbes' offer of her remodeled farmhouse for a honeymoon home. Roger could have brought himself to accept this hospitality,
which would have involved very little outlay on anyone's part; but Emily
liked Vermont better in the winter than in the summer and Roger never
could have spent large sums in travel for which the money was supplied
wholly by his bride.

During the final days of their engagement, when he and Emily were
taking one of their frequent walks together, he had steered her in the
direction of Joy Street and paused before the house which he had already
eyed surreptitiously several times since the Christmas Eve when he had
first seen it. The "For Sale" sign was still in the window and, as Emily did
not immediately notice this, he called it to her attention and, for a few
moments, they talked in a desultory way about the potentialities of the
house. A week or so later, she telephoned him and asked if he would go
with her to see it the following Sunday. Their inspection of it revealed an

interior which fulfilled the promise of his imagination; but, after the ubiquitous agent, who insisted on accompanying them to every nook and corner of it, casually mentioned its "bargain price," Roger recoiled from his dream with something approaching horror. He had been right in the first place; it was doubtful whether his life earnings would equal the cost of purchasing, renovating and maintaining this house. He never spoke of it to Emily again and she did not mention it to him either. Reluctantly, he suggested the Cambridge apartment as a temporary abiding place "while they looked around"; and Emily had agreed, rather vaguely for her, but still very pleasantly, that this arrangement would be all right "unless they unexpectedly found something better"; at all events, she did not think they should spoil their wonderful summer abroad by worrying about what they were going to do next. The question had not been re-opened and neither had any definite provision been made for Caroline; it was understood that she and Marion Swan had "plans" for some joint undertaking which might mean a general readjustment in her design for living.

Homer Lathrop had, of course, talked to Roger about Emily's financial status and Roger still winced at the memory of this conversation. Unsparingly, the trustee had dwelt on the disapproval with which he viewed a matrimonial venture where the wife supplied most of the money; he said he had tried to make Emily understand the grave disadvantages of such a union. Since she did not seem able to grasp these, he had reluctantly given his consent to an allowance from the trust fund which would preclude her from being noticeably shabby, or going hungry, or working her fingers to the bone. Homer Lathrop did not divulge the sum which he thought would do this, and Roger was too proud and by that time too wretched to ask; his only thought was to bring the humiliating interview to an end and, when he went to see Emily that night, it was with the purpose of telling her that he thought he should release her from her engagement, though this was already announced, that he could not inflict a life of want upon her or endure one of almstaking for himself. But she had received him so confidently and so lovingly—she had shown him with such pride the engagement presents which had already begun to come in and talked with such joy about the beautiful wedding they were to have—that he had not been able to speak the words which would have chilled her happiness and separated him from her, perhaps forever.

Well, no one could separate them now, in spite of her family's opposition and his own misgivings. With the last words of the marriage service, his antagonists had been forced to accept him irrevocably; they could not contend against him when he had become one of them. And when he had actually made Emily his wife, his own sense of unworthiness and inadequacy would be engulfed in one of triumph. Without realizing it, he was thinking in terms of security and vindication rather than in terms of rapture.

In the days before their marriage, he and Emily had sometimes sat quietly side by side for long periods, so content in the communion of their minds and spirits that they needed neither words nor caresses to complete their consciousness of harmony. It did not seem strange to him that they should do so now, enclosed in the privacy of their drawing room, while the train sped on its way through the twilight; after the turmoil of their wedding day, before the ecstasies of their wedding night, this silence, this deepening dusk, were balm to his weariness. Emily, sensitive to his mood, did not break in upon it; she was not tired herself, but she understood his exhaustion. He had benefited as much as she from the hard-won victory on that distant Christmas Eve, but still it had been hers rather than his; and she knew that the fruits of it, at all times sweet to her, had sometimes been bitter for him to swallow. Frequently she had feared he could not continue to do so. Moreover, he had not been sustained by the exhilaration which had never lessened, for her, since she learned that Old Mrs. Forbes was her ally. She had known from that moment that she and her grandmother were somehow kindred spirits; but she had also known that the elderly woman and the young man misprized each other and that perhaps they always would. Roger had never told her about his feeling in the matter; but she was so close to him that, without words, she had divined his antipathy. Old Mrs. Forbes had expressed hers with her usual brutal frankness one cool afternoon late in May when she and Emily were sitting by the fire together.

"Of course, I've nothing against that Field boy," she told Emily. "He's agreeable, he's intelligent, he's well born and well educated, he's got good principles—in short, he's a gentleman. You'd think, to hear your father and mother and Homer Lathrop run on, that he'd broken every one of the Ten Commandments and that the popular Seventh was quite possibly his favorite. I don't believe he ever broke even a piece of bric-a-brac. That's the trouble—it isn't what he's done or may do that worries me; it's what he hasn't done and never will do."

"That doesn't worry me at all," Emily replied serenely.

"I know it doesn't. And I'm not trying to make you worry. You say you want your life to be peaceful and pleasant and safe. Well, I think it will be pleasant and peaceful and safe with Roger and I think you'll be reasonably happy with him too—as long as you don't want the world set on fire and as long as someone doesn't set it on fire for you, whether you think you want it aflame or not. Right now, you imagine you're in love with Roger Field and—"

"Of course I'm in love with Roger." Emily did not hesitate to say it to herself or anyone else now. She said it proudly and confidently.

"My dear, if you had been, in the sense I mean it, you never would have voluntarily gone off to Kentucky and postponed your marriage for over a year, to prove your point. You'd have eloped, in the face of family opposition, within a week after Roger's proposal of marriage. You may not

44

care for the comparison, but falling in love is something like having labor pains. You can have 'false pains' and you can imagine you're in love. But when the real labor pains begin, you know the difference right away; you don't see how you ever could have thought you were suffering before. I ought to know—I've had six children. And it's the same with falling in love. I ought to know about that too."

"You didn't fall in love six times, did you, Grandmamma?" Emily inquired whimsically.

"Never you mind. I may tell you about that some other time—when I think you're better qualified to understand what I'm talking about than you are now. And you needn't joke about it either. It's no laughing matter. Because, unfortunately, there's no way of telling which is the real thing and which isn't until you've had a chance to make the comparison."

"Well, if you didn't think I was in love with Roger, why have you made it easier for me to marry him?"

"Because I knew you had to get this pseudo love affair out of your system. If you hadn't, there's no telling what might have happened. You'd have gone on and on building it up into a shining tower. And when it toppled over with a crash, it would have hurt you terribly. As it is, I think it may be just what you need, in the way of preparation."

"Preparation for what?"

"For life. Real life. Life in a world that *is* on fire. Your private world. Maybe everyone's world. You haven't had any preparation so far. If there ever was a girl who needed to learn by experience, it's you. I think Roger can help you to get it, without hurting you too much in the process. In fact, I'm afraid he may not hurt you quite enough for your own good. He'll always be 'considerate' and I don't mean just one thing by that either. But some other man will come along who hasn't the least idea of being considerate, in any way. He'll want you and sooner or later he'll try to get you. But not as soon as you'll want him to. Because, that time, the pain will be real."

Old Mrs. Forbes leaned over from her thronelike chair and patted her granddaughter's cheek. Then, even more surprisingly, she bent still further and kissed her.

"Don't be angry with me for telling you all this, Emily," she said with a gentleness that came as another shock. "And don't take anything I've said to mean I don't like that Field boy. I like him very much. In fact, I can't think of anyone I'd rather trust you to. I don't want you to be hurt. I only think you'll have to be someday—in childbirth and in love too. And, unless I'm very much mistaken, you'll feel, in the end, that the agony was worth while in both cases. . . . Now, let's talk about something else. What about that house on Joy Street you dragged me out to see? Would you like to have it for a wedding present? If you would, I'll buy it for you and have it all ready for you to move into when you get back from Europe. Only, don't tell Roger. Let's keep it for our secret and give him a nice surprise, shall we? And of course Homer Lathrop's got to give you more than three thousand a year to run it on. I never heard such nonsense in all my life. That wouldn't pay for your clothes—at least, it shouldn't. There, there, my dear!"

Unwillingly, Emily's mind kept reverting to this conversation as she sat silently in the dark beside Roger, while the train sped on toward New York. At last, determined to change the tenor of her thoughts, she called him by name and pressed his hand. He did not answer her or return her caress and, after a moment, she realized that he had fallen asleep from sheer exhaustion. Then, afraid that her least movement would disturb him, she sat still more quietly, thinking about the house on Joy Street and wondering where it was that she had seen Pellegrino de Lucca before her wedding day.

Part Two

JUNE, 1938, TO NOVEMBER, 1938

ROGER AND DAVID

Chapter 5

As FAR BACK as she could remember, Emily had gone to Europe every other summer, and she had also spent several winters on the Continent, in schools which encouraged their pupils to take trips during the Christmas and Easter holidays and assisted them in making their excursions illuminating and enjoyable. During the course of their long friendship, Roger had mentioned to her his own lack of opportunities for travel; but it was naturally not a subject on which he cared to enlarge and his brief, reluctant references to it had slipped Emily's mind. When he told her about the gift from his Uncle Nathaniel, which would make their European honeymoon possible, the intensity of his pleasure was so evident that she tardily realized how greatly he had missed the advantages which she had taken for granted.

"It's wonderful, darling, wonderful," she said. "I'll write your uncle tonight, the minute you've gone, and tell him how much I appreciate what he's doing for us—if I write immediately, like that, he'll know I'm not just being polite, that I'm really delighted. Let's see—you say you don't have to go back to work at the office till the Tuesday after Labor Day. That means we can have two whole months abroad, besides the time we're at sea, if we go on the new *Normandie*. Why, we can do a lot in that length of time! And Roger, what would you think of taking my new car, so that we can be perfectly independent? I mean, about traveling wherever we like, whenever we like. We wouldn't have to go straight to Paris from Le Havre on the boat train; we could work our way slowly down through the Norman towns and along the coast of Brittany to La Vendée and Le Bordelais and then to Auch or Avignon. Afterward, we could go on to either Italy or Spain, whichever we'd prefer. We could—"

She stopped, aware that she was saying the wrong thing. Roger had not interrupted her, but she could tell, from his expression, that he did not want to go roaming around the Continent in her car; he wanted to feel that all the facilities for this trip were furnished, directly or indirectly, by him. Moreover, he did not want to seek out remote exotic places of which he had hardly heard; he wanted to take the beaten track which had long

49

since ceased to enthrall her, because it was so familiar to her, but which he had vainly yearned, for years, to follow, so that he might have the same easy acquaintance with good old Anglo-Saxon landmarks that his companions possessed. Later, she confessed her mistake to her grandmother.

"I smoothed it over right away," she said. "I don't think I hurt his feelings—not really. I said of course that what I'd suggested was just one way of spending our time—that there were lots of other ways and that we'd have fun, planning itineraries and then discarding them for better ones. I got the atlas and asked Roger to map out an entirely different kind of a trip."

"Very sensible of you, Emily. And I suppose his plan was to take a Cunarder, because he's always heard Cunarders have such a wonderful record of reliability. Then, of course, you'd go straight to London, and after you'd been to the Tower and Westminster Abbey and the British Museum, he thought you might do a little touring—say to Stratford-on-Avon and Oxford and two or three of the cathedral towns. And that afterward you'd go to the Scottish Lakes, via Edinburgh. You'd travel to Edinburgh on the Flying Scot—such an excellent train, always on time to the minute."

"How did you guess, Grandmamma?"

"If I'd never had anything harder than that to figure out, I certainly would have had an easy life—and a very dull one. Roger wasn't thinking in terms of Honfleur and Quimper and Carcassonne and Urbino and Burgos—and you were. But you'll be very wise for more reasons than one to take the route Roger's mapped out—this time. Places don't really matter very much anyway to a girl when she's on her honeymoon. It's the man that counts."

"That's the way I feel about it," Emily said contentedly. "So we're sailing on a Cunarder and we're going to stay at Brown's Hotel in London. And we're leaving my car behind."

In answering her grandmother, Emily had focused her attention on the old lady's final remark; but later, she could have agreed quite as sincerely with everything that had been said. Her honeymoon was a very happy one; and it was not until Roger himself confessed, after several exceptionally grim and gloomy days in Glasgow, that he would welcome a change from Brussels sprouts and drizzly weather, that Emily realized these had begun to pall on her too. By then, there was not time enough left to do much on the Continent; but a rapid change of plan enabled them to have a whirl in Paris and an interlude of sheer enchantment at Ravello before taking the *Vulcania* home; and it was while they were stretched out, at ease, in the sunlit privacy of the little verandah leading off their cabin, that Emily told Roger the secret she had kept so well until then.

"I've got a wonderful surprise for you, darling. We don't have to bother

Caroline or start a more or less hopeless search for an apartment. We've got a house of our own."

"A house of our own! What are you talking about? Where? What kind of a house?"

"That house on Joy Street you liked. Grandmamma's giving it to us for a wedding present. She's been having it fixed up for us while we've been gone —that is, she's been having basic improvements made, like a better heating system and more plumbing. Nothing in the way of interior decorating— she's left that to us, so we could suit our own tastes. But we're to send all the bills to her. And stay in her house while we supervise the final papering and painting and that sort of thing. She's going to stay late at Manchester-by-the-Sea this fall, so we'll be by ourselves on Louisburg Square."

"Emily, you must be joking. It couldn't be true. It's too—it's too—"

He was unable to go on. Emily moved closer to him and put her arms around him.

"It is true. I wouldn't joke about a thing like that. It's all right to joke about little things. But not about things that really mean something to us. Oh, Roger, we've been awfully happy this summer, haven't we? It's been perfect—in its way. But after all, it was just a prelude to our real life together. Now we're going to have that—on Joy Street. And it'll get better and better all the time."

He held her to his heart, believing her.

Nothing marred the pleasurable excitement of their return or disturbed the serenity of their stay on Louisburg Square. Roger resumed his work at the office with zeal and enthusiasm and, from the very first, Emily took immense pride and pleasure in her own house and devoted herself, with intelligence and industry, to its organization and embellishment. Every evening, when Roger came home, he found that she had made it a degree more livable and attractive than it had been the day before. Fresh frilled curtains appeared in the bedrooms and richer draperies on the ground floor; the well-rubbed mahogany in the dining room was brightened by an array of wedding silver; the library furniture was arranged and rearranged until it was placed in the way most conducive to complete comfort. And one afternoon Emily led her husband to the spacious linen closet and, throwing open its double doors, revealed pile after pile of snowy sheets and pillowcases and towels, gartered with satin-covered elastic to insure perfect regularity, and scented with small bags of lavender nestling between each pile.

Roger felt such manifestations of housewifery delightful and found convincing ways of showing his appreciation to Emily. But secretly, he was even more pleased with the tact and consideration she showed by consulting him about all matters in which he might logically take as much interest as she did. During the years which Old Mrs. Forbes had spent in foreign courts, she had accumulated such "numerous treasure" that even the immensity of the house on Louisburg Square would not hold it all, especially as it had not been permitted to displace family heirlooms. Roger and Emily would be saving her money, she assured them, if they would give "space to some of this junk, which was cluttering up almost an entire floor at the Boston Warehouse." Consequently, much to the annoyance of Officer Tupperty of the Joy Street Station, traffic was several times blocked by great vans which disgorged their contents into the Fields' house, only to return, a few days later, to cart away the rugs, furniture, paintings and objets d'art which, after careful deliberation, Roger and Emily had jointly decided were least suited to their needs and tastes. Meanwhile, the bride and groom had spent exciting and rewarding evenings while they chose among the rich varieties of household equipment and adornment so lavishly placed at their disposal.

Emily's obvious eagerness to meet and, if possible, to forestall all his wishes emboldened Roger to speak of his own modest possessions and to say that perhaps a few of these would also fit into the Joy Street house. There were not many—his mother's silver had gone to Caroline, of course, and apparently there had not been much outstanding furniture on either side of the family. But there were a good many books, some of them first editions, he thought, and a few really fine etchings, which belonged to him; also some other odds and ends which Caroline did not care for—a china tea service, a spool bed with matching bureau and chairs, a very old pastel of a little girl playing with her puppy. . . . Emily answered with enthusiasm. Of course she would love to have his things in their house, she told him; she did not see why she had not suggested it herself. But somehow she had assumed that if there were anything he wanted to bring there, he would have told her so long before this, of his own accord.

Roger brought as many of his possessions as he could in his old ramshackle Ford and arranged for the carting of the rest with a drayman who operated one of the few remaining forlorn, horsedrawn vehicles in Cambridge; and Emily dropped everything else she was doing to devote herself to the disposition of his belongings. When he came home, the night after their arrival, she was waiting for him behind a tea table set with his service.

Why, it was spode, she told him; she could not understand how Caroline could help admiring it. But after all, that was their gain. Of course they must not use it every day; it was far too valuable. But on special occasions and this one time, just for the two of them. . . . After tea, she led him upstairs to a hall bedroom which they had previously used only for storing suitcases; these had now been relegated to the attic and the spool furniture was all in place. The pastel hung over the tiny mantel and Emily had somewhere found braided rugs to put on the floor and an old-fashioned porcelain powder box, with twin perfume bottles which went with it, for the bureau.

"I've come back to look at all this at least a dozen times since I got it fixed," she told her husband. "If you like it as much as I do, I'm going to use it for our very best spare room. I haven't done anything with the books and etchings yet. I thought we'd hang the pictures together, after dinner, and that maybe you'd take over the books."

After everything was in order, Roger recognized that, in its realization, the house on Joy Street had far surpassed his vision of its potentialities, when he had first become aware of it, on Christmas Eve. It had dignity and spaciousness and beauty; but it contained no rigid chairs, no somber hangings and no overpowering family portraits. Through care and taste, Oriental rugs, Italian furniture, Russian ornaments and a heterogeneous collection of books had been assembled to create a surprising degree of harmony; and if Emily's decisions in regard to these had now and then been influenced by her frequent conferences with her grandmother, the expert hand of Old Mrs. Forbes had never been obtrusive. Sunlight streamed in on freshly polished floors, pleasant wallpapers and glistening white paint; and the perfect cleanliness of the house did not detract from its easy cheer. In the evening, when the curtains were drawn, there were always open fires burning behind shining brasses; and dinner came hot and hearty and abundant to the polished table in the candlelighted dining room.

The gloom of the Gloucester Street house had been perennially deepened by "servant troubles," and Emily had not been without secret misgivings lest she should fare no better than her mother when it came to a question of domestic help. Old Mrs. Forbes' impeccable staff had been assembled during her years of foreign sojourn and every member of it had relatives who would gladly have augmented its numbers. But the immigration laws which Homer Lathrop found so deplorably lax were still sufficiently restrictive to make such additions complicated. A niece of Pearson, the butler, did succeed in penetrating to New England. But though her cooking had been satisfactory to the scion of a royal family in whose exalted household she had previously seen service, she had not succeeded in meeting the culinary standards of even the least exacting Bostonian who had employed her; and Emily, while feeling certain that she was available, shrank from approaching her. When she finally did so, Lizzie Pearson's calm assumption that she would have at least two scullery maids at her disposal and a sitting room to which the humbler domestics would have access only through her condescension, put an end to the interview, which had become equally haughty on both sides; the allowance which Emily had finally wrested from Homer Lathrop, while much ampler than he had originally intended to give her, was not elastic enough to provide for scullery maids; and, on this occasion, Old Mrs. Forbes merely snorted with indignation when Emily referred the matter to her.

"Whoever is fool enough to engage an English cook deserves a lifetime fare of Brussels sprouts and sago pudding," she said unsympathetically. "Everyone knows that only butlers and parlormaids and children's nurses come from England." Her statement was so sweeping that, for the moment, she seemed to exclude even diplomats, manufacturers and men of letters from the traveling population of Great Britain, though of course this was not actually her meaning. "You may have proper food if it is prepared by almost any Continental, without the help of scullery maids; and she will have too much energy and pride to spend hours sitting around. Private parlor indeed! Personally, I prefer a Pole or a Dane, but that is a matter of taste and there are exceptions to the general rule. Romans and Russians often make very good servants too."

Unfortunately, there were no Poles or Danes, or even any Romans and Russians visible on the horizon when Roger and Emily prepared to move into their house on Joy Street. Emily, who was facing the prospect of her first interview at an employment agency in much the same spirit of mingled fortitude and fear which would have marked her delayed approach to a dental chair, confessed her apprehension to Roger.

"Why, perhaps I could help you find someone," he said, speaking with the pleased surprise which always marked his train of thought when he discovered that he actually had, or could, contribute something tangible to their design for living. "I don't know what Deirdre's doing now, but I could find out."

"Deirdre?"

"Yes. She was our general maid for years. She left us after Father died, when we sold the Brookline house. Of course Caroline and I couldn't really afford to keep a maid, so I suppose it was just as well. But Deirdre'd been with us ever since I can remember and I took it for granted she always would be. It's never seemed the same to me without her. She and Caroline kept having arguments, though. I ought to tell you that."

"What kind of arguments?"

"Oh—about going to Mass. Deirdre's very devout. And how many pounds of butter we used per week—she's rather extravagant. And whether she ought to have so much company—she's got an enormous family. So one day she left—just like that—and Caroline said it was good riddance to bad rubbish. I'm not so sure. Deirdre's a good plain cook and she can turn off a lot of laundry work too—never acts as if that weren't part of her job. Besides, I think she must feel something the way I do—that she really belongs to the Fields. She's never stayed in any one place long since she left us. I know, because we've been asked so many times to give her a reference. But I don't think she's ever been discharged. I think she's left all those other families because she's been restless."

"When can you get in touch with her?"

"Why, right away! I've always kept her mother's address—so that I could send her little presents, you know, Christmas and Easter."

"Is she awfully old by now?" Emily inquired, her heart warming toward Deirdre at the same time it warmed afresh toward Roger at the thought of the "little presents," knowing he must have gone without something himself in order to buy them.

"She can't be young, of course. But she probably isn't nearly as old as she seemed to me these last few years. Let's see—I can remember back to the time I was five and she was young and pretty then. I'm twenty-five now. Why, she can't be a day over fifty, if she's that much! And she was always strong as a horse."

Deirdre came to see Emily the following evening and their mutual understanding and admiration were immediate. Deirdre—stocky, vigorous and collected—was not working; she hadn't liked her last job so well, she said, implying that this would not be the case with the next one. Sure, she could start in right away—in the morning if Mrs. Field wanted her to. And sure, she had a niece who could help out too. Maybe the niece, Ellie her name was, couldn't come till the next week, but Deirdre could manage all right alone until then. With just two in family and a fine new kitchen and all, it would be nothing but child's play.

She left without mentioning the subject of wages and Emily did not bring it up either; somehow it seemed out of harmony with the tenor of their talk, and both instinctively felt it could be quietly and satisfactorily settled later. But as Deirdre reached the door she turned and, with one rough, capable hand on the knob, delivered herself of a single pregnant remark.

"And can I ever wait to see the look on Miss Caroline's face when she finds me, that she turned out, in this grand house of yours!"

As it happened, Deirdre was denied this satisfaction, for Caroline learned of the unwelcome presence indirectly. She had already critically inspected the kitchen several times, while the Joy Street house was in the process of reconstruction; and, since none of her suggestions for its improvement, though courteously received, had subsequently been followed, she decided to indicate her disapproval of her headstrong sister-in-law by refraining—temporarily—from giving her the benefit of further advice. Doubtless, when Emily realized how many mistakes she was making, through being deprived of such helpful guidance, she would turn contritely to its source, unless prevented by pride. Meanwhile, it was ridiculous, as well as lamentable, in Caroline's considered opinion, that a girl like Emily, barely twenty-two years of age, should be allowed to have her own way about practically everything—about getting married, about spending large sums of money, about living on an extravagant scale in a pretentious house. Caroline did not see what Homer Lathrop must be thinking of, to permit such a succession of follies; she quite understood why so many persons felt old Mr. Forbes must have been in his dotage when he was persuaded to select Homer as a trustee. Not that Russell Forbes, who mingled indiscriminately with all kinds of disreputable politicians, would have been any better; and as for that gambling nonentity, Sumner Thayer . . . ! Caroline could not adequately express, even to herself, the degree of contempt which she felt for Emily's father and this

55

sweeping disparagement included Emily's mother. She was not contemptuous of Old Mrs. Forbes; even Caroline could not dispose of the formidable matriarch by looking down on her. But unfortunately Roger had been right in his assumption that Caroline would be even less pleased with his engagement to Emily than the Forbes' and the Thayers. She was averse to wedlock for him on general principles; but, if marry he must, eventually, she knew the kind of girl he should choose for his own good; and this mythical maiden—preferably a docile orphan—bore no resemblance whatsoever to the flesh-and-blood reality with which he had permitted himself to become entangled. However, after the engagement was announced, Caroline nobly sought to be silent on the subject of her brother's fiancée and she might have tried to be equally charitable about Old Mrs. Forbes, had she not happened to hear that this outrageous woman was highly amused by her own judicial attitude.

"No doubt," Old Mrs. Forbes was quoted as saying, "some desiccated ladies-in-waiting from The Steppes criticized the conduct of Catherine of Russia. But the poor, futile creatures went on *waiting* all their lives—to get Catherine's leavings."

The coarseness of this comparison, as well as its arrogance, made Caroline feel there was no reason why Old Mrs. Forbes should be spared denunciation in the most emphatic terms of which a well-bred Bostonian was capable. She was always careful to add, "Of course, Emily is not in the least like her grandmother." But in what passed for her heart she was not so sure. Every now and then, she had the terrified impression that unless Emily were promptly checked and suppressed, she might develop certain traits which had characterized the fabulous Evelina. Emily was already far too self-assured and self-assertive for a girl of her age and Roger showed no signs of checking and suppressing his wife, or even of wishing to do so. He adored her so blindly that, apparently, she seemed to him perfect, just as she was.

Caroline told herself that it was her duty to see that her brother's life was not completely wrecked, if she could help it; with this end in view, she made frequent visits to the house on Joy Street during its organization. When the bridal couple was actually installed there, she appeared promptly at teatime, and was chagrined to be admitted by a neat, rosy-cheeked maid in a spotless uniform, who beamed upon her with great good will and ushered her competently into the library, announcing that Mrs. Field would be down right away. A shining samovar was already singing beside the pleasant hearth; and almost immediately Emily appeared on the circular stairway, humming a gay little tune. Caroline, who had always righteously refused to wear anything merely because it was becoming, observed, without admiration, that her sister-in-law had on a long crimson robe which floated out behind her as she moved quickly along. Wide lace ruffles edged the elbow sleeves and square *décolletage* of this garment, which Caroline knew would now be classed as a hostess gown, but to which she herself referred as a wrapper and considered inappropriate for anything except bedroom wear; and the entire effect of it was not only costly but exotic.

"How nice of you to drop in!" Emily said pleasantly, as she submitted to Caroline's solid kiss and returned it lightly. Emily did not care much for stereotyped kisses as a form of greeting between women, but she had quickly discovered that Caroline, though she derived no pleasure from such caresses, considered them an essential part of correct family ritual. "Roger isn't home yet, but I think he will be, any minute. Let's have some tea right away, shall we? And then some more, made fresh, when he does come. That'll give us an excuse for second cups."

She seated herself beside the samovar, lighted a cigarette and leaned back luxuriously in her chair. Caroline did not smoke and had impressed on Emily her opinion of this "filthy habit" so forcefully that the latter did not proffer her the cloisonné box from which she helped herself casually. She crossed her knees and Caroline observed that the hostess gown, though very long, was "suggestively" cut. It was not actually too low or too tight; but it revealed Emily's lovely white neck and emphasized the lines of her figure in the artful way which only a skillful dressmaker could effect. Emily, apparently quite unaware that her costume was an affront to her sister-in-law's sense of decorum, began to chat pleasantly and inconsequentially. Caroline interrupted her.

"Where did you get that maid?" she demanded.

"Ellie? She's cute, isn't she? Roger found her for me."

"You don't mean to tell me that with everything else he has to do, you're sending Roger out to employment agencies?"

Emily laid aside her cigarette and rearranged the folds of her crimson robe. "I don't 'send' Roger anywhere, Caroline," she said quietly. "He goes wherever he likes, whenever he likes, as far as I'm concerned. But he hasn't gone to any employment agencies yet—at least to my knowledge. He knew Ellie before we were married. Or rather, he knew her aunt very well, and he knew Ellie in a vague way, as one of Deirdre's nieces. You must have seen her around sometimes too."

"You don't mean to tell me that the maid who opened the door for me was one of that gang of grimy, runny-nosed children that Deirdre had around all the time?"

"I suppose she must have been. Hush—here she is now with the tea."

Beaming more proudly than ever, Ellie entered with the tray and set it down on the small mahogany table beside Emily. Mindful of the injunction that the spode was to be saved for special occasions—among which Ellie saw no reason to number a visit from Miss Caroline Field—the maid had not used this; instead, she had surprisingly selected a silver-gilt service which harmonized so well with the samovar that she guessed, and rightly, that the two had some previous connection with each other, without having any idea of their value, which Emily had so far neglected to tell her, supposing such an explanation to be superfluous. Having silently checked everything on the tray to make sure there were no omissions, Ellie departed to return with a well-laden muffin stand. Then she stood back and awaited further instructions, respectfully but eagerly.

"Thank you very much, Ellie. I'll ring if I want anything more," Emily said, nodding in easy dismissal. "How many lumps of sugar, Caroline? And I forget whether you like a spot of brandy."

"Then you haven't a very good memory. I never touch alcohol in any form. And I've told you over and over again that I consider it the ruination of good China tea to put anything in it."

"I'm sorry. Will you have a scone? Or did you tell me something about those that I've forgotten too?"

"I prefer toast, but I don't suppose it's convenient—"

"Of course it's convenient. That's here too." Emily reached to a lower shelf of the muffin stand and uncovered a deep dish. "There's plum cake too, if you like that. I thought of the scones first because Deirdre makes such good ones."

Caroline set down her cup so quickly that it made a sharp, clicking sound against the saucer. "You don't mean to tell me—" she began. But this time Emily interrupted.

"Yes I do. Deirdre's here too. I think she's wonderful."

"You won't, after she's left you to get your own breakfast while she goes to Mass and runs up bills whenever you don't watch her like a hawk and keeps the kitchen cluttered with her shiftless family."

Emily inspected the cigarette she had put aside, chose a fresh one from the cloisonné box, lighted it and began to blow rings. "I never liked hearty, early breakfast myself," she remarked. "I'm awfully relieved to find that Roger doesn't either. I can't imagine anything worse—well, anything much worse—than being married to a man who expected you to be down in the dining room, all dressed for the day in a tailored suit, at seven-thirty; and then having grapefruit and oatmeal and bacon and eggs and, quite possibly, griddlecakes brought to you in courses. We have a tray in our bedroom, at eight-fifteen, weekdays. That gives Roger just time enough to get to his office at nine without hurrying. He's clocked himself, walking across the Common, and it takes him exactly twelve and a half minutes. Of course, he's dressed before the tray comes up, but I don't dream of doing so until after he's gone. Sundays, we just ring, whenever we feel like it—tenish. Deirdre hasn't even mentioned Mass to me. I suppose she goes and gets back before we need her. Anyway, we haven't had to get our own breakfast yet."

"Just wait until the newness wears off," Caroline said warningly. "After all, you've only just started." She had instinctively recoiled at the reference to "our" bedroom and she was horrified to hear that a young, healthy girl like Emily indulged in the slothful habit of breakfasting in bed; the fear that Roger's sterling character would be undermined by lax influences rose to torment her again. Then she had another harrowing thought. "No doubt, you're paying Deirdre perfectly fantastic wages," she added accusingly.

"No doubt."

"What do you mean, 'no doubt,' Emily?"

"Why, probably the same thing you did! I haven't discussed wages with her yet. I haven't had time."

"*You haven't had time!* You lie in bed half the morning and then you say you haven't had time to settle a vital point like a servant's wages!"

"I'm trying to concentrate on essentials. The first essential, in my opinion, was to get the house running, comfortably and pleasantly. I think it is. I'm very happy here. I believe Roger is too."

She glanced about her with obvious contentment. Caroline followed the glance grudgingly. There was no denying that Emily, in spite of her inexperience, had somehow produced a very pleasing effect. But after all, this was not so strange when one considered that she had all that loot of her wicked old grandmother to draw on, besides spending money like a drunken sailor herself. And she was disturbingly pretty, in that clinging crimson robe, with those ruffles of old lace fluffing out around her arms and shoulders. She had a great deal more color than when she was younger and she seemed to have filled out a little, which was becoming too; she had been rather too thin before. Caroline could only hope that these beguiling curves which had begun to appear did not presage anything more than a slight increase in weight. It would really be too disgusting, if so soon. . . .

"Doesn't Roger have a key?" she inquired, cutting short her own train of thought as she heard a step in the hallway and saw Ellie hurrying toward the front door.

"Yes, of course. Apparently, I have another visitor."

"But surely you wouldn't be 'at home' yet."

"Of course I would be. I haven't had any callers before. But evidently—"

"I couldn't help overhearing what you were saying. And I'm delighted to learn that you are 'at home.' Your grandmother thought you might be. I've just been making my party-call on her. I'm sorry it was so long delayed, because I really appreciated her invitation to your wedding reception. Also her suggestion that I might try my luck at finding you in too."

At the sound of a strange voice, Emily had instinctively risen. Caroline sat still, watching her, as she moved gracefully across the room and held out her hand to David Salomont.

Chapter 6

HE CAME FORWARD with all the assurance of a welcome guest, the fresh-ness of his face and the breeziness of his bearing in no way suggesting that he had been through a grueling day; Emily could not help noticing the contrast to the telltale signs of fatigue which Roger failed to conceal when returning from the office. On the other hand, something about the superb cut of David's clothes and the spotlessness of his starched linen reminded her of the way in which Homer Lathrop always managed to appear, whatever he had been doing and no matter how long. Roger not only looked tired when he came home, he looked rather rumpled. Of course, he could not afford to patronize costly tailors and haberdashers, as Homer did, and as David apparently did too; but this faculty of looking both vigorous and immaculate was not, Emily realized, merely a matter of physical strength or ample funds. It was a special aptitude which Homer and David had in common and which Roger unfortunately lacked.

As Emily greeted David with cordiality, Caroline stiffened in her chair. Matters were at a pretty pass indeed if a presumptuous Jew could come, uninvited, to her brother's house—in her brother's absence—and be made welcome. She acknowledged his presence without speaking and with the barest possible inclination of the head. But the gesture lost some of its effect, because David forestalled her with the mocking quality of his own greeting.

"I'm sure you wouldn't remember me, Miss Field," he said. "I was only one of the wedding guests who belong in the category of those brought in from 'the highways and byways.'" Having made this announcement, he appeared to forget her entirely and, after accepting a cup of tea from Emily, looked about him with obvious appreciation. "What a delightful room! Roger's been bragging all over the office about his bride's accom-plishments as a domestic organizer. But I didn't realize that she'd have so many museum pieces at her disposal. That's as fine a Gaugengigl as I ever saw, over there, and I don't know that I ever saw one more advantageously placed. And this is the 'missing' tea service from the Winter Palace, isn't it? Where did you get all these treasures—and learn what to do with them?"

"My grandmother helped me," Emily replied readily. "At least, the etchings came from Roger's family. But it was Grandmamma who suggested hanging 'The Intruder' on that particular wall space and lighting it the way I have. And she's loaned me lots of other things—among them the tea service. It was given her when Grandpapa was Ambassador to Russia, about thirty-five years ago. I never knew before it was supposed to be 'missing.'"

"Oh, yes, it's had quite an interesting history. I'll have to tell it to you sometime."

Sometime when he isn't hampered by the presence of a third person, Caroline said to herself bitterly. *Not that he seems much inhibited now. In a minute, he'll ask her how much she thinks it's worth.* But she was mistaken. Instead of asking Emily, he told her.

"I believe it's valued at something like eight thousand gold rubles," he remarked. "But that's a conservative estimate. I must tell my stepfather I've seen it. He'll be terribly jealous of me."

"Is your stepfather especially interested in such things?" Emily inquired, offering the scones.

"Well, he's an antique dealer, catering to the luxury trade. So he keeps himself informed. He certainly would give anything to see this room," David added, helping himself to the scones and looking around again with mounting admiration. "I'd like to bring him here sometime."

"I'd be very pleased if you would. If you let me know beforehand when to expect him, I'll see if Grandmamma wouldn't join us for tea. She could tell him so much more than I could about the things she's loaned me. She's lame, so she doesn't go out a great deal any more, but I'm sure she'd enjoy talking with your stepfather."

"And of course he'd give his eyeteeth to meet her," David said enthusiastically. "He could go to her house if it wasn't convenient for her to come here—and come here himself, of course, beforehand or afterward. I'll wire him tonight about your kind suggestion. I know he'll come right over from New York unless he's tied up with a sale or something."

"Perhaps it would be just as well, Emily, if you would find out when your grandmother is free and whether she feels equal to making new acquaintances at this time."

Caroline spoke freezingly. Only her sense of duty constrained her to stay in the same room with this common, pushing person. But she did not feel she should leave Emily alone with such an obnoxious creature. There was no telling what might happen.

"I'll telephone and ask her. It won't take me but a minute. Did you go to the game last Saturday, Mr. Salomont? Caroline didn't and I'm sure she'd love to have you tell her about it."

David had not been to the game, having remained at the office all day

61

working on a libel case which, to him, was far more provocative than football. However, he had been to the recent opening of *Porgy and Bess* and proceeded to dissect it expertly, unabashed by Caroline's terse statement that she had previously heard it was disgusting. When Emily returned to the library, he leaped up to greet her with the satisfied air of a man who has just engaged in a singularly stimulating conversation.

"Miss Field and I've been discussing the drama," he said. "I have found her viewpoint extremely illuminating. . . . I hope you have a good report for me about your talk with your grandmother?"

"She'd like very much to meet your stepfather. In fact, she thinks she may have met him already. Is his name Morris Brucker?"

"It certainly is! Did she say when and where—"

"Budapest first. St. Petersburg afterward. I gathered that was another interesting story, though she wasn't too definite as to time. But apparently they didn't lose touch with each other until '14, when the war broke out. They haven't met since he settled in New York and married. But anyway, she'd be glad to have him come in for a cocktail, after he's been to tea here, any day next week except Friday."

"So that's still sacred to the Symphony! Well, more power to her! I'll get in touch with the old man and drop by again to give you his answer. . . . No thanks; not that they aren't the very best scones, but scones don't happen to be among my major enthusiasms. They're not in the same league with the *Schnecken* my aunt makes. She won't give away the recipe, but probably your cook could figure out how to make them, if she tasted one. I'll ask Dad to bring some over from New York with him. Well— sorry I can't wait to see Roger. I'm having an early dinner with the Stockbridges in Chestnut Hill. Probably Roger's told you that Ellery Stockbridge's slated to be president of the Third National Bank next January. No? He's one of our most promising clients. But he's a little on the stiff side. Just the sort of man that outsiders seem to feel is typical of Boston. Good night, Miss Field. I really think you ought to reconsider and go to see that play."

Roger arrived barely five minutes after David had left, so there was not much chance, during the interval, for Caroline to impress Emily with her disapproval—especially as Emily seemed willfully bent on being pleasant and was, moreover, preoccupied with the prospect of Roger's impending arrival. She heard his key turn in the latch before Caroline detected any such sound and ran out into the hall to meet him. The next sounds were easily identified, even by Caroline, and there was a considerable delay before Roger and Emily came into the library. Roger was smoothing his hair and Emily's pretty color was heightened.

"Hello, Caroline," Roger said and kissed her too. "How are you? Emily says David's been here. Sorry to have missed him. But I'm usually later leaving the office than he is. He has his own secretary who polishes off all his odd jobs and I have to wait for poor old Miss Riley to finish everything Mr. Mills gives her before she does my work. Half the time, when I ring for her, she just appears in the doorway long enough to say, 'I can't come in now, I have eight more pages to do for Mr. Mills.' That happens even when Mr. Mills is riding me for a memo. But of course I don't rate anything better and David does."

"I haven't the slightest doubt that David Salomont would gladly leave some poor, overworked girl to 'polish off his odd jobs' while he goes out on the town," Caroline rejoined. "He seems at liberty to make any number of engagements. He's about to get in touch with his stepfather—a New York antique dealer—about coming over here for tea any day next week except Friday, and as soon as he gets the answer, he's going to 'drop in' and report to Emily—presumably also at teatime."

"Well, that's fine," Roger replied. "I hope I won't miss him again. I think he's about the most brilliant man I ever met—and one of the most versatile. No matter what subject crops up, it seems to be right down his alley. I don't see how on earth he ever got hold of so much varied information."

"Perhaps his stepfather's wealthy customers gave him helpful hints when he was helping behind the counter. Or maybe it was his aunt, in her kitchen. It seems she excels in cookery. I have no doubt she'll soon be added to this cozy little circle David Salomont's assembling around your tea table. Speaking of cookery, Emily tells me you've taken Deirdre back."

"Yes, I was lucky enough to find her free. She's doing a grand job too—at least, Emily and I think so. Better stay for dinner and see for yourself."

Caroline rose, buttoning the jacket of her severe and rather shabby suit. "No thank you," she said. "I really had quite enough of Deirdre's rich, indigestible food before I discharged her for wastefulness. Besides, you have dinner so late that I should miss half the Lowell lecture if I stayed. I don't see how you keep such hours, even if you do have breakfast in your room. I can see that it's telling on you, Roger. You look very tired to me. And you seem to be coming down with a cold. Don't forget that your colds always settle in your chest. One of these days you'll be having pneumonia, if you're not more careful. Good night, Emily. I suppose it's useless to tell you that Roger ought to go to bed at once and keep completely quiet until he's better."

Unfortunately, Caroline's predictions about the symptoms of a cold proved to be correct; but the nature of his work prevented Roger from taking proper precautions to arrest their development: he was first too warm in the subway and then too chilled in the elevated, while on his way to the Middlesex Clerk's Office at Lechmere; he got drenched by a northeast rain while searching Somerville for a witness. By the time he did take to his bed, he was really ill for several days. Therefore, to his great regret, he missed both David's second call and Morris Brucker's visit. However, Emily's detailed accounts of these served to while away some of the tedium of his illness, though they did not compensate for her temporary absences from his side.

"David has only just left," she told him, returning a little breathlessly to his sickroom an hour or so after Ellie had announced that Mr. Salomont was in the library. "He brought us some of those *Schnecken* his aunt makes. They really are wonderful and I kept eating more and more of them, so of course I kept drinking more and more tea too. And then we got to talking. . . ."

"About his stepfather's visit?"

"Yes, partly. Mr. Brucker's coming over from New York next Saturday. I called Grandmamma and she said that would be fine. Uncle Russell was on the line when I first tried to get her, fussing about the election, and you know he goes on forever. That was another thing that delayed me. But most of the time David and I were talking about Morris Brucker—not just about his visit, but about what he'd meant to David and David's mother. One subject seemed to lead to another. . . . Did you know there were different kinds of Jews, Roger?"

"Why, of course there are different kinds of Jews, just as there are different kinds of Gentiles—good, bad and indifferent!"

"Yes, of course. But that's not what I mean. Do you know the difference between a Sephardic Jew and an Ashkenazic Jew?"

"No, I can't say I do. I don't think I ever heard of either."

"Well, you see!" Emily exclaimed triumphantly. "The Sephardim are the descendants of the Portuguese and Spanish Jews, who were about the most important people on the Iberian Peninsula at the time the Moors were driven out, and they've always felt superior to the Ashkenazic Jews, who came from northern Europe. David's father was a Sephardic Jew."

"Was he?" Roger inquired, without much interest.

"Yes. And his mother wasn't. She married above her, as the saying is. She was very proud that such a cultured man as Rafael Salomont wanted her for his wife. And she really cared very greatly for him. But she found it hard to live up to his intellectual standards. He knew seven or eight languages, several of them dead ones—read all the Greek plays and poems in the original for pleasure. He had any number of degrees and corresponded with scholars all over the world. He was always preoccupied with higher things and—well, I guess she had a very affectionate nature and would have been happier if her husband had been a little more demonstrative, though David didn't say that in so many words. But he did say that nearly all the money there was, except what got put aside for his education, went for books and worthy causes, never for good times and nice clothes and holiday trips, and that his mother missed such things when she was young and pleasure loving. David respects his father's memory very highly; but I think, in a way, his stepfather means more to him—not just because he's had a much more comfortable, happy life himself since his mother married again, but because he believes his mother's been happier too. Morris Brucker's given her everything in the world she could possibly want. He thinks the sun rises and sets on her head and he lets her see he feels that way. Besides, he's more her kind anyhow than her first husband was."

Roger, who failed to find any of this especially intriguing, made no immediate answer. Emily did not seem to notice the omission; she was pursuing a train of thought that was new to her.

"It's nice, isn't it, that David should be so fond of his stepfather? I didn't think people were, usually. And it's nice, too, that his mother should be so happy in her second marriage. I never supposed, either, that there was much romance in those. But the way David talked, I could see that a woman might sincerely love two men, in entirely different ways, at different periods of her life—enough to marry them both, I mean. And that she might find life more exciting all the time, in spite of growing older, if she had the kind of husband who told her how much he loved her and how beautiful she looked to him. David says his mother really is very beautiful still. He made me feel I'd like to see her. I'm sorry she isn't coming over to Boston with Mr. Brucker."

"Did you suggest it?"

"No, because I didn't know how Grandmamma would feel about it. I thought perhaps she'd rather see Mr. Brucker without his wife. You see Grandmamma. . . ."

Emily left her remark unfinished and Roger did not urge her to continue. He had become more interested in her observations as she went along, but they were vaguely disquieting to him, and he did not feel that a discussion of Old Mrs. Forbes' characteristics would be any less so. If encouraged, Emily would probably next voice the conclusion, which it took no great perception to reach, that her grandmother, in spite of her age, was not averse to proving her undeniable powers of attraction for almost any male who came within her orbit, and that she could do this more conveniently when unhampered by the presence of his wife, if he had one. To be sure, Old Mrs. Forbes had married only once; there was nothing in her history which would help to develop a train of thought about second marriages. On the other hand, no one supposed, for a moment, that her husband had been the one love of her life. Indeed, it was common knowledge that she had not lacked opportunities to remarry, even recently, and also that she had fascinated any number of admirers while her husband was still living. Though she had never caused an open scandal, Roger could not help believing that this was due partly to adroit management. Altogether, it was better to let the subject of romance drop. . . .

It was inevitably revived, however, after Morris Brucker's visit. According to plan, the antique dealer came to Joy Street with his stepson, and snatches of animated conversation and echoes of hearty laughter from the library below reached Roger in his sickroom. The voices became clearer

65

as Emily and her visitors came out into the front hall. She called up to Roger and he could tell from the way she sounded that she was enjoying herself very much.

"We're off to Grandmamma's, Roger. . . . Anything I can do for you before we leave?"

"No thanks. Tell Mr. Brucker again how sorry I am to miss him. David too. Have a good time, all of you."

He was very hoarse, it hurt him to raise his voice and a fit of coughing followed the effort. But the others were already outside by that time, so he was not self-conscious about the racket he made, and presently the sound of their footsteps on the brick pavement died away in the distance, as they went on up the Hill. Almost at the same moment, the clock struck five, and he told himself that Emily would surely be back by six, that they would still have an hour together before she went down to dinner and Ellie came up with his tray. He tried to read, but his eyes smarted and watered, so he gave up the attempt and lay in the dark, listening for Emily's return. This was so long delayed that he began to fear something untoward had happened, and it took real will power on his part not to pick up the bedside telephone and call Old Mrs. Forbes' house. Seven o'clock came and with it Deirdre instead of Ellie, bearing a tray designed to be tempting—broth in a covered bowl of Chinese porcelain, hot buttered toast, ice-cold milk, a custard that slipped smoothly down his sore throat. Deirdre snapped the folding legs of the tray into an upright position and placed it firmly on Roger's knees.

"If you had two good mouthfuls of that fine dinner I sent up to you, Mr. Roger, I wouldn't know it from the looks of your plate when Ellie brought it down. She don't dare speak up to you, the poor young girl. But I do. And I'm staying right here till you lick that platter clean."

"Your food's wonderful, Deirdre, just as it always was. But I've got such a splitting headache—"

"Offer it up, Mr. Roger, offer it up! That's what I do when my rheumatism almost gets me down and I yell right out with the pain of it. But, at that, I don't starve myself."

Deirdre had turned on the lights and it was clear that she did not intend to budge until Roger had eaten everything on the tray, under her watchful eye. He did so haltingly and without tasting any of it, and when he had finished and Deirdre had gone, he unfolded the *Evening Transcript*, which she had brought at the same time with his supper. Election time was nearing and Russell Forbes, he knew, was worried about his Senate seat. Roger felt he should find out how things were going in the campaign, but he did not really care much, and when he found nothing on the front page, he did not search any further. Then the telephone rang and he snatched it up. But it was not Emily calling; it was the doctor, inquiring how he was.

"Sorry I couldn't get in this afternoon, Roger, but I got caught in a

66

jam. Couple of real emergencies. I can look in on you tonight if you want me to. How's the temperature?"

"A hundred and one point two at four o'clock."

"Well, that's not bad. Still coughing a good deal?"

"Just about the same. I don't get much sleep. I'm afraid Emily doesn't either."

"I'll send you a stronger sedative. Take a capsule every hour and two if you're still restless by midnight. See you the first thing in the morning. Or, as I said, I'll be glad to come tonight if you want me."

"No, tomorrow'll be fine. But it does bother me to talk much. So long."

He did not want the doctor butting in when Emily finally did get home. And surely she would be there any minute now. But he waited and waited and still she did not come. . . .

He had almost dozed off when he was suddenly aware of her presence and sat up with a start, to see her standing beside him, her eyes shining, her dimples deepened as they always were when she was especially pleased about something. She put her arms around him and hugged him ecstatically.

"I've had such a good time!" she exclaimed. "Morris Brucker is the greatest fun! Not especially good looking, in fact, sort of shriveled, but the best company, amusing and lively and very, very witty. You should have heard him and Grandmamma sparring! He said that when she was first in St. Petersburg, she used to go to his shop very often and that they had wonderful talks together, while she made selections from his stock; but then he lost her as a customer, because all the grand dukes gave her so many presents that she didn't need to buy anything more from him. So then, he had to invent ways of getting her back, he said, because he missed her company so much. He kept teasing her while they were talking about old times and she simply loved it. I don't know when I've seen her in such high spirits."

"Did anyone tell the story of the missing tea service?"

"No one told the story, but Grandmamma and Mr. Brucker both referred to it in a cryptic way. And finally, he took a little package out of his pocket and told her that, since there were no more grand dukes, he'd ventured to bring her a present himself. She undid the package and there was a signet ring in it—a man's ring with a great carved emerald; I think the carving was the Russian double eagle, though I couldn't see very clearly. She didn't say a word, just sat and turned the ring over and over, and then she put it on and looked at him—and Roger, there were tears in her eyes!"

"But you never heard the history of the ring either?"

"No. There was something mysterious about the whole meeting, something a little uncanny, even though everyone joked so much. It didn't seem a bit like a Boston party. It seemed a lot more like an encounter that might happen in the Balkans, for instance."

"What do you know about encounters in the Balkans?"

"I don't know anything. I'm just imagining. But I loved everything about the evening. I thought it was all terribly exciting. Grandmamma still had that ring on when I left and she told Mr. Brucker she thought he'd better stay to dinner, it was getting so late. I think she must have meant all along to ask him, because she said they would have borsch, and I haven't known her to do that in a long time. But she didn't ask David and me to stay."

"So David brought you home?"

"Yes. We had a good time walking up the Hill and trying to figure out the story about the ring. Of course, David does know the one about the tea set. He said there wasn't time to tell me between Louisburg Square and Joy Street—it wasn't as if this were a warm summer evening when we could loiter along. We really did have to hurry, there was such a nip in the air. I thought of asking him to stay to dinner here, so that he couldn't use lack of time as an excuse. I think he half expected I would."

"I'm rather glad you didn't. Not that I want you to be tantalized indefinitely by curiosity. We'll ask David some other time. But I've missed you a lot, darling."

He did not say he hoped she would not leave him again while he was ill or that she would not entertain any more visitors until they could do this together. But she realized this was how he felt and, fearful lest her own excellent health might have made her insensitive, she reproached herself for having been lacking in tenderness and devotion toward him. During the next few days she redoubled her efforts to keep him comfortable and to divert his mind, remaining with him constantly; and eventually, on his own initiative, he again brought up the subject of company.

"What would you think of giving a little dinner, darling?" he asked.

Emily had been reading aloud to him from *Drums Along the Mohawk* but, with the coming of twilight—the hour which they found increasingly companionable—she had laid aside the book and was sitting quietly beside his bed with her hand in his. She answered with enthusiasm.

"Why, I'd like to! As a matter of fact, I'd been meaning to suggest it myself, as soon as you were well enough."

"I'm well enough now to plan. . . . David seems to feel welcome here already. I'd like to have Brian and Pell feel the same way. Incidentally, do you remember asking me, the day we were married, how Mr. Cutter happened to run across Pell?"

"Yes, and you told me you hadn't the least idea."

"I didn't have then. But since, I've found out. Would you like to hear?"

"Of course I would."

She sounded not only interested, but eager. Roger was delighted that he was now able to answer the question she had asked so long before. It had troubled him that all he could say was, "I haven't the least idea," when she asked him the first time.

"Well, when he got through studying law at Northeastern, he opened a little office with his shingle in the window, on the ground floor of the same house where he has a room on the third story. . . . I've told you he lives on Joy Street too, haven't I?"

"Why no, you haven't! How nice that he's a neighbor!"

"Well, you couldn't really call him a neighbor. He lives on the other side of the Hill, opposite the police station. It's way down near Cambridge Street. I don't believe you've ever been that far."

Emily, who took a walk every day as a matter of course, admitted that this was true. "I'll go down there tomorrow morning though," she added.

"Good idea—you'll be amazed to see how the street changes once you're over the crest of the Hill. Of course, Pell isn't in that spare little office I was talking about, any more. I can tell you just about what it was like though. There was a sign in the window with the words, ATTORNEY AT LAW, NOTARY PUBLIC, after his name. And the office had just a few pieces of beat-up, old, secondhand furniture and Pell's diplomas on the wall—the one from the parochial high school and the one from Boston College and the one from Northeastern. I'm sure he couldn't have afforded to keep a secretary all day, but he'd probably have had one part time—mostly the time when he had to be out himself, so someone would be there if a client happened to come in. This secretary might have been one of his relatives. He lives with relatives. That third-floor room of his is in their tenement."

"He hasn't moved then? I mean his living quarters?"

"I don't think so, but that's not the point. The big shot who owned this tenement wanted to get Pell's relatives out for a tenant who would pay higher rent, and since the lease still had some time to run, he needed an excuse for breaking it. Well, on some saint's day or other, the Italians had a nice, comfortable family party and in the course of it they put away quite a lot of Dago Red along with their pizza and made a lot of happy noise. So the realtor brought eviction proceedings, claiming that the party was a lot wilder than it really had been. He gave the case to Cutter, Mills and Swan."

"Whereupon Pell defended the Italians, I suppose."

"And how! He won their case for them hands down and Mr. Cutter decided then and there that he was exactly the sort of chap they wanted for the new group of juniors. But to get back to where we started: I thought we might invite Brian and David and Pell here all together, so none of them would think we were singling him out from the others."

" 'That's a good idea, said the tiger.' Did you want to have the dinner stag?"

"And give up having you around? Never, if I can help it!" He leaned over to make the statement more emphatic. "No, I thought we'd better ask three girls too—Caroline and Marion Swan and anyone else you'd like."

"Caroline was pretty rude to David Salomont the other day," Emily said doubtfully. "Do you think we ought to risk having her snub him like that again?"

Roger laughed, and though the laugh ended in a cough it was an untroubled one. "Don't worry about that. David's more than a match for Caroline. He can tell her off any time he likes."

"Well, there's Caroline to think of too. Do you believe she'd consider it a compliment to be asked to dinner with David Salomont? And remember what she said about Deirdre's wonderful food!"

"She'd be very much hurt if we didn't ask her to our first dinner, no matter who the other guests were or who cooked it. Ask her anyway, darling, if you don't mind. If she says no, you can always ask someone else."

He began to cough again and Emily said they mustn't talk any more about the dinner just then, but that she would speak to Deirdre about it the first thing in the morning; afterward, she would bring him two tentative menus so that he could choose between them and make other suggestions. She was sure, if Uncle Sherman knew they were going to have their first dinner, he would send them some game from the Cape. And there was Uncle Homer's famous cellar on which he had told her to draw at any time. He knew all about vintages and, frankly, she didn't yet. But she intended to learn. When it came to the way the table ought to look, she was on firmer ground; she was sure that nothing could be more suitable than her point de Venise cloth and her Sèvres service.

Roger so highly approved both the menus which she submitted to him the following day that Emily was obliged to choose between them herself after all; and he assented to her every suggestion in regard to the dinner. There were several reasons why the choice of her cousin, Priscilla, for the third girl seemed to him wise: it would have indicated a lack of delicacy to ask Uncle Sherman for game if no member of his immediate family were invited to share it; as it was, Sherman could bring Priscilla and the ducks to Joy Street at the same time and he would, of course, be urged to remain for tea. At the moment, this gesture of hospitality would be adequate—no one expected a young couple to make their first formal dinner too much of a family party. Then there was another consideration: if Priscilla, who was now seventeen, were to come out the following year, it was high time for her to have a little preliminary social training; she and her brothers and sisters had run wild among the cranberry bogs far, far too long. Roger had noticed her trapped look at the wedding and he also recalled that, strangely enough, this had been less marked when David Salomont tried to engage her briefly in conversation. To be sure, as far as Roger could tell from the distance at which he had observed them, she

70

had responded mostly in monosyllables; and he would have thought, off-hand, that David was the last sort of person who could have helped to put a girl like Priscilla at her ease. Nevertheless, Roger had retained a very definite impression that such had been the case. In response to Emily's suggestion, he mentioned this, and said he thought it would be a good plan to put David and Priscilla side by side at table. Emily agreed and from that point they went on to discuss the table plan.

"I think we ought to put Mrs. Putnam at your right and Mr. Putnam at mine, don't you, Roger? After all, they're older people. We ought to pay them a compliment."

Inwardly, Roger had been less enthusiastic about Emily's selection of the Putnams than over her choice of Priscilla. Mr. Putnam was a third husband who had appeared tardily on the scene; Roger had nothing against him, and was indeed rather sorry for him; but he did not seem likely to provide stimulating conversation at a dinner table. Mrs. Putnam, on the other hand, always talked too much and sometimes drank too much; her stories frequently verged on the vulgar. But her appearance was undeniably striking and her breezy manner was not without its own boisterous attraction. Moreover, her family background, like her husband's, was "good" and on this account much had been forgiven her by people who had forgotten the details of her earlier marital adventures or had been too young to hear about them when they occurred. The fact that she was extremely hospitable, and entertained lavishly in her large house on Louisburg Square had also contributed to the forgetfulness of a considerable group, even though this did not include Homer Lathrop. Roger had been to a few of her prodigal parties, so he was prepared to acknowledge his social indebtedness to her when Emily mentioned this; and, little by little, he came to feel that his bride had been right in wishing to include the Putnams on the dinner list. They were not too highbrow to mingle readily with his fellow juniors; Mrs. Putnam would help to make things go; and since there was a social debt to be paid, probably the sooner it was out of the way the better. . . .

"Well, we've got that far. Mr. Putnam at your right and Mrs. Putnam at mine. Who goes on our left?"

"I thought I'd put Pell on mine. He's been with Cutter, Mills and Swan longer than the others, hasn't he?" Then, as Roger nodded his assent, obviously feeling that this seniority entitled Pell to a certain precedence, she went on, a little hurriedly, "And Marion on yours, I should think. After all, if it hadn't been for her, you probably wouldn't be connected with the firm at all."

"No, I suppose I wouldn't—that is, not if Caroline and Marion hadn't got so chummy. And of course I can't have Caroline beside me."

"I thought I'd put her between Pell and Brian. It couldn't possibly be any worse than putting her beside David and there's just a chance it might be better."

"I guess you're right again. Well, let's have a look at the plan, the way it's shaped up now."

Emily handed him the sheet of paper on which she had drawn a large oval surrounded by small circles, each with a name scribbled against it. Roger regarded it approvingly.

"Hostess, Mr. Putnam, Miss Forbes, Mr. Salomont, Miss Swan, Host, Mrs. Putnam, Mr. Collins, Miss Field, Mr. de Lucca. . . . Yes, that seems to work out very nicely. But since the party's all planned now, can't we take a little time off? It's a long while since you've given me a kiss."

Chapter 7

EVERYTHING CONTINUED TO go propitiously with the preparations for the dinner party. All the prospective guests accepted their invitations. Ellie repolished the already shining silver and reverently took down the most precious porcelain from the highest pantry shelf. Deirdre found that another buxom niece, named Dolly, was free to accommodate on the night of the dinner, and busied herself with the concoction of various delicacies. Flowers for the decorations were delivered at just the right moment, not so far ahead of time that they would lose their first freshness and not so late that Emily would have had to hurry with their arrangement; and when Sherman Forbes arrived with Priscilla and the ducks, he was in such rare good humor that Emily derived more enjoyment from their brief chat, over the teacups, than she had ever experienced in previous contacts with him.

"Quite a nice place you've got here," Sherman had said, looking about him approvingly. "Sorry Sue didn't come with me. I'd have liked to have her see it too. But, doing all her own work, it's hard for her to get away from the Cape."

"I know," Emily replied, without adding, as Old Mrs. Forbes would have done, that she also knew that there was not the slightest need for Sue's intensive domesticity. "But I'd love to have her. Perhaps she'll come some other time, Uncle Sherman."

"Well, perhaps. . . . Of course, we've got to do something about Pris, sooner or later."

"Yes, of course. And I'd be glad to help, Uncle Sherman. I mean, naturally Grandmamma will want to give Pris her coming-out party, but—"

"To tell you the truth, I'd be just as well pleased if she did. You know Sue and Mother have never hit it off and Pris shies like a frightened filly every time she sets eyes on Her Imperial Highness. But if the kid could stay with you and Roger—"

"We'll have her here a lot this winter, Uncle Sherman, and see how it works. Then, in the spring, we'll ask her how she feels about her coming-out party—her and Grandmamma both. We wouldn't want to hurt Grandmamma's feelings."

"You wouldn't want to dent the Rock of Gibraltar, I suppose. But we'll let that pass. I hope you'll enjoy the ducks. If you want any more, just tell me. Of course, the season doesn't last long, but there are ways and means. With one lawmaker in the family, there ought to be a law-breaker too, just to balance things, oughtn't there? . . . Well, I must be pushing along. Compton's a good man, but we're likely to have a hard freeze this evening and I want to make sure he's overflowed the ditches. I generally stay up all night to look after such things myself. Bring Roger down for a week end sometime soon. Do you both good to see how the other half lives. I'll tell Sue about your offer. She'll appreciate it. So do I."

He departed in great good humor, leaving his niece in equally high spirits. She took one last look at the perfectly prepared dinner table, assured herself that the pantry was equally well ordered and started up-stairs. Priscilla had gone straight to her room, declining her cousin's offer of tea and saying she wanted to unpack. Emily had assured her that Ellie would do the unpacking, but Priscilla had looked so frightened at the sug-gestion that Emily had not insisted; now she decided to see how the poor girl was getting along before she herself began to dress. As she mounted to the second story, she was already busy with expansive plans for the following year.

There was no immediate answer when she knocked at the door of the little guest room where Roger's spool furniture had been installed. She opened the door part way, to be confronted by the sight of Priscilla, struggling into her bridesmaid's dress. One of its fastenings had caught on her bra and she stood, half smothered in lace and tulle, frantically trying to free herself, her back and head bent, her hands wrenching at the refractory hook. Stifling a laugh, Emily released her and pulled the dress down to its proper place, inevitably observing, while she did so, that Priscilla was beautifully built and that her skin, where it had not been ruthlessly exposed to the elements, was unusually soft and white. It was too bad she did not know what to do with her hair or what to put on. Her tight red curls were uncombed and the bridesmaid's dress, which had been so suitable for an ebalorate June wedding, would have looked en-tirely out of place for a small autumn dinner, even if it had retained its first freshness. But the tulle was now limp and the lace torn in several places. Evidently, the dress had been carelessly put away after the wedding and not even inspected again before it was tossed into a suitcase and brought back to Boston that day.

Emily experienced a momentary feeling of irritation because Priscilla had not been provided with something smart and seasonable in satin or velvet. This would not have necessitated so much as a special trip to town, for, with her figure, Priscilla could have stepped straight into any standard-sized model; an earlier start that morning would have been all that was necessary. And certainly expense was no object; if Priscilla had bought out a specialty shop, either Sherman or Sue could have paid the bill without wincing. Really, it was time somebody else in the family took hold and Emily was quite prepared to do so. But she knew she must proceed cautiously. She would have liked to offer Priscilla one of her own dresses, then and there, but this would hurt the girl's feelings and anyway, they would have been far too long, for Emily was the taller of the two. She did not even dare offer to mend the torn lace. Priscilla, still a bit breathless after her struggle, looked at her cousin with miserable eyes and put a piteous question to her.

"Emily, do I have to go down to dinner? Couldn't I have it up here on a tray, the way I had my tea?"

"My dear child, you've come on purpose for the party!"

"I know. But I didn't want to. I wouldn't have, if it hadn't been for keeping Daddy company when he brought the ducks. I don't like parties any better than he and Mummy do."

"Isn't it too soon to decide? You haven't been to many parties yet, have you? I really believe you'll like this one. And David Salomont would be terribly disappointed if he didn't see you again. You remember him, don't you? You and he had a good time together, at the wedding."

"Y-e-e-s, I remember him. But I don't believe he remembers me. And I don't believe he wants to see me again, even if he does. I couldn't think of anything to say to him before. He must have thought I was a Dumb Dora. I am too. I won't be able to think of anything to say tonight either."

"Don't you worry. David will do the talking, just as he did at the wedding. And he does remember you, truly he does. He told Roger he was looking forward to seeing you again."

Instead of appearing pleased at this information, Priscilla's expression became more terrified than ever. Emily was afraid that if she left her, the girl might actually lock herself in her room and decline to come out.

"Listen, Priscilla, it would help me a lot if you'd go down to the library right now. You're dressed already and I haven't so much as started to change. What's more, Roger isn't even in the house yet. If one of the guests happened to come early—"

"You mean I'd be all alone down there with some perfect stranger? Oh, Emily, I couldn't! Please—"

"It would only be for a few minutes. And one of us has got to be downstairs. You can turn on the radio—there's an awfully good program beginning at seven-fifteen. If a guest comes early, you can pretend you're so absorbed in it that you don't want to be interrupted."

"I don't like the radio. I never listen to it. I don't even know how to turn those knobs and things. . . . You haven't got a dog, have you, Emily? A dog would help a lot."

"No, I'm sorry. I haven't got a dog. Deirdre has a cat though. Would you like me to get Deirdre's cat?"

"No, I hate cats."

"Well, there's nothing else I can offer you from the animal kingdom, but I'll come down to the library with you and turn the radio on for you. You can make believe you like it, can't you?"

With less gentleness than she habitually showed, Emily propelled Priscilla, still protesting, down the stairs, installed her in the library and fairly fled to her own room. She was really short of time now, Roger was still absent and she knew the doorbell would be ringing any moment. Presently it did ring. If that were only David. . . . But it was not David. It was Caroline, who had come with Marion. Caroline's harsh voice penetrated to the second story.

"We're not to take our wraps upstairs? Are you sure? You look like a new maid. Probably you don't know. I always go upstairs."

"Please ma'am, I'm Deirdre's niece, Dolly, accommodating for the dinner. And Mrs. Field said, the ladies in the powder room, the gentlemen in the cloakroom."

Dolly sounded almost as frightened as Priscilla had, but her high-pitched voice also had a penetrating quality and it was clear that she was standing up to Caroline. Marion said something that was evidently conciliatory, though just what it was Emily could not hear, for Marion's tones were more subdued. Then the two guests were apparently ushered into the library and Emily's heart smote her, thinking of poor Priscilla. Emily had pulled on her dress hastily and now she was snapping her bracelets. Next would be her earrings, then just a dash of perfume and she could go down. She was screwing on the second earring when the doorbell rang again and Mrs. Putnam's hearty laugh sounded through the hallway.

"Who'da thunk it? Little Em'ly blossoming out like this, givin' dinners n'everything. Are you there, Em'ly? Oh—she hasn't come down yet. Why hello, Roger—are you invited to this party too? So's Jasper, so's Jasper. You remember Jasper, don't you? He's my husband and he comes to my parties, just like you're coming to Little Em'ly's. Only I make him come on time!"

If Mrs. Putnam's greeting to the returning master of the house were a sample of what could be expected of her throughout the evening, it had certainly been a mistake to invite her. But thank heaven, Roger was home at last, and evidently one of his fellow juniors had arrived at the same moment, for Emily could hear another male voice. Then there was a slight delay, suggesting that the host was apologetically introducing guests to each other before he came racing up the stairs. He and Emily met on the threshold of their room.

"I'm terribly sorry, darling. It's the same old story. Mr. Mills wasn't through with Miss Riley and I had to wait for her. There was a draft of a will that simply had to be finished tonight. But I thought of course you'd be ready."

"I would have been, except for Priscilla. I practically had a knock-down-and-drag-out fight to get her on the scene at all. Tell you about it later. I must dash now. . . . Who besides the Putnams came in at the same time you did?"

"Pell."

"Oh—I hoped it might be David. Well—hurry, won't you, Roger?"

"Of course."

He had unbuttoned his vest and undone his tie while they were talking and now he went hastily along, pulling off his coat. For the first time since their marriage, they had not even exchanged a kiss after a day's separation. Emily flew on down the stairs, dropping an earring she had put on with such speed that she had fastened it insecurely. It fell in front of her, exactly where she could not see, and she was obliged to stop and search for it. When she finally found it, she screwed it almost savagely into place and rushed along, reaching the bottom step just as Dolly opened the front door to admit David.

"Oh—I am glad to see you! Now everything will be all right."

"Of course everything will be all right. What do you mean?"

"I can't stop to explain now. Come on in with me!"

She had intended to greet her guests, rather formally, in the drawing room, where she had arranged the flowers and studied the lighting with the greatest care. But Priscilla had not stirred from her place by the radio and everyone else had naturally drifted out to the library. As Emily welcomed them all in turn, she noticed that the ash trays already indicated careless use, and that the company had that expectant and slightly thwarted look, suggesting that drinks have been too long delayed. Leaving David, who had competently made the rounds with her, to cope with the situation, she hurried to the pantry.

"You may begin serving the cocktails right away, Ellie. You'll have to manage alone. Dolly can't leave the door. Mr. Collins isn't here yet."

"Shall I just set the tray down and go back for the canapés, ma'am?"

"Yes—yes—I guess you'd better. Then, of course after Mr. Collins does come and you have Dolly to help you, you can both circulate, the way we planned."

"Would you just taste the Martinis for me, ma'am? Mr. Field said he would, to be sure they was all right, but he hasn't, and you know he's always made them himself before."

"Yes, I know. But I'm sure they're all right. Anyway, I can't stop, Ellie, I simply can't. And Mr. Field isn't downstairs yet. You must bring the cocktails right in."

Strange that Ellie, who had been so cheerful and capable up to that night, had apparently sensed that everything was not going as it should and had caught the prevailing malaise. Well, it could not be helped, and when Dolly was released, probably the two cousins would manage very well together. In the library, an atmosphere of stiffness still prevailed.

Caroline and Marion were seated side by side on one of the sofas which stood at right angles to the fireplace, Mr. and Mrs. Putnam on the other. Priscilla was still cowering in her corner. David had not rescued her; apparently he had started to do so when Mrs. Putnam had waylaid him, for she was leaning in his direction, telling one of her shady stories, while Mr. Putnam sat mute and uncomfortable beside her. Pell, graceful and attractive in spite of his ill-fitting clothes, was standing near Marion, talking to her quietly. His slight, but evident shyness was not unbecoming; it rather added to his appeal and Marion was responding to him more or less adequately. Caroline, like Mr. Putnam, sat in silence, but her silence, instead of being shamed, was grim.

Roger and the cocktails arrived almost simultaneously, and when he had taken charge of the mixer, and begun to dispense drinks with a hospitable hand, the strain in the atmosphere slackened. The Martinis were very good, after all; so were the canapés which Ellie brought in their wake— the small squares of toast thickly overlaid with caviar, the beaten biscuits stuffed with Virginia ham, the piping hot sausages wrapped in crisp bacon. David had successfully eluded Mrs. Putnam and reached Priscilla in her corner, Mr. Putnam had wandered over toward Caroline and said something about the weather to which she took no exception, and Marion and Pell seemed increasingly at ease with each other. Emily sat down on the sofa beside Mrs. Putnam, allowing the lively lady to rattle on, while she continued to glance from Roger, making his welcome rounds with the mixer, to the clock, whose hands now pointed to eight-fifteen.

She had told Deirdre she was sure they could count on getting to the table promptly at eight, with the guests invited for seven-thirty; and here was Brian Collins three quarters of an hour late already! What was worse, when he did come, he would want a drink—two or three of them, to judge by the way he had guzzled champagne at the wedding! The ducks would be utterly ruined, those beautiful ducks which Sherman had brought to her with such pride and which Deirdre by this time would have cooked to a turn! As for the soufflé, that would have to be omitted altogether. Deirdre had told Emily that she could keep one from falling for fifteen minutes, by putting a little tapioca in the mixture; but no one could keep a soufflé from falling for half an hour. . . . The next time Roger passed near her with his mixer, she whispered to him.

"Don't you think you'd better telephone the Collins' house? There must be some mistake."

He nodded, set down the mixer, which Mrs. Putnam immediately picked up, and went out to the rear hall. Emily, listening now instead of watching, caught only fragments of what he was saying. When he returned to the library, his expression was troubled. He spoke to Emily in a low voice.

"I talked with his mother. She said he left home more than an hour ago."

78

"Well, he had to come all the way from South Boston!"

"That doesn't take an hour, dear. It doesn't take half an hour even. I'm afraid there's been an accident."

"There's no way we can find out, is there? What shall we do?"

"I hate to sit down without him. It would be so awkward if he did turn up, for him to find us halfway through dinner. Couldn't we wait fifteen minutes longer?"

"Yes, I suppose so."

The poor ducks! The ill-fated soufflé! Well, anything was better than hurting Roger's feelings, when he was upset already. Emily was both watching and listening now—watching the clock again, listening for the telephone as well as the doorbell. But, by making a great effort, she managed to keep her mind on her duties as a hostess too. Adroitly, she shifted Pell to a place beside Mrs. Putnam, waiting for a chance to do so when she would not break in too abruptly on his conversation with Marion. Then she asked Marion to make room for Mr. Putnam between herself and Caroline—the sofa was such a large one, it was a pity not to have it used by three persons! Using this same persuasive argument, she drew David and Priscilla from their corner, saw Priscilla ensconced beside Pell and herself engaged David in small talk. The clock struck the half hour.

"I wouldn't worry about Brian if I were you," David said reassuringly. "He'll turn up all right."

"Roger's worrying about him. I'm not. I'm worrying about my dinner."

"Then I wouldn't worry about that, any longer."

"Evidently I don't have to. Dolly's opening the front door right now."

Her voice betrayed her relief; but this was short-lived. When the portieres parted, Brian Collins was revealed wearing a salt-and-pepper suit and red tie. However, this was not the worst; below his disordered hair, his face was flushed and his normally keen eyes were glazed. He looked about him and laughed loudly.

"Well now, a real party, is it? I thought it was going to be just us boys, getting together for a fine poker game, or the like of that. I've got glad rags myself at home, believe it or not, but I never bothered putting them on."

"We were getting worried about you, Brian," Roger said, still speaking in a troubled voice. "I telephoned your house and your mother told me you left home over an hour ago. Did you have an accident?"

"Accident? Accident? Never had an accident in my life. You did say seven-thirty, I remember that now. But then I knew you were always late getting home yourself, so I just stopped in to chew the rag and drink a drop with my cousin, Tim Tupperty, around the corner from the station. You ought to get to know Tim yourself, might come in handy sometime. Matter of fact, he does know you, halfway, seeing as he was one of the traffic cops at your wedding. What's more, he swears you must be the swell he pried loose from a drunk that latched onto you Christmas Eve."

79

"Unless you'd like another drink, Mr. Collins, we'll go out to dinner now. You're taking my sister-in-law, Miss Field. David, will you take Priscilla? And Mr. de Lucca, I have to separate you and Miss Swan after we get to the dining room, but you can have the pleasure of each other's company that far. Mrs. Putnam, you lead off with Roger, of course, and Mr. Putnam, you and I'll bring up the rear."

It was inexcusable to have said "another," Emily knew that. But she was angry, so angry that she had been obliged to force herself to give the conventional directions. Only that one word had come out spontaneously. She hoped that Brian Collins had realized its significance—and that Roger had not heard it. But anyway, she was not sorry for it. That clumsy clown, spoiling her dinner, not only because the food would be ruined on account of his lateness, but because he had insulted them all by his loud clothes and his tipsy talk! She understood now why Russell Forbes and Homer Lathrop and other men she knew so despised and hated the Irish. She had been prepared to like Brian for Roger's sake, she had even told her bridegroom on their wedding day that she did like this "flannelmouthed Mick." It had been a colossal lie. . . .

She did not blame Caroline for sitting so rigidly beside him, turning her head away. Emily would have done the same in her sister-in-law's place. But Brian Collins appeared quite undisturbed by Caroline's avoidance; indeed, he seemed to have found such a kindred spirit in Mrs. Putnam that he had promptly dismissed Caroline from his mind. During the long wait for his arrival, Mrs. Putnam had consumed a number of drinks herself; she was now in top form.

Nothing had happened to the soup; Deirdre had not been defeated there by Brian Collins. The clear green turtle was strong and hot, perfectly seasoned—and perfectly served. Now that Ellie had Dolly with her, she was more like herself again, as Emily had hoped she would be. Emily looked down toward the other end of the table, beyond the flowers and the silver birds and the tall epergne with its overhanging fruit, and saw that Roger and Marion were chatting quietly and contentedly. Priscilla and David were also getting on very well. Conscientiously, Emily applied herself to Mr. Putnam, leaving Pell free for Caroline. But the generous gesture was wasted. Caroline was now so obviously affronted that she would not talk to anyone. When the vol-au-vent of sea food came in, as unspoiled as the soup and complemented by Homer Lathrop's excellent Chablis, Emily relaxed a little and turned to Pell, giving voice to the bewilderment which had plagued her for so long.

"I'm ever so glad you could come tonight. And do you know, I have the strangest feeling that I've seen you before."

"But you did. At your wedding."

"No, I mean before that. It puzzled me when I saw you that day too. I've kept wondering about it. I'm annoyed with myself because I can't remember when and where it was."

"Then I must put an end to your annoyance. It is not suitable that lovely ládies should be annoyed, especially without reason. You saw me Christmas Eve, on Louisburg Square. I saw you too."

"Christmas Eve—"

"Yes. You were waiting for someone, I imagine—was it perhaps Roger? I think it must have been, for I saw him later too—on Joy Street, near this very house. At all events, you were standing in the bay window of your grandmother's drawing room, beside a big Christmas tree. You had on a golden-brown velvet dress and you looked very beautiful. But then I am sure you always look very beautiful."

Pellegrino made the remark about her beauty in the same calm, dispassionate way that he had said everything else as he helped himself to the overdone duck. So spoken, the words did not constitute a compliment, only a statement of fact. Emily realized this; nevertheless, she colored with pleasure. Of course, Roger had told her many times that she was beautiful, but that was because he was in love with her, which gave the declaration value, but no authenticity. If Pellegrino de Lucca thought she was beautiful, she really must be—a conclusion far from displeasing. Moreover, Roger expressed such appreciation only in moments of intimacy, when he and she were alone. He never could have made such a statement as Pellegrino's in the course of dinner party small talk; it would have caused him to feel shy and self-conscious even to try.

"Why, I was standing in Grandmamma's window waiting for Roger!" she said, tasting the duck which, unfortunately, so far fulfilled her worst fears that even the Pommard could not redeem it. She decided that perhaps it would be better to make no direct rejoinder to Pellegrino's final remark, much as she wished that she could have spoken in the same natural way that he did about her looks. Besides, her curiosity was still only half satisfied. "But where in the world were you?" she asked impulsively.

"Outside, in the street. With a group of my friends. We stopped beside the steps of your grandmother's house to sing. I think it was *Adeste Fideles* we sang there."

"*Adeste Fideles!* Of course! Then you were—" She checked herself suddenly. She could not say, "You were the man who made me think of Michelangelo's David, because you were so strikingly handsome." Yet the statement would have been no more candid and direct than the one he had just made about her beauty. Neither could she say, "I kept noticing the snowflakes on your hair," because it would indicate too close observation of a stranger, though now that the incident was recalled, she remembered those glistening crystals and those glossy curls very vividly. Pellegrino's hair was much more closely cut now; it still turned up crisply at the edges, but the curls were gone. Probably someone at the office had dropped a hint. . . . Yes, and she remembered what Homer Lathrop had said, "Some of those worthless Italians from St. Leonard's!" Illogically, since she was now more than prepared to agree with Homer about Brian, she wondered whether her trustee would still think Pellegrino worthless, since the young Italian had been taken into one of the best law firms in Boston after winning an eviction suit brought against the relatives with whom he lived. Then, perhaps the girl who had been with him on Christmas Eve, that lovely, lovely girl whom he had kissed, was just a relative, someone he took for granted, though it certainly had not looked that way. "You were the song leader," Emily continued, rather lamely and tardily. "And your singing was marvelous. I remember it all perfectly."

"Well then, you do not need to keep searching your memory or to be perplexed any longer. The puzzle is solved."

He smiled and half turned toward Caroline on his other side. Evidently he considered the reminiscence closed. Emily was not yet ready to do so, however. The salad had come in and there was no soufflé with it. Deirdre's cheese soufflés were really something out of this world, and now they must forego one, all on account of that unspeakable Irishman, who was guffawing at that very moment, oblivious of all the damage he had done or unconcerned by it. To be sure, Deirdre had shown great presence of mind. She had substituted *pâté de foie gras* and it was excellent. But that in no way exonerated Brian Collins.

"I remember both you and your song very well now," she said. "It was terribly stupid of me not to place you before. I don't see why I didn't."

Pellegrino turned toward her again. "But there's no reason why you should have," he said quietly. "After all, you saw dozens—probably hundreds—of street singers that night. And you weren't really paying much attention to them anyway. You were watching for Roger and your thoughts were on him. It was different in my case. I did not see dozens of beautiful girls dressed in golden-brown velvet, standing in bay windows beside Christmas trees. The vision of you was unique."

"But you had a very beautiful girl with you! I remember her perfectly too!"

Even before she finished speaking, Emily realized that Pellegrino's pleasant expression was becoming vague. He shook his head slightly, as if it were his memory which was now playing tricks.

"There were five or six girls in our group that night, as I recall it, and probably they were all pretty. It seems to be quite a habit with young Italian girls. I wouldn't know which one you mean."

"Why, you must! She was a great deal more than pretty! And besides—"

Again Emily checked herself. She could not say, "And besides, you had your arm around her all the time. Besides, she put up her hands to stroke your cheek, and when she dropped her shawl, you picked it up and wrapped it tenderly around her again. Besides, you and she kissed each other." As a matter of fact, she could not say anything, for the simple reason that Pellegrino had put a conclusive stop to their unfinished conversation by turning wholly away from her and beginning one with Caroline, who was no longer able to remain withdrawn in the face of his quiet persistence. But Mr. Putnam was hopeless. Across the void created by his silence, Emily listened to David and Priscilla.

"I don't know the first thing about raising cranberries. Tell me."

"Well, a cranberry bog isn't really wet—that is, not most of the time."

"Isn't it?"

"No, just in midwinter, when the waters have been released from the reservoirs to overflow the ditches. After that, of course you can't tell a bog from a pond until spring. But the cranberries are there, all safe, underneath."

"I'd like very much to come and see your bogs."

"Oh, would you really? You mean, when we're harvesting next fall? It is something of a sight then, with the men moving along among the bright green vines, on their knees, with their scoops in front of them, and the red berries tumbling over each other until the scoops are full."

"Do I really have to wait until next fall for an invitation? I thought maybe you'd ask me down for Thanksgiving dinner this year and let me help make the cranberry sauce."

Well, that combination at least was working out better than Emily had even dared to hope. David, who was so brilliant himself, was not talking down to Priscilla; in the kindest possible manner, he was drawing her out—which, after all, was the best possible way of revealing how brilliant he was. The champagne was bubbling up in the glasses now and the "rock rice" with hot raspberry sauce, a super ice cream which was one of Deirdre's own inventions, was being passed. In another ten minutes, Emily would be able to give the signal to leave the table, and this time she would lead the way straight into the drawing room, shepherding Mrs. Putnam—who was now as drunk as Brian—Caroline, Marion and Priscilla along with her, and quickly admonishing Roger to keep the men in the library as long as he could. But before Ellie and Dolly were halfway around the table, Mrs. Putnam's booming tones sounded through the pleasant, expectant hush which had followed the complimentary reception of Deirdre's pièce de résistance.

"Who do you suppose I ran into on the Square the other night, Em'ly? That scoundrelly antique dealer, Morris Brucker! And what do you think he had the nerve to tell me? That he'd just been having dinner with your grandmother!"

"But he had. They're old friends. He came over from New York on purpose to see her."

Emily spoke with a calmness that was no less effective because it was forced. David, who had looked up at the mention of his stepfather's name, now turned quietly back to Priscilla. But the pleasant hush had suddenly become a strained silence. Then Mrs. Putnam laughed.

"Well, do excuse me! Of course I didn't know. I used to spend a lot of

83

money with Brucker myself, when he first opened up that fancy shop of his in New York—not that I ever knew him socially. I stopped going to him because I found out he was a faker—claiming all that loot he had came right out of the Czar's palace! Some of it may have, but if it did, I bet he stole it, and there was a lot of junk in with the good stuff. Besides, he was getting away with murder, the prices he asked."

"My grandmother has some of the things that came out of the Winter Palace too, Mrs. Putnam, and I can assure you—"

"Oh, I know she didn't steal! She had other ways of getting what she wanted—and how! And maybe Brucker didn't exactly steal either. After all, I guess he's reasonably honest—for a Jew."

Emily had precipitately risen and with her everyone else at the table, except Mrs. Putnam and Brian. David was still talking quietly to Priscilla when Caroline, with a frozen expression, accepted Pell's arm and Roger offered his to Marion. Mr. Putnam, oblivious to his hostess, plunged in the direction of his wife, reaching her side just as Brian seized her by the shoulder.

"Shut your trap!" he shouted. "You think I'm going to let you sit there and insult my friends? I can tell you that old Forbes gal may have had her moments, but she never was the bitch you are. Something else: David's dad is as straight as they come and his money's a lot cleaner than yours. I know, see? You'd better take my word for it and say you're sorry!"

Chapter 8

THE HORRIBLE FAILURE of her first party was not only a severe blow to Emily's pride, it was a source of very genuine distress to her, on Roger's account. She had never doubted her ability to be helpful to him, and she visualized this helpfulness in terms of tact toward his associates quite as much as in terms of tenderness toward himself. Yet her *savoir-faire* had not sufficed to save the dinner from disaster.

With a dexterity which suggested previous practice, Mr. Putnam had managed to get his wife out of the house before Brian's outburst could result in a serious altercation; Pell was similarly successful in dealing with Brian. Immediately after their removal, Caroline remarked cuttingly to Roger that of course it would be unthinkable for her and Marion to remain when such a scene had taken place; and though Marion tried to soften the statement with gentler excuses, it was obvious that she was also glad to escape. Neither Roger nor Emily made any effort to detain them; and with the group reduced to David, Priscilla and their hosts, the tension in the atmosphere slackened. David glanced at his watch.

"It seems to be a little on the late side for a show," he said, as casually as if there had been some previous question of going to one. "But what about dancing for a while? We'd hit it just about right at the Copley."

The suggestion proved a godsend. The festive atmosphere of the ballroom at the Copley Plaza precluded any sort of serious conversation; and, by the time they finally started home, they were all much too tired for any. David said good night at the door of the Joy Street house, after suggesting to Priscilla that he might take her to a matinee the following afternoon and drive her back to the Cape afterward, with dinner along the way—an invitation which she accepted with mingled shyness and astonishment, not untinged with delight. Then, as if fearful that either Roger or Emily might try to dissuade her from going out unchaperoned with a comparative stranger, she bolted to her room and stubbornly remained there. When they reached the threshold of their bedroom, Roger and Emily paused, by mutual impulse, and put their arms around each other, saying almost the same thing at almost the same time.

"Let's not try to talk about it until morning, darling."

Secretly, each thought that morning would not be a good time either, because Roger would have to hurry off to the office and Emily would still be drowsy; and secretly, each was glad that this was so: the longer the evil moment could be put off, the better. After Roger had left, Emily tried to go back to sleep and had almost succeeded when Deirdre appeared, staggering under the weight of an enormous azalea plant, which she claimed, not without reason, was too heavy for Ellie to carry. She then proceeded to hang around until Emily had read the attached note from Mrs. Putnam, who was just too sorry for words that she had made such an awful break the night before. Of course she never dreamed that Morris Brucker was any relation to David Salomont, who was most attractive. In fact, she never dreamed that David was a Jew. She didn't think anyone would, if it weren't for his name, and she hadn't caught that. Even if she had, she might not have recognized it as Jewish, because all the Jews she had ever heard of were named Cohen or Levy or something like that. Jasper said that Salomont was a very fine old Portuguese name, but just the same she thought David ought to change it, the way so many Jews did. Then he'd be invited everywhere. And anyway, she was going to ask him to dinner at her house and make up for her awful faux pas. Naturally, she would expect the Fields, too, and she would call up very soon and fix a date. And she was most affectionately. . . .

Emily tore the note into small pieces and tossed them into the scrap basket. "There isn't any message," she said. "You needn't wait, Deirdre. And, if it isn't too heavy for you, take that hideous plant to the kitchen."

"Sure and it's a fine, handsome plant, Mrs. Field. Why wouldn't you be wanting it yourself?"

"I don't, that's all," Emily said, speaking a little sharply to Deirdre for the first time. "And by the way, if Mrs. Putnam calls up, say I'm not at home. Tell Ellie that's what she's to do too. And don't disturb me again. I'm trying to get some sleep. I don't feel well."

Deirdre departed, bearing the plant and sniffing slightly. It was clear to her that this was no time to argue with the lady of the house, or even to suggest that she might "offer up" her alleged indisposition. Emily did not go back to sleep, but she lay still for some time, dwelling resentfully on the showy plant and the tactless note; simultaneously, with feminine inconsistency, she told herself that if Brian Collins had been possessed of a single saving grace, he would have sent her some token of apology. Eventually, conscious of her lack of logic, and slightly amused at it, she dismissed both offenders from her mind and settled down to hard thinking along more objective lines. Obviously, dinner parties were not the best means of bringing alien elements harmoniously together; it would be folly to attempt anything more along the same line. On the other hand, she could not admit herself beaten after her first attempt to make the house on Joy Street a center of good feeling and a place where better understanding could be promoted. She must keep on trying until she had found the right solution for the problem, and she wanted to find it for herself, without help or advice from anybody.

The daily walks which she took as a matter of course seemed to furnish the best opportunities for reflection. During the beautiful days of Indian summer, she frequently cut across the Common to the Public Garden and, sitting down near the little lake, where she and Roger had ridden on the swan boats together when they were children, deliberated the questions which troubled her. The crowds that thronged the Garden did not distract her; their character had changed very little through the years and she took their presence for granted. Gradually she realized, however, that there were fewer and fewer people crossing the bridge and wandering along the gravel walks, fewer still reading and resting on the park benches. The men who sold balloons and pinwheels had disappeared, the swan boats had stopped running, the fountains no longer played and the flower beds were covered with burlap. The babies in the perambulators, wheeled by smartly caped nurses, were so bundled up that only the tips of their noses were visible between their woolly bonnets and their knitted blankets; and the nurses began to have a chapped, chilled look which their prim head-dresses accentuated. Chilled herself, Emily abandoned the Garden.

After that, she most frequently walked along the crest of the Hill to Louisburg Square, going by Mount Vernon or Chestnut Street and returning by Pinckney, for no better reason than the vague feeling that this was the natural way to proceed. Nothing on any of these streets interested her particularly; their attributes—the big gray stone church, the large buildings which served as headquarters for various important organizations, the fine old houses still occupied by private families and those of less prosperous appearance which were divided into apartments or let, room by room, to transient lodgers—had the same elements of familiarity as those of the Public Garden, without the latter's appeal to her. Several of the fine old houses belonged to friends of hers, and she knew they would welcome her at any time she cared to drop in; but she was not in the mood for general visiting. She did go, occasionally, to see her grandmother; but though Emily could have confided in Old Mrs. Forbes more easily than in her mother, the fact that such a confidence would have been an admission of failure, instead of a revelation of success, kept her silent on the subject of her problems. She wanted to wait until she could speak not only candidly, but pridefully. More than once when she had started out with Old Mrs. Forbes' house as her intended destination, she went instead to the chapel in St. Margaret's Convent; but somehow Homer Lathrop's cynical remark to the effect that he hoped she was not "seriously interested in religion," that such an interest was "just a passing phase," which almost every girl went through, kept coming, unbidden, to the forefront of her consciousness. If the sensation of peace and the seeming awareness of Divinity which came to her almost instantly after she entered the chapel, tranquilizing her and uplifting her as long as she remained there, were only part of a "passing phase" she could not depend on them for succor and support. She wanted to believe in their permanence and reality; but her faith in them had been undermined and she could not. One morning, when she was leaving the chapel, she did so with the sorrowful knowledge that she was not going back there unless and until her doubts about the validity of her feeling for it had been stilled.

Since the one time when her curiosity about Pell had taken her over the crest of the Hill, Emily had never again surveyed the northern slope of Joy Street; she had felt afterward as if she had been too inquisitive and was slightly ashamed of this. Pell's noncommittal answers on the night of dinner had increased her conviction that she should not pry into his private life, however much this intrigued her. But the day after her decision about the chapel, having hesitated for a moment as to the direction she should take for her constitutional, she started down the unfamiliar thoroughfare. In most ways, it seemed just the same as it had been before: there were still lines of dingy laundry flapping in the breeze and dirty scraps of paper blowing about. The fire escapes were still cluttered with rubbish and the garbage cans still stood, unemptied, on the corners. But the district was now unredeemed even by the evidences of neighborliness which had given it some stray aspects of cheer when she had seen it the first time. There were no more men sitting in their shirt sleeves beside open doorways, passing the time of day with each other, no more women leaning out of upper-story windows and gossiping, in a leisurely manner, with other women, leaning out of other windows. It was too cold for that now. Traffic was heavy and trucks, taxicabs and delivery wagons impeded each other's progress as they swarmed down the Hill, the drivers honking their horns and shouting and swearing at each other. The battered brick sidewalks were crowded, too, by pedestrians for the most part laden with heavy bundles or miscellaneous small packages, who seemed to have caught the feeling of urgency from the drivers, and who pushed and panted as they went along. But neither the drivers nor the pedestrians were really part of the locality; only the children playing with their rubber balls in the concrete courtyard which separated the Peter Faneuil School from the street seemed to belong there.

Emily stopped by the iron railing which served as a fence for the yard and watched these children. Evidently it was recess time, but they did not seem to be taking advantage of this to play any real games; they simply bounced their rubber balls, caught them, and bounced them again. Sometimes a ball, thrown with unusual force or revealing unexpected resiliency, soared beyond a child's reach. Then he pursued it. But he entered into no competition with his fellows, he kept no score of his successes; he merely went on and on, futilely bouncing his ball.

While Emily stood wondering what profit or pleasure there could be in such a pastime, a ball skimmed over the iron railing, struck the uneven pavement and rebounded into the crowded street. Before it had touched the sidewalk, a little boy rushed through the gate after it; but he did not catch up with it in time to prevent the second bound. He leaped from the curb and darted directly in front of a plumber's truck.

Above the wail of locked brakes and screaming tires, there was a loud shout, followed by lesser cries and by the honking of horns. Then the tumult ended abruptly in terrible silence.

The child had been struck, but not run over; he lay on his side and from underneath his head a tiny stream of blood trickled slowly over the pavement. Emily reached the small, limp form at the same moment that the driver jumped down from his seat. The silence had ended as abruptly as the tumult and there was confusion of sound again. Emily, with her horrified gaze on the prostrate child, was dimly aware of another girl kneeling beside her and of two tall, blue-clad figures looming directly behind her; then of a single voice of authority in the midst of the babel.

"Don't touch that kid, any of you. We'll have First Aid here in a minute and it's for them to say what to do. Jim, get through a call for an ambulance on the double and put one of the other boys at the corner to untangle this traffic jam. And let's have less noise around here. Stand back there, every one of you, except the driver and these two. Now let's see your license, bud."

The driver thrust a shaking hand into his hip pocket and from this extracted a worn wallet which he opened with fumbling fingers. While the policeman inspected the proffered license, the frightened truckman jabbered excitedly.

"Jeez, officer, I just turned into Joy from Myrtle, I was still in second. Brakes okay too, or I couldn't have stopped like I did. But that kid come out in front of me from nowhere."

"That's true, officer. The little boy was running after his ball."

Emily had turned from the child to look up at the remaining policeman. He answered her tersely.

"You saw it happen, did you, Mrs. Field?"

"Yes. I was standing by the fence, watching the children play," she replied quickly, without even noticing that he had called her by name. "This little boy ran right in front of me, so close that I tried to catch hold of him. I couldn't, he went so fast. But do you mind if I take a look at him? I've had some experience in nursing."

"One of them Gray Ladies?" The question was contemptuous.

"No. Nurse's Aide and Frontier Service in Kentucky."

"Okay. Go ahead. I guess you can't hurt him anyway."

Emily turned back to the child and put her fingers on his thin wrist. Then she gave a little cry of gladness.

"I can feel his pulse. It's slow, but it's steady."

Another shout went up from the crowd which, though it had retreated, had not dispersed and had, indeed, increased in size. The children had not gone back to their schoolrooms when a bell announced the end of recess, and they were trying to edge forward and get a glimpse of their stricken playmate. Two or three plainly clad, bespectacled teachers, conscientious and troubled, were trying to restrain these unruly youngsters and, at the same time, determine for themselves the gravity of the accident. Both men and women, in various stages of dress and undress, had streamed out of the tenement houses across the way and were gesticulating frantically as they talked rapidly and disjointedly to each other in several strange tongues. The driver of the repair truck, mopping his brow, gave vent to a string of oaths expressive of thanksgiving. The policeman raised his hand.

"I said less noise around here. On your way, everyone who doesn't live in these parts. I still don't want the kid moved. He may be alive all right, but that's not saying no bones are broken. And move along, the rest of you. Except you, Mrs. Field. . . . And you, miss. Did you see this happen too?"

The officer was now addressing the second kneeling girl. With her hand still on the little boy's wrist, Emily turned again and again she gave a little cry, this time one of surprise. She had been slow to identify Pell, but now recognition was immediate: the girl beside her was the same one who had been with him on Christmas Eve. There was no mistaking that rare, madonnalike type of beauty. . . .

"No, not everything from close by, like the lady here," the Italian girl was saying, speaking rather haltingly. She had a sweet voice, but she spoke with a strong accent and it was evident that she had to grope for the right words. "I was standing at the window. I live right there, across the street." She motioned in the direction of a tenement house and once more Emily was struck with the grace of her movements. "I know the driver is telling the truth. I saw Pietro run after his ball too. It was a new ball and—"

"You the kid's sister?"

"No, he's not a relation. But—"

"You went through the crowd like you'd been shot out of a gun. If I hadn't 'a thought you was his sister or something, I wouldn't 'a let you stay. What's the rest of his name?"

"Danielli. And please let me stay, even if he isn't a relation. I know him very well. His mother is our neighbor. She goes out to work, so we try to help her take care of him."

"Who's 'we'?

"My mother and my brother and myself. Pietro's mother will think we did not take good care of him this time and. . . . Couldn't I please put my shawl over him at least? It's so cold and he's so little."

The girl's sweet voice ended in a low sob. The officer spoke more gently.

"Sure, that's a good idea. And look, he ain't dead. He ain't even bleeding any more. And kids like him has got nine lives anyway. At that, I guess I'd better take your name as a witness of the accident. What is it? I know your address already."

"Simonetta de Lucca."

She was absorbed in arranging her shabby shawl so that it would cover Pietro as completely as possible. She did not even look at the officer as she answered.

"Simon—you'd better spell it."

She glanced up and tried, docilely enough, to do as she was told. But the letters of the unfamiliar alphabet came so slowly and indistinctly from her lips that the officer had difficulty in following them. The pencil with which he was writing in a small book moved more and more slowly and then came to a stop.

"Perhaps I can help," suggested Emily. "S-i-m-o-n-e-t-t-a d-e L-u-c-c-a. That's right, isn't it?"

"Yes, that is right. I thank you very much, lady."

Evidently Simonetta felt no astonishment because her name was known to a passer-by and no curiosity as to how this happened. Her passive acceptance of the fact struck Emily as strange until she realized she had hitherto accepted the officer's recognition of herself in almost the same matter-of-course way and that she was no longer inclined to do so.

"Would you need to use my name too?" she inquired as casually as possible.

"Could be. But of course I knew that already: Mrs. Roger Field, and I know your Joy Street address too. No reason why you should remember me. In case it would be handy for you to get in touch with me later on though, I'm Tupperty, Tim Tupperty. . . . Well, have a look here now, will you?"

Emily and Simonetta both followed the direction of the officer's pointing finger. The little boy whom they had, momentarily, ceased to watch with the same closeness that they had at first, was stirring uneasily, but with no indication of pain. After first moving his shoulders slightly, he flung out his arms and drew up his legs, turning restlessly from side to side, as if he found the pavement uncomfortable. Then he opened his eyes and looked up into Simonetta's face, putting his hand to his head as he did so.

"What happened?" he asked in a puzzled whisper.

"You ran after your ball, caro, and you forgot to take care. A truck was coming and it hit you."

"But I'm all right now, except my head hurts a little."

As if to prove that what he said was true, Pietro pushed away the shawl and tried to sit up. Officer Tupperty put a restraining hand on his shoulder.

"Not so fast there. It's a fine scare you've given us all and I'm not so sure that we're out of the woods yet, but there's the ambulance coming now and we'll find out."

The shrill sound of a siren drowned out his final words and the crowd scattered as the ambulance tore down the Hill and came to an abrupt stop.

Two policemen leaped from it, nodded to Tim Tupperty and, bending over Pietro, inspected the cut on the child's head.

"Just a surface wound," one of them said encouragingly. "A touch of Mercurochrome and a bit of Band-aid will fix that up in no time. Don't worry, sonny. It won't hurt you none. But we're going to take you along with us, see, just to make sure there's nothing else wrong."

"Where to?"

"Over to M. G. H., right around the corner. You'll like it there."

For the first time, Pietro's under lip quivered and again he looked appealingly at Simonetta.

"Can't I go home with you, Etta? You could take care of me."

"I could try, caro. But I think perhaps this time I should go with you instead of taking you with me. You will let me go with Pietro to the hospital, will you not, *signori?*"

"The kid's mother works out," Tim Tupperty said in an undertone. "This girl and her family look after him."

The officer, who had finished putting the Band-aid neatly into place and, with his companion's help, taken a stretcher from the ambulance, nodded again.

"Sure. She can go along. Now, if you'll just lie still, sonny, me and Ned'll roll you over on this nice little number and we'll get going."

"Couldn't I go to the hospital too, Mr. Tupperty? I'd like to be of some help if I could."

"And say, officer, now that we know the kid ain't hurt bad, couldn't I get going too? There's a big leak in the house where I was headed and the whole place'll be flooded if I don't fix it pretty damn soon."

The two requests came almost simultaneously. Tim answered the plumber first.

"Okay. I can always get hold of you if I want to. Just wait for the ambulance to clear. . . . You couldn't do anything if you did go to the hospital, Mrs. Field. Probably they wouldn't even let you see the kid. This De Lucca girl, she's different—like his own folks, you might say, even if they aren't really related."

The ambulance shot off, making the same shrill sound with which it had approached, and less noisily, but almost as speedily, the repair truck followed down the Hill. As she walked away in the opposite direction, Emily was conscious of curious glances and whispered comments from the onlookers who still lingered in the street. However, nobody spoke to her and she went home feeling not only shaken, but rebuffed. The incident added to her general state of unrest. The next day she went to the hospital, where the receptionist received her coldly, and told her that it was against the rules to give out information about the patients, except to members of their immediate family. The following week she went to the tenement house where the De Luccas and the Daniellis lived, but there was no answer at the Daniellis' flat, and the middle-aged woman who answered her ring at the De Luccas' either spoke practically no English or pretended that this was the case. Eventually, Simonetta appeared, apologetically. She was sorry she had not been able to come to the door immediately herself, she said, but she had just gone out on the fire escape to bring in the laundry. Yes, Pietro was doing very well—in fact, he had already left the hospital and was back in school. The X rays had revealed no broken bones and the cut on his head was healing rapidly. It was very kind of the lady to inquire, but no, he needed nothing. She spoke with the utmost politeness, but she did not ask Emily to come in and there was a certain unmistakable finality in the way she said good-by.

Emily continued to worry about Pietro and to wish she could do something to improve his lot. The fact that he had escaped injury once did not mean he would always do so, unless the conditions under which he lived changed for the better; and these were no worse than the conditions under which dozens—hundreds—of other children dwelt, who were her neighbors. If Simonetta would have accepted her as a friend, she might have found a way of reaching out to these children; but Simonetta, in spite of her grave courtesy, had made it very clear that she did not wish to continue the chance acquaintance. Emily thought of appealing to Pell, but was prevented by pride. After all, there was a limit to the number of rebuffs she could accept.

Nevertheless, Simonetta herself had become an increasingly enigmatic figure and as such, an increasingly provocative one. De Lucca was not a common name among the Italians of Boston and, in any event, Emily knew that Pell lived with relatives. Simonetta had spoken of a brother to Tupperty; but she could not have been referring to Pell when she did this —or at least, so Emily persistently told herself. Conceivably, he and Simonetta might be cousins, brought up like brother and sister, though there had been nothing to suggest such an unromantic relationship in their attitude toward each other. To be sure, marriages between cousins were by no means rare among the old Boston families; but such marriages did not occur, as far as Emily knew, either between young men and young girls who had lived all their lives under the same parental roof, or between young men and young girls who loved each other so passionately that they embraced, with abandon, on the street—and still went unwed, year after year. Yet Pell and Simonetta were doing both these things. It was puzzling, it was shocking, it was almost abnormal—at least, it was certainly puzzling, and it would have seemed both shocking and abnormal were it not for the inescapably spiritual quality in the beauty of the two young Italians. It was impossible to associate evil, much less depravity, with either Pell or Simonetta. . . .

There remained Tim Tupperty, whom Emily could have dismissed easily enough from her mind if it had not been for his connection with Brian Collins. In that case, there was no question about the relationship; the two proudly proclaimed themselves cousins and they were boon companions to boot. They drank and gambled together; probably they did worse, to each other's ribald amusement. Tim Tupperty doubtless owed his position on the police force to some form of political graft, or else profited by this position to practice graft himself. And what was true of Tim Tupperty must be correlatively true of Brian Collins. His connection with the firm of Cutter, Mills and Swan must be due to favors received; and he must be taking advantage of the freedom from suspicion which the firm gave him to line his own pockets and those of his innumerable relatives. Emily despised him and she could not understand why she did not stop thinking about him.

It was all very different from what she and Roger had planned. She did not want Brian for a friend and Pell did not want to be hers. Only David was friendly and he did not need her friendship; she had never met anyone so self-assured and so self-satisfied. It was all very puzzling. She was sorry she had decided never to return to St. Margaret's Chapel. Whatever Homer Lathrop thought, she could not help feeling that if she had gone there long enough, she might have found understanding and wisdom as well as peace.

Chapter 9

ONLY ONE PERSON gauged the degree of Emily's distress or guessed some of the reasons for it. Emily's parents had continued to make their headquarters in Dublin throughout the autumn, so the "horrible little Gloucester Street house" was still unopened and unoccupied; and, in any case, Emily had never felt sufficiently close to her mother to confide in her easily, nor had Eleanor Thayer ever revealed much initiative in regard to her daughter's problems. But Old Mrs. Forbes, with a mercy she would have shown no one else, while making no direct allusion to the girl's perturbed state of mind, adroitly sought to divert Emily's thoughts.

"What are you doing about the first Waltz Evening?" she inquired when the two were lunching together, without guests, according to their not infrequent custom.

"I don't know. I hadn't thought much about it. The invitation only came this morning."

"Then you haven't made any plans for dinner beforehand?"

"No. I don't seem to be in just the right mood for giving dinners."

"No one expects a bride to keep giving dinners all the time, or to devote herself exclusively to philanthropy. People in your set ought to be giving dinners for you. Naturally, your father and mother can't do anything, as long as they unreasonably stay on in the country and, even if they were here, they couldn't do much in that horrible little Gloucester Street house; what's more, I don't want to foster the idea that I've got a monopoly on you. But Homer Lathrop gives very nice dinners at the Somerset Club, as you must remember. The food's very creditable there. Of course, those private dining rooms on the second floor are about the last word in gloom, but they do have a certain cachet. I think it would be highly suitable for Homer to give a small party at the Somerset Club before the first Waltz Evening."

"I hope you won't suggest it to him if he doesn't come across of his own accord."

"Why not? Will you please tell me, Emily Field, how there could be a better time to make suggestions to a thoughtless man than when he doesn't do anything on his own initiative?"

Emily laughed, and when she did so, some of the strain within her eased. But, as she reached for a cigarette, without making any immediate answer, her grandmother asked her another question, meanwhile twisting around the signet ring which she now wore constantly.

"There isn't any special reason, is there, why you're not interested in dancing? A reason that you thought you might tell me two or three months from now when there wouldn't be any need of it? In other words, to quote Maurice Hewlett, I hope you'll proclaim your condition before your condition proclaims you."

"I would, if there were anything to proclaim. But there isn't, I'm sorry to say."

To her intense chagrin, Emily blushed as she spoke. Her grandmother, observing her critically, realized that the girl's annoyance over the failure of a dinner party did not wholly account for her perturbed state of mind; she was acutely disappointed because there was, as yet, no prospect of a child.

"Well, don't talk as if you were verging on change of life," Old Mrs. Forbes said briskly. "After all, you're only twenty-two and you haven't been married six months yet. Most brides are very thankful when things turn out this way. In fact, nowadays a good many of them are pretty careful to see that they do."

"I know. But I wasn't. I'm not. Roger and I want children—several children. And when husband and wife both feel like that, don't you think it's—well, reassuring if—if—"

She was not only blushing now, her voice was trembling too. She reached for a glass of water and found that her hand was shaking.

"If a girl begins to lose her breakfast before she's home from her wedding trip?" Old Mrs. Forbes inquired tartly, so that Emily would think she had not noticed. "Why yes, I suppose it is 'reassuring.' But it certainly doesn't add to the glamour of the situation."

"I'd rather have the reassurance than the glamour. And some girls never lose their breakfast. Somehow, I don't believe you did, Grandmamma."

She was speaking and acting more naturally again, Old Mrs. Forbes observed with relief. She was distressed herself when Emily was troubled, though she would never have been able to make anyone believe it, and indeed would not have wished anyone to do so. Her relief increased as Emily went on talking more and more normally.

"I'll call up Uncle Homer myself. I was going to anyway. I need some more money. That's the worst of a spring trousseau—it doesn't provide for things like fur coats and my old one is a sight. It wouldn't ever do to wear for a Waltz Evening. Thanks, Grandmamma, for the lunch—and the good advice—all you gave me and all you didn't. I don't know which I appreciated more."

Homer Lathrop put no obstacles in the way of a new fur coat, even when Emily told him she thought it had better be mink this time—mink was so practical, you could wear it for anything and everything. Moreover, he was most receptive to the suggestion of a dinner at the Somerset Club before the first Waltz Evening—his only regret was that he hadn't beaten her to the draw, as of course he should have done. They discussed a guest list, first over the telephone and then over a cup of tea. Roger, coming in from the office even later than usual, found them deep in a conversation into which he entered himself without much spirit. He too had been troubled by the fiasco of the first little party; and the fact that he had found it difficult to discuss this with Emily added to his distress. He had supposed that they would always talk everything over freely; that such discussions would not only result in a solution of problems, but in closer and closer communion. Yet nothing had been solved in regard to his relations with his fellow juniors, and suddenly Emily seemed remote from him, as she sat there talking with Homer Lathrop on a subject, which, because of his lateness, required explanation before he could enter into the conversation at all. He was very tired, he was not in the mood to welcome a guest—above all a guest who treated him with condescension in his own house. He did not want to go to dinner at the Somerset Club and he had always detested the Waltz Evenings. But he could not put these feelings into words. Instead, he had to say it was very kind of Mr. Lathrop, that he was most appreciative and that he thought a Waltz Evening would be just the right occasion for Emily to christen a new mink coat. (A coat which he was not buying for her, the sort of coat he probably never could buy for her.)

If he had not felt so uneasy about his progress at the office, his mood might well have been different, or he might have been able to throw this off on his return to a comfortable home and a cheerful wife. But, day after day, he was dispatched on errands, charged with delivering or filing papers which he thought could just as well have been mailed, and sent to look up information which, in many instances, he could have obtained more easily and quickly by telephone. He could not escape the suspicion that some trips were more or less invented to occupy him. Most of his time in the office was spent in looking up doubtful points of law, and when he had finished with these, they appeared no less doubtful than when he had begun. He was allowed to write letters demanding the payment of overdue accounts, to draft simple contracts and to prepare briefs. But none of his drafts was accepted as a finished product and none of his work was creative.

His feeling of frustration was intensified by the general atmosphere of the office. Instead of finding this stimulating, he found it disheartening. Everything about it seemed oppressive, from its physical attributes to the rigid protocol by which the three seniors, the two partners whose names did not yet appear in that of the firm and the four juniors were firmly placed above and below the salt. It was logical, of course, that Mr. Cutter and Mr. Mills should have fine corner offices, with windows on two sides, and that Mr. Swan, who came next in seniority, should occupy quarters almost as spacious, though less light and airy, between the two; also that Elliot Berkeley and Cyrus Fletcher, the two subordinate partners, should have the benefit of daylight, even though the library and the conference room, which were on the same open side of the building, necessarily left them somewhat cramped. But it seemed to Roger that somehow it should have been possible to redeem the cubicles occupied by the juniors and the clerical staff from the same stuffy gloom which pervaded the long central corridor into which all the individual rooms led, beyond the elevators, the switchboard and the small reception hall. A fresh breeze blowing through, a square of sunlight on his desk, would have worked wonders for his morale. So would a word from one of his superiors to the effect that it was a matter of regret that they did not have more to offer their juniors in the way of creature comfort, but that plans for the future included improvement along those lines, in keeping with their general policy of progressiveness. . . . Meanwhile, they hoped there were compensations.

There were no compensations, nor was there anything especially progressive about the general policy of the firm, as far as Roger had been able to discover. Neither had he found much evidence of those "idealistic standards" about which he had heard so much beforehand; and nothing he had heard or seen had helped him to overcome his depression and sense of futility. As a matter of fact, he still felt as if he hardly knew the senior partner, who came in on a late train from Chestnut Hill every morning, and left early, at least three afternoons in the week, to go rowing from the Union Boat Club. Roscoe Cutter was a big man, with abundant iron-gray hair and a ruddy countenance, who spoke in a loud voice and bore himself like a motion picture actor cast as a ship's captain. Almost everyone in the office was afraid of him and he was not above taking advantage of this fear to achieve desired results from his subordinates. But his blustering manner took on a different quality with the officers of his corporate clients, to whom he was always hail-fellow-well-met and never the big bully; while among the boon companions with whom he regularly rowed were the most important of these clients. The only time he had summoned Roger to his office, he had been preoccupied with adding coal to the fire, which he kept burning brightly under a stone mantel decorated with a heraldic design. This fireplace, one of the few still operating in the building, was obviously a source of great pride to Mr. Cutter and it was only belatedly that he remembered he had sent for Roger to file a revised list of the Acme Wool Company's directors. Occasionally he dispatched a memorandum, which was typed and delivered by his secretary, Miss Elsie Smythe, an angular, elderly spinster. But, after dispatching such a communication, he usually forgot that too.

Roger found himself thinking enviously of Bradford Olcott, a classmate who—as he tardily discovered—had been offered the job which he now held himself. Brad had turned it down and struck off independently to a small city in Vermont where he had opened his own office. He had written Roger jokingly about his first case: a farmer's wife was suing her husband for divorce because he had spanked her. The spanking, so the farmer claimed, had been administered only after his stubborn spouse had declined to press his pants, and this was freely admitted; but it next transpired that the reason the man wanted his pants pressed was because he was taking the hired girl to a chicken pie supper at Odd Fellow's Hall!

Roger had smiled rather ruefully when he first read this letter and he had reread it a number of times. Obviously, Brad's first case had been humorous rather than rewarding; but it was his own case and he had won it. He had not spent all his time acting as someone's errand boy or poring over old statutes in books which were, literally, as dry as dust. And it might be twenty below zero in Vergennes, but the air had a sparkle as well as a sting to it and the white snow was dazzling in the sunshine. Roger, who was seeking to resolve an intricate point in a minor bankruptcy case for Mr. Mills, found his thoughts straying from the dull subject to dwell with increasing envy on Bradford Olcott's invigorating freedom. If he had only come to regard Mr. Mills himself with more respect, Roger would have been less prone to such mental insubordination. But he had found absolutely nothing to admire in the evasive character of this plausible and pretentious attorney. He resented the frequent absences of Mr. Mills on unexplained business trips and the cavalier fashion in which he shunted the detail work of his own cases onto the desks of the hapless juniors, especially as the suits were of petty nature. Most of all, Roger resented the adroit way in which Mr. Mills assumed all the credit for such cases, when these were won by his subordinates, and shifted all the blame on them when the cases were lost.

"Old Artful Dodger's the only one who brings in chicken coop litigation," David grumbled to Roger one day when they were in the library together. "He can smell a penny from here to Pawtucket, so he never says no to a case, even if it's a suit to recover the value of a cut clothesline. Then he slips the work to us. But he takes the cut of the fee for himself, because it's 'business' he brought into the firm. One of these fine days. . . ."

Recalling David's outburst, Roger smiled faintly. He was still seeking to resolve that intricate point in a minor bankruptcy case for Mr. Mills, and the task was one on which he had already spent more than two hours, apparently without getting one whit closer to the desired goal. Unless he could achieve something definite in the way of progress within the next few minutes, he would have to stay late at the office again; and this was the night of the first Waltz Evening, when he and Emily were to dine at the Somerset Club with Homer Lathrop! The shrill summons of his telephone broke in upon his mood of dismay.

"Mr. Mills wants to see you in his office," the switchboard operator informed him.

Roger knew exactly what would happen next. He would be chided for "devoting so much time to a simple matter of elementary practice" and asked how much longer he would require. He would then be reminded that he was not being asked to prepare a brief for the Supreme Court and told that, in Mr. Mills' day, it was presumed that a Harvard graduate could at least look up the Index in Corpus Juris. Probably he should have asked advice from David, who was so much more quick witted and more experienced than himself, or even from Mr. Swan, the only one of the three firm members about whom Roger found nothing to resent and who had treated him kindly while regarding him somewhat absent-mindedly. Marion's father was a scholarly, stoop-shouldered man, perpetually in need of a haircut, who found his principal diversion in the dinners given by the Club of Odd Volumes. He was generally acknowledged as the office savant in spite of the fact that, for some unexplained reason, he had gone to Amherst instead of Harvard. David called him "The Great Brass Brain". . . .

Well, it was too late to think about help from that quarter now. Roger hastily gathered together such notes as he had assembled in the bankruptcy case and, papers in hand, entered Mr. Mills' commodious corner office.

"I'm afraid I'll need a little more time in going over this, sir," he began. "You see, I've found what may involve the receipt of technical preference by our client on at least one transaction."

"Eh? Bankruptcy? What the devil. . . . Oh, yes, of course, to be sure," Mills replied. "Forget that for the time being. And don't labor it to death when you get back to it. Prepare a proof of claim and worry about the law when it comes up. Meantime, first things first."

He pulled a bound folder from the litter of papers on his desk and extended it to Roger in the manner of one bestowing largess. His pale lips parted over his yellow teeth in an ingratiating smile.

"Got a real job for you, my boy. Want you to take over for me in a jury trial that comes up in Salem this very afternoon."

"But, Mr. Mills—"

"I know, I know," Mr. Mills admitted graciously. Having rid himself of the folder, he smoothed back his thinning hair, adjusted his costly tie, and went on with increasing fervor. "Short notice and all that sort of thing. Reason for it, though. Expected to handle the matter myself. It's my own case, you see. Then, not ten minutes ago, Van Pick called me from Bennington and says he must see me up there at once. Head of one of the hydroelectric companies that furnishes current to the Boston-Edison. Some sort of hitch in a subcontract that will have to be ironed out right away. Can't be in Bennington and Salem at the same time."

"But how can I argue a case before a jury this afternoon, when I've never even heard of it until this minute, Mr. Mills? Can we get a continuance, under the circumstances?"

"Doubt it. Trouble is, it's been continued a couple of times already.

Last time it was to be reached I had to leave for Philadelphia. The way it happens, sometimes. No harm asking for another continuance, of course. But afraid it won't be granted. 'S why I'm counting on you to step in for us. Know you'll give it all you've got. . . . File right here. Study it on your way to Salem. Can't stop to explain. You've got one train to catch, I've got another. Let's get going!"

Again Roger smiled ruefully as he left Mr. Mills' office and strode along the corridor to his own last-and-least door. "The Artful Dodger's a great one to give 'pep-talks,' " he muttered to himself. "You'd think I was the sub, called from the bench when the fullback's been injured. To save the game and all that. . . ." Then he realized, quite abruptly, that this was it. His first jury case. His real opportunity. Better than Brad's. The big chance. Well, he would show them. He would show them all. . . .

"Hello there! What are you throwing out your chest for?"

David, who had just emerged from the elevator, looking, as usual, fresh, complacent and unhurried, regarded Roger with a tolerant smile not untinged by condescension. He had noticed the same expression on David's face before and he had never resented it; David had a right to his feeling of superiority. But though Roger still felt no resentment, he was slightly embarrassed, for the first time, in his friend's presence; evidently he gave himself away too easily.

"Well, really, Dave, I wasn't . . . I mean. . . ."

"Don't mind me. I'm only kidding. You did look rather on the exalted side, though. What's coming off? Anything special?"

"My first jury case. . . . This afternoon, too. Got to catch a train for Salem."

"Oh, no, not that! Anything but that, Rog. Not the Hart thing, is it?"

Defiantly, and already fighting a feeling of deflation, Roger nodded.

"So the Artful Dodger's at it again. He's been called out of town for some very important consultation, I'll bet. Wanted to go up to Salem and argue this himself, but simply had to meet this other sudden appointment? Wasn't that it?"

Again Roger nodded, his feeling of deflation growing.

"It's a god-damned crime, what that gold-bricking bastard gets away with. Let me give you a quick run-down on this thing, so you'll at least know what you're up against. It was Pell he worked it on the last time, and Pell managed to get a continuance."

"That's what I thought I'd try to do."

"I don't think you'd have a prayer for it. Not this time. You see this case hasn't any business in the docket of a firm like ours. It's some chap who runs a sea food restaurant, and who hasn't paid his bills. He's being sued for them. The Artful Dodger met him at the time he was putting through a lease for the restaurant. We represent the realty brokers who handle the property. When this Hart was sued, the only lawyer he could think of was our Mills, so he came up here. Instead of sending him off to someone who would handle that sort of thing, Mills took the case, dictated a routine answer to the declaration and then promptly forgot it. . . . Pell saved Mills' hide once by getting a continuance, and apparently he forgot it again till this very afternoon, though it's dollars to doughnuts Miss Riley gave him a memo on it in plenty of time. Now he's dropping the hot potato in your lap. . . . Well, best of luck. But don't take it to heart if it goes against you. You've got three and maybe four strikes on you already."

The "exaltation" was entirely gone long before David finished; but Roger was still grimly determined to "show 'em" when he reached the North Station, boarded the cinder-grimed local for Salem and found a seat behind a fat woman who was absorbed in a motion-picture magazine and a small boy who was greedily sucking a Hershey bar. Then he buried himself in the file, finding, the further he went into it that he had more and more cause for concern. If Mr. Mills had neglected the case, as it became increasingly clear that he had, then the defendant, Hart—Roger's first client at a jury trial—might not even have been notified to appear in court. There would not be time to locate him in Beverly, where he had his place of business, and still be present when the case was reached. Momentarily, this handicap appeared to him insuperable. But, as he forced himself to study the faltering and inadequate list of payments, Roger caught what he hoped was an inspiration and scrawled a motion on ruled white paper, hurriedly finishing a duplicate as the train slowed down at his stop.

Emerging from the fantastic gray castle with which the Boston and Maine shelters its Salem tracks, Roger waited until his train, blowing steam through the station, had snortingly started up again and disappeared into the tunnel under Salem's busiest street. Then he approached the guard who had been holding a "Stop" sign to prevent automobiles from passing in front of the engine and asked the way to the courthouse.

"Go up the grade beside the tunnel and turn to the left when you come to the church. After that, you'll see it on your right."

Hastily obeying directions, Roger found his turn, entered the gray stone courthouse and, following the signs pointing to "Courtroom," hurried up the stairs. As he had feared, he was none too soon; the place was already sparsely occupied by scattered groups, the men in dungarees and windbreakers, the women in heavy drab coats with straggly fur collars. He had a blurred impression of white walls and a fine portrait; then of jury seats on either side of the bench, into which, on the left, men were filing from a door beside the bench. The clerk was already at his desk, fiddling with a little barrel-shaped drum. A gray-haired, poker-faced judge in a loose black robe entered briskly and everyone stood.

"Court is open. Be seated," intoned a deputy sheriff.

Chapter 10

As ROGER UNEASILY took a seat within the rail, he looked searchingly in every direction for someone who might answer Mr. Mills' description of his client. There was no such person in sight. His anxious glance next fell on the clock. Its hands pointed to three-twenty and he knew Court would sit only until four. He was therefore confronted with the grim realization that if his client, who was the only witness he could summon to testify, did not turn up, he would have to stall until the hour of adjournment came. It came as a shock to him that the outcome of his first case before a jury hinged not upon his knowledge of jurisprudence, but upon his ability to kill time. If the Court recessed before the case went to the jury and the proceedings were therefore continued until the following morning, he might have a chance of finding his client, of effecting a settlement out of court and of winning after all.

"Wholesale Sea Foods Corporation against the Beverly Lobster House!" the court clerk intoned.

"Plaintiff," promptly answered a thin, impatient-looking man in an Oxford gray suit.

"Defendant," added Roger, taking the table in front of the jury box.

Plaintiff's counsel approached Roger and offered his hand. "I'm Fleeney," he said.

"Field," responded Roger.

"Your first time here?" Fleeney asked in a penetrating whisper.

"Yes, sir."

Fleeney cleared his throat.

"Your Honor," he proclaimed oratorically, so that all prospective jurymen would hear. "May I present Mr. Field—of Boston."

"You gentlemen ready for trial?" the judge inquired, after a perfunctory nod at Roger.

"Yes, your Honor," said Fleeney emphatically.

"I have a motion, if your Honor please," said Roger, "to amend the defendant's answer by setting forth that the last payment on account constituted an accord and satisfaction."

"Had you notified Mr. Fleeney?" asked the judge.

"No, your Honor, I must confess I drew this motion on the train, and apologize for its appearance."

"Any objection, Mr. Fleeney?"

"I don't wish to appear unduly technical, may it please the Court, but I think this comes very late. I am ready to try the case on the present pleadings, and although I am confident I could meet this defense, I was not expecting it or prepared for it. Surely my brother is well aware that a payment on account cannot, as a matter of law, operate to extinguish an undisputed claim."

"This claim is disputed, if your Honor please," urged Roger, "and always was. That is why we are here. If my brother should need time to assemble evidence on this point, he will probably have an opportunity to do so before tomorrow morning."

The judge sighed. "Well, all right. I'll allow it. Witnesses all here?"

Two men and two women, who had been sitting together, rose in the rear of the room.

"My client has been delayed by an important engagement," Roger explained, the palms of his hands beginning to sweat, "but he should be here any minute."

"He certainly should," said the judge. "Go ahead, Mr. Clerk."

The clerk handed each lawyer a typed list, whirled his little barrel and, after stopping it, slid open a panel and pulled out a card. Roger scanned the list before him, which set forth the talesmen's names, addresses and occupations. He realized that he could draw out the proceedings to a considerable length by challenging some of these prospective jurors for cause. But the names were all unfamiliar to him. He could think of no reason to argue that any of the men who were being called could not render an impartial verdict. Of course, he also had the right to some peremptory challenges; for the life of him, however, he could not remember how many.

"If any of you is related to either party or has any interest in this case, or has expressed or formed an opinion, or is sensible of any bias or prejudice therein," the clerk was telling the prospective jurors, "you should say so now and step down."

No one said or did anything.

"Plaintiff?" asked the clerk, in a bored tone.

"Content," said Fleeney.

"Defendant?"

Roger cast another hasty glance at the list. Number Three came from Beverly—he might have heard rumors about the Lobster House.

"The defense challenges Number Three."

The man stepped down. Another was called and took his place. Eagerly as he desired to prolong the opening gambit, Roger decided not to offer another challenge for fear that only one was allowed. He did not want to reveal his ignorance of routine court procedure, even on the chance of securing further delay. If Fleeney would only make a long opening statement, as Roger earnestly hoped he might, the case might yet be put over until morning. But when the clerk handed Fleeney the sheaf of pleadings, the attorney merely rattled through the papers and almost instantly began to speak.

"This is a simple case. The plaintiff sold and delivered the lobsters in question, as we will show. The defendant only partly paid for them. . . . Mr. Edgerly!"

Roger cast a dismayed glance at the clock. Fleeney's opening had consumed no more than a few seconds, and the first witness was already making his self-conscious way to the stand. However, the court clerk intervened at this moment, halting the trial until all witnesses had been put under oath in unison. With satisfaction, Roger watched an entire minute slip by. Now he would have to think of a technical objection which could be argued at length, perhaps in connection with something that might crop up during the ensuing point counterpoint of questions and answers.

"Your name?" began Fleeney.

"Stanford Edgerly."

"Your address?"

"Edgerly Building, Main Street, Beverly."

"Your business?"

"President and treasurer of Wholesale Sea Foods Corporation."

"Have you done business with the defendant, Beverly Lobster House?"

"I have."

"I show you a bundle of slips. What are these?"

"These are delivery tickets. When we get an order, it's put on one of these, and when it's delivered, the purchaser signs here at the bottom."

Roger saw his opportunity and seized it. He was on his feet with an objection which he did not expect the Court to sustain, but which would give him an opportunity to argue at some length that the documents themselves were the best evidence of what they contained and that it therefore did not matter what this or any other witness might say was in them. He spoke hesitantly at first, but with growing assurance as he went on. It was true that Fleeney did not even accord his argument a reply, but looked inquiringly at the judge, who droned, "Overruled!" as though bored by something unworthy of serious consideration. But Roger noted with satisfaction that the hands of the clock now stood at ten minutes of four.

"Your witness," Fleeney said casually.

Roger's fleeting moment of triumph was gone. He experienced a sensation of emptiness. He would have to cross-examine Edgerly now, and if he made a good job of it, he could keep the man on the stand until well past adjournment time. But what could he cross-examine him about? His testimony had been a simple, almost elementary recital of a few facts. Against what point of that chronicle could any attack be directed? What was there to break down? In something like desperation, he began to lead the witness through a review of the testimony he had just given on direct examination.

"You said Mr. Hart telephoned his orders for lobsters?"

"That's right."

"You said you knew and recognized his voice on the phone?"

"Yes."

"And that's how you knew it was Mr. Hart calling?"

"That wasn't the only way. He'd usually say something like: 'Stan, this is Irv Hart. I've got a mob coming here Friday night. Send me double the regular order, quick.' "

"And you wrote it down on one of these forms in Exhibit A?"

"Yes."

"And it was you who sent out the order?"

"I gave the orders, yes."

"You didn't drive the truck, did you?"

"No, Sam did," said the witness, pointing to the man who had been sworn with him.

"So you were not present when these lobsters were delivered?"

"No."

"And you yourself didn't see Mr. Hart, or anyone else, sign a single one of those receipts introduced here, did you?"

"No, but I know his signature, like I said."

"Now there were times, weren't there, when Mr. Hart complained about the lobsters you say you sent him?"

"I don't seem to remember any."

"You mean you are perfectly sure, testifying under oath, that there was no time when Mr. Hart in some way told you that the lobsters you sent him were not satisfactory?"

"I can't think of any."

The early dusk of a somber autumn day was closing in. A bailiff rose and turned on the lights. One by one, the attorneys who had been seated within the inclosure rose and tiptoed from the courtroom, secure in the knowledge that they would not be asked to start a trial so late in the day. But Roger was aware he could still lose if he did not use every minute until four, and perhaps a little beyond, if it appeared the case could thus be closed. Looking at his file, he persisted in his efforts to break down Edgerly's testimony.

"Isn't it a fact that, on the Monday after the Fourth of July, he called you up and said he'd been getting complaints from his customers that they'd been sick?"

"I object!" exclaimed Fleeney, instantly on his feet.

"What's the matter?" asked Roger, effectively concealing his gratitude for the interruption.

"If my brother wants to, he can prove the customers at the Lobster House got sick. But, your Honor, I object to this question directed to the witness, who can't possibly know what made them sick, in an effort to hurt my client's reputation here."

"Counsel will come to the bench," directed the judge; and, when they had done so, he admonished them in low tones. "I must remind you gentlemen that this sort of argument is to be addressed to the Court, so the jury cannot hear, as you both know perfectly well. See if you can't ask your question in some other way, Mr. Field."

"Yes, your Honor."

The lawyers returned to their tables and Roger resumed his cross-examination.

"Now, Mr. Edgerly, don't you remember Mr. Hart talking to you about the quality of your lobsters on the Monday after July Fourth?"

"Yes, I guess I do, now you speak of it."

"Will you tell the jury, as nearly as you can remember, what your conversation was?"

"Well, I called him on the phone at the Lobster House—that is, I called their number and asked for him, see, and he comes on and I say, 'Is that you, Irv?' and he says, 'Yes,' and I say, 'Irv, this is Stan, and Irv, your account is getting too big. You've got to realize I have my own pay roll to meet and I'm not running a bank down here,' I says. 'You can't expect me to keep sending you lobsters, Irv,' I says—"

"What did he say?" broke in Roger, hastily.

"Well, that was when he said the lobsters weren't so good—after I jumped on him to pay me for them."

"And he did send you a payment the next day, didn't he?"

"Yes, he did—but not all he owed me."

"And he did say some of the lobsters were dead, didn't he?"

"Yes."

"Did he say how many, or how many pounds?"

"No, he didn't. He just said some of them, like I told you—after I wanted my pay. But they weren't dead—that was just a stall. Them lobsters was okay—crawling around like nobody's business."

The judge leaned forward. "We'll suspend here."

Everyone stood. The sheriff intoned, the judge vanished, the jury dispersed. Roger gave a deep sigh of relief and, gathering up his papers, began stuffing them into his brief case. When he looked up, he saw Fleeney standing beside him.

"See here! Are you really going on tomorrow? Why don't you let me have a judgment? If you've got a defense, I wish you'd tell me what it is."

"I've told you already," Roger replied doggedly. "Edgerly and Hart agreed that last payment should settle the account, because the lobsters weren't satisfactory."

"Okay, okay. See you in the morning."

Roger watched his opponent out of sight with a mounting sensation of triumph. He was far too excited to feel fatigue and, in spite of his long fast, he was not conscious of being hungry. Though all the cards had been stacked against him, his first desperate efforts at trying a case had not ended disastrously; even David Salomont, even Roscoe Cutter himself could not have stalled more successfully than he had. His nervousness, his lack of self-confidence, his sense of inferiority were all gone. Never again would he feel intimidated by a nondescript jury; never again would some small-town lawyer be able to browbeat him. He had proved that he could hold his own against any and all of them. Of course, he must still find Hart; but first he would take time out to get to a telephone and tell Emily. . . .

Tell Emily? Tell her what? If he had suddenly been kicked in the stomach by a mule, the sense of shock would hardly have been greater. He could tell her about the jury trial, of course. But he would also have to tell her that he was delayed in Salem, for how much longer he had no idea. He had placed in jeopardy the Waltz Evening which was to make up for their own disastrous dinner. . . .

He located a pay telephone in the basement, secured some nickels from a bored clerk, and called his house. The answer was so immediate as to suggest that Emily was already awaiting a call from him. He swallowed hard.

"Hello, darling. I'm calling to say that I'm in Salem on a jury trial."

"At last! That's what you've been hoping and hoping for, isn't it?"

"Yes. And things have gone pretty well, so far—a lot better than I expected. I'm feeling awfully good about that. The hitch is, I don't know just when I can get home."

"You don't mean you're afraid you can't get here in time for dinner? Why, Salem is only—"

"I know. And of course I could easily, if I could start for Boston right now. But I've got to see my client first. I haven't even met him yet and I don't know where to find him."

"Roger, it's terribly important that you shouldn't do anything to offend Uncle Homer."

"I realize that. But this case is still more important. The job has to come first. You know that, don't you, dear?"

There was no immediate answer. "Don't you?" he persisted.

"Yes, I suppose so, but—"

"Listen, Emily, every minute we spend talking is going to make me that much later. You know I'll get there if I possibly can. Wish me luck. Good-by."

He hung up, looked in the telephone book for Hart's number and dialed again. There was no answer and, after a moment or two, his nickel was returned. His feeling of triumph was gone now. Suddenly he knew that he was inexpressibly empty and tired, that he wanted food and drink and rest. But he must keep on trying to locate Hart. Evidently, neither he nor any member of his family was at home, and the Lobster House seemed the only other probable place where the elusive client might be found. This being the case, the next step was to take a taxi and get to Beverly as rapidly as possible.

Roger discovered, however, that taxis did not cruise hopefully through the streets of Salem after dark in search of stray fares, and eventually he walked all the way back to the station before finding one. The drive to Beverly also consumed far more time than he had anticipated and, when he reached the Lobster House, he was informed that Mr. Hart, though expected, seldom came in before six. Of course the gentleman could wait if he wanted to. He was welcome to a seat in the restaurant whether he ordered dinner or not. But Mr. Hart kept his private office locked. . . .

Roger hesitated. With a good meal inside him, he probably would feel better. On the other hand, if he stayed in the restaurant, Mr. Hart might continue to elude him. He decided in favor of a dingy passageway outside the private office, where he reviewed the file in the feeble light that came from a solitary bulb. He had read it through several times when the outer door to the passageway opened, and a heavy man, wearing baggy trousers and a tight-fitting coat, came lumbering in Roger's direction. He was in need of both a shave and a haircut, but he would not have been bad looking if his expression had been less ill-humored. He glanced at his visitor in a surly way and without speaking. Roger stepped forward.

"Mr. Hart? I'm Roger Field. I've been trying that lobster case in Salem."

"Who? Oh, that one. Well, what about it?"

"We were reached this afternoon and you weren't there. I had to stall— drag out my cross-examination to kill time—till you could get to court. Didn't you hear from our office?"

"Oh!" Mr. Hart said again, without making any direct answer. Then, as if struck by a sudden thought, he added, "You don't mean you expect me to go to Salem tomorrow?"

"Why, yes, Mr. Hart. This is your case. I'm trying to win it for you and you're my only witness."

For the first time, Hart smiled. "Shucks, boy! You're okay, but I can't spare the time. Lots coming up tomorrow. I'm about through for today, though. Here, come on into my office. Sit down. Have a cigar. Have a drink."

He unlocked the door and stepped inside, switching on the light to disclose a cluttered, roll-top desk, a swivel chair, and a couch covered with a dingy "throw" which had once been gaudy. Roger followed him, but declined the invitation to be seated.

"I'm sorry, sir, but I'm in rather a hurry. My wife and I are going to a dinner tonight. So, if you will just be kind enough to glance over this testimony with me—"

While Roger was speaking, Hart had leaned forward to push a button and he now interrupted his caller by giving an abrupt order for Scotch and soda to a waiter who appeared in the doorway. Then, tilting his chair back, he smiled more and more expansively.

"Don't worry about your dinner, boy. Never any harm being a little late to shindigs women are mixed up in. Lord knows such things last long enough anyhow. And look, there don't have to be any testimony. I've hocked my house, and the bank's letting me have cash enough to hand those dopes half what I owe them. What's more, business is holding up so good this fall, I'll be getting my creditors off my neck by June. Then next summer, I'll really be making dough. I'll just call Stan up and get him to drop the whole thing. He'll be glad enough to do it when he hears about the ready money."

"But Mr. Hart, I think with the case pending, this sort of thing ought to go through Mr. Fleeney, especially with the trial actually going on."

"Maybe, maybe. Was Edgerly there?"

"Why, yes, of course. He was on the stand most of the afternoon— after we were reached, that is."

The waiter reappeared, bearing the Scotch and soda. As he poured out whisky with a lavish hand, Mr. Hart good-naturedly admonished his caller.

"Loosen up, boy. I wangled a roll out of the Third National this afternoon and you've been showing up that fourflusher, Edgerly. We can both do with a little of this stuff. Here's mud in your eye!"

Tardily seating himself on the dingy couch, Roger accepted the proffered glass and slowly drank a little from it. Then he set it down on the floor beside him. It was unbelievable to him that his client, his very first client, whose standing as a substantial citizen and whose commercial salvation had been entrusted to him, Roger Field, when both were endangered, and who had now been at least temporarily rescued, should be shrugging aside everything that seemed of such vital importance. Yet that was what Hart seemed to be doing. He said they didn't need to look over the testimony. He said he was ready to "drop the whole thing." Roger tried again to make himself clear.

"Mr. Hart," he said earnestly, "I want to be sure you understand exactly what I did do in court. I had an entirely new idea. I got your answer amended to say that your last payment was in accord and satisfaction, so that it would settle the whole thing. It looked to me, from our file, as if that was what you intended, after they shipped you so many bad lobsters. If you could come and testify to that, we might be able to beat them."

With a reproachful look, Mr. Hart poured more Scotch into Roger's glass and refilled his own, which was already empty.

"That's nice of you, boy, and don't think I can't appreciate all you're trying to do. But I don't like trials and I don't want to get up on the stand and give some smart-aleck lawyer, like Fleeney, the chance to make a monkey out of me. You get hold of him right now, on the phone, and tell him he can have half his claim in cash, if that's your idea. It isn't a bad one either. If you clean this thing up tonight, then you and your little woman can go ahead and have all the fun you want, and I can forget about the whole damn business."

Reluctantly, Roger fumbled through the directory and, reaching for the telephone on his client's desk, called Mr. Fleeney's house. A childish voice answered.

"Is Mr. Fleeney there?" asked Roger.

"Who?" said the child.

"Mr. Fleeney," repeated Roger, trying not to sound impatient. He covered the mouthpiece. "Some little girl, I guess," he explained to his client.

"Ask her if her daddy's home," suggested Mr. Hart, sighing audibly at Roger's inexperience.

"Is your daddy home?"

"No?"

"Is her mom home," prompted Mr. Hart.

"Is your mom home?" repeated Roger.

"Yes."

"I want to talk to your mom," begged Roger, inwardly writhing, but forcing himself to speak patiently. There was a long interval of silence. Then he heard the closing of a door, approaching footsteps and finally, a woman's voice.

"This is Roger Field, Mrs. Fleeney," he explained. "I've been trying a case against your husband in Salem and he wanted to discuss settlement with me this afternoon. I couldn't do so then, but I can now. Have you any idea when he'll be home?"

"Might be almost any minute."

"Then I'll come right over to your house, if I may, and wait for him."

"That's the way to talk," Mr. Hart said approvingly. He opened the top drawer of the desk, took out a checkbook and, breathing hard, began to write. Then, as he ripped out a check and handed it to Roger, who was already standing, hat in hand, he added, "You just dangle this in front of Fleeney's nose and I bet he won't be able to resist it. But understand, he's got to take it or leave it, just as it's written. So long!"

Once in a taxi again, Roger fought against the temptation of going straight to the railroad station. To be sure, the end of the whole wretched business seemed at last to be in sight. But nervousness overwhelmed him again; fatigue and depression engulfed him. He doubted whether he had the stamina to cope with a shrewd, hard-boiled customer like Fleeney when in a state of such physical and mental exhaustion. His doubts increased when he found that Fleeney was still absent from home. Mrs. Fleeney, a somewhat slatternly and vaguely unpleasant woman, received him rather suspiciously, but ushered him into a room furnished with a parlor suite, upholstered in green brocatelle, and told him to wait. Then she disappeared, saying she must put her little girl to bed, and Roger sat interminably on the stiff sofa trying, without much success, to focus his attention on the tinted enlargements of family photographs which hung on the walls. At last a key turned in the lock and the front door opened.

"Hi, Molly! Any supper left?"

The voice was unquestionably Mr. Fleeney's. Footsteps above hurried toward the stairway.

"Sure I have supper for you, warm on the kitchen stove," Mrs. Fleeney called down. "But there's a Mr. Field in the parlor, waiting to see you."

A short silence, plainly indicative of displeasure, followed this announcement. Then Mr. Fleeney strode into the parlor, frowning.

"Well, what now?" he inquired abruptly.

"I'm sorry to bother you at home, Mr. Fleeney," Roger began apologetically, "but I thought you seemed interested in a settlement. So I talked to my client to see if we could avoid going forward tomorrow morning. I'm pleased to report that I have a check right here for half Mr. Edgerly's claim."

"On account?" Fleeney inquired grimly.

"Why, no. In full settlement." As he spoke, Roger held out the check. Fleeney shook his head.

"You can't get rid of me so easy," he said. "If you want to hand me that now and get me notes that will come due in the early summer for the rest, I'm willing to ask Edgerly to take a chance on them. Otherwise, I want a judgment, as I told you this afternoon. As a matter of fact, come to think of it, I'm scared of notes from Hart, with all the other creditors he has after him. But I'll give him until after July Fourth to pay the other half."

"I'm sorry, Mr. Fleeney. This check is all I can offer you. I hope very much you'll accept it. But Mr. Hart said you could take it or leave it."

"Oh, he did, did he? Well, you can tell him I leave it. I'll get my judgment and put his joint into receivership."

"Mr. Fleeney—"

"Look here, you're wasting your time and mine. You'd better get on back to Boston."

There was no mistaking the finality of his words. Roger put the check slowly back into his pocket. "May I use your telephone?" he asked tonelessly. The dull, depressing feeling that he seemed destined to spend endless periods in telephone conversations which, after all, served no useful purpose, rendered the request doubly difficult. But he knew he could not start back to Boston without making an effort to get in touch with Hart again.

"Sure. There it is on the hall table. But, if you don't mind, I'm going in to supper. Good night."

"Good night."

112

Roger gave the number of the Lobster House and listened to the repeated ringing of the telephone. Finally, a gruff male voice answered.

"May I speak to Mr. Hart please?"

"He's gone."

"Gone! Where can I reach him?"

"I dunno."

"Listen, my name is Field, Roger Field. I'm Mr. Hart's attorney and it's important to Mr. Hart that I should get in touch with him tonight. Can't you find out where he is?"

"Look, Mr. Field, I'm just the cashier. I'd like to help you, but all I can tell you is Mr. Hart left and I'm sure he's not coming back tonight."

"Well, would you write down a message and leave it on Mr. Hart's desk?"

"Sure."

"Say, 'Mr. Field called. Be in court at ten.' "

"I got it."

"Thanks. Good night."

He hung up the receiver and sat still for a moment. Savory odors drifted into the chilly hallway from the kitchen beyond and he wondered, vaguely, what sort of people would permit a cold and tired caller to leave their house, while they sat in a warm room, enjoying appetizing food, without asking whether he would care to join them. But he did not dwell on the thought after he had pulled himself together and gone out into the street. A drizzly rain was falling and again there was no taxi in sight. Turning up the collar of his coat and buttoning this more closely around him, he walked to the station, where he found that a train had just left; so he paced up and down the platform until another came along, nearly an hour later. Then he climbed aboard and sagged into a seat, utterly discouraged.

Mr. Mills had, no doubt, expected him to lose the case, but not to antagonize both his opponent and his client. Mr. Fleeney was ready to try the case to the end and seek a receivership; Mr. Hart would be angry at his failure to persuade Fleeney to settle. And, as for Emily, whom he had not even tried to reach again, knowing she would have long since left the house. . . .

He became aware that the local, which had been lurching toward Boston, was slowing down. Then it stopped altogether. He rubbed the window near him with his hand, but could see no lights outside, except at a distance. Whistles blew, first from the engine of his train and then from another, farther away. A brakeman, carrying a lantern, hurried through the car, ignoring the efforts made by Roger and the other scattered passengers to question him. Roger sat a few minutes, his concern growing, and finally went out on the platform. At the foot of the steps stood the brakeman.

"Better stay up there, mister," he warned.

"Can't I get off?" begged Roger.

"Not unless you want to get wet."

"I don't mind getting a little wet, if I can just get home."

"Yeah, but you wouldn't get home, and your widow might be sorry."

"Why, what's the trouble?"

"Drawbridge stuck open. We're on a trestle. Better go back in and keep your shirt on, mister."

The lights grew dim, the car turned cold, then the steam came banging back on; but the little train stood still over the tidal inlet whose traffic had indirectly balked the railroad. Roger heard occasional shouts and saw an occasional lantern. At last the ancient locomotive sighed, struggled, and started across the draw, which somehow had been wheedled back into place. A few minutes later, it bustled into Boston.

Roger stumbled down the steps, hurried through the station concourse and climbed into a taxi, which wove its way through the maze of one-way streets on the Hill till it deposited Roger before his door. He let himself in quietly, kicked off his rubbers in the vestibule and flung down his hat and coat on the nearest chair. It was Emily's custom to leave a room pleasantly lighted, even when they went out; therefore, it came as no surprise to him to see that the library was not in darkness. But he was puzzled by the murmur of voices. He pushed back the portieres and walked in.

David and Emily were seated close to the fire, so absorbed in what they were saying to each other that neither was instantly aware of his entrance.

Chapter 11

FOR A MOMENT, Roger had the strange feeling that he was the interloper, that it was David who really belonged there in the library, beside the fire with Emily. He tried unsuccessfully to suppress it as both preposterous and morbid, and went forward, making an effort to speak cordially and naturally; but the sickening sense of intrusion became stronger and stronger. Emily had not come quickly into the hall, to welcome him home with a loving caress, the way she had always done before; instead she sat very still, her white dress dazzling against the crimson of her chair, her lovely face almost expressionless. David, on the contrary, leaped up, holding out his hand and exclaiming, "Hello there! You have had a day of it!" before Roger himself could think of anything to say. Yes, it was as if David were the host, as if he were the outsider and as if Emily did not belong wholly to him any more.

"You're right. I have had a day of it," he answered wearily. Even his voice did not sound like his own, just as this room did not seem like his own and Emily did not seem like his own. He turned away from David and looked at her, hoping for help, and she did not give it to him. He knew this must be because she could not, for some reason that he did not understand, and that he ought to help her out. Perhaps it would be better if he asked her to tell him what she had done, rather than to go on trying to tell her what he had done. Perhaps he should ask her how she happened to be sitting in their house on Joy Street, his and hers, alone with David Salomont, instead of being at the Copley Plaza with a group of their old friends. After she had told him that, everything would be all right. It was because she sat so still, because she did not smile or speak that everything seemed so strange and sickening. Well, he would ask her. But David spoke again before he could frame his question.

"Your loss was certainly my gain," David said, still with great good cheer. "Emily was kind enough to call me up and ask me to fill in at Mr. Lathrop's dinner. Naturally, I was delighted to do so. Then, after dinner she decided she'd like to come back here and wait for you, instead of going on to the Waltz Evening. She didn't want to miss you when you did get home. So we've been sitting her beside the fire talking—why, for almost a couple of hours now! I don't know when I've enjoyed myself so much. I'll run along now though. By the way, how'd you make out in Salem?"

"Well, that's a long story—"

"Then it'll keep till morning."

"I have to go back to Salem in the morning. The case isn't closed yet."

That wasn't the thing to say. He ought to have thanked David for filling in, he ought to have said he was glad his friend could keep his wife company through a long and disappointing evening. But he didn't feel grateful to David, he wasn't glad to find him with Emily in the library. He hated him. And that was puerile and senseless. David had done the right thing at the right time, just as he always did. The right thing? The kind of thing that got him ahead. . . .

"Good night. Emily. Thanks again for everything."

"Good night, David. Thank you for everything."

Well, she had spoken at last, she had smiled at last. Now everything would be better. But everything was not better. David had gone over to the chair where Emily was sitting and put his arm around the back of it. He did not touch her and yet, as he bent over her, the effect was that of a caress offered and accepted. He stayed there for a moment looking down at her, not saying anything more, not needing to. Then he straightened up and shook hands with Roger, still speaking cheerily, and afterward he was gone.

The front door closed behind him with a bang. Emily rose and came over to Roger, putting her lovely arms around his neck.

"Darling," she said gently. "Darling, I'm so sorry you've had such an awful day. I couldn't seem to say anything before David, but now we're alone, we can have a good talk. First though, you've got to have a drink and something to eat. Ellie's left everything ready, in the pantry. Please sit down and rest, while I get it for you."

He was too tired to protest, too tired to say she must not wait on him, or that he wasn't hungry, or that all right, he would get the whisky and sandwiches himself. Emily brought them in, quietly and expertly, and set them down on the table before him. She filled two tall glasses with ice from a thermos bucket and poured out two drinks, a stiff one for Roger and a light one for herself. Then she uncovered the sandwiches, folding back the damp napkin to disclose a tempting array topped with crisp sprigs of parsley. Roger drank slowly, and as the warmth of the whisky filtered through his veins, he began to take slow bites from a sandwich. But all the time he kept thinking, *Emily's treating me as if I were a child who needed her care, not as if I were a man who could take care of her. If we had a son, this is the way she would act toward him. She wouldn't act this way toward David, if he were her husband. She wouldn't need to. He*

116

wouldn't come home, half dead, hours later than she expected him. He'd manage to be around whenever she wanted him, he'd always be a credit to her. . . .

"After you telephoned, I called up Uncle Homer and told him I was afraid you couldn't make the dinner, that perhaps he'd better ask one of his old friends to fill in," Emily was saying soothingly. "But he wouldn't. He said of course you'd make it." (There it was again. Homer Lathrop had said of course he'd make it. Men like Homer Lathrop and men like David Salomont didn't give out half an hour before a formal dinner.) "Then he called me back at seven, just to assure himself you'd got home. When he told him you hadn't and that I had no idea how to reach you, he said in that case, I'd have to find someone to fill in—he couldn't." (Yes, and I know just the way he said it. You're trying to spare me as much as you can, Emily, you're trying to make this easy for me, but I know. I know Homer Lathrop told you again just what he thought of me, he intimated you'd made your own bed, in spite of all he could do to prevent you and now you'd have to lie in it. He wouldn't help you out. Couldn't? Of course he could have! He could have asked any one of a dozen old fogies, snoozing around in big leather armchairs, right at his elbow in the Somerset Club, but he wouldn't. He dared you to find someone in our own crowd, at seven o'clock, to come to a seven-thirty dinner, the night of a Waltz Evening. He never thought you'd ask a Jew to the Somerset Club.) "Well, I tried to think and think fast. I thought first of Pell. But I remembered you said he didn't own dress clothes, that he hired them when he needed them. Besides, there's no telephone listed in his name."

"Oh—so you did try to call him after all?"

"No. I—I knew that already. You see, after you told me about the way he'd lived, the way he got his start, all that, I was terribly interested. Don't you remember, you asked me if I'd ever walked all the way down Joy Street, on the other side of the Hill, and I told you I hadn't? But I did, the next day. And before I started out, I tried to find Pell's name in the telephone book, so that I could look for his house and see exactly what sort of a place he lived in. And he wasn't listed."

"I see." Vaguely and illogically, Roger felt relieved to learn that Pell and not David had been Emily's first choice in her dilemma. He took another drink, and though his glass was nowhere nearly empty, Emily poured a little more whisky and put another lump of ice in it. "You didn't think of Brian, I suppose," he asked, biting into his sandwich again.

"Brian! That uncouth, clowning Mick! I certainly didn't."

"Don't talk like Homer Lathrop, Emily."

"I'm sorry, darling. I didn't mean to. But you haven't forgotten, have you? That ham actor entrance, that awful red tie, those terrible stories—"

"No—no. Of course you couldn't risk having anything like that happen a second time. I'm afraid we're not going to make much headway with

117

the plan we had—you know, about having our home a center of good feeling, a place where better understanding could be promoted."

"Well, we will yet. You'll see. It's just because you're so tired, Roger, that you think we can't—eventually. But, in the meantime—"

"In the meantime you couldn't ask Pell to fill in because he doesn't own dress clothes and you wouldn't ask Brian because he wouldn't bother to wear them unless he felt like it. And you faced a major crisis because your trustee was short one man for a dinner party on account of your husband's unavoidable absence."

For the first time since their marriage, he was speaking to her sarcastically and bitterly, as he had on the evening when they became engaged. But if his tone surprised or hurt her, she gave no indication of it. Instead, she went on speaking in the same soothing way as before.

"In the meantime I thought perhaps David was my best bet. I had no idea where he lived or how quickly he could get here. But of course he is in the telephone book. And he got here in no time at all. I don't see how he managed, dressing and everything. He lives on Aspinwall Avenue, way out by Coolidge Corner. But he said he was used to doing things on the double."

"There's no doubt about that."

Again he spoke sarcastically and again she disregarded his sarcasm. "You should have seen Uncle Homer's face when I walked into the club with David," she said, almost gleefully. "I hadn't called him back myself —Ellie did that for me—and he understood her to say I was bringing a Mr. Sulloway. Of course he thought it was one of the New Hampshire Sulloways and he was terribly pleased—it seems there was a Sulloway in his class who was quite outstanding and he leaped to the conclusion that this was a son or a nephew of that one, who happened to be in town and whom I'd had the good luck to get hold of. He took me aside as soon as he could and asked me if I'd gone crazy. He said, 'You can't take that fellow with you to the Waltz Evening, Emily. You'd never be asked again if you did.' "

"I hope you told him, in that case, your own social position must be pretty shaky."

"No-o-o. I didn't think it was the best time and place to start an argument. I'm planning to have that later. I told him I wouldn't dream of going to the Waltz Evening without you, that I was coming back here to wait for you, as soon as the dinner was over, but that I'd taken him up on his dare."

"So you knew it was a dare, when he told you to find an extra man?"

"Of course. And did I turn the tables on him? David was the great success of the evening. He dominated the dinner. I don't mean he did it by trying to monopolize the conversation or being aggressive or anything like that. But he was so entertaining that everyone wanted to listen to him and so attractive that no one could help looking at him. Before we came away, several people had asked him to drop in for cocktails and the Amorys had invited him to Sunday dinner. I could see that Uncle Homer was fairly foaming at the mouth with rage."

"Well, evidently we can drop our philanthropic plans as far as David's concerned. He'll be pretty well launched after tonight."

"Why, I hadn't thought of it that way! But I guess he will be."

"You can be damn sure David's thought of it that way. I only hope he's properly grateful to you."

Roger set down his glass and laid his half-eaten sandwich beside it. "I seem to be pretty well bushed," he said. "Let's get upstairs, shall we? No—don't bother with the tray. I'll take it back to the pantry myself."

The spaciousness of the Joy Street house permitted the use of a hall bedroom as a dressing room for Roger, and this dressing room included in its equipment an Empire day bed. It was Caroline's belief—or at least her hope—that Roger slept there, and not in the enormous sleigh bed, which was the main feature of the large, luxurious chamber that adjoined the dressing room. As a matter of fact, he had never done so, even when he was ill, and he and Emily had often joked about the alleged advantages of separate apartments for married couples, while lying cozily side by side. Now, for some reason that he could not define, Roger felt that he wanted to be alone, that solitude would mean even more to him, in his exhausted state, than the nearness of his beloved. He undressed slowly, wondering just how he could tell Emily this without hurting her feelings, wishing that it were possible simply to close the door between the two rooms and lie down between the clean sheets, under the warm blankets, burying his head on the soft pillows without a word of explanation or excuse. But he felt sure this would wound Emily deeply and that was the last thing on earth he wanted to do, especially when she had been so understanding and so kind, first in the face of his inadequacy and then in the face of his ungraciousness. He went to the threshold and paused there, hoping that the right words would come.

Emily was already in bed, but she had not turned on her side, with one arm under head, as she generally did when she was beginning to grow drowsy. If she had been, he might have gone back into the dressing room and stayed there a few minutes longer, puttering around among his possessions, until she was still sleepier or actually asleep. Then there would have been little or no need for explanations; she would not even have missed him until later. But she was sitting up, with two pillows behind her, her soft hair hanging in two long braids over her breasts. Above the lace of her nightgown, her skin was luminous. He had never seen her when she looked more lovely; yet at the moment he did not desire her. He wanted only to say good night and leave her. But when she saw him, she smiled; and her smile, like her eyes, was welcoming. She held out her arms.

"Dearest," she said. "Dearest—"

He could not deal another blow to her pride, he could not let her know that he did not want her. The conviction of this was so strong that it impelled him to assume an urgency he did not feel. Her instant acquiescence, her passionate response, betrayed the degree of her own yearning and her own need. . . .

Long after she had at last gone to sleep, Roger lay wakeful and wretched beside her, dwelling on this new revelation. He had grown up in the belief that in his marital relations a gentleman was always "considerate" and he had scrupulously lived up to his code. Now, for the first time, he realized that Emily had wanted ardor rather than tenderness, that she had expected domination rather than reverence. Since this was so, he had failed her in another way from the beginning. . . .

Throughout the darkness of the night, these thoughts persisted. He knew now why he had felt that she treated him like a child instead of a man when she was sorry for him; it was because he had treated her like a child instead of a woman when he made love to her. And while he dwelt upon the bitter knowledge, wondering how best to act upon it in the future, the unwelcome image of David Salomont reared itself before him. It was no longer merely the image of a man who would always be a credit to his wife, who would always take care of her instead of needing her to minister to him, who would always do the right thing at the right time, the thing which helped him to forge ahead. It was the image of a man who would have been a lover as well as a husband, a master as well as a mate. Yet again, a man whose seed would have been as fruitful as his sovereignty was supreme, who would have begotten a son in the first consummation of union.

The hatred that Roger had felt for David earlier that night welled up within him, choking and suffocating him. And it was no longer the hatred of a man for another more successful and brilliant than himself; it was hatred for a recognized rival, who would have won a desired woman for his wife if he had been first on the scene, and who might still hope to win her for his mistress, if she were not the embodiment of loyalty and steadfastness. . . .

Thank God, Emily was loyalty itself, steadfastness itself. On that score he had no anxiety. The anxiety was all for his own inadequacy. But that did not make him hate David Salomont the less.

He would have hated him more if he had known the story of the evening in its entirety.

Part Three

FEBRUARY, 1939, TO JANUARY, 1940

ROGER AND BRIAN

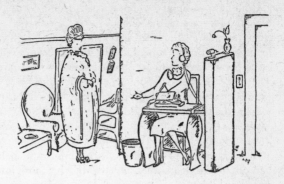

Chapter 12

"... AND PARTICULARLY, without limiting the generality of the foregoing," Cora Donlon typed, copying carefully, "all claims, contracts, demands, choses in action and rights under instruments both negotiable and non-negotiable, shall and hereby are conveyed, assigned, set over and transferred unto the grantee and assignee hereunder; provided however. . . ."

"From your preoccuation, young woman, I gather that the latest book banned in Boston has just been bought in Quincy for the law library of Cutter, Mills and Swan, but that strict orders have been issued against removing it from the premises—that is to say, from within easy reach of the senior partners. Therefore you are copying its more salacious passages so that you may enjoy them with your intended this evening."

Cora Donlon, the harried receptionist, who sat at the switchboard near the elevators, a typewriter stand beside her, had looked up with a start as soon as the formidable visitor began to speak. As she found no suitable opening for interruption, however, she waited for the tirade to end before attempting to say anything in self-defense and then going on to the usual routine questions.

"No, I was just making a transcript," Cora said. She spoke patiently and politely, according to her habit; still, she did not intend to let the unjust accusation go unanswered. "I do try to watch the board and the elevators while I'm typing, but sometimes the wording of a document's so complicated that it's hard for me to follow and then. . . . But I'm very sorry. May I help you?"

"You may show me the way to Mr. Field's office, if you can leave the switchboard and the elevators and the typewriter that long."

"I think Mr. Field and Mr. Salomont are in conference. But I'll be glad to find out," Cora said. She still spoke patiently and politely and, at the same time, she reached to plug in a jack and ring Roger's cubbyhole. "Who shall I say is calling, please?"

"You needn't say. I can see Mr. Field's name on the door over there at the right. If I'd only noticed it in the first place, I wouldn't have had to waste all this time."

Cora jumped up and then sat down again, shaking her head and biting her lips. In spite of the difficulty with which she moved, the immense elderly woman, who leaned heavily on a cane and was wrapped from head to foot in a fur unfamiliar to the receptionist, would reach Mr. Field's office before she could be stopped, since it was only a few feet distant. The best Cora herself could do was to let him know someone was on the way. Roger was indeed deep in discussion with David at the moment, though their argument could hardly be characterized as a conference.

"Look, Dave, this boy who was in here with his parents has just escaped from an insane asylum. He and his wife ran a filling station. Along comes a flashy salesman. The wife waits on him once in a while and falls for him. Between them, they railroad the husband into an insane asylum and—"

"My son, you just haven't been around. You can see that in the movies any day. Different trimmings, but the same old geometry. I wouldn't touch that case with a borrowed clothes pole. And if you'll take my advice, you won't either."

"I'm not sure I want to take your advice. This isn't a movie. These are real people and they're in a jam. They need a lawyer and besides, I. . . . Why hello, Mrs. Forbes! I'm awfully glad to see you! Won't you sit down? You remember Dave Salomont, don't you? Excuse me a second, while I catch that call."

"Never mind the call. It's just to tell you I'm here, which you've already found out for yourself. And of course I remember David Salomont. How's your stepfather, David? Tell him we still have good borsch on Louisburg Square. . . . What are you and Roger quarreling about?"

"Oh, that wasn't a quarrel! Roger was just telling me where to get off. Quite right too. I keep forgetting he's a big boy now. Could I take your coat? And thanks for the invitation. I'll call up Dad and see if some night next week would be convenient. Right now I have to get on my horse. Good-by, Mrs. Forbes. So long, Rog."

Mrs. Forbes, adjusting the sable wrap which, a quarter of a century earlier, had represented the ultimate in elegance and which she had never seen fit to have remodeled, settled her imposing person in the least uncomfortable chair available and permitted her penetrating gaze to rest upon David as he took his easy departure. Then she turned to Roger, who was still standing, his expression rather tense, beside his desk.

"Is there more to this than meets the eye, Roger?"

"I'm not sure I know just what you mean, Mrs. Forbes."

"Well, I've had the growing impression for some time now that you and David Salomont weren't hitting it off as well as you did at first. You're not jealous of him by any chance, are you?"

"There's no reason why I should be, is there?"

"Just that he's making a name for himself pretty fast as a lawyer and attracting a good deal of general attention besides. More than you are.

Not that I feel there's any reason why you should be jealous of him on that account, as you say. Especially as you've got so much that he'd give his eyeteeth for and won't ever get. There's a balance about these things. But sometimes young fools don't have enough sense to realize that. Incidentally, David made a good move, leaving those weird relatives of his who live way out on Aspinwall Avenue and setting himself up in a bachelor apartment on Lime Street. Very attractive he's making it too, so I hear. But of course you've seen it for yourself."

"No, I haven't been to his apartment. He's asked Emily and me there twice—I believe he's giving a series of small suppers—but we had something else on both times. And right now, you know Emily's awfully busy with rehearsals for the Vincent Club Show. She's in the Drill again and she's doing a lot of work on the lyrics besides."

"Yes, I know. Well, I didn't come here to talk about the Vincent Club or about David Salomont and his various successes. I've got other matters on my mind."

"I'd feel very much complimented to have you tell me about them, if you would."

"Of course I would. I've just said that's what I came here for. But I wish you wouldn't stand there, as if you didn't feel quite sure you had a right to sit down in your own office—provided a little hole in the wall like this can be called an office. It looks more to me like a store-closet where old furniture's been relegated."

Mrs. Forbes' glance now wandered about the cubbyhole, taking in its distasteful details—the battered desk, the drab walls, the dingy rug, the dirty window, the torn shade. When she brought her gaze to rest on Roger again, he had seated himself and, looking slightly less strained than before, was attentively awaiting her pleasure.

"Your father-in-law, Roger," she began without preamble, "is behaving very badly. I want you to take measures to stop him."

Roger, who had always secretly felt that Sumner Thayer was more sinned against than sinning, and who could not imagine what new dereliction was now being laid at his door, wisely waited for Old Mrs. Forbes to go on.

"When the Gloucester Street house was closed for the summer, after your wedding, this was done exactly as it has been for twenty-five years. I mean the silver was put in the bank and the rugs were sent to storage and the furniture was slip-covered—that sort of thing. And since I didn't care about using the Dublin house this last summer, I was glad enough to have Sumner and Eleanor go there. I said they were welcome to stay as long as they liked. Naturally, I didn't suppose they'd like it there in the wintertime."

Roger murmured something which he hoped sounded vaguely sympathetic. His ear, which was quicker than his speech, had caught the omission of the word "horrible" before "Gloucester Street house"; and, as this was the first time, within his memory, that the term of opprobrium had ever been left out of any such reference by Old Mrs. Forbes, he realized that this might be portentous. But he knew better than to risk a premature comment. He was also well aware that it would not do to say that the climate and general living conditions were no more rigorous in New Hampshire in the wintertime than they were in Vermont, where Elizabeth Forbes betook herself whenever she could steal the time from her Bryn Mawr teaching, and where Emily loved to go also; or that Dublin probably had as much to offer in the way of diversion as Cape Cod, where Sherman Forbes so stubbornly remained. On the face of things, it looked to him as if Eleanor Thayer, on whom her mother had so long been able to keep a stranglehold through Emily, had been freed by her daughter's wedding and had made good her escape from maternal domination, as her sister and her brothers had done before her. But this, it appeared, was not the cause of Old Mrs. Forbes' grievance, or at least not the primary cause.

"Of course, Eleanor hasn't been in Dublin much since October," she went on. "She's been here, there and everywhere with those vapid Southern friends of hers, as you and Emily must know. And whenever she's come to Boston, she's stayed at the Chilton Club—well, you must know that too. It didn't strike me as strange at first, because of her perpetual servant troubles. You know how your mother-in-law harps on servant troubles, Roger. She doesn't seem to realize that it's a dead giveaway of her own lack of executive ability. Besides, it's the most tedious topic on the face of the earth, except the horrors of gynecological operations and the bright sayings of one's children. You'd think, to hear some women talk, that a special feature of their anatomy made them the prey of scheming surgeons, and that they never gave birth to an infant that wasn't either a prodigy or a paragon. The only proper place for such women is a padded cell."

Again Roger murmured a vague agreement. He was beginning to wonder if his first surmise had been wide of the mark and to cast about in his mind for a logical connection between gynecology and his father-in-law's delinquency.

"Well, as I was saying, it didn't seem to me strange that Eleanor should stay at the Chilton Club when she came to Boston without Sumner, or even that she *did* come without Sumner—until she kept on doing it," Old Mrs. Forbes continued. "But she's done it too often. And she's acted more like a fool than usual when she has been here. I'm not going into that—at least not now. But yesterday, I asked her pointblank when she and Sumner were going to open the Gloucester Street house again and what do you think she told me? That they weren't *ever* going to open it again! That they were both sick and tired of it! She said they'd meant for years to get rid of it as soon as Emily was married, and that if they'd only had a good offer for it, they'd have sold it. Well, they haven't had an offer for a sale. But they have had a chance to lease it for five years to some dentists who do extractions and all that sort of thing! There are three of these quacks who work together and they would remodel it into an office building and start making X-ray pictures and pulling teeth just as soon as they could get their equipment installed. And Sumner and Eleanor would take the rental money from the house my husband gave his daughter as a wedding present and live abroad on it! Sumner says he's willing to live with Eleanor if she'll go abroad. He says he'll never live with her in Boston again after the way she's acted—well, as I told you before, that's neither here nor there for the moment. And where do you think they're talking about going? To the shabby, stupid little place on the Riviera, where Letty, Russell's ex-wife, lives with that crazy fiddler! Sumner and Eleanor have actually been in correspondence with Letty and she says she's found them just the place—a villa on a hillside where the terrace is simply overhung with geraniums. *Geraniums!*"

Old Mrs. Forbes paused for breath and drew her outmoded wrap a little more closely around her massive shoulders. Then she rummaged in her elaborate handbag and, producing a fine, embroidered handkerchief, blew her nose rather more loudly than a personage of less exalted position would consider ladylike. This time, Roger knew he must say something as promptly as possible, and still not so quickly that he erred in discernment through haste. After all, his first guess had *not* been too wide of the mark and this was encouraging; but there were quite a few gaps in Old Mrs. Forbes' story and somehow these must be filled in with guesswork. Obviously, it was his mother-in-law, rather than his father-in-law, who had really been "behaving badly" and, until he knew just how badly and in what way, there was not much he could say along those lines. He had probably better concentrate on the subject of real estate, now that the horrible little Gloucester Street house had suddenly become both a symbol of family unity and of family dissension.

"I don't wonder you're upset about all this," he said earnestly. "And I can't tell you how pleased and touched I am that you've come to me about it."

"Well, after all, you're in the family now," Old Mrs. Forbes replied, speaking more briskly again and replacing the embroidered handkerchief in her bag. "I don't believe in washing dirty linen in public, if it can be helped. The point is, can it? I mean, are you capable of handling a case of this sort?"

"I'll have to know a little more about it before I can be sure," Roger said cautiously. "But so would any lawyer. And I'm afraid there isn't anything that could prevent Mr. and Mrs. Thayer from selling their house, if they wanted to, because it's theirs. But I'm not so sure they can lease it —that is, for use as a dental parlor or any other business purpose. The zoning ordinances may prevent it. I'd have to check and see just how they affect the area where the—" He caught himself just in time. He had almost said, "horrible little Gloucester Street house" himself. "Where their property is located," he continued. "In that case, I think quite possibly they could be enjoined from doing what would be so distasteful to you."

"You do? How long would it take you to find out?"

"Not long. I could let you know by tomorrow at the latest—that is, if something else wasn't suddenly sprung on me that I had to do for the firm."

The telephone rang and Roger picked up the receiver. "Hello—why hello, dear! How's the rehearsal going? Oh, that's too bad! . . . Well, of course, if you think you ought to. Yes—yes. Good-by." He hung up and turned toward Old Mrs. Forbes. "Emily says everything's at sixes and sevens with the show."

"It always is, at this stage," Old Mrs. Forbes replied, with something like a snort.

"Well, Emily seems to be worried about it. She thinks she ought to go home with Marion, after the rehearsal, and work on the lyrics. She'll have dinner with the Swans."

"What do you do with yourself, the nights she stays out to dinner?"

"It isn't *nights*, Mrs. Forbes. This is almost the first time."

"It won't be the last," Old Mrs. Forbes said conclusively. Then she added, more hastily than was her wont, "What I mean is, she'll be putting a lot of work into these rehearsals and those lyrics during the next few weeks and I'm glad of it. She's dropped out of the general picture pretty completely since she got engaged to you, Roger. Not that I'm blaming her for that either. I think that Frontier Nursing idea of hers was excellent; and no one expects a brand-new bride to spend her time ushering at a lot of dull fall functions, like the Baker Guidance Center Lectures and the Children's Museum Benefit and the New England Antiques Exposition. She's got more exciting claims on her time. But after all, Emily was in Kentucky a long while and on top of that, you and she went off to Europe. Then, when she finally got back to Boston, she didn't even go to the Junior League election and she used to be one of the vice-presidents. She was too busy going in for good fellowship in a large way. Now she's learned you can't hurry things like that and she's got to think of Priscilla, as she very properly said before I reminded her of that. Sue and Sherman aren't going to do anything to pull that poor little unbroken filly away from the cranberry bogs and your father-in-law and mother-in-law won't either. So Emily and I have got to take matters in hand."

"I know. Emily's spoken about it to me and I'd be glad to have her do anything that would help Priscilla. I like the poor kid a lot. Besides, I think Emily gets a kick out of being in the Drill anyway, and I want her to do the things she enjoys. I always have. I'd hate to think she'd drop out of the picture on my account."

"Well, she thought the game was worth the candle and she still thinks so. That being the case, I wouldn't worry about it, if I were you. But you ought to have some independent interests too. Have you ever thought of joining the First Corps Cadets?"

"No—but it might not be such a bad idea."

He turned again, this time toward the viewless window. Old Mrs. Forbes allowed a moment to elapse without further comment. Then she picked up the thread of her previous remarks.

"I intended to have a word with the head of the firm, about interrupting your work for me, before I left here, in any event," she said conclusively. "That is, if you felt you could handle the case. And I see that you can. But there was also something else on my mind. I have not finished talking to you about Sumner. He is not satisfied with saying that he will never come back to Boston and live here like a gentleman. He has been making trouble for me with the tax authorities."

"The tax authorities?"

"Yes. That property of mine in Dublin isn't handled by the Federal Street Trust Company, like most of my belongings. It couldn't be, as I understand it, because it isn't located in Massachusetts."

"Then I hope someone else has been handling it for you. You shouldn't be bothered with anything like that."

"Of course I shouldn't. But I have been. That's what I'm coming to."

Again Old Mrs. Forbes opened her handsome bag and this time she extracted from it a sheaf of papers which she laid on the corner of Roger's desk.

"Probably you've thought of that Dublin property in terms of the big house where you've been to visit," she announced. "As a matter of fact, I control quite a good deal of real estate around there. Some of the farms I rent out and I hold heavy mortgages on some others. A New Hampshire realty firm handles the revenue from both for me and just sends me the checks. It's always been a very convenient arrangement. I've no fault to find with it. But there's one place I've never rented. It's stocked with fine Holsteins and run as a model dairy farm, in connection with the big house. Dairying was quite a fad of my husband's; he said cows helped him take his mind off his diplomatic associates, they always looked so peaceful, lying around and chewing their cuds, instead of blowing up about every trifle of protocol and all that. I understand how he felt. So I've always kept them. At quite a cost. Not that I've begrudged it or had to scrimp in other ways to do it. I've enough money to indulge a hobby for cows. But they cost a good deal more in the course of a year than I got from all the farms I rented out and all the mortgages I held."

Roger, who remembered the model dairy as a highly ornamental part of the rural landscape, said he could well believe this.

"Well, five years ago, the foreman died. He was the old-fashioned type —you could depend on him to do just the same things, year after year. Then Sumner persuaded me to let a youngster who had just graduated from the State Agricultural College take over on shares. And the first thing

I knew, this boy had started selling certified milk and making money for both of us."

"But you didn't object to that, did you? He asked you if it would be all right to sell the milk, didn't he?"

"Yes, he asked me; he said there was an 'ever-growing demand for dairy products'—something of the sort. I didn't pay much attention to him—I haven't spent a great deal of time in Dublin of late anyway. But then *he* began sending me checks."

"Yes?"

"Well, I didn't report them as income. I didn't see any reason why I should. Talk about balancing the budget! The sum total of those checks didn't make a dent in the accumulated deficit of that dairy farm. But this white-headed boy of Sumner's reported the money he'd sent me on *his* farm returns. And the next thing I knew, here was a revenue agent walking straight into my house, in spite of everything Pearson could do to stop him, and reminding me that I'd made no report on this item of my revenue! As if I needed any reminder! I knew all the time I hadn't."

"So you said—"

"I was perfectly polite to him at first. I told him that the trifling gain he was talking about was offset more than a hundred times by previous losses. But he seemed to take a very pessimistic view of my figuring. He kept telling me that 1936 was the only year he was interested in and he went on talking about those checks from the dairy until I wished I'd never seen a cow. So I decided to go straight to headquarters. You know the old French proverb, 'Au Sauveur et non pas à ses saints.' "

Roger, whose French was limited to what he had learned at Milton Academy, nodded his head sagely without too far committing himself.

"So I telephoned Franklin Roosevelt right then and there. He was charming, the way he always is, wanted to know why I hadn't been to Washington lately. I told him I hadn't found any place to stay that suited me, since Russell sold his house and went to live at the Carlton—really, the mania my children are developing for selling their houses ought to receive some kind of special treatment by alienists! So then Franklin said, what about coming to the White House for a week end—he thought they could make me comfortable there. I think I'll go—it's quite a while since I've stayed at the White House. It never seemed to occur to Franklin's immediate predecessor to ask me there and I used to enjoy it very much. No doubt I would again. However, the invitation didn't take care of the tax matter. Franklin said he'd have to turn that over to Henry and—"

"You mean Henry Morgenthau? The Secretary of the Treasury?"

"Yes, I suppose so. But the agent left after I telephoned Franklin and so I thought he'd decided to drop the whole thing and that I could just let the matter slide. But right on top of Sumner's announcement about the dentists, in come these papers."

Old Mrs. Forbes leaned forward and shoved the papers which she had previously placed on the corner of Roger's desk a little nearer to him. Irrelevantly, he noticed that the great signet ring, which Morris Brucker had given her, was now the only one on her right hand, though her left was still laden with diamonds; and the observation revived the dormant curiosity which the gift had aroused when it was made. Conscientiously striving to dismiss this from his mind, he picked up the papers and scrutinized them.

"It doesn't surprise me that these have puzzled and disturbed you, Mrs. Forbes," he said, speaking quite sincerely. She was by no means the first person of more than average intelligence whom he had seen thus baffled and consequently thus upset; and women particularly, however quick to grasp the *raison d'être* for many of the law's workings, usually seemed to have a blind spot when it came to tax matters, just as they usually saw no reason why they should not smuggle, however meticulous they might be in other matters of honesty. There was, nevertheless, one aspect of the present difficulty which he himself did not find quite clear.

"I think I understand the root of this trouble, Mrs. Forbes," he said at length. "And if I do, we ought not to have too much difficulty getting rid of it. But I still don't quite understand why the Federal Street Trust isn't looking after this for you."

"Neither do I. That's just what I said to myself. But when I asked Mr. Adams, he replied that the Federal was only responsible for administering the trust funds established by my father and my husband. And, as I told you, the New Hampshire properties don't come under that; in fact, none of my real estate does. And all Mr. Adams, who is obviously in his dotage, could suggest was that I refer the tax matters to Fiske, Ford and Gibbons. But those whited sepulchers declined to have anything to do with my problems, on the ground that they represented the trust and that there might be a conflict of interests. They didn't say whose interests and it's quite evident they weren't thinking about mine! All they did was to ferret out a tax accountant who heaped more reproaches on me and, on top of everything else, in came that green form!"

Old Mrs. Forbes glared at the offending document lying on top of the other papers, and then pushed them still farther away from her with such force that they fell, scattering, to the floor. The great emerald in the signet ring glittered with the sweep of her hand. Roger, resolutely glancing away from it, retrieved the papers and put them on the other side of the desk, beyond his caller's reach.

"I'm very sorry you've had so many things to bother you," he said calmly, "especially as it seems to me that most of them were unnecessary."

"Unnecessary! Do you mean to tell me these miscreants have been persecuting me merely for the fun of it?"

"No, I don't mean that. But I do mean there's no reason why one person—let's call him Mr. X for the moment—couldn't handle everything for you, if you would authorize him to do so. Then the Federal Trust and the New Hampshire Realty and your white-headed manager would report all receipts to Mr. X instead of to you. He would turn the money over to you as it was received, withholding a certain percentage in each instance. This percentage would be deposited in a special account, so that as each income tax payment fell due, there would be cash on hand to meet it in full. Mr. X would also prepare your tax returns for you in proper form, handling the whole thing for you and relieving you of all responsibility. It might be a very good thing if he went over your personal checkbook with you, say once a quarter, to keep track of deductible items of expense. Otherwise, he'd never have to bother you."

"It really could be handled that way?"

"I don't see why not. Anyhow, I'd like very much—"

Again the telephone rang and Roger picked up the receiver.

"Hello," he said. "Yes, Mr. Mills. Yes, the rug is at my house right now. Yes, I'll take it there early tomorrow morning—you know Court isn't sitting today. Yes, I do believe we have about an even chance of winning, but the difficulty is. . . . Yes, sir, of course you may count on me." He had managed to speak evenly, betraying neither annoyance nor agitation at the inopportune interruption. But, as he turned from the telephone to face his caller once more, his words came with a rush. "What I was trying to say, Mrs. Forbes, was just this: I'd like very much to have a try at handling your affairs for you myself, if you'd let me. I know you must feel I haven't had much experience. But I'd do the very best I could for you. Not just because you're Emily's grandmother either. But because you're about the grandest person I've ever known and I'd be proud to be of service to you."

He stopped abruptly and, for a moment, they both sat very still, looking at each other. But, as they did so, Old Mrs. Forbes found nothing in Roger's earnest and direct gaze which would cause her to doubt that every word he spoke was true and he found nothing in her appraising glance except astonished respect. She rose, gathering her sable wrap around her.

"No, don't come with me," she said emphatically, as he hastened to rise also. "I prefer to go alone. As I told you, I want to have a few words with Roscoe Cutter before I leave this building and I am not interested in having a third person present at the interview. . . . I suppose that rug you were just speaking of on the telephone is the same one Emily's been telling me about—some filthy, moth-ridden old rag that you've been dragging home every night lately."

"It isn't quite as bad as that, Mrs. Forbes. It has been sort of a nuisance, taking the thing around in taxis and elevators, I mean. But it is a vital exhibit in a suit, and a court officer wouldn't accept responsibility for it. So I've had to lug it in and out of court. You see, our client bought it as an Oriental and then some friend of his, who knows more about rugs than he does, told him it was no such thing. So the purchaser holds up payment and the dealer sues and the purchaser brings countersuit. The whole thing hinges on what representations or misrepresentations were made. And of course the rug—"

"You get Morris Brucker to testify that rug is no more an Oriental than the dirty little mat under your feet and it'll be the end of the whole matter," Old Mrs. Forbes broke in, speaking with all her former briskness.

"Why, I could do that, couldn't I?"

Roger spoke with admiration not untinged by amazement. The feminine mind was certainly a baffling instrument. It was not more than ten minutes since his visitor had revealed a completely blind spot in regard to taxes. Yet now, with startling swiftness, she had shown him the solution of a problem with which he had been vainly grappling for several weeks.

"Of course you could," Old Mrs. Forbes went on, as if that question were so easily settled that it did not require further discussion. "Well, I suppose you've got to see that rug case through, since you've started on it. But after you've won it, I don't want to see you trying any more cases like it. If you're going to look after my property, you're not going to have time to drag rugs around. What's more, I don't want my personal legal advisor to be the butt of all kinds of wisecracks from taxi drivers and elevator boys—as I don't doubt you have been. It was bad enough when you went chasing off to Lynn to catch lobsters—well, somewhere and something of that sort. But this is worse. I intend to tell Roscoe Cutter just how I feel about it. I propose to be represented in a dignified manner."

Roger started to speak and then refrained from doing so. As far as he knew, the agent from the Department of Internal Revenue was the only person who had ever succeeded in defeating Old Mrs. Forbes through argument, and he was inclined to believe that history was not likely to repeat itself in that respect—certainly not in this particular instance. It would not take Roscoe Cutter long to realize that the Forbes account was worth all the lobsters and rugs which could be dragged into the Middlesex Superior Court, not only in prestige but in cold cash.

"Incidentally, as I am going to keep coming to this office, I should like to be greeted by a receptionist who is a receptionist," Old Mrs. Forbes continued, pausing on the threshold. "That poor girl out there doesn't have a chance to do a good job. Her typewriting gets interrupted by the buzzer and while she is attending to that someone gets out of the elevator. She has entirely too much work to do and evidently her salary is also quite inadequate. Her dress looks cheap and she needs a permanent and a manicure. I also think that a few square meals might improve her color and her figure. Not that I am suggesting you should take her out to dinner, while Emily is busying herself with the Vincent Club, though some such thing might not be a bad idea. Be that as it may, I may as well talk to Roscoe Cutter about his receptionist while I am bringing other details to his attention."

The door had hardly closed behind Old Mrs. Forbes when Roger snatched up the documents she had left on his desk and plunged excitedly into his tax project. He was soon so completely immersed in it that he did not realize the afternoon had slipped away, until the door of his office slowly opened and Brian, having first peered around with an air of great caution, entered on tiptoe, his battered felt hat in his hand. Laying this and his brief case down on the chair earlier occupied by his associate's new client, he salaamed deeply several times.

Roger laughed, throwing down the pencil with which he had been figuring and pushing aside a sheaf of loose-leaf account sheets.

"Cut it out, Briny. What's got into you?"

"As if you didn't know! And realize that everyone else in these here parts must know by now. Why, the grapevine's been so busy it's had to put out new tendrils!"

Roger laughed again. "Sit down and let's talk about it. This is a pretty big thing, Briny. I'm going to need lots of help and I'm counting on you for some of it. Of course, I've already got in touch with a couple of accountants and called the tax office for copies of all requisite forms, but I think I ought to set up a separate account next. Don't you think I should discuss this at the bank?"

"Of course. And I'd go straight to Ellery Stockbridge. You know he's president of the Third National now and I don't need to tell you he's one of our best clients. Not that he's a patch on what Old Lady Forbes will be. Jeepers creepers, what a windfall! And am I glad you've got it! Of course, you've had something coming to you for a long time—but who'da thought it would be this size? When the news first got around that the old lady was here, everyone thought it was just a family visit; but when she walked into the Artful Dodger's office and began to tell him off, you could have heard the commotion if you'd been on the Common. Naturally she asked for the Ruddy Oarsman first and when she found he'd already left for the day—and why—were there ructions? At that, I believe it's all to the good that the Artful Dodger's the one she finally pounced on. He could see the shekels rolling in and piling up with a clearer eye than the R. O. even if that old so-and-so has the skin breezes love to blow on. . . . Look, you're not trying to telephone Stockbridge tonight, are you? Cora has long since departed for the home of the honest working girl, which hereafter may be slightly less humble than in the past, thanks to the firm's new benefactor. The bank's been closed for hours."

"Good grief! I had no idea it was that late!"

"Time to call it a day and then some. You and I are closing up the joint this evening. There's something I've wanted to get off my chest for a long while, so I thought—"

"Shoot!"

"Well, I guess there isn't any graceful way for a man to admit he's made a damn fool of himself. Or any easy way either. But that's what I know I did and I'm sorry as hell. Honest to God though, I didn't set out to mess up your wife's dinner party. When you asked me to your house, I really did think it was for an evening with the boys, like what we'll be having at home tonight. If I hadn't, I wouldn't have come dressed like a bookmaker and I wouldn't have stopped for a couple of quick ones with Tim. I wouldn't have—"

"Say, let's skip it!" Roger found Brian's obvious sincerity moving and his embarrassment contagious. Determined not to show this, he blurted out in what was meant to be a casual tone, "It was just one of those things."

"Well, I'm glad you realize I wouldn't go in for clowning on general principles. But what about your wife?"

"Why, Emily—" Roger began. But his tone failed to carry conviction. Brian interrupted him.

"Don't bother to go on. I know she thinks I'm as crude as they come. I'm sorry about that too, because I like her and I wish she liked me. If you'd just tell her tonight for me that if there's any way I can show her—"

"Why don't we just forget the whole thing?"

"You mean you don't want to ask her—"

"It's not exactly that. But I couldn't tonight, anyway. She won't be home until late and then she'll be dead tired. She's been rehearsing all afternoon for the Vincent Show, and she telephoned awhile back to say that something didn't quite come off in one of the lyrics, so she's going to Marion's to see if between them they can't fix it up. It's very important for them to get it just right before tomorrow. I'll be dining in solitary state when I get home—if I ever do get home with all the work I've still got ahead of me here."

Roger motioned, half proudly and half desperately, toward the pile of papers which littered his desk. Brian shook his head.

"You can't straighten all that out at a sitting, no matter how hard you try."

"Well, I've got to keep on trying anyway. And not just to straighten out this tax deal. There's another job Mrs. Forbes wants handled too—matter of fact, it was the one she spoke of first and I haven't even made a start on that, because I got sidetracked. Look here—you don't happen to know anything about the zoning setup in the area around Gloucester Street, do you?"

"Well, I know this much: I know my uncle, Barney Garvin, is secretary to the Zoning Board of Appeal. And I know he can fix things so that any ten blocks beyond the golden streets of heaven would be off limits to the saints. Would that help any?"

"Would it help? How soon. . . . I mean, would it be convenient for you to introduce me to your uncle sometime, so that I can ask him which side is up?"

"Sometime? He's coming to our house tonight. He always sits in on our little poker parties. Why don't you come along and meet him right now, instead of 'dining in solitary state'? It's a foul night, but you won't get any wetter going to South Boston than you would going to Joy Street. The whole family'd be tickled to death to have you take potluck with us and all your zoning troubles would be fixed, but good, before the first bluff of the game had been called. What do you say?"

Chapter 13

It took Roger and Brian something less than half an hour to reach the Collins' house from the offices of Cutter, Mills and Swan; but Roger realized afterward that no previous journey had taken him into territory so unfamiliar.

To be sure, he had long been acquainted with the first part of their route, which took them to Scollay Square—past the Old State House, the famous steaming teakettle which served as a trade-mark for the Oriental Tea and Coffee Company and the mammoth pipe marking Erlich's Pipe and Tobacco Store. The lights of the Old Howard were murkily revealed beyond the big snowflakes which melted as they fell, and diners were streaming out of Patten's Restaurant, their umbrellas interlocking as they opened them. While Roger and Brian waited to get across to the subway entrance, they were liberally spattered by slush from the tangled traffic; and even when the lights changed to permit their passage, cars coming down Tremont Street and turning into the Square made their progress hazardous.

All this was in the realm of frequent and familiar experience to Roger; neither was there anything strange about plunging down into the subway and fighting for a place on a train. He had done that for years already. But he had never before taken a car marked "City Point"; and when this emerged from the subway at the corner of Shawmut Avenue and Broadway, the feeling of strangeness began.

The City Point car crossed a bridge which seemed to surmount railroad tracks and then plunged up and down a succession of small hills, its progress mildly suggestive of a ride on a roller coaster. This plunging motion rendered any scrutiny of the route doubly difficult, and this was already obscured by the early dusk and the big snowflakes. However, as nearly as Roger could make out, they were passing through a business district where small shops and large signs predominated. Eventually, Brian signaled to the conductor and nodded to his guest.

"Car turns off Broadway here," he said. "We have to walk a little over a block. I'm sorry it's such a foul night. But you don't mind, do you? It'll be nice and warm after we get there."

"Of course I don't mind. I'm interested in seeing this section of the city."

" 'Parts unknown,' eh?"

"Well, I didn't mean that exactly," Roger replied in some embarrassment.

"I know you didn't—at least, not offensively. And maybe you'll have a happy surprise, at that."

The guess was correct. Roger knew that Brian's people were well to do; but he had assumed that some strange attachment must have caused them to cling to the quarters their immediate forebears had occupied as immigrants, for he had never thought of South Boston except in terms of drabness interspersed with squalor. Therefore, he was amazed to see that the houses on the hill they were now mounting were not only sizable and substantial, but that hardly any of them gave any evidence of a rundown condition or of multiple occupancy. At the top of the hill, a large park stretched out expansively to the left and facing it, in addition to a block of rather distinctive brick houses, their long flights of steps railed with ornamental ironwork, were several detached residences of imposing proportions, typifying the Victorian Era, and set in ample, well-landscaped grounds. The big snowflakes had now changed to slanting rain and the houses looming up beyond this gave a general effect of enduring solidity and spaciousness; their long, lighted windows bespoke good-fellowship and good cheer. Brian closed his dripping umbrella and ran rapidly up the steps of the largest and handsomest house in sight, proclaiming his presence in a ringing voice at the same moment that his key turned in the latch.

"Hello, everybody! Where are you all keeping yourselves? Come see who I've brought home to supper!"

A radio in some room beyond was blaring a tune so loudly that Roger wondered how Brian could possibly make himself heard above it, especially as the noise it made was only part of a general tumult. Nevertheless, there was an instantaneous response to his greeting. A small child with a big pink bow atop her fiery red curls came bounding into the hallway, followed by two young girls only slightly more subdued as to coloring and movement. All three flung themselves upon Brian with outstretched arms and shouts of joy and, while he was tossing the youngest one up in the air, a gangling boy, a thickset young priest and several older persons, all beaming broadly, appeared on the scene. Brian set the little girl on her feet and, still holding her close to him, began his introductions.

"Easy now. You don't want to scare our visitor off with all your ructions. He's not used to the like of this. Roger, this small hellion here is Queenie. And right behind her Della and Doreen—my other sisters aren't home. Bearing up to the rear of them is my collegiate brother Ray and my clerical brother Mat and still farther off, Himself and Herself.

And yes—I thought so, Uncle Barney Garvin. Folks, this is my friend, Roger Field."

Having observed that this presentation was producing the desired effect, and that everyone was, in turn, greeting Roger with reasonable adequacy—Queenie suddenly very shy, with one finger in her mouth, Della and Doreen bobbing quick little curtsies, Ray shaking hands in pumplike fashion and Father Mat doing so with a firm grip—Brian responded heartily to the backslapping of his father and his uncle, kissed his mother resoundingly, and then held her at arm's length, looking at her admiringly, before kissing her again.

"Is it any wonder now I don't want to get married?" he inquired, looking over his shoulder at Roger. "My old man got the last of this kind. That's why Uncle Barney's still a bachelor too. Isn't it, Uncle Barney?"

"Will you hush your nonsense, Brian, and bring Mr. Field on into the sitting room? We were just having a little drink before we sat down to supper. He could do with one too, I'm sure."

"Maybe he wants to go to the bathroom first," suggested Queenie, removing her finger from her mouth and transferring it, after she had spoken, to a curl which she proceeded to wind around it.

"Now maybe he does, darling, at that," Mrs. Collins said dotingly to Queenie, meanwhile casting a reproving glance in the direction of the two older daughters, who were tittering. "You show him where to go, Ray, and we'll have his drink ready for him when he gets back."

The drink, with which Father Mat promptly presented him, was so good that Roger was persuaded, without much trouble, to have a second one. The assembled family was now in the sitting room, forming an uneven circle; and though the radio was still going, Brian had turned it down to something resembling normal volume, so that casual conversation could proceed in a more or less natural tone, though nobody seemed to feel any compulsion to create small talk. The large square room lent itself readily to companionship; and Roger was so pleasantly aware of the overstuffed sofa's comfort that he hardly noticed the upholstery of pressed plush, the Axminster rug, the chromo of the Sacred Heart, flanked by family portraits, or even the rather gory crucifix hanging above the mantelpiece. Both Brian's father and his Uncle Barney gave such an immediate impression of good will and geniality that he found it difficult to associate either one with crooked politics and generally shady practices, in spite of all the tales he had heard to the contrary, and Father Mat's conviviality came as a great and welcome surprise. But it was Mrs. Collins who affected him most profoundly. She sat calmly in a large armchair, her face benign above an ample figure and a nondescript dress, her expression suffused with such genuine loving-kindness that he could not take his eyes off her. The hands which lay loosely clasped in her lap, unornamented except for a wide wedding band, were rough and wrinkled, and her thin gray hair was brushed back from her brow without any attempt at studied arrangement. But looking at her, he felt the force and the beauty of maternity as never before in the course of his life.

Eventually Mrs. Collins rose, saying she must see to the steak and signaling Della and Doreen to go with her. Brian, making a sign to his uncle, withdrew to the farther side of the room and engaged him in earnest, but low-voiced conversation, of which Roger thought he could guess the purport. Ray, spreading open a well-thumbed textbook, asked Father Mat if he would mind going on where they had left off; and soon thereafter Roger caught, intermittently, the cadences of vaguely remembered passages from Virgil. Mr. Collins, lifting Queenie onto his lap, shifted his chair a little nearer their guest.

"As Briny told you, two of our daughters aren't here tonight," he said genially, stroking Queenie's curls as he spoke. "I'm sorry they wouldn't get to meet you—but then, you'll be coming again, now you've found the way here, and we're lucky enough to have them both near by. Not to talk of the luck of having Mat right at the Gate of Heaven Church. It'll be a sad day for us when the fledglings start leaving the nest, but we've got to expect it sooner or later. Meanwhile, Sheila's a teacher at St. Brigid's School and Katie lives right across the way from the Carney Hospital on Thomas Park—as pleasant a place as you'd ever wish to see, right where she can look at the monument out of her front windows and the water out of her back ones. Like as not, you know just where I mean."

Expressing regret, Roger said that he didn't.

"Well, we'll take you there too, one of these fine days, as soon as Katie's got her strength back. She's just had her fourth in five years, and a fine boy it is, and she with plenty of milk and all and all. There was a bit of trouble when he came, I don't rightly know just what, except maybe he was too big. Everything's all right again now, but they're keeping her at the hospital longer than common; and Terence, that's her husband, goes up there to be with her, after he gets through his day's work, and stays till they kick him out. No doubt you've found out for yourself how these hospitals treat the poor young fathers nowadays, as if they didn't have a right in the world. I take it your wife's lying-in too?"

"Why, no," Roger replied, ashamed to realize that he was flushing. "So far, we haven't . . . I mean, Emily's quite well, thank you. But she had a —a rehearsal for a benefit and I was at rather loose ends until Briny—"

"Well, now, it's a fine thing when young women don't give up their church work just because they've married," Mr. Collins remarked heartily. "And those that aren't blessed with babies haven't the excuse of those that are." Having groped for the probable reason why Roger had not brought his wife with him and guessed wrong, he was glad that another suitable explanation of her absence had so quickly been given. "Well, Terence will be coming along soon—he won't fail us for poker, even if he does miss out on the steak. A grand boy he is, one of the best. I don't know what I'd do without him in my business. Of course, any father's proud to have a son of his go into the Church or into the law. But when a man's two eldest both leave him in the lurch that way, in a manner of speaking, and his third isn't through with book learning by the time his father needs him. . . . Why, then it's a great thing to have a son-in-law stepping right into the breach!"

Roger agreed that it must be and Mr. Collins, having insisted that their drinks needed a little freshening, said that he would like to tell Briny's friend a few things about the contracting business later on in the evening, but that, meanwhile, it was Queenie's turn to talk. Queenie was in the first grade already, would Mr. Field ever believe it now? And she spoke pieces. Maybe she would speak one for him. At this point, Queenie put her finger in her mouth again and, nestling up against her father, retreated behind her curls. While he was still trying to tempt her, with appropriate bribes, to demonstrate her talents as an elocutionist, Della appeared in the doorway and announced that Doreen was just bringing in the steak.

There was an immediate surge to the dining room, which led out of the room where they had been sitting, and Father Mat asked a quick, cheery blessing, as everyone gathered around the long table which was covered with a white cloth. Mrs. Collins was already ensconced at one end of this table, with two well-heaped, smoking hot vegetable dishes before her. Mr. Collins took his place at the opposite end, and began to carve the steaks, which were spread imposingly over a huge platter. They were nearly three inches thick, broiled to a turn and garnished with crisp onion rings. When he had placed a generous portion on one of the plates piled in front of him, this was passed down the table to Mrs. Collins, who flanked it with mounds of mashed potatoes and string beans and then sent it along again, repeating this process until everyone had been served. Meanwhile, milk, butter, jelly, pickles and hot rolls had been circulated from the sidelines. For a few moments, the requirements of healthy appetites effectually put a stop to the flow of talk and remarks were limited to requests for another roll, more butter and a second helping of beans. But, by the time the vegetable dishes had been refilled and more steak brought in, hunger was sufficiently appeased so that conversation gradually became animated again.

"How'd you make out in basketball practice this afternoon, Ray?"

"Not so hot. Somehow I couldn't hit the hoop for missing."

"You made up your mind about that dance yet, Della?"

"Well, I've decided to go. But I haven't made up my mind who with."

"There's the telephone ringing right now. Maybe that'll help you decide."

Della dashed out of the dining room, to return a few minutes later with heightened color and an unconvincingly demure expression. Ray nudged her as she sat down.

"How's good old George doing?"

"It wasn't George."

"Well, how's good old Jim doing?"

"Leave your sister be, Ray," admonished Mr. Collins. "Like as not, it wasn't a boy at all."

"Oh, yes it was!" Della announced hastily, unwilling that their guest should suppose she would attach enough importance to a call from another girl to absent herself so long from table. "It was Tom Kelleher."

"That character!"

"He isn't a character. He's—"

"That'll do about Tom Kelleher for the present. And I'd be just as pleased, Della, if we could have a little less talk about boys from you. It wouldn't hurt any if you didn't go to quite so many dances and gave more of your time to the Children of Mary. Now Mr. Field was telling me, just before supper—what was that church work of your wife's you were talking about, Mr. Field?"

"It isn't church work, exactly," Roger said, again conscious of visible embarrassment. "It's the Vincent Club."

"And something to do with the good sisters of St. Vincent de Paul, no doubt," Mrs. Collins said hopefully and pleasantly.

"Well, no. You see, a long time ago there was an actress named Mrs. Vincent and—"

"An actress!" exclaimed Doreen. "That's what I want to be."

"Over my dead body," observed Mr. Collins tersely. "But you might let Mr. Field go on, at that."

"I believe she was very much admired, very much beloved," Roger continued, his embarrassment increasing. "At all events, when she died, one of her admirers—a Miss Caroline Staples—wanted to give money toward a worthy memorial for her. And she—or somebody acting for her, I'm not sure which—asked Phillips Brooks if it would be all right for an actress' name to be connected with the dispensary maintained by Trinity Church."

"Who's Phillips Brooks?" Ray inquired.

Barney Garvin groaned. "And you on the Honor Roll at school!" he said indignantly. "Phillips Brooks's been dead some fifty years now, you dope—and well I remember how the whole city grieved when he was taken, though I was just a young boy then. He was one of the best that ever came out of New England, and one of the finest Christians, God rest his soul, if he was a heretic. He'd been rector of Trinity Church and he was Protestant Bishop of Massachusetts at the time Mr. Field's talking about. I could have told you something about this Vincent Club myself and the good work it's done, but I didn't know the background. Go on, Mr. Field, if you haven't given up because you think you can never get in a word edgewise in this house."

"I'm afraid I'm boring some of you. But you asked me—"

"That we did, Mr. Field, and we want you to go on, like Barney says,"

Mrs. Collins interposed warmly. "What did this fine great man say when those nice ladies asked him would it be all right?"

"He said, 'Why not? She was a good woman,' " Roger answered, with a grateful glance at Mrs. Collins.

"You see! And so then—"

"Well, after some more money came in, from various sources, the Vincent Memorial Hospital was incorporated. But there still wasn't enough money to run it. So then a small organization was formed to give annual entertainments—hospital benefits."

"There! I said all along it must be a good work!" Mrs. Collins announced triumphantly. "And this Vincent Club your wife belongs to—it's that small organization grown big, isn't it now?"

"Yes. It's quite big. And it puts on awfully good shows every spring—singing and dancing, like in a musical comedy, you know. Then there's the famous Drill. That began as the 'March of the Baby Blues' with twelve girls in it. Now there are sixteen. A girl can't be in the Drill unless she's tall and —well, very good looking. She doesn't belong anyway of course, unless—"

He stopped abruptly. He could not say, "She doesn't belong unless she has all the right qualifications. The Vincent Club does do good work, important work. But it's very exclusive. A girl can't belong just because she wants to do good work or because she has a talent for singing and dancing or even just because she's pretty and pleasant, like Della and Doreen. She's got to be elected to membership and she's chosen largely because of her social standing. Not wholly, of course. She's got to have the other attributes too. But they wouldn't help if she *didn't* have social standing." Suddenly, it seemed to him very strange that he should be telling these hosts of his, who had lived in the same city where the Vincent Club had been giving shows for nearly fifty years, not only what it did, but what it was. Barney Garvin knew something about it and probably Brian did too, though Brian had been exceptionally quiet throughout the conversation. But none of the others had ever so much as heard of it, unless so vaguely that they did not remember, and most of them were only listening out of politeness now. Yet Roger himself had always thought it was so important! Even Old Mrs. Forbes, who was hard to impress, thought it was important enough for Emily to devote practically all her time to it, for weeks and weeks, not because the Memorial Hospital would benefit by this, but because it would mean that Priscilla might have a better chance of being elected to the Vincent Club next year. He looked down the table at Mrs. Collins, who still sat smiling benignly and, as he did so, he became aware, as never before, of the limitations to the standards imposed by his own set and suddenly he felt vaguely ashamed of them. Then, incongruously, he also became aware of Queenie, beating on the table with her fork and speaking shrilly.

"I ate up my meat and potato a long time ago. I want my dessert."

"Of course you do, darling. We all do. Mr. Field's been telling us a nice

143

story and we didn't want to interrupt. But Della and Doreen are going to change the plates right now. And guess what's coming next!"

"Ice cream?" inquired Queenie hopefully.

"No. Guess again."

"Chocolate chiffon pie?"

"Right you are. And Mother's going to cut you a great big piece!"

The two teen-agers cleared the table quietly and quickly. Roger noticed that Della looked rather smug and Doreen slightly sulky; it did not take any great powers of perception to guess that Della was gloating over her obvious popularity and that Doreen would have felt better if she too had also received a telephone call. But their respective moods did not interfere with their efficiency and two coffeepots, two chocolate pies and the indicated cups and plates to take care of these made their prompt appearance. The telephone rang again and, though Doreen hastened to answer it, she returned to the dining room looking sulkier than before, with the announcement that it was for Uncle Barney. His absence was prolonged and, during the course of it, Queenie abandoned the last few crumbs of her pie and began to rub her eyes.

"The sandman must be around here somewhere," Ray announced with a prodigious wink. "Want Ray to take you upstairs piggyback, dearie?"

Queenie squirmed in her seat. "No. I don't want to go upstairs."

"Not even if Mat and Briny make a chair with their hands?"

The suggestion came from the vigorous young priest. The brothers rose, grasping their own left wrists with their right hands and each other's with their left. The "chair," having thus been formed, they swung their arms back and forth invitingly. Queenie, visibly tempted, but still hesitant, half slid from her seat and then slid back on it again.

"Too bad—Queenie'll have to walk upstairs then. I want some more pie and Terry'll be coming any minute now, hellbent for poker."

Brian made as if to go back to his own seat and Queenie immediately slid all the way from hers.

"No, no, Briny! I do want to ride on the chair! But you'll have to wait till I kiss everybody good night."

She bestowed moist smacks, supplemented, in several cases, with big hugs, on everyone in the assembled group, though she hesitated for a moment when she came to Roger. Then she wriggled herself into place on her brothers' clasped hands and put her arms around their necks. They straightened up and marched out of the room, singing: "Come, little queen, in your flying machine." At the top of the stairs, Father Mat interrupted the song to call down to Mrs. Collins.

"I'll hear her prayers, Mother. Don't bother to come up."

"Two years already, she's undressed herself," Mrs. Collins told Roger proudly. "But sometimes she skimps a bit on her Hail Marys. You know how it is with a child. Mat'll take care of that all right though. And I'll have a look at her later on, when the girls and I have done the dishes and you men are having your poker game. . . . Well, Terence! Briny was just saying you'd be along any minute now. Meet his friend, Roger Field, that we're lucky enough to have with us tonight. Would you have a bite of pie and a sip of coffee while you're telling us about Katie and the baby?"

Terence Lenahan acknowledged the introduction in the same hearty way that the others had done and, falling in with his mother-in-law's suggestion, took the chair vacated by Queenie. "We'll be getting him and Katie home day after tomorrow," he said in conclusion. "I was thinking of speaking to Mat about the baptism."

"He'll be down in a minute, when he's finished hearing Queenie's prayers. . . . Well, Barney! It wasn't any bad news, I hope, that kept you so long at the telephone?"

"No, not what you'd call bad. But I've just heard that it looks now as if the legislature might go along with the Governor on those cuts he wants made in the budget. If it does, there won't be enough cash to go around. Not that I'm really worried. But could be Shaun and Terence won't get all they thought they had coming to them on the new highway contracts and I'd be sorry if—"

"Well, there'll be no bids submitted tonight and no contracts let, either," Mrs. Collins observed with what was apparently never-failing cheerfulness. "So why not put the whole matter from your minds and get started on your poker? . . . You'll be going with Shaun and Barney and the boys to the den, Mr. Field," she added, rising to indicate that supper was now over. "Maybe I'll see you again later on, if your game doesn't last too long. I'll be in the sitting room for a while, listening to the radio, after the girls and I get the table cleared and the dishes done. But the chances are I'll be abed and asleep long before you cash in the chips. So I'll bid you good night now, just in case, and tell you I hope it won't be a month of Sundays before you find your way here again."

Roger's expressions of appreciation for her hospitality were cut short by the obvious impatience of the other men to begin their game; in fact, Barney Garvin and Terence Lenahan, who were discussing with Father Mat the Cardinal's visit to Rome, had already strolled out of the dining room with the priest before Roger left it, accompanied by Mr. Collins and Brian. After they had crossed the hall and entered the back parlor, which, like the front parlor, was more dimly lighted than the other rooms, and gave no impression of impending occupancy, Mr. Collins paused and glanced about him with pride.

"When I was a newly married man, Barney and I and the whole of our gang used to have our poker games in the dining room," he said. "But after the family got bigger, that meant taking the leaves out of the table every Monday night and putting them back again every Tuesday morning. So, when I bought this house, we set up our poker table in the back parlor. Then, along came Terence, courting Katie, and either we had to pull the sliding doors to, between the front and back parlors, or have them hearing everything we said or else us hearing everything they said—and I don't know which was the worst! Besides, it was harder tugging at those sliding doors even than taking leaves out of a table and putting them back again. Then all the youngsters wanted to have parties, if you please, using both parlors and crowding the poor old men out. So I made up my mind it was time Barney and I had a room we could call our own and I built on this den. There was plenty of land, what with a corner lot and all and the ell being narrower than the front of the house. I still didn't shut off any light from the kitchen, because this den of mine's no deeper than the pantry—and that's still got light on one side, as we'll show you later on. Now take a look and see if you don't think I did a good job!"

The thought flashed through Roger's mind that the pantry must indeed be immense if this "den" which flanked it did not extend beyond its limits in depth. But he politely focused his attention on the addition which was obviously a source of great satisfaction to his host and which, architec-turally, bore not the slightest resemblance to the huge Victorian double parlor where they were standing and from which it led. It was beamed and wainscoted in fumed oak and furnished to match in the so-called "mis-sion style" which had been popular at the turn of the century. The walls above the wainscoting were covered with burlap and hung with diplomas and group photographs of young men in various stages of athletic undress; and, above a gas log, a mantel was profusely decorated with silver cups. In the center of the room was an immense circular gaming table, its green baize center rimmed with inlaid wood, which was recessed into compart-ments for individual supplies of chips. Comfortable swivel chairs were drawn up around this luxury item and Barney Garvin, Father Mat and Terence Lenahan, who had now stopped talking about the Cardinal and were discussing the gold mine which ex-Governor Curley had recently bought in Nevada, were already leaning against three of these. Their eager-ness to "get going" was even more obvious than it had been in the dining room; nevertheless, Roger rightly sensed that Mr. Collins would appre-ciate some expression of admiration from their guest, even if this involved a slight delay. Wishing he knew whether the room itself, the silver tro-phies, or the elaborate gaming table was the source of the greatest pride to the greatest number, he strove to make his enthusiastic comment as inclusive as possible.

"I should say you *did* do a good job!" he exclaimed. "This is a man's room all right—the kind every house ought to have!" Momentarily, he felt a twinge of conscience; it was certainly not the kind of a room he would ever want in his house. But the pleased look on Mr. Collins' genial face encouraged him to go on in the same vein, even if this did mean stretching the truth. "In fact, it looks as if you'd done all kinds of good jobs," he added, nodding first in the direction of the silver cups and then toward the diplomas, "and that certainly is some card table! I don't think I ever saw such a beauty."

146

"Well now, I can't take credit for the trophies and the degrees," Mr. Collins admitted. "Those are the boys'. But since I didn't have any of my own and we were all going to make use of this den together, I asked them, wouldn't it be a good idea to put them here, where we could all see them, instead of in their bedrooms. Mat was quite a boxer—still is in fact. He'll be getting you down to his community center one of these days when he's giving his boys a tryout—his poker winnings keep them in gloves." Roger, following Mr. Collins' glance in the direction of the priest, saw that Father Mat had now divested himself not only of his coat, like the other men, but of his clerical collar, and that he was briskly rolling up his sleeves to reveal muscular and hairy forearms. "And Briny was captain of the baseball team at Holy Cross—didn't he ever tell you?" Mr. Collins went on with increasing pride. "As to the gaming table, maybe I can take credit for that. It was a present from the men who've helped me put the Collins Contracting Company on the map. They gave it to me on the twenty-fifth anniversary of the day when I started out for myself, with only a couple of helpers on the job. Now I've got fifty."

"From what Uncle Barney's been saying, I think maybe we made a mistake not to get in on this gold mine, Dad," Terence broke in, with a note of regret in his cheery voice. "Especially if those rumors about a cut in the budget are true, as I'm afraid they may be. Once Saltonstall gets started on this damned economy program—"

"Even if he does, the less we have to do with gold mines, away off in Nevada or some such place, the better," Mr. Collins announced decidedly. "All too often they turn out to be gold bricks instead. And I understand they're calling this one Curley's Luck—which hasn't been any too good lately, more's the pity! Besides, you heard what Herself said, bless her heart—there'll be no bids submitted and no contracts let tonight. So we might as well forget about economy and Republicans and all such blights and get on with our game. . . . You don't know our ways yet, Mr. Field, so you may not have noticed that here's bourbon and Scotch and, praise the saints! a bottle of Bushmill's on the sideboard over there. You'll be helping yourself as the spirit moves you, I hope, the same as the rest of us will."

As a matter of fact, Roger had already observed the prodigal display of whisky, which was supplemented by a thermos bucket, presumably ice filled, a pitcher of ice water, bottles of soda and ginger ale and tall glasses. As he took the place now indicated as his, Barney Garvin stripped the jokers from a new deck and riffled the cards skillfully, while Brian measured out six stacks of chips.

"Ten dollars each okay with everybody?" he asked. "Ten-cent ante and fifty-cent limit—table stakes—dealer's choice—everybody antes for draw, only the dealer for stud—and whoever gets caught bluffing loses the pot."

Uncle Barney passed the cards to Shaun Collins for a cut and then began to deal them swiftly.

"First black jack wins the deal," he said, but, just as he spoke, the knave of clubs fell, face up, before Brian, who swept the deck into a neat pile and began to shuffle.

"Plenty of beer on ice in the pantry if you'd rather have that than whisky, Mr. Field," Shaun Collins remarked expansively.

"No thanks. You said I might see the pantry later on and I'd like to, immensely. But no beer could touch this Bushmill's!"

"Sure we'll be showing you the pantry. Herself would never forgive us if we didn't. It's her pride and joy now that she's got it fixed up just the way she wants it, with a ten-foot electric refrigerator and a stainless steel sink with double drainboards and all the rest. . . . What'll it be, Briny?"

"Stud, of course, Ould One."

"I suppose my father-in-law'll be hushing me up again," Terence remarked in an aside to Roger, "but all this talk about budget cutting does get me down. Here's the United States Senate passing an appropriation bill of nearly two billions and, at the same time. . . . Who, me? No, I won't stay in, not even for a white one. . . . And at the same time Saltonstall. . . . Of course, we ought to know what to expect in Washington, with a stuffed shirt like Russell Forbes for a junior senator, but it does seem as if here in Massachusetts—"

"Mind your manners there, Terry, or Roger'll think we're a lot of bog-trotters. He's had the great privilege of acquiring Russell Forbes as an uncle by marriage."

"Gosh, I must have known that, but I'd forgotten if I did. No offense, I hope?"

"Of course not. I've hardly met Senator Forbes and I'm afraid I don't know anything at all about politics, local or national."

"That's because you're concentrating on law, which is what I ought to be doing. Now I'd like nothing better than to dabble in politics a bit on the side, beginning right now by running for the City Council and gradually working up to something big—like taking Russell Forbes' seat away from him, for instance."

"Will you hush your mouth, Briny? You too, Terry. How can we keep our minds on the game with all this foolish chatter going on? Just because you're out—"

The complaint came from Barney Garvin. Brian, as well as his father, had followed the example of Terence by dropping out in the second round, so only his uncle, Father Mat and Roger were left to call for the final card of the deal.

"If it's like that," grumbled Barney after Roger had raised his bet, "I'd better try for a cheap look. I'll call, but just to keep you honest. Let's see the last one, Briny."

Brian flipped a card across the table to his uncle, then another to Roger, and put the balance of the deck aside.

"Your king-ten's still high," he reminded his uncle.

"Check the bet to Mr. Field," said the latter.

"Go on, bet him," urged Terence.

Roger shook his head. He had been rather appalled at the size of the stakes, accustomed as he was to bridge at a twentieth point. Though by no means a poker addict, he realized he might easily lose thirty or forty dollars in this friendly game, but he had seen no way in which he could reasonably do anything about it.

"I'll check it too," he said. "Mine's a pair of nines."

"That's good as gold," Uncle Barney sighed. "All I had was a hole ace, and my king topped anything you had showing. . . . Deal, Shaun."

Brian's father passed the cards to his son for a cut.

"Draw," he announced. "Jacks or better to open."

"I'll open for two and I'm warning the rest of you not to come in unless you've got prospects, because mine's pat," Father Mat announced.

The priest was a type definitely new in Roger's experience. Yet, once recovered from his first surprise, he found Father Mat greatly to his liking. It had come to him as something of a shock that a clergyman should be built like a coal heaver; that, having asked grace before meat, he should deliver himself, a few minutes later, of a hearty "Damn!" and that after supper was over, he should settle himself in a swivel chair, a brimming glass conveniently placed beside him, and play poker in his shirt sleeves. But gradually it had all come to seem natural and proper. Roger found himself losing his earlier sense of constraint and when the deck came to him, he flipped a white chip into the center of the table, dealt each player a card, face down, and then another, face up. "First ace bets," he reminded Brian. The latter cautiously lifted one corner of his hole card and peered beneath it.

"Might as well keep the ribbon clerks out," he announced cheerfully. "It'll cost you guys five to see the next card."

He looked a bit chagrined as all the others, even Roger, stayed with the hand. This ultimately became a spirited match between Brian and Roger, in which the latter's three sixes beat Brian's two pairs.

"Me and my big mouth!" Brian conceded ruefully. "I should have shut up about the ribbon clerks. . . . Well, anyway I win the deal."

"You didn't expect to get the winning hand when I was dealing, did you?" asked Roger, and Brian flashed him a quick, approving grin.

"Wolf in sheep's clothing, eh?" he retorted. "Maybe we'd better search you for chips and extra aces, at that."

"I ought to know what's going to happen to me when I sit down to the cards with one of these I-don't-hardly-even-know-the-game fellers," Barney Garvin grumbled. "You'd think I'd be gun-shy by this time. But no, Uncle Sucker always comes back, asking the boys please to skin him pretty. That's me all over."

"Yeah, too bad about you," gibed Brian. "They tell me that down at the Athletic Club you sent all the boys home for fresh money last week."

" 'Tis a slander, indeed," retorted Uncle Barney. "I may have won a few dimes. No more. And I am like to lose them three and four times over to this innocent from Joy Street who has come down here to spoil the Egyptians."

"Incidentally, that's not all he came down for, as I hinted to you before supper," Brian remarked. "He's got a zoning problem you might give him some advice on."

"Advice is cheap enough," observed Shaun Collins.

"Tell him about it, Rog," urged Brian. "Meantime, we'll all stop and have a drink, just to keep you from fleecing us while our attention's distracted."

"Why, it's like this," Roger began a bit diffidently. "My wife's grandmother, Mrs. Forbes, came in this afternoon to ask for my advice. I'd like very much to be helpful to her, if I could. Briny thought you would know whether I could do anything for her. It seems that her daughter, Eleanor —my mother-in-law—and her husband want to lease the house where they've lived ever since their marriage to a firm of dentists and Mrs. Forbes finds this a very distasteful prospect."

"What's wrong with dental parlors?" asked Father Mat bluntly.

"Why nothing, really," conceded Roger. "But Mrs. Forbes is an old lady of very decided views and she can't bear the thought of having a family possession, such as a house that her late husband gave his daughter for a wedding present, become a commercial establishment of any kind, maybe with a big, tooth-shaped signboard swinging in front of it and a glass case full of dentures beside the doorway."

"Where is this house now?" asked Barney Garvin, pulling at his pipe and releasing the smoke in a trickling cloud.

"Number sixteen Gloucester Street—near Marlborough."

Garvin nodded. "I know the block well. It's a residential area and, if you like, I can have the word passed down to the painless pullers that the Commissioner won't give them a permit. That'll knock a hole in the deal big enough to drop the Notre Dame squad through without touching the sides."

"I can't think of any way to do the trick more neatly," Roger agreed heartily. "And I don't know how to thank you enough, Mr. Garvin. I didn't have any idea—" He had started to say, "I didn't have any idea it could all be handled so simply." Opportunely, Brian interrupted.

"Now that's as good as settled, let's get on with our game," he said. "Here, let me freshen that drink of yours, Uncle Barney. Whose deal is it, anyway? Yours, Ould One? Well, deal it out then and let's see if we can win back some of this greenhorn's ill-gotten gains."

Chapter 14

Two HOURS LATER, as Roger went quickly up the steps of his house, whistling softly, but jubilantly, he could not help thinking of the night when he had returned from Salem, so completely discouraged that he could not seem to take heart, even when Emily received him with loving-kindness and revealed her passionate yearning for him. How much it would have meant to him then if he could only have known that within three short months he would have begun to prove his worth, both to her family and to his firm, and that, instead of inviting her compassion, he could claim her praise! He knew that from now on his status with Cutter, Mills and Swan would be vastly improved; the problem about the Gloucester Street house was as good as solved already; and on top of his big day at the office, he had spent an evening in a way so gladdening to him that the glow of its prevailing good-fellowship warmed him still. Last, but by no means least, he had in his pocket almost seventy dollars that had come from his winnings at poker—the first money which had ever come to him easily and pleasantly. And he had already made up his mind what he wanted to do with it: he would ask Emily to choose a brooch or a bracelet or some other trinket which could be bought within such a sum, and then they would have a little celebration the night she wore it for the first time —dinner at the Ritz and a show afterward. He had never given her a present like that or taken her out on the town like that. He had never been able to afford it. Now, at last, he could, instead of choosing seconds from a pushcart of flowers or stopping at a drugstore for a pound of candy.

He was still whistling as he turned his key in the latch, but suddenly remembering that it was very late, he suppressed his impulse to call out to Emily. She might very well be asleep by now—in fact, she should be, after her long, hard rehearsal and her session at the Swans'. To his amazement, the portieres of the library instantly parted and Emily, still in street clothes, came hastily toward him.

"Roger!" she exclaimed. "Where on earth have you been? What happened? I've been worried to death!"

"Why, I'm terribly sorry, darling," he said soothingly. "Didn't Ellie tell you that—" he broke off. His departure from the office had been so precipitate, his invitation from Brian so unexpected, that he had entirely forgotten to telephone and say he would not dine at home.

"Ellie said she hadn't heard a word from you. Deirdre kept your dinner warm for hours and both she and Ellie sat up until I got home. Then I telephoned every place I could think of. And no one else had heard a word from you either. Caroline's been worried to death too."

"I'm terribly sorry, darling," he said again. He put his arms around her and kissed her in the usual fond way that marked his home-coming; but though she returned his embrace, something was lacking in it, and he suddenly realized that there was an element of annoyance in her anxiety. As far as he knew, Emily had never been annoyed with him before—at all events, he had never been aware of such a feeling on her part. Distressed that she should have it now, and with reason, he tried, quickly, to explain.

"I had a pretty full day at the office. Your grandmother came in and offered me a wonderful piece of work. I was awfully pleased—pleased and proud and—well, rather touched that she should show so much confidence in me. So, after she left, I plunged right into this new job and I didn't realize how late it was until Brian came in and reminded me."

"But I telephoned the office too! I've telephoned there over and over again. And I never got any answer!"

"Well, of course you wouldn't have got any answer there after about quarter of seven. I didn't mean we'd just left. I meant we left after normal closing time."

"But where have you been ever since?"

"I've been at Brian's house. You see, he came into my cubbyhole to congratulate me and—well, talk to me about something that had been on his mind a long while. Then, on the spur of the moment, he asked me to go home to supper with him. I was knocked for a loop by this suggestion of your grandmother's anyway, and then this invitation of Brian's came as a complete surprise too. In the general excitement, I just plain forgot to telephone I wouldn't be home to dinner. . . . I'm terribly sorry, darling," he said for the third time. "I wouldn't have worried you, purposely, for the world, you know that. And I'll try to make my peace with Ellie and Deirdre in the morning. It shouldn't be too hard."

They had continued to stand, with their arms around each other, in the hall, and now Roger tried to draw Emily closer to him and to kiss her again. To his bewilderment, she stiffened slightly.

"Of course I'm very glad that Grandmamma's given you some important work to do," she said. "Perhaps if it's important enough, Mr. Mills won't make you go on dragging dirty rugs around. I certainly hope so."

As she spoke, she cast a resentful glance at the offending object which lay beside the hall table. Roger laughed.

"It *is* important enough. My dear, allow me to tell you that you are now gazing on that priceless Oriental for the last time."

"I'm very glad. But I still don't understand why you should have been so excited over an invitation from Brian Collins that you'd forget everything else. I shouldn't think you'd have even wanted to go home to supper with him, after the way he acted here."

"It wasn't just the invitation. It was the combination of everything. But I did want to go home with him. . . . Perhaps I can explain better if I don't have to do it standing here in the hall. I've been hoping for the last five minutes that you'd invite me into the library—at least."

His tone was now light and loving. But Emily did not respond to this either.

"I think I'd better call up Caroline. Or that you had."

"I will. Where shall I look for you afterward? Upstairs, downstairs or in my lady's chamber? I confess to a preference for the latter."

"All right. I'll meet you there. And while you're telephoning, I'll go tell Deirdre and Ellie you're home. They've been worried too."

Caroline kept Roger on the telephone for some time, in spite of his efforts to cut her short; she too was feeling injured. When he reached the big bedroom, he was relieved to find its atmosphere somewhat less tense than that of the hall, though it still fell short of his anticipations. Emily had taken off her tweed suit and put on a pink cashmere dressing gown trimmed with small silk loops, which, while not especially alluring in style, at least suggested relaxation. She had lighted the fire and was stretched out on the chaise longue near it. There was, of course, no room for Roger beside her, but there was an easy chair on the opposite side of the hearth and a well-laden tray stood on a near-by end table. Emily was smoking and had already made herself a nightcap.

"I didn't fix a drink for you, because I didn't know whether you'd want one. But everything's right there."

Her tone was perfectly pleasant. Nevertheless, Roger thought he caught the implication that the reason he might not want another drink could well be that he had already been abundantly supplied with them throughout the evening. He decided to disregard it.

"Well, I'll fix myself a light one for the sake of sociability. . . . Emily, I think we ought to have Bushmill's in the house. I believe I like it even better than Scotch."

"Bushmill's?"

"Yes. It's an Irish whisky. I've had it before tonight, but I'd forgotten how good it is."

"All right. I'll get some tomorrow."

He moved his drink and sat down, wishing that she would ask him some more questions, so that he would know where to begin. Instead, she went on quietly smoking her cigarette and sipping her drink. He decided that the only thing to do was to plunge into his subject.

"You said you didn't see why I wanted to go home with Brian Collins, after the way he acted here. Perhaps I ought to begin by telling you he's very apologetic about what happened the night of our dinner. That was what he'd been wanting to say to me for so long. He'd stayed overtime on purpose, because he never seemed to get a chance before."

"I should think he could have managed, if he'd wanted to very much. I should think he'd have apologized to us both."

"Well, as he said himself, there's no easy way and no graceful way either for a man to admit he's made a damn fool of himself. But he knows that's what he did and he's sorry as hell. When we asked him here, he really thought it was for an evening of poker with the boys, like what they were having at his house tonight. If he hadn't, he wouldn't have stopped for a couple of quick ones with Tim Tupperty and he wouldn't have come to a dinner party dressed like a bookmaker. I'm quoting almost literally. Afterward, he said he knew you must think he was about as crude as they come, and he's sorry about that too, because he likes you and he wishes you liked him. He ended up by saying he hoped I'd tell you tonight that if there were any way he could show you. . . . I was afraid I wouldn't have a chance to tell you tonight. I thought you'd be so tired when you got home you wouldn't feel like talking. I'm glad you weren't—glad the rehearsal didn't whip you down and glad I've had a chance to tell you right away what Briny said."

"I am tired. But I'm not sleepy and now that I'm not worried any more. . . . Is that why you're so late, because you've been 'having an evening of poker with the boys'?"

"Yes. But first we had supper with the family. Not the whole family. Two of Brian's sisters, Sheila and Katie, weren't there, one because she belongs to a teaching order and the other because she's just had her fourth baby. Terence Lenahan, the proud young father, wasn't there either for the whole supper; but he came in for the tail end of it and for poker. He's in the contracting business with Mr. Collins and they think the world of each other—besides, their association's been tremendously successful in a financial way. Even without the absentees, there was quite a gathering around the festive board—Mr. and Mrs. Shaun Collins and their teen-age daughters, Della and Doreen, and their six-year-old daughter, Queenie, and their son, Matthew, who's a very husky priest, and their son, Ray, who's a collegian of sorts, and of course their son, Brian, and Mrs. Collins' brother, Barney Garvin, apparently something of a political power—and me. That makes ten, doesn't it? Just the same number we had for our dinner. And there wasn't a servant in sight, or any sign of confusion or commotion either. It was a wonderful supper too—great, huge juicy steaks and lots of well-cooked vegetables and rolls and chocolate pie that really melted in your mouth."

"It doesn't sound like a very imaginative menu."

"It wasn't. It was just plain good. I don't believe the people who ate it are particularly imaginative either. They're just plain good too."

"Including the contractors who've been tremendously successful in their line and the great political power?"

"Look here, Emily, you're not trying to pick a quarrel with me, are you? I know that contractors, especially Irish contractors, are all supposed to be crooks; but there must be some who are reasonably honest, just to keep up the law of averages. And Barney Garvin's making it possible for me to do something your grandmother was afraid couldn't be pulled off. It certainly isn't any worse, at least in my book, to grant a favor of that kind than to ask it!"

Roger rose, setting down his drink, stooped to poke the fire somewhat harder than its condition necessitated and then, straightening up, stepped closer to the chaise longue. He looked down at Emily, who was staring at him incredulously, with an expression he had never seen before.

"Anyway, when I said they were just plain good, I wasn't thinking so much of the successful contractors and the great political power. I was thinking mostly about Mrs. Collins, who's had eight children and kept them all close to her, not just physically, but mentally and spiritually too. That's something no woman we know has done or could do." He paused, suddenly realizing that Emily would interpret what he had said as a thrust at her grandmother, whom she adored, and of whom, as a matter of fact, he himself had grown extremely fond; and such a thrust would seem to her like insult added to injury, coming, as it did, on top of his veiled allusion to the relative ease with which she and Mrs. Collins had ten persons to dinner. Then he plunged on, with a comparison which was not even indirect; Emily might be resentful, but so was he.

"Mrs. Collins is beautiful too," he said. "I don't mean the way your grandmother must have been beautiful once. I mean her spirit shines through. Her eyes are lovely and her smile and her voice. If either you or I had had a mother like that, we might have amounted to more ourselves. All her grown children are doing something that counts in the world, and the others will too, as soon as they're old enough. What have I done, compared to Father Mat and Brian? And what have you done, compared to Sheila with her teaching and Katie with her babies? And still you look down on the Collins', you don't want them for friends, you don't even want me to have them for friends! Well, that's just too bad, because I'm going to be friends with them! I'm going to their house as often as I please and I'm going to have them here too, as often as I please!"

"I've done nursing and you know it! And it isn't my fault I'm not going to have a baby—you know that too! You'd better stop insulting my family —after all they've done for you! You can go and see your precious Collins' whenever you like—I don't care! But I won't go with you and I won't have them here in my house!"

Emily had leaped up and was facing him again, not in half-allayed anxiety and mild annoyance and complete bewilderment as she had downstairs, but in deep resentment and unreasoning mutiny. He seized her arms, gripping them hard, not with the compulsion of passionate love, but with its ugly counterpart of passionate anger. The primitive male instinct to overpower a rebellious woman by sheer physical strength had been roused, without warning, from civilized dormancy. Then, suddenly appalled by the realization of the violence to which he had come so close and the injustice of which he was already guilty, Roger released his angry hold and gently encircled Emily's waist.

"Forgive me, darling," he said tenderly. "That is, if you can. Of course you've done things that count—I do know it. Your nursing's just as important as Sheila's teaching and lots of other things besides that she hasn't done. You're wonderful. I don't see how I could have said what I did. I don't see how I could have made such a comparison between you and Sheila, or between you and Katie either. I know it's a terrible disappointment to you that you haven't a prospect of a baby yet. But of course you will have a baby—just as many as Katie's had. And you'll be a marvelous mother. Your children will be willing to go through fire and water for you —just as I am, even if I don't show it. Please believe me. Please say you forgive me."

He bent his head, but she had already buried hers on his shoulder and he could not reach her lips. Then he felt her body trembling against his and heard her sobbing. More and more appalled, he tried to comfort her with caresses and whispered endearments. When she finally raised her tear-stained face and answered him, it was with contrition equal to his own.

"I'm just as much to blame as you are," she said, between sobs which were beginning to subside, but which still shook her intermittently. "I've been hateful to you ever since you came in. But I was worried, terribly worried, for hours. And when I found I needn't have worried, after all, somehow I wasn't just relieved; I was piqued too. I don't see why. It was unreasonable. It was—it was small."

"No it wasn't, dearest. It wasn't at all unreasonable. And of course you never could be small about anything. It was very careless and stupid of me not to telephone. You had a right to be annoyed."

"I didn't either. You can't be expected to think of every little thing, when you've got big things on your mind. What if Deirdre and Ellie did keep your dinner hot and wait up for you? That's what they're here for, to make you comfortable. I can't do it all by myself, because I'm not capable, like the Collins'."

There was no sarcasm in her tone now, only genuine humility and regret. Roger, bringing her closer to him by the slight pressure of one hand, stroked her hair with the other. The trembling of her body had ceased, and he could feel its softness and warmth through her dressing gown. Her hair was very soft too and there was a fragrance about it. . . .

"Of course you're capable," he murmured. It seemed a silly thing to say, because at that moment he did not care whether she was capable or not. He was thinking how lovely she was, and how much he wished they could stop talking and bring this senseless quarrel to an end through an embrace in which mutual forbearance and mutual forgiveness would emerge so naturally into mutual fervor that no words would be needed to express their feelings toward each other. But he knew that Emily was not ready for such an embrace yet. He knew that she must unburden herself, little by little, of everything that was troubling her, before she could accept the release of self-abandonment.

"I've been small about Brian too," she went on. "I knew all along he felt the way you say he does. But I wanted him to tell me so. I wanted him to humble himself and then I would have been gracious and condescending. And when I found out he'd told you instead, I was jealous. I was jealous because you'd had such a good time without me too. You have no idea how terrible it is to be jealous."

"Yes, I have, dear. I've been jealous lots of times. I guess everyone is." Fleetingly, he thought again of the night he had returned from Salem and found David alone with Emily. But he was not jealous of David now; he knew that Emily had never been so wholly his as she was at that moment.

"Really?" She looked up at him again and this time, when she did so, he kissed her mouth. "Of course I want Brian to come here," she said, when he gave her a chance to speak again. "That's what this house is for, isn't it? I mean, we didn't get it just for ourselves. We got it for our friends too. *All* our friends. Yours and mine both. Anyway, your friends are my friends. You'll ask Brian here right away, won't you? Brian and all his family."

Roger laughed, contentedly. "Well, not all his family, at one fell swoop. I'm afraid that would be too much of a good thing. And I won't ask him, right away. It would be a little too pointed if I did, wouldn't it? He'd know that we'd talked this all over. He might even suspect that we'd quarreled."

"But we've never quarreled before! We're never going to again!"

"No, of course not. But Brian's pretty shrewd, you know. I think it would be better to wait a week or so and then suggest that I might give a poker party here—something like the one he thought he was coming to the first time."

"You mean—just men?"

"Yes, just men." He did not remember telling her once that he did not want to have a stag party and she did not remind him. "After dinner. More or less on the spur of the moment. Some night when you have to work on lyrics again."

"Then I wouldn't even be here?"

"No. Except probably you'd get home during the course of the evening and look in on us to say hello. Then, the next time Brian came—"

"Yes. Yes, I can see how it would all work out. Simply and naturally and pleasantly. And I've been making mountains out of molehills all winter. I must be the dumbest girl you ever knew. And the meanest. I should think you'd hate me. I should think you'd want to beat me."

"You know you're not dumb or mean either. You know I don't hate you. You know I'm crazy about you. But maybe I ought to tell you. . . ." He had been on the point of saying, "Half an hour ago I did want to beat you. Well, not beat you exactly. But I saw red for a moment. I wanted to hurt you as much as you were hurting me and I couldn't think of but one way. . . ." Then he realized that such a confession would be pointless. It would not take away his own sense of shame and it would needlessly startle and shock Emily. Besides, the moment for which he had been so patiently waiting had come at last. Having fully unburdened her heart, she would now be ready for rapture. There was no more need of words.

"Maybe I ought to tell you again how much I love you," he said. "Or maybe I'd better just try to show you."

Chapter 15

AFTERWARD, EMILY SAID several times that it was almost worth while to quarrel, because, unless you quarreled, you could not make up, and making up was undoubtedly among the most wonderful things that it was possible to do. Roger did not altogether agree with her. He was amazed and disturbed to find how hard it could be to forget words spoken in anger, either by himself or by his wife, and the memory of them continued to pain him. But since obviously Emily did not have the same sad experience, he wisely did not mention his own.

Besides, the next months were so pleasant and profitable, in almost every way, that he realized he should not tempt fate by asking too much of it. As he had foreseen, his status at the office took a turn for the better after Old Mrs. Forbes had been there to consult him professionally; but he would not have dared to hope for such an immediate improvement as the one which took place. The mere mention of Morris Brucker's name proved sufficient to settle the question of the alleged Oriental: the seller backed down on his pretensions and the buyer, having paid a fraction of the price originally demanded by the unscrupulous merchant, contentedly took home his rug and, because of his triumph, was quite undisturbed over the fact that the sum charged by Cutter, Mills and Swan for handling the case would now have to be counted in with the rug's price. Indeed, he shook Roger warmly by the hand, assuring the astonished young lawyer that henceforth all disputes having the slightest legal tinge would immediately be referred to him.

Shortly thereafter, Old Mrs. Forbes, accompanied by her faithful maid, Doris, and accoutered with a Victorian bottle bag, a hatbox and two immense suitcases, departed for her week end at the White House. She was already in a mellow mood over the news Roger had brought her from Barney Garvin; and she returned much gratified at having been asked to prolong her visit by several days and pleasantly stimulated by the congenial atmosphere of Washington. Her mood mellowed still further when she learned that her tax difficulties should soon be a thing of the past and that her other financial affairs were already in order. Roger had filed a letter of protest concerning past taxes, in order to gain access to the capable conferees in the office of the Internal Revenue Agent, and had prepared the return currently due on a basis revised for her benefit. He had also opened the bank accounts and established the bookkeeping methods necessary to carry out his control of her funds, and deposits were being made and expenses met in an orderly fashion. Practically all his time during her absence had been put into the details necessary to achieve these results, and again, Cutter, Mills and Swan charged a substantial sum for services rendered. On this occasion though their distinguished client paid their bill without a murmur, her check was enclosed in a note which stated that she assumed all charges were divided on a percentage basis and that her grandson would benefit by such a system. It was so obvious that this assumption was based on her wishes, and that therefore her continued favors would be based upon it also, that Mr. Cutter summoned Roger into his handsome corner office, and looked up from the fire which he was industriously poking long enough to state that the time had now obviously come for a second raise, and that Mr. Field might also expect a percentage from the payments received from Mrs. Forbes.

Greatly encouraged by the radical change in his prospects, Roger was emboldened, in spite of David's outspoken disapproval, to persist in his efforts to help the unfortunate fugitive who had appealed to him the same day that Old Mrs. Forbes had come to the office and that he had first gone home with Brian. He was not naturally superstitious, nor was he given to attributing any special significance to chance happenings. Still, he could not help feeling that he should look upon a day which had brought him so much good fortune and marked a turning point in his career as one which he ought to single out for a special effort in behalf of a man far less fortunate than himself. The next time Brian stopped by his cubbyhole after office hours, in an obviously sociable mood, Roger broached the subject which David had dismissed in so summary a fashion.

"I've got something riding me, Briny," he said. "David told me to skip it, but I'd much rather—"

"Spill it? Go right ahead."

"Well, a youngster came to see me—about our age really, I guess, but he seemed a lot younger. His parents brought him. He'd escaped from the Rhode Island State Mental Hospital—said his wife railroaded him there with the help of a flashy salesman who'd become a regular customer—a damn sight too regular—at the filling station this kid ran on Route 1."

Roger paused, half afraid of an equivalent to the jeer about "the same old geometry." Instead, Brian sat down and, taking out his pipe, inquired, "Where's this boy now?"

"He's here—I mean in Boston."

"And where are the salesman and the farmer's daughter—I suppose she is a farmer's daughter?"

"I don't know. Briny—don't you start taking me for a ride too!"

160

"Okay. But didn't your boy take a crack at the salesman on his way out of the state of Rhode Island and Providence Plantations and into the Commonwealth of Massachusetts?"

"I didn't ask him."

"You better. And how did he get out of the asylum? Who sprung him?"

"He said he did it by himself: jumped out of his window onto a roof and slid down a spout from there, at night."

"Sounds too easy."

"Perhaps, but it might happen to be true. So now what? If I don't tell on him, I may be letting a mental case wander around to his harm and that of other people. If I do tell, I've violated professional confidence."

Brian pondered in silence for a few moments, puffing away at his pipe. "You can't go back on the poor simp now," he agreed at last. "Did these people favor you with a retainer?"

"No. I didn't ask for any. Now don't say, 'Then you can just drop it.'"

"I'm not going to. Do you think I'd have you miss a fine scrap with the salesman? Sane or insane, the boy shouldn't lose his wife and his filling station both; not as easy as that, anyway. And I think I see a way to start things going so that he won't. Just get the boy's father and mother to have him examined by a psychiatrist here. If the psychiatrist says he's nuts, he should go back to the nut house. If the psychiatrist says he's not, you've got a legitimate reason, and probably an effective one, for keeping him out. Go on from there. Get a retainer, and if these people start coming in and piling up your time, bill them. You'll take good care, that way, of the boy and yourself too."

"I might, at that," Roger said gratefully. "I don't know how to thank you, Briny. I've been turning this darn thing over in my mind so long, without any results, that I'd begun to think I was going crazy myself. But now—"

"Wait a minute," broke in Brian, "what's the name of this salesman Romeo?"

"Gosh, I don't know," admitted Roger.

"You find out," advised Brian, "and I'll see if the Boston Police or the State Police ever heard of him. You know lots of guys who pretend they're salesmen are nothing but small-time holdup artists who go for small stores open late, filling stations run by women, all-night lunch wagons—those places. If you could get something on this bird and show him up to the girl for what he really is and persuade your boy to let bygones be bygones between himself and the little woman, you might fix the whole business. I still want to see him do a job on the salesman and get back his girl."

As it turned out, Brian had come very close to rescuing Roger from the horns of a dilemma in the course of that one short talk. Roger found that, once he vigorously went on from there, the solutions of the problems the case presented came more easily than any of them had foreseen. The Boston psychiatrist, called into consultation, said there was nothing wrong which could not be remedied by a reasonably normal life at home and at work; and these again became possibilities when Brian's investigation revealed that the salesman was not only "wanted" in Massachusetts for various petty thefts, as Brian had predicted, but also for the nonsupport of his own wife in Brockton. The erring Rhode Island lady, confronted with these facts, and weary of having the salesman demand the bulk of the filling station receipts along with her personal favors, welcomed her forgiving husband back. The Rhode Island authorities, cautiously approached, disclosed that they had held the boy only for an observation period, which had almost expired when he so impatiently departed, and that they were glad to have his case solved with so little trouble to themselves and his room available for another more needy patient in their overcrowded hospital. The grateful parents appeared, promptly and without solicitation, with their savings bank book, which showed a balance of four hundred and eighty dollars, modest deposits being widely spaced over a period of years. They were sorry they did not have more to offer, they said, but they would like Mr. Field to take as much of this money as he felt he should. Personally, Roger would have preferred to take nothing; but he knew this would hurt their pride, and also that Mr. Mills, who hitherto had brushed him off every time he tried to discuss the case, would never consent to such an unremunerative arrangement. Leaving the apologetic and conscientious couple in his cubbyhole, he barged, unannounced, into Mr. Mills' office; demanded and secured an immediate hearing; and stated that he thought a hundred dollars, from which he was more than willing to forgo his percentage, was the outside sum that should be charged for the case he had just settled. Having made this unequivocal announcement to his startled superior he succeeded in compromising for two hundred, which was doing much better than he had expected.

Roger's financial advancement and his progress in self-confidence and initiative at the office were paralleled by an increasing number of outside activities which varied his interests and widened his outlook. Monday poker with Brian and Brian's relatives became a regular though not an inflexible part of his schedule: it was understood that if Emily wished to make other plans for that evening in which, almost automatically, he should be included, he would be available; otherwise, he went straight from the office to the Collins' house or Brian came to his. The first postprandial game on Joy Street proved generally enjoyable; and Emily's brief, incidental appearance was obviously regarded as a compliment and not an intrusion from the viewpoint of the guests, while from hers, it was an agreeable if novel episode. Thankfully, Roger realized that the strain between her and Brian had slackened of itself and that neither pressure nor artifice was necessary to bring about better mutual understanding. The next time that it was "his turn to shout," he asked Brian to come home to dinner with him, in the same casual way that Brian asked him to the big house in South Boston. Brian accepted with a spontaneity which suggested genuine pleasure at the invitation; and after that, his presence at the Fields' table on poker nights was taken for granted, both by them and by him. The other men continued to come in later, but the slight remaining diffidence on their part was also on the wane; Roger knew that it would not be long before this was overcome. Meanwhile, Brian had achieved the status of family friend.

Roger had never been privileged to enjoy such a friendship before and, next to the fulfillment of his love for Emily, he found it the most enriching experience of his life. His father, in a fond but ineffectual way, had tried to make his schoolmates welcome in his boyhood home; but this, lacking the presence of a wife and mother, had lacked so many other vital elements as well that most of the youngsters Roger knew preferred to seek diversion elsewhere. After Mr. Field's death, Caroline had discouraged company, at first with the pretext that it was "unsuitable" for her and Roger to "entertain" while they were in mourning, and later on the grounds of "expense" and "extra work." Roger had lived at home all through college and law school because it admittedly cost less that way— in cash; Caroline never knew how much it had cost him in kind.

Now, at last, there was no question of unsuitability, of extra work or expense; he could entertain as much as he chose. Though Emily had been sincere in deploring her own lack of capability, she actually had great potential gifts, both as a housekeeper and as a hostess. Not the least part of her largess to her husband had been the creation of a home which—as she herself had said from the beginning—was designed and intended for the pleasure and profit of their friends as well as themselves. She had blundered in her first attempt to make it a center of good feeling; but that, Roger assured her, with sincerity equal to her own, was his fault more than hers; it was he who had suggested a formal dinner party to begin with. Besides, she had learned her lesson now; she knew that her grandmother was right in saying that it took time to achieve results along the lines she had so greatly at heart.

She had long spoken, without constraint, of that first dinner party and, as time went on, she did so less and less seriously, characterizing it as "silly" instead of "disastrous." But she had never referred again to the first Waltz Evening, except to tell Roger how pleased and proud she was when Fleeney belatedly accepted her husband's suggested compromise. In spite of her silence however—possibly because of it—she had given a great deal of troubled thought to the incident which had put an abrupt end to her spontaneous reception of David as a habitué of the house.

As she had freely told Roger on his return from Salem, David had dominated the group at the Somerset Club, charming all Homer Lathrop's other guests, besides saving the situation for her. In asking David to go home with her afterward, she had primarily desired to pick up the gauntlet which her trustee had thrown down; but while also sincerely feeling that she could not have a pleasanter companion to while away the time until Roger's return, she had not thought of David as a stimulating, much less as a disturbing, presence. She had always had her fair share of masculine attention, but she had never been an enchantress like her grandmother and she wholeheartedly loved her husband; the idea that she might have a passage at arms with David or any other man had never entered her head.

This had still not occurred to her when she returned to the library from the pantry, after assuring herself that everything was in readiness for Roger's substantial refreshment when he came home, late and tired, and that the makings of a drink were available for David whenever he chose to have one. Meanwhile, David had turned on the radio to an inviting musical program. He bowed to her with mock solemnity as she re-entered the room and then, straightening up again, smiled at her engagingly.

"There's no reason why we shouldn't have a dance of our own, is there, just because I wouldn't be acceptable at the Waltz Evening?" he inquired; and, almost before she could answer, "Of course there isn't!" he had swept her into his arms.

She had danced with him before, the night of the dinner that she was still characterizing as "disastrous"; but then she had been tired and dispirited and angry; and though he was not the cause of her weariness or her depression or her anger, they had precluded her from entering, with any zest, into the diversion which he had so opportunely suggested, or from recognizing anything outstanding about his ballroom qualifications. Besides, they had danced at a hotel, where the noise and the crowd and the setting had all combined to deprive the experience of intimacy or special significance. Now everything was different. Her mood was triumphant, because she had thwarted Homer Lathrop in the effort to humiliate her; she was grateful to David for helping her to do this and—though still objectively —she appreciated the charm which had enabled him to win everyone over. The amplitude of her drawing room, which opened out of the library, offered sufficient space for a turn and yet its atmosphere was one of privacy and seclusion. Although David's suggestion had taken her by surprise, the surprise was an agreeable one.

Almost immediately she was aware that he was far and away the best waltzer with whom she had ever danced; presently, of a vague wish that the music would go on and on; then of the magnetic attraction of their united motion and physical proximity. Rather startled, she murmured something inconsequential and unconvincing about not being able to keep up with such an accomplished partner. David laughed lightly.

"Nonsense! Of course you can. Didn't you ever dance before? I mean really? Well then, it's high time you learned—it'll do wonders for you. Don't stiffen so—just relax and float along. It's a marvelous feeling."

"Yes, I—I know. Just the same, I think we'd better stop."

"You mean you're not enjoying this?"

"Of course I'm enjoying it. But—"

She tried, ineffectually, to disengage herself. David laughed again and drew her closer to him, in a way that was both compelling and intoxicating. After that, she ceased to think of release. In fact, she did not try to think at all. As the music rose to a crescendo, David bent his head and, pressing his face against hers, kissed her on the mouth.

Instantly she wrenched herself free and confronted him, trembling and incoherent with rage. He walked over to the radio, switched it off and then, opening her favorite cloisonné box, helped himself to a cigarette and lighted it. When she paused, breathless, in her tirade, he spoke with the utmost calm.

"I'm sorry you feel that I insulted you. I certainly didn't mean to. I felt as if a kiss were a suitable climax to our dance, that's all."

"You know we shouldn't have danced in the first place."

"Wouldn't you have danced if you'd gone to the Waltz Evening?"

"Yes, of course. But not—not like that."

"I said I didn't believe you'd ever really danced before. I told you I thought it would do wonders for you to learn. Well, it has—already."

"You've made me so ashamed that I don't see how I'm ever going to look my husband in the face. If you call that doing wonders for me—"

"Emily, if you'll excuse me for saying so, you have a tendency toward exaggeration. You and I have both had a very gratifying evening—very exhilarating. We've spontaneously celebrated our mutual success in an extremely pleasant way, with perfectly normal consequences. I'm sorry you feel impelled to talk as if we'd committed adultery."

"I feel impelled to say I'm sorry I ever let you into this house."

"Very well. I won't come here again, if you really feel that way. But are you sure?"

"Of course I'm sure."

"You're not going to lie to me, are you? Are you sorry we've had such good times, sitting in front of the fire together while we had tea? Are you sorry you went with my stepfather and me to your grandmother's house when he took her the signet ring? Are you sorry I suggested going out on the town the night of that dreadful dinner? Are you sorry I came to your rescue tonight? If you can say yes to all that, looking me straight in the eye, I'll leave here this minute and I'll never come back."

Without answering, Emily sank down in one of the big chairs flanking the hearthstone and put her hands to her face. David seated himself opposite her and quietly awaited her answer.

"No," she said at last, without looking up, "I'm not sorry for any of that. I shouldn't have told you I regretted ever letting you into this house. I did exaggerate. I've—I've enjoyed everything you've mentioned. But that doesn't mean I'm not ashamed of what's just happened."

"Didn't it occur to you that something of the sort might happen sooner or later—as a result of the rest?"

"Of course not. I thought we were just friends. I thought you were Roger's friend. I thought you were—"

"A gentleman? Emily, if you say that, it'll be the last straw."

"But I did. I thought—"

"Didn't you ever think of me as a man? Didn't you ever think of yourself as a woman?" David asked. He spoke slowly and still very calmly; but somehow he made every word sound ominous. "All right, let me tell you something: from now on you'll know that two people like you and me don't ever stay 'just friends.' You'll recognize my kind of a man when you see one. You'll know he's a potential lover. Eventually, you'll want him for an actual lover. What's more, you already know—at last—that you're a woman and not just a lady."

It was at this moment that Roger had parted the portieres and come into the library, to find David and Emily so absorbed in what they were saying to each other that they did not even hear his approach.

During the ensuing months, Emily had never seen David alone again. If Roger thought it was strange that his fellow junior no longer dropped in at teatime, he did not say so. In fact, he mentioned David very little and he tried, conscientiously, to overcome his instinctive antagonism, telling himself that it was both unworthy and baseless; but he did not succeed in completely rooting it out. The office association between the two was pleasant enough, except for an occasional slight clash, as in the case of the Rhode Island fugitive; and, not infrequently, they formed part of the same downtown luncheon group; but Roger found plausible pretexts for declining invitations to the handsome new apartment on Lime Street and he did not suggest that David should join the weekly poker parties. He did mention these to Pell; but he accepted, without insistence, Pell's simple and straightforward statement that he could not afford to play poker. Early in the spring, Roger joined the First Corps Cadets and, shortly thereafter, asked Pell why he did not do the same. This time the suggestion was accepted, and frequently they walked together from Joy Street to the armory where the drills were held and home again afterward. Roger's admiration for Pell's character and ability increased all the time; but he did not try to force the status of hail-fellow-well-met upon the young Italian, since this was obviously unwelcome; it was Brian who had become his intimate and, with every new day, this friendship meant more to him than it had the day before.

With increasing frequency, they consulted each other about cases and thrashed out moot questions; and it was not only through the weekly poker games that their companionship developed and flourished outside of office hours. In the intervals while cards were being shuffled and drinks freshened, Roger became aware, during March and April, of more and more references from the Collins family to Tom Yawkey's Red Sox. As a result of this new consciousness, he realized, with astonishment, that Cora Donlon was also concerned, in this case about the fate of the "Fenway Millionaires"; and that people in elevators, shops and streetcars were predicting opening line-ups. Soon it began to appear as if the population of Greater Boston were divided between those who worshiped the ground upon which Manager Joe Cronin trod and those who so far misprized him they felt sure that, given his job, they could handle the team much better.

Roger had long taken for granted regular attendance at the football games in which the Harvard varsity team played a conspicuous, though, unfortunately, often a losing role. From the earliest days of their courtship, Emily had expected him to have season tickets and to keep Saturday afternoons free for the matches in various stadiums and the correlative cocktail parties afterward. But, until Brian took him in charge, it had never entered his head that professional baseball loomed much larger in the minds of many people than any college contest. Now he began to understand that this mounting fever—which at first appeared to him almost a childish preoccupation with what a few men, equipped with balls and bats, were doing in Florida—involved not only immense local pride, but a genuine appreciation of the dramatic value the national game had achieved in its hundred years' progress toward almost universal popularity; and he was moved as well as amazed by the feeling of brotherhood it aroused among its devotees in all walks of life.

Mr. Cutter, to whom such understanding and such emotion had never come, could see no logical connection between wanting to row from the Union Boat Club and wanting to attend a ball game at Fenway Park; so there could be no question of leaving the office early and going to the season's opener, which came on a fine Friday afternoon. But the proverbial enthusiasm of a convert burst all bounds when, on a Saturday late in April, Roger and Brian finally watched the Red Sox hit their way to victory with the venerable Connie Mack at the head of the defeated opposition.

After that, Saturday baseball became almost as much of a regular habit as Monday poker; and, in between, besides the drills at the armory with Pell, there were luncheons at Durgin-Park's or Thompson's Spa, which were allegedly shared by the juniors for the purpose of continuing shop talk, but which actually took on an increasingly convivial atmosphere. Emily did not resent any of these new interests; she herself was increasingly preoccupied with Priscilla, who was at Joy Street more and more, and with her housekeeping, which seemed to demand a great deal of her time. Dolly had now been permanently added to the domestic staff, but larger and larger numbers of guests were coming to the house. These added responsibilities were obviously enjoyable rather than burdensome to Emily; and Roger's own sense of well-being was disturbed by only two aspects of the general situation. The first was the attitude of Emily's parents. Roger had long since ceased to resent their opposition to his marriage and the fact that, once this had actually taken place, their manner toward him had been civil, if not cordial, had helped him to forget past grievances. But they were both displeased when Old Mrs. Forbes turned over the management of her financial affairs to him, completely shutting Fiske, Ford out of the picture, as far as she was concerned, and they betrayed this; when the further news leaked out that Roger had been instrumental in blocking the lease of the "horrible little Gloucester Street house," their displeasure flamed into anger.

They did not reveal these feelings simultaneously, during the course of a family conference, as they would have done in the past; their estrangement, though it did not have the status of an official separation, was sufficiently established so that they almost never appeared in each other's company; and though they both went to the house on Louisburg Square and—less often—to the one on Joy Street, they did not do so together. Roger had regarded Old Mrs. Forbes' remarks to him on the subject of her daughter and her son-in-law as a professional confidence, and had not spoken of it, even to Emily, when she herself brought up the matter.

"Grandmamma says she's told you Father and Mother aren't getting on so well," she remarked, as casually as she could, on one of the increasingly rare evenings when they were alone.

"Yes. I'm very sorry."

"So am I. Especially that they should choose just this time to blow up. After all, they've gone along a good many years without worrying about incompatibility—or anything worse. Mother just went her way and Father went his—or rather, Mother went her way and Father sat at home and moped. I don't blame him; he's always had a cheerless sort of life. But, after letting Mother have her head so long, I think he might have done it one more year—until Priscilla really got under way. It won't help her any if there's a family scandal right now."

Roger was conscious of the slight irritation he always felt when the subject of Priscilla's debut was treated as one of paramount importance. But he had never voiced this irritation.

"Is there really a question of scandal?" he asked, also speaking as casually as he could. "Don't tell me, of course, if you'd rather not."

"Not any more than there has been in a long while. To put it bluntly, Mother likes men. Probably you wouldn't think so, to look at her—she's so completely the classic Bostonian type, even more so than Aunt Elizabeth. You'd think it would be just the other way. Because, after all, Mother did marry young and she's always moved in mixed society, while Liz is an old maid and spends a lot of time way off in a lonely farmhouse when she isn't teaching at a girls' college. As a matter of fact, I don't believe Mother's ever gone off the deep end. I hope you won't misunderstand me when I say I don't believe it's so much a matter of principle with her as that she simply hasn't got the kind of courage it takes to do that. Now I can see that Grandmamma might have had."

"Yes. Yes, I understand what you mean. Of course I know you wouldn't speak about either of them this way to anyone but me. And I think it's very sad that you haven't more respect for your mother. I mean that she hasn't given you more cause to respect her."

The vision of Mary Collins, benign and beautiful as she sat surrounded by her adoring family, came, as it so frequently did, unbidden to his mind. But he had never made the mistake, a second time, of comparing her audibly with Eleanor Thayer. He waited for Emily to go on.

"But she does love to skim over thin ice," Emily continued. "So Father finally said he wouldn't put up with it any longer. He's self-conscious even about going to his club because he thinks people are gossiping. And he hasn't much of anything else to do, now that's he resigned from Homer Lathrop's brokerage firm. Not that he does much when he goes to the club. If he played cards, it would be different. But he promised Grandpapa he never would again after his college gambling debts were paid. And he's kept his promise all these years. It must have been awfully hard for him. I think he deserves a lot of credit."

"So do I," said Roger heartily, thinking with gratitude of his pleasant poker games. It soon became evident that Emily had been thinking about them too.

"Do you know, I wouldn't be surprised if your poker games didn't have something to do with Father's feeling about you?"

"You mean because everything was fixed up with Barney Garvin in the course of one?"

"Yes, partly. But only partly. I think that, perhaps, without actually knowing it, he's jealous of you for having such a good time. We've agreed that jealousy can be a terrible thing. If he were playing poker himself, with that crowd that does it regularly at the Algonquin. . . . Of course, poker wasn't his game and the Algonquin isn't his club. But you must see what I mean."

"I do. And I'm sorry about that too. Of course Uncle Barney and the Collins' and I would be delighted to have him join us any time, if it weren't for his promise. I wish you'd tell him that."

"I will, thanks. And it might please him. But it wouldn't help to release him from his promise and, after all, he isn't as adaptable as you seem to be. He might not get on as well as you do with Barney Garvin and the Collins'."

"Don't you think he'd have got more out of life if he'd been more adaptable?"

"Of course I do. I think Father's had an awfully empty, futile life. As far as that goes, Mother has too. So she's kept aimlessly pursuing something she hasn't found. Now Grandmamma's different. She's had everything."

"And made the most of everything she did have. But we seem to have strayed from the main subject. You began by telling me that your father and mother weren't getting on so well—which of course I knew already. Did you have anything special in mind that we might do about it?"

"Well, I thought perhaps as you'd blocked this lease business, you might think of something else that would bring them in money. They can't live in France without any."

"It's pretty hard to live anywhere without any, isn't it?"

"Oh, Roger, you know what I mean! Now that Father's resigned his position with Uncle Homer, their joint income is pretty limited, especially since Grandmamma has stopped supplementing it. Grandpapa left almost everything to her—except for my trust fund—you know that too. Apparently he adored her to the day of his death. Mother and all his other children got mere pittances from his will. And Father didn't have much more—outside of his salary, I mean."

"Would you like me to try and see what I could do about leasing the Gloucester Street house to some desirable tenants?"

"No, Father and Mother have gone back to their original plan of trying to sell it. They want to get rid of it for good."

"All right. Shall I try to sell it?"

"Do you think you could?"

"I could try. Fletcher's been saying his wife wants to live in town for the winter, now that the children are school age, and perhaps if your father and mother would let it go at a bargain. . . . Maybe you'd better sound them out, since I'm in their bad graces. Meanwhile, I should think your grandmother could be persuaded to let them go on staying in Dublin —that is, to let your father go on staying there. Your mother spends most of her time visiting anyway."

"Well, Grandmamma might, at that. Especially as she doesn't want to stay there herself. She wants to take Priscilla to Europe. Priscilla doesn't want to go, but Uncle Sherman and Aunt Sue have actually agreed to it. They still won't do anything for her themselves, but they've begun to see that somebody must."

There it was again, that annoying subject of Priscilla's debut. Once more Roger suppressed the impulse to express his irritation.

"About selling the house. I think maybe you've got something there," Emily said thoughtfully. "I'll sound Father and Mother out, as you suggest. And I'll ask Grandmamma about Dublin. Incidentally, you wouldn't mind having Priscilla come and spend the rest of the spring with us, would you?"

"Of course not. I told you last fall, when you first spoke of it as a possibility, that I'd be glad to have her. I like Priscilla very much. But I don't especially like—"

He wished that it did not seem advisable, quite so often, to leave statements unfinished even when he had begun them at all. He knew he must not say, "But I don't especially like the way you're all trying to railroad her into doing something she doesn't want to do. Suppose she doesn't 'make' the Junior League and the Vincent Club? Lots of wonderful people don't even know they exist and don't care if they do know. Suppose she doesn't get asked to all the right parties or have a whirl at the ones she does go to? She may turn out to be a one-man girl, the way I was a one-girl man. It does happen. And there hasn't been time for the one man to come along yet. She isn't ready for one. Suppose she is gun-shy? She'll get over it, if you'll give her a chance. Just a year or two might make a difference, if she could develop naturally. I was shy myself, I know she must really suffer. Why don't you let her alone?"

He should not say all this and he did not, as was so often the case. But afterward, as was less often the case, he was glad of it. For, as it turned out, Priscilla proved to be his second source of disturbance that spring, and he would have been the last to recommend that she be allowed to go her own way. He was thankful that no one could lay her willfulness to his door.

Chapter 16

SINCE PRISCILLA HAD not attended a major private school, it was impossible for her to obtain the official status of a debutante upon her graduation from one of these. It was therefore decided, through general family conference, that it would be well for her to come up from the Cape early in the spring, settle down at the house on Joy Street and gradually drift into the current of the proper preliminaries to a formal entry into society. In this way, she would—or should—be well established when everyone began to go away for the summer, at which time Old Mrs. Forbes would take her to Europe, inviting some girl, whom she had found particularly congenial, to accompany them. In order to have the free months for his honeymoon, Roger had been obliged to mortgage two ordinary vactions, instead of one, as had originally been suggested; and this meant that, except for brief week-end excursions, and slightly longer ones over the Fourth of July and Labor Day, he and Emily would be in town all summer. Neither of them regarded this as any hardship. Their house was cool and airy; they enjoyed it increasingly and had no special desire to leave it; and the city and suburbs offered a sufficient variety of diversion to make them feel that they would not miss those which were unavailable. But, as Old Mrs. Forbes pointed out, they might be satisfied to attend the "Pops" at Symphony Hall and the concerts at the Shell on the Esplanade, to play tennis at the Country Club and to sip mint juleps on the Ritz roof; but none of this would advance Priscilla's chances of making the Junior League. On the other hand, if she went to a court at Buckingham Palace and the girl who went with her would have been unlikely to receive a "command" to accompany her on this grand occasion, had it not been for the good offices of Old Mrs. Forbes, that would make all the difference in the world. So would an entree at various exclusive embassies, where Old Mrs. Forbes was always more than welcome; in France, the season did not end until after the Fourteenth of July; they could still get in on the feverish finish of that, even if they went to England first and stayed for Ascot. In Italy, every noble portal swung wide open at the dowager's approach. To a lesser degree, visits at several romantic and historic villas and *palazzos* might very well be helpful. They would leave Boston early in June and return in September; with this schedule Priscilla would have gone to several important luncheons at the Chilton Club and one or two outstanding house dances before they sailed; and they would still reach London in time for the last Court. They would be back early enough for her to attend the Ushers' dinners on the North Shore, dances at the Essex County Club and the Myopia Hunt Club and the correlative week-end parties.

For fear of mutiny, the details of this schedule were revealed to Priscilla only by degress; but to everyone's amazed relief, she made no objection to any of the activities proposed. Without argument—indeed with every appearance of amenity—she arrived at Joy Street on the appointed day; unpacked her belongings in a manner indicative of expecting prolonged occupancy of the small spare room with the spool furniture; and, apparently quite on her own initiative, remarked that she supposed she ought to go shopping, because she did not have enough clothes to last "until she got to Paris." As nothing had been said to her on the subject of *grande couture* by any member of the family, this suggestion was as gratifying as it was mystifying; and she immediately embarked on a campaign of spending which seemed, even to Old Mrs. Forbes, somewhat staggering in its proportions, financially speaking, but which certainly left nothing to be desired from the viewpoint of suitability and fashion. She did not resist advice and she did not stipulate that she should go on her shopping expeditions unaccompanied; but it was soon obvious that she needed surprisingly little guidance. The wardrobe she selected during the shopping expeditions, on which she started out alone, contained exactly the right proportion of extremely well-tailored tweeds and serges, superlatively smart silks, prints and linens and a collection of evening dresses which varied in hue and design, but which were uniformly gauzy, girlish and bewitching.

With thoughtful foresight, Roger had realized that Priscilla might want to have a horse available and had arranged to have one stabled for her at the Dedham Country and Polo Club, where Emily still kept up her membership, though she had done very little riding since her marriage. This gesture was much appreciated, as several other young girls kept horses there and Priscilla found agreeable companions. Roger had also realized that she would be less homesick if she were not deprived of the pleasure she took in sailing, and had paved the way for her membership in the Community Boat Club. This organization, the first of its kind, had been started two years earlier under the leadership of Joseph Lee, Jr., an outstanding Bostonian whose primary purpose had been to make the advantages of sailing available to persons who would not normally be able to enjoy them. Two boats had been built, by hand, on the roof of his house, which provided the nucleus for a public sailing playground. The following year, great impetus was given the movement by the dramatic appearance on the Boston scene of Arthur Peterson, a cowboy from the West, who became fascinated by the mechanics of sailing, hitherto unknown to him. By the end of that season, several more boats had been completed by volunteer labor, and building operations had been moved from Mr. Lee's roof to a West End philanthropic center. The current season had opened even more auspiciously, in spite of temporary difficulties because of high water and consequent violent altercations with certain members of the Boston Police Force, who kept displacing the boats from their moorings at night, only to find that, the next morning, the members of the club had sailed them back and moored them where they had previously been. Roger, who, thanks to Brian, was by this time on very good terms with Officer Tupperty, discussed the question with him and, in due course, it was laid before Police Commissioner Hauptman and reached the ears of Governor Hurley. An amicable arrangement was then duly reached by means of which the club members could keep their boats at the Pinckney Street landing. Their number increased with almost incredible speed and colored sails began to make their appearance among the white ones which were already adding an alien element of grace and charm to the sober Charles. Two of the new boats had been built by the Burroughs Newsboys; two others by members of the Y.M.C.A.; Pell had built one and equipped it with bright red sails. Indeed, it was a chance glimpse of him, leaving the Pinckney Street landing with the beautiful girl whose name, because of Pietro's accident, had been tardily disclosed as Simonetta de Lucca, but whom he still never mentioned, that gave Roger the idea of initiating Priscilla into the new club, which not only included, but welcomed members of all classes. She rewarded him by a show of sincere and affectionate gratitude and took immediate and frequent advantage of his action by getting out on the water almost daily. She chose yellow sails for her boat and handled it so expertly, thanks to long practice at home, that she very quickly commanded attention. Often she went out alone, saying quite candidly that she preferred to do so; when she did invite anyone to go with her, David was usually her chosen companion.

Neither Old Mrs. Forbes nor Emily had ventured to hope that Priscilla would make much of an impression at the Empire Dance or the Freshman Jubilee, and were therefore agreeably surprised to find that she was able to more than hold her own on both of these occasions. They had taken it for granted that she would do better at the pseudorustic barn dances which were featured among the spring festivities, the synthetic Hofbrau on Stanhope Street and the four-course picnic suppers on Buzzard's Bay. They had likewise felt almost certain that she would ride in the Memorial Day Horse Show; and, with this in mind, had decided somewhat hesitantly to include Elliot Berkeley among the guests at the first dinner given in Priscilla's honor, which, because of the greater prestige which would inevitably be attached to it under these circumstances, was scheduled to be held at Old Mrs. Forbes' house instead of Emily's. It was when this dinner list was submitted to Priscilla for inspection that she asked her first disturbing question.

"Aren't you going to ask David Salomont to the party?" she inquired with genuine surprise.

"Why, no. We hadn't thought of doing so. You see, he's older than the crowd you're going with and—"

"He isn't any older than Elliot Berkeley, is he? I thought he was younger."

"Well, he is, a little. But we made an exception, in the case of Elliot Berkeley, because we thought you might find him especially congenial, on account of his interest in horses. We asked Caroline so that there'd be an older girl too."

"I found David very congenial all winter. He's spent several week ends with us on the Cape and we all like him a lot. Besides, he invited me to supper at his apartment just as soon as I came up to Boston and it was a wonderful supper too. We haven't asked him back yet. I think we ought to."

Old Mrs. Forbes and Emily, who were seated facing Priscilla, on the opposite side of a large flat-topped desk where various lists were spread out, exchanged glances which, though fleeting, did not escape Priscilla's notice.

"You're right, Priscilla, and we will," Old Mrs. Forbes said reassuringly. "You may ask him here to dinner any night you like next week."

"Him and who else? It ought to be a party."

"Well, we'll have to think who would be con—"

"I don't see why you're so worried about people being congenial. David's a very good mixer. I know the Stockbridges like him and the Amorys. They've told me so."

"Then we'll ask the Stockbridges and the Amorys to the party. But how did the subject of David Salomont happen to arise between you and the Stockbridges? Or between you and the Amorys?"

"Joan Amory and her beau had the next table to David and me at the Ritz last Saturday. We went there to a late lunch after I finished my shopping. He went shopping with me too. And Olivia and Faith Stockbridge were starting out in their sailboat from the Community Boat Club just as David and I were starting out in mine day before yesterday. We went back to David's apartment for a drink afterward. And all three girls have called me up to tell me how attractive they thought he was."

Again Old Mrs. Forbes and Emily exchanged glances, but this time there was nothing fleeting about the looks they gave each other. Then Emily spoke with an obvious effort at restraint.

"But, Priscilla, you never told us you were shopping or lunching or sailing with David Salomont. And you know you're not supposed to drink at all until after graduation."

"You never asked me who helped me choose my clothes or who took me out to lunch or who went sailing with me. I'd have told you if you had. And you acted as if you weren't much interested in David Salomont any more. Every time I've started to talk about him you've changed the subject. I didn't understand why, because, after all, he was your friend and Roger's before he was mine. His stepfather's a friend of Grandmamma's and I met David here at her house for the first time."

All this was so unanswerable that neither Old Mrs. Forbes nor Emily attempted an immediate reply. While they were busily considering the best counterattack, Priscilla continued her line of argument.

"Besides, as I'm not graduating anywhere, how can I wait until afterward to drink? And I don't think that rule amounts to much. Most of the other girls have begun too—not in bars yet, of course, but at each other's houses. Gin, mostly. Someone told me that when you came out, Emily, girls weren't drinking anything but sherry, and that when Mother and Aunt Eleanor came out they weren't drinking anything at all—that at dances there were two kinds of punch, one for the men and one for the girls, and that at dinners there was champagne, but that the girls made gestures to show that their glasses shouldn't be filled. Well, things have certainly changed. We drink Martinis when it's cool and rickeys when it's warm. It was really hot the day we went to David's apartment and he made us lovely rickeys."

"Did Faith and Olivia tell their mother that they went to David's apartment with you?"

"I don't know. I suppose they did if she expected them home at a certain minute and she asked them why they were late. And I don't suppose they said anything if she didn't. I don't see why they should. Girls can't keep running on and on about every little thing they do—their families would be bored to death. And women with a lot of children don't bother to keep asking every one of them where they were every single minute of the night and day, do they? I shouldn't think they would. I shouldn't think they'd have time, if they have anything else at all to do. I know Mother doesn't. She's too busy pulling worms out of the ground herself."

"Priscilla, you've simply got to be more careful. The next thing you know, you'll overhear something, while you're under the drier after your hair's been set, or in a powder room or in a—"

"Of course I'll overhear something. I can't help doing it all the time. I overheard one woman say she'd married off three of her daughters to members of the Porcellian Club and that she was sure she'd have equally good luck with the fourth. Then I overheard that she hadn't. Is that the kind of thing you mean?"

"I mean you'll overhear that you're running all over town with David Salomont, that you're even letting him choose your clothes and going to his apartment without a chaperone for drinking parties. And presently, the things you've overheard will get around, because other people will overhear them too, just as you heard that about the Porcellian. And the next thing you know, you'll find yourself left out of the parties you'd especially like to go to, because David isn't the sort of man—"

"Isn't *what* sort of man? He's well educated, isn't he, even if he did go to Columbia instead of Harvard? He knows how to dress, doesn't he? Anyway, he goes to Littlefield, just like Uncle Homer. He's got wonderful manners and he knows how to talk—he can talk about *anything*, in three or four languages, not just a little feeble French. He's been all over the world, he knows people everywhere—people who've *done* things. And he's got terribly important relatives in Spain and Portugal. He's the best dancer I ever saw. He can even tango. He's good-looking, he's amusing, he's charming, he's—"

"Priscilla, I am sure that David Salomont would be very much complimented to know that you have such a high opinion of him. But it really isn't necessary for you to rise to his defense quite so vehemently. Neither Emily nor I would dream of denying that everything you've said is true."

Old Mrs. Forbes had now recovered from her surprise and gathered her forces. Instead of warning or reproving Priscilla, like Emily, she spoke with the utmost suavity.

"All Emily means," she said, "is that there are a lot of very stodgy, stupid people in Boston who don't know how to appreciate a young man like David Salomont, for the very reason that he *is* so much better educated and more widely traveled and more sophisticated than their own sons and the callow youths who went to college with them and who represent about all there is in the way of available material as beaux for their daughters. The Stockbridges and the Amorys may be exceptions to the general rule—I hope they are. Anyway, we'll soon find out. But, taken by and large, the parents of the girls you're meeting now and that you'll be thrown with next winter wouldn't welcome David Salomont because he's different. They'd recognize this without recognizing the reason that he's different is that he's superior and they'd resent it—perhaps unconsciously, but they would, just the same. And it would harm his prospects very much if he aroused antagonism in such powerful quarters right now. Because those quarters are powerful. And they can be vindictive—just as the women who heard that mother say she'd married off three of her daughters to members of the Porcellian Club felt vindictive and proved it. The fourth one married a nobody. Thinking as highly of David Salomont as you do, I'm sure you wouldn't want to do anything that would jeopardize his career—especially when he's made such a brilliant beginning, when there's no reason why he shouldn't rise to great heights in his profession."

"No, of course I wouldn't. But Emily wasn't talking about David's career. She was saying—"

"What Emily says usually makes sense," Old Mrs. Forbes announced, including both girls in the smile which had lost so surprisingly little of its charm with the years. "But this time it didn't—at least, as far as I was concerned. Of course you can listen to Emily if you want to. But if you listen to me, you'll follow a rather different course of action. You won't stop seeing David Salomont, but you'll see him quietly—at this house and at Emily's. As often as you please. You'll ask him to small parties, in which you'll include such people as the Stockbridges and the Amorys that you know like him too. But you won't insist on including him in groups where there might be the least chance of antagonism to him, and you won't so much as hint that anyone outside your own family should ask him to a party. Let the suggestions come from the other side—they'll have a great deal more weight that way. Does what I've said make sense?"

"Yes, sort of."

"Very well. I don't see any reason at all why you and he shouldn't go sailing together—that is, if you go with other young men too, as I assume you do, and if you don't ask David too often. I'm sure you don't want to give him the idea that no one else is available or that you're trying to monopolize him—nothing makes a young man fight so shy of a girl as he does if he gets either of those ideas in his head."

It was now obvious that Old Mrs. Forbes had really begun to strike home. She pressed her advantage.

"There's a silly, old-fashioned notion that very young girls ought not to go around alone with men to hotels, or accept invitations to their apartments, unless they know that older persons are going to be present. All this hasn't anything to do with David personally; it applies to everybody. And in Boston, more's the pity, men don't often help girls choose their clothes. So I'm going to back Emily up there. But you've got enough clothes for the present and with all the other things you have to do, and two private houses available, I should think you could wait for the tête-à-tête luncheons at the Ritz. And I'd like very much to see David's apartment myself. I understand it has a great deal of distinction and I'm not surprised. I'll go there with you whenever you like—that is, unless either one of us has something even more exciting to do. Of course, we haven't a great deal of time before we start for Europe and we have got a pretty full calendar. But there ought to be a few free evenings. Let's see. . . ."

Nothing more was said about David Salomont that afternoon; and Priscilla made no comment when her grandmother told her that she had been able to improve their reservations by taking an earlier sailing for Europe than had originally been intended. They were going on the *Normandie* instead of the *Ile de France*, which was one of those things which should be "even more exciting." The small dinner which included David as well as the Stockbridges and the Amorys was a great success and so was the larger one at which none of these persons were present; therefore, no occasion for unfavorable comparison arose between the two. Both the Stockbridges and the Amorys had already invited David to their houses, before Priscilla appeared on the scene, so there was nothing forced about the fact that they should do so again, now that she had become a logical part of it; and, upon exploring the situation, she discovered that there was no lack of young men who were delighted to accept her invitations to go sailing with her. She also discovered that her grandmother's presence gave both a substance and a sparkle hitherto lacking in David's entertainments, without in the least detracting from their individuality and charm; and she now felt free to invite him as often as she liked—without running the risk of appearing to attempt monopoly—to both Louisburg Square and Joy Street.

David, it appeared, felt equally free to avail himself of these invitations; and it was thus that, quite innocently, Priscilla proved a source of disturbance to Roger. For, though she was the ostensible attraction, he was convinced that she had furnished a convenient pretext for the resumption of David's visits to Emily. What was even more to the point, Emily was convinced of the same thing—so thoroughly convinced that she broached the subject to David one evening when Priscilla had gone sailing with someone else and he strolled in, clad in immaculate Shantung, with the idea of asking her whether she would care to drop in at Zero Hereford Street for a predinner drink. Emily, who had waited for just such an opportunity, felt that the time and the place were now both propitious. Having done everything she could think of, with marked success, to give the atmosphere of the house comfort and culture, combined with elegance, she had more recently turned her attention to the back yard which, like most back yards in Boston, had hitherto been an unsightly and neglected area. However, it did possess one natural advantage—a good-sized tree of heaven which, as the spring advanced, provided pleasant shade; and with this as a focal point, Emily planned and planted a small garden, complete with brick walks and flower beds bordered by miniature box, a few Japanese quince and syringa bushes and even a little fountain. She had never done any gardening before, since, in common with most Bostonians, she had neither the taste nor the talent for it which are second nature to Southern women; and she was amazed and enchanted to find that her plants not only survived, but throve, and that the erstwhile dismal "dump" had become a pleasing terrace. She equipped it with painted iron furniture, upholstered in bright denim, and gay matching parasols; and, on warm afternoons, she abandoned the library and began to serve tea and tall drinks from a metal table covered with a cloth embroidered in cross-stitch and well supplied with all necessary utensils and ingredients.

Roger was inordinately proud of the success of her experiment and spontaneously revealed his own enjoyment of it, which encouraged Emily to make more and more use of the little garden. She was already ensconced there, becomingly dressed in cool green, and painstakingly following the directions for knitting Argyle socks—another recently acquired accomplishment—when David appeared on the scene; and, after coupling her suggestion that some gin rickeys would taste good with the comment that she knew they would be much better if he made them, she led up to the point she wished to make by circuitous and what she believed were tactful means.

"Almost everyone I've talked to lately seems to be making vacation plans," she said. "What about yours?"

"Well, of course I have to spend two weeks at Camp Smith, and that won't leave me much time to do anything alse, if I can't fix up something with the Artful Dodger. But I hope I can. After all, Roger got a whole summer off for a honeymoon, by slaving straight through the previous one and mortgaging the one after. I ought to be able to strike as good a bargain as that, if not a better one."

"I don't seem to know about Camp Smith or why you have to go there."

"Camp Smith, my dear girl, is in Peekskill, New York, and I have to go there for so-called duty in the field, because I am a reserve officer, holding a commission as second lieutenant in the National Guard. While I was in Columbia, I joined the officer candidate's school of New York's Twenty-seventh Division."

"You did! I didn't know that before."

"The subject never came up before. I didn't know you were especially interested in me as a reserve officer. Now that I see you are, I am pleased to inform you that, for more than a year and a half, I attended the o.c.s. one night for theoretical work and another night every week partook in the training schedule assigned to my company; and then, in addition to all this and the duty in the field, I took correspondence courses. My written examinations were read and graded at Fort Benning, Georgia."

"Why at Fort Benning, Georgia?"

"Because that's the infantry school. The Twenty-seventh is an infantry division. And the headquarters of this other school I've been talking about are at the Seventh Regiment Armory, which is the proud treasure house of said regiment, an outstanding landmark in the great city of New York and, what is more, the proud possessor of one of the best bars in that metropolis."

Emily laughed. "That's all very impressive. Proud to know you, Lieutenant Salomont. . . . And if you can drive a bargain with the Artful Dodger, what else would you do this summer besides 'duty in the field'?"

"I think I'll probably go to Venezuela. The Grace Line has replaced the old Red D Line ships with some very snappy new *Santas*. So the trip there and back ought to be an extremely pleasant one now, what with buffet luncheons beside an outdoor tiled swimming pool and dinner in a white-columned dining room whose high, arched ceiling rolls back to reveal a starlit sky."

"Please stop. You're making me green with envy."

"You don't look green. Your coloring's lovely—and it gets still lovelier when anyone pays you a well-deserved compliment. You're almost the only young lady I know who hasn't lost the gentle art of blushing. Well, about Venezuela. In addition to the pleasures of the voyage on the *Santa Paula* or the *Santa Rosa*, I can look forward to others in Caracas. Some of my father's relatives, that we used to visit regularly when he was alive, have a rather nice place there. A house of the Spanish-Colonial type, that they've owned for generations. It's in the old part of the city. Nothing much to look at from the outside, just a couple of grilled windows and a wide passageway in a blank, one-story façade, but inside there are endless rooms around a succession of patios—five of those, if I remember right. Mother's always kept in touch with the family and my stepfather gets on well with them too. Mother and Dad thought they'd like to go to South America for a change and they've suggested that I should go with them."

"It sounds wonderful," Emily said, wondering why David could not have had some relatives of this kind in Boston instead of the kinsfolk of his mother, with whom he had stayed at first, and with whom he seemed to be rapidly losing touch.

"Well, yes. Caracas is a very pleasant city. And of course these relatives of ours have a *quinta* in the country too—I wouldn't know how many acres. But I do know there are three girls in the family. I haven't seen them in the flesh for a long while, but they sent us pictures of the wedding party when their brother was married and they were all bridesmaids. I must say they were quite easy to look at. That picture rather influenced my decision about a vacation; it made a very favorable impression on me."

"No doubt you'd make a very favorable impression on them too," Emily said, delighted that she had been provided with such an advantageous approach to the subject she wished to discuss. "You certainly have on Priscilla."

David smiled, with a slight deprecatory shrug.

"It's nice to know I have the unqualified approval of some member of the family," he remarked.

"I don't see why you say that. I understand from Priscilla that you've visited on the Cape several times this past winter, so I gather that Uncle Sherman and Aunt Sue must have approved of you too. And I'm sure Grandmamma's been just as nice as she could be to you."

"I have the impression that Mr. and Mrs. Sherman Forbes act on the principle of live and let live and apply it even to the very young," David replied. "And of course I benefit because Old Mrs. Forbes is grateful to my stepfather on account of Feodor."

"Feodor?" exclaimed Emily, diverted in spite of herself. "Feodor who?"

"Romanoff. But of course grand dukes didn't use their surnames. Surely you know that. And I believe your grandmother always called him Freddie anyway."

"I haven't the least idea what you're driving at."

"Surely that doesn't worry you? It's so seldom you seem to know what I'm driving at. If I didn't know you were really a very forthright person, I might be tempted to put it down as a pose. But because you are, I know lack of comprehension is just a characteristic of yours. Like exaggeration."

Emily flushed and bit her lip. "We were talking about Priscilla," she said. She spoke rather severely, partly because she resented the indirect allusion to her passage at arms with David and partly because she was dying to hear more about the Grand Duke, whose existence had been definitely disclosed to her for the first time, and about whom she had long felt a consuming curiosity, as, of course, David was well aware.

"Excuse me. I thought it was you who was talking about Priscilla. I don't particularly wish to discuss her. But I strive to please. What more did you want to say?"

"Only that she seems to have what's commonly called a crush on you and that I hope you won't take it very seriously. Of course she's a great deal too young to know her own mind."

"I thought you'd already found out I never take things of that sort very seriously. And I might add it isn't only girls in their teens who sometimes don't know their own minds—though sometimes they do. But occasionally girls in their twenties don't either."

Emily flushed again and turned away. There was no use trying to spar with David. He was a great deal better at it than she was.

"Incidentally, my mother and stepfather are planning to give a party in honor of Old Mrs. Forbes and her young charges the night before they sail," David went on. "It might be good. You and Roger better come over to New York for it too. You could take in a few shows at the same time."

"It's very kind of you to suggest it, but I don't believe Roger can leave the office. He's got an awful lot of important work on his hands."

"Yes, things have certainly changed since your grandmother took over that situation."

"It's very unfair of you to give Grandmamma all the credit. Roger settled that Salem case long before there was any question of handling her affairs."

"That didn't prevent him from getting the 'Oriental' rug to drag around, did it? You know as well as I do that your grandmother turned the trick. . . . Well, I hear there's going to be a new errand boy at the office now that Roger's no longer available."

"A Greek? Or an Armenian?" Emily inquired, rather cuttingly for a girl who was supposed to be interested in furthering better relations among alien groups.

"No," David replied imperturbably. "Stanley Lyman, the boy Priscilla's out with now—the right parents, the right address, the right school, the right college, the right clubs—and I hope enough brains to skin through the bar examinations. Of course he stammers, like so many Bostonians, but, luckily for him, all the exams aren't oral. . . . I think Priscilla knows her own mind to the extent of deciding not to marry him."

"What makes you think he wants to marry her?" Emily inquired, somewhat startled at the idea that Priscilla was already having serious suitors,

"Well, in spite of the handicap imposed by his stammering he goes around telling everyone who will listen to him that he proposes to her regularly twice a week. . . . His volubility on such a subject will give you an idea of his mentality. . . . If Roger can't get away, why don't you come over to New York without him?"

"Because I'd rather stay at home than go anywhere he can't go with me."

"If you came to that conclusion on the basis of one kiss, that must have made quite an impression on you."

"I don't care to discuss the episode in question with you, David."

"Well, I didn't want to discuss the question of Priscilla. But, as I said, I strive to please. You might strive to please too once in a while, Emily. You'd be ever so much more lovable if you did."

"*More lovable!* What makes you think I want to be more lovable?"

"Don't you?"

"No. Roger loves me very much, just the way I am. That's all I care about."

"Oh! I thought you were interested in love of fellow men, like Abou ben Adhem."

"I am. But that's not. . . . You told me yourself that certain kinds of people couldn't. . . ."

"I thought you didn't want to discuss that episode, Emily."

"I don't— And I'm not going to stay here and let you badger and bait me any longer." She rose precipitately. David, who remained seated, spoke more soothingly.

"I don't want to badger and bait you. But you don't give me any choice. You prod me into it. I can't imagine why. You don't act this way with Brian."

"Brian never gave me any reason to—to feel antagonistic toward him."

"He didn't? What about his behavior the night of that famous dinner?"

Emily sat down again, on the edge of her chair. "Well, I admit he was very offensive then. But he's apologized. He's shown he was sorry. He and his family have been very kind to Roger."

"And very useful to him. Yes, I know. And I know he's a very different type from me and all that. He may very well be the sort who thinks it's a sin to kiss his best friend's wife—probably taught so by the Church which, as far as I know, was the first organized group to extol continence. Certainly the Jews never did. You remember the good Old Testament verses about the quiverful and the fruitful vine, don't you?"

"Ye-e-s. But those referred to married people. I don't think the Church ever said that married persons—"

"Wait a minute. The Catholic church does approve of large families—if it didn't, it couldn't afford to single out at least one or two from every big brood for the celibate life. But if you'll read up on the lives of married saints, you'll find they were mostly widows and widowers or that, if their spouses were still in the land of the living, they'd taken a 'voluntary vow of chastity,' like St. Cecilia and her husband, for instance. And the preference has certainly always been for virgins—especially for virgins who were eager to be martyred rather than married. Read *Sacred and Legendary Art* and go right down the list alphabetically. St. Agatha, St. Agnes, St.—"

"I have read *Sacred and Legendary Art*. And I've been to Rome over and over again and seen the places where those poor girls were martyred. You seem to forget that Grandpapa—"

"Oh, no, I didn't forget about Grandpapa. I never have the chance, between all the money he left, which is now coming in so handy in Roger's profession, and the ambassadorial prestige, which is doing so much to handicap poor Priscilla. But where were we? Oh, yes, as I was saying, Brian probably thinks it would be a sin to kiss you and what's more, he probably doesn't want to—a helpful combination of circumstances. I can't very well apologize, the way he did for being crazy drunk, because I don't see any reason why I should. I don't think it was wrong to kiss you and I'm not at all sorry I did. In fact, I'd like very much to kiss you again, in spite of the fact that you're not especially lovable—you're very attractive nonetheless. Someday I shall. Meanwhile, if you make any further objections to my perfectly innocent attentions to Priscilla, I shall draw the inevitable conclusion. You're not the only person who can draw conclusions."

"I don't see that you need to draw any special conclusions."

"I didn't see that you needed to either. But you did. And the conclusion I shall be forced to draw is that you don't want me to give that poor trapped kid a good time because you're jealous of her. You think that someday I'll make love to her—if I haven't already. And you'd much rather think I was dying to make love to you again—if you can call what I did the first time making love. It wasn't really. But the next time I kiss you—"

"You're not ever going to have a chance to kiss me again."

"Would you like to bet on that?"

"Yes. I'll bet on it. Whatever you like."

"All right. I'll take you up. But not right now. All our most interesting conversations seem subject to interruption. If I'm not mistaken, the luck of the Irish is about to intrude upon our delightful solitude à deux. Isn't that his special signal?"

David was quite right. Brian was jiggling the old brass knocker which Emily had attached to the new door that had been cut through the brick wall at the side of the transformed back yard, so that visitors could enter there, instead of through the old rear door, leading into the alley, where trash cans were perforce placed. It was Monday and, as usual on poker nights, Brian had come straight to Joy Street from the office. Emily hastened to let him in and greeted him with even greater cordiality than was her habit.

"Hello, Emily! I thought I'd find you here," he said, "that's why I didn't bother to go through the house. Hello, David! Gosh, you always manage to get through earlier than any of the rest of us, don't you? Is it good luck or good management?"

"Both in about equal proportions. And apparently Roger is still the one to shut up shop, in spite of the favorable turn of fortune's wheel."

Brian had nodded, almost casually, to Emily as he came in, without shaking hands. Now, without paying much apparent attention to David, he draped his rumpled coat over the back of the nearest chair and sank back on it, throwing his hat on the ground and wiping a moist brow.

"It's hot," he said unoriginally. "Yes, thanks—but not one of those numbers made with gin, if you don't mind. I'm allergic to them—probably a hang-over from the time I had to mix the damn stuff in the bathtub. I haven't the same allergy to rum—a planter's punch would be fine. But that would take time and I need something that would hit the spot right away. Why not just whisky and plain water? With lots of ice, but not too much plain water."

Emily laughed and followed directions. Brian, without rising, reached for his drink and, having taken one or two satisfying swallows and drawn a deep breath, turned back toward David before draining the small remaining amount of liquid from his glass.

"To comment on your comment, Pell is shutting up shop tonight," he announced. "Roger has gone out to Beverly. He said he'd be along as soon as he could."

"What, more lobsters?"

"No, Rolls-Royces this time."

"Rolls-Royces?"

"Yes. We've brought suit against a man who has six of them. He's quite a character—writes poetry that is privately printed, and has the flowers in twenty-four vases changed every day, simultaneously, in his four houses and his two apartments. One of the houses is in Beverly and one of the apartments at the Ritz and, according to Roger, they're really something. But the Rolls-Royces are this bird's special pride and joy. Two of them are just alike, except that one's gray and the other brown. When he's in Boston, he has those brought around to the Newbury Street entrance of the Ritz every morning and, after surveying them carefully, decides whether he's in a brown mood or a gray mood."

"Briny, you're making this up as you go along."

"It's the gospel truth. Most precious of all to this distinguished gentleman is the car he designed himself—red leather cushions, lots of brass, that sort of thing. Really splendiferous. Lord knows what he's spent on it. He's a very free spender. But somehow he's apt to overlook his monthly bills for considerable periods. He overlooked one for fourteen thousand dollars' worth of jewelry so long that the unpaid jeweler asked Cutter, Mills and Swan to sue him for it. We attached the Beverly estate, but we were the fifth plaintiff to do that. Then we attached the Berkshire estate, where we were only third, but that didn't look so promising either. And Roger said, why not go after the cars?"

"Smart boy! So then?"

"So then he started for the Beverly estate with a writ and a sheriff and lo and behold! there was the special number enthroned in the garage. This was locked, but the sheriff boosted Roger in through a window, and Roger managed to unfasten the door from the inside. So then the sheriff appointed Roger keeper, and he sat calmly resisting the blandishments of a lot of agitated servants, who had discovered the presence of the intruders by this time and were sure the owner would blame them for what had happened. Roger said he'd explain it wasn't their fault; but meanwhile the sheriff telephoned a public garage in Beverly and asked them to send a tow car to take the Rolls-Royce away—he and Roger had both tried to see whether they could drive it, but it had so many fancy gadgets on it that they decided against the attempt. So Roger just sat in it and steered to Pride's Crossing, where it's safely in custody. He called me up and told me about it when the deed was all done. I'm afraid we won't get much for the damn car, on account of its weird design—maybe two or three thousand. But anyway that's a start in the direction of the fourteen and Roger's rung the gong again."

"I thought Roger wasn't to have any more of those chicken coop cases," David remarked, when the general merriment had subsided.

"He doesn't have to. He wanted this one. And I could see how he would. I'd have asked to take it on myself if he hadn't beaten me to the draw. I'd have had a good laugh too, seated in state on those red leather cushions, surrounded by all those frantic servants wringing their hands while I sat with my arms folded, and then riding through the streets, amidst gaping and guffawing crowds. I could hear Roger chuckling all the time he was telephoning. . . . Just the same, I hope he isn't late for poker. Can you pinch-hit for him until he gets here, if he is, Dave?"

"Thanks for the compliment. But I've got a dinner date. In fact, I ought to be on my way right now. I've kept thinking Priscilla would be along any minute and I wanted to have a word with her about that bon voyage party—I'm to call my mother about it at midnight. Well, I'll catch up with Pris somehow and somewhere before then. . . . Sure you can't get over to New York for the great event yourself, Emily?"

"Yes, I'm very sure."

"Sorry. Well, so long. Tell Pris she shouldn't have let Lyman cut me out today and that I'll make them both pay for their bootleg sail, one way or another."

He brought his empty glass back to the table and set it down on the tray. Emily said good-by without looking up; she did not want to risk meeting David's eyes after what he had said that afternoon, especially in the presence of a third person; it might be too much of a betrayal. He paused briefly, almost as though expecting some further word or at least some sign from her, but when none was forthcoming, he did not linger beside her. With a passing compliment on the growth of her tulips since he had last observed them, he strolled toward the new door in the side of the brick wall, paused again for a moment and then went out, latching the door carefully.

"He will, you know," Brian observed, making sucking sounds with the ice which was all that remained of his drink.

"For heaven's sake, Brian! Stop making that noise! Give me your glass and let me refill it! He will what?"

"Make them pay for it. That is, if he wants Priscilla himself. And it wouldn't surprise me if he did."

"Nonsense! He thinks she's just a kid." Emily spoke with authority. But there was a queer feeling of suffocation in her throat, and she was afraid that her voice did not sound entirely normal.

"It's hard to tell just what David thinks. Or why other people think they know what he thinks. For instance, Cora Donlon is under the impression that he has a crush on her."

"Cora Donlon?"

"That's the name. The receptionist at our office."

"The receptionist at the office?"

"Yes. Of course, she's crazy. David isn't thinking—that is, not seriously—in terms of office receptionists. Cora ought to listen to what every good Irish mother tells her daughter if the girl starts going out with a Jew—that Jewish boys take Irish girls out on the town, but they don't marry them. They marry Jewish girls. I've heard my mother tell every one of my sisters except Queenie that and, no doubt, she'll be telling Queenie in the near future. Quite right too. But perhaps poor Cora has no mother to guide her, as the old saying went."

"Well, Priscilla isn't a Jewish girl."

"No. And David may be the exception that proves the rule. None of his new friends seems to be Jewish. Not that they seem to be Irish either, with the exception of Cora, and I doubt if he looks upon her as a friend."

"You mean—that he's not the type of man who stays just friends with a girl, that he's always a potential lover?"

"You sound as if you were quoting, Emily."

"Why, I was! How did you guess?"

"Wasn't very hard. And yes—that's what I did mean. Not that it's anything for you to worry about, of course. Say, you have done a grand job with this garden. Let's take a turn, shall we, before it gets any darker? I want to have a look at those tulips myself. And the pansies too."

They were still strolling up and down the diminutive walk, deep in conversation about flowers, with which it appeared Brian's mother had always had great success, when Roger came in, half an hour later. Emily ran to meet him with a glad cry of welcome and Brian stood by, grinning, while the young couple embraced. Afterward they all three sat down while Emily mixed fresh drinks and went into gales of laughter over Roger's adventures with the specially designed Rolls-Royce. Both men fell in heartily with Emily's suggestion that they should have a picnic supper. There was some cold roast beef left over from Sunday dinner, Emily said, some strawberry ice cream left in the freezer too; Deirdre would whip up a salad and make cheese sandwiches. Then there were those candlesticks with hurricane shades that had been among the wedding presents and had never been used; Ellie could get them down from the top shelf in the pantry—this would be a grand time to try them out. If they liked having supper this way, they could do it often throughout the summer. Deirdre and Ellie could have the same evening off and Emily could prepare everything herself.

The rest of the poker players and also Priscilla and Stanley Lyman arrived more or less simultaneously, before Roger and Brian and Emily finished supper. Uncle Barney and Father Mat had both eaten, they said; but Shaun Collins and Terence Lenahan confessed that they had been kept late at the office and that they could do with a bite along with their drinks; as for Priscilla and Stanley, they were frankly ravenous after their sail. Somehow the cold roast and the salad were stretched to feed everyone who was hungry and Brian went to Mary Pazalt's and brought back more bread for sandwiches and "store ice cream." Presently, everyone was hobnobbing with everyone else as if they had known each other all their lives. Eventually, Priscilla and Stanley said they must leave to get ready for a dance in Concord and the poker players repaired to the library. But Emily sat for a long time in her little garden, looking at the stars, wondering if she dared to ask her grandmother about the Grand Duke Feodor, and why David thought she was not lovable, and what she should do to prevent him from making love to her, and why he should imagine for one moment that she should be jealous of Priscilla. But it was so quiet and pleasant in the garden that, though she pondered these things, she did not worry over them. She felt happy and at peace. . . .

She was still sitting there when Roger came to tell her that the poker players were gone and that he had won twenty-five dollars, which they would blow in at the Ritz. He also said that there had been no chance to tell her about it when he came in, with so many people around, but he had another piece of good news for her—he had pulled off the sale of the Gloucester Street house. The Fletchers were so delighted with the location, which was what they had long hoped for in vain, that they were more than willing to put up with the inconvenience of the house itself. They had actually made him a very advantageous offer, on their own initiative; he had not been obliged to press them at all.

"What's more," he went on, "when I telephoned the good news to your mother, what do you think she said? That she had entirely forgotten about Commencement."

"Commencement?"

"Yes. You don't mean to say that you have too? Emily, I wouldn't have believed it of you! When your father'll be celebrating his twenty-fifth."

"Why, I *had!* We've had so many other things to think about! But I don't see how Mother could have."

"She doesn't either. And of course she doesn't want to miss any of the festivities—settling in the Yard with the other reunioners and marching in the parade to the stadium and all the rest of it. Homer Lathrop is Chairman of the Reunion Committee. And President Conant and Governor Saltonstall are both going all out to give their old classmates the glad hand. The President's giving a reception for the reunioners at his house in the Yard and, of course, the Governor's going to lead the parade, besides providing a buffet supper for everyone who wants to come to Chestnut Hill, between the all-day picnic in Swampscott and the class Pops. Your mother says it's such a long time since Massachusetts has had a governor who was a gentleman, she really feels everyone in his own class should stand by him—his own social class, that is; not just his class at college."

"Grandmamma has always said Roger Wolcott was a gentleman," Emily remarked thoughtfully. "That makes one other."

"Yes, but that was a long time ago, wasn't it? After all, if we went back farther still, there were a few more—a man named Hancock, for instance, and two or three named Adams. Anyway, your mother feels she should take a stand for Governor Saltonstall, and of course she couldn't do it—that is, not as a reunioner—if she and your father made their separation official. She's talked it over with him and he sees her point. He agrees that they ought to be seen at Commencement together, and if they do that, they might as well see Priscilla through too. In fact, I wouldn't be surprised if, eventually, they wouldn't be almost sorry they sold the Gloucester Street house, especially as your father's practically decided he may as well resume his connection with Homer Lathrop's office. But, of course, there's always the Chilton Club and the Somerset Club. Incidentally, your father's going to try to put in a good word for Fletcher with the Membership Committee of the Somerset Club. It seems that next to having a house in town, on one of the side streets, it's been his greatest ambition to belong and every year he's felt more and more thwarted because he didn't make the grade."

"So it's beginning to look like the best of all possible worlds to Father and Mother again and they're even ready to hold out a helping hand to their fellow creatures?"

"Well, things certainly do look better than they did a while ago. But I wouldn't go quite so far as to say that. After all, everyone can't be as happy as we are."

There was an undertone of amusement in his voice, as there had been throughout the conversation. But he also spoke as if he too were happy and at peace, which was not strange, because he also felt that way. It had never even crossed his mind to be troubled or jealous when he came home and found Emily and Brian alone in the garden together.

Chapter 17

BEFORE THE MONTH was out, the sale of the Gloucester Street house had been consummated to the satisfaction of all concerned, and the Class of '14 had celebrated its twenty-fifth reunion in a manner befitting the best traditions of Harvard College. Perfect weather had prevailed throughout Commencement Week, Harvard won the baseball game against Yale, and the paraders, led by the Governor who was also a gentleman, presented a striking sight in their fanciful blue blazers and variegated headgear. Eleanor Thayer's slight misgivings about the congeniality of the reunioners with whom she and her husband might be quartered in the Yard proved to be groundless; they were Philadelphians of unimpeachable background. With such a generally satisfactory setup, it was not strange that she should find the way toward complete reconciliation with her husband smoothed; in fact, only one jarring episode threatened the uniform serenity of its progress.

Though there had been no dickering concerning the price to be paid for the Gloucester Street house, and the sum total offered by the Fletchers was substantial, a comparatively modest amount was paid to bind the bargain. It was understood that, as soon as the Thayers had removed all their belongings, and the Fletchers were free to take possession, a much larger sum was to be paid; then the balance in the early autumn. This arrangement suited everybody. Unfortunately, however, Eleanor and Sumner Thayer failed to discuss the way in which the first payment was to be spent and to reach an agreement concerning this beforehand. Eleanor, who, like her husband, had been handicapped by straitened circumstances during their separation, did not feel that her wardrobe was in any way worthy of a twenty-fifth anniversary celebration; as soon as she knew that two thousand dollars was so opportunely available, she went to Miss Ruby's and ordered a complete new outfit which cost almost that entire amount. Then she went back to Emily's house, where she and Sumner were dining that night, taking with her a dazzling array of samples.

"Don't you think these are gorgeous?" she asked, spreading them out with pride before her husband, her daughter and her son-in-law. "I really let myself go, for the first time in years. Some of the models are more Mamma's type than they are mine, but I felt in the mood for them somehow. Miss Ruby says that red-and-white print is one of the most striking things she has imported in a long time."

"You don't mean to say you've been ordering clothes at Miss Ruby's?" Sumner inquired, in horror-stricken tones.

"Yes, I do. Why shouldn't I?"

"Because her prices are simply astronomical. With your excellent figure, you could have gone to Stearns' or any other good department store and got whatever you needed, ready made."

Eleanor's frame of mind was not such that she could be placated by compliments to her figure. "I wasn't in the mood for Stearns' or any other good department store," she said, rather testily. "I wanted to go to a place like Miss Ruby's. Why shouldn't I? I had two thousand dollars to spend."

"But you didn't. I spent them myself this morning."

"*You spent them yourself this morning!*" The tones in which Eleanor echoed her husband were as horror stricken as his had been a moment earlier. "Why, you couldn't have! On what?"

"I bought a cemetery lot at Mount Auburn. It's worried me for a long time because we didn't have one of our own. And when this large sum unexpectedly became available I went straight to the office building and saw the manager. I was very fortunate to get a lot in such an advantageous location. It's right between the Hem—"

He got no further. His wife, who had responded to the first part of his announcement with a groan, had now begun to scream hysterically. Emily, who was doing her best to soothe her mother, cast a withering glance at her father and made signs for him to be still. Roger, coughing so violently as to suggest that he had another attack of bronchitis, precipitately left the room.

When he returned, still clearing his throat, and carefully carrying a glass of water, which he offered his mother-in-law, she was still unable to take it from him. Her screams had subsided, but she was groaning again and, between groans, she uttered incoherent reproaches.

"Two thousand for a cemetery lot!" she kept repeating. "And I was so happy to think that, after going around practically in rags for years, I was going to have some decent clothes! Now I'll have to go back, the first thing in the morning and tell Miss Ruby that I can't have those imported dresses after all. I can just see her face when I do it. I can just—"

"Mother, of course you won't have to do anything of the kind. Of course I can help you out. I can lend you enough to pay Miss Ruby something on account and then you can pay her in full when the Fletchers make their first big payment. It isn't as if you weren't going to have plenty of money coming in, very soon too."

"But I had plans for all of it and now your father has spent two thousand on a cemetery lot; it's easy to understand why Papa felt Sumner Thayer shouldn't ever be trusted with money and had all yours tied up. But things have come to a pretty pass when a mature woman has to borrow money from her own daughter. Any man who would go out and squander two thousand on a cem—"

"Well, you were out squandering that much on clothes at the same time, Eleanor. I don't think you ought to be so bitter about it. You act as if I had committed another extravagance, like gambling. You were the extravagant one. As I said before, you could perfectly well have bought your clothes from Stearns', but everybody has to have a cemetery lot. We'll have ours long after the clothes are all worn out. And as I tried to tell you, it's one of the very best still available at Mount Auburn—small, but then we don't need a large one. And right between—"

At that point, Roger began to cough again and this time, when he left the library, it was for a much longer period than before. In fact, he did not return until Ellie came in with the cocktails. By then, Emily had succeeded in patching up some sort of a peace between her parents. He never inquired exactly how she had managed to do it.

Final courts at Buckingham Palace were later than usual that year, because of the visit which the King and Queen made to the United States. This was a matter of considerable regret to Old Mrs. Forbes, partly because it did not give her as much time as she had anticipated for the festive finish of the season in France; and partly because she could find no plausible excuse for the earlier sailing on the *Normandie* when Priscilla went to the office of the French Line herself and returned with the information that they could have better accommodations toward the end of June than they could have toward the end of May. Moreover, this would permit her attendance at the Harvard-Yale Boat Race, which was undeniably an advantage. However, before the month was out, Old Mrs. Forbes, Priscilla and Olivia Stockbridge, accompanied by the faithful maid, Doris, and Clark, the equally faithful chauffeur, had departed for Europe, and soon thereafter, Brian, Pell and David went off successively on their vacations. Their absence, inevitably, meant more work for Roger and both he and Emily began to take his lateness as a matter of course, and to accept the fact that he would usually be too tired to go anywhere in the evening, after an abnormally long day at the office, even if they could put sufficient dependence on his departure from there at a certain hour to permit the making of definite plans. However, they continued to enjoy their garden and, on week ends, they usually went either to Manchester-by-the-Sea or to Dublin, where Old Mrs. Forbes had instructed Roger to "keep an eye on how things were going." Less frequently they visited Sue and Sherman Forbes on the Cape, finding an unexpectedly warm welcome whenever they did so; and, stealing one extra day, they went for the Fourth of July to Elizabeth Forbes' old brick farmhouse, in Vermont, where she was already contentedly installed for the summer.

Emily had always understood her aunt's love for the place and Roger had come to share this. The house, built when the early settlers of the region had their own kilns and made their own bricks, stood foursquare on a small rise of land which sloped in front to a country road with a magnificent view of the White Mountains beyond the Connecticut River and, in the rear, to a large pasture with a small brook meandering through it and wooded foothills hemming it in. The nearest house, very similar in build, was situated around a bend, about a quarter of a mile away. Most of Elizabeth's land was worked on shares by a family of prosperous farmers, named Randell, who lived there, and who also supplied her with milk and chickens, plowed and harrowed her garden and harvested her orchard for her, "winter boarded" her two horses, and "lent a hand" with housecleaning in the spring, closing up in the fall, and other work as needed; but their mutual relations, though cordial, had never reached the point where dropping in on each other was habitual. The village was two miles away, and though this lay on the direct route to the mountains, the main highway which went through it by-passed the back road; its tranquillity and solitude remained almost complete.

Elizabeth, with the Randells' help, had dammed the brook, thus providing herself with a summer swimming pool and a winter skating pond. The slope at the rear of the house furnished a natural toboggan slide, the pasture an ideal range for snowshoeing. Emily and her contemporaries, as well as Elizabeth and her college cronies, had always vastly preferred the simple facilities thus assured, and the seclusion in which they could be enjoyed, to the centers where rural sports, especially winter sports, had been featured and commercialized. Emily had formerly found the summer, when Elizabeth spent most of her time gardening, less consonant with her own ideas of vacationing than the winter, though a daily swim in the pool, and a ride over the hills or through the old logging roads in the woods, filled in several hours agreeably; but now that she had begun to take an interest in growing things herself, she could appreciate what her aunt had accomplished and felt disposed toward having a share in the further development of the grounds. The house had long been untenanted when Elizabeth bought it for a song, and only a few clumps of lilac and sweetbrier had survived its abandonment; but an old diary, overlooked when its former occupants had tired of its serenity and joined the general exodus of the period toward the west, referred to moss roses, cinnamon pinks and Johnny-jump-ups bordering and beautifying the central path in the vegetable garden; to hollyhocks rising against the brick of the façade; to sweet peas, surpassing in variety and profusion any that the neighbors could raise; to asters that defied the frost way into the fall; and to petunias encircling a vanished summerhouse. Elizabeth had planted all these flowers again and had even erected a new summerhouse of latticed wood. Since she had mingled imagination with skill, she had done much to re-create the blossoming pattern of a bygone day. In the brief intervals which Emily spent there, she took increasing pleasure in helping to expand her aunt's design.

What was true of the land was also true of the house. Both the ground floor and the one above it were bisected by a central hall with two large connecting rooms on either side; over all was a spacious attic and underneath a well-built cellar. A small ell, surmounted by a shed chamber, jutted out at right angles from the main house and led directly to the barn and woodshed. Elizabeth had transformed the ell into modern service quarters, which were efficiently occupied by a dour-looking, but faithful Scotchwoman, named Jenny Griffin, who went uncomplainingly back and forth between Bryn Mawr and Vermont whenever it suited her employer's convenience. Elizabeth had also installed a furnace, and shut off the front end of the upper hall to enclose a bathroom; but except for these concessions to comfort, convenience and cleanliness, she had leaned over backward to restore the original atmosphere of her home and capture suitable appointments for it. Until Emily made similar experiments and achieved similar results on Joy Street, she had tolerated rather than shared her aunt's rhapsodies about the discovery of beautiful boards under layers of gray paint, and chimneys that "drew" to perfection, in spite of the fact that the fireplaces they served had been closed to permit the installation of "airtights." But though she felt none of her grandmother's impatience with the recital of such details, she had failed to understand why anyone, especially anyone of Elizabeth's unquestionable intelligence, should find them thrilling. That the discovery, under the eaves of attics, at noisy country auctions and in small, unpretentious antique shops, of gate-leg tables, ladder-back chairs, and mahogany four-posters should prove rewarding seemed to her slightly more comprehensible; so did the fortuitous find of the missing plates to a set in a favorite pattern of china, a hooked rug which would exactly fit an uncovered space, or a patchwork quilt which looked as if it had been made on purpose to give the needed tone to a slightly colorless room. However, it was only since her marriage that she had delighted in poking around to search for such items herself, and had shared Elizabeth's enthusiasm when they were installed where they obviously belonged.

During the week end lengthened to include the Fourth of July, Emily found herself taking almost as much pleasure in the hours she spent with Elizabeth in the house and garden as she did in the hours when she and Roger went swimming and riding together. Roger was just recovering from another attack of bronchitis, which seemed even more severe than its predecessors, probably because it was so unseasonable. He really felt more like stretching out in a hammock, with a pile of books and a pitcher of orangeade beside him than like making any physical exertion. The realization of this robbed Emily of her own zest for exercise; of course she could go swimming and riding alone, and once or twice she did. But she did not stay out very long. She was soon back on Hollyhock Hill, as she had christened her aunt's place, weeding contentedly around the moss roses, which were still at their prime, or discussing with Elizabeth the possibility of further improvements and embellishments for the house.

"I don't see why you don't put in another bathroom at the rear of the upper hall, the way you did at the front," she said one day, after Roger and Elizabeth had inopportunely collided several times. "It would be different if you never had any men here."

"Well, I'll tell you. I've never wanted any kind of veranda in front, because, in the first place, it would spoil the looks of the fan door and in the second place, it would be suggestive of the horrible old idea that you must share your private life with everyone who was passing by—not that there's much passing here, thank heaven, but you know what I mean. After all, we are pretty near the road."

Emily said she understood and waited for Elizabeth to go on.

"On the other hand, I've thought that my next improvement might be a double gallery in the rear—something like those they used to have on ante bellum houses in the Deep South, but with simpler columns. If I did build such a gallery, naturally I'd want to have a door leading out on it from the hall. We couldn't see the mountains from there, but we could see the pasture and the brook and the foothills. Of course you've always slept in the front of the house, so perhaps you don't realize that there's a lovely view in the back too, if you don't think of it in connection with the mountains; but I chose a rear room for mine on purpose, because I could look out on the pasture and the brook and the foothills and they seem so friendly and intimate."

While they talked, the two had been sitting in Elizabeth's bedroom which faced south and west. Emily rose and went to one of the west windows, which provided a limited outlook on the scene Elizabeth had described and gazed at this with awakened understanding of its charm. Then she went out into the hall, measured its width appraisingly with her hands and turned back to her aunt with shining eyes.

"Why, Liz, I think that's a wonderful idea! A long door, divided in the middle, so that when it was opened, you could look out through its entire width! I can see just how it would be. You're right—this western view is lovely too. I hadn't half realized it before. And we can always see the mountains from the doorstep and the lawn and the garden—from the summerhouse too. But so often it's too cold to sit out there, especially in the evening, and this gallery would give shelter and get the warm afternoon sun. It would be wonderful for Roger. I can't help worrying about this recurrent bronchitis of his."

"He's been examined, of course?"

"Yes, of course. And Dr. Blaine says there's no cause for alarm—whatever that may mean. I *am* alarmed though. I suppose it's silly of me, but

I'd have been happier if Roger hadn't gone out in the summerhouse today, even if there isn't a particle of wind and it is July! Now, with this double gallery. . . . He wouldn't even have to go over the stairs, if he weren't feeling well!"

"Then you're reconciled to doing with one bathroom when you come here to visit?"

Emily wrinkled her brow. "No-o-o. Not quite! You know I always want to have my cake and eat it too! Why not put one between your bedroom and the southeast guest room, taking a slice off each? Of course it would make them both a little smaller, but it isn't as if you were thinking of using yours as a double room, or as if you often needed to use the other that way. You'd still have the two big connecting bedrooms on the other side!"

"You do love to make other people's plans for them, don't you, Emily? But—well, yes, I think it might be done. Of course I don't want to spoil the proportions of the rooms, or upset my scheme of decoration. We might measure though."

Elizabeth took a yardstick from her bureau drawer, putting her hands on it with such ease as to suggest its frequent use; then, methodically, she began to measure, and to jot down her findings on a small pad of paper which she took from her bedside table. Emily watched her eagerly, but she did not interrupt her or make any further suggestions. Though she hoped to overcome her aunt's hesitation, she respected it; she appreciated the symmetry of the rooms' proportions and she knew how much time and thought had gone into their decoration. Elizabeth had furnished each one differently, but in such a way that they all harmonized with each other. In her own room and the adjacent guest room she had put the gaily painted "cottage furniture," which, during the first part of the nineteenth century, had succeeded the more austere mahogany and maple then the vogue. In the northeast bedroom, which Roger and Emily called theirs, she had one of the rare candle-flame four-posters and a dresser to match; and, in the connecting room behind it, twin sleigh beds, which were rarer still, at least in that size. These were her special pride and represented the results of a long search; but she had insisted that, owing to the limited number of her guest chambers, there must be one where she could put two unattached persons together, in case of crowding, and she had been triumphant when she found the perfect pair of "sleighs."

"I think I can do it," she said at last, referring to her jottings, "and I'm going to better your suggestion. I'm going to make a little passageway, with a bathroom on one side—it can be ventilated through the attic—and a clothes closet on the other. Then no one will be locking anyone else out, as they're always sure to do when a bathroom has two doors. And I need more closet space anyway. I think, while I'm about it, I'll make the same arrangement downstairs, between the library and the dining room—a lavatory and a coat closet would come in very handy too.

197

Of course it will mean some repapering and the fireplaces will be the least bit off center, but I don't think that matters very much. I'll enjoy overseeing the work while I'm here this summer and I'll have the rear gallery put on at the same time. It'll be all finished when you come back for Labor Day. But don't you dare suggest anything like this on the other side of the hall! I'll have hard enough work matching the heaven and hell hinges on two doors without trying to do it on three and you know the paneling on the other's much more elaborate."

Emily laughed and promised that she would suggest no more changes. As a matter of fact, she had no wish to make others. She would have been loath to sacrifice any of the spaciousness of her room and she admired the door—for some inexplicable reason more elaborately wrought than any of the others in the house—which led to the adjoining chamber quite as much as Elizabeth did. Leaving her aunt still absorbed with the measuring stick and the little pad, on which she was now making sketches, Emily went out to join Roger in the summerhouse and tell him all about the wonderful improvements they would be seeing on Labor Day.

He answered, lazily, that he thought the place was almost perfect as it was, but that if she and Elizabeth were bent on gilding refined gold and painting the lily, he supposed there was nothing he could do to stop them; as far as he was concerned, he hoped they would let him lie still and enjoy the view in peace. Falling in with his mood, Emily sat down on the ground beside the reclining chair in which he was stretched out and, clasping her hands around her knees, gazed across the intervening hills and the valley where the Connecticut River wove its peaceful way between fresh fields, toward the White Mountains beyond. A slight mist was rising from the meadows, which veiled them without hiding them; but above it, there was almost perfect clarity; and when the sun set behind the wooded foothills at the west, everything seemed covered with a delicate sheen of glory. There were a few sounds—a cow lowing in the distance, a bird singing in a near-by apple tree, a cricket chirping on the wide granite steps which led to the front door. Then everything was silent as, one by one, the stars came out. . . .

Yes, it was perfect as it was—perfect to sit there, in the gathering darkness, with her head against Roger's knees and his hand on her hair. This was exactly the sort of perfection she had meant when she had said she did not want the world to be on fire, that she wanted it to be peaceful and pleasant and safe and that she wanted to share her place in it with Roger Field. All her perplexities, all her worries, were relegated to another sphere when they were together like this. She did not feel troubled or curious about anything or anybody. She forgot that she had wondered about the Grand Duke's ring, that she had been concerned about Pietro's accident and piqued by Simonetta's elusiveness; she had even forgotten that Priscilla had become a problem and that a passage at arms with David always ended in her defeat. Things like that seemed so far away and so unimportant, here and now. Of course, it was very pleasant and peaceful in the Joy Street garden too, but it was not perfect; it did not give the same feeling of complete detachment that this did. As Roger said, it was unimportant whether Elizabeth made any changes on the place. In fact, it seemed rather a shame that she should toil all summer, instead of sitting quietly in the garden like this. Only of course Elizabeth had no one to sit in the garden with her—at least, no one who counted. That made all the difference. She had said to Emily once, "I love this place so much that I would give up teaching and stay here all the time, if only—" Then she had flushed and she had not finished her sentence. But Emily knew she meant, "If only I had someone to live here with me. Some man whom I loved and who loved me." Suddenly, Emily felt very sorry for Elizabeth, who had never known the fulfillment of love and who had never sat in the dusk with her head against her husband's knees and his hand on her hair. But presently she ceased to feel sorry, because such complete contentment filled her being that there was no room for anything else. She was conscious of only one thought: that she and Roger were together. And of only one wish: that they might stay on and on like this.

Of course she knew they could not, but at least they could return to this perfect place over and over again. It would always be there waiting for them. They would come back to it very soon—in September. . . . But, as it turned out, they could not. Roger and Pell, as members of the First Corps Cadets, were sent to Camp Edwards the first two weeks in July; and in view of David's absence, which had not only covered his duty in the field at Camp Smith, but had been prolonged to cover his desired trip to Venezuela, work at the office inevitably piled up. Then late in August, the news from France became suddenly disquieting and Roger felt impelled to cable Old Mrs. Forbes, urging that she and her charges should return to the United States immediately. Her answer, somewhat delayed in reaching him because of mobilization, indicated that she felt this might have been put off a few weeks, even if it were eventually inevitable, so that she might have come home when she planned to do so and had suitable reservations. However, she displayed her usual faculty for ignoring or surmounting the disagreeable and the seemingly impossible with amazing good results: she secured the luxurious shipboard accommodations reserved for the American-born wife of a French nobleman, who had intended to visit her native land, but elected to remain with her husband in this hour of danger. A week later, the triumphant old lady arrived in New York with her granddaughter, her banker's daughter, her maid, her chauffeur, her car and all the clothes she had ordered against the coming season, both for Priscilla and herself—not to mention a considerable sum of money which, because of her shortened stay, she had not required.

By this time, Europe was at war, and world conditions, though not yet chaotic, were admittedly menacing. David and Brian had already made plans of long standing for the Labor Day week end and Roger had a preliminary hearing in an equity case coming up Tuesday morning—the most important entrusted to him so far. Besides, he did not feel justified in leaving Pell to grapple alone with any problems which might unexpectedly arise, even if he had been in the mood for Hollyhock Hill just then. He urged Emily to go there without him, knowing how disappointed both she and Elizabeth would be by her failure to do so. But though the disappointment was real enough, Emily was not in the mood for Hollyhock Hill either. The memory of the radiant evening which she and Roger had spent in the summerhouse together had become much more vital to her than her eagerness for material improvement; though she was still interested in seeing these, she wanted to do so with him. Besides, if she had gone to Vermont, she would have missed the home-coming of her grandmother and Priscilla; she wanted to hear the account of all their exciting adventures, without any delay.

They were both well, both in high spirits and both inclined to regard their precipitate departure from the scene of impending conflict in the light of a lark. In like measure, Old Mrs. Forbes was insistent that no change should be made in their program for the autumn and winter except, if anything, to crowd it more full of festivities than she had originally planned. She did not actually say, "Après nous, le déluge," but it was implicit in all her actions and her attitude was by no means an isolated one. Both the debutantes and their elders realized that this year might well be the last when the supply of suitable escorts from Harvard remained undiminished and were determined to make the most of the opportunities furnished by this provident university while they still survived. Priscilla was immediately caught up in a whirl.

It began with a Sunday luncheon, given by Emily and Roger at their Joy Street house, a function very lavish of its kind, but almost immediately eclipsed by the elaborate dinner which Old Mrs. Forbes gave on Louisburg Square. This dinner preceded the ball at the Somerset where the ballroom had been transformed, under her directions, to suggest the terraced garden of a great Italian villa, with the façade of this forming the backdrop and fountains gushing in the foreground. Dozens of beautiful brocaded hangings, hundreds of changing multicolored lights and thousands of tropical flowers were used in the scheme of decoration, while the feast that followed the dancing carried out the illusion of medieval magnificence. Nothing had been done on such a scale in Boston within the memory of its proudest dowager, and there was widespread murmuring that something simpler would have been in far better taste, especially when presenting a harum-scarum little girl from Cape Cod. But none of this murmuring was done within earshot of Old Mrs. Forbes; and even the most critical were bound to confess that the harum-scarum little girl from Cape Cod was proving much more adaptable than anyone would have supposed possible, a year earlier.

In the wake of her own ball at the Somerset, Priscilla went to countless other hotel balls, to country club balls and hunt balls; to dances at the Chilton Club and at the Duxbury Yacht Club; to cocktail parties, supper parties and theater parties; to football games and hockey games. She poured at innumerable teas; she ushered at morning musicales. As if Boston and its smarter suburbs did not offer sufficient diversion, she was rushed off to an Assembly in Philadelphia, to the Bachelors' Cotillion in Baltimore and to the coming-out party of Hall Roosevelt's daughter, Eleanor, at the White House. Having promptly become a provisional member of the Junior League, she began her volunteer work at the Perkins Institute for the Blind and the Canton School for Crippled Children, and also attended the requisite course of lectures at Zero Marlborough Street where the League had its headquarters. It was after she had gone to several of these that she betrayed a marked lack of appreciation.

"If all those girls sitting on those hard, straight-backed chairs in that pinky ballroom are really the cream of Boston society," she remarked caustically to Emily, "I shudder to think what the skim milk is like. Some of them don't wear either hats or stockings; they are really rowdy looking; and two or three of them have voices that grate like a file. The girls in that group aren't actually snooty; they're too unaware anyone else is around to do any high-hatting. They just get together in a little huddle and talk tweedily on and on."

"There are just a few of that type, Priscilla."

"There are plenty. Then there are the girls who go to the other extreme. Their hats match their dresses and their bags match their shoes; never the other way around. They do less talking and more watching than the others, as if they didn't feel quite sure what was expected of them and wanted to see what someone else would do first. Most of them knit, very neatly, all sorts of useless-looking little doodads."

"Priscilla, it's very ill-bred to talk this way about your friends. Very—very ungrateful."

"They're not my friends. I never said I wanted them for my friends and I'm sure they don't want me for theirs. Most of them look down on me because I don't fit in with either type. Of course, there are a few other outliers besides me and some of them are nice; good-looking too, Olivia and Faith and Joan for instance. But mostly the independents are the ones who have on too much make-up or don't have their hair washed often enough; they're usually either the worst dressed or the best dressed too. Then there are some whose clothes just seem to be held together with casual pins here and there and some others who keep breaking out into French all the time, so that everyone will know they've had the advantages of foreign sojourns."

"If Grandmamma heard you talking like this, she'd just about die."

"Oh, no, she wouldn't! It's exactly the sort of thing she says herself. Only she doesn't say it about the provisional Junior Leaguers of this year. She doesn't want anything to 'go wrong.' But give her time! A little later, when she isn't hampered, she'll say things that will make your hair curl."

Except for occasional captious comments of this character, it was not until after the League's Christmas performance at the Peabody Playhouse, in which she took a leading part, that Priscilla showed any further signs of surfeit. Then, unexpectedly, as she did so many things, she voiced sudden discontent.

"I've been to all the luncheons and done all the ushering I can stand. I'm pretty well fed up on dancing too. I see the same stupid sophomores night after night and my feet have spread so I've had to buy bigger shoes. When things get that bad, it's time to stop. I want to do something different for a few days at least. If I don't, I'll go crazy."

"Just what do you mean by different?" inquired Emily, laying down her pen and trying to speak patiently. She had been balancing her checkbook, which she liked to do promptly and regularly, when Priscilla burst in upon her and she would have preferred not to be interrupted just then. In fact, she was getting rather tired of her cousin's continued presence in the house—if the word "presence" could be used in connection with someone who constantly darted in and out, who thought nothing of getting home from a dance at five in the morning, or starting out breakfastless for a Junior League lecture after coming back from New York on a milk train. Probably habitation would be the better word. Yes, she was getting rather tired of Priscilla's habitation. . . .

"I've never been to Hollyhock Hill," Priscilla was saying. "That ought to be different."

"Yes, it is. . . . Well, I don't know Elizabeth's plans, but I can ask. When would you want to go?"

"Next Thursday."

"You seem to have this pretty well thought out already. Do you want to be alone, like Greta Garbo, or do you want a big boisterous house party?"

"I don't want either one. You wouldn't let me stay there all alone, would you? And there isn't room for a big noisy house party, is there? I want you and Roger, of course. And Olivia."

"No men, except Roger?"

"Naturally. Don't hurry me so, Emily! I heard Roger talking to Brian about Hollyhock Hill the other night, and Brian said that he'd never been to a place like that, that he'd give anything to see it. I think he meant what he said. I think he'd probably like Hollyhock Hill. And Olivia isn't interested in anyone special just now. She's had a row with her high-particular, as she calls him. And she isn't snobbish. She'd be polite to Brian."

"Damn white of her, as Brian would put it himself. Yes, I've heard him say he'd like to go to Hollyhock Hill too and I'd be glad to ask him. I think Elizabeth would be glad to have him. You knew he'd just been elected to the City Council, didn't you?"

"Yes, I heard Roger talking about it and saying it was just the first rung of the political ladder—that he was sure Brian would get to the Senate someday which is what he wants."

"Well, I wouldn't go so far as that. Our senators are pretty firmly entrenched and after all, one of them's my uncle, so naturally I wouldn't want to see him defeated by an Irishman—not that I dislike Brian. . . . Would I be hurrying you—or prying into your affairs or doing anything else I shouldn't—if I ask whether you're interested in anyone special just now and what man you had in mind for yourself?"

"I want to ask David."

Emily pressed her lips together and, picking up her pen, placed it in an upright position, ran her thumb and forefinger down its length and, turning it over, repeated this process several times. She had not seen David alone since the spring evening when he had told her he was not sorry he had kissed her once and that he intended to do so again, in spite of the fact that he did not find her particularly lovable, adding that he gathered she was jealous of Priscilla. Emily had considered his conduct on that occasion even more outrageous than on the night he had first upset her, because it seemed more studied; and she was thankful that he had apparently drifted completely away from her orbit and that Priscilla had evidently been so occupied with more eligible young men that she had ceased to give him a thought. It came as a distinct shock to Emily to find that she was mistaken in the last assumption.

"Why David?" she asked noncommittally.

"Well, he and Brian are great friends, aren't they? He and Roger too, for that matter. I keep having to remind you that I first met him through Roger. But I've seen hardly anything of him lately. And I've missed him a lot. If he went off in the country like that, with us, we could be together all day and every evening."

This was undeniably true. Emily told herself that the reason she resented it so much was because David was such an unsuitable companion for Priscilla.

"Somehow, I don't believe David would care for Hollyhock Hill," she said cautiously. "I don't even know whether he can skate."

"Of course he can skate. I've been skating with him. He's a wonderful skater. He skates just the way he dances."

"I thought you said you hadn't seen anything of David lately," Emily remarked, closing her eyes to the mental vision of David, skating just the way he danced.

"I ought to have said, hardly anything. Of course I see him once in a while. After all, he's one of my best friends. Besides, we used to go skating a lot on the Cape, a year ago last winter."

"I didn't know you considered David one of your best friends."

"Yes you did too. You like to pretend you don't, that's all. I can't see why. It isn't as if you were a girl and wanted him yourself."

This time Emily did not lay down her pen; she threw it down.

"It certainly isn't," she said almost sharply. "All right, I'll telephone Elizabeth and if she can manage a house party over the New Year week end, I'll speak to the others. . . . Was there anything else you wanted to talk to me about just now? If there isn't, I'd really like to finish balancing my checkbook, so I can pay this month's bills. I'm late getting to them as it is."

"I don't see why you bother to balance it. You know you have plenty of money in the bank. And it wouldn't matter, even if you were overdrawn. Olivia says she heard her father telling David that the Third National has a list of people who are always overdrawn and that the cashiers have instructions not to annoy any of them. The bank knows it's safeguarded by the trust funds these people have. Even if you don't have a trust fund, the cashiers are very considerate, when they're told to be. I happen to know. I'm overdrawn more than a thousand myself right now. I just bought myself a very snappy ermine jacket. I was sick and tired of that old squirrel number. It looked like something left over from your time."

Emily did not reply; she did not trust herself to do so. Assiduously, she bent over her accounts.

Chapter 18

ELIZABETH EXPRESSED HERSELF as delighted when Emily telephoned. She had rather wanted to invite Mark Merriweather, who taught biology at Dartmouth and who had recently lectured at Bryn Mawr, to spend the New Year's week end at Hollyhock Hill; she had hesitated because—well, just because she had. Since the others were coming, she would get in touch with him right away. He could sleep in the library on a foldaway bed —now that she had a closet and a lavatory connecting with it, thanks to Emily's insistence, it was perfectly feasible to use it that way. She would put the two girls in the southeast guest room and the two other men in the "sleigh" room; of course Roger and Emily would have their candle-flame room as usual. She had liked both David Salomont and Brian Collins so much, when she met them at the wedding, that she had been really sorry not to see them again; she was sure they would all have a fine time together. Of course they would not make too much work—Jenny was with her as usual and Una Randell would come in whenever they needed her for dishwashing and cleaning. There was any amount of snow, the tobogganing would be wonderful. And she would have the pond cleared off. She had not been skating, because it was not much fun, all alone. But she was sure the ice was inches thick. . . .

Olivia, Brian and David all expressed themselves as equally delighted, when the invitation was extended to them and Roger, if anything, seemed even more pleased. He genuinely enjoyed Hollyhock Hill himself and he had deeply regretted Emily's disappointment over their failure to go there for the Labor Day week end; he hoped this would make up for that to her. The trip began most auspiciously with the departure of Priscilla's party—as they had all agreed to call it—on a snow train from the North Station, in a car jammed with other young people equipped for similar outings with snowshoes, skis, skates and a miscellaneous collection of bulky and unwieldy outer garments. Presently, card games were in progress, lunches were being shared, thermos bottles filled with coffee and flasks filled with whisky were circulating freely and several groups had burst into song. Long before the train had slowed down at the Junction, which served the twin villages on either side of the Connecticut in that locality, everyone was on terms of great good fellowship; and, when Priscilla's party left this jovial company and descended to the platform, they were followed by shouts and cheers which echoed through the frosty air until the train puffed slowly away and the group that had been left behind was already stowed into the old-fashioned sleighs, liberally equipped with jingling bells, which Elizabeth had sent to meet them.

The sleighs swung immediately into the back road where the snowplows had not penetrated and, for several miles, while the bells jingled and the horses jogged easily along, the members of Priscilla's party gave themselves up to the quiet enjoyment of an experience which was new to more than half of them. Then the lights on Hollyhock Hill came into view, shining warmly through the cold glitter of the night; and everyone was piling out of the sleighs and saying here, let me take that, and have you got my skates with yours, and all the other customary, inconsequential things. There were big fires in all the fireplaces, the house was as warm as toast and gaily decorated with Christmas greens and Elizabeth had on a red dress; there was color in her cheeks to match it too, color that neither Roger nor Emily had ever seen there before; and Mark Merriweather, her biology professor, who did not seem too professorial or too elderly either, was helping everyone with bags, and saying how about hot buttered rum or would somebody rather have plain toddy and seeming and acting like the most genial of hosts. And next there was one of Jenny's fine suppers, a big ironstone tureen full of corn chowder and chicken pie and hot rolls and a huge baked Indian pudding. . . .

By the time they had finished coffee, Emily was so sleepy that she wondered whether she could keep awake long enough to get out of her clothes before she tumbled into the candle-flame bed. Roger was equally drowsy and they were soon fast asleep, with their arms around each other for extra warmth and comfort. It was not until they waked the next morning, with the sun streaming into their room, that Emily, cuddling closer to her husband, smilingly reminded him that they were supposed to be the chaperones of the occasion, and that they had not even made a pretense of finding what the others were up to before they tumbled off to bed themselves.

"Why, Liz is the chaperone, isn't she?" Roger inquired unconcernedly. It was certainly very pleasant in this bright, warm room and this big, soft bed and he saw no reason why he should give anyone except Emily even a passing thought.

"Go on! She has a beau of her own now! And am I glad, after all these years! We're the old married couple, lending respectability to this gay gathering, darling."

"Aren't you glad of that too?"

"Glad we're lending respectability?"

"No, I don't give a hang about that. Glad we're a married couple. It's rather nice to be married, I think."

"Yes, I do too. But remember that at Hollyhock Hill we go downstairs for breakfast. And even if there is another bathroom now, we've got to share ours with Brian and David."

Brian called through the connecting door. "These walls are thin—better be careful what you say. But if it's of any interest to you, Dave and I washed long ago—as much as we're going to for the present. So don't use that as an excuse for staying in bed half the morning! And can't you smell that bacon? To think that a poor bead-rattler like me can't have any, on a Friday, no matter how early he's up, and that you might have all you wanted, if you'd only take the trouble to come and get it, you lazy heretics!"

Fragrant aromas were indeed stealing pleasantly through the house, and Roger and Emily did full justice to their share of the excellent breakfast when, belatedly, they joined the others round the dining-room table and good-naturedly responded to the jokes made at their expense—though some of these jokes were rather broad, in Emily's opinion, considering the presence of Priscilla and Olivia. But she took them all in good part, except David's low-voiced remark, "*On se lève tard pendant la lune de miel—et on se couche tôt.*" She thought the quotation inept as well as indelicate; after all, she and Roger were not honeymooners; and it was natural that the combination of a long, noisy train trip, a sleigh ride through crisp, cold air, a warm house and a hearty supper should have made them sleepy and that their slumber should have been peaceful and prolonged. She was astonished to learn that everyone else had gone skating the night before in the moonlight and had stayed up for hours, entranced by David's execution of fancy figures; also that intermittent tobogganing had already been going on that morning too. She hastened to get bundled up and go outdoors herself; and from then, until the sun went down behind the foothills in a blaze of rose, radiantly reflected on the distant snow-covered mountains, she did not come into the house at all, except for dinner. Then she was amazed to find that she was already tired and sleepy again.

"I must have been using a lot of muscles that I don't, ordinarily," she said by way of self-excuse, bending over to rub her shin in order to prove her point.

"Nonsense! You use all those muscles, every day, climbing up and down Joy Street on your constitutional!" David answered. "You don't mean to say you're going to welsh on the skating again tonight?"

"I'm not welshing on anything," she answered indignantly. "But I don't see why I should keep on doing things, when I'm tired. Roger's tired too."

"Oh, of course, in that case! But we were all hoping you'd join us tonight. We're going to have a small bonfire, so you wouldn't be cold. And I can take down a bench. You could sit on that and rest if you found you couldn't keep up with us."

"You don't need to talk as if I were a thousand years old. Of course I'll come skating, if everyone else is going. I didn't know everyone was going last night."

"I did open the door a crack and tell you so," Brian interposed. "But you must have been sound asleep already. Myself, I just stumble around on skates. Why don't you and Roger and I go down to the pond for just a little while and then come back to the house and get our well-earned rest, leaving the others who don't work as hard as we do to their childish pastimes?"

She looked at him gratefully; there was really something very pleasant about Brian, after you got to know him. But his kindly suggestion did not serve to counterbalance David's taunt. Determined to show him that she could stand up under long hours and violent exercise as well as anyone, she went early to the pond, and was already gliding quietly over it, hand in hand with Roger, when Priscilla and David came down the slope which led to it. The moon was shining brightly and, in the light of it, Priscilla's scarlet-clad figure stood out with almost startling brilliance against the snow. David had his arm around her, presumably to steady her over the slippery surface and steep descent, and they were looking at each other and laughing. Brian, who, as he himself remarked, "simply stumbled around on skates," made his way clumsily over to Roger and Emily and nodded toward the pair on the hill.

"Olivia's given me up," he said good-naturedly. "But those two are certainly making a go of it, aren't they?"

"Looks that way," agreed Roger. "Here, you and Emily have a try. You'll find she's a good teacher—in fact, she taught me on Spy Pond years ago. Not that she gives what you'd call a dazzling performance, but it's pretty smooth, at that. She'll have you in better form before you know it. I'll go and take on Olivia. Talk about making a go of it! Liz and her prof don't seem to know that there's anyone else on the ice."

Emily accepted Brian's hands in place of Roger's without comment. Her eyes were still on Priscilla and David, who had now reached the pond. Briefly, David knelt to help Priscilla change her stadium boots for her shoe-skates and put on his own; then they were off together, cutting figure eights, playing leapfrog, separating and meeting, waltzing, locked close together. It was a beautiful exhibition. Mechanically, Emily gave Brian a few stereotyped directions and showed proper patience when he revealed no skill at following them; but as soon as he suggested that they should go and sit down by the fire, she readily agreed. He piled more logs on it, and they bent over it together, enjoying its cheerful glow. Then, as Emily glanced up, she caught his arm.

"Oh, Brian, look!"

He followed the direction of her enchanted gaze. Above the wooded foothills, streaks of translucent radiance were rearing into the sky, some mounting evenly and steadily in even bands of various widths, others rising sharply only to fall suddenly, as if their points had failed to penetrate the heavens. The night, which had been beautiful before, had suddenly become magical as well. Brian gave a low whistle, followed by an exclamation of wonder, not unmixed with awe.

"Gosh almighty! What would those be? Not really northern lights, that you read about?"

"Of course. You don't just read about them, you know. They exist. But they're rare around here. I haven't seen them many times myself. And never as bright as this. Look! They're mounting higher and higher all the time! And they're not all white any longer. They're getting more and more brilliant every moment!"

It was true. The bands had risen to a height where they were almost converging and their edges had become iridescent; between these, the daggerlike points, no longer falling in defeat, pierced the summits of the sky with flaming tips. The manner in which these multicolored rays slanted toward each other gave them the effect of striving to meet and make a dome; and gradually this lustrous mass took shining and complete form overhead. Equally rapt, equally awed, Brian and Emily sat gazing at it, both unaware that, in the excitement of the moment, she had let her hand slide down his arm, and that their fingers were now tightly interlocked. They were still thus absorbed when David swung gracefully up to them, alone.

"Quite a sight, isn't it?" he said agreeably. "I've seen lots of northern lights before, of course, in the places that are most famous for them. But I have to admit I never saw anything to beat that domelike formation of light. It gives real meaning to the expression 'vault of heaven'—I haven't thought there was any before. . . . Well! You two have been in such a daze that you haven't noticed our number is now reduced. Olivia actually doesn't like northern lights; she's heard they're an omen of some sort. The things girls hear—and that they believe! I've heard myself that the lights sometimes forebode a storm, just when you think the weather's exceptionally fine, but I never put any stock even in that, much less in an old saw that disaster was on its way. . . . Anyhow, Miss Forbes and Roger have taken Olivia up to the house and she's going to bed. The others said they'd be back in a few minutes and that they'd bring a thermos of hot chocolate with them—sounds good to me. Meanwhile, the prof's taken advantage of his lady love's absence to make up to Priscilla. If you really don't want to skate, Briny, you won't mind if I lure Emily away from you, will you?"

"Not if luring's what she wants. I'm going to go right on sitting here. What I'm looking at beats any skating I'll ever do."

Emily was inclined to feel much the same way. But as Brian made no effort to detain her and David was smiling engagingly, she told herself it would be pointed to decline and permitted David to raise her to her feet. As they glided away, she understood almost instantly what Priscilla had meant by saying that he skated in the same way that he danced; the ease and grace of his movements made them seem not only natural, but inevitable. Emily felt a surge of pride in the consciousness that her own performance was worthy of his, even before he voiced his approval of it.

"You're really an excellent skater. I had no idea."

"Have you made up your mind I don't do anything especially well?"

"On the contrary. You do a great many things exceptionally well. You're very capable. You know it and so do I. I never said you weren't. All I said was, that you'd never really danced, until I made you, and that you weren't especially lovable, but that you might easily become so, under the right influence."

"I'm afraid you and I haven't the same ideas about what constitutes a good influence."

"Very possibly not. But couldn't we discuss that some other time? It really seems too bad to bicker just now. It's a night in a million. You were enjoying it a lot with Briny—you were even holding hands with him, though I don't believe you realized it or that he did. I supposed the Irish were more impressionable. But that's beyond the point. The point is that you could enjoy it a lot more with me, if you'd only let yourself. Come on, make a bargain with me!"

"What kind of a bargain?"

"Just that if you don't denounce me all the time, I won't do anything to deserve it. We'll simply skate—and look at that great dome of light."

His tone held no suggestion of sarcasm now and none of sensuality either; it was merely pleasant and persuasive. Emily found it amazingly easy to listen to. They circled the pond a few times, passing Priscilla and Merriweather, who were circling it in the opposite direction, and nodding gaily each time they did so. Then, by mutual, unspoken impulse, they began the execution of simple figures which gradually became more elaborate. As they finally paused, both breathless, David crowned his compliments with a question.

"You wouldn't like a race to wind up with, would you?"

"A race! What kind of a race?"

"We don't need to stay on the pond. The ice is solid on the brook a long way up beyond the dam and it's clear of snow to the end of the pasture. Priscilla and I raced on it last night."

"Who beat?"

"I did."

"Well, I'm not going to let you beat me!"

She was off with almost unbelievable speed, so fast indeed that her head start gave her considerable advantage. The pond, formed by the dam at the northern end of the pool, narrowed into the normal channel of the brook at the southern end; from there on, it took its natural curving course and had less and less width; but, as David had said, the ice was completely clear and solid. Emily skimmed over it, still keeping her lead, and she did not stop when she heard David begin shouting to her. She could not hear his words, only his voice, and she did not feel that words mattered. The only thing that mattered was that she was winning the race, that she could skate faster than David, that she was doing something Priscilla could not do. . . .

Then suddenly she was conscious that she had hurled herself against something hard and unyielding, something that hurt almost unbelievably, something against which she could not prevail. After one terrible moment of pain, the shock of it stunned her. Again she was conscious of David's voice, but not of his words, as she went down hard on the ice, twisting one foot underneath her.

He had tried to warn her of the solid fence, forming the boundary line between her aunt's land and the Randells', and he had been too late.

Chapter 19

ALMOST INSTANTLY, EVERYONE was crowding around her, questioning her solicitously and trying to lift her up. David, who had been close behind her, of course reached her first; however, Brian, for a man who was clumsy on skates, got there surprisingly soon and so did Priscilla and Merriweather; Roger and Elizabeth, who had just come down the hill with the hot chocolate, were delayed while they put on their shoe-skates again. This had been done fast too; but, by the time they reached the fence, Emily was sitting on the bank of the brook, supported by both David and Brian; she was involuntarily reaching down to rub her injured foot and trying hard to suppress the little moans of pain, which, in spite of her efforts, kept escaping from her lips.

"Here, take a small swig of this," Brian said helpfully, extracting a silver flask from his pocket and unscrewing the top. "You've been telling all these people you're a convert to Irish whisky. Just show them now."

Obediently, she tried to swallow, gagged and then tried again, as he continued to hold the flask against her trembling mouth. A little whisky dribbled down her chin and he wiped it off with a handkerchief which he had also whipped out of hiding, so quickly that no one else saw what had happened and further embarrassment was not added to Emily's pain. When the whisky had done its good work, she looked up at the anxious faces encircling her and tried to smile.

"I—I think I'm all right now," she said. "I'll just get on my feet and then—"

"Indeed and she'll do nothing of the sort, will she, Roger? That must have been a bad tumble you took, and you've a sprained ankle, if nothing worse. You couldn't skate now to save your soul, and you'd be crazy to try to walk. Besides, you'd freeze to death while you sat here and waited for us to bring your boots. Roger and I will just make a chair for you, the way he's often seen me do for Queenie, and we'll have you back at the house in no time."

Emily shook her head and, in spite of Brian's warning, tried to stand,

212

only to sink down again with a cry which she did not even attempt to suppress.

"Brian's right, darling," Roger said soothingly. "I'm sure he and I can carry you all right. If you'll just put your arms around our necks—"

"You two carry her part way and then let Merriweather and me take over," David interposed. "I'll feel terribly if I don't do anything to help, especially considering that I suggested this wretched race—which Emily won, let me tell you! Talk about being fleet of foot! And of course she's very slender too. But you'll find her heavier than you think."

"Is that so?" Brian inquired, a trifle caustically. "And how would you be knowing how much Emily might weigh? If you had five sisters, like I have, all of them teasing their brothers to give them rides, you'd have learned something about the heft of girls and how much you were good for. Now then, young lady—"

"Roger hasn't had five sisters," David retorted. "It's a long way back to the pond, let alone to the house. There's no use being stubborn. Besides, since I'm to blame—"

"Roger's had a wife, which is more than any of the rest of us men around here has been lucky enough to get, and I'll bet my bottom dollar she'll be no burden to him. I'll thank you kindly to just skate off with Priscilla, the way you have been doing. If you and Mr. Merriweather will just go ahead too, Miss Forbes, Roger and I'll have more gangway. We can always call for help, if we need it."

Brian had assumed control of the situation with such ease and ability that no one except David questioned his right to do so. The skaters started back toward the pond with Brian and Roger, carrying Emily, bringing up the rear, and the others casting backward glances to make sure everything was going all right. Brian had not overestimated his powers and he laughed and joked as they went along; but though he was apparently still in good spirits, the accident had depressed everyone else. No one looked at the northern lights any more or spoke of gathering around the little bonfire to drink hot chocolate. By common consent, the skating party was over. When the pond was reached, the shoe-skates were hurriedly changed for boots and the ascent of the hill began. Roger was very tired by this time and Emily knew it; the realization added to her distress. But she also knew that it would humiliate him to acknowledge publicly that he did not have Brian's powers of endurance and she kept turning her head toward him, whispering that she was sorry she had made so much trouble, while Brian, in a louder voice, kept saying, well now, they were almost there. They were both rewarded by the triumphant look on Roger's face when Emily was finally lowered onto the candle-flame bed.

"There! And didn't I say all the time we could do it?" Brian inquired with a broad grin. "Not that I'd call you thistledown, Emily, but you might sneak into the featherweight class at that. Now, if Miss Forbes has got some Epsom salts in the house, I bet it would do that foot of yours a lot of good to soak it in a strong, hot solution. . . . I don't suppose there's much chance of getting a doctor from the Junction this late at night, is there, Miss Forbes?"

"Oh, country doctors are used to being called at all hours of day and night, in an emergency! And we don't have to send as far as the Junction to get one—we have a very good doctor in the village. But it is pretty late and I do have the Epsom salts—I was going to suggest them myself. I think, between us, Roger and I could make Emily pretty comfortable for the night, if the rest of you will get out of the way and let us see what we can do for her. Then we'll send for Dr. Ives the first thing in the morning."

An exchange of good nights was accompanied by many expressions of sympathy and assurances that, of course, Emily would soon be right as rain again. Then, one by one, the unrelated guests departed, leaving Elizabeth in charge, with Roger to help her. Priscilla found that Olivia had already fallen asleep and that she was rather resentful at being waked; she reminded Priscilla of what she had said about northern lights bringing bad luck and Priscilla retorted, rather snappishly, that no one but a nincompoop would imagine that northern lights had anything to do with bumping into a fence—as far as that went, no one but a nincompoop would do that either. The exchange of comments in the "sleigh" room was not any more complimentary. Once out of Emily's presence, Brian's apparent good humor evaporated and, in brief, ugly terms, he upbraided David as a damn fool and then some; David was obliged to remind him, in tones which were nonetheless angry because they were low and controlled, that Brian himself had said the walls between the rooms were extremely thin and that doubtless Roger and Emily, and Miss Forbes too if she were still in there with them, would overhear every word that was being said. Only Mark Merriweather, in the peaceful isolation of the library, was wrapped in contentment, as he lay in his foldaway bed, which he had unfolded and made up himself; he sipped a nightcap and read a detective story which he put down from time to time, in order that his thoughts might wander more freely on the pleasant and promising nature of his courtship.

He was also the only person who, the next morning, appeared to have completely recovered from the effects of the previous night's misadventure. Roger, Emily and Elizabeth had all been very late in settling down and had all slept badly, Emily because of pain, Roger because of weariness and anxiety, and Elizabeth because of the troublesome feeling that her little house party, which had started off so auspiciously, was not going to continue in the same convivial vein. Olivia and Priscilla had resumed their bickering when they awakened, and Brian and David were scarcely speaking to each other. In spite of Mark Merriweather's geniality, breakfast was far from being a successful meal; and, as the doctor arrived before it was over, everyone felt impelled to await his report before beginning the day's sport. Nothing but a bad sprain, he announced cheerfully, when he came downstairs, to the rather grumpy group assembled around the library fire. He had bandaged Mrs. Field's ankle now, but the Epsom salts had been a good idea. He thought it would be well to repeat the soaking process in the evening and then put the bandage back on again. Miss Forbes could do it; she was deft about such things. Of course Mrs. Field was feeling the effects of her fall in other ways than merely because of the pain in her ankle; she had had quite a shock and he had given her a mild sedative. The quieter she kept, the better off she would be. A few days' rest in bed was essential; but this would fix her up, he was sure. He would look in on her again the next day. As he was going out of the door, he returned to say he also thought it would be just as well if Mr. Field did not exert himself very much; Mr. Field looked rather shaken too and was obviously suffering from exhaustion. . . .

When the overworked, conscientious little doctor had left, Elizabeth, speaking with more sprightliness than she felt, said that now they would make plans. What about snowshoeing? No one had gone snowshoeing the day before or the evening before that; so far, everyone's time had been taken up with tobogganing and skating. Rather half-heartedly, it was agreed that snowshoeing would be a good plan. So Olivia and Brian, followed by Priscilla and David, went tramping off across the pasture in the direction of the foothills. Elizabeth said she must stay at home to be near Emily and see to her household, in case anything were needed, and Merriweather wanted to finish the detective story he had begun the night before. When the others returned for dinner, which, like all the rest of the meals, was excellent, Elizabeth was a little vague on the subject of Emily's progress and Merriweather equally vague as to the outcome of the mystery; but both were in very good spirits, and the long walk through the snow seemed to have had a beneficent effect on the frayed tempers of the others. However, they had had all the exercise they wanted; they were going to spend the afternoon playing bridge.

"Why not skate again and postpone the bridge?" Elizabeth asked. "It's a beautiful day again, but the barometer's falling. Tomorrow may not be so pleasant."

Nobody wanted to skate, so the bridge table was brought out and the game went on and on. Everyone had eaten rather too heartily and eventually everyone felt logy in the warm room which, by this time, was hazy with cigarette smoke; there were no real outbursts of ill-humor, but it was evident that tempers were on the point of fraying again. An unexpected call from Bradford Olcott proved a welcome diversion. He had motored over from Vergennes, with heavy chains on his car, bringing with him his plump, rosy-cheeked wife—a Vermonter who had been his first secretary —and their plump, rosy-cheeked son, a husky youngster not quite two years old. Considerable time was spent in removing the layers of coats, sweaters and mufflers in which the visitors were bundled; but once they were settled before the fire with the others, Bradford regaled them all with stories which Roger precipitated by asking if his visitor had tried any more cases which revolved around unpressed pants.

"No, but I've had others to equal it. Just lately I tried to defend a man who claims his state of health is so poor that he can't take a full-time job. His family lives under very unfavorable and primitive conditions—in fact, his children have to carry water half a mile and get fuel when and where they can. However, he is not in such a condition that he can't go deer hunting and the day after the season closed, he trailed a buck over two miles through rough wooded country. At the end of that time, he caught up with it and wounded it in the right leg with a shotgun. The scattered pellets nearly tore the leg to pieces, but somehow the buck managed to keep on and, later that afternoon, was taken by an archenemy of my client, who shot with a rifle."

"And then what happened?"

"Then a bitter feud developed between the two men as to who owned the deer. The public authorities were notified and then neither man would have anything to do with it, each claiming that it belonged to the other. My client was brought into court on information supplied by his rival and, eventually, entered a plea of guilty for taking deer out of season. He had no money to pay his fine and was committed to jail for thirty days. I think his wife was really very happy to have him out of the way, even for this short period, but the neighborhood was greatly upset at the added work piled upon his unfortunate children and, eventually, he was released."

Elizabeth urged the Olcotts to spend the evening, but they had a long drive before them and presently the complicated process of putting on the layers of coats, sweaters and mufflers was resumed and they took their cheerful departure. After they had gone, the torpor which had previously permeated the atmosphere threatened it again; and when Elizabeth said there was to be a baked bean supper, followed by dancing at the village hall that night, and that perhaps some of her guests would like to go, the card players agreed with alacrity that it would be a good idea; they were more than ready to get out of the house again. But once more their hostess excused herself from going with them; Emily had slept a good deal during the day, but now she was restless; the sprained ankle needed to be soaked and rebandaged and Roger had no experience in such matters. Besides, Roger, as the doctor had said, seemed very tired himself.

"And as I said, he had no business trying to carry Emily all that distance," David reminded her. "He wouldn't have done it, either, if you hadn't practically dared him to, Briny."

"You're a great one to talk about dares. If you hadn't dared her to race with you, no one would have had to carry Emily. Not that I wasn't glad to do it."

"I have a feeling those two aren't getting on so well together," Elizabeth confided to Merriweather, when the foursome had departed for the dance. "Or the two girls either. I'm terribly sorry. I thought they all seemed so congenial at first."

"Well, anyway, Roger and Emily are congenial. Obviously, they're a very devoted couple. And you and I are pretty congenial too—aren't we, Beth?" He had never called her that before. No one had ever called her that before. She looked at him, coloring with surprise and pleasure. The name, as he said it, was more musical than she had ever thought her name, or any other, could be. While she was pondering on this, he said something that surprised and pleased her still more.

She told Emily about it the next day, after the soaking and the bandaging were over. The sheets had been changed too and Emily, who had been sponged off with tepid water and Old English Lavender and clad in a fresh nightgown, was lying back among her pillows, looking and feeling very much better than she had the day before—so much better, in fact, that if Elizabeth had not told her this exciting news, she might have found the hours dragging, for Brian, who had got up at an unearthly hour and gone off by himself to Mass at the Junction, had now persuaded Roger to come downstairs and play poker.

"Oh, Liz, I'm terribly glad! I can tell, just by looking at you, how happy you are! And I think Mark's just as nice as he can be! When are you planning to be married? Will you let me be your matron of honor? Are you going to give up teaching and live here all the time, the way you've wanted to?"

"How can I answer so many questions all at once? Nothing's decided yet—after all, it was only yesterday. . . . I'd love to have you for my matron of honor. Though of course, at my age, it'll be a very quiet wedding."

"What do you mean, at your age! Honestly, Liz, you don't look a day over twenty-five at this moment."

"Well, I am a day over twenty-five—a good many days. It must be the happiness you were talking about that makes me look younger. Because I am very happy. And I think we'll be married in June, as soon as college closes. About living here—well, I'm not sure. You know how I feel about Hollyhock Hill. If I'm home for Decoration Day, when the apple blossoms and the lilacs come out at the same time, and the garden is full of peonies and syringa, I think it's most beautiful then. If I'm here for Columbus Day, when the hills are all ablaze with crimson and gold and the asters are defying the frost, I think it's most beautiful then. Once I came up in the very early spring, and the Randells had brought some Mayflowers and put them in a small glass bowl on the library table. They seemed so welcoming that the next day I went out in the woods, to get more Mayflowers myself, and I found lady's-slippers and Jack-in-the-pulpit and wake-robin too. I came home and filled every vase in the house with them. They're the kind of flowers that belong in Vermont, that are part of it. Do you know what I mean?"

"Of course I do. I wish I could have gone walking in the woods with you when you found them, Liz."

"We'll go into the woods together some other spring. . . . Then I came here once when there'd been an unseasonably early fall of snow. It melted very rapidly. But, in the meantime, it was spread like frosting on the top of the grass, which was still bright green, and lay like powder on the leaves, which were still brilliant red and gold. The sun sparkled on it. And the mountains were dazzling in the distance."

"It must have been a wonderful sight."

"It was. But it isn't only the things I see here that I love. I love the smell of boiling sap in the spring and of newly cut hay in the summer and of rising wood smoke in the autumn. I love all the country sounds—the ones that are made by whippoorwills and wind in the pine trees and sleigh bells and the ones that are made by frogs and turkey gobblers too. I love the mountains and the river and the valley and the pasture and the brook and the foothills. I love the little white church with its lovely small spire in the village and the quiet old houses clustering around that and the village hall and the public library and the general store. I love the sort of people who live in those houses. They're sincere and intelligent and kindly. They do more thinking and more reading too, along with their hard physical labor, than almost anyone at Bryn Mawr. And yet they always have time to be neighborly with each other. They're not neighborly with me, but I think they would be if I lived here all the time, if they didn't still put me in the class with 'summer people.' Anyhow, I'd be willing to risk loneliness. I love everything about the place so much that I could be happy with very little human companionship. I wish I could stay here all my life. I—I hope when my time comes, I can die here—in my own room, with the firelight flickering and the sunlight streaming across my bed. I want to be buried in the little cemetery on the hill, with white birches screening my grave. I want—"

She stopped, her voice trembling. But she had spoken after the manner of one in whom certain wellsprings, long sealed, had at last been released, and Emily knew that the reason Elizabeth could do this was because of Mark; apparently when a woman found that the man she loved also loved her, it transfigured her life in every way, it made of her a new being. Emily did not try to answer Elizabeth; for a moment, she could not. And then, after that moment, Elizabeth went on, speaking calmly and collectedly again.

"Well, to answer your question, of course I'd like to live here all the time and Mark thinks he would too. But he wouldn't be content to live on my money. We'd have to think up a way he could earn some—writing, perhaps, or teaching locally. And I'm not blind to the fact that Hollyhock Hill is terribly quiet—terribly remote. Perhaps, after a while, a normal, active man wouldn't be satisfied with such an uneventful, unstimulating life. On a day like this, for instance, you almost feel as if you weren't in a real world, any longer."

She rose and went over to the window. The dancers had reported that it was "spitting snow" when they came in late the night before; now the snow was falling steadily, though very quietly. There was not a breath of wind and, as the flakes fell, they clung to the branches of the trees, transforming them into fairylike boughs, and mantled the ground with a covering smooth as white satin.

"I don't think I ever saw it so beautiful," Elizabeth said in a hushed voice. "I suppose I must have. I suppose it just looks that way to me because I'm so happy. Can you see it from bed, Emily? If you can't, let me get your dressing gown and help you hobble over to the window."

"I can see pretty well. But I'd like to see better. And my foot hardly hurts at all any more. I think I could even bear my weight on it, if I tried."

"But you mustn't try. You know what Dr. Ives said—several days. You won't mind staying here several days, will you, Emily?"

"You know I won't. You know I never could stay on Hollyhock Hill long enough to suit me. I feel almost the same way about it that you do, though I couldn't put my feelings about it into the same words."

She accepted the dressing gown which Elizabeth held out and, leaning on her, limped over to the window. For several minutes, they stood there together in silence, gazing out at the quietly falling snow, and at the still, white, remote world which it had created.

"In some ways, I think this is even more wonderful than the northern lights," Emily said at last. "You're right, Liz—it never was so beautiful before. It isn't just because you're happy that you think so. I think so too. But then, of course, I'm happy too."

After a little, when Elizabeth left—to "see to the housekeeping" as she put it, smilingly disregarding her niece's correction, "to see Mark, you mean"—Emily drifted off to sleep. Once or twice she half waked, but the feeling of drowsiness, mingling, as it did, with the release from pain, was delicious; she did not try to combat it. When she finally roused to greater consciousness, she saw Roger sitting beside the bed and realized that the reason she saw him dimly was not only because she was still sleepy, but because the room was in semidarkness. He leaned over and kissed her.

"You slept straight through dinner, darling," he said. "Liz and I both came and looked at you several times, but you were having such a wonderful sleep that we hated to disturb you—we knew you needed rest more than anything else. I'll see about getting you something to eat in just a minute. But first, I think I ought to tell you some rather bad news—no, not bad exactly, but disappointing. At least it's disappointing to me and I'm afraid it will be to you. I think I ought to start back to Boston."

"Why, I thought you didn't have to be there until Tuesday morning!"

"That's right. But if I don't leave tonight, I'm afraid I won't be there Tuesday morning. The storm's getting worse by the minute. Listen to that wind!"

Instinctively, she sat up as if by doing so she could hear better; but the movement was superfluous. The wind was blowing hard and, though it was fitful, so that the sound of it was at some moments much louder than others, it was not at any moment wholly still. Looking beyond Roger toward the window, Emily could see that the branches of the trees, which had been so beautiful in the quietude of their white covering earlier in the day, were now waving about, dark and naked again. The ground was different too; in places there were bare patches and in others the snow was piling up to uneven heights. The smoothness, the exquisite uniformity were all gone.

"The barometer's still falling and the radio says that a blizzard's on the way," Roger continued. "I can't risk getting stuck here. That equity case of mine is the one that's coming up January second. You know how important that is to me personally, as well as to the firm."

"Yes, I do. Well, I suppose it can't be helped. And I suppose I've got to lie here, like a good girl, until this miserable ankle's really well."

"Of course you have. And you won't be lonely. I'm the only one who can't afford to take a chance. Mark's vacation isn't up until next week and neither Briny nor Dave has anything especially urgent on the calendar. Besides, Stanley Lyman's there to run errands, you know. It isn't like the old days." They looked at each other, smiling. They could afford to smile now at the recollection of the days when Roger had been the errand boy. "Briny's going to drive me to the Junction, right after an early supper," he continued.

"Wouldn't one of the Randells do it?"

"Liz telephoned and they said they hated to be disobliging, but the snow's piled so high in front of their barn already that they'd have hard work getting a sleigh out of it. And Briny doesn't mind anyhow. He says he rather likes a storm, just the way he likes a fight. I don't believe David and Mark feel that way about it. I notice they're rather hugging the fire. Besides, neither one's ever driven a horse. This is the machine age, you know—except on the back roads."

"Just the same, I love the back roads best, don't you?"

"You bet! And I'm not worried about you because I'm leaving you in such good hands. Even if the doctor can't get here tomorrow, Liz will look after you all right. And your ankle's ever so much better already, isn't it?"

"So much better that I'm sure I could walk on it, if I had to."

"But you don't have to and you'd better not try. Promise!"

"All right. I promise."

"Good. Now I'll go down and look into the food situation and then I'll come back and throw some things into my suitcase."

He reappeared, five minutes later, carrying a well-laden tray. "I thought

I might just as well bring this myself," he said. "Una went home early, because of the storm, and though Jenny's willing enough she has quite a household on her hands. Besides, I've got to get busy on my packing right off. Brian thinks we'd better not stop for supper, that we might as well snatch something at the Junction—there's a diner of sorts by the station. . . . I guess he's right at that. Those seven miles didn't seem very long four nights ago. But it will be different tonight. . . . If I forget some of my things, you can bring them with you. Well, good-by, dearest. I do hate like hell to leave you, especially on New Year's Eve. This is the first time we've been separated since we were married—do you realize that? But it won't be for long, and we'll try to make up for lost time, even if we can't see the New Year in together."

He had talked disjointedly while he was throwing things into his suitcase. Now he bent over her again, kissing her fondly. David called from the hall below.

"Briny's shouting to you from outside. He can't seem to make you hear. But he's ready and raring to go."

Roger snatched one more kiss, picked up his suitcase and hurried out of the room and down the stairs. Emily could hear hasty farewells and the jingle of sleigh bells, but not distinctly. The wind was blowing harder now, the panes in the old windows were rattling and there was a whistling sound in the chimney. Elizabeth came up for her tray, bathed and bandaged her ankle again and smoothed out the bed; but she did not seem disposed to stay and talk and Emily, guessing the reason, was glad to release her. Elizabeth had brought an old cowbell, which she placed on the bedside table, and said she would leave the door into the hall open; she said she was sure she could hear Emily, even above the storm, if her niece rang and called loudly enough. Emily thanked her, but confessed an aversion to open doors; anyway, she was sure she would not need anything; certainly she would not want any supper, after that late, enormous dinner Roger had brought up. Very well, Elizabeth said; she would leave the cowbell, but she would not insist on the open door or on supper either. She could look in at bedtime and bring some hot Ovaltine and sandwiches. In the meanwhile, there were books within reach, and she noticed that Emily had brought some knitting; she would put that within reach too.

Emily thought the knitting was a good idea. She rearranged her pillows, disposed herself comfortably among them, and took the half-finished sweater from the cretonne bag with wooden handles. Her thoughts as she knitted were, for the most part, agreeable. She was very pleased about Elizabeth and Mark. She had always thought it a shame that anyone as nice as Liz should not get more out of life and now Liz was going to. Emily counted up and realized that Liz was not forty yet, that she might even have one or two children. Emily had a momentary pang at the thought of her own continued childlessness, but it did not last. Of course she was going to have children eventually. It was just as well, saddled as she had been with Priscilla, that there was not a baby in the house too. . . .

She was not worried about Roger. Briny would get him to the Junction all right and they would have their companionable snack in the diner and then Roger would catch the midnight as it came through from Canada and be in Boston early the next morning. Deirdre and Ellie and Dolly would look after him all right until she got back, which would be within just a few days, anyhow. In a way, she was not sorry to have a good rest. It had been rather a wearing winter. . . .

She was glad that Priscilla was really launched now, that the girl had "made" the Junior League and the Vincent Club and done all the other things for which Emily had been obliged to assume responsibility, because of Sue's shiftlessness. Well, she was not going to be responsible for Priscilla any longer; the girl could go her own willful way. Not that it was doing her much good, at least as far as David was concerned. . . .

When Elizabeth came back, with the Ovaltine, and wished her Happy New Year, Emily was amazed to learn that it was so late. She had not looked at her watch; she had been preoccupied with her contented thoughts and her knitting. Elizabeth was delighted to find that she was feeling so much better, that she was not minding the storm. It was really very bad now, the worst one Elizabeth could remember. Brian had telephoned from the Junction; he and Roger had made it, all right, but they had had hard work getting there. He had decided that he would not try to come back to Hollyhock Hill that night. There was a tourist home of sorts near the Junction, which had an old stable attached to it, where he could put the horse and sleigh; he and Roger had noticed it on their way north. He thought he could manage to get that far, but he knew it would be foolhardy to attempt to get any farther. He had found it hard enough to get a call through.

"I'm afraid he won't have a very comfortable night. And I'm sorry he missed seeing the New Year in with the rest of us—we've been making popcorn and toasting marshmallows in front of the fire. Just the same, I think he was right to stay where he was."

"So do I. And I don't believe Brian minds a little discomfort. Good night, Liz. I know your New Year's going to be happy."

"Good night, dear. Don't hesitate to call if you need something. If you can't make me hear you, or the girls, I'm sure David would, and he could come and get me. Remember, he's right in the next room."

"Yes, I remember."

But she had not remembered until that minute. In the midst of all her pleasant meditation, she had not once thought of David, except in connection with Priscilla's futile pursuit of him and of her own easy victory over him—a victory which had really been worth the price of a bad fall and a painful ankle. It had put him in his place at last and done away with his assumption of superiority. For the first time, she had seen him when he was not self-assured and self-satisfied, but humble, contrite, alarmed. Even his wish to help Brian and Roger carry her had been set aside. All this had been extremely gratifying to her.

Now that her wish to bring him to such a pass had been fulfilled, however, and that Elizabeth had innocently reminded her of his nearness, she began to think of him in other ways: of his skating, which, as Priscilla had said, was so much like his dancing. Of his charm—of his magnetism—of his virility—of his kiss. . . . And now he was in the next room, alone, because Brian could not get back that night. And she was in her room, alone, because Roger had been forced to go away. And David had told her that sometime he would kiss her again, that sometime he would really make love to her. He had said that and he had meant it. . . .

She lay in the dark, thinking of all this, her heart thumping in her breast. She did not try to dwell on these thoughts, as she had on the earlier ones; they came unbidden and unwelcome and she tried to suppress them. But, in spite of her efforts, they persisted, as so many of her unbidden and unwelcome thoughts had done in the past: her concern about Pietro; her curiosity about Simonetta and the Grand Duke; her antagonism to Brian; her realization of failure because the house on Joy Street had not become the center of good feeling she had visualized. All these had been unwelcome thoughts too. But they had not been sinful, unless her antagonism to Brian had been sinful, because it was uncharitable and, after all, she had never wished Brian any harm. Now there was no doubt at all in her mind that her thoughts were sinful. She knew they were. Because suddenly she realized that she wanted to have David kiss her again, that she wanted to have him make love to her. She thought she knew what his love-making would be like—vehement, possibly even violent. But the thought of such violence did not frighten her; it fascinated her. And this fascination had no kinship with her feeling for Roger. She did not even think of Roger in connection with her wickedness. Her shame was for her own sinful desire. . . .

She sat up in bed again, reaching in the dark for her dressing gown. She would go to Elizabeth, she would say she was afraid of the storm after all, she would ask if Elizabeth would not come and sleep in her bed or let her stay in Elizabeth's. She did not want to turn on the light, for fear it would shine through the cracks in the old paneling of the door which connected her room with David's. If he saw a light, he might call to her and ask if anything was the matter and then, even if she said there was not. . . . No, she would not turn on the light. She would grope her way to Elizabeth's room in the dark. She would try to walk in spite of her promise to Roger. It was better to break such a promise than to risk staying where she was, a moment longer, alone with her sinful thoughts. . . .

She slid from the bed, tried her injured foot on the floor, winced and drew back. The noise of the wind had become a howl, the rattle of the windowpanes a succession of sharp, rapid sounds, the whistle in the chimney a ceaseless moan. The snow was beating against the house, and suddenly it swirled down through the fireplace and across the room, in a series of small, glacial gusts. At the same moment, the door into David's room blew open.

Emily now had only one thought: to reach the door and close it quickly. If David were already sleeping soundly, he would not know it had blown open. But if he woke and realized what had happened, he might think she had opened it. He might not think of the wind. He might believe that she had opened it as a sign. There was no telling what he might think— or what he might pretend he had thought. Or rather, it was all too easy to tell.

It did not occur to her that he would hear the door blow open at the same moment she did, that he would hasten to close it too, that he would hope to keep her from being wakened by its banging. But with a conviction as compelling as hers—that the door must be closed immediately—he had leaped out of bed and rushed toward it.

They reached it at the same moment, meeting on its threshold.

Part Four

AUGUST, 1940, TO MARCH, 1943

ROGER AND PELL

Chapter 20

Despite the disrespectful nickname of Artful Dodger, bestowed upon him by his juniors, Cleophas Mills was a man who always referred to himself as a worker, with the unmistakable implication that he alone bore the burden and heat of the day in the firm of Cutter, Mills and Swan. He deplored Mr. Cutter's preoccupation with rowing and Elliot Berkeley's enthusiasm about horses. He resented the fact that Brian had roused Roger's interest in baseball and that David went skating and sailing with Priscilla Forbes. Pell escaped his censure only because, with characteristic reserve, Pell never disclosed what sports, if any, attracted him.

Cultural pursuits, unconnected with the law, seemed to Mr. Mills less reprehensible. Nevertheless, he considered the pleasure which Mr. Swan took in the Club of Odd Volumes sophomoric rather than scholarly, and ridiculed the little green cloth bag in which his patient partner was wont to transport rare books from his Marlborough Street residence to the club's headquarters on Mount Vernon. Social position seemed important to Mr. Mills; but he felt there should be some way of maintaining it with a minimum of amenities and with practically no diversions, and he admired Cyrus Fletcher's adroitness in doing so. To be sure, Mr. Mills made no objection when his wife invited a few of her old friends to tea; but if she gave a ladies' luncheon, he was likely to frown when the bills came in and inquire sarcastically whether such lavish entertaining were really necessary. As far as possible, he limited his attendance at dinners to the banquets which unfortunately formed an integral part of Bar Association meetings, but where the more serious speeches—especially his own speeches—partially atoned for the otherwise jocose atmosphere.

When it came to the subject of vacations, his sentiments were even stronger. He saw no reason whatsoever why Roscoe Cutter should spend a month in Bar Harbor every summer, much less a month in Palm Beach every winter. He actually went so far as to say he was glad that the European War had prevented Harold Swan from making a fool of himself over the Shakespearean Festival in Stratford-on-Avon; but taken by and large, the subject of war was also distasteful to him, and he saw no reason why three of his juniors should go rushing away to camps every year for two weeks' duty in the field—David to Camp Smith, Pell and Roger to Camp Edwards—especially since there was not the slightest reason for so-called preparedness on the part of the United States. If these juniors insisted on doing such ridiculous things, certainly they should not maneuver to get additional time off, as David had done the previous summer, when he wanted to visit Venezuela. In this respect, Brian was the best of the juniors; he had been heard to say, rather belligerently, that he was not interested in fighting England's battles, and he had good-humoredly remained on the job so that David could go gallivanting off to South America. To be sure, he had forestalled a similar suggestion this year, by saying that if David ever got another extra month's leave, it would not be on his time; and he had led Roger astray by making him a poker addict, no less than by turning him into a baseball fan. Brian had his failings too. . . . As to that poor simp, Stanley Lyman, he was completely hopeless. They would have to get another errand boy and another cat's-paw. Now Roger Field was conscientious and intelligent, but he was a plodder by nature. If he had been left alone—if Old Mrs. Forbes had only come direct to one of the senior partners with her problems and her millions and if, on top of her precipitate action, that old skinflint, Nathaniel Sears, had not consulted his nephew about the Boston and Maine Bond Reorganization and rewarded him for his advice out of all proportion to its worth—Roger might still be making himself useful in the humbler capacities for which he was so eminently fitted and there would be no need of any further addition to the staff, with its correlative expense. But Roger Field had been taken out of his sphere; he was getting farther and farther away from it all the time. The next thing anyone knew, he would be expecting to try some really important case. And now that he was on a percentage basis, in addition to his salary, what would soon become of Mr. Mills himself, at this rate?

Now that Mr. Mills thought of it, Brian Collins also presented a financial problem. A few days earlier, looking even cockier than usual, the impudent Irishman had imparted a piece of news which began in a very auspicious fashion, but which ended on a note of gloom, as far as Mr. Mills was concerned. "You might be interested to learn that my old man's roping in contracts to build filling stations for the New Moon Oil Company," Brian had briskly informed his superior. "These Moons used to sell their product through a distributor, but now they're starting a new setup with their own district manager. They're leasing and buying locations right and left and they're going to build stations on them. Now, I ask you, who could get their licenses and search their titles for them, better than the boy who's already done such a good job for a superduper construction outfit whenever he was needed?"

"Are you referring to yourself?" Mr. Mills had asked. He spoke stiffly, but the mental arithmetic he had been doing while Brian talked had resulted in some very pleasing figures.

"None other. Someone must have suggested my name. Of course I can't imagine who."

Brian gazed at the ceiling. Mr. Mills smoothed back his thin hair and coughed.

"So you have been selected as the Boston attorney for the New Moon Oil Company?"

"That's right."

"Well, I—I suppose I should congratulate you. I do congratulate you."

"Thanks. I thought maybe you'd be pleased."

"Yes. I appreciate the importance of such a choice. I suppose it will be satisfactory if you receive your usual cut of the firm's business?"

"Not entirely. I thought this time the cut might be somewhat larger than usual—edging up a little closer to the cuts you get, for instance."

"I'd have to discuss that with Mr. Cutter and Mr. Swan. As you know, it wouldn't be in line with our usual practice."

Brian did not reply; he continued to gaze at the ceiling. But somehow Mr. Mills felt that this gaze was not as meaningless as it appeared.

"Well, I'll see what can be done," he said eventually. "No doubt, we can manage matters so that you will receive some sort of recognition for your services, either in cash or in kind."

"Did you ever hear about the letter Colonel Thomas Johnson wrote to Eleazar Wheelock?" Brian inquired.

"I can't say I ever did. What have Colonel Thomas Johnson and Eleazar Wheelock to do with the subject under discussion, may I ask?"

"Nothing much, perhaps. But I like the story. It seems that the good old Colonel furnished most of the lumber for the original buildings at Dartmouth College, but that afterward, whenever he sent in a statement to the first president, Eleazar responded with a long, flowery letter, lauding the great services Thomas Johnson had rendered in the American Revolution and in the subsequent development of the Upper Connecticut Valley. At last the Colonel, instead of sending another statement, wrote the President a letter which contained just one line: 'I thank you for your compliments, but I would prefer the cash.' Eleazar Wheelock paid up."

"Where did you hear this story?"

"Mark Merriweather told it to me. He's a professor at Dartmouth. This correspondence is carefully preserved in the archives there."

"I never heard of Mark Merriweather or of Colonel Thomas Johnson either, for that matter."

"Well, Mark Merriweather's quite an authority on biology and, incidentally, he's Elizabeth Forbes' fiancé. He's about to become a member of that powerful clan. Thomas Johnson founded one himself, as you'd probably find out if you ever spent much time north of Boston. I assume you've heard of Dartmouth College and Eleazar Wheelock?"

"Of course I've heard of them. But I don't see what your story has to do with the present situation. It seems to me to constitute a *non sequitur*."

"Does it really now?" Brian inquired with interest, momentarily shifting his gaze from the ceiling to Mr. Mills' face.

There was a short silence, which Brian did not seem to feel in the least awkward. Mr. Mills finally broke it. "I see," he said. "Well. . . . It is a great mistake for a young man to think that money's everything in life. But, as I said before, I'll see what we can do about it. In fact, I will go so far as to assure you some additional remuneration in this instance. You're not to take it as a precedent, of course."

"Of course not, sir," Brian had responded. But Mr. Mills had not felt so sure.

He sat thinking irritably of all this one very warm day in August, when Mr. Cutter was disporting himself at Bar Harbor and Mr. Swan, disheartened by the impossibility of visiting England, had retreated to the Congressional Library to do research for a paper which he expected to deliver the following winter. Several matters had already come up since their departure, for which Mr. Mills had been obliged to accept the responsibility of decision, not to mention putting in considerable time; and though in theory all this was his delight, in practice it irked him greatly. Miss Riley, his secretary, had inconsiderately chosen the same time to fall ill; and Miss Smythe, Mr. Cutter's secretary, who was pinch-hitting for her, did not understand his ways or cater to his tastes; she could not even read his handwriting. He felt injured as well as irritated, and he had just decided that there was no use in killing himself, if no one else was going to do any work at all, when Elliot Berkeley unceremoniously entered his office.

"I'd like to have a few words with you, if you don't mind," Elliot said, drawing up a chair which he had not been invited to take.

"Well, as a matter of fact, I was just about to go home," Mr. Mills replied, half rising from his own seat. "How about tomorrow morning? I've a very crowded schedule, but I think I could manage a few words—if that's really all you want—around eleven-thirty. Of course you should check with Miss Smythe first to make sure nothing unexpected has come up."

"I've got a pretty full schedule myself. I assume Mr. Cutter told you that I'm leaving."

"Leaving!" echoed Mr. Mills, sinking back in his chair. "Leaving for where? I thought you said you wanted to take your vacation in the fall, so that you could go to Middleburg, or some such place down in Virginia, for the hunting. It's out of the question for you to take a vacation now. It's—"

"I'm not talking about taking a vacation. I'm talking about leaving the firm for good. I've had a very attractive offer from the Southern Railway.

230

One of their vice-presidents, Randolph Carter, has written asking me to join its legal staff. Incidentally, I first met him in Middleburg, at a hunt breakfast—astonishing the number of acquaintances you make at hunt breakfasts."

"I'm not interested in hunt breakfasts!" barked Mr. Mills. "I am appalled at what you are telling me. I may say I think it is entirely out of reason that you—"

"Randolph Carter and I found we had a lot of interests in common besides horses," Elliot Berkeley went on imperturbably. "One thing led to another and we got to be pretty good friends. Now Carter makes it clear that if I do a good job, I'll be in line for general counsel. I told Mr. Cutter about all this the day after I got Carter's letter. He gave me the usual brush-off—said we'd talk about it later, that he'd confer with you, all the old stuff. Then, also as usual, he apparently forgot all about it. But, after thinking this offer over, I decided to accept it. I have accepted it. I found I could have my headquarters in Richmond during the winter and I'd enjoy that—it's a very pleasant city. Saturday'll be my last day here, and as that's only a half day, we actually haven't got much time left. I thought perhaps I ought to speak to you about the cases for corporate clients that I'll have to leave still pending. After all, I've been acting as clerk for them, and you might get into a tangle if you didn't know what was cooking."

"Of course we'd get into a tangle. I haven't seen your records for some time, but I've no doubt they're in very poor shape. We'd probably need to have several long conferences before we could get matters straightened out to such a degree that we could give our corporate clients satisfaction. And I haven't the time for several long conferences before Saturday. You can't leave then, Berkeley. It's outrageous that you should even suggest such a thing, at the eleventh hour like this."

"I've just told you that I gave Mr. Cutter fair warning several weeks ago. It's not my fault that he forgot to tell you. I am leaving Saturday. But I'm perfectly willing to work every evening until then, beginning tonight, if you want me to. That's what I said I'd like a few words about—as to when and how much you thought you'd need me. Don't forget I've got to attend to some matters of my own too. A man can't go off and leave a big house, fully staffed with servants, and a stableful of horses unless he makes some arrangements for the future."

"It's impossible for me to consider remaining here tonight. I've been feeling the heat very much and—"

"All right. Tomorrow night? Friday night? Whatever you say."

Mr. Mills sighed, thinking of the cool seclusion of his suite at the Puritan, to which he customarily retired undisturbed throughout the summer months, after his family had left for Nantucket. "Very well. Tomorrow night," he said in tones of resignation.

"Okay. See you then. Five-thirty until we've made enough progress to call a halt, I suppose."

Berkeley rose, pushed back his chair and started out of the office with as little ceremony as he had entered it. At the doorway, he ran into David, who was approaching with a letter in his hand.

"Hello, Berkeley! Don't knock me down. I wasn't intending to do you any harm. I just want to have a few words with—"

"David, I'm in no condition for further conversations tonight," broke in Mr. Mills. "I'm feeling very far from well and I'm also very much upset. I'm starting for home immediately and I shall go straight to bed. I'm not at all sure that I'll be able to come to the office at all in the morning. But, if I am, possibly around eleven-thirty—"

"Just as you say, Mr. Mills. But I got a letter from the Adjutant General of the Army in the afternoon mail and I thought—"

"The Adjutant General of the Army!" repeated Mr. Mills angrily. "Why on earth should the Adjutant General of the Army be writing to you?"

"Well, I believe that the Judge Advocate General requires the services of a few young lawyers who've had reserve officer training. You know I trained at the Seventh Regiment Armory while I was at Columbia, and apparently my record's been examined and found satisfactory, both then and since. This is the second letter I've had from the Adjutant General. The first one merely said that consideration was being given to ordering me to active duty in the Army of the United States, with my consent, for the period of one year, and requested that I reply, by endorsement thereon, advising as to my availability for subject duty. It further requested that I indicate the earliest practicable date of availability. I didn't think it was necessary to mention the first letter, because there was nothing definite about it. But of course I answered immediately that I would be available any time. I'm not sure just what my duties will be, but no doubt that'll be very quickly explained as soon as I get to Washington."

"As soon as you get to Washington!" Mr. Mills shouted, the echo much angrier this time. "May I ask what made you think you were free to start off for Washington at the drop of a hat, just because an interfering old busybody like the Adjutant General writes you a couple of letters? They're probably nothing but forms, anyway. No doubt the clerk who mailed them out with several thousand others expected you'd just drop them in the wastebasket."

"They don't sound that way to me. I brought the second one along, so that you could see for yourself what's in it."

David extended the envelope and Mr. Mills snatched it from his hand. Elliot Berkeley, who was finding the conversation extremely interesting, lingered in the doorway; it was clear to him by this time that Cutter, Mills and Swan were about to lose not only one of their junior partners, but their most brilliant junior, at practically the same time.

WAR DEPARTMENT
The Adjutant General's Office
Washington

2nd Ind.
5 August 1940

IN REPLY
REFER TO   AG 201, Salomont, David
(7—21—40)

SUBJECT: Active Duty

TO   : 1st Lieutenant David Salomont, AGD-Res.
40 Lime Street
Boston, Mass.

1. You are advised that you have been accepted for active duty in the Army of the United States, for a period of one year from date of Special Orders.

2. You will report for assignment to The Office of the Judge Advocate General on or about 1 September 1940. Special Orders confirming subject assignment will be issued.

3. Further acknowledgment is not required.

By order of the Secretary of War:
ALLEN W. GULLION
Major General
The Adjutant General

"You'll have to say you can't go, David," Mr. Mills said authoritatively. "If Elliot Berkeley weren't deserting us at this crucial time, of course I'd be glad to release you. But he's just told me he's leaving on Saturday. If he'd given us even a little more notice—"

"I've told you over and over again that I gave all kinds of notice!" Berkeley snapped, stepping back into the room. "It isn't my fault that you big shots don't get together as often as you should."

"I was under the impression that you and I had terminated our conversation, Elliot, and that you had left. At all events, I would be much obliged if you would leave now," Mr. Mills said acidly. He paused and, picking up the offending letter again, appeared to give it his full attention. Nevertheless, he was well aware that Elliot and David were exchanging glances, and that though Elliot then left the room, he did not do so until the glances had ended in a wink.

"I'm sorry, Mr. Mills, but I don't seem to feel the same way about this letter that you do," David said courteously when the door had closed behind Elliot. "I've already said that I will go. I did that after I got the first letter. What's more, I think I ought to get to Washington as soon as I can. I think I'm needed there."

"You're needed right here. We can't lend our juniors out to every pompous government official who suddenly decides to enlarge his department."

"I'm sorry, Mr. Mills," David said again, still speaking very courteously. "I don't like to leave without your approval."

"It isn't a question of my approval. It's a question of my consent and I won't give it."

"Then I'm afraid I'll have to go without it."

"If you do that, you'll leave for good."

"Do you really mean that, Mr. Mills?"

For a moment, Mr. Mills hesitated. He was aware that he had gone too far; David Salomont was not only a very brilliant and promising lawyer, he was a singularly personable, gifted and versatile young man; and these attributes of his were great assets to the firm. If his connection with it was severed, this might well represent a great loss, not only now, but in the future, for he was bound to make a success of almost anything he undertook. But, having taken a stand, Mr. Mills could not, with dignity, retreat from it.

"Yes, I really mean that," he said tersely.

"Very well, sir. I'll try to leave everything in good order. Shall I discuss unfinished business with Mr. Fletcher?"

"You'd better sleep on this, David."

"I would, ordinarily. But this doesn't look to me like an ordinary situation. And it isn't as if I didn't know the rest of the boys would take care of things all right. They're a fine bunch. Good night, sir."

"Good night," muttered Mr. Mills.

Without waiting to sign the letters he had dictated that morning, or to put his cluttered desk into even a semblance of order, Mr. Mills picked up the brief case which he always carried from force of habit, whether it contained anything of importance or not, and hurried out of his office on the very heels of his insubordinate junior. He was still very angry, and he was also in a state of amazement not untinged by humiliation. Within an hour, two persons whose activities he was supposed to control had eluded him, and one of them had successfully defied him. Nothing like this had ever happened to him before; and when Roscoe Cutter had left him in charge of the office, the senior partner had certainly not foreseen that such an emergency would arise, or that he, Cleophas Mills, would not be able to cope with any that did. He knew that Cutter, who probably could have done no better himself, would blame his partner for the turn things had taken, and he dreaded the long-distance call which he knew he must make without delay. But he was determined to escape first; in his disturbed state, he visualized the entire staff as barging in upon him and forcing him to face unpleasant facts of one sort or another. He rushed down the corridor without glancing into the juniors' offices, and rang the elevator bell, having omitted his usual brief good night to Cora Donlon, who had been carefully protecting him from calls all day and who still sat patiently at the switchboard. Once in a taxi, he began to breathe more freely, for there he was free from intrusion; but its crawling progress through the congested evening traffic added to his sense of irritation. After reaching his suite at the Puritan, he took a stiff drink, which helped a little, though not as much as he thought it should; and the dinner he ordered from room service and swallowed in solitary state was tepid and tasteless. He knew that once he had finished it, he could no longer put off the evil moment of telephoning Roscoe Cutter.

It was some time before the senior partner could be reached, and meanwhile the operator persisted in reporting every twenty minutes that Mr. Cutter was still out and that no one knew when he might be expected home. At last, something after midnight, the connection was made, though imperfectly; and it was at once obvious to Mr. Mills, from the quality of Mr. Cutter's voice and the difficulty with which he grasped details, that the latter had passed a convivial evening, imbibing freely rather than wisely, and that he did not wish to be bothered with business matters.

"I don't hear you very well, Cleophas. Can't you let things ride until morning?"

"In the morning, you'll be out in some boat," Mr. Mills responded ungraciously. "I've been hours getting you this time. I can't spend my life waiting around for you to come home. Why didn't you tell me Berkeley was leaving?"

"Oh—that! You don't mean to say you've called me up at this hour just to tell me Berkeley's leaving? Why, I've known that for a month already!"

"Well, I haven't. You didn't tell me."

"Must have slipped my mind. But there's nothing serious about it. He shouldn't be too hard to replace. We can talk over the question of his successor when I get back instead of at this—"

"But he's leaving Saturday!"

"Saturday? You don't mean *this* Saturday?"

"Yes, I do. That's exactly what I mean. Who's to take over his corporate cases?"

"Well, let me think that over. I was under the impression that Berkeley wasn't leaving until next month and I supposed we'd have plenty of time. . . . But I'll give you a ring. Around noon tomorrow. No, not around noon. I will be out on the water then. But sometime later in the day. I shan't be going out tomorrow evening, because we're having company ourselves. I'll find a way of excusing myself for a few minutes. I can be sure of reaching you at the Puritan in the evening, I suppose? And I mean reasonably early in the evening, not at this—"

"You'd better listen right now to the rest of what I'm trying to tell you. David Salomont is leaving too."

"I thought he'd had his vacation."

"He isn't leaving on a vacation. He's leaving to enter the office of the Judge Advocate General."

"Oh—well, I heard rumors Gullion was going to rope in a few smart youngsters. So he's gone after David, has he? In a way, that's a compliment to the firm, quite a compliment. And, after all, it's just a temporary arrangement. The other juniors can handle his cases for him all right while he's gone. It won't hurt them to work a little harder."

"But that's what I'm trying to tell you. It isn't a temporary arrangement. He's leaving for good too."

"The hell he is! Why, he can't be! This organization plan of Gullion's is just to start some wheels rolling. It isn't designed for a permanent setup."

"Yes, but the point is, I told David he couldn't go and he defied me."

"What do you mean, he defied you?"

"He said he was going whether I gave my consent or not. So I told him if that was his attitude, he could go for good."

"Listen, I said before I couldn't seem to hear you very well. Now I'm darn sure I'm not catching what you're saying. You never would have been such a damn fool as to tell David Salomont—"

"I'll thank you not to talk to me that way, Roscoe Cutter. I used my best judgment and my judgment was that we didn't have room for any junior in our firm who wouldn't do as he was told."

"Gosh almighty, it won't be many years before David Salomont will be telling you what to do. You get hold of him right away, you tell him you've reconsidered, you tell him—"

"He's proud as Lucifer—you'd think, to hear him talk about those Spanish ancestors of his, that he was a Mayflower descendant—it won't do any good to tell a man like him anything like that now. Even if I were willing to eat my words, which I'm not."

"Good God, Mills, can't I leave the office for five minutes without having everything go haywire? It doesn't matter much about Berkeley. A few weeks more or less won't make any difference in the long run, as far as he's concerned. I guess Fletcher can take over some of his corporate cases and Brian the rest. But when it comes to Dave, that's something else again. We've got to keep him."

"If you feel that way about it, why don't you take the next plane to Boston and straighten things out yourself?"

"Well, of course I would, if it weren't for other commitments. But I've got some irons in the fire right here in Bar Harbor and—"

"Then we'd better drop the subject of David Salomont and go on from there. Because I'm not getting down on my knees to any Sheenie."

"I wouldn't use that term in speaking of David Salomont if I were you, Cleophas. You might forget yourself and do it at the wrong time. Remember, you wanted to try the experiment of having different groups represented in the firm and—"

"I never wanted to do anything of the sort. That was something Swan dreamed up and you give him the green light. If you'd listened to me—"

"All right, if we'd listened to you, we'd have had several stammering Stanleys, and maybe one more hack like Roger Field."

"I don't see that we're getting anywhere with all this name calling."

"Neither do I, but you started it by calling Dave a Sheenie."

"All right, I'll end it by asking whether we shall just split up Mr. David Salomont's work among the other juniors of whether we shall give it all to Pell and Roger? If Brian takes over most of the corporate cases, he won't have much free time."

"If Brian takes over most of the corporate cases and does a good job, we might do worse than take him into the firm, in Berkeley's place."

There was a short silence, interrupted by the operator, who broke in, asking, "Are you through?" Cutter spoke again.

"No, we're not through. Hello—hello, Cleophas! Can't you hear me? I said we might take Brian—"

"Your voice does seem to be rather thick, but I can hear you all right. I was just turning over in my mind what you'd said. There's no doubt that Brian's the best of the lot. Of course he plays poker and he likes his whisky—"

"Good God, you're not inferring that he's a gambler and a drunkard, because he enjoys an evening of cards with his family and keeps a bottle of Bushmill's in the house! Or are you?"

"I don't think it behooves a reputable attorney to engage in games of chance or to indulge in liquor except for medicinal purposes, and if that shoe fits you can put it on."

"And you can go to—"

"We'll be disconnected on account of your language if you're not careful, Roscoe. As a matter of fact, I started to say that I've been thinking myself that it might not be a bad idea to take Brian Collins into the firm. If he's kicked upstairs, he may not make so much trouble about some other things."

"What other things?"

"Well, he wants more money. He's been pestering me. Everyone's been pestering me lately, Roscoe. It's got under my skin. That's why I speak sharply once in a while. But I don't know that we could do any better than Brian, on short notice. Everyone's getting so panicky about this European War that things are tightening up all along the line."

"I found that out quite a while ago. Well, we might as well consider

237

the question of Brian settled then. Of course, we'll have to go through the motions of consulting Swan and Fletcher. You talk to Fletcher the first thing in the morning and get hold of Swan by long-distance. Just tell them what's happened. They won't raise any objections. Hell, they can't, now that Briny's brought in the New Moon Oil Company. It does leave Pell and Roger holding the bag. I'd say we'd better give Pell the building encroachment case and let Roger do whatever he can with Jerry Donovan's case. There's no use counting on Stanley for anything special—he'll have to keep on doing errands. And we'll have to take in another junior, if we can find one. But don't let's try to settle anything else at this hour. The rest can wait. I'll call you up tomorrow evening to find out how Swan and Fletcher reacted to everything. And of course we won't say anything to Brian until I get back. But he's as good as in, right now."

A week from the following Monday, the working day began with a strangely altered setup in the firm of Cutter, Mills and Swan. Brian was engulfed in minute books and stock records, and he was doing this intensive study in the pleasant office recently vacated by Elliot Berkeley. The severity of his labors was relieved not only by the comfort in which he worked, but by the agreeable consciousness that, as soon as the preparation of new partnership papers had been completed and new signatures affixed, he would be a junior partner in an important law firm—before he was thirty. He dwelt on all this with pardonable pride, both in his private thoughts and in his companionable talks with Pell and Roger, which he usually began by saying, with a broad grin, "Now any time I can do something for you juniors, just tell your Uncle Briny. He hasn't forgotten that he was young and struggling once himself."

"All right," Roger retorted one day. "The poor young strugglers, yourself among them, have said over and over again that it would help them to bear their lot with better grace if the big shots would only say it was a matter of regret that they didn't have much to offer their juniors, in the way of creature comforts, but that their plans for the future included improvement along these lines. We've gone on, hoping against hope, but those improvements have never materialized. Of course Pell has moved up to your cubbyhole now and I've moved to his—with Dave gone, I was able to take two intermediary steps forward, instead of one, thank the Lord. But the big shots don't deserve any credit for that." He paused briefly, dwelling on the change brought by David's departure, with a degree of satisfaction that was not caused only by the fact that he himself now had a better place to work in; he was also doing this work without being needled in one way or another; and though neither of them had put the feeling into words, he was aware that, for some unknown reason, Brian shared his satisfaction to a certain degree. Only Pell had been genuinely sorry to have their brilliant and engaging associate leave them. "What I'm getting at is this," Roger continued. "Couldn't you suggest to the Artful

Dodger that a few partitions might come down? After all, he keeps telling us that he hasn't got a prayer of finding another junior this fall, that we've got to put our shoulders to the wheel, et cetera, et cetera. So why not have the four cubbyholes made over into small offices, neat but not gaudy? Pell could actually get two windows that way; and though I wouldn't have but one, I'd have enough space to turn around in and to put my books. I'd like to see poor Stanley get a few extra feet too. I've got just as good a memory as you have, Uncle Briny."

"I think you've got something there, my boy—not just about the matter of money, but about the matter of partitions. I'll take it up with the Artful Dodger the first thing in the morning—around eleven-thirty. Of course I'll check with Miss Riley first, to make sure nothing unexpected has come up," Brian remarked, grinning more broadly than ever. "And if he tells me he doesn't see how he'll ever get the work done, what with the scarcity of materials and labor, not to mention the exorbitant price of everything, I'll ask him did he never hear about the firm of Collins and Lenahan and what is the use of that close connection if you never get the good of it, begorra?"

Brian was as good as his word and his word accomplished wonders. There was no use in doing a patchy job, he said, now that they were started on it. When the old partitions were torn down and new ones differently located, some of the wall space would have to be repainted anyhow, so why not all of it? And not the dingy gray it had hitherto been, but a clear, warm cream. The floors would inevitably suffer from the debris falling on them, so those would have to be sanded and varnished; and meanwhile, the four dingy old rugs could go to the Olson Company in Chicago and be made over into three bright, clean ones. ("I guess we'd better not go in for Orientals, eh, Roger?" Brian inquired blandly.) Of course the electric wiring would all have to be shifted around; and when the new outlets were put in, somehow it was very hard to adjust them to obsolete fixtures; therefore, these were replaced with new ones, which gave pleasant and abundant light. And while the carpenters were puttering around anyway, they might just as well knock a few bookcases and cupboards together; there were some odds and ends of lumber that no one had known just what to do with. And now that everything else was spick and span, why not refinish the scratched-up desks, install some chairs which would contribute to the comfort—and hence to the generosity—of clients—and hang new window shades—for, as far as that went, no one knew what had become of the old shades. Some careless workman must have thrown them out with the trash, which was really where they belonged. . . . But there was one feature on which Brian said he had set his heart, but which he saw no way of adding to the mounting list of improvements: the absence of fireplaces in the cubicles made it impossible for him to place a heraldic design which combined the arms of the Medici and the Borgias over a mantel of Pell's and one which would suggest those of the Aldens and the Bradfords over one of Roger's. If he could only have done this, so he insisted, he could have ushered Mr. Cutter in to see his completed handiwork with entire satisfaction on the return of the Ruddy Oarsman from Bar Harbor.

Meanwhile, Mr. Mills winced and groaned as the work progressed, but his actual protests were feeble. If he had been driven to it, he would have been obliged to admit that the charges made by Collins and Lenahan were reasonable and the improvements on the premises very great. In an unbelievably short time, Pell and Roger were settled in more commodious and attractive quarters than any juniors hitherto associated with Cutter, Mills and Swan; and, thanks to Roger's reference to memories, Stanley Lyman's comfort and convenience had not been overlooked in the course of the improvements. He was most touchingly grateful, especially when he learned that Roger was responsible for the betterment of his lot; and he was quite content to run the firm's legal errands, without looking for anything more important to come his way. As for Pell and Roger, the now adjacent position of their offices almost automatically lent itself to a furtherance of their already congenial relations and the community of their interests. Besides, they, no less than Brian, both had cause for satisfaction in these days and this served to promote harmonious feeling, as well as to stimulate earnest endeavor. Pell was busily superintending a survey in his encroachment case and Roger, who had been told to do whatever he could with the Jerry Donovan case, had leaped into this with both feet. Their offices were now side by side, for Pell had been moved into Brian's cubicle, and Roger into Pell's; so they kept dropping in on each other to discuss their respective cases and, almost automatically, they went out to lunch together. Sometimes Brian went with them, but more often he snatched a sandwich while he studied his minute books.

Meanwhile, David had not only taken leave of the firm, but had also been engaged with various other leave-takings.

Chapter 21

IN SAYING THAT he would try to leave everything in good order, David had been entirely sincere. The same standards of perfection for which he had been conspicuous both at Columbia and at the officers' candidate school, and which governed the least significant of his social and athletic accomplishments, would have deterred him from inviting criticism after his departure from the firm, even if natural pride had not done so. When his interview with Mr. Mills was over, he returned to his cubicle, closed the door and settled down to several hours of hard work. It was nearly nine o'clock before he finally locked the drawers of his desk, having arranged the few remaining papers on top of it in neatly clipped piles, labeled with care for easy reference in the morning. The other offices were long since deserted, the gloom of the long corridor unrelieved except for a glimmer from the reception hall beyond. But, as he stepped out into this, he saw that Cora Donlon was still seated beside her quiet and unwinking switchboard, her normally busy hands lying loosely clasped in her lap, the precise part in her well-waved hair seeming preternaturally white against its darkness because of her bent head.

"For heaven's sake, Cora!" David exclaimed. "What are you doing here at this hour?"

She raised her head and looked at him with swimming eyes. It was obvious, from the redness of her swollen face, that she had been crying for a long while.

"It isn't true, is it?" she asked brokenly.

"Isn't what true?" David inquired. With characteristic quickness, he had now guessed why Cora was still at the switchboard and why she was upset; and, like most men, he was antagonized and not moved to sympathy by the sight of tears. But, having recovered from his first astonishment, he spoke calmly and rather coolly.

"That you're going away," Cora sobbed.

"Yes, since you ask, it is true. But I didn't know Mr. Mills had made an announcement to that effect already."

"He hasn't. But you were in his office when Miss Smythe took in the day's letters for him to sign. He didn't look up and she thinks he didn't even notice her. She thinks you didn't either. But she couldn't help overhearing—"

"Of course I saw her when she came in with the letters, and I realized she must have overheard something. But I didn't realize she'd feel she'd got to broadcast everything she'd overheard. I should have though—she's done it before. One of these days Miss Smythe's going to find herself out of a job, if she isn't careful. However, that's neither here nor there. You haven't sat here all this time, have you, just to watch for me to come out and ask me whether what Miss Smythe thought she overheard was true or not?"

"Please don't be angry with me, Mr. Salomont. I simply couldn't bear the thought of—"

"I'm not angry, but I'm slightly annoyed and rather puzzled. I always thought you were a very sensible girl, not at all the type who would cry over a silly rumor or wait around for hours to spring questions on a tired, hungry man."

"But it isn't a rumor. You've just said yourself it was true. And I didn't mean to annoy you, Mr. Salomont, really I didn't. I just couldn't make up my mind to go home until you told me. But I will now. I know you must be tired and hungry. It was very thoughtless of me to delay you."

She rose, reaching for her hat and her handbag, which lay on the small table beside her, and walked toward the elevator, without pausing to apply fresh make-up. David stepped in front of her.

"See here," he said, "you're not going out looking like that, are you? If you do, everyone who comes anywhere near you will know you've been crying."

"It doesn't matter. The elevator man certainly won't notice, and there's no one else left in the building now but you and me. I'm going straight home and I live alone. As you know."

"I've got a much better plan," David rejoined, ignoring the last part of her remark and speaking less coolly. "You must be starving to death too. And I know what you'll do if you go home alone now. You'll go straight to bed without any supper, and you'll cry some more—just from sheer exhaustion and emptiness of course. Why don't you come home with me instead? That is, after you've fixed your face. Because you're mistaken in supposing the elevator man won't notice. He's just as good at putting two and two together and getting five as Miss Smythe is. If you go away from here looking like Niobe, when there's no one else left in the building but you and me, he'll imagine the worst, even if we carefully space our separate departures half an hour apart. And I'm sure neither of us wants to stay here that much longer. Come on, let's see if you can put on make-up in the same record time that you can put through calls. Then we'll taxi right over to Lime Street and have a couple of long cool drinks with canapés alongside. By the time we've finished with those, Ramón will have some kind of a supper whipped up for us. He's really very good at that sort of thing."

Cora hesitated. Her mother had indeed given her the advice of which Brian had spoken to Emily, and had further cautioned her that she should never, under any circumstances, go except as one of a group to a bachelor's establishment. However, her hesitation was only momentary. David had several times taken her out to dinner at pleasant, inconspicuous restaurants where the food was excellent, and, as she had rather ungraciously reminded him, had been to her apartment, where she had done her best to make ready-mixed drinks and canned products attractive and appetizing. But he had never before invited her to go home with him; and the grapevine, which Miss Smythe so carefully nurtured, had brought her numerous alluring accounts of the décor, the service and the cuisine at 40 Lime Street. These accounts had not only piqued her curiosity, they had roused her envy of the fortunate beings who were encouraged to share these delights with David Salomont whenever they chose. Among these privileged persons—also according to rumor—was Miss Priscilla Forbes; and this young lady had returned to the Cape, as soon as the social season was over, with the flat announcement that she was through with Boston for good and all. Cora could not understand how any girl in her senses could be so indifferent to her opportunities. Heartened by the engaging smile, which had displaced the abnormally blank expression with which David had first regarded her, she swiftly applied powder and lipstick, smoothed her still-tidy hair, and assured herself that she had tilted her hat at its most becoming angle. She was just drawing on her spotless white fabric gloves when the elevator, which David had summoned, appeared to receive them.

"It was awfully good of you to stay this evening and help me out, Miss Donlon," David said as they stepped inside. "I don't know how I could have possibly managed, if you hadn't, with all that stuff which was suddenly dumped on my desk." Then, as the doors of the elevator opened on the ground floor, he nodded, first to the operator and next to her. "So long, Tom. Don't let them treat you as if you were a lawyer and make you work until all hours. . . . Good night, Miss Donlon. Thanks again."

Cora understood that she was to turn in the opposite direction from the one David took, and though she did this with no apparent vacillation, her progress toward the side door, where she knew he would rejoin her, was not an altogether happy one. She knew that if he had been escorting Miss Priscilla Forbes, he would have done so not merely openly, but proudly; and the very fact that his technique with her was different indicated some cause for uneasiness, as well as some cause for resentment. She had practically decided to tell him that she had changed her mind and was going straight home after all when she was aware of his hand lightly placed under her elbow and of his easy guidance toward the exit.

"We're in luck; there's a taxi right now," he said, hailing it; and, once they were inside, he added, "Too bad the parking problem's so bad. If it weren't, I'd go to and from the office in my roadster—I can't seem to acquire the Boston passion for walking, just for the sake of walking. . . . Well, all that'll be different in Washington—like lots of other things. No doubt I'll have a parking place allotted to me. . . . But I'll tell you what: we'll take a spin around Jamaica Pond later on, if you like. A pleasant breeze always seems to spring up there in the evening, for some reason. You haven't seen my new roadster, have you?"

"No, I haven't," Cora said. She was aware that this statement, as well as the one she added—"But I'd love to"—was entirely superfluous. David knew perfectly well that he had never before invited her to take a ride in his new roadster; as for the prevalence of a pleasant breeze after sundown, in the vicinity of Jamaica Pond, he had not learned about that in her company either. But she wisely decided that he was not the type who would take kindly to either reminders or reproaches, having already discovered that he was not the type who took kindly to tears. Although he had said he was not angry when he found her still at the switchboard, the annoyance he admitted had certainly been very close to a stronger feeling. At that, she was not sorry she had waited for him; if she had failed to do so, she would not be on her way to his apartment now. And by this time, the thrill of the experience was so great that she was quite ready to overlook its other potentialities.

The proximity of David, as the taxi jerked its way along with sudden starts and stops, was, of course, the major reason for her pleasurable excitement; but everything he said added to this, and even the route taken by the taxi increased her sense of an unfamiliar and stimulating experience. Normally, when she left the office, she took the near-by elevated to Roxbury; now, while the meter registered a mounting expenditure on the part of her escort, David pointed out various noteworthy landmarks: Goodspeed's secondhand book store, where, he said, he often went to see what he could pick up and where he sometimes located real treasures; Mr. Swan, he observed, with a slight sarcasm which was lost on Cora, was not the only person in the firm with a penchant for odd volumes. The wooden shutters of the famous shop were now securely locked from without, and the shelves which stood on the street, at either side of the front door, had been prudently emptied against the night; but Cora could picture David looking in at the windows and fingering through the contents of the shelves, swiftly selecting the best there was to be bought. The Old South Meeting House and Newspaper Row were the next points of interest; and Cora listened enthralled to a brief résumé of the characteristics of both Congregationalists and journalists. Soon, the taxi was passing through the tunnel beneath the State House; then, with a sudden spurt, it shot down Mount Vernon, across Charles, and finally drew up, with a jolt that almost threw her off her seat, at 40 Lime Street.

This was a small, spruce house with a façade, which, as Cora first peered at it, seemed to consist mostly of a huge, brightly painted door, though this was flanked on either side by a grilled window, and she was presently aware of larger windows overhead, and of a brick superstructure. Nevertheless, the immense entrance was both puzzling and fascinating to her; and, after alighting from the taxi, she stepped back on the pavement to look at this curiosity, while David was paying the driver. When her host stepped briskly forward, taking a key from his pocket, she turned her questioning gaze on him.

"Didn't I tell you that my house used to be a stable?" he inquired. "You know, don't you, that nearly all the old families who lived on the Hill had their own private stables near by?"

"No," murmured Cora, whose natural orbit had not included old families who lived on the Hill.

"Well, they did. And now these stables have almost all been converted into houses—of course, in the meantime, they usually changed hands too, some of them many times. A few are occupied by their owners and others are rented. I thought I was very lucky to be able to rent this one—it's been very well restored. That big door you're staring at was the old carriage entrance. The victorias and broughams and what-have-you and the horses, too, of course, were kept at street level; the living quarters for the coachman and his family, if·any, were above."

"But I thought you had just an apartment!"

"Well, I do usually speak of this place that way, we're so accustomed to using the term for a duplex in New York; and the old stable isn't half as big as the apartments my people and most of my friends live in. But it's been quite attractively adapted to modern conditions. You'll see!"

The big door swung open noiselessly at the turn of his key, and he drew back to let her step inside. In the tiny foyer, a beautiful old lowboy, surmounted by a mirror, stood directly opposite the entrance, and at right angles to this was set a love seat, upholstered in red brocade. The polished surface of the lowboy was bare except for one strange golden ornament in the middle; and again Cora paused in puzzled awe.

"Lovely, isn't it?" David asked, picking up the ornament and holding it almost caressingly. "It's a very old, very rare kovsh—about the finest one I know of. My stepfather gave it to me for a graduation present when I finished at Columbia."

"What is a—? I didn't even understand what you called it."

"K-O-V-S-H. It has somewhat the same significance that a loving cup has for us. Look, it's engraved with the Russian double-headed eagle, in the midst of conventional floral motifs." He turned it over, still caressingly. "Even the bottom of the bowl is repoussé work and shows the double eagle too. The finial's engraved with the same device."

"It's the handsomest thing I ever saw. But everything you're saying about it's Greek to me, Mr. Salomont."

"Russian, you mean," he said good-humoredly. Though Cora's admiration was completely incomprehensive, there was something about its intensity which was very gratifying to his pride. "Would you like me to translate the inscription for you?" he inquired.

"Translate it! Do you mean to say you can read Russian?"

"Yes, of course. This inscription says: 'By the grace of God, I Elizabeth, the first Empress and Autocrat of all the Russians, hereby award this *Kovsh* to the merchant of the first Moscow guild, Feodor Feodorov, son of Bogdann, for his demonstrated efforts and patriotic devotion in fulfilling contracts to supply the army and which army he will continue to supply with the same zeal and energy for six years beginning with the year 1752.' I don't know how it happened to get into the possession of a much later Feodor, who was a descendant of this same Empress Elizabeth. But anyway, that would be another story. Come on, let me show you some more 'handsome things.' And here's Ramón waiting to find out what you want to drink. His gin rickeys are very good. All right, Ramón, two gin rickeys and some canapés, in the drawing room."

Cora had not heard any approaching footfalls, and when David referred to "Ramón," she turned, with a start, to see a dark-faced, gray-haired man servant, dressed from head to foot in spotless white, standing at the top of the short flight of steps opposite the brocaded love seat. He bowed, without speaking, and vanished as unobtrusively as he had appeared. David, placing a guiding hand under Cora's elbow for the second time that evening, identified Ramón as they mounted the steps in his wake.

"Ramón and his wife, Soledad, were my father's servants. They worked, for a pittance of course, at the students' boardinghouse where he lived when he was at the University of Salamanca and they begged him to bring them with him when he came back to the United States. He and my mother were already formally engaged, so somehow he found the wherewithal to do it, and they never left him, even through the lean years when he couldn't pay them anything. Soledad died long ago, but Ramón stayed on with my mother after her second marriage, and when I set up housekeeping here, he asked permission to join me. He's getting old, of course; however, he's still an excellent servant. And entirely discreet—you needn't be afraid that he'll gossip. . . . Well, what do you think of this room?"

The short flight of steps had taken them to a small landing where they now stood. A narrow staircase wound upward from one side of this and, in front of them, another short flight of steps led to an immense room which stretched out before them in cool, inviting spaciousness. The carpeting and the curtains draping the long windows at the farther end were a soft shade of green; some of the furniture was upholstered in this same color; the rest was covered with chintz, which was figured in green and lemon on a white ground. Near the windows stood a grand piano and above the marble mantel hung the portrait of a striking dark woman, wearing modern evening dress. The other paintings, disposed at intervals over the cream-colored walls, were evidently very old. The lamps were made of pale porcelain, their shades of old parchment. Several vases, filled with yellow roses, were scattered about on the incidental tables; so were a few beautifully bound books, some miniatures in glittering frames and some small silver boxes. Cora's exclamation of admiration was as spontaneous as her reverential attitude toward the *kovsh*.

"Of course in winter, none of the furniture's slip-covered," David explained. "But it's all brocaded, except for those few pieces done in plain green, and it looks a little oppressive, in its natural state, during hot weather. That's why I liked the flowered chintz. I can't seem to understand why most Bostonians use colorless linen for slip covers instead. But I suppose neutral and conservative traditions are hard to buck. . . . Well, shall we go and sit down? I'll take you upstairs later. I've a paneled library and a dining room and kitchen on the second floor, and bedrooms above. I haven't any garden to show you though, unfortunately—the buildings behind us here are so close that the owners apparently thought it wasn't worth while bothering—another attitude typical of Bostonians. There's really space enough for a tiny terrace off this room, and more steps leading down to a little plot of greenery that would add a great deal to the property. I've been meaning to develop the theme myself, but I haven't had time, and now, of course, there'd be no point in it."

He motioned her to a seat on a big chintz-covered sofa, offered her a cigarette from one of the silver boxes and lighted it for her. Then, taking one himself, he sat down opposite her and, except for a few inconsequential remarks, allowed her to accustom herself to the strangeness of her surroundings without disturbing her thoughtful observation of them. Ramón reappeared, bringing tall, tinkling drinks on a silver tray and a prodigal supply of canapés on a silver platter. Having first carefully arranged these on a little table, which he set down in front of his master, he next placed a coaster, a small porcelain plate and a tiny embroidered napkin beside Cora and offered her a glass and a canapé. Afterward, glancing toward David and receiving an almost imperceptible nod in return, he withdrew while maintaining the same silence as hitherto.

"You're beginning to look better," David said approvingly, when Cora's first drink was about half gone, and she had eaten several small toasted cheese squares and open-faced cucumber sandwiches. "Try some of these caviar canapés too. I think they're especially good. My stepfather still gets his caviar direct from Russia, Communism or no Communism." Then, as Cora, who was not accustomed to caviar, nibbled at the proffered canapé in a rather gingerly fashion, he went on, "Of course you always look very nice—that is, when you're not crying or directly afterward. All the classics to the contrary, no girl's really attractive then."

His smile was still so engaging that the implied reproach had no sting to it. Cora, who was feeling as much better as she looked, smiled in return.

"I know. I won't ever let you see me looking like that again."

"Don't let *anyone* see you looking like that again. Especially any man.

It isn't a peculiarity of mine, you know, to resent seeing a normally pretty girl disfigured. It's an almost universal masculine trait. And you're so exceptionally pretty, Cora, generally speaking, that it seems rather a pity for you to go out of your way to be unattractive when some nice young man happens along."

Again making a wise decision, Cora refrained from saying that she was not especially concerned about the impression she might make on any nice young man, but that she was very much interested. . . . David rewarded her by giving her a brief résumé of the office situation on his own initiative.

"As a matter of fact, you ought to congratulate me. I've been rather hoping that something like this opening in Washington might come my way. I don't especially care for Boston and, even if I did, I don't think Cutter, Mills and Swan represent the best it has to offer. Of course other firms have approached me, since I've been there, but I've been a little wary of severing the connection, until I was certain I was making a change for the better. Now I'm dead sure that's what I'm doing."

Cora gazed at David with increasing admiration, not unmixed with awe. She had never before heard of anyone who did not especially care for Boston, and the consciousness that other cities might exceed it in charm and opportunity opened new vistas to her. Moreover, the thought that anyone employed by Cutter, Mills and Swan should not be gratified by this connection had not crossed her mind; and the intimation that still more important firms might be in a position to lure members of its staff away from it was also a novel one. She knew that Brian Collins and Pellegrino de Lucca felt that they had received signal marks of recognition when they had been invited to come to it as juniors; and the grapevine had not once suggested that the association had failed to fulfill their every expectation. She was less well informed about Roger Field, who, as far as she was concerned, did not matter much anyway, or about Stanley Lyman, who mattered still less; but now that the question had arisen, she dismissed it easily, with the certainty that they also considered themselves very fortunate. Only David Salomont was so advantageously placed that he could pick and choose where he would go and what he would do.

"Then you wouldn't have stayed with us long anyway," she said thoughtfully, helping herself to a few more excellent canapés and taking another long, refreshing drink.

"That's right. If I hadn't gone to Washington, I'd probably have gone to Detroit. There's a lot of activity in Detroit and a lot of money too. But it's a gray, gloomy sort of city, a good part of the year. Whereas Washington's delightful. I don't know any place I'd rather be than Washington."

David drained his glass and signaled to Ramón, who was hovering close by, that it was time for refills.

"Of course that doesn't mean I won't ever come back here," he said.

"I'd do that, in any case, just for the hell of it." He did not identify "it"; but Cora knew he meant he would come back, after his temporary work in Washington was finished, as a junior partner in some firm like Fiske, Ford; and that when he met anyone connected with Cutter, Mills, though he would be completely courteous, as usual, he would contrive to give an impression of detachment not only from his former associates, but of superiority to them. "I rather like this place too," he said, looking around him with appreciation. "And I've got a long lease on it. I don't think I'll try to sublet. I think I'll hang onto it, just in case. . . . For instance, I might get sent over here, occasionally, from Washington, and, if I were, it would be pleasant to feel this was all ready to step right back into. Of course, I'll get myself something in Washington too, or Alexandria more likely—one of those quaint little old houses on Queen or Prince or Duke Street. When I do, you'll have to come down and see that too, Cora."

Cora, now well along on her second drink, said she thought that would be heavenly, and meant it.

"You know, I wouldn't be surprised if I could get you a job in Washington too," David went on. "There must be any number of places where they'd be only too glad to have a girl like you. Would you be interested in going to Washington, Cora?"

She had been on the point of setting down her glass temporarily. She knocked it over, breaking it and spilling its contents. David spoke to her reassuringly, easing her embarrassment.

"Don't worry about that. Ramón will have it cleaned up in no time and bring you a fresh drink—you'd hardly touched that one. Afterward we'll have supper and then we'll see how the breezes are, around Jamaica Pond. That'll give us plenty of time to talk about Washington and all kinds of other things. I'm glad you waited for me, Cora. Otherwise, it wouldn't have occurred to me that you might be free. And you're certainly helping me to spend a very pleasant evening."

By the following afternoon, everybody at Cutter, Mills and Swan had learned, through legitimate channels, that David Salomont was leaving the firm and, one by one, different members of the staff had come to his cubicle, in the wake of Cyrus Fletcher, to express their regret. These visits, while gratifying—especially in the case of Mr. Fletcher—constituted a series of interruptions which seriously interfered with David's purpose of putting everything in the best possible order, in the least possible time. In this light, he rather resented them; as far as he was concerned, his association with Cutter, Mills and Swan was already relegated to the realm of past experiences. Nevertheless, he did not fail to notice that, whereas Pell paid him a long and almost ceremonial visit, Brian merely stuck his head in the door with the terse remark, "Hear you're off to Washington to take charge of things there. Hope they appreciate you," and, up to five o'clock, Roger had not been near him. David found himself involuntarily dwelling on this omission, and wondering whether it had any special significance, when Roger, looking even more wilted and disheveled than he usually did at the end of a warm day, appeared on the threshold.

"I've been trying to get in here all the afternoon," he said apologetically. "But I've been going around in circles. That Jerry Donovan case is certainly something! You know the background of it, I suppose?"

"I don't believe I do," David answered, in a tone which, civil as this was, unmistakably indicated that he had neither the time nor the inclination to hear it now.

"Well, I won't go into it," Roger responded. He had not failed to catch the implication; but, as a matter of fact, he had not wanted to tell David about the Jerry Donovan case. He talked to Pell about that and Pell was always a ready listener; he had no need of any other. Besides, he was very tired; he had only wanted to explain what he feared might have appeared like a discourtesy. "I seem to have reached the point where I can't make any more progress until I can find out how some stock was held and I've got a devilish headache. So I'm starting for home earlier than usual. But I didn't want to go without telling you that the news about your leaving was quite a shock. Your absence will make a great difference here, David. No one can possibly take your place."

"Oh, nuts!" David answered. Roger's gravity, though indubitably sincere, lacked an essential element not unlike the one David had missed in Brian's offensive jocularity; neither one had voiced the regret otherwise universally expressed.

"I mean it, I really do. All the rest of us know we're not in your class, Dave, when it comes to brains."

"But you still think I'm not in yours, when it comes to certain other qualifications, don't you?"

"I didn't say that, I didn't even think it," Roger answered wearily. He did not want to start an argument any more than he wanted to start a detailed analysis of the Jerry Donovan case. "Of course I felt like telling you how much you'd be missed," he went on, determined not to take umbrage at David's attitude. "I know you've been told that so many times already today that you must be tired of hearing it. Just the same, I wanted to say it too."

"Well, thanks a lot," David said. He was slightly ashamed of his retort about class; Roger Field really was a well-meaning kind of guy; it was a pity that his good intentions did not prevent him from being a blunderer and a bore. David's twinge of remorse was not sufficiently strong or lasting to prevent him from picking up the brief with which he had been engaged when Roger entered, and, looking at it attentively again, as a signal that time was passing and that he still had a great deal of work to do.

"Also," Roger persisted, "I wanted to ask you if you wouldn't come up to the house some evening before you left. I know you've got a lot ahead of you, but I thought perhaps we could have some kind of a little farewell party that you'd enjoy. If you would—"

"It's nice of you to think of it, but I do have a lot to clean up here. I expect to work late every evening this week."

"Then perhaps a midnight supper rather than a dinner?"

David tossed the brief back on the desk. "Have you consulted your wife about this party?" he asked, rather dryly.

"Why, no. Of course I didn't hear, until this morning, that you were leaving. And I haven't telephoned Emily at all today, I've been so busy with the Jerry Don—"

"Then don't you think it would be a good idea to find out whether she'd like to have it before we try to make any plans?"

"Well, I can telephone right now, if you like. But I know it isn't necessary. Emily enjoys having company and she's always liked you very much. We've seen hardly anything of you lately, because you've been in such demand elsewhere. And I know she'd be very sorry if you went away for an indefinite absence without giving us a chance to offer you some sort of hospitality."

He was already reaching for the telephone on the desk as he spoke. David put out a restraining hand.

"Please don't think I'm not appreciative," he said, speaking more graciously than before. Darn it, there was something rather moving about the unshakable, persevering courtesy of this colorless Bostonian. "But, as I said before, I have got a lot to do here. I told that bastard, Mills, I'd try to leave everything in good order and I meant it. You know yourself what it's like to break off in the middle of a job. It usually means you have to start all over again, at the beginning. And it's also usually impossible to tell just when you'll finish it. If I knew you and Emily were having a party for me, I'd keep looking at my watch, every half hour or so, to make sure I wouldn't be late, and I'd end up with the whole evening practically lost. As you say, I have been to a good many parties recently and that's always what happens. Besides, we'd be up till the wee small hours and I'd lose most of the next morning, to all intents and purposes, because I wouldn't be hitting on six cylinders."

"Of course, if you feel that way—"

"I'm sorry, but I do. However, if you'd let me, I'd just like to drop in on you some evening after I have finished. Then I wouldn't be under any strain. I could stretch out in a big chair beside the fountain in that pretty little garden Emily's made and imagine I was one of my ancestors back in Granada—well, anyway, I'd feel just as important and know I was in just as pleasant a place. And we could have a good long talk and a couple of nightcaps and still get in a decent night's rest."

"All right. Since that's what you'd prefer. . . . It doesn't seem like showing you any special courtesy and we'd like to; but it is pleasant in the garden these summer evenings. I'll tell Emily to expect you. We're nearly always home—it seems more sensible than to go tearing around looking for a better place. There just isn't any. Good night, Dave. And best of luck."

"Good night. Thanks again."

Roger went out, leaving the door open, as he had found it. Nobody kept doors closed these days; it was much too warm. Just the same, open doors led to distractions and David wanted none of these; he wanted to concentrate. As he picked up the brief again, he could hear Roger's footsteps in the corridor, Roger's good night to Cora at the switchboard, Roger's greeting to the operator as the elevator door slid open; and these sounds were unwelcome out of all proportion to their apparent importance. The footsteps were slow, almost dragging; they suggested extreme weariness. Of course the warm weather and the lack of a proper vacation could be partly responsible for that. In addition to his fortnight at Camp Edwards, which certainly could not be classed as a holiday, Roger had been offered only one week's absence from the office, which he and Emily had spent at Old Mrs. Forbes' place in Dublin; and doubtless various problems regarding the model dairy had been laid before him there. Even so, he should not be as tired as he seemed. David himself was not in the least tired, and he had not been given a proper vacation either, because of the extra time he had taken off the summer before in Venezuela. If Roger were weary now, when the office was fully staffed, he would certainly be continually exhausted after the almost simultaneous departure of Elliot Berkeley and David Salomont. David could visualize Roger as he would look if he were continually exhausted, and it was not a cheering picture. . . .

Weary or not, of course Roger would have to stop and say good night to Cora. Courtesy was part of his code; he would be polite on his deathbed. David, who could, when he chose, be charming to a degree which Roger never could hope to achieve, could also be brusque when it suited his purpose, or completely neglectful of all amenities when he was not in the mood to observe them. He had been brusque with Cora the previous evening, before he decided that it would be better if he were kind. Roger would not have acted as he did, either to begin with or later on. He would have been moved by Cora's tears and he would have tried, immediately, to comfort her. However, he would not have forgotten for one moment that he was married to Emily. But then, Cora would not have cried if she had found out that Roger was going away; the news would have left her entirely indifferent. So, after all, there was no sense in wasting time on reflecting how Roger would have acted under the conditions which confronted David.

A little smile played around David's mouth as he recalled these. He had told Cora the truth when he said she was helping him to pass a pleasant evening; once she had stopped crying, she had been just the sort of companion he required then—not only undemanding, but touchingly grateful for whatever attention he chose to show her; he had been faintly amused by such humble appreciation. The degree of admiration which his establishment had evoked, and the terms in which she had expressed this, were pleasantly amusing too; he had not realized that such naïveté still existed, in a grown girl. It was rather refreshing. So was the way in which she had responded to his suggestion that they should go for a drive around Jamaica Pond before he took her home. Obviously it did not occur to her that the drive might take them farther afield, or that it might serve any ulterior purpose. For a girl who had been on her own since a tender age, there was still something surprisingly virginal about Cora, something surprisingly sweet. . . .

All this was delightful to recall. But, just as Roger's courteous good night to Cora had revived these agreeable recollections, so the sliding doors of the elevator revived the mental picture of the operator's expression when David had thanked Cora for staying late to help him at the office and said he would be seeing her in the morning. He would not put it past an elevator operator to develop a sixth sense about such sayings, which he must have heard voiced not infrequently. It might be just as well to give the man a farewell present when he, David, left for good. Not enough to look like bribery or concern about blackmail, of course; but just enough to make sure that Cora would not be annoyed by any insinuating remarks or surly demands after he had gone. Though, as far as that went, he thought it was quite possible that Cora might soon be leaving too, that he really could find a place for her in Washington. . . .

Hang it all, he did not seem to be making much progress with that brief. Instead, the train of thought which Roger had evoked went on and on. David found himself following those slow footsteps across the Common, where the Frog Pond would be full of noisy little urchins from the slums, splashing about and shouting at each other; then up the steep incline to Joy Street, where the shade from the now top-heavy trees would fail to mitigate the heat which rose from the brick pavements. It would not occur to Roger to take a taxi home, no matter how tired he was; like most Bostonians, he would walk as a matter of course. Pell would walk with him and they would talk about the Jerry Donovan case; he and Pell were seeing more and more of each other these days. And when he reached home, he would find the house—darkened to keep it cool—shorn of its rugs and draperies, with its ornaments put away and its furniture slip-covered in colorless linen, because all this was also in conformity with established Boston custom. But at least he would not go on over the crest of Beacon Hill, like Pell, and end up in a small suffocating tenement. . . .

Apparently Pell had nothing to live on but his inadequate salary, or he would have left that dingy district long before. No influential relative had ever demanded that he should be put on a percentage basis and, of course, that skinflint, Mills, would never have done it of his own accord; and apparently Pell was supporting not only himself, but the shrewish middle-aged woman and the beautiful girl with whom he lived and who had figured in the suit which got him his position. Of course the beautiful girl was his mistress—if she had been his wife or his sister or his cousin, he would not have been so silent, not to say secretive, about her. As far as that went, there were plenty of places where he would not have felt it incumbent on him to be silent, much less secretive, about an illicit relationship. But Boston was not among them. . . .

Doubtless Pell did not begrudge what it cost him to keep his mistress, in spite of his meager means. David had seen her, once or twice, when Pell was sailing with her and David himself was sailing with Priscilla; and he was more than ready to admit that a mistress with a face and figure like hers would compensate for a good deal—though not, as far as he was concerned, for living in a tenement. But then, he would have found some way of making enough money to get out of the tenement, which, for some strange reason, Pell had not. It was also strange that Pell, being the kind he was, had not married this girl he lived with. He was definitely the pious type, much more meticulous in the practice of religion than that clown, Brian Collins. It was not in character for a devotee like Pell to live in sin; if carnal cravings proved too strong for such a man to resist, he usually limited them to those which could be authorized by a so-called sacrament, and identified them by numerous offspring. If David had not seen Pell with that beautiful girl, whom he never mentioned and to whom he never presented his friends, he would have set the Italian down as a celibate. . . .

But his errant thoughts had now taken him past the point to which Roger's slow progress would finally have brought him. He would not have gone on with Pell to the tenement on the farther side of Joy Street, no matter how deep they might have been in conference when they reached the crest of the Hill, for the simple reason that Pell would not have invited him to do so; and though Roger very probably would have asked Pell to stop in for a drink, the chances were that Pell would have gone straight on home to his beautiful mistress. So after Roger had washed up, in the ground-floor lavatory under the front stairs, he would have continued on to the garden which Emily had made out of the back yard and he would have found her there. Emily was another meticulous person, though not, as far as David knew or believed, about religion. But she had been brought up to assume that all properly conducted wives awaited their husbands' homecoming behind a well-appointed tea table, and she would very seldom fail to do this—never without an apology and a cogent reason.

David's thought had skirted the subject of Emily for some time, but now they were definitely focused on it. He did not consider her colorless, as he did her husband. In fact, he felt sure she had potentialities for passion and, somewhat intermittently, he had been tempted to explore these. He had been attracted to her from the first; and the consciousness that she had also been immediately attracted to him struck him as a feather in his cap, considering both her conservative upbringing and her newly wedded state. Her unfeigned indignation at the first advances he had made to her, and her refusal to compromise with her conscience by seeing him afterward as if nothing had happened, also impressed him favorably; conquests which were too easy had very little significance, and the compliance which seemed rather touching, in the case of a girl like Cora, would have seemed merely cheap to him, in the case of a girl like Emily. Even after their every chance meeting resulted in a passage at arms, he found this stimulating rather than annoying; in spite of the fact that he could always carry off the honors in an argument, he could not do this so easily as to make it tame; and he recognized the mutual antagonism which became stronger and stronger with the passage of time, as a vital element in mutual attraction. It was sincere enough, in both cases; but it was the kind of opposing force which often ended in sudden assault on one side and sudden surrender on the other.

When he had told Emily that someday he would really make love to her and that she would be glad to have him, this was what he had meant; and over and over again afterward, he had dwelt on the vision of her first instinctive recoil, of her gradual acquiescence and of her ultimate rapturous response. Yet, when fortuitous circumstance had fairly flung her into his arms, he had not seized upon the chance to make the vision a reality.

He had often tried to explain convincingly to himself exactly what had caused him to act as he did when he and Emily had met, on New Year's Eve, at the threshold of the door which connected their rooms. The actions themselves had been simple enough and seemingly spontaneous. He had immediately put his arm around her and he had also instantly realized that, if he had not, she would have fallen; she was already reaching toward the jamb for further support. Then he remembered her sprained ankle and knew that it must be hurting her horribly.

"Hold onto that jamb for a moment and let me get both my arms underneath you," he said. "Then put your arms around my neck and I'll have you back in bed before you can say Jack Robinson."

"The door—" she began.

"Don't you worry about the door. With this gale, I'm surprised it wasn't blown right off its hinges. But I'll take care of that as soon as I get you fixed up. Now then. . . . Who says I can't make a chair, without anyone to help me too, even if I didn't have five sisters—for which I thank the good Lord! And I can make a pretty good job of carrying you by myself. I'm glad of a chance to prove it to you!"

She had obediently encircled his neck, as soon as she was aware of his two supporting arms, but he could feel the trembling, first of her fingers, and then of her whole body. The room was bitterly cold; probably she was half frozen, in her lacy nightgown and her silk robe. This conviction was strengthened when he realized that her teeth were chattering too. She was not the sort of girl to be frightened by a storm—or by a man. But somehow he resented the quivering of her body; strangely, it robbed this of allure. When he laid her down on her bed, so easily as to indicate that it had cost him no effort to carry her, he would not even have kissed her if it had not seemed abrupt to leave her without some sort of a casual caress. But the kiss was only a light one on her brow.

"If I remember rightly, you were told to stay in that bed for three or four days and give that ankle of yours a chance to get well," he said, looking down at her in much the same way that he might have looked at a child of whom he was rather fond, but whom he found rather troublesome. "I hereby charge you not to get up again until that nice little village doctor gives you permission. If you hear any sounds that frighten you, ring that cowbell Liz left with you. It ought to wake the dead; certainly it would wake her. But I promise you the door won't blow open again. Its banging isn't going to be one of the things that might disturb you."

Though David was by nature an analyst, he was still balked, nearly eight months after the occurrence of this episode, in his attempts to resolve the reasons for his behavior. Emily's trembling could not in itself have been responsible for this, though it was undoubtedly a contributing factor; and akin to it was the crippled condition which was also vaguely distasteful to him. As a perfectionist, even more than as a sensualist, he instinctively felt that bodily beauty should be unblemished to insure enjoyment of it against disillusionment. The conquest he had visualized had been one of a proud and glowing woman, not a shivering, broken one.

Of course there might have been other reasons too. Although he had also visualized such a conquest as having been consummated through sudden mastery, he had been convinced that the justification for this would have been Emily's unconscious craving for domination, once her initial resistance was overcome. A deliberate approach would have defeated its ultimate purpose, for, given time to reflect beforehand on an act which she would have inevitably called by the ugly name of adultery, she would certainly have withstood it—and would have thus remained unfulfilled. He was not partial to precipitate forcefulness as such; he saw in it only a means to an end. Indeed, if there had been a question of dealing with a different type—less puritanical, more sophisticated, a little older, a great deal wiser—he would have preferred to savor gradually all possible degrees of intimacy before arriving at the ultimate one. And he certainly would never have wished to take advantage of some abnormal condition like illness or fright or to use the violence of a storm as an excuse for driving passion. The proud and glowing woman he had pictured would have become his because her desire for him was as uncontrollable as his for her, and because he had been able to divine the exact moment at which her natural defenses would give way. Such overwhelming mutual desire and its eventual assuagement through splendid fulfillment would have needed no extraneous or artificial raison d'être.

There was perhaps still another explanation for his withdrawal. He had never yet experienced a sense of guilt after the satisfaction of any appetite and it did not seem likely that he would now begin to do so; but there was a disturbing, though slight, possibility of this. He might successfully dismiss the thought of Roger most of the time, but he could not do so all of the time; and Roger, whom he might designate as colorless, he still could not designate as negligible. He had long since guessed, of course, that Roger did not like him, and why; but this dislike had not prevented the plodding, tired man from coming in to tell David that he would be missed, from offering him farewell hospitality and from wishing him Godspeed. There was something so essentially fine about Roger Field that it illumined his otherwise unprovocative person and all the humdrum tasks he performed; it also illumined his attitude toward his wife and his relationship with her. If David beclouded this attitude, or undermined this relationship, the consciousness that he had done so might be persistently disturbing for a long while.

Even if there had been no question of Roger, there remained the question of Emily herself. There was no doubt whatsoever that if she were unfaithful to her husband—and that was the way she would put it—however great her transitory rapture, her permanent sense of guilt would be much greater. And if the act of adultery were repeated, the consciousness of grave culpability would not only soon be almost unbearable, as far as she was concerned; it would also communicate itself to David, in such a way as to destroy all pagan delight in possessing her.

Little by little, he had come to at least one definite realization: if he and Emily had allowed themselves to be engulfed in mutual passion, they would almost inevitably have succumbed to it again and yet again. Their attraction for each other was too strong to find easy or swift appeasement; indeed, it was quite possible that it might grow stronger and stronger with every secret meeting, for a long time. Conceivably, under the right tutelage, Emily might became a *grande amoureuse*—indeed, the more he reflected on it, the more clearly David could see her potentialities in this role, which he believed her grandmother had played with both daring and magnificence. But she could never be a light of love; though she might be sinful, she could not be casual. Perhaps some submerged instinct had warned him of this and kept him from kindling flames which he could not extinguish. . . .

Yet, as he sat thinking of all these things, that warm August evening after Roger had left him, he suddenly knew that it would be very hard to say good-by to Emily. As long as they were in the same city, where it was possible to seek her out at any time, it had not been too hard to resist the temptation of doing so. Besides, for a period, he had been inclined to regard the abortive quality of their meeting on New Year's Eve as more or less significant; whatever the reasons, and however sound, that he had not taken her that night, the fact remained that she had not proved irresistible to him on an occasion when everything had conspired to make it easy for him to do so. Therefore he had argued, more or less successfully, that she must have begun to lose her attraction for him, and of course that was all to the good; any emotional involvement would have been very awkward. But now the image which rose before him in the gathering twilight was unexpectedly lovely: the fine, abundant, fair hair so simply and yet so effectively arranged. The white brow with its serenity which the rosy, deep-dimpled cheeks pleasantly belied. The beautiful brown eyes which complemented, at times, the forehead's calmness and, at others, the dimples' merriment. The finely formed nose and warm red lips. The slender neck firmly set above sloping shoulders. The rounded waist below the bosom curved to such slight but such exquisite fullness. The long sweeping lines of thigh and leg, never provocatively revealed, and all the more alluring on this account. The small shapely hands and feet. It was the portrait of a lady that he saw, highly bred, delicately nurtured, intelligent, sensitive and refined; but it was also the revelation of a woman ready for love and ripe for motherhood, whose capacities for great emotional experience had never yet been fully tested and whose barrenness was a reproach and a waste.

"Good God!" David exclaimed, unaware that he was speaking aloud until after he had done so. "Am I falling in love with that girl? Really in love? Have I fallen in love with her already? Is *that* the reason I couldn't. . . ."

It was unbelievable and yet, apparently, it was true. The feeling which now swept through him bore no resemblance to any which had previously caused him to embark on a passional adventure. If anything, it was stronger; but it was also compounded of elements which had hitherto been altogether alien to him in connection with passion: tenderness, respect, admiration, sympathy, understanding, a longing to protect as well as to possess, an awareness that integrity must be the cornerstone of any enduring relationship, a consciousness that physical communion was incomplete unless it were beatified with spiritual communion.

How long he sat alone in the darkness, grappling with his new-found knowledge and his overwhelming emotion, he never knew. But when he finally left the deserted office and went home to his empty house, it was with the conviction that before he left the city he must see Emily and tell her what was in his heart. He could not leave her believing he did not care. He would not leave her without telling her of the strange revelation that had come to him of a new heaven and a new earth.

Chapter 22

HE FOUND HER, as he had hoped he might, in the little garden and, as he had not dared to hope, alone. Although he did not make an informal entrance, the way Brian would have done, through the side gate, Ellie, who answered his ring at the front door, admitted him and led him straight through the house, without announcing him. He had been there so often in the past that she took his welcome for granted; as a matter of fact, she herself was extremely glad to see him, after his long absence. He had impressed Ellie very favorably from the beginning.

There were three small lanterns in the garden, one over each gate and one over the entrance to the basement; and though the light they gave was pleasantly dim, it would have sufficed for some kind of handiwork, and even for desultory reading. But Emily was stretched out in a long chair, her hands empty. Somehow the sight of these unoccupied hands recalled Cora's, the night David had found her waiting for him at the switchboard, and the recollection was not a happy one. However, it was followed by a pleasanter impression: Emily radiated perfect health and abundant vitality; she led an extremely active life and these activities took many different forms. But she never gave the effect of haste or flurry; and she had the gift of appearing to be at leisure, whenever such an appearance was desirable, and the still greater gift for real repose, whenever there was no special reason for a display of energy. Cora's idleness was abnormal and would have stirred his pity, because of its underlying causes, if it had not roused his wrath instead; Emily's tranquillity was an intrinsic attribute, which made her doubly appealing to him.

She had not risen or even turned when the door from the basement opened, and it was obvious that she had at first assumed the intruder upon her solitude was only Ellie, bent on some trivial errand. Then, as the sound of his footsteps betrayed the newcomer as a man, she looked up and swung her feet to the ground.

"Why, David!" she said in a startled voice. Then, quickly regaining her composure, she added conventionally, "How are you? Won't you sit down? What can I offer you?"

"I'm very well, and I'd like very much to sit down," he said, drawing up a chair and suiting his action to his words. "But I don't care for a drink just now, thanks. Perhaps a little later. . . . Didn't Roger tell you that he very kindly offered to give a party for me, and that I said I knew I'd have to work late at the office every night, so I'd rather just drop in, like this?"

"Yes, he did. But I don't think he expected you quite so soon—or else he forgot to tell you that this is his regular drill night. He telephoned about half-past six to say that he wouldn't have time to get home, that he and Pell would get a bite of supper downtown somewhere and then go straight on to the armory."

"I see. . . . Yes, he did forget to tell me. Or rather, I suppose he thought I knew which night he drilled. I should have, he's been doing it so long now. But I didn't."

He was suddenly very eager that she should know he was telling the truth, that glad as he was to find her alone, she should not believe he had deliberately elected to call on an evening when he knew her husband would be absent. The feeling was so strong that he could not resist the impulse to put it into words.

"You believe me, don't you, Emily?"

"Yes, I believe you," she said rather hesitantly.

"You don't sound as if you did."

"But I do, really. Perhaps I sound as if I didn't because the reason I do isn't especially complimentary to you and unconsciously I betrayed that."

"Will you tell me what it is?"

"If you're sure you want me to. But the giveaway wasn't merely unconscious; it was involuntary too. I'd rather not say anything that will sound resentful, or—or like an attempt to rehash anything that's over and done with."

"I promise you I won't misinterpret anything you say."

"Well then, I believe you didn't make a point of coming when you knew Roger wouldn't be here, because, if that had been what you wanted, you'd have done it long ago."

"I see. And I think your reasoning's very logical, Emily. I'm not in the least offended by it."

"I'm very glad."

As if she felt nothing further needed to be said on the subject, or indeed on any other, for the moment, she relapsed into silence. David, however, felt that she had provided him with an opening, which, while not ideal, at least made it possible for him to approach, without too great abruptness, the subjects he wanted to discuss.

"I can be completely sincere too, Emily, though you may find that harder to believe. And I'm going to be. I didn't deliberately choose an evening when I knew I'd find you alone; but I have hoped there would be one, sometime before I went away, because I wanted to have a talk with

260

you, and it isn't the kind of talk to have in the presence of a third person. Any third person."

"You mean what's generally called a heart-to-heart talk?"

"Exactly. In a very literal sense."

"Do you think there's any reason why you and I should have such a talk?"

"Yes, I do. I thought so before, and the way you ask that question makes me a good deal surer of it. I don't want to leave Boston feeling there's any misunderstanding between us."

"What makes you think there is?"

"I don't *think* there is. I *know* there is. I'm surer of it every minute."

Again Emily did not answer. David saw that, after all, it would be necessary for him to plunge into his subject.

"I told you once, Emily, that sometime I was going to make love to you again, really make love to you, and that you'd like it."

"I'm sorry, but if you start talking that way to me, David, I'll have to go into the house. I can't stay here and listen to you."

"Please don't go into the house. Please stay and listen to me. Because what I'm going to say is important, terribly important, to both of us."

"I don't think it can be. And even if it were, I wouldn't want to listen to it. I've got to think of what's important to Roger."

"This is important to all of us. Please, Emily! I'm not going to try to make love to you. I'm not going to say anything that will make you feel you're disloyal to your husband while you're listening. I just want to explain certain things to you. Won't you even give me a chance to explain? I won't take any longer than I have to."

She had already risen when she said that she could not stay and listen to him. Now something in his tone, more than in his actual words, impelled her to sit down again.

"It's like this," he said, seizing upon her hesitation. "I did mean what I said when I told you that someday I'd make love to you, I did think perhaps that I could get away with it, once anyway, perhaps often. I won't go into all the reasons why I thought so—probably you can make a pretty fair guess, when it comes to that. I don't think it's necessary for me to explain what I meant by 'love-making,' either. That's beyond the point anyway. The point is, I was mistaken in what I said. I found I couldn't."

"You mean you found you didn't want to."

She was speaking scornfully now and, once more, she made a slight movement, as if she were about to leave him. Again the swiftness and sincerity with which he spoke deterred her.

"I want you to get this absolutely straight, Emily. I didn't want to, the night of the storm. You're right, that far. I didn't want to take advantage of a series of circumstances like your accident and Roger's departure and a banging door to stage the setting for a glorious adventure. It wouldn't have *been* a glorious adventure under those conditions. Can't you see that?"

She turned her head away and, for the first time, he leaned forward and reached for her hand. She did not draw it away, but there was no responsive pressure as he took it in his.

"Can't you?" he persisted. "Don't say yes, if you can't; but don't say no, either, if you don't mean it."

He had to wait for his answer, but when it came, it was the answer he wanted. "Yes," she said at last, "yes, I see that. I didn't before, but I do now."

"And don't you feel better, since you do understand?"

Again she hesitated, but it was obvious that the hesitation was occasioned because she was turning the question over in her mind and not because she was trying to evade the issue. Then she looked up at him. "Yes," she said, with a note in her voice that was very like surprise, "yes, I do feel better. I suppose—well, I suppose my pride was hurt when you left me the way you did. You'd told me you wanted me and I believed you; and then when I realized you didn't—that you didn't want to enough to take advantage of a situation like that one, I couldn't help thinking. . . . But I do feel better, David, I do understand your viewpoint now. However, you still haven't explained—"

"I'm going to. I can't explain more than one thing at a time. But after that night on Hollyhock Hill, I began trying to think things through. I myself didn't understand very well, at first, why I'd instinctively acted the way I had and I wanted to find out. I also wanted to find out what—well, what the whole score was. I think I've done it, but it's been a long slow process. And a hard one. Because I didn't stop loving you, Emily. I began."

She looked up at him with the same startled expression that had marked her greeting and drew a quick breath. But she did not try to free her hand.

"It wasn't love before," he went on with convincing earnestness. "It was strong mutual attraction at first and then—we're going to be absolutely honest with each other, aren't we?—it was something much more powerful and passionate than that. Something that's a normal and vital part of love between a man and a woman. But only a part. By itself, it isn't really love."

"No, I suppose not," Emily said in a low voice.

"Don't misunderstand me now, either. When I really began to love you, that vital part of my feeling for you didn't disappear. Nothing's happened to weaken it. But it took its natural place among all the other elements that make up love. And when it did that, I realized we mustn't let our strong mutual attraction get out of hand. I realized how you'd feel—afterward. How I'd feel afterward, if I knew you were weighted down by a sense of guilt on account of me. I couldn't bring shame and suffering to you, Emily. And you would have been ashamed, you would have suffered."

"Yes," Emily said, almost in a whisper.

"So—I take back what I told you before. I'm not going to make love to you. You wouldn't have been glad to have me—that is, not for long. I'm saying something else instead. I can't go away without saying that, either.

262

I'm saying that I love you. I think I have a right to tell you that. I don't think I'd have a right not to tell you. If things had been different, if they ever could be different. . . . But they aren't. They can't be. Probably it's better that they shouldn't be. Roger's a great guy. You knew that when you married him. You still know it. He's your kind. He's worth ten of me. . . . And that's all I wanted to tell you before I went away. Good-by, Emily."

He raised the hand he had been holding to his lips and then he released it quickly and walked rapidly toward the garden gate. As he was lifting the latch, he turned, and Emily knew that if she had held out her arms to him then, he would have come back, that he would not have been able to help it. But instead of holding out her arms, she bowed her head. She wanted to be sure he would not see the yearning in her face. She did not think he could, in the dim light, but she had to be certain. She heard him say, "Good-by, Emily," again and this time she thought he added, "Good-by, darling." But she was not sure, and if he did, he was already half outside the gate. Then he was gone.

The next day Roger told David how sorry he was that he had forgotten to mention the weekly drill; it was very stupid of him, he said. But he had thought of something else—it was stupid of him not to have suggested that in the beginning too: they could have a Sunday party at the Joy Street house. Surely David would not have to work all day Sunday?

"No," David answered readily. "But I'm going down to the Cape for the week end. I'd planned to, before I knew I was leaving for Washington, and I can't very well change the arrangements now."

"Of course I wouldn't ask you to. But you're not sure yet exactly when you're going to Washington, are you? Perhaps there'd be another week end before—"

"No, I'm not sure yet just when I'm going. But I have to get packed up sometime. And, as a matter of fact, I'm more or less expected down on the Cape every week end. Not that there's anything arbitrary about it. But it's become sort of a habit."

Roger did not stress the feasibility of a Sunday party any further and David did not again refer to week ends on the Cape. As a matter of fact, while it was true that these had become more or less of a habit with him, it was also true that there was nothing "arbitrary" about them and he did not take them very seriously. Priscilla's family had made him very welcome from the first time that he went to their wide-spreading, gray-shingled house, with an old figurehead over the entrance, and he had found this a pleasant place to visit as well as a convenient center for both summer and winter sports. It had been built as a cottage, but it had gradually been enlarged, by the addition of miscellaneous wings, gables and dormers, to accommodate a growing family and an indeterminate number of guests. In the process it had lost any semblance to a definite architectural design which it might once have possessed; on the other hand, it had achieved a certain individuality which gave it haphazard charm. Its low-ceilinged rooms lacked order and convenient sequence, but age had mellowed their furnishings and softened the colors in their draperies. Its lawns were unkempt, but flowers of every description blossomed all about it; honeysuckle and trumpet vines clambered over its sides to the roof, and rambler roses framed its doorways and overhung its windows. Even the picket fence which rather superfluously hedged in its grounds from the road which led nowhere else was garlanded with bloom from early spring until late fall. Its complete isolation precluded it from the changes which the character of the little towns, once so quaint and quiet, had undergone with the influx of tourists; it stood on a narrow promontory, overlooking a small cove partially enclosed by dunes, and its cranberry bogs separated it from the nearest village.

There was a sailboat for every member of the Forbes family, and these were conveniently anchored in the cove, so that anyone who wanted to go out on the water could do so almost at a moment's notice. David had known how to handle a boat moderately well when he first went to the Cape and, with characteristic dexterity, he rapidly achieved the status of an expert. He could not be persuaded to pick blueberries from the tall bushes which flourished in such prodigal abundance on every side, or to meander, either on foot or on horseback, through the sandy lanes which transected the long stretches of scrub pine; indeed, he found it hard to understand why anyone should delight in these unchallenging pastimes. His attitude was also scornful toward the summer theaters and the resorts overcrowded by pseudo painters and writers, and still more contemptuous toward the Gift Shoppes and "the secondhand furniture stores which called themselves antique shops." On the other hand, in addition to the sailing, he greatly enjoyed the swimming, the fishing and the hunting; and he found skating on the flooded cranberry bogs one of the most zestful sports in which he had ever engaged. It made little difference to him whether Priscilla, her parents, or the younger members of the family—Stillman and Donald, who were both teen-agers, and Charlotte, who was only ten—were his companions in the pursuit of these, though special aptitude in any direction was an attraction to him. Therefore, Sue, as an outstanding yachtswoman, Sherman, as an outstanding shot, and Priscilla, as an outstanding skater, each had a special appeal. But he could have a good time on the beach with the children too, and the trips which he made between the soignée, transfigured stable and the sprawling, weather-beaten house, in his silent, powerful roadster, were agreeable intervals also.

He came to love certain colors on the Cape—the pink bloom of beach plum in the springtime and of bouncing Bet in the summer; the rich red of the scrub oak and the purplish splendor of the cranberry vines in the fall. He learned to listen for song sparrows and to watch for red-winged blackbirds and he could do this most effectively when he was unaccompanied. There were also other sights, which he found he could savor more completely when alone: the marshlands, with their tall cattails and waving sedge grass and quiet inlets of water; the bayberry and juniper trees, rising above stony pastures and the low walls made of the stones cleared from these; the dripping water wheel by the old sluiceway at Brewster and the still older windmill at Eastham; the rows of patient Portuguese, kneeling almost as in prayer, above the cranberry scoops with which they painstakingly combed the great bogs; the two church spires, separated by the width and greenery of the town, rising high above the road as this approached Truro. . . .

When it came to the stories of the Cape, however, he did not want to read these, alone, from a book; they lost something that way. He wanted to listen while someone who had known them for a long while and who had told them over and over again already, thereby learning to tell them better, told them to him. Priscilla was a good storyteller. Very often, after an immense dinner, in which cranberry juice cocktails, quahog chowder, baked stuffed bluefish, clam pie, hot biscuits spread with beach plum jelly and berry pie had figured largely, he and she would wander out over the dunes and then they would sit side by side on the sand and she would tell him stories. . . .

"Do you know the story of the Mashpee Baby, David?"

"No. What kind of an infant is a Mashpee Baby?"

"Well, it really ought to be an Indian baby, because Mashpee is the name of an Indian tribe. There are still some Mashpee Indians left on the Cape—not many, but a few. However, this was a white baby. It is always called the Mashpee Baby though, because it was found in the Mashpee Woods, near Cotuit."

"Found? What do you mean by found?"

"I mean just that. Some friends of ours were motoring down from Boston and they stopped in the Mashpee Woods to eat a picnic lunch. While they were eating, they heard a strange cry. It kept on and on. At first, they thought it must be a bird's cry, but, as it happened, they are people who know a lot about birds and presently they realized that no bird had a cry just like that. So they started to look around and one of them found a little pink bootee. Then they knew there must be a baby somewhere in the woods. They looked and looked and finally, they found her— a beautiful little girl baby, only two or three months old. She was clean and plump and daintily dressed; but her poor little face and hands were a mass of mosquito bites. You know how bad the mosquitoes can get down here sometimes."

"I'll say I do. I found it out to my cost the one time you made me go blueberrying with you."

"As if anyone ever made you do anything you didn't want to!"

"Well, we'll let that pass. Certainly no one ever made me do anything

I didn't want to twice. . . . What next? I mean about this poor mosquito-bitten baby?"

"Well, there isn't much more to tell, because no one ever found out very much. Our friends got the police and a doctor. The police started hunting for the baby's mother and the doctor took the baby to a hospital. The mother had disappeared completely and the doctor said the baby would have died if she hadn't been rescued just when she was. . . . It's strange, isn't it, that our friends should have stopped just when and where they did to eat their lunch? It's hard to believe that it was accidental."

"What do you think it was?"

"I think it was providential. Don't you?"

"No. I'm not much of a believer in providence."

"Well, you don't have to be much of a believer to believe that."

David was not interested in discussing questions of faith, still less in anything connected with the supernatural, which he classified under the scornful, general term of "demonology." Priscilla knew about this aversion and changed the subject, after telling him that the story had attracted so much attention that, after every attempt to find the mother had failed, the baby had been removed from the Cape to a hospital somewhere else, lest so much publicity might prove a bad thing for her in the end. Priscilla did not know what had happened after that and David said it might be interesting to find out. He thought, rather idly, that someday he would try to do so and occasionally, when he was driving down to the Cape, he took the road through the Mashpee Woods, though this was out of his way. He would have been very indignant if Priscilla or anyone else had said he did this because the story had seemed to have any special significance for him; still more indignant if she or anyone else had found out that when he was in the Mashpee Woods he sometimes raised his head and listened, and that it startled him if he heard the sudden note of a bird. . . .

The day after David told Roger that he could not come to a Sunday party, because he was going to the Cape for the week end, he did not go around by the Mashpee Woods; he had barely time to reach his destination, by the most direct route, for dinner. After dinner, when Priscilla suggested that they should walk along the dunes, he agreed readily enough; but they did not walk very fast or very far. Presently he said that he had always heard that the climate of the Cape was extremely relaxing, and he had decided that this might be true, especially in early August after a hearty dinner. He would rather lie down on the sand and listen to a story than to walk any farther.

"I don't think this is the right day for me to tell you a story. I think instead you ought to tell me more about your plans."

"Very well, I will. Not that there's much more to say. I wrote your father a note about them and I talked to the whole family about them all

266

through dinner. Which, incidentally, gave everybody but me a chance for second helpings."

"You don't need second helpings, leading the sedentary life you do. Now, if you would only get out and walk or ride—"

"Priscilla, if you start lecturing me, I won't tell you anything about my plans."

"All right. Then I won't tell you a story, either."

"You win. Go ahead with your story."

"Have I ever told you about the Moon Cussers of Dangerfield?"

"You certainly never have. Who are the Moon Cussers and where is Dangerfield?"

"The Moon Cussers have been dead a long while—almost two hundred years, I think. They were called that because they had to do their evil work in the dark of the moon. So when the moon was bright, they cursed."

"I see. And Dangerfield?"

"Well, that's disappeared too, except on some very old maps. But from what I've heard, it wasn't far from here. The sailing ships used to come into the harbor there, through a long narrow channel. That is, they used to head for there. But very often they didn't get to Dangerfield."

"Why not?"

"Because the Moon Cussers would steal out, when a sailing ship was due, and change the signal lights marking the channel. Then, there would be a wreck and the captain and crew would leave the ship to save their lives. But the Moon Cussers would go aboard it and loot it."

"Why, the captain could say that the lights must have been changed!"

"Of course he could say so. But how could he prove it? The lights would be all right again the next night. How could he make anyone believe the wreck hadn't been due to his own carelessness? He had to be careful."

"I see," David said again. "Were these Moon Cussers your ancestors, Priscilla?"

"Probably. I don't believe all my ancestors were the kind you're supposed to be so proud of, the ones who read the Bible most of the time and make you eligible for the Colonial Dames."

David laughed. "Do you know, Priscilla, there's something rather refreshing about you?"

"By that you mean I'm sort of a joke. Well, I've told you a story, haven't I? Now I want to hear about Washington."

She listened, without interruption, to everything he said, but she made no stray comments on her own initiative along the way; and finally she was silent for so long that he said jokingly, "A penny for your thoughts, Pris."

"They're worth more than that."

"A nickel then."

He reached in his pocket, brought out a handful of loose change and, selecting a coin, tossed it smilingly into her lap. She picked it up and turned it over several times, still without speaking.

"Look here, no cheating. That nickel had a string attached to it."

"All right, you asked for it. I was wondering whether I couldn't go too."

"Go too! Go where?"

"To Washington, of course."

"My dear child, whatever would you do in Washington?"

"I could do just the same things I did in Boston, couldn't I, if I had to? They must be just about the same in one place as in another."

"What do you mean, just the same things?"

"Why, going to teas and cocktail parties and dances and meetings of the Junior League. There's a branch of the Junior League in Washington. There must be. It couldn't escape just because it's the capital."

"But you hated doing all those things in Boston!"

"I know. But you seemed to think I'd need some kind of an excuse to go to Washington. I'd be willing to do all those things over again if I could go. The muffin-hounds from the State Department can't be any worse than the sophomores from Harvard."

"Probably they aren't. However, I didn't realize you had any special yen for going to Washington."

"I didn't have before. But I have now."

"Why?"

"Because you're going to be there, of course. What makes you ask such a silly question?"

"I didn't think you were such a silly girl. I thought you were quite sensible, for your age."

"You're talking now as if I were about ten years old. That's not the way you talked to Emily about me. You told her I was old enough to know my own mind."

"Excuse me. If Emily reported that conversation to you, she must have done so inaccurately—quite unintentionally, of course. What I said was, that the fact a girl was only in her teens didn't necessarily mean she didn't know her own mind—that some girls knew their minds younger than others."

"Well, I'm one of those that makes up her mind young."

She spoke calmly, but conclusively. Involuntarily, David sighed. He felt that he had been through quite enough with Cora without having to go through somewhat the same thing, as far as Priscilla was concerned. Not that Priscilla was the type who wept and made scenes, or who could be placated by a flattering invitation to supper and the vague offer of a job. On the other hand, she was not so easily guided, either. She was very definitely not only one of those who made up her mind young, but who made it up for herself.

"Where could you live in Washington?" he inquired, feeling, even as he did so, that the question was inadequate, that doubtless Priscilla had this all figured out by now. He was quite right.

"You seem to forget that I have an uncle in Washington. Isn't it just as logical that I should live with an uncle in Washington as with a cousin in Boston?"

"No. Emily has a very nice house, with plenty of room for you. Your Uncle Russell's lived at a hotel, since his wife left him."

"Yes, and Grandmamma thinks that's a very poor arrangement. She's said so over and over again. If I went to live with Uncle Russell, he'd get another house. I could be his hostess."

"My dear child, I don't like to discourage you, but I'm afraid you're a victim of 'vaulting ambition which o'erleaps itself and falls on the other.' From all I've heard, it's quite a job to be a successful senatorial hostess."

"Maybe. But I think I could manage. And if I couldn't, Grandmamma could come down and help me out. There's nothing she'd like better. She adores Washington."

This was undeniably true. David, who had begun by being mildly annoyed, was fast becoming appalled. Priscilla had this thing far too well mapped out.

"What makes you think your uncle would like to have you live with him?" he asked, again conscious of inadequacy.

"Well, Emily really didn't want me to live with her. She put up with it because she thought it was part of a proper pattern. So would Uncle Russell, if he thought so. Grandmamma could convince him that it was."

This was also undeniably true. David could visualize Russell Forbes, who was no match for his mother when it came to determination, as already domiciled in a handsome house near the embassies on upper Massachusetts Avenue, entertaining lavishly and launching a debutante niece on the Washington scene, with the help of an efficient social secretary. It was as good as half done already.

"You don't seem to like the idea," Priscilla remarked, in the same calm, conclusive way she had spoken before. "I've got another one. But I'm not sure you'll like that any better."

"Let's hear it anyway. I might."

"Then let me repeat that you mustn't say, later on, that you didn't ask for all this. The other idea is that you and I could get married."

"Why, you pert little baggage!" he exclaimed, abruptly attempting to veil his consternation, which was becoming very real, in something like levity. "The idea of making advances to me like that!"

"They're not improper advances. You can't say I asked you to have an affair with me. I wouldn't be at all interested in an affair. I think they're rather messy, almost always. But I'd like very much to marry you. It isn't a new idea. I've had it quite a while already. But I'd have probably waited a little longer for you to get the same one, if you hadn't been going away. You would have in course of time and any girl would rather have a man propose to her than to do the proposing herself."

"Priscilla, I don't want to hurt your feelings, but you're mistaken. I think you're a perfectly grand kid and I'm very fond of you, but I'm not in love with you. There's not the slightest chance that I ever will be."

"I don't see why you're so sure."

"There are quite a number of reasons. I don't think it's necessary to go into them. But even if there weren't, I wouldn't ask you to marry me."

"Why not?"

"Because I'm a Jew."

"I don't see what difference that makes. I'm not interested in your religion."

"It isn't a question of my religion. As far as that goes, I haven't much of any religious belief."

"Well, I knew that already. What *is* the question?"

"I'll have to put this to you pretty crudely, Priscilla. I'll have to mention things Jews don't often talk about—that Lord knows they don't like to talk about."

"All right. This time *I* asked for it."

"I wouldn't think it was fair to subject a girl like you to running the risk of having the kind of treatment she might get if she were married to a Jew."

"I still don't know what you're talking about."

"You don't? No, you don't know what it's like to be told there isn't any room in a half-empty hotel. But I do. You don't know what it's like to find you can't buy, or even rent, a house in a 'restricted' area. But I do. You don't know what it's like to be automatically barred from membership in a club. But I do. You don't know—"

Unconsciously, he was speaking more and more vehemently. Priscilla interrupted him, with a vehemence that matched his own.

"Maybe I don't know, but I don't care, either. What difference would it make if there were some hotels where we couldn't stay and some areas where we couldn't live? There are plenty of other ones, better ones too, where we could! What do you care about stuffy old clubs? I shouldn't think anyone would *want* to belong to them!"

"It's all very well for you to say that, because you've never been face to face with such conditions. If you had, it would be different. You'd have something to go by. You've been running around here on the Cape, practically without shoes on, all your life; you've never even had a decent education. But the minute you reach marriageable age, you're hauled out of the bogs and given a little surface polishing and dolled up in Paris clothes—and welcomed into the best society! Do you think my cousin, Rachael Rosenberg, who lives on Aspinwall Avenue, could ever get an invitation to the Empire Dance or become a member of the Junior League? You know damn well she couldn't! But she's been all over the world, she graduated *cum laude* from Vassar, she dresses beautifully, she's a beauty herself, she—"

"You ought to have told me about her before, you ought to have brought her to see me. I'd have made Grandmamma and Emily invite her to things."

"You'd have made! Who wants to be invited because someone has insisted they should be? Do you suppose for a moment I didn't see through your maneuvering, as far as I was concerned? Even your grandmother wouldn't invite me to her house, except when she had a hand-picked guest list. I'll give her all the credit that's coming to her. She didn't hesitate because she thought I couldn't hold my own with the best of them. She did it because she wouldn't risk having the 'best' insult me, the way that bitch, Putnam, did."

"David, I had no idea you felt this way."

"How else would you expect me to feel?" he asked savagely. "Do you know there are certain resorts where I couldn't even call on you more than once? If I did, you'd be asked to leave the hotel."

"I'd be only too glad to leave such a hotel. But I didn't know there were any."

"Well, take my word for it that there are. Because I've been to one. I called on a girl. I—I wasn't in love with her exactly, but I might have been, if I hadn't had this experience in the nick of time. What do you think she said to me? 'I like you ever and ever so much, David, and so do my mother and father. You don't seem to us like a Jew. But you'll have to make allowances for the management, because of course most Jews—' "

"I hope you knocked her over."

"No, I didn't knock her over. I just walked out of her suite—and out of her life. I took her out of mine. But don't get the idea her viewpoint's an isolated one. I've had almost the same thing said to me over and over again. And then there are the people who don't think I'm 'different'—not that I want to be, you understand. I'm proud of my heritage. But did you ever notice Caroline Field's face when she's looking at me and thinks nobody's watching her?"

"Yes, but it isn't fair to take Caroline as typical."

"It isn't? Why do you suppose I left Aspinwall Avenue? Did you think it was because I wasn't happy with my cousins who live there? I was very happy. But I was also just as isolated as if I'd been on a desert island—as far as anyone I needed to know in Boston was concerned. My cousins realized it just as well as I did. They urged me to move. Not that I wasn't welcome in their house. I was more than welcome. But they wanted me to get ahead. So they helped me find a made-over stable on Lime Street, and my stepfather furnished it for me, and my mother let me have an old family servant to give the final touch to the right atmosphere. And now some of the 'best' people do come to my parties. Enough of them so that I am getting ahead—now that I've thrown my cousins overboard, now that I'm about to leave Boston."

"David, I can't bear to have you talk like this, I can't bear to have you sound so bitter. I don't understand—"

"I said you wouldn't understand, because you've never been in my place. But you'd understand all right if you were married to me. You'd understand if you had a child with my name. It's one of the oldest, most illustrious names in the world. It's derived from the name of a great king. I'll never change it, the way lots of Jews change their names, after they've had surgical operations performed on their faces, so that they won't be turned away from hotels and restricted areas. I'm proud of it. But when I pass it on to my son, I want his mother to be a woman who's been through the same sort of experience that I have, one that'll take it as a matter of course that the poor kid's got to face exclusion, who won't suffer when she finds he can't get into some preparatory school where his name's been entered ever since he was born and where all his cousins slide in on greased wheels. I'll make a bet with you: I don't suppose your parents have entered one of your brothers at any school, because they don't seem to think 'book learning' matters. But ask them to send in Stillman's name to whichever preparatory school they imagine is the best. Now, in August. And see if he isn't enrolled there in September. And let me make the same try for my cousin, Abel. It's dollars to doughnuts, Stillman, who can hardly read and write, will get in, and Abel, who's been an honor student for six years already, won't."

"David, I think you ought to be fair. All the boys who go to those schools have to take examinations. If they don't pass, they don't get in— or the girls who go to the same kind of schools, either. I couldn't have got into the Winsor School on any kind of a bet. But I'm not stupid, honestly I'm not. I suppose I seem stupid to you, because you're about the brightest person who ever lived. But I'm as bright as the average. I know I'm ignorant, but I can learn. I'll study hard, I'll surprise you."

"A fat chance you'll have to study hard, if you're running around all the time with those muffin-hounds, as you call them. A damn good name for them too."

"Yes, but if I married you, I wouldn't be running around with the muffin-hounds. I could study all the time—most of the time anyway. But I'd learn to be a good housekeeper. I'd make you comfortable. And I could have a baby too. I wouldn't mind at all if he couldn't go to the same school his cousins did. Anyway, how do you know he couldn't? How does anyone know what's going to happen twelve or fourteen years from now?"

"Nobody. That's another reason I wouldn't marry you. There's a war on and unless I miss my guess, it won't be very long now before the United States is in it. There hasn't been any doubt in my mind what was going to happen, not since Hitler sent his troops into the Rhineland, and neither France nor England did anything to stop him, because they were so damn jealous of each other and so afraid of each other. The sooner I can get in a war against that archcriminal, the better I'll be pleased. That's why I went to an officers' candidate school in New York. That's why I'm jumping at this job in Washington. It may make just the difference between being in at the kill and doing some of the killing—or maybe getting killed myself—and getting stuck at some camp in the Middle West as an orderly in a military hospital."

"You'll never be an orderly in a military hospital, David."

"You're damn right, I never will be. Because I've taken good care not to get caught by waiting for the draft that's bound to come. But Brian Collins may find himself emptying bedpans. Serve him right too, with all his talk about England's war. He's never heard of Hitler's war, apparently."

"Yes, he has, David. I can't stand it not to have you fair, when I lo— care for you so much. But it doesn't touch him as closely as it does you."

"I'll say it doesn't. He's one of a large family and they're all well and prosperous and safe. I'm one of a large family, too, even though I'm an only child. I have any number of aunts and uncles and cousins. My stepfather and my mother, and other relatives in this country, have done everything in their power to get those people into the United States. My relatives are pretty powerful—they haven't lacked money, they haven't lacked influential connections. In a few cases, they've been successful."

"Tell me about them."

"Well, one of my uncles is a rabbi. Two years ago, his synagogue was destroyed, together with virtually all those throughout Germany, and he was taken to Dachau, along with most of his congregation. He was finally released, but the Gestapo kept making forcible entries into his home and asking how soon he was going to leave the country. Fortunately, the United States immigration law contains a provision that ministers, among other professional men, may be admitted here if there is a pulpit ready for them. My stepfather promptly took measures to find such a pulpit and finally came across a small southern congregation, which had never had a resident rabbi. There were only about twenty families in it but they all dug down into their pockets and, with what my stepfather could do to help, collected money enough to satisfy the American Consul that a pulpit was waiting. My uncle and his wife got over here safely, they've proved their worth already, in fact they've achieved signal recognition in several important quarters. They're on their way to become American citizens. But the rabbi's mother died in a French concentration camp, and his wife's mother less than a week after she landed in New York, as a result of the tortures she'd been through before they cut enough red tape to get her away."

"David, I—I honestly thought such things were newspaper stories. And I don't read newspapers much anyway, you know. I never dreamed—"

"It's no dream. And so far, I've talked mostly about two persons who did get away. I haven't told you about the ones who didn't—about another uncle, for instance, who'd been a colonel in the Army during the First World War, who'd served the Kaiser faithfully and been decorated for conspicuous gallantry over and over again. He'd retired and was living in Vienna, where he'd been so indiscreet as to express disbelief that the Nazis would make any serious attempt to persecute the Jews; as a proof of it, he cited the numerous 'Kruzenkreuzes' and anti-Nazi slogans that had been scribbled on the streets at night with chalk and that hadn't been removed. Shortly after the Anschluss, three members of the S.S. came to his house and ordered him to scrub the chalk marks off his sidewalk. He thought it was a practical joke; he laughed and advised the three young men to go home. Then one of them drew a gun. My uncle put on his full-dress uniform and all his medals and went out to scrub the streets. The officers stood by until he finished and then they cudgeled him to death."

"David—"

"That's the least harrowing of several similar stories. . . . And then, of course, there was the systematic evacuation of Jewish children. Twelve or more trainloads went out, taking two hundred children each time—children from six or seven years old up to adolescents. In most cases, their parents didn't even know who would take care of them, after they reached England. But there was an official assurance that somebody would and it was better to lose them than to see them degraded and abused and finally killed. So parents took their children to the Westbahnhoff and waited for the train on which they were to travel to the Hook of Holland and thence across the Channel. The waiting room was dim and stifling. Once in a while, there was a loud cry or subdued sobbing; but mostly there was terrible silence. Finally, the gates leading to the tracks were opened, and the children streamed through to the cars assigned them. The parents were held back by ropes and, after the scramble for seats had subsided, the children stuck their noses out of the windows and tried to wave good-by. They were so closely packed together that there was no room for them to lie down on the hard wooden seats; some of them lay on the floor, some tried to sleep sitting up. The journey to the Dutch border lasted twenty-four hours, and during that time the children had no food, except the little they had been able to bring with them. But there was no more crying; there were not even any complaints."

"David, how did you know all this?"

"One of those children is now my adopted brother. My stepfather never had a child of his own. He wanted one and I'm glad he's got one of those. The child's never heard from his own parents since he left Germany. No doubt they've both died a horrible death by now." David broke off abruptly. "I'm sure I don't know why I told you all this. I'm sorry. I ought not to have done it."

"Of course you ought to have done it. And I'm not sorry. I'm very glad. Because people don't talk about things like that to just anybody. They only talk about them to people they like a lot and trust a lot."

"I do trust you a lot, I do like you a lot, Priscilla. I told you before that I'm very fond of you and I meant it. But I'm not in love with you. You wouldn't want me to marry you if I weren't in love with you, would you?"

274

"You might fall in love with me afterward."

"I just tried to explain to you, without using any more brutal language than is absolutely necessary, that there may not be any 'afterward.' I mentioned in passing that I might be one of those who got killed. You don't want to run the risk of being left a widow, do you? A very young widow, with a Jewish name and maybe a half-Jewish baby, and no one to try and make up to you for the discrimination I've been telling you about?"

"Of course I don't want to be left a widow, because I love you and I want to live with you all my life." A few minutes earlier, Priscilla had still shrunk, with typical New England reserve, from using the word "love." But she was making rapid progress and she now brought it out boldly. "Just the same, I'd rather be your widow than not marry you at all. And if I had a baby, I could fight for him, even if I had to do it alone. I wouldn't let him suffer from discrimination. Maybe it would be a good thing if a girl from an old Boston family put up a fight like that. Perhaps it would make at least a few people see how un-American it is to discriminate, in the ways you've been talking about, how it puts us almost in the same class as the Nazis."

"Well, supposing I wasn't killed. Suppose that instead I came home blind? Or without any arms and legs? Or not a whole man in—well, in some other way, if you know what I mean?"

"Of course I know what you mean. You're talking to me again as if I were about ten years old. We could show our love differently. And if you were blind I could read to you, couldn't I, and take care of you? It wouldn't be hard; you could have a seeing-eye dog to help me. And I suppose you've heard of such things as crutches and artificial limbs. Anyway I have. You could manage. We could manage."

She looked up at him, her whole being awake with love. In spite of himself, David was deeply moved. He found himself unable to resist the impulse to cup her mobile little face with his hands and, tilting back her head, look into her eyes. There were no tears in them, no despair and no sadness—only complete trust, deep devotion and unflinching courage.

"Priscilla, I'm—well, I'm terribly touched that you should care like this," he said at last. "I didn't dream that you did. If I had—" It was too late now to tell her that, if he had, he would not have sailed with her on the *Charles*; he would not have helped her choose her clothes and invited her to luncheon at the Ritz; he would not have gone to a house party on Hollyhock Hill and spent week end after week end at her parents' house on the Cape. In a certain sense, he had felt sorry for her; she had been so obviously unprepared, when he first met her, to swim in the social stream into which she had suddenly been flung. Almost instinctively, he had wanted to keep her from sinking, and he had taken a secret pride in the knowledge that it was he, whom most of the "best" people declined to receive, that had prepared her not only to survive, but to hold her own in their midst. Besides, he had found her plucky, amusing and original. It was true that she was ignorant. But he knew she was not mistaken in believing that, given a fair chance, she would be quick to learn. Meanwhile, she had the natural endowments of good sense and mother wit. He had genuinely enjoyed his association with her, and he had not been blind to the fact that she had been attracted and that she had become attached to him. But it had not occurred to him that she had really fallen in love with him, and that she would be ready and eager to go to any legitimate lengths to prove her love.

Only one trump card remained in his possession and, at last, unwillingly, he decided to play it. Still holding her face in his hands and looking into her fond and fearless eyes, he spoke with unwonted gentleness.

"Priscilla, I've told you several reasons why I wouldn't and couldn't marry you and I've tried hard to make you see that they're all good. There's one more I haven't mentioned. I don't want to mention it now. But you almost force me to. When I asked you if you'd want me to marry you without being in love with you, your answer was that I might fall in love with you afterward and you weren't frightened when I told you there might not be any afterward. But let's assume that there might be. I couldn't possibly fulfill your hopes of falling in love with you then, either. Because I'm in love with someone else."

She shook her head furiously, freeing her face from his hands. "Why, you can't be!" she cried. "If you were, you'd marry her."

"I can't."

"Of course you can. If you were really in love, you'd know all those silly objections you've raised don't amount to Hannah Cook. They just show you don't know what it means to be in love."

"The reason I can't marry her has nothing to do with the objections I raised, as far as you're concerned. She's older, she could cope with them better."

"Well, what is the reason?"

"I don't think you have a right to ask me that, Priscilla."

"Yes, I have. I have a right to ask you anything I want to, feeling the way I do about you. Is it because she's married already?"

Unbelievably, he was the one to turn away from a searching question and a searching gaze without answering. Priscilla went on relentlessly.

"Then why don't you have an affair with her?"

"Because I am in love with her. You know what you said yourself about affairs, just a little while ago, Priscilla."

"Are you allergic to divorce?"

"I haven't any very strong feeling about it one way or another—as long as it isn't granted on some trumped-up grounds. And it would have to be, in the case I'm talking about. There isn't the remotest excuse for one. The —lady I'm in love with has a kind, devoted husband. Even if she didn't have, I think she would have a strong feeling about divorce. She was brought up very conservatively, as an Episcopalian."

276

"Of course you expect me to pretend I haven't the slightest idea who this mysterious *lady* is. If you won't have an affair with her, and don't believe in trumped-up divorces, what are you waiting for? A dead man's shoes?"

The ugly question came as a shock, the greater in that it revealed a kernel of secret truth. David's vehement denial lacked weight because it lacked complete candor.

Priscilla did not ask him any more questions. She continued to look at him fixedly for a few moments and then she made an uncompromising and final statement.

"If that's the way things are, I think you'd better leave here. You can say you've been suddenly called back to Boston. Or you needn't say anything at all. You can just go. No one will care. You can be damn sure I shan't."

She turned quickly and ran. He did not try to catch up with her and he did not try to see her alone again. Neither did he tell anyone in the office that, as a matter of fact, he did not need to hurry off to Washington; he actually had thirty days' leeway, though this was discovered, only accidentally, sometime later. But, as soon as he had put all his pending cases in competent hands, and left everything else for which he was responsible in perfect order, he took his immediate departure.

Later he wrote to Cora from Washington, saying he was sorry, but that he had not been able to find a situation for her after all. He had not realized that the scene would already be so overcrowded with stenographers. He was enjoying his new work and he wished her the best of luck.

He did not write to either Emily or Priscilla at all.

Chapter 23

ROGER AND PELL had learned that unless they lunched very early or very late, their chances for shoptalk in the course of their meal were very slight. This was not primarily because the probability of eavesdropping made confidential discussion inadvisable, though of course this phase of the situation existed; it was primarily because of the general tumult during rush hours at their favorite "beanery," Durgin-Park—a tumult compounded about equally of hearty greetings, clattering tableware, scraping chairs, tramping feet, vociferous orders and voluble talk, which almost automatically rendered any serious conversation impossible. Even an early lunch did not help materially in solving the problem; before they had finished either their food or their conference, the hungry hordes were upon them; and an interruption of this sort meant that they were forced to begin all over again, because it was so hard to pick up the threads where they had left off. A late lunch was better; then the crowd gradually dispersed, instead of suddenly increasing. It was also better because they had less sense of haste while they ate and Pell, especially, liked to choose his food deliberately and savor it slowly. Though he was obliged to consider its cost more carefully than Roger, he also appreciated more keenly the relative merits of the different dishes featured on the prodigal "dinner bill" and took a more lively interest in flavorsome combinations.

The practice of lunching together, which had been only intermittent during the first year that Roger was associated with Cutter, Mills and Swan, had now become habitual; and instead of "shopping around" for good values and good food they went, nine times out of ten, by common consent, to the famous and individualistic "Market Dining Rooms," which scorned the title of restaurant but which proudly proclaimed their location "in the shadow of Faneuil Hall" and called attention to their antiquity by the caption, YOUR GRANDFATHER AND PERHAPS YOUR GREAT-GRANDFATHER DINED WITH US TOO. This was entirely true in Roger's case, as it was in countless others; and, also in accordance with time-honored custom, he showed little inclination to vary his fare from day to day. Mabel, the brisk, bespectacled waitress, who generally served them when they were fortunate enough to find their favorite place free, brought him corn chowder on Mondays, fish chowder on Tuesdays and Thursdays, and clam chowder on Wednesdays and Fridays, as soon as she had filled his glass from the enormous white china pitcher which she left within easy reach, and completely refilled the white china sugar bowl, which was already two thirds full. On the other hand, she stood patiently behind Pell while he shuffled the small pastel-colored slips which he had unclipped from the four-page "dinner bill," adorned with a drawing of the Old State House and the Old Market, as they appeared in the days of Yankee Clippers.

"Roast stuffed veal—eighty-five cents," Pell would say, reading aloud from a green slip which also bore the superscription DINNER. . . . "So I could have—let's see—a cup of onion soup first and apple pandowdy afterward, couldn't I, Mabel—at no extra charge?"

"Yes, sir," Mabel would say, with apparent interest. "Or, of course, if you'd prefer, you could have soft-shell crabs, with the same soup and the same dessert, at the same price."

This idea having been presented to him, Pell would study a pink slip. "No, I think I'll wait until Friday for the soft-shell crabs," he would say at last. Then, shifting to a blue slip, he would announce, "I might even go for some fresh sliced cucumbers, ten cents extra, to go with them. . . . You'll still be having soft-shell crabs on Friday, won't you, Mabel?"

"I'm almost sure we will, sir. But if you'll wait just a minute, I'll ask."

"All right, but hold on. . . . If I'm going to have the cucumbers extra on Friday, I ought to economize today. Of course, roast stuffed veal is a great temptation to any Italian. But I see you've got fried turkey wings for seventy-five, and kidney and mushroom sauté for sixty-five, both marked DINNER."

"Yes, sir, we have, and both delicious, I don't need to tell you."

"Indeed you don't. It's still a mystery to me how a dry goods merchant and a livery stable man should have known so much about food that they could make a go of a place like this. But that's neither here nor there, especially as they've been dead and gone these many years now. . . . All right then, it's the kidneys and mushrooms today and the soft-shell crabs with the extra cucumbers Friday. Don't forget, Mabel."

"I won't, sir."

"And don't try to bring them to me every Friday, either, the way you bring clam chowder every Friday to Mr. Field. Because some other Friday I might want broiled scrod or even a salt cod dinner."

"I know, sir. You can depend on me."

At that stage Mabel would depart, beaming broadly, for, as she often told her fellow waitresses, Mr. de Lucca certainly had a nice way with him. And Pell would start buttering the corn bread, which had appeared in the wake of the white water pitcher and the white sugar bowl, even before Roger's chowder, and ask, "Well, what's cooking besides my food?"

The question was companionable rather than curious. The Jerry Donovan case had been "cooking," to the exclusion of almost everything else, as far as Roger was concerned, ever since Brian had been promoted to the position of junior partner and been nominated in the primaries for the state legislature and David had left to enter the office of the Judge Advocate General in Washington. And, throughout the intervening weeks, Pell, recognizing Roger's absorption, had willingly and attentively listened to everything he had to say. Pell knew the background of the story by heart now: Jerry Donovan was a salesman for the Somerville Electric Appliance Corporation; his company had first held out on him and then fired him; afterward they had sued him for back pay. When Pell, having heard this much, inquired tersely, "How come?" Roger had given him a fairly complete picture of the situation.

"Well, he got his job with these people during the Depression, when they had a small outfit and very little cash. He needed the work and it wasn't hard to persuade him that, though he wouldn't get much of a salary to start with, he still wouldn't be badly off because he'd get a five per cent cut in the profits from sales. He didn't stop to think much about details until the year was over and he was handed a check, along with a brief statement showing the profits as so and so. After that, the checks for his cut kept getting bigger and bigger all the time. Then finally, in 1937, the company began giving Jerry quarterly checks on account for his share of sales and one after the end of the fiscal year to balance. He thought things were fine until he overheard some office gossip about 'rigged books.'"

"Oh—ho," Pell had said at this point, partly because it seemed about time for some kind of a comment, and partly to call Roger's attention to the fact that the two straw-hatted, white-aproned market men, who had been sitting at the next table, had just risen and gone out, so that almost the entire side of the dining hall was now empty except for themselves. This meant that Roger could talk quite freely, for Mabel had already supplied them with more than they could possibly eat at one sitting, and she would not return with the check until they motioned to her. It was not the policy of the establishment to hurry its customers.

"The Somerville outfit was expanding fast by this time," Roger had gone on, nodding to show that he had understood Pell's signal. "But every time a new line of goods was introduced, a new corporation was formed to handle it—one for toasters, one for waffle irons and so on. Finally, Jerry asked the treasurer what happened to the profits these subsidiaries were making, and after that, he began to get the run-around every time he questioned one of the big shots. Then, while he was on his vacation, he got a letter telling him he was through. As if that weren't bad enough, he was sued for the return of his last quarterly check."

A group of tourists had come in, peering about and calling to each other. "I'm all out of breath, going up those steep stairs, aren't you? But anyhow, isn't this the quaintest place? Look at those enlargements over the cashier's desk, just like at Antoine's in New Orleans." . . . "Yes, but the kitchen isn't in plain view there, the way it is here. I want to watch them cooking my boiled dinner." . . . "What do you mean, boiled dinner? You're just like every other Westerner, you think New Englanders live on boiled dinners and baked beans. What you want to try is some broiled lobster. That's really tops." . . . "Let's sit here, shall we?" . . . "No, this is a much better place." . . . "Well, the table doesn't matter—they're all alike anyhow. It's the food that counts. Say, miss, can you wait on us?"

Pell had watched the group with mild amusement and had tried to catch Mabel's eye and then Roger's; he would have liked to exchange understanding glances with them. But Mabel had already begun to pour water from a white pitcher and Roger had not even noticed the diversion, because he was too intent on his story.

"I tell you Jerry was pretty sore when he first came into the office and asked if Cutter, Mills would take the case. It was given to Berkeley and he told me something about it at the time; when he turned over his papers to me, I found he'd brought suit for an accounting of the 'profits.'"

"Who represents the corporation?"

"Towne and Locke."

"And you have to make them throw snowballs at you, so that you'll get something to throw back?" Pell had inquired thoughtfully, drawing patterns with an unused knife on the red-and-white-checked tablecloth.

"That's it. The appliance company isn't telling anything it doesn't have to about those profits. And so far, I haven't been able to find out how they figured in taxes, insurance and so forth. But Jerry's sure the treasurer has changed the system, so that the big shots get larger salaries than they used to and the subsidiaries aren't counted in at all. These could have made plenty in their own lines without Jerry's knowledge, because they may not have appeared as part of the sales 'profit' in the parent company's books. Don't you agree with me?"

Pell had agreed with him and there the discussion had ended for the moment, since it was high time for them to return to the office, and only the most disjointed talk was possible while they picked their way among the bales and crates cluttering the sidewalk around the market, and dodged the vans, trucks and horse-drawn vehicles which bore down upon them on the cobblestoned streets. But Roger had reverted to the case again and again, at their lunch hour, and Pell had continued to listen with the same patient interest which he had revealed from the beginning, though Roger had still not been able to find out how the profits figured in "taxes, insurance and so forth." Then, one day when they were respectively consuming gingerbread with whipped cream and baked Indian pudding with ice cream, Roger suddenly pushed back his plate.

"Pell, I've got an idea."

"All right, spill it."

"The appliance corporation may have just been trying to gyp Jerry, but

I don't believe so, any longer. I think the big shots were after plenty for themselves, and trying to turn the gravy into capital gains for a low tax besides. It wouldn't surprise me if I had a minority stockholders' suit on my hands!"

Pell made no immediate answer. Instead, he pushed back his own plate and began to draw patterns on the checked cloth, as he so often did when he was thinking something over.

"Would it surprise you?" persisted Roger.

"No. It wouldn't surprise me exactly. But I'd have to know a little more about it before I could give you an opinion."

"I can tell you a little more about it right now. Jerry's kept picking up a few shares in the company, hoping to be in the top management himself sometime. Now he's afraid he never will, because he believes the outfit has the stock rigged, so that the present management gets all the gravy and the little fellows and the stockholders get the short end."

"I see."

"It could be done, for a while anyway, couldn't it? I mean by manipulating the subsidiaries and shuffling the stock around?"

"Yes, I believe it could. . . . Roger, I think that's the Governor just going out. I think he's trying to bow to you."

Roger half rose in his seat and returned the salutation, but he did so as briefly as was consistent with courtesy. "I think it *has* been done. I think the subsidiaries *have* been manipulated, I think the stock *has* been shuffled around," he said impulsively. "If I can show that the top men did this for their own profit, I've got 'em! I'm going straight to the State House to look at those subsidiaries. After that, I should be able to draw a bill of complaint which will give me access to their corporate records. Then we'll see whether those practical businessmen have been working for their stockholders or themselves!"

Roger's investigation at the State House consumed the greater part of the afternoon; and when he had secured a sheaf of abstracts, he hastened back to the office to digest these and put them in workable order. He was still struggling to arrange them in their most significant form when Pell appeared in the doorway with the warning that they would have barely time to snatch a sandwich on their way to the armory if they were to get there for the special announcement which they had been notified would be made that evening.

It was extremely brief and to the point: the Cadets were unofficially told that induction into the Army was imminent and that married men might be excused upon request.

The evenings were already beginning to be cool and it was now the exception rather than the rule that Emily waited in the garden for Roger's return on drill nights. On the other hand, she seldom went to bed before he came home; he generally found her in the library, reading or knitting beside the open fire. Therefore, he was surprised to find that the library, though, as usual, pleasantly lighted against his return, was empty. He turned out the lights and went upstairs, only to find their bedroom and his dressing room vacant also. He had talked with her over the telephone late that afternoon, to say that he would not be home to dinner, and she had said nothing about going out; he had almost decided that the unexpected arrival of some guest had taken her to the third floor, when Emily opened, from within, the door leading into one of the unfurnished rear rooms behind their own quarters and came toward him.

"Hello, there!" he said, going forward to give her the fond kiss which was still his habitual form of greeting. "What are you doing? Pursuing mysterious sounds which might mean there are robbers in the house?"

"No. As Mr. Cleveland said to Mrs. Cleveland, when she told him she thought that was the case, 'My dear, they are all in the Senate.' I was merely pursuing a train of thought."

"Yes? Is it a secret one? Or are you going to share it with me?"

"Of course I'm going to share it with you. I've been looking over those back rooms and wondering how you'd feel about having me fix up one of them as—well, as a sort of boudoir. After all, you have your dressing room and I haven't anything that quite corresponds to it. I've taken it into my head that I'd rather enjoy doing so. Not that it's important."

For a moment he did not answer. When he had first looked at the house, from the outside, he had visualized it as having double drawing rooms on the ground floor and an immense second-story library, like Old Mrs. Forbes' house on Louisburg Square. Emily's decision that one drawing room was enough for their needs, both present and future, and that the library should be located directly behind this had resulted in the impression that she was saving the rear rooms on the second story for nursery purposes. Later this impression had been confirmed in loving and intimate words. But it was a long time since the subject had been brought up and now, in Emily's suggestion of a boudoir, Roger caught the implication that she thought they were never going to need a nursery. He tried to suppress his own pang of disappointment and to make up for his hesitancy by heartiness.

"Why, of course! I think the idea of a boudoir's quite amusing. Traditionally, the décor's rather voluptuous, isn't it? Cupids and divans and all that sort of thing? I don't believe there are many boudoirs on Beacon Hill."

"No, I don't either. And I hadn't visualized that sort. Just something rather chintzy and cozy and feminine. Perhaps I should have said an upstairs sitting room."

"Well, after all, 'what's in a name?' I know you'll make it very attractive, whatever you call it, and I do think you should have a room that's essentially yours and not ours, just as I have. I don't see why neither of us thought of it before. But since, at the moment, there isn't any furniture,

283

chintzy or otherwise, in this future sitting room of yours, let's use our bedroom for one, shall we? I've turned out all the lights downstairs and there's something I want to talk to you about."

"You haven't had bad news, have you?" she asked quickly, as he put his arm around her and guided her toward an easy chair.

"Well, I don't suppose it could be called good. We were told at drill tonight that the National Guard's to be inducted into the Army."

"Does that mean war—war for the United States?"

"Not necessarily. That is, I don't think so. But it certainly means the international situation is getting worse instead of better. With the exception of married men, the members of the First Corps Cadets are instructed to report for medical examinations on their next drill night. Married men may withdraw from the Corps if they want to before the others go to Camp Edwards for intensive training, prior to being shipped off somewhere else."

"And that's what you wanted to talk to me about?"

"Yes, darling. I want to know how you feel about having me withdraw."

"How do you feel?"

"I'd feel terribly ashamed to do it. It isn't as if you were dependent on what I earn for support. You've got plenty to live on. And it isn't as if— well, as if we had a family. I think when there are children—"

Suddenly he saw those empty rooms at the rear as Emily had seen them, suddenly he realized her need for making them less vacant, even if she did so in a seemingly frivolous or futile fashion. Children gave a purpose to marriage which no unfruitful union possessed; they might even justify a man's desire to remain at home, as long as possible, though his country was preparing for war. But without children. . . .

"Of course you know I'm going to tell you to go. Of course you know I'd be ashamed too, if you didn't. You're right in saying it might be different if you had to support me or if we had a family. But since you don't, since we haven't—"

There was a break in her voice. He knew it was not because she was afraid of what might happen to him; it was because she was afraid that she would never have a child. He put his arms around her, comforting her, as he had done so many times before, telling her, as he had told her so many times before, that it was too soon to give up hope—and knowing, as he did so, that his words carried no conviction, because he had given up hope himself.

The army doctor, who was making one chest examination after another, laid down his stethoscope and scribbled a few lines on the card, labeled FIELD, ROGER, that lay before him.

"You say you've been subject to bronchitis, Sergeant?"

"Well, I've had it several times—a number of times."

"You've been seriously ill with it?"

284

"I wouldn't have said 'seriously.' But then, of course I'm not a physician. I wouldn't know whether that was the right word. I can ask my own doctor."

"It won't be necessary. I'm sorry to tell you that when I examined you the râles were quite pronounced."

"The râles?"

"Yes. Abnormal sounds accompanying the normal respiratory murmur."

"But those aren't serious, either, are they?"

"They can become so at any moment. You quite obviously have chronic bronchiectasis. There's also a slight heart murmur in addition to this respiratory murmur. I shan't be able to pass you."

"You mean—I can't go to Camp Edwards with the others?"

"I'm sorry," the doctor said again. But he was already glancing toward the next man. There were a great many young men to examine and it was already very late. He was extremely tired. He had put in a hard day, as had all the other specialists.

Roger had put in a hard day too. He had been working intensively on the Jerry Donovan case, in which he had his new bill of complaint almost ready to file. He knew he would put in still harder days, while he continued to work on it. No one would suggest that he was not well enough to do that. And he would not be able to talk the case over with Pell any longer. Because Pell would be at Camp Edwards. He had been examined before Roger and had been passed without question.

Chapter 24

PELL CAME UP to Boston several times during the weeks that he was at Camp Edwards and dropped into the office to see Roger. He never stayed long, partly because he realized that Roger was hard pressed for time, and partly because he himself did not have much time to spare. He seemed to be in good health and in good spirits and his uniform set off his natural good looks to great advantage. From Camp Edwards, his outfit was ordered to Camp Hulen and it was some months before he returned to Boston on brief leave.

In the meantime, Brian, like every other man of his age, had of course registered for the draft, but he had viewed the requirement almost airily; it was ten to one, he told Roger, that his number would never come up and that, if it did, this would only mean he would have a few weeks of pleasant outdoor life, such as David had previously enjoyed at Camp Smith and Roger and Pell at Camp Edwards. He had always pretended to be somewhat sniffily superior to their duty in the field; while he was admittedly too young to be old, he was also too old to be young, and boy scouting was for boys. He was a man now, doing a man's work, which, as far as he was concerned, was legal work; though it might have been medical work or clerical work or any other kind of adult male work, if he had made a different choice of a profession; and then, of course, there were politics on the side. . . .

As a matter of fact, though Brian thought he was entirely sincere in referring to politics as a side issue, he had been preoccupied with them since early fall when he had been nominated in the primaries. His registration for the draft had not affected his campaign and he had won, hands down, against a burly tavern keeper. In January, he took his seat in the General Court and, from then on, his presence in the office was necessarily subject to the interruptions caused by his attendance at the legislative sessions of the House. The senior partners and Cyrus Fletcher could not effectively object to this course of action on Brian's part, partly because, in spite of his many absences, he continued to handle, with brilliance and dispatch, the corporate cases which had been entrusted to him and partly because there was no one available to take his place, or even to supplement his intermittent labors. Other established lawyers had their hands full too, because, one by one, their own juniors were leaving them, either to enter government departments in Washington or officers' training schools; and the new crop of legal talent was swallowed up in much the same way. Not only all promising graduates of both major and minor law schools, but practically all those whose qualifications were far more doubtful, were scattering to the four winds, instead of gratefully remaining fixtures in Boston. They should be thankful, Mr. Cutter told Mr. Mills irritably, whenever the latter complained about Brian's breezy ways, that they could be sure of anyone who was efficient and who was not crazy to be off here, there or anywhere.

Sometimes, when Mr. Mills' grumbles became growls, Mr. Cutter added they had also better admit that Roger Field was turning out to be a good deal more capable than they had originally had any reason to expect. He had brought in the Sears account as well as the Forbes account, and neither of those was small potatoes; he was looking after any number of minor cases successfully, without asking for help or advice from anyone; and he was not doing at all badly with some major ones—for instance, the Jerry Donovan case, which was now ready for hearing. Besides, no one could say that Field was not a worker; he did not even go out to lunch any more, unless he were entertaining a client, now that De Lucca's absence had automatically put a stop to those long talkfests the two used to have at Durgin-Park. He ordered milk and sandwiches sent in from Schrafft's and had a snack whenever he saw the chance; this saved him a whole hour at noon. And it was generally he who shut up shop at night. Evidently his wife—and his servants—did not care what time dinner was served.

This was quite true. Emily's attitude throughout this trying period was sympathetic, understanding and helpful; and, to a remarkable degree, she had the co-operation of her household staff. She had laid the situation before Deirdre, the morning after Roger had come home with every vestige of color gone from his face, and had told his wife, in a tone which he managed to keep steady only by making his statement brief, that he had not passed his physical examination and that this meant his rejection by the Army. And Deirdre, after stooping over to stroke her cat, Kilkenny, and then wiping her eyes with the corner of her apron, had said sure, it would be hard on the lad to see his friend Mr. de Lucca go off without him and all and all, especially now that his friend, Mr. Collins, was that busy he couldn't play much poker any more; but still he was man enough to offer it up.

"His disappointment, you mean, Deirdre?"

"What else? You can offer up a kick in the teeth or a thrust in the heart the same as you would a pain in the chest, can't you now? From what you've been telling me, Himself has got all three to offer up."

287

"He doesn't have pain in his chest, Deirdre—that is, except when he has those bad attacks of bronchitis, every year or so. But it seems those sounds the doctor hears—"

"And if those sounds the doctor hears are that bad Mr. Field can't go down on the Cape with his friend, then will you tell me this please: how is it those same noises don't keep him from going to the office every day of his life and toiling and moiling until all hours and coming home looking like the shade of himself?"

"It isn't supposed to be as hard on a man, physically, to work in an office as to train at a camp, Deirdre."

"But they let him go to the camp before!"

"Yes. But then it was just—well, not just fun exactly, I don't mean that. They took it seriously, just as they really drilled, down at the armory. But they didn't do it with the idea that they were getting ready for war. Now I'm afraid they will. I'm afraid the training's going to be a good deal harder—a good deal more intensive. And the army doctors who were examining the men must know this; they have to rule out the ones who couldn't stand up under hard training."

"And are these doctors going to say just how many hours in the day and just how many days in the week a man who can't stand up under training at a camp can stand up under work at an office?"

"No, Deirdre, I'm afraid they aren't. I wish they were. But wishing won't make it come true. So all you and I can do is to make sure, when Mr. Field does get home from the office, no matter how late it is, we won't give him the feeling that he's put us to any trouble. Because he would worry if he thought he had. And we've got to spare him all the worry we can. We've got to make him comfortable and keep him contented."

"We can make him comfortable by giving him a hot, tasty dinner and getting him into a nice soft bed, with a pretty young wife to keep him company," Deirdre said decisively. "But whether that'll keep him contented, now that his friend's gone, is something else again, and that you know very well, Mrs. Field. He'll have to offer it up, as I said before, or he'll be eating his heart out. But that I'll do my share to keep him comfortable, that you know too, though I take it very kindly you've talked to me the way you have about his trouble and all and all. As for the girls, if either of them lets a yip out of her about extra work or late hours, it's the back of my hand she'll be getting."

"If you think a slight raise in wages—"

"Well now, I never was one to say no to an extra dollar, nor any of mine, as far as I know. You'll do as you think best about that. But it's my guess that Dolly and Ellie won't be after money the way they'll be after men of their own, before it's too late to get any, or maybe a different kind of job—one that would get them out of nice clean uniforms and into dirty overalls, most likely," Deirdre concluded, with a touch of scorn. "But we'll cross that bridge when we come to it. If there's nothing more on your mind right now, Mrs. Field, I'll be seeing to that galantine of chicken we were talking about for Mr. Field's dinner, before we got on the subject of doctors and wars and the like, bad cess to them."

There was nothing else Emily felt she should say to Deirdre at the moment; in fact, having made her point about the late dinners, Emily was impatient to be on her way to Louisburg Square. She had seen less than usual of her grandmother lately, and she had missed the tête-à-tête luncheons with the old lady, which had come to mean as much to her, in a different way, as the luncheons with Pell at Durgin-Park had come to mean to Roger. Early the previous spring, Old Mrs. Forbes had decided to put her house in Manchester-by-the-Sea at the disposal of two English friends, Lady Sylvia Hayworth and Lady Violet Kendall, on the condition that they would take charge, not only of their own grandchildren, whom they had brought to Boston with them, but of as many other refugee children as the place would accommodate. The English ladies, who were sisters, had readily agreed to the arrangement and it had worked out extremely well; but this was due not only to their good will and good management, but to the keen oversight of Old Mrs. Forbes—whose remarkable executive ability showed no signs of diminishing with the years —and also to her substantial underwriting. Now the number of English children who had been sent, unaccompanied, to Boston by desperate parents was so great that the house at Manchester-by-the-Sea, spacious though this was, could not begin to hold all whom the English ladies wished to take under their wing, and for whom Old Mrs. Forbes would have been glad to provide shelter, food, fuel and clothing. Consequently, she had decided that the place in Dublin must be used for a similar purpose, and since no more English ladies were available, she saw no reason why her daughter, Eleanor, who had not occupied herself intensively with either British War Relief or American Friends of France should not at least look after a few quiet, harmless children. In vain Eleanor protested that no children were quiet and very few harmless; they were by nature noisy and destructive. Old Mrs. Forbes kept welcoming more and more English refugees to Dublin, where she herself had spent the major part of the summer, leaving Eleanor in charge of them during the course of her own occasional excursions to town. She had been considering the adaptability of the house on Louisburg Square for still more refugees, when the question arose as to its possible suitability for other purposes. The number of Bostonians who had both large houses and ample domestic staffs at their disposal was diminishing with almost as much rapidity as the number of promising young lawyers; and when Emily came into her grandmother's library, after her talk with Deirdre, she found that Old Mrs. Forbes was, at first, disposed to discuss the relative merits of taking in half a dozen more children and of providing bountiful dinners to inductees on several stated days every week, rather than to listen attentively to Emily's personal problems and comment wisely on them. In the face of her granddaughter's monosyllabic answers, however, she soon realized that Emily's visit had a definite purpose and adroitly shifted from one subject to another.

"Apparently, a good many changes have been taking place at Cutter, Mills while I've been in New Hampshire," she said briskly. "Roger wrote me that Elliot Berkeley had decided to hunt around Middleburg instead of around Hamilton for the present. Of course Roger didn't put it just that way, but that's what it amounts to. I knew Elliot would find some excuse for fading out of the local scene after Priscilla turned him down. I don't think it ever occurred to him that she wouldn't jump at the chance of marrying him. He's regarded himself as the Greatest Catch in New England Waters for so long, and been so encouraged in this belief, that it isn't strange he should sulk in his stables for a while. But he'll get over it."

"It never occurred to me that he *had* proposed to Priscilla."

"I've always thought you were a reasonably intelligent girl, Emily, considering the limitations of your upbringing. But the number of things that don't occur to you is appalling. It doesn't take psychic powers to see that Priscilla is the sort of girl who gets a good many proposals. She's no siren, but she has the bounce of a rubber ball and men like that. She's turned down Stanley Lyman and Elliot Berkeley and several others I know of, which means there must be at least as many others I don't know of. But that's neither here nor there, as far as Cutter, Mills is concerned. I dare say that bold-faced young Irishman, who has plenty of bounce himself, will do very well in Elliot's place. He probably won't devote any more time to politics than Elliot did to horses; and though I've heard he's a little on the thirsty side too, I doubt if he'll let a bottle of Bushmill's stand in the way of his progress, the way Elliot so often did with a case of bourbon. Brian Collins is too ambitious to make a mistake of that kind; he wants to climb. One disadvantage of starting on the top rung of the ladder is that there's no incentive to climb any higher."

"I wouldn't have said Elliot Berkeley was on the top rung of the ladder."

"Wrong again, which makes twice in one morning and that's too often. He was on the top rung of the only ladder he cared about—he was born with a golden bit in his mouth and his dam and his sire were both registered thoroughbreds. Law was just a side issue for him. And it isn't for this Collins boy, keen as he is to get from the State House on Beacon Hill to the United States Capitol. . . . Well, we're still not catching up very fast with the news. Roger also wrote me that David Salomont has preceded Brian Collins to Washington, in a somewhat different capacity from that to which the latter aspires."

"Yes, but I don't believe Roger's written you the latest news, because he only heard it himself last night. He was turned down when he took his physical examination at the armory."

"Turned down! Why on earth should he have been turned down, I'd like to know? He's a perfectly healthy young man, barring an occasional cold, and when you can show me a Bostonian, except yourself and myself, who doesn't sneeze and bark half the year, you'll show me a white blackbird."

"Well, the army doctor seemed to think those colds were more serious than we'd realized. He said Roger had chronic bronchiectasis, whatever that may mean. He wouldn't pass him. So now Pellegrino de Lucca, who was passed without the slightest question, is starting straight off for Camp Edwards and Roger is left holding the bag at Cutter, Mills."

"Without anyone to help him except that Lyman boy?"

"Mr. Mills says it isn't possible to get anyone to help him."

"Cleophas Mills always has some sort of an excuse for not doing anything he doesn't want to do. He thinks he can get away with giving one young man the work of four and pocketing the equivalent of the extra salaries. I'll have a talk with him myself and I warrant that when I get through with him he'll see things in a different light. Don't you worry about Roger. . . . I suppose you are worrying about Roger?"

"Of course I'm worrying about Roger. He hasn't had a real vacation since we went to Europe—just those weeks at camp for duty in the field, which didn't do any good, as things have turned out, and those short visits in Dublin, when he spent hours every day going over farm figures."

"Why don't you and he go to Hollyhock Hill for a little while? Elizabeth and Mark will be leaving there pretty soon, and you and Roger could have it to yourselves. Heaven knows that must be restful, from all I've heard. As you know, I've never seen the place myself and never want to. But you and Roger have always liked it there."

"Yes, we used to, very much. But it had changed somehow, the last time we went there. I don't think it's especially suited for house parties."

"I wasn't suggesting you should have a house party. I was suggesting—"

"I know. But I think of it now in connection with a house party, because there was one the last time we were there. And I think of it in connection with Mark as well as Elizabeth. It was different when there was only Liz to consult. They may be intending to go there for some week ends during the fall—they both love the autumn coloring. Or they may be intending to loan it to friends. I don't like to ask for it, so soon again —you know I only did before to please Priscilla. And I made a lot of trouble when I was there over New Year's."

Emily rose and walked over to the bay window. Then she stood for some minutes looking down on the little park, where a few leaves had already turned from green to gold and a few more had already fallen on the grass. Her grandmother made no attempt to call her back to the fireside. Old Mrs. Forbes did not pretend to have psychic powers herself; but she had felt certain for a long time that a sprained ankle, a bad storm and the inevitable disintegration of a house party's initial hilarity were not alone responsible for Emily's unenthusiastic and uncommunicative attitude regarding the holiday outing which had begun so auspiciously. Not that she seemed in any way to begrudge Elizabeth her happiness. On the contrary, Emily had insisted that there should be no references to an "autumnal" romance and that the wedding should not be shorn of any of the splendor which would have automatically surrounded a younger bride. It was due to her insistence that Elizabeth had been married in an ancestral wedding gown, made of embroidered crepe, now ivory colored with age, which had been brought from China on a clipper ship, and all the rose point lace which the "fabulous Evelina" had worn herself, but which had been adjudged too sumptuous, in its entirety, for a modern girl of Emily's type. Thanks to her, Elizabeth had presented an unforgettable picture of old-time elegance and dignity; and the ceremony, which had taken place by candlelight in Old Mrs. Forbes' drawing room, transformed for the occasion into a chapel, had been one of equal beauty and distinction. Emily herself, dressed in rose-colored satin of the same period of the China crepe, had been second only to the bride as the center of attraction, not only in her role of matron of honor during the service, but as the motivating spirit throughout the reception which followed; her grandmother had watched her with admiration untinged by envy, feeling, for the first time, that her own power and personality would not be buried with her, but would survive in her favorite grandchild. Furthermore, it was Emily who had made the arrangements for her aunt's delightful bridal trip to South America, while everyone else was lamenting that Europe was out of the question; it was Emily who had welcomed the newly wedded couple to her own house on their return, and who brought her grandmother the great news that Elizabeth was already "expecting," before Elizabeth could summon courage to do so herself. ("A case of nine months and ten minutes if I ever heard of one," Old Mrs. Forbes had said succinctly; but she had been highly pleased, just the same.) It was even Emily who had written to the Dean at Bryn Mawr, explaining the situation, and saying that while naturally Mrs. Merriweather would keep on with her courses until midyears if the college authorities would like to have her, on the other hand, she would understand perfectly if. . . . And it was Emily who had made all the arrangements for Elizabeth's confinement, which, it had been agreed, after a family council, should take place in Boston; because when all was said and done, Elizabeth was not in her very first youth, and if there should be complications, which of course no one foresaw, there was no hospital on earth to compare with the Boston Lying-In and no doctors who could hold a candle to the obstetricians who staffed it. (For a long while, Old Mrs. Forbes had held out stubbornly, saying she would greatly prefer that the baby should be born in the third story front room of her house on Louisburg Square, as Emily had been, and as all her own children had been, except, of course, the ones who had been born abroad; and again it was Emily who had persuaded her grandmother that nowadays even very aristocratic babies, the offspring of parents whose social standing was unimpeachable, were born in hospitals.)

While Emily stood looking out on the little park and the falling leaves, Old Mrs. Forbes sat thinking of all this and told herself again that there was certainly something about that house party which had never been explained to her. Emily's attitude toward Hollyhock Hill was entirely at variance with her general attitude toward Elizabeth and Mark; and Old Mrs. Forbes, who was not without a normal share of curiosity, would have given a good deal to solve the mystery. However, she sat, twisting her signet ring around on her finger and asking no questions, and finally Emily turned away from the window and came back to the fireplace.

"Besides, I couldn't persuade Roger to take a vacation right now," she said, quite as if there had been no break in the conversation. "He knows he's needed at the office and that's all there is to it."

"Well, if that's the way he feels about it," agreed Old Mrs. Forbes. It was seldom she said anything which she knew to be so inadequate. "But don't worry about Roger any more than you can help," she went on. "He'll be safe at home anyway, and what's more, you can be thankful you won't have anyone else to worry about, if we do get into this war. You haven't a brother or even a cousin, of draft age. No one you care about will be in danger—"

She stopped suddenly. Emily had turned swiftly and gone back to the window again. But not before her grandmother had caught a glimpse of her face. . . .

The signet ring slipped from Old Mrs Forbes' finger and fell to the floor. Emily heard the slight, sharp sound that it made as it struck the hearthstone. She turned once more and saw it lying there and also saw her grandmother stooping over, trying to retrieve it, and failing because of her lameness. Emily crossed the room and picked it up and when she returned it to her grandmother, the old lady replaced it carefully on her finger and sank back in her chair. Then she raised both hands and drew the girl down beside her.

"There," she said, "there, my dear. Tell me all about it. You'll feel better afterward. And you needn't be afraid that I won't understand."

Chapter 25

OLD MRS. FORBES habitually made her lameness the pretext for urging the Proprietors of Louisburg Square to hold their annual meetings at her house, undeterred by the fact that she knew her neighbors must be well aware of the many activities she pursued in spite of this handicap. As the hostess on such an occasion, she could do more to direct the tenor of the gathering and control its length than she could as a guest; she could also choose the type of refreshment to be served, when the disturbing questions which agitated the Proprietors had been settled and—with the exception of Sister Mary Theresa, who returned to St. Margaret's Convent, which she represented at the meeting, immediately thereafter—these ladies and gentlemen relaxed while spending a social hour in each other's company. Old Mrs. Forbes realized that no one would be at ease while deciding whether the cobblestoned pavement should be replaced by modern surfacing; whether an attempt should be made to persuade the City Council to clear the Square with a snow plow, even though it was not classified as a Boston street; or whether the park should be equipped with children's sandboxes and seats for the aged and improved by brick walks and a fountain. But when these questions had been voted upon and, as far as possible, dismissed, there was nothing, in her opinion, which did so much to efface the rancorous memory of divided viewpoint as a bountiful buffet, in which the vintage champagnes which reclined in her cellar and the old rum which was stored in her attic both played a prominent part. She had always maintained that the reason no amicable agreement had been reached, regarding the number of cars each owner could park in the Square, was because this matter had been discussed at a meeting where ginger ale, scantily spiked with very inferior whisky, and crackers, spread with rat cheese, had constituted the only offerings!

Nevertheless, now that she was regularly entertaining selectees from Camp Devens three times a week, she could not logically complain when a meeting was called for one of these nights, and her next-door neighbors, Mr. and Mrs. Drummond, pointed out that the dear boys would not be through dinner at the usual time of gathering, which was eight o'clock.

The Drummonds were sure that Mrs. Forbes would not wish her guests to hurry over their meal, or to be deprived of the pleasure they found in staying on afterward for cards and dancing. Leaving Emily and Roger, whom she often pressed into service, in charge of the selectees on the night of the meeting, she made her disgruntled way, with Doris' help, to the Drummonds' house, saying that she would telephone when she was ready to return.

The selectees and the young ladies who had been invited to help entertain them were still making merry in the drawing room when the call came through and Emily, who took it, instantly realized that her grandmother was about to leave the meeting of the Proprietors in an even greater state of indignation than she had gone to it. Accordingly, Emily whispered to Roger that she thought he had better go for the old lady himself, instead of sending Doris, and that she would await their return in the library. Then, excusing herself to the selectees and their partners, who nodded toward her absent-mindedly without paying the slightest attention to what she was saying, she went up to the library, and assured herself that the fire was burning brightly and that there was just the right amount of light in the room. She realized how wise she had been to avert further cause for displeasure on the part of Old Mrs. Forbes, when she heard her grandmother sputtering as she painfully mounted the stairway and vehemently interrupting Roger while he sought to soothe her. When she finally sank down in her thronelike chair, still wrapped in her ancient sable cloak, she became actually explosive.

"Whoever decided that the owners of the houses on this Square should maintain it for their mutual advantage, and placed its management and upkeep in the hands of a committee, with power to act for all, certainly lacked prophetic vision!" she exclaimed. "Of all the garrulous, stupid, silly human beings that it has ever been my misfortune to encounter—"

"Why, Grandmamma, you've said yourself, over and over again, that Louisburg Square was the last stronghold of the aristocracy. You've said nothing would induce you to live anywhere else. You've said you thought those old City Fathers who organized the Committee of Proprietors a hundred years ago did a much better job of planning for local upkeep and policing than any present-day politicians would ever dream up. You've said you thought Mr. Dorr was an excellent Chairman of the Committee, and that even if he weren't, at the end of a year—"

"Don't stand there telling me all the things I've said before, as if you were reciting them out of a book. I don't care what I've said before. I'm telling you now that if I ever had to sit through another session like the one tonight, I should certainly have an apoplectic stroke. From here on, the meetings will be held in this house, selectees or no selectees!"

"They seem to have taken it over, rather completely, for the moment," Roger remarked, as loud shouts of laughter, supplemented by raucous strains of jazz on the radio, reverberated through the house. He went over

295

to the folding doors leading into the hall and closed them carefully; but the sounds of conviviality still penetrated to the library. "However, you know you're not obliged to keep on having them here, Grandma," he said. "You didn't agree to do it for any specified length of time."

It was only a short while since he had begun to call her Grandma and hitherto her expression had betrayed her pleasure over the fact that he no longer stood in awe of her, whenever she heard him speak to her in this way; it was less stilted and somehow sounded more affectionate than the form of address which her own grandchildren had been taught to use, and she liked it. But now, if she noticed it, she did not show this.

"I'll keep on having those boys here as long as there's any need of it," she retorted. "And, judging by the latest news from abroad, I should say that might be quite a few years. But I'll see to it, that hereafter, Ralph Dorr doesn't call a meeting of the Proprietors on the same night that I'm having selectees to dinner."

"Well, I think that might be a good idea," Roger said, still speaking soothingly. "But you haven't told us yet what upset you so."

"I was upset to start with. I didn't want to go to the Drummonds' house. I knew just how it would be, ginger ale with a thimbleful of bad whisky and—"

"Yes, but before you got to the ginger ale and the bad whisky—"

"Well, I certainly thought I was on time. I still think so. The Drummonds must keep their clocks fast. Anyway, when I got to their house, there was only one chair left, a very uncomfortable one at that, between Sister Mary Theresa and Mrs. Putnam!"

Involuntarily, Roger and Emily glanced at each other and then glanced away again. The vision which Old Mrs. Forbes had conjured up of herself, dressed as usual in rich brocade and overloaded with jewels, between Mrs. Putnam, who was doubtless clad in something scanty and smart, and Sister Mary Theresa, cloaked in gray and veiled in black, was too vivid for them to share without visible merriment.

"Then, no sooner had we settled on appropriations for upkeep during the coming year," Old Mrs. Forbes went on, "than Mrs. Putnam said she thought it would be a good thing if there could be more wildlife in Louisburg Square."

This time Roger took refuge in coughing, as he had when his father-in-law and his mother-in-law began their heated argument regarding the relative merits of an outfit from Miss Ruby's and a lot at Mount Auburn. Old Mrs. Forbes was not deceived by the cough, but neither was she placated by it.

"I hope you'll put it down to both my credit and Sister Mary Theresa's that neither of us told Mrs. Putnam, *sotto voce*, that she herself was supplying all the wildlife Louisburg Square could stand," Old Mrs. Forbes said, with something like a snort. "She went on to explain that what she meant by wildlife was squirrels."

"Squirrels!" Roger and Emily exclaimed together.

"Yes. A special kind of brown, Spanish squirrel. She thought we ought to import a pair and then let nature take its course."

This time Roger neither averted his gaze nor coughed. He laughed outright and Emily laughed with him.

"It's all very well for you to treat it like a joke. In my opinion, it's no joking matter when a group of adults, assembled for business purposes, can't find anything more important to discuss than squirrels. And Mrs. Putnam's suggestion about the brown squirrels from Spain only marked the *beginning* of the discussion. Mr. Drummond immediately said he couldn't help feeling such an importation would be a great extravagance. You know he's the one who always serves ginge—"

"Yes, we know all about that, Grandma. Did he have a counter-suggestion?"

"I should say he did. He wanted to know why we couldn't just buy a bag of peanuts and mark a trail with those from the Common to Louisburg Square. He said we'd have all the squirrels we wanted here, in no time! And Mrs. Putnam said yes, but they wouldn't be *brown!* They wouldn't be *Spanish!* They'd be just *Common* squirrels. And everyone roared, as if her silly pun were the wittiest thing that had ever been heard."

Roger and Emily, who were also "roaring," attempted no other immediate response. "So the committee eventually voted to import the brown, Spanish squirrels?" Emily inquired at last, wiping her eyes.

"No, thank heaven, it didn't. I've always thought that Mrs. Dorr was a good deal of a bird-brain, but I must admit that, this time, she saved the day. She suddenly gave a small shriek, and I thought she had seen a mouse or something, when I heard her asking the chairman—her husband—if he had forgotten that two thousand crocus bulbs had recently been planted at either end of the park, and if he didn't know that squirrels—*all kinds of squirrels*—ate crocus bulbs!"

Old Mrs. Forbes sank back on her thronelike chair, at last loosening her sable wrap. "So then *I* said, 'Well, of course that settles it. We can't have any squirrels in Louisburg Square.' And everyone agreed. But if it hadn't been for Mrs. Dorr and her crocuses, that committee would still be talking about squirrels. And afterward, no one was in the mood to discuss anything serious. The question of whether we should support the Beacon Hill Association and other civic groups didn't even come up. Now if the meeting had only been here, I could have spoken to Mr. Dorr beforehand and reminded him how important it was we should talk about that. It was sidetracked last year too. And as it was, I couldn't catch his eye. I couldn't make him hear me. He's failing very fast. We certainly should have a new chairman. But of course nothing was done about that, either."

"It's a shame, Grandma. I don't wonder you're upset. You're right—it would be better if the meetings could be here. We'll have to see about arranging it that way next year. . . . Yes, Pearson?"

The aged butler had opened the folding doors so quietly that Old Mrs. Forbes had not heard him, though no one would have ventured to suggest that perhaps she herself might be getting deaf. Pearson acknowledged Roger's question with a bow, but his answer was addressed to the chatelaine he had served so faithfully for nearly fifty years.

"If you please, madam, Mrs. Field is wanted on the telephone."

"What did you say, Pearson? Mrs. Field?"

"Yes, madam."

"Did you ask who was calling?"

"Yes, madam. It was Mr. Merriweather. It seems he was speaking from the hospital and—"

Emily leaped up and rushed across the library to the instrument which was conveniently placed on the big desk, though no bell rang there. She picked up the receiver and spoke breathlessly.

"Yes, Mark. Yes, this is Emily. . . . Oh, Mark how wonderful! Yes, she's right here. I'll tell her instantly. . . . It does? You have? Don't go away, I know she'll want to call you back. . . . Elizabeth has a baby boy," she said, turning from the telephone. "Born about an hour ago. She was hardly sick at all—they didn't even have time to let you know she was on her way to the hospital. He weighs nearly eight pounds—not quite, but nearly. And they've named him Archibald Forbes after Grandpapa—that is, they'd like to, if you approve. Of course they'd call him Archie, or maybe Forbes. You want to talk to Mark yourself, don't you, Grandmamma? Wait, I'll bring the telephone right to you. The cord's plenty long enough."

Old Mrs. Forbes took the instrument with hands that trembled a little. Emily noticed that her grandmother's hands were not beautiful any more, that the joints were becoming enlarged and the nails misshapen. But they were powerful hands still; they carried the weight of their rings well and it was seldom that they shook. The fact that they were shaking now betrayed no weakness, only great emotion.

"Well, Mark," Old Mrs. Forbes was saying, and her voice also shook a little, "well, you certainly have taken me by surprise. I was expecting that we'd all be in a state of suspense for several days, worried to death about Elizabeth and unable to dismiss her suffering from our minds. What do you mean, they don't do things that way any more? Women still have babies, don't they? At least you say Elizabeth's just had one. . . . Oh, is that so? We'll discuss it later. . . . If she's had such an easy time, I should think she could be moved over here pretty promptly. She can? Why, yes, I'm pleased to hear it. I'm very much pleased. I'll see that everything's prepared for her right away. And of course I'm pleased about the name, though I don't know that the poor child will be. It never occurred to Sue and Sherman to name either of their sons after his grandfather—naturally it wouldn't. I'll see about having a porringer marked immediately. What's that? You think he won't need a porringer for a while yet? In our family, Mark, we always order a porringer as soon as a child is born—lots of them say the first taste they can remember is a mixture of oatmeal and silver polish. If it's a boy we enter him at Groton then and there—not that we've ever thought Dr. Peabody would make any difficulties for us. Well, give my love to Elizabeth. And congratulations! Good night, good night!"

She replaced the receiver and handed the instrument back to Emily. Then she looked around her—at the book-lined walls, at the long, richly draped windows, at the great Persian rug on the floor and at the portrait of herself, when she was young and beautiful, hanging above the mantel.

"Another Archibald Forbes in this house!" she said slowly. "Well, he'll have a goodly heritage." She paused and looked around her again and Emily knew that she was seeing not only her immediate surroundings; in her mind's eye, she was visualizing everything in the house from the hand-blown bottles, filled with mellow rum, in the attic, to the great bins of vintage wines in the cellar. Finally she reached for her cane, and, waving away Roger's helping hand, she made her way over to the window and stood looking out of it, not almost unseeingly, as Emily had done six months earlier, but with observant pride. "It's a good thing we Proprietors haven't given those scalawags down at the State House a chance to spoil this Square," she said, in a tone of great satisfaction. "If we had, we wouldn't have been able to keep it the way it is for the children who are coming along. The next time we have a meeting, I'm going to vote for those sandboxes. And I'm sorry I said what I did about the brown, Spanish squirrels. I'm sorry we're not going to have them, whether they eat crocuses or not. A little boy would have liked to watch squirrels in the Square when he stood like this, looking out of the window!"

Ten days later Elizabeth was discharged from Richardson House with little Archie and for the next month Old Mrs. Forbes was in the seventh heaven of delight. Not that she admitted this; on the contrary, she constantly voiced distrust and disapproval of the latest methods in the care and feeding of both new-made mothers and newborn babies. Overjoyed as she was to have Elizabeth installed in the third story front bedroom, she did not think her daughter should have even "dangled her feet over the side of the bed to test her strength," much less have moved from one place to another, so soon after she had given birth to a child. She was gratified that Archie did not have to be a bottle-fed baby, but when she learned that breast feedings were soon to be supplemented with tomato juice, she declared that none should ever be given to the poor defenseless infant in her house; she would not be responsible for seeing him doubled up with colic. Elizabeth's decision to take him home to Hanover, when he was less than six weeks old, raised her dark suspicions. In spite of her daughter's assurance that she was quite equal to taking up the reins of housekeeping again, and that she did not think it was fair to deprive Mark of the pleasure he took in his son—whom he had been able to see, so far, only on week ends—Old Mrs. Forbes was convinced that her ultimatum about the tomato juice was responsible for the untimely departure. She said all she could to prevent it, stressing the severity of the New Hampshire climate at that season, and hinting darkly that Elizabeth would lose her milk if she undertook so much; then what would happen, with summer coming on? It was ten to one they would not be able to find a formula which would agree with Archie. Besides, Old Mrs. Forbes had no confidence in the dairies around Hanover, which catered primarily to rugged athletes of college age, who could—and did—drink almost anything, though milk was not the most conspicuous single item of their choice. If the poor child were to be moved at all, he should go to her own farm at Dublin, where she could guarantee the products of the model dairy. But it would be much better for him to remain right where he was for several months more. Had Elizabeth forgotten that there should be a christening? Old Mrs. Forbes would like to make quite an event of that. Of course everyone was saying that the number of parties should be cut down, because of the European war. But a christening was not really a party; no matter how many guests you invited or how much champagne you served, it was still a religious ceremony.

Elizabeth agreed to the christening, stipulating only that it should take place somewhat sooner than her mother thought advisable, and invited her Uncle Russell and Homer Lathrop to act as godfathers and Emily as godmother. The ceremony, performed by the Episcopal Bishop of Massachusetts, took place in the baptistry of Trinity Church; and Archie covered himself with glory, both by his exemplary behavior and his engaging appearance; the ancestral christening robe, made entirely of Valenciennes lace, which had been worn by five generations of Forbes babies, was extremely becoming to him. The function, which followed the baptism and which was naturally held at Old Mrs. Forbes' house, indubitably bore a certain resemblance to a party. But no one seemed to enjoy it the less on that account and, as she said, it had a certain pious trend, since it served to bring the family together as nothing else would have done. In this respect, she was undoubtedly right; even Sue and Sherman came up from the Cape, leaving the cranberries to their fate for two days and a night. All four of Mrs. Forbes' living children were actually under her roof simultaneously, for the first time since Elizabeth's wedding, and there was no apparent friction, either between any of them and their mother, or among themselves; though Russell's attitude was characteristically pompous, though Sherman persisted in using colloquial speech, though Eleanor remained detached and superior, none of this resulted in irritation, as it often had in the past. Somehow Elizabeth's radiant happiness redeemed and transfigured it all; everyone found it impossible to be ill-natured in the face of her glowing good will.

When the last guest had departed, Old Mrs. Forbes persuaded Elizabeth to go and rest and she herself withdrew to her own ponderously furnished bedroom, summoning Emily to go with her—not, she insisted, that she was in the least tired, but the best feature of a par—that is, of any special occasion, was the fun of talking it over afterward. She permitted Doris to help her change from an elegant brocade dress to an equally elegant brocade negligee, and consented to having a few of the diamonds she had been wearing restored to her immense jewel box of tooled leather. Then, settling herself on her chaise longue, she proceeded to discuss various aspects of the christening which admittedly had very little to do with its religious significance.

"Priscilla told me she was going to Warrenton for the Gold Cup. Did she tell you?"

"No. I didn't have much chance for a talk with Priscilla. She was surrounded all the time."

"Yes, she certainly doesn't seem like the same girl she did three years ago, at your wedding. Do you remember how she looked in that yellow tulle bridesmaid's dress? As if someone had caught her and held her while she was forced into it! Of course yellow isn't her color anyway. And how she retreated into a corner and stayed there until David Salomont lured her out of it?"

"I remember. . . . Perhaps if she's going to Warrenton that means she's softening a little toward Elliot Berkeley. He's probably responsible for the invitation."

"I haven't the slightest doubt of that. But Priscilla doesn't look to me as if she were softening toward anybody. On the contrary, there's a hard line around her mouth when she isn't laughing and I don't like it. I've also noticed that her wisecracks are getting sharper all the time. They used to be amusing, but good-natured."

"Maybe she's just growing up."

"Maybe. . . . I was glad that Brian Collins came. He's good-natured, heaven knows. In fact, there's something rather likable about him."

"Yes, there is, once you get to know him."

"I overheard part of his conversation with your Uncle Russell. He'd been to the luncheon at the Chamber of Commerce when Knudsen talked about defense and labor relations here, and to the meeting at Symphony Hall, where Frank Aiken spoke about Eire's neutrality policy, from the viewpoint of De Valera's defense minister. He made quite intelligent comments on both. He seemed very well informed on national and international affairs."

"He makes it a point to be. He has his eye on Uncle Russell's seat in the Senate."

"He has? Well, Russell had better look out. A smart, up-and-coming youngster like Brian Collins might really give him some trouble. Russell's still priding himself that he was against the League of Nations."

"Brian would have been against it too, if he'd been old enough to know anything about it. He's talking about 'England's war' right now."

"He won't much longer, now that things have come to such a pass that the United States has had to send Marines to guard the American Embassy in London. You can't drop a hundred thousand bombs there, as the Germans just did, without hitting some Americans in the process; and Americans don't take kindly to being hit by German bombs. But we'll let Brian Collins find that out for himself. . . . Incidentally, I sent invitations to both David Salomont and Pellegrino de Lucca. You might tell Roger. Naturally, I knew they couldn't come. But I thought perhaps it would please him to have me do it."

"I'm sure it would, very much. He misses Pell terribly. And of course Pell couldn't possibly have come all the way from Texas. But I shouldn't think it would have been any harder for David to come from Washington than it was for Uncle Russell."

"Senators aren't subject to military discipline, Emily; soldiers are. Don't forget that. And David sent Archie a beautiful present—a complete couvert of repoussé silver; the cup is gold lined and gold bordered and the knife and fork and spoon are all gold trimmed. It must be very valuable and very old. David wrote me a nice letter too. I thought perhaps you'd like to see it. I put it over there on my desk."

A number of letters were rather carelessly piled on one side of the big blotter; the envelope with the letterhead of the War Department lay by itself in the middle of this. Emily glanced at her grandmother, whose expression was completely blank. Then she picked up David's letter and read it through slowly.

Dear Mrs. Forbes:

I can't tell you how much I appreciate the kind and thoughtful invitation to little Archie's christening. Already, in the short time since I've been in Washington, I've come to feel I'm living in another world, one of indecision and confusion. Your letter, so indicative of your deep feeling for the established order of things, so emphatic in the determination it reveals that this order shall not be changed in its essentials, or undermined by war and rumors of war, took me back, even if all too briefly, to the world you live in—one that is still stately and gracious and composed. If I had been told, a few years ago, that anything could make me homesick for Boston, I would have laughed. But your letter did exactly that. To be with you and your family on such an occasion as this christening would really be to go home again (even though Thomas Wolfe says one can't!) and I should like to do so while the old values that have survived so long, thanks to you and people like you, are still fundamentally the same. For, though I hate to say it, I know that can't be much longer. Inevitably, in spite of everything you can do, the order will change and give place to new.

Having said all this, which I hope you will not feel is too much beyond the point, I must now say, most regretfully, that I can't come. It's virtually impossible to get leave. And, even if by some near miracle I could get it, I wouldn't feel that I should. The office of the Judge Advocate General—here commonly called the JAGO—which, as you know, I left Boston to enter, is the best military assignment for a lawyer—now. But though, technically, we're not in the war yet, in my opinion it is only a matter of time before we will be, and the sooner the better, again in my opinion. We know on which side we belong and the die is cast. I don't see how we can stay out of the shooting and we're not ready for it. (One pays a great penalty for not being militaristic in a militaristic world!) So I don't want to slacken my efforts toward helping to get ready, even for a single day; and, as soon as we are ready, I want to be out of Washington and on my way 'Over There.' My chances for that will be a lot better if I can prove my usefulness here first. I know you'll understand.

Of course I'm writing you confidentially, so I may as well go a step further and say I believe you understand that there are other reasons, which have nothing to do with the war, why I think it is better for me not to come back to Boston, and, more specifically, to a family gathering in your house, right now. I've said certain good-byes and, once that's been done, it's better not to unsay them, unless and until all the circumstances connected with such farewells have changed, including the feelings of the persons involved. I'm one of those persons and my feelings haven't changed; there's still a certain tightness inside of me that hasn't had time to loosen. And, as far as I know, there's been no change in circumstances. Enough said.

I never knew Washington well before and, in some ways, it's to me a bewildering city—overgrown, overcrowded, top heavy with government bureaus, essentially unorganized and therefore becoming daily more disorganized, just when organization is most needed. Our own politicians are preoccupied with an infinite deal of nothing, when they should be fearlessly facing the issues which may mean either the salvation or the destruction of the world. (I don't mean there aren't any real statesmen that are doing just that; but they seem to me few and far between.) The British and the French are here in great numbers and more are coming every day—angling, begging and buying when they have no luck with the angling and begging. I don't blame them. I think we'd do the same if we were in their shoes. As a matter of fact, they take part of their tone from the general atmosphere—everyone here wants something and is after something, by fair means or foul. It's 'Gimme, gimme, gimme!' with very little of 'What can I give?'

I've got delightful living quarters, which is a great piece of good fortune, because there's a terrible housing shortage. But I had a mental picture, before I came here, of exactly what I wanted; so I went after it and got it. (Which is, not infrequently, the case, in my experience, when you do know what you want and do go after it!) The lovely thatched cottage of my dreams is a tiny house in Alexandria, one of a block on Lower Prince Street, that looks more like a stage setting, representing Colonial architecture, in a small southern city than the reality of such architecture in such a setting. My house, like all the others near it, is really perfect of its kind, both inside and out; and, as I have my father's old servant, Ramón, who was with me in Boston, here to look after me, I'm extremely comfortable and come home to a good dinner every night that I'm not invited out to one, which, I'm glad to say, is pretty frequently. War or no war, the Washington dinner party still reigns supreme as the greatest indoor sport. I don't need to tell you that people not only really live in their houses here, but, by preference, entertain in them too. I'm not sure whether the comparatively small number of restaurants is cause or effect. But whichever it is—and again, as I don't need to tell you—Washington is certainly not a city of restaurants, any more than it is a city of theaters. It is a city of official cocktail parties and excellent home-cooked dinners with wonderful conversation afterward and that provides all the entertainment anyone needs. It's also a city of whispering, maneuvering, tattling, declaiming— a city that's still having growing pains, that's naïve in spite of its imagined sophistication, that's beautiful in the same way an adolescent is beautiful, though he insists on pretending to a maturity and a mellowness that he hasn't achieved. And I may add, rather inconsequentially, it is a city of stenographers. These girls come from every state of the union, they have the map of America in their faces. I'm sorry for them, in a way, because they're naïve and adolescent, too, and won't admit it. And they're not having too easy a time or too wholesome a time, either. Yet, I know they wouldn't be elsewhere. Any more than I would. I'm sorry that the secretarial field was already so crowded when I got here that I couldn't find a place for a girl at Cutter, Mills who wanted terribly to come. I'm afraid she's very much disappointed and she'd be still more disappointed if she had any idea of what she missed. This is not just our capital any more. It's the capital of the world. And who wouldn't choose to be a part of world history in the making?

Well, I've rambled on long enough and probably bored you to death. (No, I don't believe I have, either. I both hope and believe you enjoyed my random comments.) Again, let me say how sorry I am—in one way! —that I can't be at the christening and how glad I am—in another!— that I'm just where I am. Under separate cover, I'm sending a small gift that I hope will please your honoree's parents, even if he himself doesn't appreciate it at present. It's another specimen of that Russian handicraft for which I know you have a certain penchant. Let's hope your excellent taste will be inherited!

My best—in the usual sense—to everyone in the family, of course. To you my sincere and devoted homage.

David Salomont.

"I thought you might be interested in it," Old Mrs. Forbes remarked, as Emily replaced the letter in its envelope without comment and laid it carefully back on the middle of the blotter. "I was."

"I was too, of course. It—it was very kind of you to ask me to come to your room, so I'd have a chance to read it."

"I asked you to my room to talk over the par— the christening." Old Mrs. Forbes said sharply. "And some other things. . . . Elizabeth persists in going to Hanover next week. But she says that, as soon as college closes, she's going to Hollyhock Hill."

"Well, I should think she would. I should think she and Mark could have a very pleasant summer there."

"No doubt. . . . She also says that she hopes you and Roger will make her a nice, long visit. I think you ought to do it. For her sake. And also for Roger's. He wants to go there too."

"Did he tell you so?"

"Of course he told me so. You don't think I'm making this up as I go along, do you? He told me so yesterday when he came here to go over my personal checkbook with me, as he does regularly four times a year now. You know about that."

"Yes, I know about that, but I didn't know about how many other things you talked about on the side."

"We talk about a good many. Roger's a good listener when I get started on something that really interests me. And he isn't a bad talker, either, when he gets started on something that really interests him. In fact, he talks well on quite a variety of subjects, and he reaches some very intelligent conclusions, because he gives careful thought first to everything he talks about, instead of just rattling along for the sake of hearing his own voice, like most young men nowadays. I may as well admit to you, Emily, that Roger is turning out to be more of a person than I expected, when I first discussed him with you. Not that I think, even now, that he'll set the world on fire. But, as you very reasonably remarked, on the occasion to which I am referring, you weren't concerned with a fiery world—then."

Emily made no reply. She could not think of one that was especially apt and Old Mrs. Forbes did not seem to expect any. Instead, she reverted to the subject previously under consideration.

"If Roger wants to go to Hollyhock Hill, Emily, I think you owe it to him. Just as much as you owe it to him to stay in town all summer, when he can't get away. You're very conscientious about that."

"I try to be conscientious about everything, Grandmamma."

"I know you do. If I didn't, I wouldn't make such a point of this. Roscoe Cutter has got to give Roger a vacation this summer. He realizes it. He kept poking the fire all the time I was talking to him, but he finally admitted it."

"I didn't know you'd talked to Mr. Cutter about a vacation for Roger."

"There are lots of things I do that you don't know about, Emily. And lots of things I've done!" Old Mrs. Forbes smiled suddenly, and Emily saw how beautiful her grandmother's face still could be, momentarily, when she smiled. But Emily also noticed, as she had the night Archie was born, that there was no beauty left in the hands, which had once been so shapely and white. They were growing gnarled, and veins bulged on the backs of them, instead of making a delicate blue tracery; the knuckles on the once-tapering, rosy-tipped fingers were enlarged, so that it was hard to get rings over them, and the nails had a brittle, lined look. These were the hands of an old woman, and while Emily sat looking at them, watching as her grandmother twisted the signet ring around on her misshapen fourth finger, the girl suddenly shivered a little. When people grew old, this meant that it would soon be time for them to die; and it came as a shock to Emily to realize that perhaps the day was not far distant when she could not go to her grandmother's room like this. And then the world would be a very different place. . . .

"I won't ask you to tell me about all the things you've done," she said, trying to speak lightly, "that is, I won't ask you about all the naughty things you've done in the past, if you'll promise not to do too many things behind my back in the present. And since you've bulldozed Mr. Cutter into giving Roger a vacation at last, and wrung an admission from Roger that he wants to go to Hollyhock Hill, I'll go there with him. I agree with you that it's very silly of me to stay away from there forever just because—"

"I didn't say anything about your being silly. I think you're fairly sensible, on the whole. But incidentally, there's something else I've been meaning to tell you—something that seems rather strange, but that happens fairly frequently: when there hasn't been a baby in a family for a long while and one finally arrives, it often has a little cousin almost before you can say Jack Robinson. Why, I knew one chit of a girl who married a man a lot older than herself—he and his brothers were all in their forties. The brothers had been married for years and their wives had never had any children. This girl had a baby right away, just like Elizabeth— and before another year was out, both those middle-aged sisters-in-law of hers had babies too. One of them had twins! You mark my words, we'll be having another christening before long."

Mr. Cutter did not go back on his word. He had promised old Mrs. Forbes that he would give Roger Field a vacation and he knew he had to do so. But he had not said exactly when this vacation would be granted and in June, he observed, with satisfaction, that Roger, while attending faithfully to office routine, was also working so intensively on the Jerry

Donovan case that any interruption would really have been unfair to him. This case had developed in numerous unexpected ways: having started out as a suit for Jerry's cut in the profits, Roger had next found it advisable to bring a stockholders' suit, as he had told Pell over the luncheon table at Durgin-Park. Then, realizing how long imminent trial and ultimate appeal might take, and how little chance there would be of a satisfactory settlement even then, he made an effort, which proved successful, to organize the small stockholders of the Somerville Electric Appliance Company. The second suit had roused them, and, instead of submissively handing their proxies to the officials as heretofore, they turned them over to Roger. By the time the meeting opened, he controlled more than half the voting shares, and thus could make Jerry Donovan an officer of the new board, and himself its clerk.

The revolutionary meeting had taken place late in the season, because of several attempts on the part of the company's previous management to have it postponed; and its aftermath, while highly gratifying to the new board, involved Roger in the necessity of winding up superfluous subsidiaries, closing out unprofitable lines and preparing for the negotiation of war contracts. July and August, as well as June, were consumed in this manner; and it was not until just before Labor Day that the chaos had been resolved to such order that Roger felt the general situation could do without his legal supervision for a few weeks. When he so advised Mr. Cutter, the senior partner could find no sound reason for disagreement.

Roger was really glad it turned out like that, he told Emily; didn't she remember they had hoped, two years before, that they might get to Hollyhock Hill for Labor Day? Then they had been disappointed. Well, now they would make up for it.

He sincerely believed this when he said it; but this time it was Roger who spoke with conviction and Emily who knew he was mistaken; their positions were reversed from the period after their first quarrel. He had visualized them as recapturing that sense of peace and detachment which had pervaded them both in the early summer, when they first went to Hollyhock Hill together; she realized that the peace of the world had been rent asunder, and that there could be no complete peace for anyone again, until this was restored to those who had suffered from the loss of it. Neither could there be detachment, for the same reason. To all appearances the old brick house facing the quiet valley and the eternal hills beyond was as remote from tumult as ever; but a subtle change had come over its atmosphere, which betrayed its tiny part in a tangled pattern. Mark and Elizabeth, instead of being wholly absorbed in each other and their baby, read the newspapers avidly, listened to the radio intently and discussed their duty with troubled faces. Elizabeth had remained at Bryn Mawr until midyears, because the college authorities had pleaded so insistently for more time to fill her place; but she had said that her resignation at that time was final, that her husband would not countenance their further separation, and that she must give all her time in the future to him and her child. However, though her connection with Bryn Mawr was now definitely severed, she kept receiving urgent communications from school boards in the vicinity of Hanover. The young principals of local high schools had either gone to officers' training camps or been selected by the draft; the schools hunted high and low to find other young men to take their places; if Mrs. Merriweather could only see her way to pinch-hitting for the absentees, it would really be a patriotic service. . . . "You can't, Elizabeth. It's out of the question. Why, you're still nursing the baby." . . . "I know, Mark, but the feedings are coming farther apart now, and it'll be getting cooler pretty soon. Archie could have one bottle feeding." . . . "Well, of course you must follow your own conscience in the matter. But, after all, I've taken over two younger men's classes at Dartmouth. It seems to me that's enough of a contribution for one family. And we've had so little time to ourselves, Elizabeth, we're going to have so little." . . .

Whether they actually heard these conversations or not, Roger and Emily were conscious of them, and very often they were drawn into such discussions and asked to give their opinions. They did not sit out in the sunshine or before the open fire, for long hours at a time, while they conversed; they talked while they worked. Both the young male Randells were already at camp and Una was helping her father with his chores. This meant that none of them was available at Hollyhock Hill just then, though Mr. Randell had promised that he would manage somehow to do the fall plowing later on and that he would winter-board the horses. Meanwhile, Mark and Roger did the stable work with the awkwardness of inexperience and also with the resultant fatigue. Elizabeth and Emily, who were both accustomed to gardening, insisted that they could do this alone and usually won their point; but there were often controversies about mowing the lawn.

"It isn't a woman's work. You know that perfectly well, Elizabeth. And anyway, you shouldn't get overheated."

"It won't do me any harm to get overheated, Mark."

Usually Emily won this point also. She was obviously very strong, in spite of her slender build, and it did not exhaust her to mow the lawn; if she sat down to rest afterward, this was not because of fatigue, but because she wanted to be with the others, who all had more need of rest after their labors. Then Mark told her and Elizabeth what he had said to Roger while they were feeding the horses, and Elizabeth told Mark and Roger what she had said to Emily while they were weeding the garden; and though these conversations went on and on, they all boiled down, in the end, to the same thing: Mark did not want Elizabeth to go back to teaching and she thought she ought to do so, because it was the only contribution she could make to the defense program. . . .

So far, Emily had not been troubled because she was not making more of a contribution to the defense program, but now she began to give this matter conscientious thought; and she was very definitely troubled about Roger. He woke up in the morning, saying he felt fine, that he could lick his weight in wildcats, if he had to; but by noon he was slowing down and long before evening, he had given up all pretense of making further mental or physical effort and gone to sit, with an unopened book in his hands, in the summerhouse, or to lie, with half-closed eyes, in the hammock on the terrace. When Emily went to sit beside him at such times, he did not put out his hand to take hers, or to stroke her hair, and then share the silence with her. He looked up every now and then and spoke anxiously of conditions at the office.

"I hope that building encroachment case of Pell's doesn't get reached for trial before I get back. I know more about it than Briny does, because he and I didn't talk things over, the way Pell and I did. It's fairly well down on the list, but unless a case is in the first half-dozen, you never know . . . I wish that trustee of Mrs. Sims' would resign of his own accord, instead of making me show him up. There's no doubt at all that he's incompetent and I'm very much afraid that he's dishonest too; but I hate to think of all the dirty linen he'll make me wash in public, if he doesn't quietly fade out of the picture."

Sometimes, even before Roger spoke of these problems of his own accord, they obtruded themselves upon him. Presumably, his whereabouts were unknown to his clients; but sometimes these were so insistent that Stanley Lyman, who had been told to "use his best judgment" about revealing the fact that Roger was at Hollyhock Hill, felt that he should do so. Then Jenny Griffin would appear in the kitchen door and shout loudly in the harsh voice which was so at variance with her great kindness.

"Boston calling, Mr. Field. It's very urgent."

Roger would force himself to get up and try to hurry toward the house, and then a long conversation would ensue, rendered doubly difficult because the connection was so bad.

"This is Hawkins, William D. Hawkins, speaking. As my lawyer, I want you to tell me if I haven't any rights as an American citizen." . . . "Did you say any rights? Of course you have rights. I don't follow you." . . . "Well, then can the city of Boston send truckloads of men to take down the iron fence on the corner of my property and make ready to remove most of the lawn, just because some poll up at City Hall thinks it would help relieve traffic conditions?" . . . "I'll have to ask Mr. Lyman, at my office, to consult the statutes on that, Mr. Hawkins. I don't have the Massachusetts General Laws here with me. I'll talk with him on the telephone and I'll also talk with one of our junior partners, who has very good connections at City Hall. If anyone can help you out, he can. I'll let you know later what he and Mr. Lyman have to offer."

Such a series of calls would be long and laborious, and afterward, Roger would feel he should write one or more letters, confirming the telephone conversation; then these letters had to be taken to the Junction, so they would catch the night mail. When that had been done, all Roger wanted was to tumble into bed.

Once or twice the clients did not telephone. They arrived, unannounced, by car, bringing their families with them. The tradition of hospitality was strong among the Forbes'. Elizabeth felt that she should invite the clients and their wives and children to remain for lunch or supper, according to the time of their arrival; if the company was not too numerous, she even felt that she should offer lodging for the night, since there was no good inn anywhere near. Almost invariably, her invitations were accepted. Then the quietude of Hollyhock Hill was completely dissipated. The clients' children chased each other around the garden, trampling the zinnias and the asters; jumped in the hay, scattering it over the barn floor as they shouted to each other; or insisted on wading in the pond, after their parents had disclosed that they did not know how to swim. The clients' wives asked endless questions about Elizabeth's antiques, and wondered if they could not be taken somewhere to purchase similar ones, while their husbands were "talking law"; or else they wanted to play bridge all day. The clients themselves propounded questions which could not be solved without reference to office files and various legal authorities.

"My wife's sister's getting very impatient. You know it's several months now since she decided to get a divorce." . . . "It's several months since you told me she wanted to get a divorce. But I haven't yet succeeded in finding a precedent indicating that her husband's conduct would enable her to do so. I'm still searching for one, but I can't do it here." . . . "Well, I thought perhaps you wouldn't mind running up to town for a couple of days. After all. . . ."

Roger did mind, but he went with his client to Boston, where the angry sister-in-law was awaiting them, ready to pour a long list of grievances, for the third or fourth time, into Roger's unwilling ears. He renewed his search for precedents, but it proved futile, the Commonwealth of Massachusetts having failed to provide means of convenient release for all disgruntled spouses. The drive back to Hollyhock Hill, where the client had left his family during his absence, took place in stony silence, except for an occasional remark directed at Roger's inadequacy. But relations were not sufficiently strained to prevent the acceptance of hospitality for another night. . . .

"I don't see why people can't let you alone. They didn't bother you this way two years ago," Emily said at last, indignantly.

"No, dear. Two years ago I hadn't taken over the Forbes and Sears accounts, or organized that minority stockholders' meeting in the Jerry Donovan case. Almost nobody knew there was a lawyer named Roger Field. Now quite a number of people know it."

310

"Then the more successful you are, the more of this sort of thing we've got to expect?"

"I'm afraid so. But you wanted me to be a success, didn't you, Emily?"

Of course she wanted him to be a success. Of course she wanted people to feel that Roger Field was the most promising young lawyer Cutter, Mills had ever taken into the firm, one of the most promising young lawyers in Boston. She wanted him to justify, in everyone's eyes, the faith to which she had held so fast, just as he had already done so in her grandmother's eyes. She also wanted people to stop talking about David Salomont's brilliance and the great loss his departure had been to the firm, and to talk instead about Roger Field's soundness and reliability and the great asset he had become to the firm.

Resolutely, she tried not to think about David. She was glad there was so little time to go swimming, because the pond reminded her of him; she did not see it as warm and blue, under the September sun; she saw it as cold and glittering, under the northern lights. She was glad there was so little time to go riding, because the horses reminded her of David; she did not see them ambling quietly along under the saddle; she saw them trotting briskly to the sound of sleigh bells. Most of all, she was thankful that the nights were so clear and still; if there had been another storm, if a door had blown open again. . . .

Roger realized nothing of this inner conflict; he realized only that Emily's loving-kindness had deepened into solicitude, that she supported and comforted him and ministered to his every need. But he was more and more troubled as the days went by, because he too was finally forced to see that they could not recapture that sense of peace and detachment which had once pervaded their beings at Hollyhock Hill.

"You're not having any fun at all, darling. It's a rotten shame."

"I didn't come here to have fun. I came here so that you could have a rest. And you're not getting it. That's much more serious."

"I'm getting some. But I do seem to feel tired all the time. And I keep thinking about poor Stanley struggling alone at the office."

"Stop thinking about him. And the next time someone tries to get you on the telephone, let me answer. I'll say I don't know where to find you. It won't hurt my conscience at all. It won't hurt my conscience to turn away a client from the door, either."

"I can't let you do that, Emily. Anyway, perhaps there won't be any more telephone calls, perhaps there won't be any more inopportune visitors."

But he knew, even while he was talking, that there would be. And finally, the morning mail brought in this letter:

Dear Rog,

   Well, I might have known that the draft would catch up with me sooner or later. Last Thursday I got one of those Cordial Greetings from the President, which, being interpreted, means that, within a fortnight, I must be on my way to Camp Devens, where I will be tossed into a uniform, inoculated, and otherwise pushed around as I begin the grueling process of thirteen weeks' basic training. It also means that you'll have to start back to Boston as soon as you get this letter. I hate like hell to say this, but I don't need to tell you there just isn't anyone else to take over.

At this point, I'm so sore, I don't know whether I'm sorrier for myself or for you.

My best to Emily, Elizabeth, Mark and the heir of the Radcliffes.

Yours,

Briny.

Chapter 26

BRIAN HAD ALREADY departed for Camp Devens when Roger returned to the office, and the confusion in which he had left his desk was a striking contrast to the perfect order that David had achieved. For the next few days, Roger was fully occupied with the attempt to cope with this chaos. Even after the papers had been sorted, the scrawled notations which, in many instances, were all Brian had left in the way of records, were incomplete and illegible. His secretary, Rose McCarty, did her level best to help with them and so, to give him his due, did Cyrus Fletcher. But when none of them could decipher Brian's hieroglyphics and impatient clients kept calling to know when they were going to get results, Roger mailed the untidy scratch pads to Camp Devens with an S O S for interpretation.

Brian usually responded as promptly and as effectively as could be expected; he was, in any case, proving to be a much better correspondent than either David or Pell. To be sure, until Pell left for Texas, he had dropped in at the office fairly frequently, so there had been no special reason why he should write letters during that period; but there had been very few from him since. And there had been only one from David, which was addressed to Mr. Cutter, and which related to a technical matter whose solution had eluded the senior partners, but which David had stumbled on by a fortunate chance through an acquaintance he had made at an official cocktail party. Briny, however, wrote brief, breezy, profane letters, which somehow seemed to lighten Roger's labors to a degree out of all proportion to the importance of their contents.

Dear Rog,

I have now been assigned to the reception center, someone having made the startling discovery that I have the mental qualifications for such an honor. I am thus relieved of the physical torture to which the Army in its wisdom first subjected me. On the other hand, it has now obliged me to submit to the anguish of being forced to say, yes, sir— no, sir—sir—sir—sir all day long to a bunch of wet-eared and milky second lieutenants, none of whom look or act as if they were really all there and some of whom are the worst sob's I ever ran into. I'm now beginning to see that Dave and Pell really do have the edge on me, and that they had sense enough to know that they would, a long time before I woke up to that fact myself, which proves—if any such proof were necessary—that they are a lot smarter than I am and always were. Incidentally, though I'd like to hear how they're getting on, I'd hate like hell to see them, since I'd now have to sir the living bejeezus out of them if I encountered them in uniform. . . .

There were several letters in this vein. Then one in quite another came in:

Well, and have you heard the great news or may I be the first to congratulate myself in your presence? The Army, in that infinite wisdom which I mentioned before, has now ruled that all of us draftees—only of course it is stressed that we shall be called selectees—who are twenty-eight years and over shall be released to the E. R. C. (which, being interpreted, means the Enlisted Reserve Corps) and sent home. Evidently a great fear has arisen that the infirmaries will be filled with men confined to their beds by the maladies peculiar to old age and babbling with senile dementia, or that we will trip over our long white beards while we are drilling.

Be that is it may, I bless God, His angels and His saints, that I was twenty-eight on Michaelmas, so even if I got under the wire by the skin of my teeth, still I did it, and if that isn't the luck of the Irish for you, then begorra, I'd like to know what is?

However, there's one catch to this, as there is to most things that look like luck at first glance: I am still subject to immediate recall as an infantry corporal of the United States Army. (Did I tell you before that, because of my superior education, cultural background, immense wealth, varied accomplishments and winning personality, I have been promoted to that proud rank?) Therefore, though you may expect to see me—and you may bet your bottom dollar it will be in civvies—at the office next Monday, I cannot assure you that you will have the pleasure of my company long; for my first act, before turning my attention to any little odds and ends of work which the Ruddy Oarsman and the Artful Dodger may dream up for me, will be to apply for a commission in the Navy. And, loath as I am to leave you holding the bag again, I hope that commission comes floating into the office on the first breeze that blows; for until said commission is actually mine, I shall continue to be subject to immediate recall to the service as an army enlisted man. The rule is that such an e. m. shall be released to accept a commission from any other branch of the armed services. But there is also a lot of flap in such cases, the Army saying we'll release him when he gets his commission and the Navy saying we'll give him a commission the moment he's released.

Well, we shall see what we shall see. Meanwhile, as I said before, I'll turn up Monday morning and do my best, before either the Army or the Navy gets me, to clear away that mess I left you to tackle alone.

Brian was as good as his word; for the next six weeks he toiled early and late, reaching the office as early as Roger did and never leaving it, except in connection with his legal work, until late at night. Even on Sundays, he went to early Mass, and was at his desk before eight o'clock. Roger, to whom churchgoing had always been a social habit rather than a religious obligation, entirely abandoned it now, and the two managed to surmount the enormous "backlog" during the long uninterrupted hours, when the office was empty except for themselves, and no telephone calls got through. But finally the Sunday came when they went home to find their families gathered around their radios with horror-stricken faces and to stare, almost unbelievingly, at the headlines in the extras, which announced the destruction of Pearl Harbor.

Brian's commission reached him by the first mail the following morning, and he rushed down the corridor, throwing on his overcoat and jamming on his hat as he went and calling out to Roger that he was on his way to 150 Causeway Street to be sworn in and to get his orders. When he returned to the office about noon, having gone straight from the Naval Procurement Office to Littlefield's to order his uniforms, he found that the second mail contained the call to serve as an army corporal. He carried the notice into Roger's office, grinning broadly.

"A miss is as good as a mile," he said, "but I'll also say, at the risk of having you tell me I'm mixing my metaphors, that it was a pretty close shave—too close for comfort, if you ask me. But my orders are to 'report' for indoctrination at Northwestern, not to 'proceed' there, so I've got a little leeway. For this next week at least, we'll go right on with the work as we have been doing, my boy."

"Except that we won't talk any more about 'England's War,'" Roger could not refrain from observing.

"Thanks for the 'we.' Come on now, let's get going. We've no time to lose," Brian answered, more soberly than was his wont.

Left to themselves, they certainly would have "gone right on as they had been doing"; for though the chaos which had confronted Roger on his return from Hollyhock Hill had now been resolved to order, and the accumulation of unfinished business greatly reduced, they were still not "even with the board." But Mr. Cutter vehemently announced that he would not permit Brian to leave without some suitable ceremony to mark his departure. Unluckily, the senior partner reminded everyone, he had been absent when David went to Washington, and Pell's departure for Camp Edwards had been so precipitate that there had been no time to arrange anything. (Naturally, Elliot Berkeley's resignation did not count in the same category; he had not left to answer the call of his country, but to further his own selfish interests.) Now, fortunately, the situation was different: on Friday afternoon there would be a cocktail party in the library, and he hoped that all persons connected with the firm, in both legal and secretarial capacities, would find it convenient to remain after hours in order to attend.

As Saturday was to be Brian's last day at the office and he had hoped to get off reasonably early for a farewell family dinner, he would have greatly preferred to go on working with Roger Friday night, rather than to stop at whatever point they might have reached—probably a most disadvantageous one—when the clock struck five. But there was, of course, no civil way of dissuading Mr. Cutter from his purpose. All through the afternoon, the corridor was in a state of commotion, while the wherewithal for the cocktail party was in the process of transportation, with attendant discussion, through the open door of the library. Several clients, who could hardly have failed to notice these festive preparations, nevertheless lingered on and on, relating their problems and woes; and several secretaries, who had been summoned to take urgent letters after four, were still riveted to their typewriters an hour later, while Cora was still further delayed by desultory calls. By five-thirty, however, Mr. Cutter had installed Stanley behind the improvised bar at one end of the library, jocosely telling him that he was now the bartender, and somewhat superfluously calling his attention to the ample supply of ice, soda and varied liquors. There was to be no skimping in the preparation of drinks, Mr. Cutter said, with mock severity, and everyone was to have as many as requested, unless and until Stanley observed that conviviality had degenerated into intoxication. Mr. Cutter next instructed Miss Smythe and Miss Riley, as the senior secretaries, to supervise the supplies on the long table in the center of the room, which was laden with miscellaneous sandwiches, canapés and hors d'oeuvres; if the guests did not help themselves freely, they must be urged to do so, he said; and the platters were to be replenished as fast as they showed any signs of depletion.

Having thus set the stage, he welcomed each newcomer at the door as if it were a long time since they had met; then, after asking for an expression of opinion on the Christmas greens, which he took for granted would be admiring, he waved his hand in the direction of the groaning table and the well-stocked bar. In spite of this great show of geniality on Mr. Cutter's part, however, and conscientious effort on the part of Stanley Lyman, Miss Smythe and Miss Riley, the party was a little slow in getting under way. Cora, with a certain show of sophistication which mystified the others, helped herself liberally to caviar canapés and ordered a gin rickey without hesitation; but Rose McCarty and most of the younger secretaries required urging to accept sandwiches, seemed uncertain what they ought to drink, and asked timidly for Cokes and ginger ale, which were lacking; then, doubly embarrassed, they huddled together on one side of the room, under the shadow of a sectional bookcase containing Massachusetts Reports, "Restatements of the Law" and Corpus Juris Secundum, while they nibbled and sipped without enjoyment. Mr. Mills, who had been categorically informed that this was an occasion when he should set aside his scruples about intoxicating liquors, and who was the more easily persuaded that this was the case because he seemed to be coming down with a slight cold, added still further to the girls' embarrassment by joining their little group and fondling them with impartial familiarity. It was not until they had been rescued by Roger, who sauntered over and encouraged Mr. Mills to favor him with some reminiscences of the last war, that the secretaries dispersed and that the general tone of the party became less strained. Snatches of shoptalk were still scattered throughout the conversation—"That's a juicy libel suit you've got on your hands, Cutter." . . . "Do you know yet when you'll get the title to the Parkview Apartments cleaned up and the papers passed, Fletcher?" . . . "Too bad we can't all have a Mrs. Forbes, Rog." . . . But such references gradually grew scarcer, as the majority of the men became increasingly ebullient; and eventually Mr. Cutter, a glass in one hand and a gavel in the other, stationed himself at one end of the long table and rapped for silence.

"Now that we have had a little welcome relaxation and some much-needed refreshment," he said, lifting his half-emptied glass, as if in salute, and then setting it down, "I think we should turn our attention to the circumstances which have occasioned this gathering. Our beloved country is at war and its young manhood has been called upon to defend it. Two members of our staff have already left us in response to this call; now a third is about to do so. To our great regret, we were unable to show the first two any special courtesy or voice our deep appreciation of their services, before their departure, because in both cases this took place under conditions which made it impossible. We hope to make up for the omission by the warmth of our welcome on their return. Meanwhile, we are happy that, in the case of Mr. Collins—*Lieutenant* Collins of the United States Naval Reserve—we have this opportunity to wish him Godspeed."

Mr. Cutter paused, to permit clapping, and the indicated response, while it did not reverberate through the library, was more or less adequate. As it died away, the senior partner reached underneath the table, and extracted from its hiding-place a large box, which had hitherto been concealed by the overhanging cloth, and which was gaily enveloped in Christmas wrappings. He placed this between two of the platters which, despite the zealous efforts of Miss Smythe and Miss Riley, now showed signs of depletion; and, resting his hands on either side of it, he continued his speech.

"My long years of experience as a lawyer have taught me, however, that words without deeds carry very little weight. Therefore, though I hope and believe that *Lieutenant* Collins would realize that we wish him all possible good luck, even if we did nothing to substantiate this expression of feeling, I have felt it best to make assurance doubly sure. *Lieutenant* Collins, will you please accept this little gift? It comes from us all as a tangible evidence that we have valued our association with you and that we look forward eagerly to its renewal. Meanwhile, those of us who are not privileged to serve our country in the same way as yourself, nevertheless recognize the obligation to do our bit by carrying on here, sustained, in the greater effort which your absence entails, by the thought of your heroism."

This time the applause was heartier. Brian stepped forward, with somewhat heightened color, and accepted the box from Mr. Cutter's outstretched hands. He did not feel sure which he was supposed to do first: open the present or respond to the speech. But he decided on the former course and, after untying several hard knots in the silver ribbon, and tearing away quantities of unexpectedly tough paper ornamented with reindeer, he came to the box itself, which was also securely tied. By this time, he was perspiring freely, and was sorely tempted to cut the remaining ribbons with a knife; but through perseverance he succeeded in getting the box open, and gradually removed from their tissue paper wrappings a dozen small silver goblets and a large matching silver cocktail shaker, suitably inscribed. Although he had tried to make light and appropriate remarks in the course of his labors, these had not been conspicuous for their wit, and the company, while conscientiously striving to maintain a collective attitude of undivided attention, was becoming somewhat restive. Finally, to the relief of everyone, himself included, Brian had an inspiration.

"I think the best way to show my appreciation for this wonderful present is to fill the shaker up right now, and ask all of you to christen it with me. Get out of my way, Stanley—from here on, I'm tending bar. What's for yours, Mr. Cutter?"

At that point, the party began to gather momentum, and when it finally broke up, everyone was not only completely at ease, but in the best possible spirits. Mr. Cutter barely caught the seven-twenty for Chestnut Hill, and there was almost no liquor left for him to take home with him.

The day after Brian left for his indoctrination school at Northwestern, Roger went to see Tim Tupperty at the Joy Street Station, in response to a notice asking for volunteers who would act as air raid wardens. Tim received him courteously, but not enthusiastically; indeed, he gave Roger the impression of having matters on his mind which seemed to him of greater importance than the question at hand. However, after shuffling several papers about and studying the charts which had been sketched on these, he said that Mr. Field might be responsible for Joy Street between Beacon and Mount Vernon; of course he would have to take a training course and participate in practice raids. Roger thanked him, as if the policeman had done him a great favor; and thereafter he visited all the houses in the indicated area, gave instructions about blackouts and saw that these were carried through, which involved considerable persuasion, since there always seemed to be someone who thought an uncurtained skylight or a glimmer around the edge of a window shade did not really count. His next efforts were along the line of preparation for bomb extinction, a duty that was complicated by the fact that some experts recommended a solid stream of water for this purpose and others a fine spray; the compromise of advising the use of one method one week, and the other the next, did not seem wholly logical, either to Roger or to the persons he was striving to instruct. But the places assigned to the sand pails, as probable danger points, were stationary, and the insignia he wore —a white helmet and a white arm band—also remained unchanged, though the latter was somewhat delayed as to issue. He tried hard to feel, when he put this on, that it had some meaning and might be of some service.

Because he was not wholly successful in this effort, he responded, as soon as he had made the necessary arrangements with his alternate warden, to Governor Saltonstall's appeal for volunteer workers at the Boston Information Center, to which, like everyone else, he was soon referring as the B. I. C. Even before Pearl Harbor, there had been some daytime activity at this center; now the airplane plotters were operating there on a twenty-four-hour basis; and since the graveyard shift between midnight to six A.M. was the hardest to supply, Roger chose to serve on this one. A big table, placed in the center of a huge, lofty room, showed the entire land area of defense, which extended from New York to Maine; and the wall, above a small gallery, was encircled by a map of the waters surrounding the coast. Roger and his fellow operators sat around the table, taking by telephone the reports which the officers who manned the little gallery received direct and then relayed. Each operator was responsible for his or her own section of the board, and accepted this responsibility with the utmost earnestness. Only the reports which the officers received and relayed broke the silence; hour after hour, the work went on, quietly, efficiently, intensively. . . .

Simple accommodations were provided at the center for operators who wished to sleep there before or after they went on duty and, as time went on, more and more of them took advantage of these. A little restaurant was opened, and frequently, workers who came on duty in the morning breakfasted with those who had been on duty throughout the night. All types were represented—rich people, poor people, elderly men, young women, prominent executives, janitors, Junior Leaguers, stenographers, shopgirls. The Director of the Boy Scouts, who had several sons in the service, came night after night; his weariness, like his anxiety, showed in his face; but he kept doggedly on. Many of the stenographers and shopgirls had put in a day's work before they arrived at the center, and snatched only a few hours' sleep either before or after the graveyard shift; they, too, went on and on. Some of these girls were preternaturally silent; others chattered incessantly when they were not at the board, bragging about their dates or telling their family troubles. One of them was engaged to a lieutenant who had been at Pearl Harbor; she enjoyed talking about his probable exploits while she watched her solitaire diamond flashing in the early morning sunlight. Another had a brother who was a gambler and who dissipated all the money his parents and his sister could earn. Both girls were equally faithful workers. Roger, breakfasting by himself, because he was too tired to talk with anyone, looked toward the ships going in and out of the harbor, and reflected, with surprise, on this phenomenal capacity for work and, with discouragement, on his own inadequacy.

For, in spite of conscientious application to his duties as an air raid warden and his operations on the graveyard shift, Roger could not escape the feeling, as time went on, that everyone else was contributing more to the war effort than he was. Brian had graduated from the indoctrination school for naval officers at Northwestern University and was now assigned to the naval station in Algiers. David was still in Washington, but he had written Old Mrs. Forbes that he might not be, much longer: the military personnel and training branch of the J.A.G.O. had received a requisition from the J.A.G.'s section of an infantry division for an officer with "certain qualifications." The J.A.G.O. was then reviewing the 201 files of all its available officers, in the rank of 1st Lieutenant; and, according to the grapevine, David had a very good chance of being chosen. If he were, he would be "put on the requisition" and the A.G. would then "cut his orders" for overseas duty. Pell had gone from Camp Hulen, in Texas, to the Mare Island Navy Yard at Vallejo, California, where the First Corps Cadets were stationed as part of the defense of San Francisco Bay immediately after Pearl Harbor; afterward, he had been sent to Camp Hahn, at Riverside, to undergo desert training in the Mojave. He still wrote infrequently and briefly, but it was obvious that he was preparing intensively for combat duty; Roger envied him far more than Brian in New Orleans and David in Washington.

His feeling of failure was intensified, not only because of what his former associates at Cutter, Mills were doing, but because almost every girl and woman of his acquaintance seemed to be doing so much more than he was, in one way or another, for the common cause. His surprise at the number of female plotters he had found among his fellow operators at the Boston Information Center, and at their endless capacity for work, was soon surpassed by his astonishment at the varied activities which were taking place in many other directions.

Dolly was the first to rouse this astonishment, for, true to Deirdre's prediction, she was impatient to "change a nice clean uniform for dirty overalls." She tried to be very fair; she gave a month's notice, instead of the requisite week, and she helped both Ellie and Deirdre with their housecleaning, so that everything would be spick-and-span, from attic to cellar, when she took her departure. Moreover, she reminded neither her relatives nor her employers verbally that Ellie and Deirdre had managed all right without her, when Mr. and Mrs. Field were first married and that, therefore, they certainly should be able to do so again. Nevertheless, her position in the matter was quite as clear as if she had voiced it. Indeed, Ellie and Deirdre both realized that Dollie felt the time was not far distant when Deirdre should manage alone, thereby releasing Ellie to do something more essential to the war effort than polishing all the silver every week and serving her employers' meals in courses.

Roger and Emily realized this also; but, with Roger's approval, Emily decided not to raise the question until Ellie herself did so; and her hesitation was prompted quite as much by consideration for Deirdre as by her own convenience. Deirdre was still strong and willing; however, she was no longer swift moving and she could not "stand the stairs"; if she did the cooking and laundry work, obviously, nothing else should be required of her. Emily pondered the feasibility of moving the kitchen equipment into the laundry, and making the kitchen into a basement dining room, overlooking the little garden. With such an arrangement, Deirdre could probably manage; for, if necessary, Emily could close the third story off entirely and herself do parlormaid's and chambermaid's work on the first and second stories. But this would mean that she could far less easily offer hospitality to homeless persons whom the war had brought to Boston and who were badly in need of it, and that she could not continue her ministrations to Roger's comfort in the same degree as heretofore. She had already resumed her work as Nurse's Aide at the Massachusetts General; and she was helping her grandmother to supervise the sock-knitting bees which were now regularly held in Old Mrs. Forbes' drawing room, where hand-turned machines had been installed. She was also giving blood to the Red Cross, with the feeling that this was another small service performed in Roger's behalf as well, for his failure to prove acceptable as a blood donor had been among his many disappointments. It was better, Emily decided, to let the domestic situation ride for the present; if and when Ellie showed signs of restiveness, there would be time enough to take the next indicated step.

So Dolly departed alone to take up her work at the Hood Rubber Company and, at the end of her first week there, reappeared at Joy Street with the announcement that she was in a car pool which included Miss Marion Swan! Elizabeth had gone back to her teaching, in spite of Mark's protests; Eleanor Thayer was spending practically all her time, most enthusiastically, at the newly organized Officer's Club and reported, with admiration, that Caroline Field was one of her ablest assistants. Roger did not take the activities of his mother-in-law and his sister too seriously. The Officers' Club, which had been established in a huge, imposing mansion, where distant relatives of his uncle, Nathaniel Sears, once resided, was, after all, a very pleasant place. A large reception room stretched the entire width of the house at the rear of the first floor and billiards and bridge were constant attractions there. Every afternoon, tea was served in the second-story sitting room, where a Gobelin tapestry lent background to the pourer, a handsomely dressed lady who was seated in state on an antique sofa, with a prodigal array of silver and china before her; and every evening there was dancing in the ballroom beyond. On cold days, wood fires burned brightly in the large fireplaces; excellent meals and comfortable rooms were provided for officers in the armed forces of the Allied Nations while they were stationed in Boston, and indeed everything possible was done to contribute to their ease and pleasure.

Without wishing to disparage the patriotism of the ladies responsible for the entertainment of these gentlemen, Roger could not believe that they found it much of a hardship. Indeed, he noticed a certain smug satisfaction in the face of his sister which he had not seen there before, and something in his mother-in-law's expression recalled her look at the time when her husband had found her behavior unbecoming to a Boston matron. Roger had been relieved to think that there was no need for further anxiety on that score; now his doubts were raised again. But it was Priscilla who gave the family its first devastating surprise.

She appeared at her grandmother's house late one afternoon when the elderly ladies who had assembled there for the knitting bee were just beginning to disperse. She accepted a cup of tea, and sat quietly to one side until the last guest had gone and only Old Mrs. Forbes and Emily were left in the drawing room with her. Then she threw her bombshell.

"I'm going overseas," she announced.

"What do you mean, you're going overseas?" her grandmother and her cousin asked simultaneously.

"Well, I asked my taxi driver—"

"What taxi driver?"

"One I happened to have in New York. I don't believe I've mentioned before that I went over there a little while ago for a short visit. I always talk to New York taxi drivers. They're very amusing and they seem to have an endless fund of information. Anyway, I told this one that I wanted to go overseas as a WAC and he said, 'You do? All right, I'll get you overseas.' He drove me to a large building on Madison Avenue and then he told me to go up the stairs and sign my name. I did it and when I came down he said, 'Kid, you're in the Army now.' And he was right. Afterward, I got a letter, telling me to go to 10 Commonwealth Avenue for a physical examination and now I have another letter, telling me to report for duty. I'll show it to you, if you like. I'm being sent to Camp Oglethorpe for basic training. But of course that's just a preliminary to going overseas."

"The whole thing sounds absolutely crazy to me, the way you tell it," Emily said, rather heatedly, while her grandmother thoughtfully examined the letter Priscilla offered for inspection. "Why do you want to go overseas, anyway?"

"What did you think I wanted to do all through the war? Pick cranberries? Or pour tea for British officers every afternoon?"

"You didn't visit the Bruckers, by any chance, while you were in New York, did you, Priscilla?" Old Mrs. Forbes asked, inconsequentially, as she handed back the letter.

"Yes, I did. I've visited them several times. Is there any reason why I shouldn't?"

"Not the slightest. . . . Shall we be seeing you again, Priscilla, before you leave for Camp Oglethorpe?"

"No, I'm going home tonight. I just thought I'd come in and say good-by."

"I'm very glad that you did, my dear. Good-by and the best of luck."

Old Mrs. Forbes sat for so long, with her eyes closed and without speaking, after Priscilla had gone, that Emily finally decided she must have gone to sleep and tiptoed out of the room. Her grandmother did not move until the front door had quietly closed. Then she reached for her cane and, leaning heavily upon it, walked up the stairs to her bedroom and crossed over to her desk. Picking up the envelope, with the letterhead of the War Department, which lay on the middle of the blotter, she drew out the single sheet of paper which it contained and read this slowly through for the second time.

Dear Mrs. Forbes,

   This is just to tell you that my hopes have been fulfilled. I have been put on the requisition and the Adjutant General has cut my orders for overseas duty.

   When I see all the poor fellows who are frozen here for the duration, to fight the Battle of the Potomac, I realize how lucky I am. I'll write you again when and as I can. I'll never forget your very great kindness to me while I was in Boston, and you've given me the feeling that you'd like me to keep in touch with you. So, as you see, I'm acting on it.

   Yours, most sincerely and gratefully,

                                        David Salomont

Old Mrs. Forbes replaced the letter in its envelope. She had meant to show it to Emily, after the knitting bee was over. But in the course of Priscilla's startling visit, she had changed her mind. Now she suddenly felt very tired. She rang for Doris and, when the maid appeared, she said she did not want any dinner. She would have just a cup of soup, after she was settled in bed. . . .

However, Emily did not lack for exciting news. When she reached home, she found that Roger had returned from the office earlier than usual, to tell her that Pell was in Boston. Roger had received a telephone call from him, saying he wanted to see Roger at once—privately. He was coming to the house that evening at eight-thirty. He said the matter was very urgent.

Chapter 27

WHEN PELL ARRIVED, Roger and Emily were in the upstairs sitting room, listening to the war news on the radio. Emily had carried out her plan of creating something "personal, chintzy and cozy" before the war had made all such improvements and embellishments seem like luxuries and extravagances; and both she and Roger were glad that she had been able to do so. He enjoyed the room almost as much as she did; it had become their preferred center, at the end of a hard day, because it had more intimacy than the library and more space for music, reading and relaxation generally than their bedroom, which they had gradually drifted into the habit of calling "Emily's bedroom." Not that Roger had ceased to share it with her, as a usual thing, but he was no longer self-conscious about sleeping on the day bed in his dressing room, if he came in very late or unusually tired. Emily, who was usually very tired herself, after a hard day at the Massachusetts General, even when she did not also give blood or superintend knitting, took it as a matter of course that sometimes he would do so; the day bed was always invitingly turned down for him, with both hot and cold drinks in thermos pitchers and sandwiches wrapped in a damp napkin, on a little table beside it. The pleasant privacy of the chintz sitting room and the quiet companionship which they shared in it had, in a sense, released them both; their marital relationship was still one of physical harmony; but it had ceased to be one of paramount physical expectancy.

Besides its value from a personal standpoint, the chintz sitting room had proven its advantages from a professional one. More and more frequently, clients who wished to see Roger on confidential or urgent matters sought him out at home; the library, where he could be sure that no one would overhear or interrupt their conversation, was an ideal place to receive such persons. It also proved a convenient meeting ground when the air raid wardens of the area needed to discuss their common problems, and for various other minor patriotic purposes. If Emily's presence was indicated for any reason, she was readily available; if it was not, she could attend, with the same meticulous care she had always given them, to the details of household management which had, perforce, awaited her return from the hospital, or balance her accounts and keep abreast of her correspondence, undisturbed by the presence of strangers.

Roger's response to Pell's appeal had been unhesitating and cordial. Of course it would be convenient for him to see Pell; in fact, there was no engagement he would not gladly have broken in order to do so; he was delighted to know that Pell was back in Boston at last, and the more time they could spend together, the better he would like it. Moreover, Pell had been specific in asking that their conference be private, with no intimation, that he wished Emily to share these confidences. She and Roger agreed that, unless Pell definitely asked for her, she would not go downstairs.

Ellie, who was still doing the dinner dishes and who had been told to expect him, answered his ring, ushered him into the library and announced his presence. He was standing at the window, looking out toward the street, with his hands behind his back, when Roger entered the room; and even before he looked around, Roger was conscious of the change in him. He had always been slender, but now he was spare; he had always carried himself well, but now he was conspicuously erect. As he turned, Roger was immediately aware of still greater changes. His skin, naturally dark, was burnt to a deep copper color; his heavy black hair was clipped so close that the last vestige of its wave was gone. Even his lips seemed to have lost their fullness; his expression, instead of being one of winning grace, was one of determination. He was as handsome as ever, and his uniform set off his trim figure to great advantage. But the troubadour was gone; this was a knight in armor.

"Hello there, Pell! Am I ever glad to see you!" Roger exclaimed, suppressing the impulse to voice his surprise. "Gosh, it's been a long time, hasn't it? What can I offer you? Scotch? Bourbon? Bushmill's?"

"Thanks, not a thing."

"Perhaps you'd rather have wine. Emily thought of that and there's some on ice in the pantry. So, if you would—"

"No, really. I just wanted to talk to you—that is, if you're sure this isn't a bad time."

"Of course not. I'm tickled to death to see you. I've been trying to get you here for a long while, you know."

"Yes, I know. I'm afraid I've seemed very unappreciative. But there have been reasons."

"I'm sure there have. You don't need to explain."

"But that's just what I've come for. I didn't want to go away without explaining. Besides, I'm going to ask you to help me. And this is my last chance. I'm through with desert training, thank God! If there's any place worse than the Mojave, it would sure be a shock to me. But I'll soon find out. I've got my overseas orders."

"You know if there's anything in the world I can do. . . . Shan't we sit down? You'll smoke anyway, won't you? And let me know if you change your mind about a drink."

Without answering directly, Pell made a gesture which indicated that he did not wish to smoke either and that he was not likely to change his mind about the drink. However, he seated himself opposite Roger, who pulled out a pipe and, after filling it and tamping it carefully, lighted it and quietly puffed away. For some moments, the silence remained unbroken, but the atmosphere seemed to become gradually more companionable and, therefore, increasingly conducive to confidences. At last Pell spoke, hesitantly.

"I don't suppose you remember the first time we ever saw each other."

"Of course I do. It was right in front of this house. You were leading a group of carolers—you and a very beautiful girl. I bumped into her, clumsy oaf that I am, and for a moment you were mad—rightly so too, because she slipped and you thought she was hurt. But fortunately she wasn't, and I convinced you I was really sorry I hadn't looked where I was going, as I lumbered along. We ended by wishing each other Merry Christmas. Then you went on up the hill, singing 'God rest ye merry, gentlemen.'"

"Yes, that was the way it was. But afterward you didn't identify me, when we met at the office and worked together."

"No, I didn't. And Emily didn't identify you either, when you came to our wedding, though she'd seen you that same Christmas Eve—seen you and been so impressed with you and your fellow leader and the singing of your group that she spoke to me about it afterward. It bothered her because she couldn't place you. I believe she told you so when you came here to dinner and that you explained to her you'd sung outside her house. It was only after she repeated to me what you'd said that I was able to identify you."

"I did tell her I'd sung outside her house, so that she wouldn't keep on being puzzled over where she'd seen me. But I didn't answer her questions about the beautiful girl who was with me."

"No, she said you didn't. And later on, when she accidentally met this girl—"

"Yes. That is what I wanted to explain to you. It's rather a long story. I hope it won't bore you."

"Of course it won't bore me. But I don't want you to think that either Emily or I meant to force your confidence or pry into your affairs. You don't owe us any explanation."

"But I've told you I want to give you one now, I've come here on purpose. At least, I've come partly for that."

"All right, shoot. I'm very much interested."

Roger settled back more deeply in his chair, still puffing companionably on his pipe. Pell leaned forward.

"The story goes back to my grandfather, Antonio Pacetti. He and his

326

bride, Bianca, with some cousins by the name of Barrata, were the first of our family to emigrate. They left Naples and settled in New Bedford during the latter part of 1890. The Barratas moved away before I came along, and I never knew Bianca, either; she lived only a short time. But she had three children, two daughters and a son—Carmela, Adelina and Nazareno. Adelina was my mother. She married a man named Felipe de Lucca. And they were both killed in an accident when I was a baby. My Aunt Carmela brought me up. She wasn't married when my parents were killed, but later she did marry. Her husband, Edmondo de Lucca, died in the flu epidemic of 1918."

"The two husbands were related, I suppose?"

"No, not at all. It was just a coincidence that their surnames were the same." For the first time, Pell smiled faintly. "It's a funny thing, but when foreigners have the same name, Americans take it for granted they must be related. But you wouldn't expect a Neapolitan to leap to the conclusion, if he met two men named Field, that they must be brothers or at least cousins."

"You're right, I wouldn't. . . . So your aunt, Carmela de Lucca, was widowed in 1918. You'd lived with her after she was married?"

"Yes—there wasn't anyone else to take care of me, because, as I told you, my grandmother was dead already. So Aunt Carmela brought me with her when she came to Boston. Edmondo de Lucca was a Bostonian." Again, Pell smiled faintly. "At least that's what he called himself. Of course most of the Bostonians you know wouldn't call him one. It's a funny thing, but they seem to think they're the only real kind—when they speak of people like Brian's, they don't call them Bostonians, they call them Boston Irish. When they speak of people like mine, they call them Dagoes from the North End."

"Yes, they do," Roger admitted. "Not all of them, naturally, but some."

"It would be most, wouldn't it? Not that I suppose Brian minds—certainly I don't. It strikes me as rather illogical, that's all. Why just take Louisburg Square, for instance! The Brahmins always think of it in terms of persons like Old Mrs. Forbes; they don't ever think of it in terms of persons like Sister Mary Theresa. Yet the nuns of her Order were the pioneer nurses at the Children's Hospital in Boston, and the wafers they make for Holy Communion are sent all over the world. Hundreds of Army chaplains are using them right now; and thousands of persons who've never heard of the 'last stronghold of the aristocracy' know about St. Margaret's Convent."

"Probably they do. Yes, of course they must."

As Pell went on talking, Roger recalled, with uncanny vividness, his efforts to explain the *raison d'être* of the Vincent Club to the Collins family the first time he had gone there to supper. Now, as then, he realized how circumscribed his environment had been when he was a boy, how greatly he had been conditioned by it in the past; and a feeling of thankfulness that it was no longer so circumscribed and so conditioned, because of his friendship with Brian and Pell, permeated his being.

"It's strange that the Brahmins don't think in terms of the Christmas carolers, either," Pell continued. "I've been one of those, you know—one of the outsiders getting a glimpse of the beauty in those old houses, instead of one of the Proprietors who lives there. And even those glimpses mean a lot to the outsiders."

"Emily's always understood that. She spoke of it the night she first saw you—the night she and I got engaged."

"She did? Well, I should have known she might. I'm glad you told me. . . . And I've got other associations with Louisburg Square too. When I was a little boy, I used to tag along every year on October 12th after a bunch known as the Italian Columbus Society, to watch the members take part in a ceremony before the statue of Columbus in the little mall. Of course, the boys from Tech, who had a club at Number Six, used to dress up the statue of Aristides the Just, at the other end of the mall, in a cap and gown once a year. But that was just horseplay. The Italian ceremony was very serious; there were speeches and wreaths and all that sort of thing. I was sorry when the celebrations were given up, along in the twenties. I suppose the Italians got tired of having the Proprietors look down their noses at a fiesta of that type . . ."

"I hope that wasn't the reason."

"It doesn't matter. Anyway, I seem to be running on and on about something that's always interested me and puzzled me, instead of sticking to the point. I got sidetracked when I said my uncle by marriage, Edmondo de Lucca, considered himself a Bostonian. He'd lived here, on the Hill, for about two years when he and my aunt were married. He'd met her through mutual friends in New Bedford whom he went to visit, soon after he landed in New York. But he was offered a better job in Boston than he could get in New Bedford, through other friends, who were also Bostonians, of a sort. In one way, the Italians and Irish are very much alike; they're clannish, they keep together, they do everything they can for each other, unless they're actually enemies, and they lay a lot of stress even on distant relationships. Perhaps you didn't fully realize this. They have their own churches and their own newspapers, their own clubs and their own cafés, and unless they really rise in the world, they cling to their own language, quite stubbornly. I know Italians who've been in this country for years and who hardly speak a word of English."

"I did realize this in a general way, but it's never happened to affect me very closely, so I've never given it much thought, any more than I had the other things you talked about."

"That's what I imagined and that's why I've stressed the point, because it may help you to understand my Aunt Carmela better. Until she was married, she and I had lived with my grandfather and my uncle, Nazareno, who's still alive and who's still single. Is this getting too complicated for you? Would you like me to draw a chart of all these relationships, and who married whom, and so on?"

"No, it's perfectly clear to me. Two sisters, Carmela and Adelina Pacetti, married Edmondo and Felipe de Lucca, who weren't related at all. Adelina and Felipe were killed in an accident, leaving an infant son, Pellegrino, and his Aunt Carmela did her best to mother this orphan, both before and after her marriage. That's all straight so far, isn't it?"

"Yes, absolutely. Then, after Aunt Carmela's husband died, she had a baby of her own—Simonetta."

Pell stopped for a moment, almost as if he were lingering over the name. But he did not seem to expect any comment and Roger wisely refrained from making one.

"It had been pretty bad, that winter of the flu. Perhaps you remember?"

"Only vaguely. I was very young then, you know. You must have been very young too."

"I was seven. But my recollection of it is quite vivid. My aunt had very little money. My grandfather sent her some for my care and clothing, but it wasn't enough even for that, much less for all our needs. He had disapproved of her marriage, so she says, and had never shown her the same affection that he had toward my mother and my Uncle Nazareno, whom she hates, and who evidently hates her. When Italians hate they do it with the same intensity that they love and the consequences are often very serious."

"But they must have some reason for doing it. Why should they hate each other?"

"Uncle Nazareno's an agnostic, like Antonio Pacetti and Aunt Carmela's very religious—almost fanatically so. She thinks my uncle influenced their father against her. At all events, as I've just said, there was very little money from that source. And her husband's job hadn't amounted to much, after all. She had hard work scraping together enough cash to pay the expenses for an impressive funeral and all the Requiem Masses she wanted, to say nothing of an elaborate tombstone. The winter of 1918 and 1919 was a very bitter one. We were cold all of the time and hungry most of the time, except when the neighbors took pity on us—which, bless them, they tried their best to do. But my aunt didn't want to accept charity. She withdrew more and more from her friends, she grew silent and morose in her sorrow and her need. But she never failed in kindness to me. And finally, spring came. And, with the spring, the beautiful baby."

Again Pell paused, smiling reminiscently.

"Of course we couldn't let the baby go cold and hungry," he said, looking across at Roger with a new light in his eyes. "So that was when I became a wage earner."

"When you were *seven?*"

"Yes. Lots of kids go to work when they're seven—not kids like the ones you knew, of course, but plenty of them that I knew. I found all sorts of odd jobs to do, during my vacation and outside of school hours. These jobs were around the market at first and most of my pay was in wilted vegetables, but those came in very handy. Later I shined shoes and peddled papers and delivered groceries. Several of the neighborhood grocery stores on the Hill are awfully good to kids who need jobs—and to lots of other people in need too. And I didn't feel the same way about our Italian friends that my aunt did. I went to them when we had to have more money than I could earn."

"Didn't your aunt even do that?"

"No. Aunt Carmela's never been the same since her husband died. Her grief over his loss was natural, of course. They'd been very happy together. But she couldn't seem to realize that many other women were obliged to endure the same sort of grief and that they surmounted it. She felt she'd been singled out for poverty and sorrow. She still feels that way. And she began by being bitter against her father and her brother and she's ended by being bitter against everyone except Simonetta and me. Of course no one could feel bitter against Simonetta."

"You've always loved Simonetta very much, haven't you?"

Roger thought it was all right for him to speak now and to say what seemed natural. Nevertheless, he was relieved when he found he had not been too precipitate in following his impulse.

"Yes. Yes, I've loved her from the day she was born," Pell answered, his words coming in a rush. "I'm glad you didn't think a boy seven years old was too young to love anybody, the way you thought he was too young to get a job. After all, the Catholic Church recognizes seven as the age of reason. And by and large, the Church is pretty wise."

"Yes," Roger agreed, wondering why there was a sudden bitterness in the way Pell spoke. "And the common law recognizes him as old enough to be capable of committing a crime. Certainly anyone who is capable of that is capable of love too."

"I'm thankful you recognize that. It makes everything else I'm going to say so much simpler. I couldn't wait to get home from school or from work to see Simonetta in her cradle. I did everything for her that I'd have done if I'd really been her brother and there'd been no one else to help our mother—fed her, bathed her, dressed her, whenever I could—not just because I wanted to help my aunt, but because I was never so happy as when I was taking care of the baby. I always thought of her as my little sister, dearer to me than anyone else in the world."

"And that was perfectly natural."

"Yes, it was perfectly natural. But I suppose it was also perfectly natural that eventually I should stop thinking of her as my sister. I suppose it was inevitable that, when I grew up, I should fall in love with her—deeply, passionately in love."

"I suppose so too. And I don't see—"

"We're own cousins. We're within the forbidden bonds of consanguinity. Unless we defy canon law, there's nothing we can do."

Pell made this statement with the finality of complete hopelessness. In the face of it, Roger was inevitably halted. His sympathy was strongly stirred, but he knew he must search for the right words in which to express it. When he finally spoke, it was with great restraint and gentleness.

"Are you sure? I don't know much about canon law, of course. But I'm almost sure I've heard of cases where there were dispensations."

"There have been. We've tried to get one. We've been refused."

"You say 'we.' I take it that means Simonetta wants—"

"Yes. She's desperately in love with me too. Sometimes I wish she weren't. Sometimes I think it wouldn't be quite so hard if she weren't. At least she wouldn't have heard our love insulted, if she hadn't pleaded for it herself. She'd never even heard the word 'incest' before. She didn't know what it meant. But she's heard it now. She knows now."

"I'm sorry. I'm terribly sorry. It's dreadful that she should have had to hear such things. But I'm sure you were able to make her understand how unjust they were, how—how unchristian. I don't care who spoke to her that way. That person shouldn't have done it."

"No, she certainly shouldn't have. It was her mother. I think she's ashamed now, but of course she won't admit it. And she can't change the laws of the Church."

"Can't they be adapted to special circumstances? Can't you appeal to a higher clerical authority?"

"We have appealed to a higher clerical authority. And we got the same answer. The very fact that we were brought up together, that lots of people have always thought we really were brother and sister—that's against us, you see. And Aunt Carmela is against us. She sides with the Church. It's a dreadful thing to say, when she's always been so kind to me, as far as everything else is concerned, but it almost seems as if she didn't want us to be happy, because she hasn't been happy herself. I've told you she's been growing more and more morose, more and more bitter, for years. The last time she went to a party was the one that resulted in the lawsuit I won, that got me my job at Cutter, Mills and Swan. You'd think that would have made her feel good about it—it made everyone else who was there feel that way. But it didn't. All she could think of was that it caused trouble and that she might have more trouble like it, if she continued to mingle with her neighbors. She won't let anyone inside her flat if she can help it—well, Emily found that out, I'm sorry to say. I haven't lived there myself since—well, since Simonetta and I realized that I shouldn't, any longer. We knew that if we kept on living in the same flat, that some night. . . . So I've lived with Mrs. Danielli and Pietro on the floor above. No one's questioned the arrangement—that is, I haven't heard anyone question it and I'm sure Simonetta hasn't either, or she'd have told me. I said I needed more space for my papers and things and Mrs. Danielli needed the money she could get from a lodger and altogether—well, I don't think it sounded too illogical."

He paused, looking to Roger for agreement. Roger nodded, not trusting himself to speak at once. Obviously, an illicit love affair had never occurred to either Pell or Simonetta as a substitute for marriage and somehow this was infinitely moving to him.

"No, I don't think it does," he said finally. "And I think if you go on applying to other authorities, sooner or later you'll find one with more understanding. Someone like Briny's brother, Mat, for instance."

"I've been to Father Mat. He's a wonderful priest and a wonderful man. He does have understanding. But we don't belong to his parish, and he doesn't have power in a case like this, in spite of all his connections."

"Well, sooner or later you're bound to find someone who has both power and understanding."

"We might, if we had time to go on trying. But I'm leaving Boston next week. I haven't any idea when I'll be back. Perhaps never."

"And you wouldn't consider—marrying out of the Church? Of course the idea of cousins marrying isn't shocking to me. I've known it to happen over and over again. Why, there are even marriages between double cousins in some of the best Boston families!"

"Yes, I know. Best by your standards. And I'm not trying to be sarcastic when I say that. I know your standards are high—if I didn't, I wouldn't be here talking to you like this. But they don't happen to be mine—or Simonetta's. We couldn't be happy if we were married without the blessing of the Church. We wouldn't even feel we were married, sacramentally, as we want to be. We'd feel we were doing something almost as bad as what that priest, who didn't understand, talked about. We'd never be happy if we did. Of course we're not happy now. But at least we don't feel guilty as well as—unfulfilled."

"So you're accepting the decision as final? You're leaving without trying to do anything more?"

"What more can I do?"

"I don't suppose you can do anything more, since you feel this way."

Again silence fell on the room and, this time, like the first time, it was Pell who finally broke it.

"Well, you see that. So I hope and believe you see why I've come to you now and why I couldn't before. Since I couldn't explain about Simonetta, I couldn't bring her here and I couldn't ask you and Emily to come and see us, even if Aunt Carmela had been willing. But now that I'm going away, now that I've found you understand, I want you and Emily to watch over Simonetta for me."

"Pell, I don't know how I can ever tell you—"

"You don't need to. You've told me everything already that I need to know. But there's something else I want to tell you—something I even haven't touched on yet, but that's all mixed up with the rest."

"If it's something I can help with—"

"It is. That is, I believe it is. . . . A little while ago, my grandfather died."

Roused to fresh alertness, Roger looked attentively at Pell.

"It wasn't in the least a source of sorrow to me. After all, I hadn't seen him in years, and I thought he'd treated my aunt very shabbily—not to mention the way he'd treated me. The sums he sent us when I was little eventually dwindled to almost nothing and then stopped coming altogether. But out of the blue arrived a letter from a law firm in New Bedford, saying he'd left me a legacy! Evidently, he'd become well to do in his old age, perhaps because he did so much penny pinching when he was younger. Anyway, this legacy's big enough to assure Simonetta's comfort if—well, if anything should happen to me. You'll be here, you could take the necessary steps to be sure that she got what she needed."

"What steps do you want me to take?"

"I want you to be the executor of my will. I want to leave everything to Simonetta outright, except what I want handed over to her right away. I'll give you a power of attorney to take care of that part. The capital isn't tied up, like in your Boston trust funds. I want Simonetta to have 'advantages,' the kind girls you grew up with take for granted. She hasn't even had any more schooling than the law requires, because her mother persisted in keeping her at home—it was just part of the general picture of withdrawal I've told you about. Of course I've taught her what I could, in odd moments, and she's very intelligent—very eager to learn. Besides, she's got natural musical talent—you knew that, because you've heard her sing. Aunt Carmela did let her do that because the singing was connected with church. But I want her to have lessons from good teachers—music lessons, English lessons, all sorts of lessons. You'd know how to arrange for that."

"Emily would. Emily would do that better than I could. Not that I wouldn't be glad to try."

"All right, have Emily do it then. Perhaps you'll talk to her about all this after I've left tonight, and then, later on, the four of us can discuss it together. . . . I'd like to know Simonetta had a better place to live in too. I don't suppose Aunt Carmela would want to leave Joy Street, but the lease on the flat really will be up pretty soon and maybe you could find something a little nearer Mount Vernon. . . ."

"We'll look into that. Of course the housing situation's pretty tight right now, but I have an idea of how we might work this thing out. I don't believe there'll be any hitch."

"Perhaps not about another flat. But there is a hitch. That's another thing I'm coming to. Aunt Carmela wasn't pleased about my legacy. She was very resentful because it was so much larger than hers. It looks to her

333

like one more example of injustice. And she doesn't want Simonetta to have 'advantages.' She thinks they'd alienate her from her mother, by putting her on a different level. That's what she feels my education's done. She thinks she should have had a substantial legacy, so that she could handle it according to her views. After all, Simonetta's her child and she's Antonio Pacetti's daughter. I'm only Simonetta's cousin and Pacetti's grandson. There's some reason on her side."

"When you put it that way, of course I can see that there is."

"So she was upset on that score. And when she found out that, besides the sum he'd left me, Antonio Pacetti had left a very flourishing restaurant and, apparently, quite a little money, as well, to his son, Nazareno—her brother and my uncle—she saw red. She said the money should have been evenly divided between herself and Nazareno, with perhaps token legacies to Simonetta and me."

"How did she find out about all this? Has the will been allowed yet?"

"No, it hasn't. Uncle Nazareno had it filed in the Bristol Probate Court, by his lawyer, Claudio Autori, and Autori had the requisite notice published in the New Bedford Standard Times and sent to Aunt Carmela and me, with copies of the will. My papers were waiting for me here when I got to Boston yesterday and I found out right away that Aunt Carmela was very angry about the terms of the will. Then today, another lawyer, named Fopiano, turned up here and persuaded her to contest it. I suppose he's filed an appearance for her already."

"Fopiano? Is he from New Bedford too?"

"Yes, he is, and I don't like what little I've been able to find out about him. I made inquiries at the Bar Association and though the secretary didn't say much, I gather Fopiano has kept bobbing up in will cases for a long time, and that he's always representing contestants or missing heirs. I don't know whether anything's actually been pinned on him; but he's not our kind of a lawyer."

"And how about this contest, from your point of view? Would you get more or less if your aunt can knock out the will?"

"Probably more. But I don't want money that way. I'd rather get what the will gives me and have it in time to do something for Simonetta. Besides, I hate family rows. I'd like to keep out of this one, as far as I can. And I'd be very grateful if you'd represent me and agree to any kind of a compromise that will keep the peace and still take care of Simonetta. I think that ought to be possible. But I'm afraid Aunt Carmela, with Fopiano telling her what to do and trying to muscle in for a big fee, will make it pretty tough for you."

"Maybe it won't be too hard if your uncle will play ball with me."

"I rather think he will. He has no use for my aunt, as I've told you. I haven't seen much of him, but I doubt if you'll have any real trouble there, especially after you've persuaded him that I feel the way I do about the restaurant."

"I'll go to see Autori right away. I don't believe he'll raise any objections if I say I'd like to talk to your uncle. . . . May I see the will?"

"Yes, I brought a copy of it to show you. It must be a homemade job, even though my grandfather used to consult Autori, too, about legal matters in connection with the restaurant. I bet he just asked Autori, casually, one day, when they were talking about something else, how many witnesses you need to have, and, after finding that out, went home and wrote this up, happy in the conviction that he'd saved at least twenty-five dollars."

Pell took an unsealed, commercial-sized envelope from his pocket and handed it to Roger, who drew from this the single typed sheet which it contained, and read:

New Bedford, Massachusetts
July 17, 1937

I know I am going to die.

I give my grandson, Pellegrino de Lucca, who lives in Boston and who has worked hard and done well, fifteen thousand dollars.

I give Carmela de Lucca two thousand dollars.

I give my beloved son, Nazareno, everything else and I want him to run my restaurant and carry on the business after I am gone.

/s/ Antonio Pacetti

WITNESSES:
  Guilio Fulginnetti
  Paul Lavaroni
  Francis J. Desmond

Roger smiled and sighed.

"He left out a lot of stuff they put in the form books, but it looks to me as if it would hold water."

"Then can you carry on from there?"

"I'll do the best I can."

"All right. I don't need to know anything more. And I don't need to do anything more, as far as this mix-up is concerned, except to draw the necessary papers and get your okay on them. I can put what little spare time I have into trying again for that dispensation. If I could marry Simonetta this week. . . ." He broke off and looked away. "Anyhow," he went on after a moment, "I'd be very happy—Simonetta and I would both be very happy—if, after you've told Emily about all this, you and she would spend an evening with us—as our guests. I'm sorry we can't ask you to the flat. But you understand now how that is. And I know of a quiet old restaurant where we'd be undisturbed. I think you'd find it very pleasant. Perhaps when I bring the papers in for you to sign, you'd tell me whether Emily would accept our invitation."

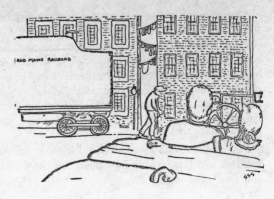

Chapter 28

ONCE HAVING BROKEN the silence and overcome the reticence of years, Pell wanted to talk on and on; and eventually he said, since Emily had been so thoughtful as to put wine in the pantry for him, he would be glad to have a glass or two with Roger before he left. This proved to be a stimulus to further conversation and it was very late when he finally said good night; but Roger found that Emily was still waiting for him in the chintz sitting room, as he expected, when he went upstairs.

"It's a long story," he said, without specifying what he meant by "it"; he took for granted that Emily would know. "Sad and baffling and—beautiful. Pell told me to tell you everything he said to me; we both felt that, if I did, perhaps you could help us lighten the sorrow and solve the mystery and keep the beauty. That isn't the way he said it, but it's what he meant. Are you too tired to listen now? The time element's very important, so if you're not—"

"Of course I'm not. I sat up on purpose. I didn't know you'd be able to tell me everything, but I hoped you'd have permission to tell me something."

They sat down side by side and hand in hand on a big comfortable sofa and, for the next half hour, Roger talked almost without pausing, and Emily listened almost without interruption. When he mentioned the impediment to marriage between Pell and Simonetta, she gave an exclamation of sympathy, and asked him, as he had asked Pell, if it were not possible to secure a dispensation.

"I'm almost sure it would be, if there were time and if we only knew which authorities it would be most helpful to approach."

"Didn't you say Pell had almost a week? Couldn't he get to the Cardinal in that length of time?"

"The Cardinal's away, on his vacation. Pell's going to try to get an appointment with his secretary tomorrow. But he feels fairly certain the secretary will say this is a matter that will have to await the return of His Eminence. And by the time His Eminence has returned, Pell will be on his way to Parts Unknown." Roger shook his head ruefully. "It seems like the irony of fate that Pell and Simonetta should be penalized because they're trying to do right. I don't know much about canon law, as I told Pell; but I'm almost sure that if Simonetta were with child by him, they could get permission to be married immediately. And it doesn't seem to have occurred to them to live together without benefit of clergy. It's really rather touching, the way Pell keeps saying that marriage is a sacrament and must be approached sacramentally or not at all. Well, to go on with the story. . . ."

The next time Emily interrupted, she did so to say that, even if Roger did not need a chart of the Pacetti relationships, she did, and she went to her desk and proceeded to draw one. When he handed her the copy of Antonio Pacetti's will, she studied it carefully and then compared it with her chart.

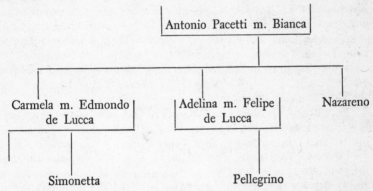

Antonio Pacetti m. Bianca

Carmela m. Edmondo de Lucca

Adelina m. Felipe de Lucca

Nazareno

Simonetta

Pellegrino

"Isn't that a very strangely worded will?" she asked at length.

"Well, of course it's an amateur job, as you'd have seen for yourself, even if I hadn't told you so. But I think it's in order."

"I didn't mean that. I mean the wording strikes me as strange. Antonio refers to Nazareno as his 'beloved' son and, even though he's done it very tardily, he acknowledges that Pell 'has worked hard and done well.' But he doesn't say anything that could possibly be interpreted as a tribute to Carmela."

"That's true. But I explained to you that there were hard feelings between them, largely on account of divergent religious opinions—or so it would seem."

"I know. But still, he was her father. I don't think it was fair to leave her so little, if the fact that they didn't agree about religion was the only thing he had against her. It seems to me there must have been other things too."

"I agree with you. And it's my job to find out what they were."

Emily continued to compare the chart and the will and, eventually, she asked another question.

"Pell didn't say anything more about his cousins, did he? I mean the

337

ones named Barrata who emigrated the same year as Antonio and Bianco Pacetti?"

"No, he didn't mention them a second time."

"Did you ask him anything more about them?"

"No. Because obviously he didn't think they entered into the picture at all. From the way he spoke of them, I don't know that he ever even saw them. I quoted him to you verbatim: 'They moved away before I came along.'"

"Well, he might have gone to visit them, mightn't he, even if they had moved away?"

"I suppose so. But if he did, I think he'd have mentioned it."

"I don't, necessarily. I think he had so many more important things on his mind that he never got back to his cousins, after he spoke of them the first time. I think it would be a good idea to ask him if his failure to say anything was accidental."

"All right, I will. But I can't do it tonight. What would you think of going to bed? It's nearly two o'clock."

"I'm willing to go to bed, but there's still one more question I want to ask."

"Then let's have it."

"I'm quoting verbatim now. When Pell said he'd like to have Simonetta and her mother live in a better place, after the lease on their flat was up, you told him you had an idea. What was it?"

"I'll answer your question by asking you one. Have you ever noticed a little old house, wedged in among the tenements, on the farther side of Joy Street? It's the only one of its kind in that locality, so I think you must have—in fact, it's almost the only one of its kind left in Boston. It's not unlike the Paul Revere house, but it's smaller. And it's really got quite a good deal of charm."

"Of course I've noticed it. And I agree with you about the charm. It's —well, I hesitate to use the word, because it's been so overworked, but that house is really quaint. It's always intrigued me. I've wished I could see the inside and the rear of it. I've wondered if there couldn't be a garden in the back."

"Well, you might have a chance to satisfy your curiosity. Remember now, I didn't say you would. I said you might. The former owner of that house died recently, and I understand her heirs aren't interested in keeping it—either it's too small for them, or they don't like the location, or something. I've heard only chance remarks and I haven't had time to find out how much truth there was in them. But I've admired the house so much, myself, that I've been meaning to ask whether you'd care to buy it, as an investment. I think it might be a pretty good one. Then, after Pell said what he did tonight. . . ."

"You will find out how much truth there was in those rumors, right away, won't you? Because it would be perfect if. . . ."

Roger agreed that he thought so, too, and they went to bed. There was no question as to where he would sleep that night. He and Emily still had a great deal to say to each other about Pell and Simonetta.

Pell telephoned again the next morning and suggested a late lunch at Durgin-Park. He had already drafted a will, he said. It was almost as simple as his grandfather's and he wanted Roger to approve it; when that was done, they would get Stanley and Rose and Cora to witness it, and that would be the end of the matter. He assumed that Roger had the power of attorney ready for him to sign.

Roger was able to give him the assurance he desired, and they ate their lunch with a mutually satisfactory feeling of picking up again where they had left off two years before, as their favorite waitress automatically brought Roger his chowder and Pell, after studying the pastel-colored slips, decided on mushrooms and kidneys. Then Pell said they had discussed his affairs all the time, the night before, and now he wanted to hear something about Roger's. So they drifted into shop-talk and chatted on, oblivious of the passing hours, until Roger happened to glance at the old clock on the wall behind them and realized, with a start, that the afternoon was almost gone.

"If we don't get back to the office presently, we'll be too late to catch Stanley and the girls," he said. "Not that I suppose it matters; tomorrow will do just as well as today. And there are a couple of things I want to ask you, after thinking over our talk last night."

"All right. Shoot!" Pell said, just as he used to when Roger was full of the Jerry Donovan case.

"You mentioned some cousins named Barrata, who emigrated at the same time as your grandparents. Have you any idea where they are now?"

"They might be in Lynn. I believe that's where they went first after they left New Bedford. But I'm not sure. And they could have moved half a dozen times since then."

"You never met them at all?"

Pell pondered for a moment. "Why yes, in a way I 'met' them," he said. "I went to visit them once or twice, with Aunt Carmela, when I was very small. I think it was in Lynn, as I just said. But I told you that, when she married, she took me to Boston with her and she never visited them after that. So I couldn't have been more than four, or five at the outside, the last time I saw them. Unless they came to my Uncle Edmondo's funeral. Now that you speak of them, I believe they did—Italians go in for funerals in a big way, just as they do for weddings. But I had my hands so full, pretty soon afterward, trying to take care of Simonetta, that I never thought of them again. I've certainly never seen them since the funeral. I don't think Aunt Carmela has, either. I'm almost sure I'd have known of it, if she had."

"Do you remember how many of them there were?"

"Not exactly. As I say, it's all very vague in my mind. I think there were a couple of women, about my grandfather's age, or maybe a little younger, and an older man. One of the women was married, so of course her name wasn't Barrata any more. I haven't the dimmest idea what it was."

"But your Aunt Carmela would know, wouldn't she?"

"I suppose she must. However, if I suddenly asked her, after all these years when the cousins have never been mentioned, she'd suspect me of some new trick. And I don't see what it would prove, anyway. Do you?"

"Maybe nothing. On the other hand, if we could get in touch with these cousins, perhaps we could find out what caused the trouble between Carmela and her father and that may have an important bearing on the case. I talked over everything you told me with Emily, the way you said I might; and Emily kept harping on the fact that differences of religious opinion shouldn't be strong enough to alienate a daughter from her father. Of course, sometimes they are. They can be terribly strong. But there's just a chance that Emily's got something. And about an equal chance that the long-lost cousins could throw some light on the subject. Isn't there a way that Simonetta could ask her mother about them, without rousing antagonism or suspicion? I should think she could get Carmela to talking about bygone days, when times were better and who the people were who made them seem so. Then Simonetta might find out something. Is that beyond the realm of possibility?"

"Perhaps not. I can speak to Simonetta about it anyway and let you know what she says."

"And of course, if Autori raises no objection, I'm going to call on your Uncle Nazareno as soon as possible. I'll see if he has anything to offer about the Barratas. He might, one way or another. Meanwhile, here's something else. If you really want Simonetta and her mother to move into better quarters. . . ."

It was obvious that Pell felt no interest in his cousins, and that he did not regard them as probable sources of important information. On the other hand, his enthusiasm about the little house was immediate and unbounded. Roger had already verified the reports that the present owners would "consider an offer" for it and were willing that it should be inspected. Before he saw Pell again, he secured the keys, which he handed over "in exchange for the power of attorney," as he jestingly put it. But when Pell came rushing back to say that he and Simonetta had been through the house, that they were both enchanted with it, and that they wanted Roger to get it for them before anyone else could snap it up, he felt obliged to urge a little patience.

"Easy there. I haven't had time to look up the title yet. I've got to make sure it's clear; and that your grandfather's will hasn't been allowed yet— in fact, you think it may be broken, and I'm afraid you're right. You haven't money enough to buy the house at present, unless you've been holding out on me and are a lot richer than I think you are. But I'll tell you what: now that I know you and Simonetta like the house, Emily and I'll go to see it. If I think it's a wise investment for her, after I've looked it over—and I'm almost sure I shall—she'll buy it, as soon as I've cleared the title; and meanwhile, she'll take an option on it, so that no one else can snap it up. Then she'll rent it to your aunt, if we can persuade Carmela to move into it. If we can't, Emily will rent it to someone else, either without a lease or on a short one. As soon as your grandfather's estate is settled, she'll sell it to you. You're bound to have enough money to buy it then, whatever happens. Maybe you'd have to put a mortgage on it, but that would be all right too. Emily'd just be running true to Forbes' family form, if she began holding mortgages on houses."

"You're making all this sound as if it were completely businesslike, but I know damn well—"

"It is completely businesslike. There's no reason why it shouldn't be businesslike and friendly at the same time, is there? Old Mrs. Forbes is always quoting some French proverb about good business methods making good friends."

"I know. 'Les bons comptes font les bons amis.' Well, we'll let it go at that. Here are the keys back. You and Emily can go to see the house before tomorrow night, can't you? Because Simonetta and I thought that would be a good time for our little party. We'd like you to meet us at the Old Venice Restaurant on Hanover Street, around seven-thirty, if that would be convenient."

"Quite convenient and very pleasant. Thank you. We'll be there."

While he and Emily were dressing the following evening, Roger asked her if she had ever been on Hanover Street.

"No. What's it like?"

"I think it would be better to show you than to try and tell you. We'll go around by Atlantic Avenue and swing into Hanover from there—that way, we'll take in quite a stretch of it. I don't suppose you've ever been on Atlantic Avenue, either. A railroad track runs down the middle of it and all the freight between the North and South stations goes that way—in fact, there's some old law, still on the books, which says a man must walk along the track in front of the freight train, waving a red flag as he goes."

"Roger, you're making this up."

"Just wait until we get down there; you'll find out whether I'm making it up or not. I bet a man will be right there, flag and all."

"I'll take you up on it. A box of candy against a box of cigars."

"You'll lose. Don't forget I prefer Corona Belvederes."

The Corona Belvederes were as good as his already, Roger said, when they started out; and they had hardly turned into Atlantic Avenue from State Street when he shouted, "Look!" Some antiquated freight cars, which had once been brightly painted, but which were now dingy and battered, were creaking slowly down a track; and a shambling, unshaven man, whose drab and dilapidated garments hung forlornly about his loose-jointed form, shuffled casually along, a faded flag, ragged around the edges, drooping from his hand. Every now and then, he raised this slightly and made a limp motion with it. Roger leaned out of the car and called after him, "Thanks for the cigars!"

The man did not even look up; either he did not hear or he regarded the salutation as unimportant. Leaving the freight cars behind them, Roger and Emily passed an old ferry, a succession of wharves and fish markets and some grim-looking warehouses. Then they turned, between a sausage factory and the Coast Guard Base, and entered Hanover Street.

"This is the main drag of the North End," Roger told Emily. "That's St. Stephen's Church, one of Bulfinch's, over on the left. It was originally an important Protestant meetinghouse, but the Catholics took over a long time ago. According to rumor, the last Protestant minister who officiated there hanged himself in the bell tower—perhaps in despair over the papist invasion."

"Roger, how on earth did you find out all these things? I'm glad I didn't make any more bets with you."

"Well, after all, I went to Milton, you know, where they really make you study. And I've practiced law a few blocks from here for more than six years now. Don't you remember that once I didn't get home at all on New Year's Day, and that I told you afterward I'd been supervising the removal of tableware and other equipment, including a bar, from a restaurant we'd closed the night before by attaching its property? You were terribly upset when you learned that the owners marched up and down the sidewalk, threatening to pull knives on us, and that the police were completely indifferent when we reported the situation. They merely replied that they didn't see the use of sending an extra officer to Hanover Street, when there hadn't actually been any trouble yet. We couldn't seem to convince them that it might be better to avert trouble than to wait until we were all stretched out with knives in our backs!"

"I certainly do remember. Do you mean to say that happened anywhere near the place where we're riding along now?"

"Sure. Over by that market where the rabbitskins and the lambskins are hanging in the window. . . . Watch out for Mondello's corner drugstore over on the right. It backs up to the yard at the rear of Paul Revere's house. The Mondello family makes a drink out of citrus fruit that they call Tamarindo. It's a dark reddish-brown, fizzless drink, very popular around here."

"Did you ever have any?"

"Yes. I come down here occasionally to get it, hot summer afternoons. It's refreshing and you can pick up a good deal of information that's quite interesting, whether it's related to legal matters or not, while you sit and sip it."

342

Their halting progress made it possible for Roger to point out one landmark after another. Traffic was heavy and complicated by the number of persons who were sitting in the streets and who merely inched their chairs back toward the sidewalk to let cars go by. Children darted hither and yon and the baby carriages were numerous. Roger was obliged to slam on the brakes in order to permit the leisurely passage of one perambulator, wheeled by a strikingly beautiful young woman, who had two older children clinging to her. Equally pretty girls, wearing bright full skirts and short-sleeved, low-necked white blouses, trimmed with cheap lace, formed laughing and chattering groups. Here and there, a couple of boys leaned companionably against a light pole munching "Guinea wedges." On the sidewalks, older people were gathered around little tables, the men in their shirt sleeves, the women in nondescript black dresses. Some of the men were playing cards; most of the women were merely fanning themselves and gossiping.

Emily looked eagerly from side to side, fearful lest any feature of this kaleidoscopic scene might escape her. "I'd never know we were in Boston," she said at last. "It doesn't seem as if we were."

"You mean it doesn't seem like our Boston. But there are lots of different Bostons, as Pell reminded me the other night. Not that I should have needed the reminder—that was one of the things you and I were going to do, wasn't it? Try to get to know the other kinds better. We don't seem to have made such progress . . . Well, we can't go into that now. There's Old Venice, right ahead of us."

Pell and Simonetta were waiting for them when they reached the restaurant, which was otherwise almost empty, and came forward to welcome them. In spite of the fact that the meeting with Simonetta had been so long deferred, there was no constraint about it. Pell now gave the impression, not only of being entirely at ease in almost any situation which might arise, but of being capable to control and even command it. His presence gave Simonetta a degree of self-confidence which she might otherwise have lacked and her slight remaining shyness became her; somehow it added to the quiet charm of her manner. She was dressed simply, but very effectively, in soft white, and Emily guessed that Pell had insisted on a new outfit for this occasion and had not only supplied the wherewithal for it, but had taken a hand in its choice.

"We thought we would sit here," she said, indicating a corner booth where the table was tastefully decorated with white roses and blue larkspur. "That is, if this would be agreeable to you." Her low-pitched voice was very pleasant and, though she spoke slowly, she did not hesitate or grope for words and both Roger and Emily noticed that her accent was almost gone.

"I think you've chosen the very best place in the restaurant," Emily answered readily. "Though it's all most attractive." She looked around, with appreciation, at the mellow wainscoting surmounted by painted panels of Venetian scenes, which had the same rich golden patina. "And

343

your flowers are simply lovely," she added, as they took their seats. "They go so well with our dresses too."

"Pell helped me choose them," Simonetta answered, glancing adoringly toward him. "He said he had noticed that you very often wore blue, so he hoped you would like them. And of course blue and white are the Blessed Virgin's colors, so it is fitting that those who are asking for Her intercession should honor Her by using them." Simonetta crossed herself, unobtrusively, then nodded to the hovering major-domo. "We have ordered an Italian dinner for you," she went on. "We hope you will like that too. But we thought perhaps you would like to choose your own drinks beforehand."

"Won't you tell us what you think would be best? What do you drink yourselves?"

"I drink vermouth and Pell used to. But now—"

"Now I like it mixed with gin," Pell said smilingly. "And the less vermouth there is in the mixture, the better I like it. Do you want to keep Simonetta company by taking your vermouth straight, Emily? Or will you join Rog and me in dry Martinis?"

"Oh, I'll keep Simonetta company. I think this would be a fine time to begin. . . . Roger and I went to see your house last night, Simonetta," she continued as the major-domo bowed and took his departure.

"My house! Is it really—"

"Well, it's going to be, of course. But I thought perhaps we could plan improvements and decorations for it together. Then I could get started on those as soon as the wartime building restrictions permit and still I'd be sure that everything I was doing was the way you'd want it later on. For instance, I like its interior arrangement, but—"

"Hasn't Roger said anything to you about clearing the title, Emily?" Pell asked whimsically. "Because, if he hasn't, I'm going to raise all sorts of objections. You should have heard him stall when I tried to talk to him. . . . Well, here's Mr. Maturo with the vermouth, both plain and reinforced. Let's drink to a clear title!"

They were still talking about the house when the antipasto was brought on, consisting of beets, celery, salami, anchovies and black olives resting on shredded lettuce; this was followed by minestrone and shrimps cacciatore. When the shrimps had been served, Maturo brought in a round, wickerbound bottle and poured a golden wine almost tenderly from it; it was Orvieto, Pell said, one of his favorites. Emily and Roger, sipping it, agreed that they did not wonder, and from talk of the wine the topic shifted to the cathedral with the glowing façade in the same city which was famous for both. Emily had spent several days of her vacation there, when she had been attending the Petite Ecole in Florence; she was glad she had not gone rushing through, like most tourists, for the cathedral could not be appreciated in the course of one hurried visit; and besides, there were many other beautiful buildings in Orvieto. But, after all, she thought that Urbino was her favorite among the hill cities. There was something about Urbino. . . .

"Do you know, you're the first American I've ever met who's been to Urbino?" Pell said eagerly. "Of course, I've never been there myself—there or anywhere else in Italy. But I'm going to start in Naples and go all over it—Simonetta and I together!"

Pell sounded so happy that Roger and Emily both wondered whether he could have had good news from the Cardinal, whether it were possible that he and Simonetta were to be married that week, after all. As if he had read their thoughts, Pell shook his head, but he was still smiling when he did so.

"Thanks to you, things look a lot better to me than they did when I came to your house the other night," he said, looking at Roger. "So I'm not going to gripe because they don't look better yet. I'll get all I can out of this week; if it isn't all I want, still it's a good deal. And when I'm on my way, I'll know I'm leaving everything in good hands. The very best."

A rear door of the restaurant opened to admit a big, brawny man, with an apron of burlap covering a substantial portion of his person, who was carrying a large block of ice in a pair of iron tongs. He crossed the restaurant unconcernedly, threading his way among the tables as he went toward the bar beyond, and nodding to the customers who acknowledged his progress with a word of welcome. In the case of Pell, the exchange of greetings was hearty, though brief.

"I don't know whether Maturo buys ice for my special benefit," Pell told Roger. "Anyway, that man's come through here with a huge chunk of ice every time I've come here to dine—which has been fairly frequently, ever since I could afford it. It's always cool here in summer and warm in winter and it's always quiet. Strange how few sounds seem to come in from outside, isn't it? Because Hanover Street is full of them, Lord knows! But this is really a restful sort of place, and not only because it isn't actually noisy. There's something about the décor and the atmosphere. . . ."

Roger agreed that there was, adding that he was surprised the place was not more crowded, but that he was glad of it; as Pell had predicted, they could talk almost as freely as if they had been in a private house. In the center of the restaurant, a lonely looking man sat reading an Italian newspaper and giving only intermittent attention to the heaped plate of spaghetti before him; in a booth on the farther side, a girl and a boy were absorbed in pizza and in each other; and two or three other couples were scattered here and there. But there were no large convivial groups and no one at all near Pell's party. The major-domo, who had removed the shrimps cacciatore and brought in scallopine and green salad, had now retreated again. Emily and Simonetta were still engrossed in a discussion of improvements for the little house, as enthusiastically as if it were already in the possession of one or the other. Roger leaned forward and questioned Pell in an undertone.

345

"Did you have any luck with the Cardinal?"

"No. His secretary received me very courteously, but said he would have to await the return of His Eminence to lay the matter before him. Perhaps you didn't know. . . . There's quite a dividing line between the Irish Catholics and the Italian Catholics in Boston. Of course there shouldn't be, any more than there should be that narrow viewpoint as to what constitutes a 'real' Bostonian, which we discussed the other night. But I can't help feeling that, if I'd been an Irishman or if the Cardinal had been an Italian—"

"I did know something about that dividing line. That's why I thought perhaps Father Mat could help."

"And so he might have, if there'd been more time. But, as you probably know, he's attending the Army School for Chaplains at Harvard right now and he's expected, in five short weeks, to cover all aspects of a chaplain's work. He receives instruction in his military duties and his pastoral duties and is taught his place and function in the entire scheme of army organization. He learns about hospital and guardhouse visitations. He also takes courses in customs and courtesies of the service and morale. Since it's part of his future duty to administer sacraments to the dying, he's taught the proper methods of locating and marking cemeteries and graves, and identification of the dead. Furthermore—"

"Good Lord, Pell, he can't learn all that in five weeks!"

"Can't he though? You should have seen what they made us learn about desert warfare in five weeks! He's darn well got to learn it and that's not the half of it, either—chemical warfare, military law, malaria control—"

"Will you please stop, Pell? I'm exhausted, just listening to you."

"Well I'm not anywhere nearly through yet. And of course, up to now, I've only been talking about the academic instruction and training. The physical instruction and training include drills, reviews, road marches— there, I don't want you to pass out. But I think maybe I've given you the idea that there simply aren't enough hours in Father Mat's days for him to take on much of anything extra right now. And he's hellbent to get into a combat zone, just as David was. He's poking quite a little fun at himself, too, saying he never thought he'd be the first of the Collins family to turn into a Harvard man! But that's neither here nor there. To answer your question, I can see there's no chance of our getting a dispensation this week."

"I'm terribly sorry, Pell. If there were only something I could do to help. . . . Perhaps there is. Not that I've any direct contacts with the hierarchy, but I've got indirect ones that might do some good. Are you willing I should try?"

"Willing! But don't worry if you're not successful. You're doing plenty as it is. You've done plenty. . . . Anything else on your mind?"

"Yes, one other thing. I want to know whether you succeeded in getting any information about those cousins of yours. Somehow I'd feel I had a clue as to why your grandfather left his money the way he did, if I knew a little more about them."

"I'm sorry, but I haven't found out a thing. I did speak to Simonetta about them and she managed to ask her mother, without having the question seem too pointed. Just the same, Aunt Carmela shut up like a clam, exactly as I told you I thought she would."

"Then I guess your Uncle Nazareno's my best bet."

"I guess he is. Sorry I haven't time to run down and pump him myself. But you can see what's keeping me here."

He looked lovingly at Simonetta and, as if conscious that his eyes were upon her, she turned away from Emily and looked at him. The gaze had the quality of a caress; and Emily, who was watching them, thought of that embrace in the street on Christmas Eve and thought, too, for a moment, that they might exchange one now, with almost the same spontaneity and lack of self-consciousness. Then she realized, with sadness, that probably they did not feel free to embrace each other like that any more, since they had come to realize both the intensity of their love and the laws which prevented its fulfillment. Probably they would kiss each other good-by, and that would be all. And perhaps they would never see each other again. . . .

The major-domo was once more hovering near by, awaiting a sign to remove the remains of the *scallopine* and bring on the *spumone*. Simonetta, rousing herself to the responsibilities of a hostess, gave him the requisite signal and he began piling up the plates and putting them on a little table at the side. As he did so, the door leading from the street was flung open, and a small, tousle-headed boy, with a sheaf of newspapers under his arm, came noisily into the restaurant.

"Evening papers!" he shouted. "*Traveler—Globe—Record!* Latest war news! U.S. PATROL PLANES SMASH TEN U-BOATS! NUREMBERG GETS IT! BRITISH LOSE THIRTY-THREE OF THOUSAND BOMBERS IN RAID! Paper! Paper!"

He darted from booth to booth, looking hopefully about in search of customers, and shifting the weight of the papers from his hip to his underarm. The restaurant was almost empty now. He had sold only two papers when he reached the booth where Maturo, having served the *spumone*, was now pouring Asti. Pell reached in his pocket and drew out a coin.

"I guess we all want papers here," he said. "Give me four, will you, buddy? Better make it five. We have an aunt at home who might like one too."

The small boy extracted five papers from his sheaf and, after wiping his nose with the back of his hand, reached out for payment. Then he stared down in astonishment at the proffered coin.

"I ain't never seen money like that before," he said suspiciously. "What is it?"

"It's a silver dollar. There aren't many of them around here. But people use them a lot in California, where I've just come from."

"I ain't got change for no dollar."

"I don't want any. It so happens that the five papers you sold me are worth twenty cents apiece to me."

"G'wan! They ain't worth but a nickel!" retorted the small boy, still more suspiciously. "If Mr. Maturo will change this money for me, that's okay. If he won't, you can give me back my papers, you cheap skate, you!"

Pell lifted his chin and laughed. "All right, here are your five nickels," he said, drawing more coins from his pocket. "But keep the silver dollar, too, for a luck piece. Mr. Maturo will tell you it's okay, if you won't take my word for it. . . . How old are you, buddy?"

"Goin' on eight and a half," muttered the newsboy. He had now pocketed the five nickels, for safety, but he still stood turning over the silver dollar with grimy fingers. It was evident he felt sure there was a catch somewhere.

"I thought you'd be around that," Pell said encouragingly. "Been selling papers a year or so already, haven't you?"

"How'd you guess?"

The question was spat out. Then, before Pell could answer, the little street Arab scurried out of the door, clutching the silver dollar. Pell lifted his glass.

"Let's drink to that kid," he said. "If our toast brings him the same good luck I've had, he'll be cracking a bottle of Asti here himself, twenty years from now, in the best of all possible company."

Two nights later, Pell and Simonetta came for a garden supper with Roger and Emily, and again Pell seemed in good spirits. They did not talk so much about the little house this time; Pell apparently regarded that question as settled, along with all questions pertaining to his insurance and will, to the allotment of his pay and his legacy, and to Roger's acceptance of his case. Instead, they talked about Simonetta's future education, which he now wished to discuss in greater detail than had been possible on the occasion of his first visit. She had a piano of sorts already, and had taken a few lessons from a broken-down old music teacher who formerly lived in their block on Joy Street, but who had died several years earlier. Since then, Simonetta had gone on without supervision and she had made a good deal of progress by herself; but Pell thought that with help she could make a good deal more. Anyhow, he wanted Emily's advice about finding a new teacher—a first-class one—and he wanted Simonetta to have a new piano, the best available under present conditions; the new teacher should be able to give advice about that.

"How would you like to go to the New England Conservatory of Music, instead of taking private lessons at home, Simonetta?" Emily asked. "Of course you'd have your new piano at home, you'd practice there. But you'd meet interesting people, you'd have the benefit of teamwork, you'd get the stimulus of competition."

Simonetta turned toward Pell and he answered for her. "I think that's a grand idea, Emily," he said heartily. "But then you're full of grand ideas —you and Roger both."

"Perhaps Mother will not permit me to go to the Conservatory," suggested Simonetta, for the first time speaking with hesitation and obvious anxiety.

"I'm afraid she won't like it. But she can't stop you, Simonetta. You're twenty-three years old. You're free to do whatever seems best to you and Pell. You mustn't let your mother interfere with your life any longer."

Roger spoke kindly, but firmly; and when Pell said, "That's right," Roger felt emboldened to say more.

"I'm afraid your mother's going to make things unpleasant for you in a good many ways, Simonetta. You see, she's so angry about your grandfather's will that her whole viewpoint's bound to be influenced by that anger; and her viewpoint wasn't very cheerful beforehand. She's going to feel that you're defying her because you haven't accepted her verdict that you shouldn't marry Pell, even if there were no question of anything else. She's never wanted you to go out to work, because she's been determined to isolate you with her; she's been satisfied to have Pell support you both. He's been able to do so and he's still able to do so—in fact, you and she can live better than you ever have on the allotment you'll get from his army pay; and if your grandfather's will is settled in his favor, you can live a great deal better. But she may take the stand that, if you can go to the Conservatory, you can get a job. Don't let her hound you into doing it. Be respectful to her always, be affectionate if you can, but assert your independence. It'll mean a great deal more to Pell, when he comes back, to find that you've learned a lot than to find that you've earned a little. I think your studies at the Conservatory will use up most of your time and strength. But if they don't, you ought to take courses somewhere else— perhaps at Simmons, perhaps at one of the good Catholic colleges. We'll see what can be arranged. But I think Emily's right—I think the Conservatory should come first, because you and Pell both love music so much. When he comes home, when you and he are married, just think what it will mean to him if you can fill the house with melody."

"You said, 'when' we are married," Simonetta began falteringly. "But—"

"Yes, I did say 'when.' I didn't say 'if.' I feel sure you and he are going to be married someday. I'm certain that when he comes home, the way will be cleared for your marriage. I don't know how yet, but somehow. Please believe me, Simonetta. I think Pell half believes me already. If I can make you believe me, he will too."

"I do believe him, Simonetta," Pell said in a low voice. "Not just half-way, either. That is, I don't see how it's going to be possible, any more

349

than he does. But I think he's going to find out. I—well, I'm practically sure of it. If I weren't, I couldn't have been so happy this week. I wasn't, when I first came home. I was in despair. But I'm not any longer. And you mustn't despair, either. You must be hopeful too."

He put his arm around her. "Tomorrow, you and I will go and choose your engagement ring," he said. "Even if I can't have you for my wife before I leave, I can have you for my betrothed. We'll plight our troth to each other, in the presence of witnesses—Roger and Emily—just as our people used to do in olden times. It will be a solemn betrothal service. After that, no one should come between us—not even your mother. Your first thought and your first obligation will be to me."

Late the next afternoon Pell brought her to the house again. Once more, she was clad entirely in white, but it was not the same white that she had worn at Old Venice. That had been very simple. This time the dress was made almost entirely of filmy lace, over tiers of chiffon. She had pearls around her neck and on her breast and in her ears; and, when she and Pell had taken their places opposite Roger and Emily in the candle-lighted drawing room, Pell drew a beautiful diamond ring from his pocket and the thought flashed through Roger's mind, with a pang of envy, that Pell had been able to do more for the adornment of his betrothed than he, Roger, had been able to do for the adornment of his bride.

"I, Pellegrino, take thee, Simonetta, for my betrothed wife," Pell said gravely. "And with this ring, I plight thee my troth. . . . Now you must say, 'I, Simonetta, take thee, Pellegrino, for my betrothed husband. And I will wear thy ring as a sign that I have plighted thee my troth.'" He waited while she repeated the words after him, and then he put the ring on her finger and kissed her on the forehead. Afterward, he looked across at Roger and Emily and smiled. "I'm not sure that's exactly the way our people used to do it," he said, "but it must be near enough. Anyhow, it's a good way. . . . We're going to drink champagne next, aren't we? I'm sure that must have been one of the features in the ceremony."

They did not see him again. This would be his last evening at home, he said, and he and Simonetta would spend it by themselves. He would make one more attempt to talk with her mother, to make Carmela see reason. He had already told her about the course at the Conservatory, so that Simonetta would not have to bear the first brunt of her displeasure over that, and he had tried to pave the way for her acceptance of other changes, such as the move from the flat. He had not made much headway, and he could see that he had now forfeited all the affection she had previously felt for him. He was sorry, for he could never forget how kind she had been to him, until the question of his marriage with Simonetta and the conflict about his grandfather's will had arisen between them. But it could not be helped. He had decided on his course and he intended to keep it. He wrung Roger's hand and told him again how grateful he was to him and how much he trusted him. And he kissed Emily and said he knew Simonetta would be safe in her keeping. Then he was gone, taking his betrothed with him.

Though they did not see him again, Roger and Emily talked of him constantly; and, late the next evening, while they were in the chintz sitting room, they were suddenly conscious of an unfamiliar sound and realized that someone was knocking at the garden gate. There had been a heavy storm in the afternoon, and there were still intermittent flashes of lightning and distant rumbles of thunder; it had been too wet for them to eat supper in the garden or, indeed, to stay there at all. Now they were startled that anyone should come to the gate in such weather and at such an hour. Then they heard a cry above the knocking and it was a cry of desperation.

"Someone must be in terrible trouble," Roger exclaimed, jumping up. "Stay where you are, Emily, until I find out."

"No, I'm coming too."

He did not hear her because he was already hurrying through the hall and down the stairs, snapping on lights as he went. She hastened after him, catching up with him as he reached the garden gate. He unlatched it and threw it open to reveal Simonetta standing on the threshold.

She was no longer clad in white and adorned with pearls. She had thrown a shawl around her shoulders and tied a scarf under her chin, to protect herself from the rain; but the effect was one of reversion to old familiar custom. Her new-found self-confidence, like her brave assumption of hope, was completely gone. She was weeping bitterly, and she threw herself into Emily's arms, abandoning herself to her grief.

"He has gone," she sobbed. "He has gone and I know he is not coming back. I shall never be his wife, for he will be killed. And my mother has turned against me, calling me dreadful names and cursing me. She has driven me away from her. I was ashamed to tell our neighbors. I had to come here. There was nowhere else that I could go."

Chapter 29

DAYLIGHT WAS ALREADY fading and a chill was creeping into the crispness of the autumnal air as Emily and Roger left the tangle of traffic in Quincy behind them and headed south. The limits of wartime speed, which they scrupulously observed, gave them leisure for enjoyment of the peaceful countryside, with its familiar pattern of neat white houses and well-tended grounds, and the blaze of fall foliage, doubly brilliant in the setting sun. They were nearly halfway to New Bedford before either of them made more than a few desultory remarks. Both had a succession of hard days behind them and were thankful for brief respite; both wanted to improve the rare opportunity for undisturbed reflection. It was very seldom, lately, that they had been motoring together. Only the fact that this was primarily a professional trip, and that their mission stood a better chance of success if it were undertaken after normal business hours, when there were fewer interruptions and less sense of pressure, would have justified the present consumption of gasoline. They were on their way to see Nazareno Pacetti, who had cordially invited them to dinner.

His lawyer, Claudio Autori, had come to Boston a fortnight earlier, for the purpose of seeking Roger's assent, in Pell's behalf, to the appointment of Pacetti as special administrator and as such, to his continued management of the restaurant, pending the outcome of the contest over the will. Roger's support of these petitions had of course weighed the scales of justice in favor of Nazareno during these important preliminary steps; and Autori had not only willingly granted permission for the interview with Pell's uncle, but had urgently advised that it should take place, in the hope that, during the course of it, Roger might elicit additional information which would stand them both in good stead against Carmela's attack. As Roger had foreseen, Fopiano had immediately begun a formal challenge of the will by filing an appearance for Carmela; and he had also contested it more specifically on the grounds that it was improperly executed and witnessed and that Antonio had been unduly influenced by his son at the time it was made. Furthermore, Fopiano was trying to persuade the probate court that these issues should be heard by a jury; and

Roger and Autori were both fearful that, if his motion for this purpose were allowed, Fopiano might be able to present a fairly plausible case, founded on the close association of Antonio and his son in the restaurant business, and on Nazareno's increasing amount of authority there.

Roger had hoped that the interview with Pacetti might take place promptly after Pell's departure. But he had of course been obliged to wait on Autori; and, when the way was clear, as far as his move was concerned, the firm of Cutter, Mills and Swan had received another body blow: Cyrus Fletcher, who had visualized more clearly than any of the senior partners the difficulties under which Roger and Stanley were laboring, and who had done his best to lighten and share these labors, was suddenly stricken with cerebral hemorrhage. He died without regaining full consciousness.

Roger had been closer to him than anyone else in the firm, both through the nature of their professional association, and through the friendly relations which had developed between Sumner Thayer and Cyrus Fletcher after the sale of the Gloucester Street house. Therefore Roger was the logical person to take over the work which poor Fletcher had so abruptly left unfinished; and he had not only felt it incumbent on him to attend the funeral, but to help arrange for this, and to offer every possible service to the widow. When he made his first visit of condolence, he found her stunned rather than sorrowful; she seemed incapable of grasping the reality of sudden death, in all its implications. The second time he went to see her, hoping to find her sufficiently rational to face the inevitable details of readjustment and legal procedure, she did indeed receive him much more collectedly. But, somewhat tardily, she bethought herself that she had not adequately enacted the role of grieving widow before and that she should do so now. Her lamentations, after first following a more or less stereotyped form, next took a peculiar turn.

"If he had to die," she sobbed, brushing her cheeks with the handkerchief which she held in one hand, while clutching a letter in the other, "I would have given anything in this world if he could have lived just one more day."

"I suppose we all feel that way, when we have a loss," Roger answered sympathetically. Her expression of sorrow had poignantly recalled his last vigil by his father's bedside and his broken, boyish prayer, "Please, God, let me keep him a little longer! I need him so much. . . ."

"I suppose so," Mrs. Fletcher admitted with a strangled sigh. "But this time, there was a very special reason. I shall never forget how kind your father-in-law was to Cyrus, never, never. This house that I wanted so much —we wouldn't have owned it if it hadn't been for Mr. Thayer."

Roger, who felt that he deserved some credit for the transaction, since he had been the first to suggest its feasibility and had afterward made all the requisite legal arrangements, refrained from comment.

"And then about the Somerset Club. You know it had been my poor husband's lifelong ambition to belong to it. And he had never made any progress at all in that direction until Mr. Thayer took a hand in the matter."

"I'm sure he was very glad to do so. I'm sure he felt Mr. Fletcher would be a great addition to the club."

"Of course he would have been—so cultured, so conservative, so informed! I don't need to go into all that, Mr. Field. No one except my children and myself realizes that more keenly than you do."

"Indeed I do realize it, Mrs. Fletcher. It was a privilege to be associated with him. I shall never forget it."

"But those stupid snobs at the Somerset Club didn't feel that way. Not until Mr. Thayer kept on and on, insisting that my husband should be invited to join. Of course your father-in-law persuaded Homer Lathrop to bring pressure to bear too. But Homer Lathrop never would have done it, if it hadn't been for Mr. Thayer. He wouldn't have gone to that much trouble. It was thanks to Mr. Thayer that the Membership Committee finally took action. But too late. The invitation was posted the very day Cyrus died. He never knew it had been sent. That was why I said, if he could only have lived one more day. . . ."

She handed Roger the letter she had been holding and covered her face with her handkerchief. While she wept, he drew from its envelope the communication, stating that, at the last meeting of the Membership Committee, it had been unanimously voted to invite Mr. Cyrus E. Fletcher to become a member of the Somerset Club.

Roger had related this episode to his father-in-law, who had listened gravely and who had obviously seen no amusing side to it. Emily, to whom Roger next told the story, had been quick to grasp its seriocomic aspects. However, she had swiftly risen to the defense of her trustee.

"It isn't fair of Mrs. Fletcher to say that Uncle Homer never goes to any trouble for anybody. He's gone to all kinds of trouble to look after my interests."

"Well, those are his, too, in a way, you know, Emily. A trust fund like yours represents a good deal more than responsibility; it also represents very substantial returns for the person who handles it. And yours isn't by any means the only one that Homer Lathrop handles."

"I know it, and I think it's all the more to his credit that he's given so much attention to mine. Besides, look how much he's contributing to the war effort. Not just money, either. He's serving on both the Draft Board and the Executive Committee of the Red Cross. And if it hadn't been for him, that Bay State Club on the Boston Common would probably have never come into existence. He visualized it before anyone else did, he went around overriding obstacles and getting contributions of labor and material. It's going up fast now. He told me just the other day he thought it would be ready to open in less than two months."

"Yes, he has put a lot into it. I wish I could have seen him making his plea before the Bricklayers' Union, after he had decided there had to be a fireplace. Somehow, it doesn't seem quite in character."

"Well, doesn't that make it all the more to his credit?"

"Of course. I wasn't trying to minimize his contribution. I just thought it had its amusing side, like Mrs. Fletcher's tale of woe. You could see that, so I hope you can see this too. All the same, I like to hear you stick up for Homer Lathrop. You're a loyal little soul, Emily, if there ever was one."

She had made no reply to this, and they had not spoken of either Mrs. Fletcher or Homer Lathrop again until they were on their way to New Bedford. Now, after an interval of relaxing silence, they reverted to both.

"We've got to do something down at the office. Everyone is run ragged and still we're not getting anywhere. There's no one to do the leg work and the clients aren't getting any kind of service. We're sending the girls on some errands, but they can't go into court—or at least they shouldn't. And they're all tired out too. Rose McCarthy almost fell asleep while I was trying to dictate to her yesterday and normally, she's as keen as they come. And half the time, Cora's late on the switchboard. Of course they're trying to do something for the war effort too. Rose is putting in odd hours at the Travelers Aid in the South Station—so many servicemen are going through there now that the regular force can't handle them. And Cora's at the USO, off and on. We try to make allowances for them. But that doesn't help us to get rid of the leg work. It was bad enough before Fletcher died. Now it's a great deal worse. He wasn't much to look at or to talk with, but he really pulled his weight."

"What about that friend of yours who went to Vermont? Couldn't you lure him back to the great city?"

"Bradford? Good Lord, he's about the only lawyer left in Vergennes! He's his own boss, but he's his own office boy too. He thought he was through with chicken coop cases a couple of years ago, but he's had to go back to them, besides keeping on with the big ones—there just is no one else to do it. If he didn't, a lot of poor people couldn't have any legal advice and help at all."

"Have you ever thought of a woman?"

"What do you mean, have I ever thought of a woman? Oh—you're talking about a female lawyer! Not if I could help it. As far as I know, almost none of the big firms in Boston has one on its staff."

"But they do in other places, don't they?"

"May be. I should think they might be all right for tax and title work. But I never saw one yet who made a good appearance in court."

"You're a hidebound old Bostonian, that's what you are! I won't make any more suggestions."

"Go right ahead. You might come up with something yet. . . . By the way, I'm sorry I couldn't accept Homer Lathrop's invitation to serve on his committee for the Bay State Club. I hope I convinced him I'd really like to. But you know what time I've been getting home lately. And with air raid practice and plotting, I honestly don't see how I can do anything more."

"I don't either and I'm sure Uncle Homer understands. He was just trying to pay you a compliment."

"Well, I guess we have to let compliments go for the present. . . . Gosh, look at that little lake! Isn't it pretty and wouldn't it seem good to get out on it for a while? Just you and I, in any old kind of a boat; but that sort of thing will have to go for the present too."

Emily looked longingly at the little lake; it was fringed with bright foliage, which was reflected on its clear surface, and this was blue and sparkling. It would indeed have seemed good to get out on the water in "any old kind of a boat." But she knew, as well as Roger, that there would be no chance for "that sort of thing" at present and probably not for a long while; and this was not only because of Roger's preoccupations, but also because of her own. The time which she and Deirdre had foreseen, when Ellie should feel she should follow Dolly to a factory, had come that fall. True, they had not lost Ellie altogether; she continued to live with them and did what housework she could after factory hours and on Saturday afternoons and Sundays when she would otherwise have been free. She was sturdier than Dolly and insisted she did not mind eighteen-hour days; but Emily, while appreciating Ellie's willingness and loyalty, knew that she could not go on at such a pace indefinitely, and was gradually reorganizing her household still further to meet changed conditions.

Her tentative plan for a basement dining room, looking out on the garden, had been abandoned, partly because it seemed unpatriotic to spend money on nonessential building materials, even when these were available; and partly because Deirdre was so unfeignedly loath to leave her familiar kitchen quarters for a transformed laundry, and so especially unwilling to be separated from the mammoth old-fashioned stove, to which she had become greatly attached and which could not possibly be moved. Therefore, she sent up breakfast on the dumb-waiter, and Emily was dressed and downstairs, ready to receive it when it reached the butler's pantry, and to take it into the same old dining room; for Ellie had already left for the factory, even though breakfast was now much earlier than it used to be. There were no more pleasant leisurely bedside meals before Roger went to the office. Emily served the breakfast herself, washed the breakfast dishes and did the chamber work and as much dusting as she could before she went to the hospital; then, on her return, she saw to the marketing, the mending and other incidental tasks. Together, she and Ellie devoted Saturday afternoons to vacuum cleaning; and Ellie laid fires, brought up wood and washed windows, a few at a time, after her later return from the factory on other week days.

In spite of their joint efforts, the aspect of the house was gradually changing from one of immaculate order and meticulous care to one of more casual comfort. Roger said he really liked it better that way; it had been almost painfully clean before; now he could put his feet on a chair and drop ashes on a rug without worrying. But Emily secretly regretted the inevitable lowering of the standards of gracious living which had been set for her when she was a girl and which she had striven so long to maintain. She still strove to do so; and because the work was a type to which she was as yet unaccustomed, it was hard for her. She had not realized before that she would use such different muscles for housework than for walking and riding; that anyone as strong and well as she was could ache all over from sheer fatigue. Besides, she knew her efforts represented a losing battle and recognized that they should, even while she continued to make them. As Dolly had intimated a year earlier, there were things much more essential now than shining silver and brass and serving meals in courses, with finger bowls and doilies.

Though she was adjusting herself to more and more physical labor and giving less and less attention to superfluous amenities, Emily worried because the house was already so cold and because she knew it would be much colder when winter really set in. The allotment of oil for heating purposes was entirely inadequate to keep the large, high-ceilinged structure at an even temperature of moderate warmth. The open fireplaces helped and she had been able to get some wood from the Dublin farm; but actually, Deirdre's kitchen, with its big stove, which they were fortunately still able to feed with coal, was the most comfortable room in the house. Emily did not blame Deirdre for clinging to it. As a matter of fact, she did not mind the cold too much herself, especially now that she was so active. But she worried about it on Roger's account. Every time he had an attack of bronchitis, it was more severe than the one before; and finally, the family doctor had taken her aside and talked to her privately about her husband's condition.

"I don't like to see Mr. Field so overtired all the time. And I wish there were some way of getting him out of this Boston climate in the worst winter months. In fact, as his physician, I'd say it was imperative. Isn't there any way you could persuade him to take more time off every week, Mrs. Field? And to go to Florida or the Gulf coast during January and February?"

"I wish there were. But you know, as well as I do, Dr. Blaine, that Roger won't leave the office, even for a day. He feels that what he's doing there, in the absence of the other juniors, is the only contribution he can make to the war effort. He's pretty sensitive on the subject. I'd only hurt his feelings, without getting anywhere, if I said anything. And after all, you're a great one to talk! You told me, three years ago, that you were going to retire, that when a doctor reached threescore and ten, he ought to give the younger sawbones a chance. And now you're plugging along night and day, doing the work of younger men, just as Roger is doing the work of healthier men."

"Well, I'm afraid there's a certain logic in what you say. But, for Mr. Field's sake, I wish you felt you could be illogical. . . ."

Emily had wished so, too, at the time this conversation took place; and now, as she sat watching the sparkling waters of the little lake, while Roger slowed down the car so that they might at least have a good look at it as they went by, she wished so still more earnestly. If she and Roger could have gone boating once in a while; if they could have got out more frequently in a car, as they were doing today, or stolen a week end now and then at Hollyhock Hill, neither of them would have been so tired all the time. And Roger had told her, over and over again, how much he would like to see the Gulf Coast. She finally decided to broach the subject.

"Well, couldn't we?" she asked.

"Couldn't we what?"

"Get out in a boat?"

"Just when?"

"Well, whenever you like."

"Whenever I *like!*"

"Well, whenever you could manage to. Because honestly, Roger, I don't believe you can go on indefinitely, without taking some time off. I don't think you ought to."

"I don't imagine Pell and Brian and David are getting much time off, do you?"

"No, but—"

"Let's skip it, Emily, if you don't mind."

Well, she had hurt him, as she had feared she might. She would not try to say anything more about getting away.

It was growing dark as they entered New Bedford and went on and on down Ashley Boulevard, between dimly lighted houses and small shops. At last they turned under the railroad; and after Emily, despite Roger's typically masculine objections, had inquired the way from several noncommittal pedestrians, they reached a side street dominated by a red neon sign on which the name PACETTI's appeared in large scroll letters. Having carefully parked and prudently locked their car, they went through the double doors of a vestibule into a large dining room, somewhat garish as to lighting and decoration, and so overheated as to be rather close. At the same time, the place was pervaded with good cheer; it was redolent with the mingled odors of herbs, spices, liquor and tobacco; and it was crowded with customers whose genial talk and hearty laughter resounded through it. Some of the clientele, obviously a familiar one, looked up curiously when Emily and Roger entered, appraising them instantly as strangers; but before they had time to ask a passing waiter where they might find their host, a short, stocky man, with wiry, iron-gray hair and noticeably fine teeth, who was neatly dressed in a dark, double-breasted suit, hurried forward to meet them and introduced himself as Nazareno Pacetti.

He shook hands with every evidence of good feeling, insisted on making away with their wraps, and ushered them ceremoniously into a small private dining room, where a table covered by a white cloth and adorned with a stiff little bouquet of paper flowers was set for three. At the moment, only a basket of bread and a carafe of water flanked the flowers; but the prodigal display of cutlery and the variety of goblets revealed the lavish proportions of the impending feast.

"Sit down, sit down," Pacetti said jovially, drawing out the chairs. "We shall eat first and talk business afterward, shan't we? That way, we'll be better fortified to face any unpleasant subject which may arise—not that I anticipate disagreement. I hope you like Italian cooking. We can't do as well for you as we'd like, hampered the way we are with rationing. But we'll do our best. And you'll come back, I hope, after the war's over and find out more about our specialties."

Roger and Emily hastened to assure him of their enthusiasm for the Italian cuisine and mentioned the excellent meal they had enjoyed at Old Venice, as Pell's guests. Nazareno nodded, with apparent interest, and said he would try to do even better for them than his nephew, but that, unfortunately, hampered as he was. . . . While course succeeded course, Mr. Pacetti, though still speaking heartily, bemoaned the trials and tribulations of a restaurateur caught in the toils of a global war; and, with the appearance of each new dish, he poured out a different wine, whose quality belied the apologies with which it was offered. The Fields found him a likable host. He reminded them greatly of Pell, for the family resemblance was unmistakable. This man was less cultured, less magnetic and less intense; but Pell's natural eagerness, his spontaneity and sincerity, his warmth, were all there. So was a singular mixture of simplicity and shrewdness, which was Nazareno's own and which was rather attractive. He gave an impression of enormous energy and great good will; and he was obviously bent on being friendly and on showing his friendliness in the way which was most instinctive, by plying his guests with food and drink. When the strong black coffee and the sweet golden Strega were finally brought in, Roger and Emily were both in a state of repletion, and their host, leaning back with a sigh of satisfaction, seemed inclined to continue the drift of casual conversation, rather than to turn to the discussion of the business which had brought his visitors to his restaurant. Roger was finally obliged to take the initiative by plunging into the subject.

"Mr. Pacetti," he began, leaning forward with one arm on the table, "may I ask how much you can tell me, of your own knowledge, about the execution of your father's will?"

"Not much, I'm sorry to say. In some ways, my dad and I were very close. In others, he kept his distance. He brought me into the restaurant when I was just a kid—first to wash dishes and then to wait on table, outside of school hours. Afterward, he kept me in the kitchen and sent me to the markets; I learned to cook and to buy foodstuffs. He took me with him when he went to get supplies and ideas. All in all, we visited a good many famous restaurants, both in this country and abroad and, incidentally, we met a good many famous persons." Nazareno smiled and, in his turn, leaned forward. "My dad was more interested in having me learn the business than he was in seeing I had a good time," he said. "I managed to do both and to pick up a fair education along the way. But I never wanted to be anything except a restaurateur. I always wanted to carry on here."

"And you always expected to? Your father expected to have you?"

"Of course. Dad kept telling me, from the time I began to wash dishes, that someday I'd be running the business. On the other hand, he didn't want to make me his partner. He wanted to be the boss, see?"

"Yes, I see," Roger said thoughtfully.

"It would have been better if he'd let me share the responsibility though, the last years of his life. He still wanted to see everything, do everything, decide everything—and he couldn't. He tired easily, his memory was tricky. Just the same, he was bound to have his own way and keep his own counsel. That was how it was with the will."

"Yes?" Roger said again. But this time the word formed a question.

"I don't even know when he made it," Pacetti went on earnestly. "Probably while I'd gone out on some errand. Anyhow, one day he showed me an envelope and said, 'This is my will. I'm leaving the restaurant to you, just as I always planned. I know I can trust you to see that our patrons get good food and sound wines and that they're treated like friends. I'm putting this in our office safe and, when I'm gone, take it out and give it to Mr. Autori. He'll do the necessary and then this place will be yours.' "

"So you're sure there was nothing sudden about his decision? And you're equally certain you didn't influence him in any way as to the terms of the will?"

"Of course I'm certain. I told you that before," Nazareno repeated, speaking, for the first time, with a touch of annoyance. "And, after he died, I did just what my dad said. I sent for Claudio Autori and took the envelope out of the safe and gave it to him. I never knew what was in the will until he told me. But I've spent my whole life working for the restaurant and my dad always meant me to have it. He wanted me to have the chance to run it my way after he was gone. Carmela is a wicked woman. Supposing she does spend half her life on her knees and fast until she's faint? What does that prove? If she weren't wicked, she wouldn't try to stop me from getting what's lawfully mine."

His tone had become more and more indignant as he went on. Roger tried to speak soothingly.

"I don't blame you for feeling the way you do. And there's no doubt

360

that Mrs. De Lucca is a very strange woman. You knew, of course, that she'd turned against Pell, after treating him like her own child for years and years. But perhaps you didn't know she'd turned against her own child too. She drove Simonetta out of her house the night after Pell went away."

"She did? What happened to the poor girl?"

"Fortunately, she came to us. And I think she's quite happy now—as happy as she can be with Pell in a combat zone. Those two are very much in love."

"Then why didn't they get married?"

"They're own cousins, you know. They can't, according to canon law, unless they have a dispensation."

"And of course Carmela would do everything she could to block that, that mean old woman. Why didn't they get married anyway? Own cousins can get married in Massachusetts. Plenty of them do. It's legal, all right."

"I know that and so do they. But they're very sincere, themselves, in feeling they must be married in the Church. They hope, in time, they can get a dispensation, in spite of Mrs. De Lucca. Meanwhile, Pell's overseas and Simonetta's studying at the New England Conservatory of Music. She has a great deal of talent and she's progressing beautifully. She comes to us two or three times a week, but she's living at Franklin Square House. For the first time in her life, she's meeting lots of nice girls her own age, with interests similar to hers. It's been a revelation to her. . . . Pell doesn't know yet that her mother was so cruel to her. We thought that should be kept from him as long as possible, because of course this isn't any time for him to have additional worries. It had been agreed that he'd write to her in our care anyway, because—well, because we wanted to be sure the letters weren't intercepted."

"What did I say in the first place about Carmela?"

"I know. And I said I understood your viewpoint. But we mustn't keep harping on that. We must try to find out why your father felt the way he obviously did about her. He didn't realize she'd try to prevent you from getting your rights; he didn't know she'd turn against her foster son and her own daughter. Can you think of any reason—any *special* reason—why he didn't leave her more in his will? Any reason that she might not mention or that we should talk over now, so that we could show it at the trial?"

"Oh, I can think of reasons. But it's for you and Mr. Autori to decide about using them."

"Will you tell me now, confidentially, what some of them are?"

"Well, one is that I stayed close to him and she didn't. She got married and went away."

"That might be a reason, but it isn't an important one. A great many girls—most girls—leave home when they get married."

"Yes, but they come home to visit; they bring their children to visit. Carmela didn't come home, she didn't bring Simonetta and Pell to see my dad."

"Did he ask her to?"

"I don't know for sure. I've told you he was a great one to keep his own counsel. But I'm almost certain he did, after her husband died, though he and I were both disgusted over the way she'd squandered money on Edmondo's funeral—we went to it, of course. He'd have paid the hospital bills when Simonetta was born. But he found out that Carmela'd put all the money he'd given her into a marble monument, and he was furious. Not that he wouldn't have wanted things done decently. My dad always wanted that."

"I'm sure he did."

"And he'd have taken it for granted that she'd want Requiem Masses said. He was an agnostic himself—well, you know that, I believe. But he wouldn't have objected to anything in reason. It was because Carmela wouldn't be reasonable, when it came to religion—" He broke off. "I don't know how far we want to go into that. I suppose we've got to watch out. There might be some fanatic on the jury."

"That's right," corroborated Roger. "We can't properly conceal anything. But there's no use in raising an issue over something that might turn one or more jurymen against you."

"Against us," amended Nazareno.

"Thanks. Against us. . . . Then you can't think of anything else, besides the fact that she was the first to make the break, and that she became a fanatic, which could have turned your father against your sister?"

"Not right off the bat. If I do later on, I'll let you know."

"Good. Now here's another question. What can you tell me about your cousins?"

"My cousins? What cousins?"

"Pell told me you had some cousins, named Barrata, who came to the United States at the same time as your parents, but that they didn't stay in New Bedford."

"Well, that's so. They moved away before I was born. Carmela might remember them. She's older than I am. For that matter, so was my other sister, Adelina—Pell's mother. I was the youngest in the family."

"I think Mrs. De Lucca does remember them. But she won't talk about them. Pell remembers them too—very vaguely. He says he went with his aunt to visit them, several times, before her marriage. But he's never seen them since his uncle's funeral. . . . You say you and your father went to that funeral? Didn't you see these cousins of yours there? Didn't your father speak to them?"

"He didn't speak to anybody. I told you he was disgusted because the funeral was so showy. He came straight home from the church. He didn't even go to the cemetery. He didn't go to Carmela's flat. I didn't know that any of the people in the church were our cousins. My dad never told me so."

"Well, wouldn't that show there was *something* strange? I mean in connection with the cousins?"

It was Emily who put the question. Up to this time, she had been an attentive, but silent, listener, looking from Nazareno to Roger as first one and then the other spoke. Now she bent forward eagerly.

"Please don't think I'm trying to butt in, Mr. Pacetti. I know men don't like to be interrupted by a woman when they're talking business. But I've been intrigued by those cousins from the beginning. I'd like to know why they moved away from New Bedford, when the only relatives they had in the United States lived here. It would be much more natural for them to stay, wouldn't it? There must be someone who could explain that to us—and someone who could tell us where they went."

"Well, supposing there was, Mrs. Field?" Nazareno said tolerantly. "What then?"

"As my wife just said, she's been interested in those cousins of yours from the beginning," Roger said, answering for her. "This happens to be the first case I've ever fully discussed with her—of course the relations between a lawyer and his client are usually confidential. But Pell wanted Emily to know everything there was to know, on account of Simonetta. And I agree that we should try to track the Barratas down—especially in the light of what you've told me about the funeral. Obviously, Pell didn't know you and your father went to it, or he'd have mentioned that, when he told me the Barratas were there. And obviously your father, who'd taken the trouble to go all the way from New Bedford to Boston, would have gone to the cemetery and the house, unless something happened to disturb him very much—to make him very angry. I'm only fencing in the dark, of course. But my guess is that something was connected with those cousins."

"And so? My dad's dead. He can't tell us what it was. Carmela's raging, she won't tell us what it was. We don't know where the Barratas are and it would be like hunting for a needle in a haystack—"

"Well, you wouldn't have any objection if Roger tried to find them, would you, Mr. Pacetti?"

"Of course not, if he's got nothing better to do. But it seems to me we've got enough else to worry over. What about this trumped-up charge of Fopiano's that the will wasn't properly witnessed? Everybody knows three witnesses are enough and almost everybody in New Bedford knows the ones my dad chose, either personally or by reputation. Fulginnetti's a foreman in one of our big paper factories. Lavaroni is an undertaker with a funeral home in a Colonial mansion that used to belong to a whaleboat captain; they've been regular patrons here for years and they've both got plenty of credit at the Citizen's Bank. As for Desmond, he could buy the old bank, any time he wanted; he's been the power behind the scenes in local politics ever since any of us can remember."

"That's fine and I'm glad to hear it. But just the same, Fopiano may have something. Mind you, I'm not saying he has, and I don't think he's by any means certain of it himself. I think he's taking a shot in the dark."

"What's he shooting at?"

"Well, as I've told you right along, I think the will's okay legally. But it was obviously homemade. If it had been drawn up in a law office, it would have recited, above the witnesses' signatures, that your father told them it was his will, and also, that he and they all signed it in the presence of each other. I'll have to go and see those three men and, if possible, get their sworn statements that this was done. Unless Autori's done it already."

"Shall I telephone him and find out?"

"Good idea."

Nazareno rose and left the little dining room, closing the door behind him. Roger reached for the coffeepot, which had been left on the table, refilled his cup and stirred sugar into it. Emily took another sip of her Strega and then set the small glass aside. "You brought a copy of that will with you, didn't you, Roger?" she asked. "Could I have another look at it?"

"Sure, Mrs. Sherlock Holmes."

He drew the document from his brief case and handed it to her. She was still studying it intently when Nazareno came back into the room.

"Autori's out of town," he said in a disappointed tone. "He didn't get any real vacation this summer, and now he's gone to New York for the World Series."

"Good for him. I wish I were right there with him."

"May be. But we'll never be able to reach him, until everything's all over but the shouting."

"It doesn't matter. You can let me know when you do get hold of him, or I can come down again if he's delayed. I'll have to anyway, if he hasn't got his affidavits from the witnesses. But I guess that's about all for now, isn't it? Unless there's something else on your mind, I'm afraid Emily and I ought to be getting back to Boston. You've given us a wonderful dinner and a very pleasant evening. As far as I'm concerned, I'd be only too glad to come back."

He glanced toward Emily, awaiting her corroboration of his move toward departure. She looked up from the will, which she had continued to hold, but she did not return it to him, or rise.

"Just a minute," she said almost pleadingly. "I want you to look at this will with me for a moment, Mr. Pacetti, if you wouldn't mind, and tell me if you don't see something strange about it."

"Mrs. Field, I've told you and your husband, a half a dozen times now, that I know there's nothing the matter with that will."

"I know you have. And I know there isn't anything the *matter* with it.

That's not what I said. I said there was something *strange* about it. I said so to Roger when I first noticed that your father spoke of his '*beloved*' son and of his '*grandson who'd worked hard and done well,*' but he didn't speak of Carmela as his beloved daughter."

"He couldn't, without being a terrible old hypocrite. He didn't love her any more than I do."

"Yes, but she was his daughter, wasn't she?"

"Of course she was his daughter."

"Then why didn't he say so? Why does he speak of his beloved '*son*' and his '*grandson*' who's worked hard and done well and only say, 'I give Carmela de Lucca two thousand dollars'? I know you always thought she was his daughter, I know he brought her up like one. But I believe he knew she *wasn't!* I believe that, when he came to die, he wouldn't pretend any longer!"

Chapter 30

THE COURTROOM IN New Bedford really bore a striking resemblance to the one in Salem, where he had tried his first case, Roger told himself. It was not imagination—or fever—that made him think so. It had the same spaciousness, the same white columns and other Colonial attributes, and the walls were hung with the same type of portrait. The chandeliers with their tall lamp chimneys, the side brackets with their white globes, indirectly revealed the progression from coal oil to gas, and from gas to electricity. But the fixtures themselves were outwardly unchanged. For more than a hundred years, this room had been the scene of legal conflict; yet the struggle had left it unscarred, even essentially unaltered.

He seated himself at one of the counsel tables, unstrapped his brief case, spread out his papers and opened his loose-leaf notebook. It was the sort of trifling preparation for trial which any lawyer made almost mechanically in a courtroom; but every move cost him an effort, and the mental exertion essential to concentrated thought was harder still.

For nearly a week now he had felt under the weather and during the last two days he had been coughing a little and running a low fever; then his head had begun to ache. Emily had begged him to go to bed and send for a doctor. He had declined, at first rather nonchalantly, and then with increasing annoyance.

"You know just as well as I do what that would mean—a postponement of the trial. And I don't propose to have this trial postponed. I've been to court any number of times when I've felt sicker than I do now and won my case even if I did have a headache. You haven't worried like this before."

"Yes, I have. I always worry when you begin to cough."

"Well, you shouldn't. A little cough doesn't amount to anything, no matter what those hidebound army doctors say. I'm taking aspirin, I'm gargling with hydrogen peroxide, I've got a pocketful of Sucrets. That ought to see me through the trial. After it's over, we'll send for the vet and he may do his worst."

"I wish you'd let me go to New Bedford with you. I hate to have you

366

go alone. It'll be a strain, however you take it. It's a tedious train trip and a hard drive."

"My dear girl, if you start thinking you ought to go along, every time I have to take a tedious train trip or a long drive, I'd better stop practicing law. At least you're contributing something to the war effort, with your hospital work. But you wouldn't be, if you began to go with me, here, there and everywhere."

"I don't want to go with you here, there and everywhere. I only want to go this once. I'm entitled to a day off from the hospital and I've always wanted to hear you try a case. Here's one I understand something about: you're trying to pull the rug from under Carmela de Lucca, somehow, aren't you, before she can pull another rug out from under Nazareno Pacetti—the one she's had hold of all this time?"

"Yes, that right."

"You see, I do understand. Besides, I'm terribly interested. Why won't you let me go with you? I'll take care of you, and I'll get a great thrill out of seeing you in action."

"Darling, you ought to know by this time that a man doesn't want anyone to take care of him while he's about his work; the time he likes to be coddled is after he gets home. And it gives most men the willies to have members of the family looking on, with bated breath, while they're doing their stuff. It does me, anyway."

"Then at least go down to New Bedford the evening before the trial and get a good night's rest."

"A good night's rest! In a hard hotel bed without enough blankets! I'd keep tossing and turning, trying to find a soft spot or a warm spot, and going over and over the darned evidence in my mind, the way I used to do when I first tried cases."

"Said he, tugging at his long white beard. All right, have it your own way. I'll stay here and keep the home fires burning—as brightly as possible under present fuel restrictions. And of course I'll be on pins and needles until I know how you've come out. But I might even have some rather exciting news of my own for you, when you get back."

Ordinarily, his curiosity would have been piqued by such a statement. But this time, his attention was hardly arrested; all his interests, all his thoughts were focused on the impending trial. Nevertheless, as he drove southward through the cold rain of a dismal March dawn, he began to regret both his peremptory refusal to let Emily come with him, and his scoffing rejection of her suggestion that he should spend the night before the trial in New Bedford. This early, hurried drive meant that his final approach to his case would be hectic; and he was no longer able to convince himself that his increasing dizziness and nausea were due only to that state of nervousness before a trial which was more or less normal and which no amount of experience could wholly banish. However, he told himself, as he had told Emily, that he had tried many a case when he felt worse; he would take some more aspirin, he would stop and get some hot coffee, and presently he would feel fine. . . .

He had taken the aspirin, he had drunk the coffee, and still he did not feel fine. Here he was in the courtroom, with the trial about to begin, and he was coughing so hard that he had been obliged to stop, while he was arranging his papers, and steady himself by holding on to the counsel table. Behind him, the crowd of spectators was rapidly increasing in size; and except that it was so much larger, this group, like the courtroom, at first glance seemed strangely like the one in Salem. There were men in well-cut coats and well-pressed trousers, and men in windbreakers and dungarees; there were women wearing smart hats and handsome fur coats, and bareheaded women with shabby jackets carelessly buttoned over their rumpled housedresses. Some of these people looked eager and some bored; some chattered unceasingly, some sat in stolid silence, and some edged away from their fellows and buried themselves in their morning papers. All this was dully familiar. But gradually Roger realized that there was another difference, besides the one of size, between this crowd and the one that had drifted in and out of the Salem courtroom: those people had felt no interest in him or his client; these people did. They were all waiting to find out what the papers he had drawn from his brief case would disclose, and how he would handle those disclosures. As the friendly janitor who had directed him to the courtroom had said, when he entered the building, word had got around that this was going to be good. Whether they betrayed their anticipation or not, these people were counting on him for excitement. They did not expect him to disappoint them.

Autori came into the inclosure with Nazareno, and shook hands with Roger; then Nazareno retired to a public bench and Autori stayed at Roger's table. Fopiano appeared with Carmela and Roger eyed them both with attentive interest. Fopiano was a small, brisk man, with more nose than either brow or chin; he alternately tugged at his coat and played with the seals on his conspicuous watch chain. Carmela's face still had remnants of beauty; but her mouth was hard and there was a malignant glitter in her eyes, as her glance darted in first one direction and then another. She was dressed entirely in black, so unrelieved and enveloping as to suggest deep mourning; a long veil hung from her small hat, her hands were black gloved and her shoes and handbag made of black suède. The appearance of the ultraconservative Mrs. Fletcher, when newly widowed, had been far less somber.

Everything followed the familiar pattern: the lawyers shook hands formally, the court officer and stenograher appeared, the assistant register took his seat at the clerk's table, and all rose as the judge came in and the crier spoke his piece. The judge, pink of cheek and white of hair, gathered his black robe about him and seated himself in his high-backed chair.

Then he greeted the assistant register, court officer and counsel, and glanced quickly at the papers the assistant register handed up to him.

"We are today hearing the motion of Pellegrino de Lucca to strike from the petition for probate the name of Carmela de Lucca as an heir of the deceased Antonio Pacetti," he announced. "This motion also asks that the Court strike her appearance in opposition to the will of the deceased." He turned the top paper over and read the notation which appeared on the back. "You may proceed, Mr. Field," he concluded quietly.

Roger rose, trying hard to stifle a cough. "I shall not make any formal opening, unless your Honor so desires," he said. "May the witnesses be sworn?"

The assistant register directed all witnesses to rise, whereupon Carmela, Nazareno and an elderly unidentified man, who was with the latter, stood up and were sworn.

"Who is that character?" Fopiano inquired of Roger, in a stage whisper, jerking his thumb in the direction of the stranger.

"You will find out in due time," Roger responded. Then he turned toward Carmela. "Mrs. de Lucca, will you please take the stand?" he said, with formal politeness.

Fopiano rose. "And make her your witness?" he asked in astonishment.

"Yes. A hostile witness. Why not?" rejoined Roger. "Of course I have no reason to fear that she will not be truthful."

Carmela, guided by directions in Italian from Fopiano, stepped onto the stand and clutched its railing. She appeared bewildered, and every now and then she glanced toward the unidentified witness with perplexity tinged by apparent resentment. Fopiano rather wordily stated that she understood Italian better than English, and asked that she be permitted to testify through an interpreter. Roger and Autori, though somewhat surprised by Fopiano's request, could offer no valid objection; and a gentle-looking little man, clad in a chocolate-colored suit, who seemed entirely ready to play his part in the drama, presented himself as an interpreter and was duly sworn.

"Your name?" Roger inquired, again addressing the witness and watching her as the question was translated.

"Maria Carmela de Lucca."

"That is your married name, isn't it?" Again Roger paused for the question and answer in Italian. Then it suddenly occurred to him that, if from his knowledge of Latin and French, he could get the drift of her answers, he might almost ignore some of the English replies and concentrate on mentally framing his next question while the interpreter repeated the previous answer.

"Yes," Carmela answered.

"And before you were married your name was Maria Carmela Pacetti?"

"Yes."

"And Antonio Pacetti left you two thousand dollars in his will?"

"Yes," she replied a third time, the single word charged with indignation.

"He came to this country in December, 1890?"

"I think so."

"And with him was his bride, Bianca?"

"Yes."

"And also his cousins, Luisa, Beatrice and Ernesto Barrata?"

"So I am told."

"By your family?"

"Yes."

Fopiano apparently felt the time had come for self-assertion. "My brother is beginning to ask questions which can be answered only through hearsay," he objected.

"I presume these preliminary questions are based on general reputation in the family, as the witness has testified," the judge answered. "Technically, she is the adverse party. You may continue, Mr. Field."

"In the next generation, you were the eldest?" Roger asked, much encouraged.

"Yes."

"And next to you in age was Adelina Pacetti, the daughter of Bianca and Antonio Pacetti and the mother of Pellegrino de Lucca?"

"Yes."

"And next to her in age was Nazareno, the son of Bianca and Antonio Pacetti?"

"Yes."

"Bianca Pacetti died when you were a small child, did she not?"

"Yes."

"So you hardly remember her, I suppose?"

"No."

"But Antonio Pacetti did his best for these three motherless children, and they were all very fond of him, I am sure?"

"Yes! yes! yes!" This time the response was almost eager.

"And he was fond of you all?"

"Sì! sì!"

"You and Adelina and Nazareno had many good times together when you were children, no doubt?"

Her answer was voluble, affirmative and reduced in translation.

"You had Christmas parties?"

"Yes, a party every Christmas."

"Birthday parties?"

"No."

"Not any birthday parties?" Roger asked, trying to conceal the fact that this answer was unexpected.

"No."

370

"You didn't celebrate birthdays in your family?"

"No, it was not our custom."

This was either an unlooked-for advantage or an unlooked-for danger. Roger decided that he could not afford to ignore it in either case.

"You mean to say birthdays were never celebrated in your family?"

"Yes. That's what I said before."

Roger hesitated. While he was trying to frame another question, Carmela volunteered an explanation.

"We celebrated our saints' days instead."

Some people in the crowd murmured and others tittered. Roger realized they considered his failure to know that it was customary among them to celebrate saints' days rather than birthdays as a mark of ignorance. Up to then, he had felt he had the spectators with him; now he was not so sure. The uncertainty was slightly disturbing, but he did not feel it was serious. Glancing at the outline he had prepared, he reverted to this.

"Well then, you did not celebrate the anniversary of your birthday, but I am correct in believing it was May 23rd, 1891, am I not?"

"I was born May 23rd, but I do not remember the year."

"A lady's privilege," interjected Fopiano.

"Well," said Roger, drawing a paper from his brief case, "I show you this paper and I ask if to you it appears to certify correctly the facts of your birth?"

Carmela looked at the paper. She hesitated and turned her glittering eyes toward Fopiano, who rose. The room was very still.

"If that is a certified copy of a record, it does not need her testimony to qualify it," he said scornfully.

"That is correct," answered Roger, showing the paper to Fopiano, "but I have a right to question her from it, just the same."

"Ah—I think the witness may be confused, your Honor," pursued Fopiano, obviously bent on protecting his client. "I believe she has seen a similar certificate in different form."

"I offer this certificate," Roger insisted, handing it to the assistant register, who took it and presented it to the bench.

"It may be marked," the judge said, handing it down again. The stenographer wrote on it and gave it back to Roger.

"Exhibit One," said Roger, "is a certificate from the records of the Commonwealth that Maria Carmela Pacetti, daughter of Antonio and Bianca Pacetti, was born May 23rd, 1891."

"Thank you," said Fopiano sarcastically. "Now that you have taken charge of the case, I shall not have to introduce my certificate."

Roger glanced toward the bench, hoping the judge would rebuke Fopiano in some way; but the judge appeared indifferent. Roger was coughing again and was appalled by his increasing fatigue of both mind and body. Yet Fopiano's remark suggested one or two leads which he knew he should follow.

"Now, Mrs. de Lucca, suppose we get back to the parties you *did* have. They were all at Mr. Pacetti's house?"

"Most of them."

"Some were at the Barratas'?"

"Yes."

"They had moved to Lynn?"

Again Carmela glanced toward the unidentified witness, who did not seem to notice that she was doing so; his gaze was steadily fixed on the portrait behind the judge's bench. Carmela's glittering eyes next fixed themselves on Fopiano, as if seeking a signal. "Yes," she said belatedly.

"And you were fond of them too?" inquired Roger, who had closely observed all this.

"Yes."

"Did you call them Aunt Luisa and Aunt Beatrice and Uncle Ernesto or Cousin Luisa and Cousin Beatrice and Cousin Ernesto?"

"Aunt and uncle."

"And what did they call you?"

"They called me Carmela, of course."

Almost everyone in the crowd tittered this time and a number shifted about. Again Roger felt that he had lost ground; again he tried to retrieve it.

"As you grew older, you spent more time with them, didn't you?"

"Yes. My mother had died and my father was very busy with his restaurant. He didn't know much about taking care of children anyway."

"Then Adelina and Nazareno went with you, I suppose, to stay with the Barratas in Lynn?"

"No, there were neighbors in New Bedford who took care of them. These neighbors would have taken care of me, too, but I liked to go visiting."

"Your Aunt Luisa had married, hadn't she?"

Once again, Carmela glanced nervously at the elderly man seated beside Nazareno. But she did not hesitate so long this time.

"Yes. One time she got married."

"But her husband wasn't at the Barratas' when you visited there, was he?"

Fopiano rose. "Really, your Honor, I want to give my distinguished brother every leeway, but I think he is straying from the point."

The judge sighed. "Are you objecting or aren't you?"

"Yes, I am."

"Sustained."

"May it please the Court," protested Roger, "if your Honor will permit me to pursue this inquiry, I think I can convince you that it is relevant."

"Very well. But try not to bring in the whole family."

"I thank your Honor. May the last question be read again?"

The question was read and translated, and Carmela, looking more and more troubled, answered vaguely that her aunt's husband was "away."

"As a matter of fact," insisted Roger, "they were divorced, weren't they?"

At this point, Fopiano began to volley objections. Not only was the question irrelevant, according to him, but this was no way in which to introduce evidence. If Mr. Field wanted to prove a divorce, he should produce the certificate.

"Very well," Roger replied promptly, reaching into his brief case, "I offer this certified copy of a decree of divorce between Leopoldo Mafalda and Luisa Barrata Mafalda."

"Just a minute," howled Fopiano.

"I thought I was following your suggestion, Brother Fopiano," mocked Roger. "Are you now objecting?"

"May I see the certificate?"

"Of course."

Roger handed it over and Fopiano glanced at it. "I still object," he said tersely.

"How can you—after calling for it and looking at it?"

"That was merely to see it while you were offering it. It is immaterial, in any case."

"I will take it de bene," the judge said, intervening. "If Mr. Field does not connect it with pertinent evidence at the close of the testimony, Mr. Fopiano, I will entertain your motion to strike it from the record."

"And Mr. Field's questions about it?" urged Fopiano.

"Those may go out, too, in that event. Now, let us get on with the case."

Roger, again encouraged, read into the record the title of the decree, reciting a divorce between Luisa Barrata Mafalda and Leopoldo Mafalda, on grounds of desertion, in 1891.

"Now," he continued, "suppose we return to Mr. Pacetti. You were, of course, greatly grieved by his death, Mrs. de Lucca?"

The witness nodded and began to sniffle.

"And went to his funeral?"

"Yes, of course." The sniffle had now become a sob, and Carmela's words were increasingly muffled. But their drift was still completely clear.

"And then you heard about his will?"

She nodded again and sobbed more convulsively. Roger waited for her to collect herself. "So you consulted Mr. Fopiano?" he asked, after an interval.

The witness nodded again and, wiping her eyes, looked toward Fopiano with a faint smile.

"Where did you first talk to him?"

"At home."

"As a matter of fact, it was he who explained Mr. Pacetti's will to you, wasn't it?"

"Yes," Carmela responded, beginning to sob again.

Fopiano rose. "If it please your Honor, the witness has been visibly affected. May we have a recess?"

Roger closed his loose-leaf notebook, replaced some of his papers in his brief case, and walked from the bar inclosure to the public bench where Nazareno and the unidentified witness were awaiting him.

"You're doing fine, Mr. Field," Nazareno said in a hearty undertone. "And when everything's all over but the shouting, we're going to have us a celebration. Ernesto here is going to be in on it, too, this time. After he's pulled the ace out of his sleeve, he'll be needing a little sustenance. I've got everything all ready, right in the same dining room where Mrs. Field showed me how slow I was on the uptake. Too bad she isn't here today."

"She wanted to come, but I discouraged her. I think now maybe I shouldn't have. . . . Well, I don't believe things are going too badly, but we're not out of the woods yet, so I don't think we should make too many plans for a celebration. Besides, I hate to mention it, but I'm feeling rather seedy. . . . Mr. Barrata, I may need to call on you fairly soon now. Don't be surprised if I do. On the other hand, I may not have to call on you at all, as I told you before. It depends on how much I can get Mrs. de Lucca to admit herself. Now that she's recognized you, as it's obvious she has, she may be either more communicative or less so—it's hard to tell. Of course she's talking to Fopiano about you right now. But I want to tell you again how grateful I am for your willingness to help. It may make all the difference."

"I was glad enough to do it, after I understood how things were. That first time you came to Lynn, I didn't. Of course my wife didn't, either."

He spoke with apologetic and convincing sincerity. There had indeed been a great change in his attitude since that first call at his house in Lynn. As Roger, after exchanging a few more desultory remarks with the cousins, went off in search of a water cooler, where he washed down ten more grains of aspirin, he found himself thinking of that discouraging episode, instead of dwelling, as he knew he should have, on his next moves in the trial. It was getting harder and harder to concentrate. He must have had more fever than he realized when he started out that morning. . . .

After poring over many city directories, he had stood, some months earlier, on the doorstep of a dingy brown Victorian house, which lay half-way between the main street and the ocean in Lynn. He had rung the doorbell and gazed with distaste at the straggly lawn and the paint flaking off the walls of the house—a boxlike structure surmounted by a mansard roof. He had thought the frayed curtains in one of the front windows parted momentarily, but no one had answered his ring and he tried again. After a considerable interval, an elderly, swarthy woman, wearing a smirched violet dress, black loafers and no stockings, half opened the door and stuck her untidy head out.

374

"What do you want?" she asked, with a scowl.

"Good afternoon. Is Mr. Barrata at home?" Roger inquired, trying to use just the right tone to make friends and influence people.

"No," she said, starting to shut the door again.

"Wait a minute!" Roger exclaimed hurriedly. "I have something to talk over with him that might interest him."

"He's not interested in buying anything, if that's what you mean," she retorted. But she partly reopened the door.

"No, that's not what I mean. I'm not a salesman. I'm a lawyer. I want to speak with Mr. Barrata about a case involving his family. If I could see him, I think it might be to his advantage."

The woman had taken the card he offered her and stood staring at it while he talked. "All right, I'll see," she said finally, shutting the door. A minute or two later, around the corner of the house sauntered an elderly, unshaven man, dressed in dark green slacks and a red and black lumberman's shirt.

"You want something?" he asked Roger.

"Yes," returned Roger, descending the steps. "You're Mr. Barrata, aren't you? My name's Field. I'm a lawyer." Again he held out a card. "I'm working on an estate and I'd appreciate it if you'd give me a little information. I think I may be able to do something for you in return."

"What estate?"

"Antonio Pacetti's. I believe he was a relative of yours and he's left a very strange will, which is giving my client trouble. I'd like to talk with you about it."

Barrata hesitated. "My wife was sure you'd try to sell us something," he said doubtfully. "But I don't know. Maybe you'd better come in, after all. Antonio was my cousin all right. Is Carmela making trouble for Nazareno?"

Well, Roger could not review the rest of that episode now. It was time to return to the courtroom. Carmela was already back on the witness stand, where a chair had now been provided for her, at Fopiano's request, on the grounds of fatigue. Her black-gloved hands were folded in her lap, her glittering eyes were less restless and her expression more secretive. Roger resumed his place at the counsel table and continued his examination.

"Tell me, Mrs. de Lucca," he said, "have you discussed your testimony with Mr. Fopiano?"

Instantly Fopiano was on his feet again. "Of course she has!" he blurted out.

"Your Honor, if Mr. Fopiano is going to testify himself, I should like to have him sworn and submitted to cross-examination."

"I am surprised that anyone from an office with the standing of Cutter,

375

Mills and Swan should ask such a question of a helpless widow!" shouted Fopiano.

"Gentlemen, gentlemen!" admonished the judge wearily. "The question was proper, even if hackneyed. You will please not intervene in the testimony, Mr. Fopiano. You will please keep to the point, Mr. Field."

"You did discuss your testimony with Mr. Fopiano?" Roger inquired, turning back to Carmela.

"Yes."

"Did you make a full disclosure to him of your family situation?"

Fopiano rose at the same time that Carmela replied in evident bewilderment.

"She claims she didn't understand the question," offered the interpreter.

"Never mind then. Did you tell him about your recent trip here?"

"She says, what trip?"

"Ask her if she didn't come here to get her birth certificate, for the purpose of introducing it at the trial," Roger said, looking toward the interpreter.

"She says, yes, she did."

"You will please address your questions to the witness, Mr. Field," enjoined the judge.

"And when you came to New Bedford, you went to the city clerk's office?"

Again Fopiano was on his feet. "Of course she did, your Honor. This is getting us nowhere. We have already introduced the certificate of my client's birth. Once is enough."

"If your Honor will bear with me," urged Roger again, "I think I can make my purpose clear."

The judge, though looking somewhat skeptical, nodded assent.

"And what did you ask for, in the clerk's office?"

"I asked for my birth certificate."

"What did you say?"

"I said I wanted it."

"Mrs. de Lucca—didn't you ask the clerk if he had a record, showing the birth of a baby born May 23rd, 1891, to *Luisa* and *Leopoldo Mafalda?*"

With a smothered exclamation, Carmela half rose and then sank back again, grasping the arms of her chair. But almost instantly, she sprang to her feet, vehemently shouting in Italian.

"She's asking how you knew that?" inquired the interpreter dramatically.

"I'm doing the questioning at this moment," Roger pursued, so quickly that Fopiano could not come to Carmela's rescue. "And I insist upon a reply."

376

There was a tense pause, unbroken by any sound in the courtroom. "She says she did," the interpreter reported at last.

"And the clerk told you he had no such record?"

"Si."

"So then you asked him if he had a record, dated the same day, of a baby named Carmela born to *Antonio and Bianca Pacetti?* Be very careful. Remember that you are under oath."

There was another long pause. But finally, she spat out the single word, "Si."

"And that is the certificate you had ready to introduce here?"

"Si."

"But you didn't know then, and you don't know now, what your name really is, do you?"

This time, she burst into genuine tears and her reply came with tragic intensity.

"No. I have never known my real name. I have never known who was really my father."

A sudden murmur arose in the courtroom, swelling gradually in sound. A sheriff rapped for order and failed to get it. The judge spoke in a voice of authority.

"The courtroom will be quiet. Proceed, Mr. Field."

"May it please the Court," Roger said slowly and distinctly. "I offer this certificate, showing the birth of a child, Adelina, to Antonio and Bianca Pacetti, in New Bedford on September 29th, 1891. I also offer the marriage certificate of the said Antonio and Bianca Pacetti, dated in Naples, November 30th, 1890."

"Your Honor, I object to these certificates, and I now renew my objection, as your Honor said I might, to all previous evidence relating to the Barrata family."

Fopiano was fast losing his self-control. The judge, who did not fail to observe this, answered even more dispassionately than before.

"On what grounds, if you please?"

"That it is both irrelevant and immaterial!"

"Before ruling on this objection, I will hear you, Mr. Field."

"I submit that these certificates are both relevant and material, as is all the evidence concerning the Barrata family. It would have been impossible for Bianca Pacetti to give birth to a child in May and to another in September. Therefore, if Antonio had been the father of a child born in May, it must have had a different mother and there is no evidence that this occurred. I therefore further submit that Carmela was the daughter of Luisa Barrata Mafalda and that, as the said Carmela was born less than six months after her mother's arrival in the United States, her father is unknown to us. Your Honor may infer from this that Antonio Pacetti registered the said Carmela as his child, in order to shield her mother, Luisa Barrata Mafalda, from disgrace, and that the father of the child was also unknown to him, as it was to Leopoldo Mafalda, who instantly left his wife upon the discovery of her pregnancy by another man. All this evidence is therefore admissible on the issue before us, namely: will your Honor allow the motion of Pellegrino de Lucca to strike the name of Carmela de Lucca from the list of Antonio Pacetti's heirs, *since she is not his daughter?*"

Chapter 31

INCONSEQUENTIALLY, AS HE started back to Boston, through rain which was fast turning into snow, Roger's first thoughts centered on the hope that he had not hurt Nazareno's feelings. Roger had tried his best to do justice to the feast prepared for him—the tender filets of beef in their rich sauce, the delicious unsalted butter, the homemade *cassata*—all the delicacies which were now so hard to come by. Nazareno must have used a great many points in order to provide them. And it was obvious that he had expected Roger to sit for a long time with him and Autori and Barrata in the little private dining room decorated with paper flowers, to linger over coffee and liqueurs and cigars while they exultantly discussed the trial and its outcome. But Roger had been obliged to excuse himself, first from eating and then from remaining. He felt very ill. He must get home as quickly as possible.

Nazareno had done his best to conceal his disappointment; he had said he understood, he had spoken and acted sympathetically. There had been nothing in his voice or his manner to betray resentment. And, even if there had been, why should Roger take it to heart? This was a day of great triumph, a day that would mark a revolutionary change in the life of the friend who had trusted him and whose battle he had fought and won. Pacetti's estate would be distributed as Pell had wanted it done; no further impediment could be placed in the way of providing for Simonetta as he had so eagerly desired. But even that was unimportant, compared to the fact that no further impediment could be placed in the way of his marriage to her. She was not his own cousin; she was very distantly related to him. Because Roger had been able to prove this, they did not need a dispensation; no fanatical mother, no indifferent priest, could prevent the sacramental fulfillment of their love. It was strange that Roger did not keep thinking of this, that he did not glory in the knowledge of it, instead of dwelling on the possibility that he had hurt Nazareno's feelings. But then, his thoughts had been inconsequential and confused all day. It was nothing short of a miracle that he had been able to conceal this inner turmoil, that he had driven his every point home, that he had dominated the courtroom.

379

He guided the car mechanically, stopping and starting almost instinctively as the traffic lights changed. Against the gray clouds, at the top of every rise, he seemed to see the black-clad figure of Carmela, as she had appeared on the stand, at first confident, then frightened, and finally violent and vindictive. But with the dark vision came the compelling knowledge that she had not been able to prevail against him. He had trapped her even without recourse to other witnesses; neither Nazareno nor Barrata had needed to testify; they had been superfluous and ineffective, after all. But it had been a tough day. Pell would understand that, not only as a friend and as a man, but as a lawyer. Pell would feel that his trust had been justified—again not only as a friend and as a man, but as a lawyer. He would write immediately to Pell, explaining everything, both about the present situation, as far as Simonetta was concerned, and about the trial, step by step. It was tremendously important that he should do this. Or was it? Did it matter? Did anything really matter except that his head was bursting and his heart pounding, that he had never felt so ill in his life, or dreamed that it was possible to be so ill and still be on a highroad, driving a car?

He was not in any condition to drive a car. He was a menace on the highroad. He hardly saw the road signs and the traffic lights any more, only that black-clad vision of Carmela. He should have let Emily come with him. Emily would have driven properly, she would have seen clearly. Emily always saw clearly. It was she who, from the first, had maintained that, once he had located the long-lost cousins, he would begin to solve the mysteries of the case. It was she who had questioned the wording of the will and grasped the significance of the missing words. She had been justified in her desire to attend the trial. If it had not been for her, its outcome might well have been different. She should have shared her husband's moment of victory, because it was her victory too.

Roger's errant thoughts returned to the day when, at her insistence, he had gone to the State House and patiently waited, among the adolescents who were seeking their birth certificates in order to qualify for war jobs, until the clerk in charge of such documents should give him the ones he sought. After his name had been called and he had gone to the counter to claim them, he returned immediately to the bench in the corridor, where he had sat for a long time already; and, using his brief case as a lapboard, he had spread the papers out before him. Then the dates attached to the dry, statistical entries of names leaped out at him, suddenly vitalized:

NAME	DATE OF BIRTH
Maria Carmela Pacetti	May 23, 1891

NAME	DATE OF BIRTH
Adelina Margaretta Pacetti	September 29, 1891

There, in those two telltale dates had lain the long-sought clue. Carmela and Adelina could not possibly be sisters. The next move was to find out what their relation really was to each other and why this had been falsified.

Slowly the pieces of the pattern had fallen into place. Ernesto Barrata, once persuaded that Roger was entitled to information and that he was trustworthy, explained a great deal: the Pacettis and the Barratas had all lived together when they first went to New Bedford, and Luisa had been married there to Leopoldo Mafalda, who had fallen in love with her at first sight. He had left her, just as impetuously, as soon as he discovered her condition. Antonio had felt sorry for her, had permitted her to remain under his roof, and had quietly registered Carmela as his child; but he had used his agnosticism as a pretext for having no public baptism; and, as Luisa's behavior continued to be scandalous, he told her that she could no longer remain permanently in his house though, for the sake of appearances, he would permit her participation in family celebrations and he would be glad to keep her child. She agreed to this arrangement, apparently without regret, and when Antonio found a job for Ernesto at a shoe factory in Lynn, the three Barratas moved away. Carmela remained with the Pacettis and was accepted as their daughter. A few of the neighbors who had, inevitably, recognized Luisa's condition and whose curiosity had been aroused by Leopoldo's abrupt departure, whispered among themselves that Carmela was Antonio's illegitimate child and that he had acted outrageously in bringing his bride and his mistress to the same place. But such gossip was quickly hushed by Antonio's obvious devotion to his wife and his growing importance in the community. The rumors were soon forgotten and Adelina and Nazareno never knew that their cousin was not their sister. However, after Bianca died, Luisa demanded that Carmela should visit her more often; Antonio consented because Beatrice was a decent woman and could be trusted to see that Luisa behaved herself while Carmela was in the house; the visits took place periodically, even after Adelina died, too, leaving a son, Pellegrino. It was Carmela herself who eventually refused to have anything more to do with her mother; she had become aware of Luisa's lapses from grace, her fanatical tendencies were already beginning to take form and her husband was a decent, almost strait-laced man. A woman of loose life had no place in their newly established home. Luisa soon gave up her attempts to force herself upon them; and it was not until the day of Edmondo's funeral that she reappeared in the midst of a general family group. Antonio had considered her presence an insult and had declined to believe that Carmela was not at least indirectly responsible for it; after that, the final break between himself and his foster daughter had come.

"And where is Luisa now?" Roger had inquired of Ernesto when all this had gradually been made clear to him.

"She and Beatrice went back to Italy before the war. You see, I finally married myself and there were too many women in the house. Of course, it is large," he added, glancing with pride around the Victorian monstrosity. "But no house is big enough to hold three women, especially if one is a respectable matron and another an incorrigible wanton. And though, as I said before, Beatrice was never a woman of ill repute, like Luisa, she was meddlesome and faultfinding. I was glad to get rid of them both. I gave them the money to go back to Naples. And naturally, we have no way of keeping in touch with them now. I am not sorry about that, either" . . .

So far, Roger would not have been able to piece the pattern together without Emily's initiative, and he would try to make up for his unfairness in excluding her from his triumph, by relating every detail of the trial to her when he reached home. But, in the course of doing this, he would also be justified in mentioning the important move he had made on his own initiative, when it dawned on him that Carmela might have gone to the city clerk's office to make sure that she had not been recorded as the daughter of Leopoldo and Luisa Mafalda and thereby automatically disqualified as a next of kin. The question which he had accordingly put to her, based on pure guesswork, had startled her into telling the truth. Emily would applaud this as an inspiration on his part. They would go to the chintz sitting room together and he would forestall her eager questions by telling her everything there was to tell. Also, he must not forget to ask her what she had meant when she told him she might have some news for him too. He should have shown immediate interest when she said that. He must have hurt *her* feelings. And he would not have hurt Emily's feelings for anything in the world. He would make her understand that. Or would he? Could he? Could he do anything except tumble into his bed and sink down and down and down into its softness and its warmth?

He hoped he could, because there were so many things he wanted to tell Emily before he went to sleep. Several times that day he had thought how much this last trial resembled his first one—in the physical aspects of the courtroom and the spectators, in his abnormal degree of nervousness beforehand, in his feeling that a successful outcome was imperative and must be won at any cost. But not for a moment had he felt that there would be any resemblance between the aftermath of the two. When he reached home that first time, he could not have talked with Emily to save his life; he had been completely exhausted. This time he was dizzy, he was perhaps getting a little lightheaded, and his persistent coughing rendered speech difficult; but he was not conscious of fatigue any more. Instead, he felt increasingly buoyant, increasingly exultant. He would talk on and on, stopping only when he was obliged to cough. And he would have Emily all to himself while he did so; he would not find an interloper on his hearth this time. Briefly, and with a sensation bordering almost on amusement, he recalled his jealousy and rage over David's unexpected presence on that long-ago night. How could he have been so crazy as to imagine, for one moment, that David was a menace to the happiness and harmony of his marriage? Why, David had hardly left the house when Emily urgently welcomed her husband to her arms, revealing a capacity for passion hitherto not only undisclosed, but unimagined! And she had scarcely seen David since then, except when circumstances which she neither directed nor controlled had brought him into her company. She had been cool to Priscilla's suggestion that he should be included in the New Year's house party. She had said she was glad he did not come to little Archie's christening. Except for that one remark, Roger could not remember when she had spoken of him; he had disappeared from their lives and Roger did not even know where he was at present. Someone at the office had said he had gone to England and Roger had felt no curiosity to learn anything more. He wished David no harm, he wished no harm to anyone; he simply did not care. It would be rather nice to hear from good old Briny once in a while, to know he was safe and getting along all right in the South Pacific—Roger had a vague impression that Briny was somewhere in the South Pacific now. But there was no hurry about hearing—any time would do. Of course he would be hearing from Pell and he was glad of that, because of the reasons for it. But there was no hurry about that, either. There was no hurry about anything, except to get home and talk to Emily.

He never knew how he reached Joy Street. He had no recollection, later on, of drawing up to the curb in front of his house and mounting the steps and unlocking the door. He had a dim impression that he called to Emily and that she answered him, but everything was very hazy, for all at once vertigo overcame him completely. When she reached his side, he was lying unconscious on the floor.

After that, there were moments of awareness. He knew that he was in his big soft bed and that Emily was standing near it. He heard the doctor saying, "There's no cause for uneasiness, Mrs. Field. Pneumonia isn't what it used to be, you know. Why, we'll have his temperature down, with penicillin, inside of twenty-four hours." Roger was meant to overhear that, he knew. But he was not so sure he was meant to overhear what the doctor said when he came the next time. "Well, of course, occasionally there *is* a case. . . . I think perhaps I'd better arrange for oxygen."

Roger did not care what they arranged for, because, in the meanwhile, Emily had told him her news and he was supremely happy. She had not wanted to say anything until she was sure, and she had been disappointed so many times. . . . But she had been examined by a famous obstetrician the morning that Roger went to New Bedford and he had told her there would be a September baby. She made a little joke, saying she was going to have a very special Labor Day all her own, and they both laughed, as if she had said something tremendously witty. At least, Emily laughed and Roger tried to; and he realized she knew that he meant to laugh and that he was happier than he had ever been in his life, even if it made him cough when he tried to tell her so.

Soon after that, Emily read him a letter that had come in from Roscoe Cutter, congratulating him on his signal success in New Bedford. Mr. Cutter was extremely sorry to learn that Roger was having one of his little bouts with bronchitis, but was glad to feel sure that the wonder drugs would have him fixed up in no time. He was not to hurry back to the office before he was really able, though they would all be glad to see him there for both personal and professional reasons. As a matter of fact, Mr. Cutter and Mr. Mills wished to discuss with Roger the possibility that he might now be interested in a partnership. Mr. Cutter really thought the time was ripe for such a discussion and he was confident that the outcome would be one of great mutual benefit. . . .

This communication, gratifying as it was, seemed unimportant compared to Emily's great news. For the first time, in more than six years, Roger did not seem to have the office work on his mind; he did not worry about the unanswered letters and the trial lists and the other papers which must be piling up on his desk, or about the telephone calls to which no one, except himself, could give proper attention. He did not worry about anything. He did not feel there was anything to worry about.

He was not supposed to see anyone except Emily and the doctor and the nurses who had mysteriously appeared from nowhere. But he promised he would not talk if they would let him see Simonetta; he would just lie and listen while Emily told her everything. Simonetta came and stood quietly by his bed, looking so beautiful that she might well have been an angelic vision. And Emily told Simonetta that she must write to Pell and say they could be married as soon as he got home. Of course Roger was going to write himself, when he was better, and Emily would write too. But Simonetta must write first. She said she would, and she tried to tell Roger how happy she was and said she knew this happiness was all due to him. Roger was very glad to have her there, but the day nurse came in and interrupted and said that Simonetta must go away, that Mr. Field must be kept absolutely quiet. And Roger thought he heard Emily say, "What difference does it make now? Why don't you let him do what will make him happy?" So he tried to tell her again that he was completely happy. There seemed to be a great deal of talk about happiness. And he thought Simonetta turned back for a moment, and said she was going downstairs to play for him, and that the doors would be left open, so that he could hear her. At all events, afterward he did hear music and it was very beautiful. He had not realized that Simonetta could play like that. It was more what he thought heavenly music might be like.

Deirdre came into the room too. She must have watched for a chance to do so when the nurse on duty was busy about something else, because Deirdre was not supposed to come, any more than Caroline was. He had heard them turning Caroline away and he was glad of it. But he had known Deirdre longer than anyone else in the world, longer even than he had known Emily. She had held him in her arms when his mother died and she had comforted him when his father died. He loved her very much and he was glad to see her beside his bed. She leaned over and kissed him and spoke just once, in her quick, kind way.

"You must offer it up, Mr. Roger. Remember what I've always said. You must offer it up."

Emily must have been in the room when Deirdre came in, because, if the nurse on duty went out, even for a minute, Emily always stayed there. She did not ever seem to get tired or anything, and she understood, better than the nurses, what he wanted and needed. He was very grateful to Emily for understanding that of course he would want to see Deirdre, whatever the stupid nurse said; he was glad Emily had put one over on the nurse. But then, she had always been understanding—understanding and loyal and loving. She had made him very happy. There it was again, that consciousness of joy. The doctor looked graver and graver, whenever Roger noticed his presence; Roger did not see why. There was nothing to be grave about. He had won his case. He was going to be a member of the firm. Simonetta and Pell were going to be married. And after all these years, he and Emily were going to have a baby.

"There isn't anything to offer up, Deirdre. You offer up misery, don't you, or can you offer up happiness too? Of course, if you can, I'd be glad to."

Deirdre did not answer him, because Deirdre was gone. He had not known when she went. Only Emily was in the room with him now. Well, he did not need anyone else. Just Emily, so that they could share his victory.

Part Five

MARCH, 1943 TO NOVEMBER, 1946

EMILY

Chapter 32

FOR THE FIRST few weeks after Roger died, Emily was mainly conscious of numbness; then she was aware only of overwhelming fatigue and uncomparable apathy, tinged with sorrow.

She did not care when her physician told her she must stop acting as Nurses' Aide and giving blood, that she would endanger her child if she did not; he was willing that she should continue to supervise the work done on the knitting machines, and to knit herself, by hand, but that was all. She did not argue when he said she should do nothing more. She did not argue even when Old Mrs. Forbes, who was undoubtedly in league with the obstetrician, said it would be much more sensible for Emily to close the Joy Street house, temporarily, than to stay in that cold, gloomy place, alone except for Deirdre. Of course, after the baby was born, it would be different; Emily would want to be in her own home then, to do things in her own way; and the house would not seem gloomy with a beautiful baby in it, nor would it be cold any more, since there would be an extra fuel allowance, for the baby's benefit. Meanwhile, Emily would be much better off in that famous third-story bedroom on Louisburg Square. Besides, Deirdre needed a vacation; she had appeared to accept Roger's death bravely, but, as a matter of fact, she had been completely crushed by it. When she had pulled herself together, Emily could take her to Hollyhock Hill, if she chose, for the warm summer months. Deirdre would get on well with Jenny, and there was plenty of room; Mark and Elizabeth were really counting on having them. But for the present. . . .

So the shutters were closed and the shades were drawn in the Joy Street house. The silver was put in the bank, the rugs in storage, and the furniture was slip-covered with clean, colorless linen. Emily went through the premises, the night before she left, to make sure everything was in complete order. At least, that was what she said. But that was not the real reason. The real reason was that she wanted to say good-by to it and this was the first thing she had definitely wanted to do, since Roger died. She started on the third story, in the small guest room with the spool furniture and the old pastel of the little girl, playing with her puppy, where

Priscilla had spent so much time; then she went past the rooms on the second story, all the way down to the ground floor—to the drawing room with its tapestries and portraits, and the library with its Gaugengigl etchings and first editions, and the dining room with its massive, well-rubbed mahogany, and next, out into the garden, where the crocuses and the forsythia were just beginning to come out. She stood there for a few minutes, wondering who would take care of it, when the later flowers bloomed, if the doctor would not let her do so. She did not suppose that it would be possible to get a gardener, and she shrank a little from the thought that weeds would grow up and choke the blossoms, that the shrubbery would become rank and the grassplot unkempt and the fountain choked. But she did not stay in the garden and, after she went away from it, she tried not to think about these things.

She left the kitchen unvisited, because that was Deirdre's domain rather than hers and she knew everything there would be spotless before Deirdre's departure; and she did not go into the chintz sitting room or Roger's dressing room, because she had found that first her numbness and later her apathy were pierced by a sudden pain whenever she did so. And she went back to her own room last of all; she knew that was where she must sleep, one more night. She was dully glad, when she lay down in her bed, that this *would* be the last night, until she had the baby there beside her. She had not thought, beforehand, that she would feel this way, but now she did. All the time she was going through the house, she had kept listening, instinctively though involuntarily, for once-familiar sounds that no longer came; and during the long hours before dawn, she kept thinking of the first night she had slept in that house, and how happy and hopeful she had been then. Deirdre had said nothing more about not being able to stand the stairs, since Roger died; in fact, she insisted on bringing Emily's breakfast up to her. And when Deirdre came in with the tray, and gave her a keen, quick glance, Emily realized that Deirdre knew she had not slept, and was thinking, as she was, of those bedside breakfasts which had been so leisurely and so joyous, when Roger and Emily were first married.

Later in the morning, Clark, Old Mrs. Forbes' elderly chauffeur, came to give Deirdre a hand with the bags and, as if he had read Emily's unspoken thoughts, said he had a nephew, Dan, who was unfortunately a four-effer, and would be only too glad to look after the garden through the rest of the spring and summer after he finished his regular day's work; perhaps Mrs. Field would like to go and sit there, warm afternooons; she could tell Dan how she wanted things done. Deirdre was to go to the house once or twice a week to air it and dust it and make sure everything was all right inside, and no doubt Mrs. Field would be going inside, too, once in a while, just to look the premises over. Officer Tupperty had promised to keep a sharp lookout for prowlers, and he was on hand, too, that morning to wish Mrs. Field well when she went off to stay with her grandmother. He thought it was a fine idea. . . . He said he would drive Deirdre to her cousin's house, in the South End, where she was going to visit while she had her vacation. It would not take him out of his way at all. It so happened he was going to the South End anyhow that day, as soon as he got off duty.

There was nothing more to do and it was time to leave if Old Mrs. Forbes were not to be kept waiting for luncheon. Emily bent over and stroked Kilkenny, Deirdre's cat.

"Your cousin likes cats, doesn't she, Deirdre?"

"Sure, she likes them fine."

"And you're not afraid Kenny'll run away, are you, when he finds himself in strange surroundings?"

"Never a bit. We'll butter his paws, in the good old-fashioned way, and he'll settle himself under the kitchen table, in less time than you could say a Hail Mary."

"All right. I'll see you some day next week. And if you want anything in the meanwhile, you'll let me know, won't you?"

"That I will. Don't you fret about me or anyone else, Mrs. Field. It's rest you need and a change, for your own sake and the sake of the blessed baby that's coming to bring new joy to this house of mourning. Your grandmother'll be seeing to it that you have them both."

"I know she will. Good-by, Deirdre."

For a moment they clung to each other. Then Emily went down the steps and got into the car. Clark held its door open respectfully and Officer Tupperty saluted from the sidewalk and Emily was driven down Mount Vernon Street to Louisburg Square.

Old Mrs. Forbes talked briskly all through their tête-à-tête luncheon, but Emily could not think of much to say, and afterward she could not think of much to do. She lay down for a little while, because that seemed to be expected of her, but she did not like to lie down in the daytime and she did not go to sleep; she merely kept still, glancing at the clock every few minutes until an hour had passed and she felt justified in getting up again. Then she watched Doris unpack her clothes, and put them neatly away on scented shelves and padded hangers, and carry off a few to be pressed and cleaned. By and by, Doris came back with some tea; Mrs. Forbes had thought that probably Mrs. Field was tired after her moving, that she would like to have tea in her room. If she would prefer to have dinner there, too, Mrs. Forbes would understand and Doris would be glad to bring it up. Emily realized she was expected to say, yes, she was tired; yes, she would like to stay in her room. As a matter of fact, she did not feel at all tired and she did not care in the least where she stayed. She knitted for a little while and read for a little while and then she went to bed because there did not seem to be anything else for her to do.

For the next month nearly all her days seemed equally aimless and equally empty. She had a number of callers, some of them very old friends, and she saw them because she could not excuse herself on grounds of ill health or preoccupation; but she would have been just as contented to remain alone. One day, Sister Mary Theresa came and, after a little desultory conversation, talked to her about the number of holy wafers which the nuns were now sending overseas from St. Margaret's Convent for the use of army chaplains.

"Perhaps you'd like to come and see the wafers being made, sometime, Mrs. Field. It's a rather interesting process."

"Thank you. I should like to—sometime."

Sister Mary Theresa hesitated. "You used to come and see us quite often, Mrs. Field. We know you've been very busy these last years, that you haven't had much time for visiting. But we've missed you very much. We hope now you're so near. . . . The chapel is always open."

"Thank you," Emily said again. But she had no desire to go to St. Margaret's Convent or anywhere else, and no intention of doing so. She thought Sister Mary Theresa understood this.

Quite often Simonetta came to see Emily. Simonetta did not try to talk to her about anything; she sat and played the piano and sometimes she sang. She played and sang more and more beautifully all the time, and she seemed to grow more and more beautiful herself, all the time too. Emily realized that she ought to ask Simonetta what she had heard from Pell, and kept telling herself that the next time Simonetta came, she would do so. Then she put it off until the next time after that. She also began to wonder, vaguely, what had happened to Carmela, and she thought she ought to ask about this. But Simonetta did not seem to expect questions and she did not offer any information on her own initiative. Emily sat still and listened to the music and that was all that happened.

Eventually her physician told her that she should be getting outdoors more and taking more exercise, so every pleasant day she walked up the Hill and sat for a little while in her garden and then walked back to Louisburg Square. On the afternoons that Dan worked in the garden, she watched him and occasionally made a suggestion. But he did very well without suggestions, so it really was not necessary to make them. On the afternoons that Dan was not working there, she sat with her knitting or a book in her hand and sometimes she worked a little or read a little, but not much. She had not told anyone about the habit she had formed of going there, so she had no reason to expect that she would be disturbed; and she was slightly startled when, one evening, someone knocked at the gate. She went to it and opened it and, to her surprise, saw her father standing there.

"I hope I didn't frighten you," he said. "I went to your grandmother's house and she told me you were here. She said she thought you might be glad to see me, so I walked on up."

"Of course I'm glad to see you, Papa. Won't you come in and sit down?"

He accepted a chair and laid his hat and gloves on the table beside it. Then he looked around him with approval.

"I'd forgotten how pleasant you'd made this," he said. "It's rather a long while since I've been here."

"It *is* a long while. Of course you've been in Dublin so much of the time—"

"Yes, of course. . . . I think it was a mistake for us to sell the Gloucester Street house, Emily."

"I'm sorry you feel that way about it. Because it did seem the best thing at the time."

"Yes, it did. And of course we're very comfortable at the Ritz. Besides, your mother's so busy at the Officers' Club that it's just as well she doesn't have to bother with housekeeping."

"Well, she never did like housekeeping, you know. Grandmamma enjoys it still. And I enjoyed it too. Perhaps tastes like that skip a generation, sometimes."

"Perhaps they do. . . . You're an excellent housekeeper, Emily."

"You mean I was. I'm not keeping house any more."

"That's just temporary. Of course you will again, in the fall. You've had a hard time. You needed a rest."

"That's what everyone said, but I don't know. . . . Would you like a drink, Papa? I haven't been in the house since I left it, but I have my keys in my purse and I'm sure there's still something in the wine closet. Deirdre comes in to clean, so I told her to keep the small refrigerator going. I think I could get some ice cubes fairly quickly."

"Thank you, Emily. A drink would be very refreshing. May I help you?"

"No thanks, I can manage all right. But I may have to do a little rummaging. You sit here and enjoy the sunshine."

She was gone for some minutes and, when she reappeared at the back door, she was carrying a well-laden tray. He hurried to take it from her.

"Just set that down for me and I'll be back presently. I found some crackers, too, and some cheese. I'm toasting them for us."

They sat for some time over their drinks and their crackers. They did not talk much; they had never been particularly close to each other, and there did not seem to be much to say. But the silence was companionable. When it began to grow dark, and Emily said she must go back to Louisburg Square, or her grandmother would worry about her, her father carried the tray back to the kitchen, and insisted on drying the glasses she washed and putting the bottles back in the wine closet. As they went out into the street together, he cleared his throat.

"I've enjoyed this very much, Emily. I'd like to do it again."

"Then I hope you will."

"I go to the Somerset Club quite often, afternoons. It's just a step from here. I could walk over, any time."

"I hope you will," she said again; and found that she meant it.

After that, they sat together almost every pleasant afternoon, until she went to Hollyhock Hill. And little by little, they found they had more to say to each other, more than they ever had before.

"Do you hear anything from Priscilla these days, Emily?" he asked one afternoon.

"She doesn't write to me, but she does write, once in a while, to Grandmamma. And Grandmamma passes on the news to me, if I'll listen. It hasn't been particularly thrilling, so far. The last I knew, Priscilla had been ordered to Camp Kilmer for overseas training and was doing K. P. duty there. The first time she was in the kitchen, she looked around for the green soap they use for dishwashing and finally found a jar of green-colored substance which she proceeded to pour into the water. The substance proved to be mint sauce—the soap was actually an orange-colored powder until it was put into the water, when it turned green. Since then, Priscilla's nickname at camp has been Mint Sauce Forbes. Wouldn't you know that would be the crazy kind of thing she'd do?"

"Yes, it's quite in character. Just the same, I think you've always been a little overcritical of Priscilla, Emily, if you'll excuse me for saying so. She's got lots of gumption, as they express it around Dublin."

"I wouldn't deny that for a minute. And I don't mean to be over-critical—of her or anyone else. She just doesn't happen to be the type that appeals to me, that's all."

"And you don't know whether she's gone overseas yet?"

"Grandmamma hasn't spoken about her lately, but she may well have. That's what she was determined to do."

"I think Sue and Sherman would be very pleased if you'd go down and visit them on the Cape, Emily. In fact, they told me so. I think they miss Priscilla very much."

"It's very kind of them, but I'm not in the mood for visiting."

"Well, I can understand that. But perhaps later on . . ."

Another day he asked her if she ever heard what had become of the young men who had been with Roger at Cutter, Mills. It seemed all right, now, to mention Roger's name, and Sumner had long suppressed the curiosity of an idle man to know what more active men were doing.

"I believe David is still in England and Brian in the South Pacific. They both wrote me when they heard about Roger, of course; but they didn't say much—naturally they couldn't on account of the censorship and they just sent brief notes of condolence anyway." Emily did not mind speaking about Roger now, either; in fact, she was beginning to find that she was quite willing to do so. "I got the same kind of a note from Pell, as far as news was concerned, but it was longer, because it was filled with expressions of deep gratitude and strong affection. Roger and Brian were good friends, but he and Pell were really devoted to each other. I know

394

when you add that mendacious touch about your usual dignified fashion."

"Well, you knew that I'd been in Manus for nearly a year."

"I knew you were there, but I didn't know for how long and I don't know what you were doing there, or much about Manus itself."

Brian struck an attitude. "Manus, my dear girl," he announced in a declamatory tone, "was one of the five finest harbors in the world until the U. S. Navy and the Seabees got hold of it, and turned it into the finest and probably the busiest port on any of the seven seas. Nobody except a few professional mariners knew much about it before the war, because the native village there wasn't a trading point. Now it teems with activity, as the saying goes. And amidst the dull monotony of the port, your humble servant here has been occupied with endless legal work, such as: one, the prosecution of malingerers who had resorted to various devices in order to escape battle duty; two, the prosecution of others who had acquired cigarettes and similar fabulously desired trade goods via what were known as 'moonlight requisitions,' and were trying to pyramid these into fortunes by swapping them with the natives for gold, pearls and other suchlike trifles."

Emily laughed again. "And what's happened to the malingerers, now that you've left them to their own devices?"

"That's somebody else's headache, for the moment. By a great stroke of luck, I cut my foot on a jagged piece of coral, while swimming off the sandy shores, and got an infection in it."

"This is the first time I ever heard an infection called a piece of luck."

"Well, you've heard it now and you have the evidence of it before you. In the normal course of events, I wouldn't have got home for six or eight months more, when I'd have been entitled to a tour of state-side duty. But the medicos took on about that infection as if I'd cut open my head instead of my foot and the brains were leaking right out of it. I tried to tell them it was the other end of me that counted, but they wouldn't listen. I don't know what's going to happen to me next. I may get shipped back to the South Pacific or I may be sent to the B Docks in Norfolk—there's a rumor going around that my legal talents are too great for confinement at Manus. While that fine technical point's being decided, I'm spending a little time in Boston, much of it, I hope, in your company. Incidentally, I've got a whole pocketful of gasoline coupons. What about a nice long drive out into the beautiful spring countryside?"

"You mean now?"

"Well, tomorrow would be just as good if there's something else you'd rather do now."

"No, I wasn't doing anything special. When you came, Papa and I were talking about Simonetta's house and wondering how we should go about getting materials and labor for its restoration."

"Simonetta's house? Go back to the beginning on that one, will you?"

Briefly, Emily explained. While she was talking, Brian reached over toward the table and unceremoniously mixed himself another drink. He heard her through, but he had begun to show signs of impatience before she made her final remarks. The immediacy of his response disclosed the difficulty he had had in restraining himself.

"Why in hell didn't you ask my old man to help you out?" he inquired.

"Your—why, I never thought!"

"For a reasonably intelligent girl, the number of thoughts you don't have is really staggering. I take it your telephone is still connected?"

"Yes, I—I think so."

"Aren't you sure?"

"No, Brian, I'm not. I never thought of the telephone when—when I left."

"Well, you must have a key with you or you couldn't have got out all these drinks. If you'll trust me with it, I'll get busy right away."

She handed him the key unquestioningly and he disappeared into the kitchen. She did not say anything to her father while Brian was gone. He returned, grinning more broadly than ever.

"My luck's holding," he said cheerily. "I got my old man and Simonetta both on the telephone, the first try. He's going to stop at Franklin Square House and bring her over here. Then we'll all go together and look over the premises—probably Terence will come along too. Mark you, I haven't any black marketing in mind. But, as Mr. Thayer told you, anything that can be done, within the law, to get a home ready for a returning veteran is all to the good in the way of keeping up army morale. I imagine Simonetta drops a line to Pell once in a while—not just microfilms or voice letters, either. She'll tell him what we're doing and he'll get a great kick out of it. He'll brag to his cronies about it and dream of it under the Sicilian stars—I suppose he *is* under the Sicilian stars by this time. If he isn't, he will be pretty soon and anyway, there are stars in Africa, too, that he can dream under. . . . When we've looked over Simonetta's house, why not come back to my house for supper?"

"It's awfully kind of you, Briny, but I haven't been anywhere yet and—"

"I haven't asked you to go 'anywhere.' I've asked you to come to South Boston. You, too, of course, Mr. Thayer. You agree with me that Emily ought to come to my house to supper, don't you?"

"Why, I—" began Sumner Thayer hesitantly. He looked from Brian to Emily, who had now bent her head and was clasping and unclasping her hands in her lap. Then he looked back at Brian again. "Well, yes," he said. "I don't think that's a bad idea at all. In fact, I think it's a rather good idea. I'm sorry I can't go myself, too, but my wife and I— well, we have another engagement. I just dropped in for a drink with Emily on my way back from the Somerset Club. I ought to be leaving. I hope I'll see you again though, Commander Collins, while you're in Boston. Perhaps you'd dine with me one of these nights."

Shaun Collins and Terence Lenahan were both very sanguine about what could be done to the little house. Simonetta listened to them enthralled while they talked about two-by-fours, sheetrock and semi-gloss. When they finally closed the door of the little house behind them, Shaun suggested that she should ride over to South Boston with him and Terence, since Brian's car was only a roadster; and without making something of a scene on the street, Emily could not object, then and there. However, when she and Brian were actually on Broadway, she tried to argue.

"You were really pretty highhanded, Briny. I was delighted to have you come to the garden. I'd be delighted to have you come again. But, as I tried to explain to you, I'm not going anywhere just now. As far as that goes, you ought not to need an explanation."

"But I do. Why aren't you going anywhere?"

"Please don't pretend to be dense. One reason ought to be pretty evident to you."

"You mean because you're going to have a baby and are beginning to show it?"

"Of course."

"Well, that's not a very convincing argument to the eldest of eight children. If my mother'd shut herself up in the house, every time she was pregnant, she'd have been in a state of intermittent incarceration for about twenty years."

"Perhaps she wasn't as self-conscious about it as I am."

"Aren't you glad you're going to have a baby, Emily? I thought, from things Roger let drop once in a while, that you wanted one very much."

"Of course I'm glad I'm going to have a baby. But——"

"Well then, don't hide as if you were ashamed of it."

If the words had not been so kindly spoken, they would have carried with them the implication of a rebuke. Even as it was, Emily flushed and bit her lip.

"You know there's another reason. It's less than three months since Roger died."

"Yes, I know that too. So what?"

"So I haven't wanted to go anywhere. I haven't wanted to see anyone or do anything. For two or three weeks, after I'd recovered from the first shock and grief of his death, I didn't feel at all. I was just—well, I was numb all over."

"And that was perfectly normal—for two or three weeks."

"Since then, I haven't been numb exactly, but I've felt exhausted."

"Which was also perfectly normal. But you don't feel as exhausted now as you did when you first began to go to your garden, to sit there talking with your father, do you?"

"No, not quite. But I don't seem to want to see anyone else."

"How can you tell without trying? You were glad to see me—or at least if you weren't, you certainly put on a pretty good act."

"I didn't put on an act," Emily retorted indignantly. "I was glad to see you. But—"

"I'm going to start counting the number of times you say 'but,' if you aren't careful. You're not in a state of apathy or exhaustion any longer. You were, you should have been. Now it's about due to be over. You ought to be in a state of expectancy pretty soon."

"Expectancy of what?"

"Well, of motherhood first, naturally. And after that for whatever else is in store for you."

"I don't feel sure there is much in store for me that's worth while."

"Nobody can be sure of anything. But I should think you had a better-than-average chance of having a good deal that's worth while."

"I'd be more inclined to believe you were right if I hadn't been such a failure thus far."

"A failure? How?"

"Well, I failed in everything I meant to do on Joy Street, didn't I?"

He slowed down the car. "We're almost to my house and I'd like to go into that, a little, if you don't mind," he said. "Suppose we drive around City Point. It's very pleasant there in the spring, especially at this time in the evening. . . . You mean you feel you failed to make your house the sort of center you and Roger planned?"

She nodded, her eyes filling with tears.

"I'd agree that first dinner party of yours wasn't a conspicuous success," Brian said, grinning again in spite of his growing gravity. "But that was mostly my fault. And I'm not sure it wasn't a blessing in disguise, at that. It more or less opened your eyes to the fact that the way to create good fellowship among alien groups and individuals isn't through Social Contacts, with capital letters, any more—if it ever was. I think it was a good thing you found that out right away, instead of waiting until you'd made a whole series of mistakes along the same lines."

"My grandmother never made that kind of a mistake. She never had that kind of a failure. She's always entertained beautifully. People have always thought it was a compliment and a privilege to be asked to her house."

"Yes, of course. But your grandmother didn't entertain with a Noble Purpose—again to resort to capital letters. She entertained spontaneously, almost instinctively, and she assumed, to begin with, that people would know how to behave in her house and that they'd have a good time there. She didn't think they'd have to be shown by tactful means how to use the right fork and what to do with finger bowls. She didn't see herself as the great white hope for making Jews and Catholics, Irish and Italians, understand each other overnight, when they'd gone on for generations without succeeding in doing so. She wasn't condescending and she wasn't presumptuous, either. She still isn't."

"And you think I am?"

"I think you were, a little. Don't you?"

They had now reached City Point and, without replying, Emily looked away from him, toward the blue waters of Boston Harbor. He reached for her hand.

"I'm not trying to hurt you, Emily, or to criticize you. I'm just trying to help you see things straight, if I can, so that you can snap out of this apathy, or whatever it is that's got you hog-tied, and go on from there to the next thing. You don't have to answer me if you don't want to. Just think over what I've said a little."

"I don't mind answering. At least, not much. I'm afraid you're right. I'm afraid I was a little condescending, I'm afraid I was rather presumptuous. But at least I wasn't—vainglorious. Please give me that much credit."

"I'll give you all the credit that's coming to you and it's a lot. Of course you weren't vainglorious. Of course everything you did was to help Roger—getting the house in the first place, making it comfortable and beautiful and hospitable."

"But still I didn't help him!"

"But still you *did!* Why, Emily, you made him completely happy! Do you call that failing? No wife could have been more loyal and devoted than you were! And you were an inspiration and a help to him in his work besides! Suppose your house wasn't the sort of center you'd planned—don't get the idea for one moment it wasn't the sort that meant most to him, in every way. *It meant a lot to me, too! It meant a lot to Pell!* You haven't thought of it in terms of those poker parties that *did* bring about good fellowship among alien groups. You haven't thought about it in terms of a medieval betrothal service, that had all the solemnity of a marriage and transfigured two persons' lives. Why don't you? Why can't you?"

"I—I don't know, Briny."

"Well, won't you try? If you will, I think you'll stop seeing the Joy Street house as a failure."

"Yes, I'll try."

"That's all I want to know, right now. If I know you're trying, it'll help me try too."

"Try to do what?

"Try to make up for my mistake—which was a damn sight worse than any you ever made or ever could make."

"I don't know what you're talking about."

"You know that I went around for more than two years talking about 'England's War,' don't you? That I didn't apply for a commission in the Navy until I was faced with the probability that I'd be recalled as an infantry corporal in the United States Army? How do you think I've felt about that, ever since Pearl Harbor? How do you think I feel about never getting combat duty—I've tried and tried for it. David tried and got it—at least he's going to have it; he's in England already, and it's only a matter of time before the division he's with will be getting into action. Pell didn't even have to try for it. He got it without trying, he's won the Silver Star already. A lot of citations I'll get for fooling around on the B Docks. And it serves me right too!"

"Briny, I had no idea you felt like this!"

"How did you expect me to feel? As far as that goes, how do you think I felt when Roger died? He was a war casualty all right—doing the work of three men besides himself, only one of them good enough to lick his boots, at that! I'd have done more for the war effort, as it's turned out, if I'd stayed in the office, too, than I've done in that stinking South Pacific port. Roger might be alive if I had! It's too bad I didn't develop a squint in one of my ugly eyes, or let my big feet get flat, or something. I finally got it through my thick head why David was hellbent to get in at the kill, and he'll do a lot of killing, one way or another, before he gets through, believe me. And Pell's the stuff that modern knights in armor are naturally made of. But what am I except a bogtrotting Irishman, who might just as well be back in the bogs, for all the good he's ever done!"

"Briny, you mustn't talk like this. You're not being fair to yourself."

"All right, don't let me hear you talk the way you have been doing, either, then. As a matter of fact, we can't either of us talk this way or any way much longer right now—we will some other time though. Meanwhile, I've got to take you to the house before the hungry hordes eat up all the scrod. There aren't any big platters weighed down with steak in our dining room any more, worse luck. But scrod's pretty good eating at that, the way my mother fixes it. You'll see."

Several hours later, when he took her back to Louisburg Square, she confessed to him that she was glad he had made her go out, that she had really enjoyed the evening with his big cheerful family. Father Mat and Ray were both overseas now and Doreen was married and living in Hartford; but Barney Garvin had become a permanent member of the household, Della's "date" was apparently also more or less of a fixture, and Queenie had brought two small schoolmates home to supper. The general atmosphere was still contagiously hearty and Mary Collins was still the personification of loving-kindness. Inevitably, Emily responded to this and, as she did so, she became suddenly conscious of release from the constrictions of the past months. When she went to bed that night, it was not to lie wretched and wakeful for hours, but to fall almost instantly into quiet and refreshing slumber.

In the course of the next week, Brian persuaded her, without too much difficulty, to go off with him on several all-day trips in his car, and he sat in the Joy Street garden with her and her father and dined with her and Old Mrs. Forbes on Louisburg Square. When his leave was almost up, he suggested that perhaps she would let him drive her and Deirdre to Hollyhock Hill.

"I'd rather not go until after Decoration Day, Briny. I want to go out to Mount Auburn by myself, then."

He nodded, understandingly, and for a minute appeared to be thinking things over. "Well, I can manage to stay here until June first, if I cut out New York, and I don't mind doing that," he said at last. "In fact, I'd much rather go to Hollyhock Hill."

"If you're sure—"

"Of course I'm sure. Look, philanthropy isn't one of my strong points. If I wanted to be night-clubbing instead of driving you around, you can be damn sure that's what I'd be doing."

Mark and Elizabeth and Archie were not coming to Hollyhock Hill until after college closed; but Una Randell, despite her heavy schedule of chores, had been over to air and clean the house and stock it with enough foodstuffs so that the early arrivals would have the wherewithal for their first supper and their first breakfast. Brian spent the night, but Emily seemed so wholesomely sleepy, after they finished their evening meal, that he did not try to have another serious talk with her; and he had to be up and away at dawn the next morning, for he had stretched his leave to the uttermost limits, in order to wedge in the Vermont trip. However, he left a little note behind him, which Deirdre brought up on Emily's breakfast tray. It had no heading and no closing and contained only two lines:

Remember you're not numb any more or apathetic, either. You're just waiting. And you've got lots ahead of you to wait for.

As one tranquil day succeeded another, Emily began to understand more and more clearly what Brian had meant, and to believe, more and more wholeheartedly, that he was right. With the quickening of the child in her womb, came a general quickening throughout her whole being, and she began to marvel that she had been so long insensible to those great forces which destroy only to rebuild. Roger would live again in his child and hers and her task now was one of preparation for this resurrection. After the child was born, she would recognize the next task and prepare to meet that. Life would never be the same as before, but it might still be full and abundant; it would not again deteriorate into dull and meaningless existence. She was very grateful to Brian because he had convinced her of this, because he had shown her how to set forth on the highway that stretched ahead, instead of sitting sadly and aimlessly by the roadside.

Although it was so quiet at Hollyhock Hill, Emily was conscious of no tedium, even before the arrival of Mark and Elizabeth and their baby. She occupied herself with minor household tasks, which relieved Deirdre, but represented no strain; she kept the house bright with flowers and did a little light gardening, so that there would be more bloom later on. She had begun to really enjoy books again and read omnivorously. Without having much aptitude for music, she found that she enjoyed playing, for her own amusement, on the old square piano; and when Simonetta came up for the week end, as she did two or three times, Emily sat for hours listening to her and remembering how Roger had once said that someday Simonetta would fill her husband's house with melody; but there was no poignant pain in the memory, only a quiet nostalgia. Simonetta brought Pell's letters with her and read them aloud, in part, to Emily. Some portions she skipped, with delicately heightened color, and Emily thought she could guess what was in those. Simonetta also brought glowing reports of the progress which was being made, thanks to Shaun Collins and Terence Lenahan, in the little old house; it would be all ready for Pell when he came home. Emily remembered the time when she had made that other house on Joy Street ready for Roger and herself and, in the light of those recollections, gave helpful hints to Simonetta about what she might do also.

They were growing closer and closer together in every way, all the time and, because of this, Simonetta told Emily many things of her own accord. She spoke of the special courses she was about to take, now that the Conservatory was closed for the summer. She had found some available at Boston University and had decided on a six weeks' session in English and history. Finally, she spoke to Emily about her mother.

"She's gone back to Lynn. Uncle Ernesto and his wife were willing she should come—they said it was time to let bygones be bygones and of course, in a way, their house seems like home to her. I don't know whether she'll stay there permanently or not; if she doesn't, she'll have a little apartment of her own near by—of course Pell would be perfectly willing to pay the rent for her, if she decided that was what she wanted to do. The lease was up on the Joy Street flat, and she's stored what few household possessions she had in Uncle Ernesto's attic. I didn't want any of them. When Pell and I move into our little house, I want everything in it to be ours. I'd rather go on living where I am until he comes back; I'm very comfortable and happy there. But I see my mother again, once in a while. In fact, I helped her move. She isn't violent and vindictive any more. Just crushed and hopeless, because she feels life has dealt her one more blow; or she would be, if her Church wasn't such a comfort to her. I'm glad it is."

"I'm glad too."

Momentarily, Emily wished that she might have found some comfort in a church, after Roger died, when she herself had felt crushed and hopeless.

She thought of Sister Mary Theresa's visit and resolved that she would call at the convent when she went back to town, if only for the sake of courtesy. But as far as she was able to visualize the situation, the only real comfort she had derived had come from Brian. He had made her see that even though life did deal out blows, it also dealt out blessings, and that the better you stood up to hard knocks, the less unendurable they seemed. He had also made her see that she was waiting for something that was worth while.

When the Merriweathers and Jenny arrived from Hanover, Hollyhock Hill became less quiet, but pleasantly so. Archie was a precocious, noisy little boy, unusually knowing and active for his age. He tore from one end of the house to the other, from one end of the lawn and garden to the other; unless he were carefully watched, he darted across the road. There was so little passing-by that this did not represent a serious menace; but it was a cause for vigilance, just the same. In so far as possible, he was encouraged to confine his activities to the rear gallery, which was well railed, and which had only one gate, that was always kept carefully latched. Emily enjoyed sitting on the gallery, watching over Archie while he played there. Meanwhile, she did a little desultory reading and knitting and glanced, every now and then, down over the terraced hill to the brook and to the pond which had been formed where this was dammed. There was no pain in the memories connected with that any longer, either. She saw it now as it really was, warm and blue under the summer sun, not cold and glittering under the northern lights. She did not visualize it in connection with David—that is, not often. Usually she saw it in connection with Archie, whom she sometimes led by the hand down the terrace to its brink, so that he could dabble his toes in the water, and listened while he crowed with delight as the tiny paper boats which she made for him bobbed up and down in the water. Sometimes she even saw it as it would look when she took her own child there, two summers hence, to dabble his toes and play with paper boats.

Then one day when she was sitting on the gallery, quietly and contentedly, thinking of all that the future still held for her, as Brian had begged her to do, she heard a little click, a sound so slight that she would not have been conscious of it, had it not been alien to all the other sounds which Archie normally made. Next she realized that, with fantastic swiftness, he had fumbled at the latch and undone it, and that he was pelting down the terrace toward the little pond which she had taught him to love. . . .

She caught up with him just as he slid over the brink. She slid in after him, drawing him back to safety, Then, unexpectedly sliding a little farther on the slippery mud beneath the surface, she suddenly stepped off into deeper water.

She tried to regain her footing, failed and sank. It was merely a matter of moments before she had regained the surface and had struggled back to the shore. The only fear she felt, in the brief interval that she was under water, was that Archie, whom she had pulled back on the bank, might elude her again. But he had been startled by her disappearance and had stood still, beginning to cry. She took him up in her arms and, after alternately scolding and soothing him, led him back to the house.

The water had not been cold, there was no reason why it should have chilled her. But because she could see that Elizabeth and Deirdre were worried, and because she remembered how she had felt, when she had vainly urged Roger to go to bed and send for a doctor, she consented to do both. The same kindly, overworked little man who had taken care of her when she sprained her ankle came to see her; he agreed that any slight sensation of chilliness which she might have had was not likely to amount to anything. But he looked more sober when she told him how she had slipped and struggled for a footing which she could not find.

"You weren't aware of any wrench when that happened, were you?"

"Why yes, I think I was, now you speak of it. But I was much more vitally aware of going under water and of what Archie might do while I couldn't see him."

"You're how far along, Mrs. Field?"

"A little over six months."

"Well. . . . Of course I'm very sorry you're not where your own physician can see you. Not that I think there's any cause for alarm—"

Again something seemed to click, but it was in her mind, this time. That was what Dr. Blaine had said when. . . . The conscientious little country doctor, oblivious of the train of thought he had started, continued calmly enough.

"But perhaps we ought to send you back to Boston in an ambulance. We'll see how you are in the morning. Meanwhile, I'm going to give you a sedative. I want you to get a good night's sleep."

They did not send her back to Boston in an ambulance and she did not get a good night's sleep. Shortly before midnight, she was seized with violent pain; and in the dark dreadful hour just before dawn, she was delivered of a premature baby. It was a little girl, and it breathed for a few minutes before the doctor laid it sorrowfully down, knowing there was nothing more he could do for it. And there was a great deal he must do for its mother, if she were not to die too.

Emily was very ill for a long while. Her recovery was retarded by her belief that, since she had lost her baby, she did not have much to live for after all. Brian, who had been assigned to the B Docks in Norfolk, tried several times to convince her that she was wrong, but he did not make much headway. He had been mistaken before, she reminded him; why should she think he was right now? He realized that she was still very weak and completely disheartened and he did not try to argue with her. He decided that probably time would do more for her than anything else, and that he should not harass her into assuming false hope and false cheerfulness. But one day she realized, of her own accord, that she was waiting again, and that her expectancy was not only hopeful, but glad.

She was waiting for David to come home.

Chapter 33

In the meanwhile, a great many other things had happened. The most important of these, of course, was that the war had ended and that, with the cessation of hostilities, a new era had begun for Emily, as it had for everyone else. Her viewpoint, like many women's, however, was personal rather than general; she was more affected by the changes which came into her own life and those of the persons whom she actually knew, than by those wrought in the lives of people in distant lands. Simonetta was radiant with joy in those days, and Emily caught the reflection of it.

For Pell had indeed proved himself a modern knight in armor. His military achievements had been both glamorous and meteoric; and Emily had shared with Simonetta the mingled excitement and pride with which his beloved had followed his progress. He had made the Sicilian campaign with the rank of major, arriving at the city of Messina in August of '43 and becoming military governor of the province of Messina not long thereafter. He had remained with the Scottish occupying forces until January of '44, receiving the honorary degree of Doctor of Jurisprudence from the University and various other signal marks of recognition; for his knowledge of Italian, and his wise and agreeable use of it had won him countless friends. Then he had been transferred to the mainland of Italy, where he was appointed governor of the province of Cantanzaro. Before getting really well established in the latter post, he had again been transferred, this time to England, with a group of selected M.G. officers, in order to prepare for the invasion of Normandy; he was next assigned as legal officer in the M.G. section of the First U. S. Army, and given the privilege of entering France with the Eighty-second Airborne Division. During the invasion, he had been wounded the second time, and the second time cited for heroism; but after thirty days he had rejoined the First Army Headquarters, made the campaign across Europe with this outfit, and been sent back to England to form part of the nucleus assembled there for the military government of Austria. When the draft for the Allied control of Austria was completed, he flew back to Italy, where part of his unit joined General Clark's headquarters and finished the European campaign over the Alps into Austria. There he served as American chairman of the Allied Legal Directorate, with the rank of colonel. His return to the United States, and his marriage to Simonetta were now only a matter of months.

The little old house on Joy Street, completely renovated, was already prepared for them to move into; even the grand piano which dominated the living room had been installed. Simonetta had bought very little furniture, because she preferred to wait until she and Pell could get that together, which she thought should not take long, at least as far as essentials were concerned. But she had purchased her kitchen equipment and, with Emily's help, gradually assembled an adequate amount of linen from the depleted supplies in the stores, selected her preferred patterns in glass, china and silver from the lines still carried, and begun to get her clothes. Somehow she had found time to do an immense amount of embroidery, drawn work and other kinds of fine sewing herself, and her growing piles of sheets, towels and underwear bore witness to her skill as a needlewoman; but Miss Ruby was making her wedding dress, Caggiula her suits, and Kakas her fur coat. Everything else was correspondingly of the best. She and Pell were to be married at St. Leonard's, and Emily and Brian were to stand up with them. There would be two wedding breakfasts, one at Old Venice, for the special delectation of Italian friends and connections, and another at Old Mrs. Forbes' house, in order that everyone connected with Cutter, Mills might be entertained in a manner which would seem more suitable to conservative Bostonians. Emily had tried to protest that this would prove too fatiguing for Simonetta and Simonetta had only laughed.

"Why, most weddings among my people last all day and far into the night!" she told Emily. "We ride through the streets with sirens blowing, we dance until the wee small hours. This will be a comparatively short, simple celebration, with just the breakfast at Old Venice, immediately after the Nuptial Mass, when we will all be really hungry; and then the party which your grandmother is so kindly giving, which will not be a breakfast at all, but a very elaborate luncheon. We will have to simplify the menu and cut the toasts short at Old Venice in order to reach Louisburg Square on time; and it will be much easier for Pell and me to slip away from there than it would have been if the festivities had continued in typically Italian fashion; everyone would have been very much astonished and a little hurt if the bride and groom had not remained until all the other guests were ready to start for home."

Not without some demurring, Emily allowed herself to be overpersuaded on this score, as well as on the plans for a honeymoon; Pell and Simonetta were not going to take a wedding journey; they preferred to go straight to their little house and Pell was going back to work at the office immediately. Brian was able to get to Boston from Norfolk reasonably often in these days, and the question of his return to the office had already been raised too; but he had been noncommittal. He would agree to go back there, as soon as he was separated from the Navy, if it could be distinctly understood from the beginning that this might be only a temporary arrangement. He made no secret of the fact that, if he were free, in time to enter the campaign, he intended to run against Russell Forbes for the United States Senate. If he won, he would be going to Washington in January of '47; he did not propose to commit himself to anything which would keep him in Boston beyond that date.

This decision might easily have caused a coolness between him and Old Mrs. Forbes, had Brian not breezily made it evident that he preferred to see Emily in his mother's house than on Louisburg Square, and had not Emily made equally evident the pleasure she took in going to South Boston. As an only child herself, who had married an orphan with an only sister, this was her first experience in a large group consisting entirely of the immediate family, and she was finding it unexpectedly heart warming. Her grandmother wisely decided that it was better not to make overmuch of an issue which would only serve to separate her from her favorite granddaughter. She had managed to persuade Emily to stay on at her house, first because the girl was really not well enough to return to her own, and next because, for the first time, Old Mrs. Forbes had pleaded loneliness and the handicap of her growing incapacity.

"I'm getting to be an aged woman, Emily. We might as well face the fact. It's almost impossible for me to go over the stairs—I haven't climbed up to the third story since I can remember, and you've probably noticed that I don't go back and forth between the first and second any oftener than I can help. Perhaps we can get an elevator within a year or so now, and probably I can hold out that long. But until then, I need you to check on the condition of the attic and the guest rooms, not to mention the kitchen quarters. I don't suspect any of the servants of shirking, consciously. However, they're all getting old too. There's no telling when they'll begin to give out, one by one. And I'm not deceiving myself; when they're gone, I won't be able to replace them. Deirdre's a great help here; it's really wonderful how she keeps going. But she couldn't manage alone in your house—you know that as well as I do. And what's the sense of trying to run two big cumbersome establishments for a couple of unattached women, when they could combine forces and keep each other company?"

None at all, Emily was forced to admit. Besides, she felt no special urge to return to Joy Street and she was honestly glad to feel that she was being of some service to her grandmother. She worked in her garden herself again now, and she and her father continued to meet there, when it was warm enough, and to enjoy each other's companionship during the late afternoons. When Brian was home on leave, he frequently joined them there. Emily kept the wine closet well stocked, and went in and out of the kitchen and pantry as occasion demanded; but she had not once been upstairs again since that night when she had walked from room to room, instinctively listening for sounds which did not come. Deirdre aired and cleaned the premises and reported that everything about them was unchanged. Emily was quite willing to take her word for it.

However, since Old Mrs. Forbes seemed to feel so strongly that someone should supervise every nook and corner of the house on Louisburg Square, Emily did this meticulously; and one day she asked Brian if he would care to go to the attic with her; she thought he might find it interesting. He did not quite see what an attic might possibly provide that would be intriguing; but he was entirely amenable to going there with Emily, if that was what she wanted him to do. So they climbed the last steep flight of stairs together and, when they reached the door at the top, she handed him a large key. As she did so, he noticed for the first time, that she had two small glasses in her hand.

"What are those for? To catch rain water when the roof leaks?"

"You don't suppose Grandmamma permits leaks in her roof, do you, Brian? Or that glasses this size would hold enough rain water to do any good, if there were one? Have a little patience, you'll see what these are for."

He unlocked the door and opened it. Directly in front of him stood rows of great hand-blown bottles, which were among Old Mrs. Forbes' most cherished possessions. The bottles were filled with rum and the neck · of each was encircled by a chain, to which a tag was attached. He bent over and inspected the nearest one.

" 'This rum was taken in this container around the Horn—1830, 1838, 1845,' " he read. "Why Christ in the mountains! It's more than a hundred years old!"

"Certainly it is. Look at some of those other labels. The old theory was that the prolonged rolling and pitching of sailing vessels improved the quality—in addition to aging, of course."

"Here's another bottle that went around the Cape of Good Hope— three of them, by golly!"

"Yes, those are supposed to be the best of all. Now you know what the two glasses are for. We'll draw up a couple of those old tavern chairs, over in the corner, and have a drink of Great-Grandfather's super-special brand."

"And did I ever tell you it was surprising, the number of things you didn't think of, for an intelligent girl? 'Twas a slander indeed, as Uncle Barney would say."

Old Mrs. Forbes' attic was not the type where cobwebs were permitted to accumulate, and broken furniture was thrust out of sight, because no one was sufficiently interested in it to have it mended. Besides the bottles, it contained a number of enormous old-fashioned trunks, which had undoubtedly once made the Grand Tour, and which Brian's imagination could easily picture as being filled with elegant wearing apparel in bygone styles, which might someday have real historical value, besides furnishing the wherewithal, whenever needed, for fancy-dress parties. These mammoth trunks were flanked by new and more practical luggage, neatly arranged to be readily withdrawn at a moment's notice. Pushed farther back were ornamental washstand sets of such fine flowered porcelain that it was easy to understand why they had not been destroyed, together with the marble-topped washstands which they had formerly graced and which, after all, made up a once-essential item in valuable bedroom suites whose other pieces were still in use and might need partial replacement. A few fixtures, with the glass globes characteristic of the gaslight period, were carefully suspended from the rafters, and it was obvious that these, too, might someday be requisitioned again; the same was true of two or three student lamps which had never been electrified. Several pieces of ponderous bronze, representing everything from stags in conflict to vestal virgins, seemed less promising; so did the Rogers' groups and other figures in Parian marble. The tavern chairs to which Emily had referred were two among a number which obviously represented a surplus supply, available, like the smart new luggage, at a moment's notice, in case of need. Brian was sure Clark and Pearson took them down to the drawing room when well-known musicians came to render chamber music before select gatherings, or when a benefit was held for some worthy and fashionable cause. At the moment, they certainly provided ideal seats for the enjoyment of entertainment conveniently at hand; and after Brian had placed them where Emily had designated, and filled the glasses from one of the bottles labeled GOOD HOPE, he leaned back, alternately sipping and sighing with satisfaction.

"Why didn't you ever bring me here before?" he inquired at length. "I'd say, without a moment's hesitation, that this is the most interesting place in the house."

"Well, at the risk of having you pull that old line about the number of things I never think of, in spite of the treat I've just given you, I've got to confess that I never did think of this before—I mean of bringing anyone up here with me. I've just thought of the attic as a place I'd got to inspect, in the course of regular household routine, to make sure it was in order. I never thought of it as the setting for a tête-à-tête."

"I'd say it had everything needed for that—seclusion, comfort, atmosphere and the means of unlimited refreshment."

"I didn't intend to have the amount of refreshment unlimited, Briny."

He set down his glass, suddenly grave. "That's not worrying you, is it, Emily?"

"Isn't what worrying me?"

"That I might drink too much?"

"No-o-o. I've always supposed you were a little on the thirsty side, as the saying goes. But that's really none of my affair, is it?"

"It might be. So I'd really like to set your mind at rest on that score. I did used to drink too much, now and again. But I've never once done it since that historic dinner party—which is another reason why you might set it down as a blessing in disguise. I've never wanted to run the risk of being as much ashamed of myself again as I was after that night. Of course when I reached that conclusion, I didn't realize I'd have a great deal worse to be ashamed of."

"Haven't you got over feeling badly about—"

"About 'England's War'? No, and of course I never shall. But at least I haven't ever had to be ashamed again of 'getting drunk and making a damn fool of myself as a result of it. I never shall do that, either. I'm pretty serious about this, Emily. You can count on it."

"I think you deserve all kinds of credit, Briny, for making up your mind to do something that must have been awfully hard for you and then sticking to it the way you have. I think—"

"I'm not trying to take any credit for it. I don't want any. I just want you to tell me you're not afraid I'll ever disgrace you."

"Briny, I just said it really wasn't any of my affair."

"And I just said that it might be. Now I'll say that I hope more than anything in the world it will be."

She had continued to toy with her glass while they talked. Now she set it down on the floor beside her, as he had done with his.

"I'm not sure I know just what you mean, Briny," she said quietly.

"You aren't? Why, you must be! You must know I've been in love with you for years! You must know that I've waited and waited for the time to come when I thought it was decent to ask you to marry me."

"But I didn't! It never occurred to me that you were in love with me. In the beginning, I thought you rather disliked me."

"*Disliked* you! I fell in love with you at first sight. But after all, you were married to my best friend!"

"I tell you, it never occurred to me,"Emily repeated persistently. The words came rapidly and she spoke with heightened color. "You didn't act as if you were in love with me!"

"How did you expect me to act? Sneak into the house when Roger was out of it and then come up suddenly behind you and throw you down on a bed?"

"No—no—of course not! Don't say such—such terribly coarse things, Briny!"

"Well, we might as well have a showdown. And, from what you've just said, I gather you expected me to do some kind of pretty violent love-making, either before Roger's death or very soon afterward."

"No—no!" Emily exclaimed again. "I didn't expect you to do that then, any more than I expected you to tell me just now that you wanted to marry me. I thought you did get to like me, after a while. And then, when Roger died and—and the baby, I thought you were sorry for me."

"I was. I was damn sorry for you. I knew what you were going through. No one could help being sorry for you who knew that."

"Well, and then you tried to help me realize there was still something ahead of me. Something worth waiting for."

"Yes. Gradually I tried to get it into your head that you couldn't live all the rest of your life with a memory. You're too young! You're too lovely! You're too—too feminine! You're bound to fall in love again. It's just as normal for you to do that as it was for you to grieve when Roger died. You're bound to have more children. You were made to have children, you'd be a wonderful mother. You can't thwart nature, the way you were trying to do. You ought to be married right now. My God, you're going to marry me, no matter what I have to do to make you! You'll be so glad, afterward, that you won't care!"

He leaped up, and, pulling her to her feet, threw his arms around her and, taking her in a viselike hold, kissed her as she had never been kissed before. It was completely useless for her to struggle for freedom; since she could not escape the embrace, she had no choice but to accept it. When Brian finally released his grip to the extent of holding her at arm's length, he looked down at her with savage joy.

"Now kiss back, darling, and then we'll really get someplace," he said, drawing her toward him again.

"No, we won't. Let me go, Brian. You haven't any right—"

"I've every right. I'm a free man and you're a free woman and I'm so much in love with you that I'm not going to wait for you another day."

"You'll have to."

"And what'll make me, I'd like to know? Not you, my dear. I tell you, all you need is—"

"I *will* make you. I won't marry you. I can't. I'm in love with someone else."

"You're not! You're just saying that because you think, if you do, I won't hurry you this way, I won't treat you like a woman who's got to be shown she's ready and ripe for mating."

"I've told you the truth, Brian. If you don't let me go now, I'll never speak to you again as long as I live. I'll never see you again. You'd better believe me. Because I mean it."

Her voice was very quiet again, as it had been a little earlier, when she told him she was not sure she understood what he meant; but now it had a more compelling quality. He gripped her elbows hard.

"You say you're in love with someone else. How long has this been going on?"

"In a way, it's been going on for years."

"You mean, before Roger died?"

"Don't look at me that way, Brian. It wasn't—I didn't. . . . I almost told you about it that day you kept saying I hadn't been a failure, that no

414

woman could be more loyal and devoted to her husband than I was to Roger. I was loyal, I was devoted. I put all my heart and soul into the effort, because I was trying to make up to him for—for what I didn't feel for him, for what I couldn't give him."

"Then he never knew?"

"No. At least, I think he was vaguely jealous, for just a little while, when we were first married, but—"

"When you were first married!"

"Yes. This—this other thing happened very soon afterward. I don't see how it could have, but it did. I loved Roger, I loved him dearly, but I didn't love him—well, that way. My grandmother tried to tell me so and I wouldn't listen. I wouldn't listen to anyone. I was bound and determined to marry Roger. And then later, I found out what it really meant to yearn unspeakably for a man, what it was to live for years and years with yearning like that unfulfilled. But Roger never knew. I'm sure of that. I'm sure the vague jealousy I told you about lasted just a little while. I'm sure I made him happy. He said so, over and over again. He couldn't have said it the way he did, he couldn't have acted the way he did, if he'd had the least doubt of my loyalty."

"No, I don't suppose he could have," Brian muttered. "I—well, I know he couldn't have." He let go her arms and stood facing her squarely. "And I know you're telling me the truth," he went on. "I know you weren't ever disloyal to him. This other thing you're talking about—it was something you didn't expect, something you didn't even know existed. This other man—does he know how you feel?"

"I think he must. Of course I never told him so. But, before he went away—"

"Before he went away where?"

"Why, he's been in the service, too, Briny. And, before he left Boston—"

"Then he had made love to you? It didn't matter to him that you were married, the way it did to me?"

"Please let me finish, Brian. He had—he'd attempted a little light love-making. Nothing like—well, nothing like what you did just now," she added, her color deepening still further. "Only one very casual kiss and a few more or less ardent remarks. The sort of thing that used to be called flirtation, I believe. I don't think I was the only woman he kissed casually and talked to that way. I think it was more or less natural for him to do so. I'm sure he was very attractive to women generally, and I suppose that type—"

"Yes. I know all about that type. In fact, we had one in our office." He broke off suddenly. "You don't mean to tell me—" he began. Then he interrupted himself again. "Go on," he said curtly, after a moment's pause.

"Perhaps you don't know as much as you think you do about that type,

Brian," Emily said calmly. "Because when this man I'm talking about really had a chance to make all kinds of love to me, when I'm afraid I mightn't have tried to stop him, he didn't do it. He had just as much to do with saving my marriage as I had myself. But before he went away, he did tell me that he loved me. He did say that if things had been different. . . . He thought he had a right to say that much. I'm not sure whether he did or not, but I know he thought so. I know he wouldn't have done it unless he had."

"And you didn't hear from him again before Roger died?"

"Never directly. Not once. And when people told me how lucky I was not to have anyone I cared about in danger, I felt like such an awful hypocrite. Because of course I was half sick with worry, because of course I read the casualty lists every day and lay awake every night, wondering. . . ."

"But you've heard from him since?"

"Yes. Naturally he wrote me a letter of condolence."

"With his tongue in his cheek!"

"Was your tongue in your cheek when you wrote me after Roger died, Brian? You say you've been in love with me for years too! Please be fair! . . . Then he didn't write me again until he'd heard I'd lost the baby."

"Well, after all, the best time to make love to a woman isn't when she's carrying another man's child."

"Brian, unless you'll at least try to be fair there's no use going on."

"All right. I'll try to be fair. At least I'll try to be what you call fair. . . . So after you lost your baby, this man, who of course is cloaked in mystery, as far as I'm concerned, started writing to you regularly?"

"No, just intermittently. And at first very impersonally. He didn't write love letters—at least not exactly."

"He didn't ask you outright to marry him?"

"Brian, I don't think you have a right to ask for so many details. The letters have been wonderful. They've made me very happy. They've given me something to live for again. Don't you remember, you said yourself you didn't know what would happen to make me feel again that life was worthwhile, but that you knew something would? Well, these letters have. They've made me content to wait. They've raised me to that state of expectancy you talked about. They've never come regularly and the very fact that I've wondered when they would come and what would be in them when they did has made them seem just that much more marvelous."

"And now you've heard that this man's coming home?"

"Yes. I had a letter this morning. He said he wasn't sure yet when he could get here, but sometime this week. He said he'd let me know. He said—oh, Briny, he said he had something very important to tell me, something that couldn't wait any longer!"

Her voice, which at first had been so quiet, then troubled and then calm again, suddenly rang out with gladness. She looked up at Brian with shining eyes.

"I meant to tell you about this today anyhow," she said. "I was all ready to when—when you interrupted me. I wanted you to know that you'd been right, that I did have something worth waiting for. I didn't bring you here to the attic accidentally or casually. I brought you because I knew no one would find us here, because we'd be undisturbed, because I didn't want anyone to break in on us while I was telling you something so important. And I thought after I'd told you, we would have a second drink—just a little one. A—a sort of toast. I didn't dream, you see, that you felt the way you did—the way you do. I'm terribly sorry, Brian. I think a lot of you. But I'm not in love with you. I couldn't be. You understand that now, don't you?"

"Yes, I understand that now."

"So of course you don't want to drink the toast? Of course you'd rather go downstairs."

"But of course I do want to drink it! Of course I wouldn't dream of going downstairs until I had."

He leaned over and picked up the two glasses that had been set down on the floor. Then he lifted one of the old hand-blown bottles with the GOOD HOPE label chained about it and poured out the fragrant old rum. This gurgled a little in its flow, and when the glasses were filled, it showed a rich warm color, one that had mellowed with long years and with much voyaging to distant parts of the world. Brian put the old bottle back in its place and, after handing Emily her glass, raised his own.

"I can't toast you personally," he said, "because then you couldn't drink with me and of course that's what I want you to do. So let's drink instead to your married happiness—with a husband who loves you better than anyone else in the world!"

Chapter 34

THE INTERLUDE IN THE attic left Emily more shaken than she would have cared to admit. After Brian left, she went to her room and, much to her own indignation, burst into sudden and uncontrollable weeping. When the storm had spent itself, she was so exhausted that, despite her scorn for daytime rests, she flung herself down on the chaise longue, and this time she did not watch the clock, to see when she would be justified in getting up again. Instead, it was only after a prolonged period that she told herself, resolutely, she had acted like a Victorian female long enough; if she were not careful, she would be swooning, the next thing she knew. She dragged herself off the chaise longue, washed her face and applied a conservative amount of make-up, tidied her hair and, taking David's letter in her hand, went to her grandmother's room.

Old Mrs. Forbes was herself so engrossed in a letter that she did not immediately look up. When she tardily realized that her granddaughter was standing in front of her, obviously waiting to speak with her, she gave a slight start.

"Why, Emily, I didn't know you were there! Don't frighten a poor feeble old lady by creeping up on her like that."

Emily attempted to laugh, not altogether successfully. "Grandmamma, you know you were never frightened by anything in your life! And as for being old and feeble—tell that to someone who doesn't know you as well as I do! You've got more energy and vitality right now than all the other women in your family put together."

"Nonsense! I can't say much for your mother, but you have any amount of energy and vitality. The only trouble is, you don't half use it. Priscilla's also got plenty—almost too much, I've thought at times. And I'm agreeably surprised in Elizabeth. Her development was certainly retarded, but she seems to be making up for lost time. This letter is from her."

"It is? May I sit down and hear the latest news?"

"By all means. I'd have sent for you in a few minutes to talk it over with you—at least I'd have sent to find out whether Brian Collins was still here, or whether you'd gone streaking off to South Boston with him."

"The way you say 'South Boston' makes it sound like 'South Pole,' Grandmamma. Brian left more than an hour ago, and I haven't the slightest intention of streaking off to South Boston or anywhere else this evening."

"Well, you sound as if you'd been quarreling. Now I have a chance to really see you, you look that way too."

"Grandmamma, you notice altogether too much. Brian and I didn't have a quarrel exactly, but it was something like that. I'll tell you about it later. Go on and give me your great news first. I suppose Elizabeth is going to have another baby."

"Yes, but that's only one of the important items in her letter. Mark's been offered a professorship at Harvard. He's resigning at Dartmouth, effective at the end of the college year, and they're leaving Hanover as soon afterward as they conveniently can."

"Well, good for Mark! I should think he and Elizabeth would both enjoy Cambridge very much."

"They'd prefer to live in Boston. And of course I'd prefer to have them. I want Archie where I can keep my eye on him. He's a handful, all right."

Old Mrs. Forbes spoke with great pride; obviously the fact that Archie was a handful constituted a source of immense satisfaction to her. With a slight pang, Emily realized that a few years earlier, her grandmother would have shown more tact and reserve in speaking to her of this. If it had not been for Archie's physical and mental precocity, Emily would probably not have lost her own baby.

"You mean you'd like to have them live with you?" she inquired, wisely refraining from dwelling on the subject of Archie.

"Well, I was thinking over the feasibility of that when you came in. Elizabeth doesn't exactly suggest any such thing, in her letter. But reading between the lines, I believe she thought of it, too, at least as a temporary arrangement. It certainly would simplify matters for her, until after the new baby's born, and while she's looking for a house of her own. . . . I don't suppose you'd care to let her have yours?"

"Why, Grandmamma, of course I'd have to think that over! I don't need to tell you that everything you've been saying has come as a complete surprise. Just what do you mean by 'let'? I've never thought of selling it or even renting it."

"You've never thought of it in any definite way since you left there, have you? Of course I did urge you to come here, of course I'm glad and grateful that you did. I'd be equally pleased to have you stay on indefinitely. But, as a matter of fact, I don't believe you wanted to go back to Joy Street. I haven't seen any indication that you did."

"No, I haven't wanted to. I've been very glad to stay here with you. It's pleased me to think that I was being of some help to you—I mean, in practical ways. It's pleased me to think I was helpful in other ways too—that I've been company for you, that you've been less lonely than you would have been without me. And you've been company for me, Grandmamma. You're wonderful company. I've always enjoyed every moment I've spent with you."

Emily leaned over and kissed her grandmother. It was not often that they exchanged caresses, in the course of casual conversation, but now the gesture was entirely spontaneous. At the same time, Emily's thoughts were racing in a new direction. If Elizabeth and Mark and their increasing family were in the house, there would hardly be room for her and there would certainly be no need of her presence. Elizabeth could attend to the "supervision" by which Old Mrs. Forbes set such store, and Jenny could take Deirdre's place in lightening the load for the old servants. There would no longer be any sound reason, under such an arrangement, for Emily to postpone her return to her own house. Yet she still felt no impulsion to go there. She did not want to live there alone, and certainly she did not want to live there with anyone else. It had been her house and Roger's, it represented a definite phase of her life which was now over, but which had been full of significance to her and always would be. She did not want to mar the memory of what it had represented to her in the beginning, and she now knew that the only way to avoid doing this would be to go forward in a new way and with a different setting. That must have been what she had subconsciously intended to do—even hoped to do—for a long while—ever since Brian had made her realize that she could. Under these circumstances, it would be selfish to keep the house empty indefinitely. She was not ready to sell it or to rent it; but perhaps she should offer to lend it to Elizabeth and Mark. Yes, that would be the sensible thing to do, the best thing for everyone concerned. She would offer them her house and she would stay where she was, until. . . .

"As I said, I'd like to think things over a little," she remarked at last. Her grandmother had made no attempt to interrupt her train of thought; but Emily realized that the old lady, with her usual keenness had, to a certain degree, followed it, as she sat turning the signet ring around on the finger, now noticeably more misshapen than it had been the year before. "Offhand, however, I'd say your second suggestion was the better of the two," Emily continued. "I think I ought to lend Elizabeth my house. I think she and Mark might enjoy it. They'd have more space and more independence if they and their children had a house to themselves than they would here."

"I've just pointed out to you that there's plenty of space here. Not that it should be necessary. You know as well as I do how many rooms I have. And I haven't interfered with your independence much, have I? Certainly you've come and gone as you pleased and I've tried to make all your friends welcome—even that Irishman who keeps plunging back and forth between here and Norfolk and who wants to pry Russell loose from the Senate."

"Of course there's lots of room," Emily said soothingly. "And you've been more than kind and considerate—to me and all my friends. Brian's appreciated your attitude tremendously. He knows he's put you in a difficult position."

"No one has ever put me in a difficult position yet," Old Mrs. Forbes said tartly. "It would take a good deal more than an upstart from South Boston to do so now. I was merely pointing out to you that, if I could be tolerant about that situation, I certainly could be as far as Elizabeth and Mark and their friends are concerned."

"Yes, Grandmamma, I understand," Emily said, still more soothingly. She realized that Old Mrs. Forbes was in a defensive mood which, a few years earlier, would have been as uncharacteristic as the tactlessness with which she had referred to Archie. "I just want to be sure you do. Pell and Simonetta are tremendously grateful too—it'll mean everything to them, having that wonderful breakfast at this house."

"My understanding hasn't suffered the same way my joints have, Emily. And I'm glad enough to give those young Italians a start in the right direction. But of course my greatest concern is for my own family. Someday this house will be Archie's. I've been meaning to tell you, for some time, that I'd decided to leave it to him, on account of his name. After all, you have your own house, and your father and mother persisted in selling theirs, so they don't deserve any special consideration. It's quite obvious Sherman and Sue don't ever intend to leave the Cape and that Russell won't ever have any children. Therefore, as long as this is going to belong to Archie someday, I think it would be very fitting to have him grow up here."

"You mean you'd rather have Elizabeth and Mark come here than to have them go to my house, Grandmamma?"

"Well, yes. I just threw out my second suggestion casually. I didn't think you'd take it seriously, when you've been so long making up your mind about anything."

"Very well. Let's forget about the second suggestion. I'll decide what to do about my house later—you're right, I have been a long while making up my mind about anything. You'll write to Elizabeth tonight, won't you, and ask her to come here? If she says yes, we'll consider that settled. Meanwhile, I had something I wanted to tell you about too. I had a letter from David Salomont this morning."

"That's not unusual, is it? I was under the impression you'd been hearing from him right along, for some time."

"I have—not regularly, but fairly frequently until lately. Now he's written to say he's coming home. He might arrive in Boston almost any time this week. And he's got something 'very important' to tell me. I'll show you the letter, if you like."

Her grandmother looked up at her searchingly. Emily's tone had suddenly changed, just as it had when she was talking with Brian, a couple of hours earlier; where there had previously been a forced quiet about it, it now rang with released joy. The expression in Old Mrs. Forbes' face changed too; it ceased to be one of defensive determination and became one of singular sympathy and understanding. It was a long while since Emily had seen that illusive look of beauty which had somehow survived the years.

"No," Old Mrs. Forbes said with unwonted gentleness. "No, I don't want to see the letter. If it's the kind you're leading me to believe, no one except you ought to see it. But I'm very glad you've got it—at last. I don't think you'll have so much trouble making decisions from now on. And I'll be very glad to see David Salomont himself, when he gets here."

The telegram, announcing his impending arrival, came in the following morning. Emily had not dared look for it so soon, in view of the previous noncommittal statement that he would arrive "some day that week." Now she devoured the message with hungry eyes.

HAVE JUST CLEARED THE POST PERIOD CATCHING FIRST POSSIBLE
TRAIN TO BOSTON PERIOD EXPECT ME LATE AFTERNOON PERIOD
DAVID

"Late afternoon" might mean anything from five onward—possibly from four onward, though Emily decided not to count on that. She had lain awake, the greater part of the previous night, trying to map out a tentative plan of action. It was all very well to say that the house on Louisburg Square was large enough to accommodate both herself and the Merriweather family; but Emily knew that such an arrangement would have intangible as well as tangible disadvantages. The household would and should revolve primarily around Archie and the new baby, and secondarily around Mark and the requirements of his important position; Emily would represent an alien element in this scheme of things. . . . The library and Old Mrs. Forbes' quarters, including the small room off her own where Doris slept, took up the entire second story. The third story, besides the famous front bedroom, which Emily had now occupied for so long, consisted of one correspondingly large in the rear, two hall bedrooms and two bathrooms; these would provide just enough space for the comfort and convenience of Mark and Elizabeth, with their two children and a nurse. On the fourth floor there was only one small room which was not used by the household staff; and though this had occasionally served as an extra guest chamber, when the house was overflowing with guests, as it so often did in the old days, it was considered more suitable for extra storage and was not designed for prolonged occupancy. Of course it could be adapted to this, if necessary; Emily tried to visualize it as it might look with fresh paint and paper, crisp curtains and some rearrangement of furniture. The "set bowl" in it could be removed and the closet turned into a small bathroom; there was another closet in the hall that probably could be cleared. It would not be conveniently near, and it would not hold much; but it would do. Emily had always felt contempt for persons who said this and that "would do"; she thought it generally meant they would not take enough trouble to have things really right. Now she found she was saying it herself. However, the prospect of living, for any length of time, in cramped quarters on the fourth story of her grandmother's house, did not appeal to her, no matter how hard she tried to visualize a trans-figured room. . . .

Well, the Merriweathers would not be moving in until September and that would give her plenty of time for readjustment. At least, she did not suppose they would be moving in until September, just before Harvard College opened. Her grandmother had not told her when the new baby was due and she had forgotten to inquire. It might very well be earlier than September and in that case. . . . She would find out right away. But perhaps it would be better for her to make up her mind, without any more dillydallying, to move back into her own house, temporarily. As soon as she had talked with David and knew something about his plans, she would climb up the Hill to Joy Street and walk in through her front door like a sensible woman. She would have Dan open the shutters and Deirdre pull up the shades beforehand, and she herself would plan to arrive in the middle of the day, when the place was flooded with sunshine. She would pass resolutely from room to room, with her head up and her eyes open for anything that might need attention and which could have escaped Deirdre's notice. She would get the silver out of the bank and the rugs out of storage, she would pack her personal belongings and go home. It was ridiculous for her grandmother to say that she and Deirdre could not manage alone in the Joy Street house, if they had to. But it was not beyond the realm of possibility that Ellie might return, if offered suffi-cient inducement. She had never become really acclimated to factory work, as Dolly had. And Dan could always lend a hand. . . .

It would have been helpful if David had been a little more definite in his letter. It had not said whether he was now about to be separated from the service, or whether he was merely coming home on leave; in the latter case, he would have only about thirty days. But a great deal could be done in thirty days. A great deal could happen—a great many wonderful things. . . .

She finally fell asleep thinking of these wonderful things and then, in the morning, came the telegram. Of course that did not enlighten her as to David's plans, any more than the letter had. But there were only a few more hours to wait, before he would talk to her about them. She went downstairs to tell her grandmother that he would be there that afternoon, and Old Mrs. Forbes was delighted to learn of this imminent arrival. In fact, she appeared to be in a generally mellow mood. She had written Elizabeth directly after her conversation with Emily the day before and

Elizabeth, who had received the letter in the morning mail, had immediately telephoned her mother, saying that she and Mark were both very grateful for the invitation and that they were happy to accept it.

"Did she tell you when she expected the new baby?"

"Yes, early in August. So they'll come down here right after college closes. That won't seem like any time at all."

"No, it's really very soon," Emily said aloud. Mentally, she added, "I'll tell Deirdre tomorrow that we're moving back to Joy Street. I'll call up the bank and the storage company. I'll have Pierce's send in some supplies."

"Have you told that young Irishman David's coming back?" Old Mrs. Forbes inquired.

"Yes. That is, I didn't mention David by name, but I said—"

"You let him know you had other interests. I knew you'd been through some kind of a scene. No doubt he knew to whom you were referring, even if you didn't mention David by name. He must have had some idea how things were in that quarter. And I never thought those two liked each other, particularly."

"No, I'm afraid they didn't. But Pell always liked them both. I'm sure he'd want David to be in the wedding party, too, if that's possible."

"Well, perhaps David will take Brian's place—in the wedding party and elsewhere. Perhaps Brian will find it convenient to stay a little more steadily in Norfolk than he's been doing lately, after he finds that David's back."

"Perhaps he will. Just the same, I'm sure he'll want to stand up with Pell, as they put it. They've been writing each other about it for quite a while now—ever since Pell knew approximately when he'd be getting home."

"And it still looks as if that would be midsummer?"

"Yes. August at the latest. Possibly earlier. And Brian hopes to be separated from the Navy before that, so he's going to campaign for the Senate. His nomination papers are already signed and filed."

Old Mrs. Forbes snorted slightly. "I don't believe it will do him much good. He'll find it's pretty hard to dislodge a Forbes from the Senate. There's always been one there, ever since I can remember."

"I know. But don't you also remember that letter David wrote you from Washington, about the changing order of things? We've got to face it, Grandmamma."

"Maybe you have. But I may not live long enough to see it. I'm not sure I want to. I've been pretty well satisfied with the old order. The new one probably wouldn't suit me as well. Anyhow, don't bother to quote from the letters David's written me. Keep your mind on the ones he's written you. That'll be more to the point."

Emily thought that her grandmother, who had seemed so radiant when she herself came into the room a little earlier, already acted rather tired;

so she said there were lots of things she needed to do, and went back upstairs. As a matter of fact, she had nothing to do except to wait for David; but she noticed that Old Mrs. Forbes tired more and more easily these days, and she wondered how well her grandmother would stand the strain of having a noisy child and a crying baby and a busy man in the house. She dreaded to think that it might be more of a tax on the old lady's strength than Mrs. Forbes realized; but after all, this visitation was what she wanted; Emily knew she had no right to confuse issues by pretending that she was trying to save her grandmother from overexertion, when she was really acting in behalf of her own selfish interests. She filled in the remainder of the morning with trivial tasks; and immediately after luncheon she did over her hair and manicured her nails and changed her dress. In spite of the current trend away from mourning, she had worn black for some time after Roger died, not because she wished to perpetuate an outworn custom, but because it had seemed to her the most natural and suitable thing to do and because it had been in harmony with her own mood. Gradually she had changed into soft grays and lavenders, again in conformity with her own feelings; but now she was wearing bright colors again, and she chose a green dress which was especially becoming, and which she felt sure David would like. He had once told her that she looked like the personification of spring, when he had found her in her little garden, wearing a green dress. He had even jested about it, saying that Botticelli's Simonetta had been the inspiration for the most famous interpretation of spring which had ever been painted; but that, here in Boston, it was not Pell's Simonetta, but Roger's Emily, who embodied the vernal season. . . .

The dress she put on now was not unlike the one she had worn that spring afternoon so long before, when David had talked about Botticelli's Simonetta. (Was it really six years? Yes, it must be—six or even seven. Well, he would have forgotten it by this time. Men did not remember little things like that; it was only women who treasured them. David would not recall either the conversation or the dress. But it made Emily happy to think of both, and to know that the new dress resembled the old one, even though he would not recognize it.) Ordinarily, she did not wear many ornaments; but now she unlocked her jewel box and studied its contents with care. The pendant of seed pearls which had belonged to Roger's mother would look well with the green dress; but naturally, she did not want to wear that. Surprisingly, her topaz earrings and necklace looked well with it, too; but she had worn those, with golden-brown velvet, on that perfect Christmas Eve which was still more distant than the spring afternoon about which she had just been thinking—the Christmas Eve which she would always keep enshrined as beautiful and apart, no matter what life held for her in the future. She closed the jewel box slowly and, for a few moments, sat turning it over in her hands. Then, for the second time that day, she went to her grandmother's room.

425

Old Mrs. Forbes was seated in front of her dressing table and Doris was putting the finishing touches on her hair. Her jewel box stood open, as it usually did at such a time, and she was lifting out one of its velvet trays and peering down into its depths with the unfeigned pleasure that she had always taken in doing so. She looked up at Emily with one of her rare, splendid smiles.

"Well, my dear—this must be mental telepathy. I was just on the point of sending Doris for you. I've been thinking, since last night—as you're not going to have this house, you should have other things, correspondingly valuable. I told you, before you were married, that I wasn't sure diamonds would ever suit you—diamonds or brocade. Now I'm beginning to change my mind, at least about the diamonds. You're developing. I might change my mind about the brocade, too, if I had a chance to find out how you looked in it."

"All right, Grandmamma, I'll buy myself a brocade dress."

"I have lengths and lengths of brocade put away," Old Mrs. Forbes informed her, speaking testily again. "I thought you knew that. For years, I've kept a standing order, at several of my favorite stores, that, whenever a new shipment came in, I was to have the first chance at selection."

"I did know that, Grandmamma. But I thought those brocades were for you."

"They were selected for me and by me, of course. But that's no sign one of them might not suit you—now. We'll have a look at them in the morning and see—it's too late to do so this afternoon. You shouldn't hurry a choice like that. You should spread the different lengths all around the room, on the bed and the sofa and the chairs, and compare them with each other at your leisure. If we tried to do that at the moment, David would probably arrive while we were in the midst of our comparison, and then Doris would have to pick up all the lengths and get them out again in the morning. But the jewel box is already open, as you can see. Tell me if there's anything you'd like to wear."

"I guess it was mental telepathy, Grandmamma. I came down on purpose to ask you if you'd lend me something. I couldn't seem to find anything in my own jewel box that I wanted to put on."

"No wonder. You've never had any jewelry important enough for the present occasion. I won't lend you anything. But I'll give you whatever you fancy. Don't look at me like that—I'm not Mephistopheles, tempting Marguerite, you know. Just your poor feeble old grandmother, who's very fond of you and very pleased to see you so happy."

Emily bent over the box, afraid to trust herself to speak, and also afraid to take out any of the ornaments it contained lest, inadvertently, she should choose one more valuable than her grandmother had meant to give her. At last, realizing that the old lady was becoming impatient, she picked up a necklace formed of a slender platinum chain, from which graduated diamonds were suspended, a large one in the middle, a small one imbedded in the clasp. Then she looked questioningly at Old Mrs. Forbes.

"An excellent selection," her grandmother said briskly. "But of course you need the proper ornaments to go with it. These eardrops were given to me at about the same time. I think they'd do very well. And for a brooch and bracelets—"

"Oh, Grandmamma, I don't need a brooch and bracelets too!"

"Of course you need a brooch and bracelets too. Don't tell me what you need. There! You look very nice, Emily! Run along now! I've told Pearson to show David Salomont up immediately when he arrives. Also, that after he gets here, you're not to be disturbed on any account whatsoever. I don't suppose you're planning to stand in the drawing room window this time, scanning the street! I suppose you'll go to the library and bury yourself in a book—or at least pretend to. I don't imagine you'll have very long to wait."

It seemed long to Emily. Soon after she had "buried herself in a book," Pearson came and told her that she was wanted on the telephone. Suppressing a cry of dismay, she ran to answer it, sure that it was David to say that he could not come after all. But instead, it was Mrs. Collins.

"And how are you feeling this evening, my dear? Well, I hope. Brian's on his way back to Norfolk, as no doubt you don't need me to tell you, but we were wondering, Shaun and I, if you wouldn't come over and have a bite of supper with us, just the same. We've got steak again, praise be, and I've just finished making a strawberry shortcake. Shaun would be more than pleased to come and get you, if your own car or your grandmother's isn't handy."

"Oh—thanks a lot, Mrs. Collins, for thinking of me. I'd love to see you, and it makes my mouth water, just to hear about the shortcake. But I'm waiting for a visitor myself, right this minute."

"Are you now? Well, perhaps tomorrow night then."

"Perhaps. May I let you know? I'm not quite sure yet how long my visitor will be in town."

"Sure and you know you're always welcome, whenever it is, but the sooner the better. I won't be keeping you now though. Good-by, my dear."

"Good-by and thanks again."

Emily hung up the receiver and went back to her reading. She thought perhaps she should have told Mrs. Collins right away that she could not come the next night, either. Even if David was only home on leave, he would be in Boston longer than twenty-four hours. . . .

It was astonishing how dull reading material could be. Emily tried the daily paper, several weeklies, a biography and a murder mystery, without finding anything that arrested her attention. Then she changed the position of several vases and slightly rearranged the flowers these contained. It was so warm that there was really no excuse for a fire, but she finally lighted one and fed it, slender stick by slender stick, to keep it alive without having it burn too brightly. The period of waiting had begun to seem both endless and unendurable, when Pearson at last opened the folding doors.

"Major Salomont, Mrs. Field."

She hastened forward, both hands outstretched in welcome, calling his name in a glad voice. She had expected that he would take her in his arms as soon as the doors closed behind the butler, but this time she was more than ready for the anticipated embrace. Instead, David clasped her outstretched hands in his, firmly rather than caressingly, and regarded her with smiling approval without drawing her closer to him.

"Emily, how lovely you look! I never saw you when you were half so beautiful!"

"You look wonderful to me, David. But of course you would, anyhow."

"And of course you would, anyhow. But you really are a great deal more beautiful than when I left. It isn't my imagination, is it, that you've filled out a little?"

"No, it isn't imagination. I've gained about ten pounds."

"Which was exactly what you needed, to have a perfect figure. And what a charming dress! . . . My imagination isn't playing me tricks this time, either, is it?"

"You mean about the dress?"

"Yes. It reminds me of one you were wearing the first afternoon I came to your garden on Joy Street, the one I told you made you seem like the embodiment of spring."

"I didn't think you'd remember. But I thought of that myself—the similarity, I mean."

"Of course I remember. I said it was Roger's Emily, not Pell's Simonetta that Botticelli would have taken for his model if he'd had a chance to choose between the two. How is Pell's Simonetta, by the way?"

"Radiant. And talk about being beautiful! Just wait until you see her!"

"I'd like to immensely. But, after all, there's no hurry. I came to see you. And it's certainly worth crossing the Atlantic to look at you. Incidentally, those diamonds add just the finishing touch to your costume. I don't think you were wearing those before."

"No. Grandmamma gave them to me today. In honor of your homecoming. She's very eager to see you herself."

"No more so than I am to see her. I'm one of her most devoted admirers. But we're going to have a talk by ourselves first, aren't we? You haven't asked me to sit down yet, you know."

"Oh! I'm terribly sorry! Of course. . . . I like this sofa, don't you? . . . Now start at the beginning and tell me everything."

She spoke with great cordiality, but with some confusion. All the time they had been standing, facing each other with clasped hands but at arm's length, she had been waiting, from one moment to the next, for him to fold her in a fond embrace, to tell her how much he loved her and to invite the response which would have been so immediate. It had made her happy to know that he thought she was beautiful, it was gratifying to find that he had remembered the other green dress and that he had noticed her diamonds; few men would have been so observing. But this did not fill her with rapture as the expected kisses and the murmured words of endearment would have done. Even the statement that he had come to see her, that all other meetings were secondary to this one, seemed to lack the ardor for which she had yearned. She felt both bewildered and frustrated, and she was not sure she had been able to conceal this, when she so belatedly invited David to be seated, after he himself had suggested it. Her feeling of bewilderment increased as he settled himself at one end of the sofa, with the obvious expectation that she would ensconce herself at the other.

"That's rather a large order, isn't it?" he inquired, picking up the thread of the conversation. "You know a good deal already, from my letters."

"Not nearly as much as I'd like to. Of course for a long while they were censored. And since then, they haven't contained much detail. . . . Naturally, I know they couldn't," she added hastily. "I realize you haven't had time to write long letters. Also, that there are lots of things it's easier and better to say than to write."

"Yes, there are. Those are the things I want to concentrate on now. . . . Is it all right if I smoke?"

"Of course. I should have suggested that right away too. And I'm sorry I can't offer you a cigarette from your favorite cloisonné box. It's in storage. But I'm going to get it out almost immediately—that and a lot of my other things. I'll have it for you in a day or two."

She smiled, determined, now that she had recovered from the first shock of his unexpected behavior, to show no more confusion and, above all, to betray no surprise or disappointment. Of course there was some explanation, which would soon be forthcoming; he must have something on his mind so important that, until he had unburdened himself, he could not be in the mood for love-making. She looked at him confidently, waiting for him to go on.

"Don't bother about the box. I remember that, too, and it was a collector's item. But I can enjoy a cigarette just as much if I take it right out of my own case."

"I don't wonder. It's a beauty."

"Yes. It's a present. I've become rather attached to it."

Instinctively, she put out her hand, supposing that he meant her to take it in order that she might inspect it more closely and admire it more discerningly. Instead, he replaced it in his pocket.

"Of course you realized it was a great blow to me when I found I wasn't going into Normandy over the beaches," he began. "But, as it turned out, I can't be thankful enough I went in with Patton instead. If I could have chosen what I'd do in this war, it would have been exactly what I did do—

429

tear through France and straight on into Germany, ripping everything out of the way as I went. There's never been anything in history to equal that campaign and probably there never will be again. I'm glad I'll be able to tell my grandchildren that I saw all of it and that I was part of it."

"I understand how you feel. And I think I know why you feel that way, too, David."

"Well, thank God for that. I hoped I wouldn't have to explain. When we actually got into Germany, when we began to lay waste to it, forging farther and farther ahead all the time we were destroying—well, that was when I began to know I was doing what I'd been waiting for, what I'd been living for—years and years and years! The only thing I regret is that we couldn't do more damage and more killing, because there wasn't time."

He spoke with the atavistic joy of a ruthless conqueror, gloating over the annihilation of a hated foe. Emily murmured something indicative of continued understanding; however, she sensed that almost any comment, at this stage of his outburst, would seem like an interruption.

"But when we got to Wiesbaden, there was a sort of letdown. There wasn't any point in going farther right then. There wasn't anything more behind to override or bomb, there wasn't anyone more to kill. We'd done such a thorough job, we damn well had to stop for a while. We were damn glad to get into decent quarters and relax. We were damn glad to see some women again."

Involuntarily, Emily drew a deep breath. So all this had been leading up to a confession—a confession such as almost any man, if he were thoroughly honest, was obliged to make sooner or later to the woman he really loved, to the woman he wanted for his wife. Roger had been the shining exception to the sordid rule. But she had always known that there must have been other women in David's life, and that though he would have been selective, in normal times, because he was naturally fastidious, the time of which he was now talking had been anything but normal. She could forgive whatever he had done, in those first weeks of letdown at Wiesbaden. No woman of the streets, no inmate of a brothel would be beyond the realm of her comprehension, in connection with David. And no such outlawed, unfortunate creature had any real connection with her, the beloved woman, with her feeling for him or his for her; such women were completely alien to the world she lived in; they could never approach it or affect it. Because this was so, there was nothing to confess. She tried to express this to David.

"I'm sure you must have been. But you don't have to tell me about that, honestly you don't."

"Yes I do. That's what I came here for."

"Why of course it isn't! You've come here because—"

She must not be the one to say it first. Until he had done so, she could not say, "You've come here because you love me and I love you, because there's no impediment any more to our love, because we're free to express it in every way." She waited for him to say this and instead, he said something else.

"I've come here to tell you that I saw Priscilla in Wiesbaden."

For a moment Emily found that, strangely enough, she could not seem to answer. When she did so, she hoped and believed that her voice sounded not only natural but casual.

"Why of course you must have! You didn't mention it in your letters and, as far as I know, Priscilla didn't mention it in hers. She doesn't write to me, but she does write to Grandmamma, occasionally. I remember now that some of the WAC were sent to Wiesbaden and that Priscilla had charge of furloughs and uniforms for a short period and that after that, she worked in the Department of Historical Archives. I even seem to remember a rather amusing letter about a funny apartment she lived in, when she left the Hotel Metropole—there were parasols and old-fashioned dresses in the bathtub, which wasn't in working order—at the apartment, I mean, not at the Metropole. But there was running water in the kitchen; in fact, it ran night and day. Priscilla couldn't stop it. I'm not imagining this, am I?"

"No, that's just the way it was. I tried to stop the water from running myself. I saw the parasols and the old-fashioned dresses. I saw a good deal of Priscilla, Emily."

"Well, I'm very glad. I'm sure you must have found her good company. Priscilla's quite amusing, when she's in the mood."

"Emily, I know you're not consciously making this harder for me. But what I've been trying to tell you—in fact, what I came here on purpose to tell you—is that I fell in love with Priscilla."

This time Emily did not attempt any answer. She sat staring at David, in dumb and horrible unbelief, and she did not resist when he leaned forward and took her hand. She was vaguely aware that the gesture was meant to be kindly, almost compassionate, but it failed in its purpose. It seemed to have no meaning whatsoever. An hour earlier, she would have said that the slightest touch from David's fingers would kindle her to ardor. Now she did not feel anything at all. She was completely numb, as she had been in that strange period after Roger had died.

"All this is so hard to say that I know I'll do it very badly," David went on. "But I've got to begin by asking you to believe that I never lied to you. When I told you I loved you, it was true—so overwhelmingly true that I felt I had to tell you, even though you were married to someone else. You do believe me, don't you, Emily?"

She still could not speak, she still could not make any immediate sign. But after a moment or two, though her lips were still pressed tightly together, she inclined her head, and he took it for a sign of assent.

"The real reason I didn't come to Archie's christening was because I thought I had no right to see you again after I'd told you. I suppose you

431

realized that, didn't you? I suppose your grandmother showed you my letter?"

Again she nodded, without speaking.

"I went overseas, still loving you. I still loved you when Roger died. I thought I ought to wait a year at least, before I told you so again. And then I heard that you'd lost your baby, that you were very ill. It didn't seem the right time to subject you to any more emotional strain. There are times when a human being can stand just so much. . . . You know that, don't you?"

"Yes," Emily murmured, at last finding it possible to frame the single word.

"By then, we were preparing for the invasion. Preparing very intensively. And I thought I'd wait a little longer. Until my declaration of love could be coupled with a sort of paean of victory. I told you I'd say all this very badly, I know I am. But you do understand, don't you?"

"Yes," Emily said again.

"After that there wasn't any time to write letters. Not the kind I wanted to write, not the kind that would have been worthy of you. But I still meant to do it, I still loved you. My God, I don't know why I keep saying I still loved you as if it were in the past. I love you *now*. As much as I ever did, in one way. But not the way I did before. Not the way I did when I first saw Priscilla again, in Paris."

"In Paris?"

"Yes, I'd seen her there, before I saw her in Wiesbaden. She was at St. Germain-en-Laye for eight months, doing switchboard work. Well, you must know all about that too."

"I know a little. Obviously I don't know everything."

It was possible to speak again. Whether it would be possible to speak without bitterness, without reproach, without telltale anguish, Emily did not know. But she would try. She must try. She must not say anything like that again. However, apparently David had hardly noticed what she said. He was now too intent on what he was saying himself.

"Of course I'd seen a good deal of Priscilla before I left Boston. I used to go down to the Cape almost every Sunday and stay at her house. And the last time I went down there, she asked me if I wouldn't marry her."

"*She* asked you if you wouldn't marry her!"

"Yes. Of course I wouldn't tell you this if she hadn't said I might. But after all, there's nothing especially astonishing about that. Any number of girls take the initiative in such matters, these days."

"Not—not girls like—"

"No, not girls like you. But girls like Priscilla. And by that, I mean what you'd call 'nice girls,' Emily. Don't make any mistake about that."

He was speaking in a different way now, more assertively and confidently. "I laughed her off," he went on. "It wasn't a very kind thing to do, because she was already in love with me then—very much in love. But

432

I thought perhaps it would be the best way to handle things. When I saw I wasn't making any headway, I tried a different tack. I told her she couldn't ever stand being married to a Jew, that she didn't know what it would mean."

"What it would mean?"

"Yes—to find she couldn't stay at certain resort hotels, or live in certain 'restricted' areas or send her children, later on, to certain 'select' schools— all that sort of inconsequential stuff. She told me it was inconsequential, but I still thought it was important—then. I told her she couldn't take it. So she set out to show me what she could take."

"And that was why she joined the WAC?"

"Partly, perhaps. And she's certainly taken plenty since then. Not so well at first. She fainted her first morning at reveille; she'd gone to a fire drill without any breakfast. And she was pretty well burned up when her wallet was rifled at Camp Oglethorpe. A good deal of stealing went on there, apparently, because troops were moving at all hours of the day and night, under secret orders, and there was no way of tracing where the money'd gone or who'd taken it. Priscilla didn't care about the money; of course she could always get plenty more of that. But there was a snapshot of me in the wallet, the only one she had, and that was left in it, torn to shreds. Evidently, she took that pretty hard. . . . You wouldn't think a girl like Priscilla would set much store by little keepsakes, would you? But she does. Why, that day out on the dunes, I offered her a penny for her thoughts and she said they were worth more than that. So I gave her a nickel. And what do you think she did with it? She had the center cut out of it and she's worn it for a ring ever since!"

"It isn't the first time, David, that a ring seems to have played a rather important part in Forbes family history."

"True enough. But there's quite a difference between an emerald and a nickel."

"Not necessarily. I wasn't talking about value; I was talking about significance. Well, as you were saying—"

"As I was saying, it wasn't long before Priscilla learned to stand up under routine, and to fend for herself. In the trip she made from Camp Oglethorpe to Lowry Field, for instance, she was assigned to a lower berth with another WAC, a total stranger, and two male lieutenants decided to share it with them. Of course there was an M. P. on the train who was supposed to see that such things didn't happen, but evidently this particular M. P. wasn't especially vigilant. Priscilla managed to fight herself free and get into another berth—an upper one. But meanwhile, she'd learned that attempted rape isn't just a legal expression."

"Did she tell you all these things herself?"

"Yes, by degrees. And as a rule, not too seriously. You've said yourself, she can see the amusing side of most things. But I gather the episode connected with my picture and the one on the westbound train were exceptions to the rule. However, she made a great joke of her voyage on the *Argentina*, where ninety girls were herded into one stateroom with bunks in five tiers. Also of an air raid that took place while she was in London at the telephone operators' school. The buildings on either side of the one where she was were bombed, but she claims she thought someone was just moving furniture around upstairs."

He paused and, for the first time, smiled with reminiscent pleasure. But again he did not seem to expect Emily to say anything, and, after a brief interlude, he went on.

"Well, I don't need to tell you that, by the time we'd seen each other once or twice in Wiesbaden, Priscilla didn't have to tell me again that she wouldn't be upset by a few examples of so-called discrimination if she married me. And she didn't need to propose to me again. I proposed to her. It was she who reminded me about you. And I wouldn't be telling you the whole truth if I didn't admit that, by then, I needed such a reminder. I'd have married Priscilla right then and there if I could have cut enough red tape to do it and she'd have had me."

"But how could she remind you about me? You don't mean to say you'd told her—"

"I'd never mentioned you by name. But the same day that she proposed to me, I'd said I was in love with someone else, someone I couldn't ask to marry me because she wasn't free. Of course Priscilla guessed whom I meant. She couldn't very well help it. And when I proposed to her in Wiesbaden, she asked me point-blank if you didn't have the right of way."

"And what did you tell her?"

"I told her that you did. How could I say anything else? Even though I'd never asked you, in so many words, to marry me, that was because of a combination and a succession of circumstances. I'd *wanted* to marry you, for a long time, and it was implicit in what I'd said to you. It wasn't your fault, either, that I didn't want to any longer. You hadn't done anything to change my feelings. It was just one of those things that happens once in a while, especially in wartime. When two people have been through a war together—well, somehow there's a bond between them that's different from other bonds. It's stronger. It has more meaning, it's bound to be more lasting. What happened as far as you and I are concerned won't happen again. From now on, if you release me, Priscilla'll be the only woman in my life."

Chapter 35

As EMILY KNOCKED once more at her grandmother's door, it was with the sensation that she was completing a cycle. Only a little more than twenty-four hours earlier, she had come to this room, her heart overflowing with joy, to say she had heard that David was on his way home. Then she had come there again, still more joyously, to ask for jewels with which to adorn herself in welcome. Now she was coming to say that he had gone out of her life forever.

Even before she saw her grandmother, she realized, from the way she was told to enter, that Old Mrs. Forbes had been waiting to receive David and his affianced in a fitting manner. Emily opened the door, to be greeted by the sight of the old lady, sitting in one of her thronelike chairs, arrayed in her most elegant brocade and literally ablaze with diamonds. Her expression, quite as much as her attire, revealed her feeling that this was a great and auspicious occasion, which she should not only bless but glorify. Again, her smile had that quality of radiance which transfigured it less and less frequently, but which still fleetingly lent her aged face a vestige of her once-matchless beauty. It faded, with the suddenness that came from foreboding, when she saw that Emily was alone.

"Where is David?" she asked abruptly.

"He's gone."

"Gone! Gone where?"

"Down on the Cape. He offered to come here with me before he went, but I thought it would be better if he didn't. I thought it would be better if you and I were alone when I told you."

"When you told me *what*?"

"What he's just told me—that he didn't come here to propose to me, that he's already proposed to Priscilla."

"Emily, he couldn't have! Not when he'd told you that he loved you! And Priscilla couldn't have accepted him, if he had! Honorable persons don't act that way. And they're both honorable persons, even if they do have their faults."

"They've acted like honorable persons, Grandmamma. They've both

435

recognized that—that David had a certain—well, he didn't actually use the word obligation. I'm thankful for that. But they both felt that way about it. They felt he was obligated to me because he had been in love with me once, because he had told me so, because he would have asked me to marry him then if—if things had been different. But things weren't different. He never did ask me to marry him. Of course I told him that there was no—obligation. Of course I told him he must cable Priscilla immediately and tell her he was free to marry her."

Old Mrs. Forbes' lips moved slightly, but no sound came from them. Emily drew up a low, square stool, covered with dark velvet and studded with bright nails, which stood in front of the fireplace, and sat down close to her grandmother.

"You mustn't blame either of them," she said. "I don't. I did when David first started talking to me about—about what had happened. I felt that Priscilla had gone after him, not just because she wanted him herself, but because she wanted to take him away from me. I felt—well, I'd felt from the beginning that was what she was trying to do. But I thought she'd failed."

"So did I," muttered Old Mrs. Forbes, "that was exactly what I thought. We'd sized her up the same way, Emily. And we were both partly right. Only, unfortunately, it seems she didn't fail."

"No, she didn't fail. But we've got to be fair to her. After all, she's tried to be fair to me. She wouldn't accept him, unconditionally, until she knew I'd released him."

"But in the meanwhile, she'd trailed him to Europe! She'd maneuvered to meet him! She'd taken advantage of war conditions, when any man's an easy prey."

"Yes, she'd done all that. But I still say we've got to be fair. I don't believe, any more, that she went after him because she was trying to get him away from me. I think she went after him because she loved him so much that she was determined to get him at any cost. I don't think any cost seemed to her too high. I—I understand how she felt. Because I've felt the same way. Only I couldn't go after him. I could only wait for him to come to me. I don't mean just because conditions were different in the two cases, either. I mean because I haven't got it in me to do what she did. I'm not her kind."

"No, you're not," Old Mrs. Forbes said fiercely. "And if you ask me—"

"Please let me finish, Grandmamma. I'm sincere in saying I don't blame Priscilla. I think her kind's very resolute—very brave—very—very splendid. I think David's kind is too. I want you to know I don't blame him, either. I want you to know that I believe he told me the truth when he said he loved me, that he loved me very much then and for a long time afterward. But he changed. How can I blame him? I changed myself, didn't I? I thought I was in love with Roger and then I fell in love with David."

"You *thought*—that was the whole trouble! I told you so at the time.

You didn't change. You just found out your mistake. The cases aren't correlative. David knew a lot more about human emotions when he told you he loved you than you did when you were married. He wouldn't have made the same kind of mistake that you did. He *couldn't* have! Either he loved you or he didn't. Either he lied to you or—"

"He didn't lie to me, I tell you, he *changed!* I tell you I don't blame him for changing. How many men are there in the world who love the same woman all their lives?"

"There are some. And, unfortunately, there are a great many women who are never really in love with but one man. I'm afraid you're one of them. That's why I don't want you to give in to this so easily. I want you to fight back, to tell David you won't release him. He'll probably live to thank you for it. If he could change as far as you're concerned, he could change as far as Priscilla's concerned. And she's young, she'll get over it. She has any number of other suitors—one of them would do for her just as well as David. But no one else will ever do for you."

"Again you're partly right and partly wrong, Grandmamma. I know I won't get over loving David, but I don't believe Priscilla will, either. And I don't believe David will change again. He said something to me that was very moving—very convincing. It was what made me realize I shouldn't blame either of them. I hope it'll make you believe so too."

"There's nothing that will make me believe it. . . . What was it?"

"He said that when two people have been through a war together, there's a bond between them that has more meaning than other bonds. He said it was so much stronger that it was bound to be more lasting."

For the first time, Old Mrs. Forbes looked away from Emily and again, though her lips moved, no sound came from them.

"So I'm not going to fight for him," Emily said quietly. "And nothing you or anyone else can say will make me change my mind about that. I've released him already. I know I'll love him as long as I live. But I don't want him for my husband any more."

Her words rang with finality. She rose, setting the studded velvet stool back in its customary place.

"David is only home on leave," she announced. "He's going back to Germany. He wants to go back there. He's had a chance to serve on Major Wallis' staff at the Nuremberg trial. That means more to him, both as a lawyer and as a Jew, than anything else that could possibly happen to him—to have a part in bringing those archcriminals, who've tortured his race and tried to exterminate it, to justice. He's had some wonderful offers from several important New York law offices already too. But he says those can wait until the trial's over—that if the openings are gone then, there'll be plenty more. Of course he's right, of course there will be. And as a man, it means more to him to marry Priscilla than anything in the world. She's about to come home too—he expects her before his leave is up. He wants to take her with him to Germany as his wife. That's why he's gone right on down to the Cape—to tell Aunt Sue and Uncle Sherman they've got to get ready for a wedding. And you'd better make up your mind that you're going down on the Cape, too, at last, whether you want to or not. Because I'll never forgive you if you don't go with me to that wedding."

The next morning, Emily told her grandmother that she had decided to move back into her own house, that she was going there at noon to check on its general condition. If no major repairs were indicated—and Deirdre had never reported the visible need of any—there was no reason why she could not get in almost immediately. The warm spring weather was a great asset; once sunshine had been let into the house again, any lingering dampness would quickly disappear. And of course all bedding would be thoroughly aired. Inside of a week, she should be reinstalled, without the slightest danger of overtaxing her strength or taking cold.

Old Mrs. Forbes did not attempt dissuasion. In fact, she was preternaturally silent in the days which followed David's brief visit. Several times, Emily thought her grandmother seemed to be on the point of bursting into expostulation. But nothing came of it. She herself was the one to reopen the subject of the brocades.

"Don't you think we'd better have that private showing while I'm still here? You said we ought to allow plenty of time for it. There aren't going to be many more long leisurely days ahead of us, with Elizabeth and me both in the process of moving and two weddings coming up."

"I wasn't sure you were still interested in the brocades. You may recall that, when I offered you one, you were planning a trousseau. Now I haven't the least idea what you're planning."

"I'm planning to wear brocade to the weddings. That's what you're going to wear, aren't you? Let's hope it doesn't get sizzling hot, all of a sudden. Because I'm going to wear it, whether it does or not. Brocade and all my new diamonds."

Again, Old Mrs. Forbes seemed to be on the point of vehement speech and again she suppressed it. The following morning, Doris spread out all the shimmering dress lengths and, as Old Mrs. Forbes had predicted, they covered the bed and the sofa and every one of the chairs, except the one in which she was sitting. Emily was obliged to resort to the stool again. But it did not take her long to make her choice, after all. She selected a magnificent pattern of green and gold and, after first draping it around her to get its full effect, folded it carefully and asked if she might have two dress lengths instead of one.

"This is just what I want for Priscilla's wedding. But I'd rather have that pale-blue piece for Simonetta's."

"Of course you're welcome to them both. I must say you've shown a great deal of taste in your selection of materials. If you do as well in choosing your models—"

438

"I'll try. Would you like to come with me to Miss Ruby's and make sure?"

Old Mrs. Forbes said she would be very glad to go with Emily to Miss Ruby's, and she seemed to enjoy the outing greatly. However, as Emily had predicted, they had no more long leisurely days immediately ahead of them and, consequently, no more shopping excursions or confidential talks. Emily was back in her own house within the time limit she had set for herself; but though she had been correct in her expectation that no major repairs would be required, countless small renovations seemed desirable and she and Deirdre were both busy from morning till night. When her father dropped in on her, late afternoons, he found her healthily tired and only too glad to sit back and rest as long as he remained with her. Over and over again, he expressed his pleasure in finding her where she was.

"It's good to have you back here, Emily. I've always enjoyed the garden, of course. But I enjoy it much more, now that the house is open too. It never seemed natural to me to see it closed."

"Well, you know what I said when you told me you regretted the sale of the Gloucester Street house—it seemed the best thing at the time. When I closed this house, that seemed the best thing. Now it seems best to have it open again."

She knew that he wanted to ask her certain questions and that he refrained, partly through natural reserve and partly because he did not want to run the risk of hurting her feelings. She appreciated his consideration, but she took advantage of it. However, when Brian burst in upon her, unceremoniously, one morning while she was dusting books, she quickly discovered that he had no similar inhibitions and that he not only meant to ask questions but to get answers. She had no luck at all in trying to stave him off with congratulations on his appearance in civilian attire, and queries made on her own initiative.

"I had a wedding invitation this morning that came like a bolt from the blue: 'Mr. and Mrs. Sherman Endicott Forbes request the honor of your presence at the marriage of their daughter, Priscilla Anne, to Major David Salomont.' What's the meaning of this, Emily?"

"Well, it sounds to me as if David and Priscilla were about to be married. Doesn't it sound that way to you?"

"Listen, I'm not in the mood for pointless jokes. Did you know David and Priscilla were going to be married?"

"Yes."

"How long have you known it?"

"About a fortnight."

Brian appeared to do some quick calculating. "I'd be a good deal surprised to find it was quite as long as that. I'd bet anything you didn't know it that day you lured me up to your grandmother's attic and induced me to guzzle down your great-grandfather's rum."

439

"Well, I said about a fortnight. I didn't count the days off on my fingers."

"But you didn't know it, that day we were in the attic, did you?"

"No, I didn't. . . . Have you been back to Cutter, Mills yet, Briny? Do they know you're already separated from the Navy?"

"I haven't been back there and they don't know it yet. I've got other things to do and other things on my mind. When you told me you wouldn't marry me because you were in love with someone else, you were talking about David Salomont. Yes or no?"

"Briny, I've told you before that you ask too many questions and that some of them are pretty presumptuous. This last one is a very good example of what I mean. I don't want to be inhospitable, but I'm pretty busy right now and I know they're still terribly shorthanded at Cutter, Mills. I think it would be a wonderful idea if you'd give me a chance to dust these books while you go down to the office and say you're ready to start work again."

"That's what you think. Do you want to know what I think? I think David Salomont is a—"

"Don't say it, Brian. Don't you dare say it."

"All right. Then give me a good reason why I shouldn't."

Either she would have to tell him, in substance, what she had told her grandmother, or she would have to let him go on misjudging and despising David. Between the two, there was no question how she must choose. She laid down the first edition she was still holding and spoke very gravely.

"I'm sorry you won't take my word for it that there is a good reason. If you ask me to take your word for something, I do it. But, since you insist. . . ."

He did not try to interrupt her simple and straightforward recital, and he did not speak immediately, when she finished it. But he looked at her with unconcealed admiration and eventually he voiced this.

"You'd have made a good lawyer yourself, Emily. I never heard a case better presented."

"I had a good case to present."

"You've almost convinced me of it—not quite, but almost. Well, I won't bother you any more right now. Go back to your dusting. I'll take your advice and get on down to the office."

A few days later, Emily asked Old Mrs. Forbes if she would like to have the Bruckers invited to stay at the Joy Street house during the wedding festivities. Elizabeth and her family would already be at the house on Louisburg Square by then, as they had purposely hastened their departure from Hanover. The Bruckers had probably expected to go to a hotel, but all the hotels were so crowded, with Commencement in the offing, that they might not be able to get suitable accommodations; Emily was sure they were accustomed to the best. As her grandmother had pointed out, of course there was no end of room at Louisburg Square; but perhaps Mr. and Mrs. Brucker would prefer to be quiet, during the brief intervals between the many parties which were scheduled, and no place inhabited by Archie was ever very quiet. . . .

"It's kind of you, Emily—kind and thoughtful. I think the Bruckers would appreciate such an invitation. I'd appreciate it for them. . . . I've never told you how I happened to know Morris Brucker in the first place, have I?"

"No," Emily replied, resisting the temptation to add, "You know very well you never did."

"Well, I might just as well tell you now, if you'll sit down with me long enough. You're hardly ever here these days, Emily. I hardly ever have a chance to talk with you. But Morris Brucker might make some reference to our—to our old friendship himself, while he's staying at your house, and it could puzzle you, if you didn't know the background."

"There's no reason why I can't stay with you today as long as you like, Grandmamma."

"I'm delighted to hear it. . . . All right then, going back to some rather ancient history, Morris Brucker's father, Hugo Brucker, was one of the greatest connoisseurs of his time. He was a dealer in works of art, almost every kind you could name, but he was much more than a dealer— or rather, much besides. He could drive a bargain with the best of them, he could ferret out an Old Master dumped in some rubbish heap, exactly the way some people go out on a lawn and come in with a handful of four-leaf clovers, when nobody else has seen even one, even after searching for hours. But he was also a man of great general culture and he loved his work and took immense pride in it. Eventually, he made so much money that he could have easily retired, but he didn't want to. His headquarters were in Berlin, but he had branches in every important continental capital and visited them regularly. His various relatives acted as local managers for his galleries, and they all learned and profited from his experience and tried to emulate him—his energy and enthusiasm were contagious. One of his galleries was in Budapest, and as soon as his son, Morris, was old enough, Hugo Brucker established him there. That was where I met them."

"Yes, I remember, the first time David came to call, I telephoned you to find out whether his stepfather could come and see you, and you told me you were quite sure you knew him already. You mentioned Budapest then."

"So I did. . . . Well, I used to go to the Brucker Galleries in Budapest fairly often. Your grandfather was minister to Austria-Hungary then and, unlike most people, we preferred Budapest to Vienna. Of course we had establishments in both capitals—in each case a great big barren *Schloss*, with nothing comfortable or attractive in it. At least there wasn't when we took them over. But there was plenty before we got through—thanks to your grandfather's money and Hugo Brucker's treasure-trove and my taste. Everyone said there wasn't another legation in Central Europe to compare with them, after I'd fixed them up."

"I'm sure they must have been beautiful."

"Well, eventually, as you know, your grandfather was promoted. He was very helpful in the Harrison and McKinley campaigns and he was suitably rewarded by being sent first to Rome and then to St. Petersburg, as ambassador. I'd lost sight of Morris Brucker, for a time, while I was in Rome, but when I got to St. Petersburg, I found he'd been promoted too. He was manager of the Brucker Galleries there and he was gradually taking over his father's responsibilities. The business had expanded still further—there were branches in London and New York that he used to visit. Hugo Brucker was a pretty old man by that time. He couldn't go here, there and everywhere any more."

"You saw a good deal of Morris Brucker in St. Petersburg, didn't you, Grandmamma? Another thing I remember is that, when Morris Brucker came over to see you, and I came here with him, you and he joked together about it. He said that, when you were first in St. Petersburg, you used to go a great deal to his shop. He spoke of it as a shop, not a gallery."

"That was just part of the joke. It was a magnificent gallery."

"Well, anyway, he said that at first you were a good customer of his, that you made a great many selections from his stock, but that after a while you didn't buy anything more, because you had so many presents from grand dukes."

"And of course that was just part of the joke too."

"Was it really, Grandmamma?"

"Why should you think it wasn't, I'd like to know?"

Emily hesitated, but only for a moment. "Partly because of the ring Mr. Brucker brought you. Partly because of something very indefinite David let drop about a grand duke named Feodor. And partly because—well, because I've felt for a long while there must have been a David in your life. I mean, someone you cared for in the same way I've cared for him. If there hadn't been, I don't see how you could have been so—so very understanding."

"There's someone like David in a good many women's lives, Emily."

"There couldn't be. Because there aren't enough like him to go around. But the Grand Duke Feodor was something like him, wasn't he?"

Without answering, Old Mrs. Forbes began to twist her emerald ring around. Emily put her hand over it.

"If he was, it—it would help to have you tell me so, Grandmamma. Because you've been so magnificent all these years. And if it's been because you lost so much, instead of because you had so much. . . . If I thought there was some chance that I. . . ."

She did not need to finish. Old Mrs. Forbes freed her fingers and began to stroke her granddaughter's hair.

442

"Yes," she said. "There's a great resemblance between David Salomont and the man I used to know, who was a grand duke and whose name was Feodor. That's enough for me to tell you now. Perhaps I'll tell you more some other time."

As it turned out, Emily did not have to wait very long to learn more. The Bruckers accepted, with alacrity, her invitation to stay with her; and the evening of their arrival, Morris Brucker himself, quite unconsciously, picked up the thread of Old Mrs. Forbes' narrative.

"It's good to see this tea service in use again," he said. "I always suspected, when it was reported 'missing' from the Romanoff treasure, that it had been previously given to your grandmother. There wasn't much she couldn't have had, in those days, without so much as lifting her little finger. There will never be another American ambassadress to equal her, Mrs. Field, in Russia or anywhere else. To see her when she was dressed for a court ball, or to watch her while she was making an entrance at some great ceremony—well, it's something to remember over the years." He paused, as if to give his words weight, and then went on, "I brought several silver-gilt tea sets, similar to this, out of Russia myself, when I decided to leave there for good. I was really in a very advantageous position. You see, my family'd been known and respected there for many years. We didn't have any political leanings, one way or another—we were just dealers—collectors. After the Revolution, we continued collecting—on a very extensive scale. It was a fascinating business. And it tied in very well with some of our other activities. I'd become an American citizen long before that, and so had several of the relatives who were associated with me. Our gallery in New York wasn't as large and important as some others had been, but we already had excellent connections in America. These were helpful to us in securing favorable concessions and starting extensive industries in Russia. But when we decided we'd operated under the Soviets as long as we cared to, we were careful to have a clause in the contract for the sale of our properties to the effect that we could take our collections out of the country with us. We got them into the United States almost intact. The only persons I know of who were equally fortunate were a couple of amateurs who happened to be ambassadors and who, therefore, enjoyed diplomatic immunity. But they'd operated on a very small scale, compared to ours."

Again he paused, as if for effect, and glanced toward his wife, who had so far sat silent, sipping her tea. Emily had glanced at her a good many times, since she had come into the library. The resemblance between her and David was very marked, in many ways; she had the same fine features, the same air of assurance, and she wore her clothes with the same ease and elegance. Emily would have liked to know whether the mental characteristics of mother and son were as nearly the same. Absorbed as she was in what Mr. Brucker was saying, she longed to talk at length with her other

443

guest too. But Mrs. Brucker continued to sip her tea in silence and her husband, who had warmed to his subject, went on, "I had a very cogent reason for wishing to make my headquarters in New York. Probably I don't need to tell you what it was. I'd been a bachelor for a long time, but I'd finally fallen in love with a very charming, very lovely lady, and she wasn't at all interested in going to Russia. She's one of those New Yorkers who feels no other place is really worth living in, even when she admits its existence at all. And then of course she had her son to consider. She wanted him to grow up as an American. I think you'll agree he's a great credit to her—a great credit to us both. I couldn't love him any more if he were my own. But we have an adopted son, too, now—has David told you that? The most extraordinary child! You'll say so yourself, when you see him."

"I'd like very much to see him. I'm sorry, I didn't know about him before. But I'll meet him at the wedding, won't I?"

"Oh, certainly! As far as that goes, you'll probably see him before that. He's staying with our cousins on Aspinwall Avenue, but the whole clan is coming to your grandmother's tonight, including my wife's relatives from Caracas, who've just arrived by air. Obviously, there's no limit to Forbes hospitality. I wish there was something I could do to show my appreciation."

"I think you've already done what meant most to Grandmamma. Do you remember that ring you brought her, when you came to see her soon after my marriage? She's worn it ever since."

Morris Brucker set down his silver-gilt cup and reached for a cigarette from the cloisonné box, which was now back in its old place. "Yes," he said quietly. "Yes, I thought she might like to have that. It belonged to the Grand Duke Feodor. Your grandmother was always a great belle, from the time I first knew her, but I do not think it was until she met Feodor that any of the homage she received meant much to her. Unfortunately, he was one of the Romanoffs, who met such a terrible death during the worst 'terror' periods, in the summer of '18. When the White Forces advanced westward through the Ural, his desecrated body was one of those found in a deserted quarry."

Everything connected with the wedding went off beautifully. It took place, on a perfect summer afternoon, in the garden of the big weather-beaten house surmounting the cliffs and the dunes; even Old Mrs. Forbes admitted that, once Priscilla had roused her parents from their lethargy, Sherman and Sue had spared no pains to do themselves and their elder daughter proud. Their younger daughter, Charlotte, was as dainty a bridesmaid as could have been found anywhere, and their two sons, Stillman and Donald, did not betray how unaccustomed they were to white flannels. As for Priscilla, she was really a charming bride. Of course she had never been a beauty, like some other girls in the family, and she never would be. But there was certainly something about her. Perhaps it was partly her expression. . . . When she raised her head to receive David's kiss, after the ceremony was over, the look in her eyes had a dazzling quality. Old Mrs. Forbes turned away, to hide the tears in her own. But there were no tears in Emily's. Whenever her grandmother, who had been watching her closely, glanced in her direction, she seemed to be the central figure in a convivial group, which usually included Brian Collins. The green-and-gold brocade was extremely becoming to her, and so was the big green picture hat, trimmed with golden roses, which she wore with it. And she had made a wise choice, in selecting her topazes as the finishing touch for her costume, instead of the diamonds. For the first time, Old Mrs. Forbes, who had always freely admitted Emily's good looks, coupled them with an adjective she had never used before. "The girl's striking," she said to herself. "She stands out in a crowd. She never used to. She can say all she wants to about Priscilla's courage. I'd still say, Emily's more than a match for her when it comes to that, and in a good many other ways too. What she's done today hasn't been easy. I ought to know."

The day had not been easy for Old Mrs. Forbes, either. She was proud of Emily, but she was sick at heart on her account too. Moreover, the old lady had made a great effort, physically, not only in coming to the Cape for the wedding, but in seeing that the bridal party was suitably entertained beforehand; Morris Brucker's outspoken praise of her unbounded hospitality had been well merited, for David's relatives, who were nearly all much more arresting than Priscilla's, had kept arriving in rapidly increasing numbers. The cousins from Venezuela, who were exquisitely turned out, and wore even more diamonds than Old Mrs. Forbes herself, were by no means exceptional among the newcomers in elegance and sophistication. It would have been unthinkable not to entertain them on a lavish scale; but she was finding entertainments of this prodigal character more and more of a strain. She was also finding, as Emily had feared she might, that Elizabeth and her family created more of a commotion in her house than she had foreseen and that this commotion was exhausting. The house was never quiet any more; she had not realized how dependent she had become upon restful interludes between the festivities which she still appeared to dominate and to which she unquestionably lent great distinction. Well, thank God, there were to be no more parties at her house for the present; and now that everything had gone so well with the wedding, now that she was sure Sue and Sherman had insisted on having the Bruckers stand in line with them and that there was plenty of imported champagne for everybody, she wanted to go home. She did not care about waiting to see the bride throw out her bouquet, since Emily would not be trying to catch it. She was not interested in watching the bridal couple start off, in a shower of rice and confetti; she could not begrudge Priscilla her happiness, after seeing that look in her eyes; but she still felt it was Emily who should have been going to Germany with David. She still wondered why he did not seem to know what he had done to Emily, she could not forget that Emily was going to love him as long as she lived. . . .

Old Mrs. Forbes extricated herself, with difficulty, from a very boring conversation with Roscoe Cutter, who kept telling her how glad he was to have Brian Collins back in the firm, and how much he regretted that, owing to the stupidity of Cleophas Mills, there had been a misunderstanding about David's return. She finally shook him off and managed to withdraw a little from the crowd, but presently Emily, who was watchful, too, came strolling across the lawn, escorted by Brian Collins. The gold roses on her hat, the gold threads in her brocade dress, glittered in the sunlight. She leaned over and put her arms around her grandmother.

"Brian has to get back to town," she said. "Something to do with this wicked campaign of his against poor Uncle Russell. Why don't you go with him? He says he'll promise not to importune you to act as his official hostess after he gets to Washington, though of course the temptation to do so will be very great. It's been a long day for you. I'll explain to Aunt Sue and Uncle Sherman that you were tired, and that you didn't like to break in on the line to say good-by. I'll come along later with Clark and explain to him too. You can just slip quietly out of the side entrance. Brian's got his car there already."

If anyone had told Old Mrs. Forbes beforehand that she would welcome the opportunity to drive away with Brian Collins, she would have denied this indignantly; but now she accepted Emily's suggestion with alacrity. "Why, that's very kind of him," she said. "And I think it's an excellent idea. But you'll come in and see me for a minute before you go home yourself, won't you?"

"Of course, if you want me to. If I find you're already asleep, I won't disturb you. In that case, I'll come over in the morning. But I'll stay till the end here, you may depend on that. I'll be prepared to tell you about cutting the cake, and what Priscilla's going-away dress is like, and everything."

Old Mrs. Forbes was not asleep when Emily tiptoed into her room, some hours later, and she immediately signified that such was the case. But she was not interested in the cake or the dress. She cut short Emily's description of them.

"Did David speak to you at all?"

"Why of course he spoke to me, half a dozen times! You must have heard him yourself."

"I don't mean that. I mean did he say anything special? Did he get a chance to speak to you alone?"

"Of course he didn't say anything special. Of course he didn't have a chance to speak to me alone. What are you thinking of, Grandmamma? A bridegroom on his wedding day!"

"I'm thinking that I hope you'll never be sorry."

"Sorry for what?"

"Sorry that David was never your lover."

"I suppose I'll have moments of being sorry. But only moments. And I'll know they won't last. I'll know I never could have been really happy if I'd betrayed Roger's faith in me. David knew it, too, from the beginning. He told me so himself—the same day he told me that he loved me."

"Well, you're right. And he was right. You and I don't belong to the breed that can take adultery in its stride, or call it fancy names. I found that out a long, long time ago."

Her voice trailed away into silence and she seemed to be growing drowsy at last. The light in the room was dim, but Emily could see that she was fumbling with her ring. She spoke again, almost fretfully.

"I can't get this off. I want to take it off."

"Why, Grandmamma?"

"Because I want you to have it. I want to give it to you tonight. I want you to wear it always—for my sake. Help me take it off, Emily. I don't want it found on my hand after I'm dead."

"But, Grandmamma, you're not going to die! If you talk that way, I'll have to send for a doctor."

"I'll never forgive you if you send for a doctor tonight. We may not have many more talks like this and I don't want it spoiled. I know I'm not going to die just yet. But I'm eighty years old, Emily. I can't expect to live much longer. I might die in my sleep, some night. I hope I do. And if I did, you wouldn't have any right to take this ring off and keep it, unless you knew it was yours. Besides, as I said, I don't want it found on my hand after I'm dead, the way it was found on Feodor Romanoff's hand when his corpse was taken from the quarry."

Obviously, she had forgotten that she had never finished telling Emily the story she had begun a few weeks earlier. She went on speaking as if she had done so.

"Just before the state funeral at Ekaterinburg, some of the minor ornaments on the bodies were—retrieved. I don't know how they happened to be overlooked when—when the massacre took place. But they were. And I've always been thankful that this ring came into Morris Brucker's possession. I wish you'd tell him so, for me, if you have a good chance."

"I will, Grandmamma. I'll be very glad to."

"Morris Brucker knew I gave it to Feodor. He had it made for me to give the man I really—the man I really—" Again her voice trailed off into silence.

"I didn't have as much strength of character as you do, Emily," she said at last. "But I was a great ambassadress just the same. Everyone thought so. Most of all your grandfather."

Three nights later, Old Mrs. Forbes died in her sleep, as she had hoped she would; and it was when she was leaving her grandmother's house to

447

go back to her own, after the funeral, that Emily remembered what Sister Mary Theresa had said—that the chapel at St. Margaret's was always open. She wondered now why she had never thought of it before—how she could have helped thinking of it before. She walked slowly across the Square and went up the steps. As she did so, she noticed, for the first time, the words graven on the arch above the door:

PER ANGUSTA AD AUGUSTA

The portress who answered her ring recognized her, though it was so long since she had visited there. "I'm so glad to see you again, Mrs. Field," she said, in her soft, sweet voice. "You've been very much in our thoughts and in our prayers. You'd like to see Sister Mary Theresa, wouldn't you?"

"Not quite yet. I just want to go up to the chapel, if I may."

"Certainly, Mrs. Field. I think you know the way. Of course I'd be glad to come along. Or would you rather go alone?"

"Yes, I do know the way. And thank you, but I would rather go alone."

She went up to the little chapel and knelt down. She did not try to pray; it was so long since she had really prayed that she knew she could not do so now. But gradually the sense of peace and the awareness of Divinity which had come to her so many years before, in this same place, permeated her being again. She raised her eyes to the crucifix on the altar.

"I have to go along alone," she murmured. "There isn't anyone left to go with me now. Unless You will."

Chapter 36

"Nothing is hard all the time; there is always an ebb and flow to trouble, just as there is to the tide."

Emily had heard her grandmother say this dozens of times. Now, when she least expected this, she found out the full force of its truth.

The terrible loneliness which had engulfed her after David's marriage and Old Mrs. Forbes' death lasted a surprisingly short while. Emily realized that this was partly because she was so busy that she had no leisure whatsoever for introspection, and very little for reflection; she believed it was also because she resolutely kept her mind on the manifold tasks which confronted her while she was performing them, and did not permit herself to dwell on personal problems, except in connection with these. The periods that she did give over to deliberation were definitely set apart from her numerous and varied activities: some time in the course of every day, she went to St. Margaret's Chapel, if only for a few minutes; and every night, before she went to bed, she devoted a few minutes more to quiet meditation.

She was conscious of no great resurgence of faith, no groping for doctrinal precepts, not even any special leaning toward religion; she made no attempt to force herself to utter prayers which did not come naturally from her heart to her lips or to study sacred subjects. But almost immediately after her desperate avowal that she had only one possible source of communion left, the conviction that she was wholly alone began to lose its terrors and its strength. It appeared that there were, after all, a number of persons to whom she mattered and who mattered to her; in the preoccupation of her thoughts which were centered on David and in the companionship with her grandmother, she had underestimated the importance of these other persons in her life. Now this became apparent, and it seemed to her that the revelation sprang from the same source to which she had appealed; by asking for Divine Sustenance, she had been granted the power to find human sustenance also.

Elizabeth was now very near her time, and though her condition gave no cause for actual alarm, certain aspects of it, including her age, indicated caution and care. She was easily annoyed and upset, which was wholly uncharacteristic of her; the discussion of details regarding her mother's estate, and the management of her household fatigued and troubled her out of all proportion to their urgency and importance. Her physician finally suggested that, unless she could be spared responsibility and relieved from making decisions, until after her confinement, it would perhaps be better for her to go at once to a hospital, where she could be shielded from importunities at the same time that she was kept under observation. She rebelled against this proposition and turned hopefully to her niece with an alternate one.

"If you'd just take charge of everything, Emily, without consulting me at all, I'm sure I'd get along all right. You could consult Mark, if you want to, and I'll agree beforehand to anything that you and he feel is advisable. But, as far as that goes, I've complete confidence in your judgment. The will's very definite anyway, and Brian's in Boston all the time now, so he can give you legal advice if you need it, though I shouldn't think you would. Between the testament and the memoranda, Mamma's made all her wishes and intentions very plain, and I don't believe any of us wants to go against them—I'm sure I don't. I'll sign a paper saying so, if you like, or if Brian thinks it would avoid trouble. And you can manage Pearson and Clark and Doris and the other servants a great deal better than I can. I'm sure I don't care which china is used for which meal or know whether the Cadillac really needs new tires or mind if all Mamma's furs don't get put in cold storage. As far as that goes, I don't care what we have for dinner or which room is cleaned on Thursday or who has Sundays off. I just don't want to be bothered answering questions about such things. I've never had to handle a big household staff and I don't like it. I'm going to reduce the staff as soon and as fast as I can. I'm worried about Archie though. With all these servants falling over each other, there isn't a capable nursemaid among them. And I can't have him waking me up before dawn and jumping all over me just now."

"I think Deirdre might make a very capable nurse. Anyway, she took care of Caroline and Roger when they were little."

"But Deirdre can't take care of Archie and do the cooking too! Besides, she's at your house now."

"I thought you said you wanted to leave details to me, Liz. If you'll really trust me with them, I'll do my very best. If you feel you can't, you'll have to go on taking care of them yourself. In the present instance, the solution doesn't seem to me hard at all: I can close my house again and bring Deirdre back here; or I can take Archie home with me and get someone besides Ellie to help Deirdre there, if necessary. But I don't believe it would be necessary. My cuisine isn't very elaborate these days and Ellie didn't live with Deirdre for years without learning something from her. We certainly can't turn any of Grandmamma's faithful retainers out in the world—they'd be completely lost if we did, and they're not going to be useful to anyone much longer. But I'm perfectly willing to take over those you don't want and try to put the others on an efficiency basis."

"I'd really rather have you take Archie to your house than to have you and Deirdre come back here. Not that I don't love you both dearly, you know that. But just having so many people around—"

"I know. And it's what I'd prefer too—to stay where I am, I mean. Now be a good girl and try to take a nap. If you don't, we'll have to hustle you off to the hospital after all."

The revision of a design for family living in the immediate future consumed a good deal of Emily's time; but it was accomplished with such surface smoothness that Elizabeth was both placated and deceived by its apparent simplicity. Deirdre made short work of Archie's tantrums. Inside of a week, he was eating what was put before him, going to bed without a light in his room, and submitting to the detested routine of bathing and dressing without rebellion; indeed, he was soon playing with great and reasonably quiet contentment in the old kitchen and the adjacent garden, where Deirdre could keep a stern and watchful eye on him. Late every afternoon, Emily read stories to him, and as often as possible, she took him walking and driving with her. The mutual antagonism which had existed between them, ever since his disastrous plunge into the pond at Hollyhock Hill, became a thing of the past, and mutual dependence and affection began to take its place.

The other domestic problems were solved with almost equal dispatch, some of them more or less automatically. Doris, weeping bitterly, came to Emily and said it was all too evident that Mrs. Merriweather did not want a personal maid; indeed—if Mrs. Field would excuse the liberty—that Mrs. Merriweather did not know what to do with one. But perhaps Mrs. Field herself. . . . Emily did not want a personal maid, either, but she thought she would know what to do with one, if such a maid were willing to undertake chamber work also. So Doris dried her eyes, and with a final sob which ended in a sigh, said that Mrs. Field was certainly getting to resemble her dear, dead grandmother more and more every day, and that it would be a pleasure to wait on her. Clark and Pearson, encouraged by the success of Doris, were the next to tell a masculine version of her story and invite a correlative response. Emily had no special use for a butler or a chauffeur, and no desire to build up an establishment into a semblance of what her grandmother's had been. But again she rose to the occasion, and the two old men moved their belongings, as Doris had already moved hers, to the top floor of the Joy Street house with an air of importance, not to say triumph. It was right and proper that Old Mrs. Forbes should leave her place on Louisburg Square to her husband's namesake, if that was what she wanted to do; but a couple of college professors would never be able to maintain it in her grand manner, no matter how much money they might have come into. Now Mrs. Field was different. She was getting to be a great lady herself. They would feel quite at home in her house, to be sure.

The rest of the staff was content to remain on Louisburg Square, particularly as the grim and capable Jenny was now doing most of the work; and everyone, but most especially Elizabeth, was delighted with the turn of events. Emily secretly derived less satisfaction from it; nevertheless, she did not fail to see that it had some rather amusing aspects.

"Talk about Victorian relics," she said to Brian one day, when he had come to confer with her about the will, "I'm probably the only woman left in Boston who's living all by herself in a big house, except for five servants."

"No you're not. We've still got several others among our clients—not many, but several. They're scattered around over the Back Bay as well as Beacon Hill. Every now and then, I'm obliged to have a session with one of them, so I know the old system still has survivors. You are the only one though that's come within my range of vision who's still young and good looking."

"Well, time will probably take care of that. Twenty years from now—"

"Twenty years from now, all the others will be 'laid away,' as they themselves like to put it, in just the right lots at Mount Auburn. And you'll be doing something quite different."

"Such as—?"

"We'll go into that later. However, for the moment, may I remind you that you're not living all alone, except for five servants. How could you forget dear little Archie?"

"I can't imagine. But I did, temporarily. Deirdre's got him so well under control that I'm hardly conscious of him."

"Except when you're reading him bedtime stories, or taking him down the Hill to make an orderly call on his mother, or driving him out to profit by the exhibitions in the Children's Museum, I suppose," Brian remarked. "But we'll let that pass for the moment too. Why don't you bring him out and park him in South Boston once in a while? My sister, Katie, would never notice the difference, if she had one more kid to look after, any more than my mother used to. As far as that goes, Mother'd be tickled to death to have him too."

"All right. I'll bring him with me the next time I come over to supper."

"Would that be tonight?"

"Why—it could be, I suppose."

"Fine. I'll telephone her in a few minutes and break the good news. Meanwhile, let me remind you that you may find those five servants handy after all. You're taking over the second breakfast for Pell and Simonetta, aren't you?"

"Yes. I knew that was what Grandmamma would want me to do. I've already told Simonetta there won't be any change at all in the arrangements, except that they'll be carried out here, instead of on Louisburg Square."

"And what about the first breakfast, at Old Venice? Are you going to that?"

452

"Oh, yes! Simonetta specifically asked me to. Didn't she specifically ask you?"

"Indeed, she did. . . . And are you still planning to stand up with her?"

"Of course. Aren't you still planning to stand up with Pell?"

"Sure and why not? So it looks as if you and I'd be seeing quite a good deal of each other, first and last. . . . Now, as for this memorandum about all that Russian stuff. . . ."

Elizabeth had been right in saying that the provisions of Old Mrs. Forbes' will were very definite. The one which Roger had first drawn for her had been changed, after Archie's birth, in order to leave him her house on Louisburg Square, in trust to his mother, as she had told Emily; but, as she had also told her granddaughter, she had taken care to see that all her other rightful heirs received something of equal value. The estate at Manchester-by-the-Sea was left to Russell Forbes, the Dublin farm to Eleanor Thayer, and stocks and bonds to the value of these, over and above what she left all the other next of kin, to her son, Sherman. Her jewelry, except for the diamonds she had given Emily, and which she quite obviously regarded as an "extra" for her favorite, was meticulously divided among her daughters and granddaughters. The household effects in her several establishments, with a few duly noted exceptions, were to remain where they were and to be regarded as an essential part of the legacies; but she desired that each of her sons-in-law, her daughter-in-law and Homer Lathrop should be permitted to choose some special piece of equipment which they particularly admired, and she hoped the enormous amount of silverware might be amicably divided without detailed instructions from her. Each of the old servants was to receive a substantial cash legacy and some small personal memento which each might select, subject to the approval of the next of kin. Several charitable institutions were likewise suitably remembered; and a legacy to Caroline Field provided Roger's sister against want, or even straitened circumstances, for the rest of her life—"since Roger Field himself, because of his lamented and untimely death, had been unable to make such provision, and because it would have been a source of anxiety to him if his sister lacked the necessities of a comfortable existence." A final memorandum, duly witnessed, was dated only a few days before Old Mrs. Forbes' death.

. . . And I desire that my granddaughter, Emily Thayer Field, shall have, in addition to the emerald ring which I have already given her, all the jeweled icons, enameled Easter eggs and other *objets d'art*, typical of Russia, which I collected while in that country; also all snuffboxes, cigarette cases, miniatures, porcelains, paintings, rugs, furniture and other articles of household equipment which I acquired while there, the same to be over and above her logical share of other *objets d'art* and household equipment. And if there be any objection to this, among my other rightful heirs, then I desire and direct that stocks and bonds, to the equivalent value, be deducted from those which the said Emily Thayer Field would normally inherit and divided among my other rightful heirs.

"There hasn't been any objection, has there?" Brian inquired, when he had dismissed the subject of Pell and Simonetta for the time being.

"No. But I don't think any of us realized how much there was of 'that Russian stuff,' as you call it. I'm sure I didn't, and I was closer to Grandmamma than anyone else was, for a good many years. I've kept coming across all kinds of trinkets, tucked away in drawers, and I think some of them may have cost a good deal. There was even an extra jewel case, in her safe-deposit box, that we'd never seen, that we didn't even know existed— and it was full of the most gorgeous things! I'd honestly feel happier, Brian, to have all those appraised—the ones we did know about, as well as the ones we didn't."

"If they're as valuable as you seem to think, it might mean you wouldn't get much of anything else."

"It wouldn't matter. You know she gave me a great deal when I got married—almost everything valuable in this house, except for some other wedding presents. And don't forget the famous trust fund. I'll never be poor."

"No, I don't suppose you ever will. But is there any reason you can think of why she should wish all this junk off on you, and leave huge houses and acres and acres of farm land and great hunks of Tel & Tel to other people?"

"There you go again, Paul Pry!—yes, there is."

"I'd like very much to know what it is. As your attorney, I have a right to make sure you're not being gypped."

"All right, I'll assure you, as my attorney, that I'm not. In fact, I shouldn't be at all surprised if this 'junk' you're fussing about wasn't worth more than the big houses and the fruitful acres and the Tel & Tel. That's why I want it appraised—I want to be sure *I'm* not gypping anybody. But quite aside from its value, I'd rather have the Russian stuff than anything else. That and the brocades. Evidently, there wasn't a memorandum about those. But since Elizabeth's willing I should take all the responsibility. . . ."

She would not tell him anything more that afternoon; and the next day, all discussion of the will and everything pertaining thereto was automatically thrust aside by the sudden appearance of Pell. Simonetta had already been informed of his imminent arrival; but instead of "telling her good news, she brought it," as she said herself, and thereafter, preparations for an immediate wedding were the only order of the day. It was not until Brian lingered on, after the second breakfast, that Emily spoke again, this time of her own accord, about her grandmother's final memorandum.

She had been greatly moved by the significance of the marriage service which had been so long deferred, and this ultimate union of the two who had steadfastly loved each other for years poignantly recalled the solemn betrothal ceremony which had taken place in her own drawing room. But her emotions had been tinged throughout with joyousness; it had been impossible to escape the contagion of the conviviality which had pervaded the Italian breakfast at Old Venice; and the spectacle of the Joy Street house, decorated throughout with white flowers and thrown open to receive a large and festive gathering, had the effect of raising her spirits still further. When Pell and Simonetta had finally gone over the crest of the Hill to their own little house, and Brian still showed no inclination to take his departure, even with the other last remaining guests, Emily found she was ready and willing to answer the question he had asked almost a week earlier.

"Do you want to sit in the garden with me and listen while I 'tell sad stories of the death of kings'?" she asked, half seriously and half whimsically.

He did not instantly recognize the quotation. "You know I'm always tickled to death to sit in the garden or anywhere else with you," he answered. "But as to sad stories and kings—isn't this a day for stories with happy endings? I should think it was. And stories about conquering heroes rather than dead monarchs!"

"You're right, in a way. But there's a story you particularly asked to hear."

He gave her a quick look. "You mean about that Russian stuff? Was that really given to your grandmother by a king?"

"No, he was only a grand duke. But I gather he was quite a regal person, just the same. I'm sure Grandmamma always thought of him as a royal lover."

"A royal—good God, of course I want to hear it!"

It was very late when he finally left the garden. After Emily finished telling him the story of Feodor, in so far as she knew it herself, it seemed natural for them to go on talking of other things, and eventually he spoke to her about his campaign.

"It isn't going to create any awkwardness for you, is it, Emily?"

"No, of course not. Except that I think Uncle Russell may be here a good deal. He's taking it more or less as a personal insult that he can't use Grandmamma's house for his unofficial headquarters. I suppose his official headquarters will be in some hotel."

"Yes, inevitably. But he wants to sleep and eat here, he wants a private secretary and a private telephone installed, he wants you to do his entertaining for him? Is that the idea?"

"More or less, I think. And I don't like to say no. I want to do everything, this summer, as Grandmamma would have done it, if she'd been alive, as she'd want it done."

"And I say more power to you! . . . Didn't I tell you you'd find a use for all those five servants yet?"

"Yes, you did. You're quite often right, Briny, about a number of things."

"Thanks for those kind words. . . . Well, just let me know when you're about to begin your role as official hostess—for your uncle, I mean. Then I'll fade out of the picture, with my usual tact and grace. . . . I suppose you can sneak over to South Boston once in a while, even if I can't come here?"

"I'd feel terribly sorry if I thought I couldn't."

"And what about the love nest on the other side of the Hill as a meeting place for us?"

Emily laughed. "I imagine the bridal couple would like that entirely to themselves for a little while, don't you?"

"Yes. But the campaign isn't going to begin right away. And after all, we can sit in the garden and they can go to bed."

Emily laughed again. "Brian, you're incorrigible!"

"Would you like me any better if I were different?"

"No, I like you the way you are."

"How much?"

"Very much."

"Enough to marry me after all?"

"Certainly not. Go home, Brian, and stop talking nonsense."

"Enough to kiss me good night, just this once?"

"No. I can't take your kind of kissing."

"You might learn to, with a little practice. I promise to begin in a more restrained manner than the last time."

"I said no, Briny. Good night."

"Good night. Thanks a lot, Emily, for telling me the sad story about the death of a king. It was the right story, after all."

The next time he came, she told him something quite different. She could not have said why she wanted to, but the fact remained that she did. She told him how she had gone, not habitually, but frequently, before her marriage and in the period immediately thereafter, to St. Margaret's; and how she had stopped going, at first because of Homer Lathrop's cynicism and later, because she found that a like cynicism had crept through her own being. Then she told him how she had gone there again, the day of her grandmother's funeral, for no other reason than because she felt entirely alone in the world and because she could think of no other place to go. Brian did not jest with her this time, or ask her inopportune questions. He listened attentively and gravely until she had finished telling him everything there was in her heart to say.

"And do you know, Briny, before I left there, I realized I wasn't alone. I don't mean—just on account of God. Of course I do believe again that

456

His Spirit is always with us, wherever we go and whatever we do, that if we seek Him we shall find Him. But I mean it was just as if He had shown me, right then, that I'd kept more than I'd lost, that there were any number of places I could still go, if I only would. *Earthly* places. *Pleasant* places. Places where I was wanted and needed, places where I wanted and needed to be, all of them with people in them who loved me and whom I loved. Do you understand what I'm trying to say?"

"I think so. Yes, I'm almost sure I do."

"It doesn't trouble you, does it, because I've found such peace and comfort in a form of faith that's different from yours?"

"I don't believe it's so very different. Why don't you talk to Mat about that someday, if it's worrying you? He knows more about such things than I do. But, if it were different—no, that wouldn't trouble me. Even though I don't know much about such things, I do know they have a way of working out."

They sat in companionable silence for some moments. Then Emily realized that Brian was not grave any longer, that he was grinning again and that there was a twinkle in his eye which was not without a spark of harmless malice.

"Do you remember that the day you took such exception to my technique as a suitor, I asked you whether you were troubled about the possibility that I might drink too much, and you said it really wasn't any affair of yours?"

"Yes, I remember."

"Well, you tempt me to make a similar answer. Why *should* I be troubled about your religion—unless it is some affair of mine? Why should you think I would be, unless you're ready to admit that it is?"

She rose hastily and walked away from him, conscious of a flaming face. He caught up with her and put his arm around her.

"Sure and it's all right, mavourneen," he said lightly. "And I was a low dog, and all the rest of it, to trip you up like that. But this time, I'm going to have just one wee kiss and nothing you'll say will stop me, either."

She did not see him alone again for some time, partly because her Uncle Russell moved in upon her almost immediately thereafter, and practically took over the house, and partly because she and Brian were both so preoccupied in different directions. Brian won, hands down, in the primaries. The only other contestant for the nomination was an old ward heeler whose bosses belonged to a now-discredited political machine; and, as he himself admitted, the cards were stacked against him from the beginning —what could he do against a rising young lawyer, whose own political backing was powerful, and who was himself a recently returned "hero" into the bargain? Russell Forbes had no opponent at all in the primaries; but when these were over, the pre-election campaign began in earnest, and both candidates were swept into the usual whirlwind of charges and countercharges, slogans and speeches, rallies and parades. While Russell established headquarters at the Copley Plaza, Brian was busy establishing his at the Ritz; while Brian made the noisy circuit of Chelsea, Lynn, Revere and East Boston, Russell delivered himself of a dignified speech in Salem; while Brian was whooping it up with his followers at Symphony Hall, Russell and his cohorts took over the Boston Arena. As Election Day approached, it became more and more evident that the contest would be very close; and Russell Forbes, who had hitherto been content to have Emily remain in the background, capably providing the setting for small private gatherings, urged her to appear more frequently with him in public.

"I'm sorry, Uncle Russell. I don't feel that I can."

"You don't feel you *can!* May I ask why not?"

"Because I'm not at all sure I believe in the principles you stand for and the way you interpret them. If I went to big public banquets with you and sat on the platform with you at rallies, it would give the impression that I did. Of course I don't suppose I could really help you anyway. I don't think I'm important enough to change a single vote. But you must think so, or you wouldn't ask me to come with you. So I'll have to ask you to excuse me."

"You don't mean to tell me you'd sit back and see that flannelmouthed Mick from South Boston take my seat away from me, without so much as lifting a hand?"

"I'm sorry, Uncle Russell, that you feel you have to talk about Brian Collins to me that way. I suppose it's part of the game to do mud-slinging in public. But Briny's a very good friend of mine. He's not coming to the house just now because he realizes it would create a certain awkwardness if he did. I realize that too. And I felt you had a prior right here, at present, on Grandmamma's account. But, as soon as the campaign's over—"

"I'm very much disappointed in you, Emily, and the company you keep. So are all your other relatives. So, incidentally, is Homer Lathrop."

"I'm sorry about you and Uncle Homer. But I honestly don't think the others are disappointed. I know Papa isn't."

"Unfortunately, your father has never seen fit to show an intelligent interest in public affairs. And lately, he's become a very doting parent. Everything you do apparently seems perfect to him, just because you do it."

"I'm very pleased and very proud that it does. I don't think I ever appreciated Papa until after Roger died. As to the other relatives, Uncle Sherman's a good deal more interested in his cranberry crop than he is in who wins the election—he claims it's unusually poor this year. Of course that's what he's been saying ever since I can remember, but still. . . . And Elizabeth's so wrapped up in the new baby, she doesn't even know there's a campaign on."

It had been on the tip of Emily's tongue to add that she was greatly

458

relieved when Mark insisted on naming the new baby after her mother, instead of after her grandmother; Emily had always intended to name a baby Evelina herself someday, and she was quite proud of herself because she had refrained from saying so. She had also been sorely tempted to remark that, as far as Homer Lathrop was concerned, he needed nothing more than her confessed interest in any man to express disapproval. But she was glad she had not said that, either, because it would have indicated a good deal more than she was ready to admit. As soon as she could, she left her uncle to cope alone with his dissatisfaction and walked over the crest of the Hill to see Pell and Simonetta.

Despite what she had said to Brian, about their natural wish to have their house to themselves at first, they had made her extremely welcome from the beginning, and when she reached there, after the scene with her uncle, Pell flung open the door, not only with every evidence of great cordiality but with obvious excitement.

"I'm so glad you've come! We were just going to telephone and ask if you wouldn't sit in on a conference."

"I'd be glad to. . . . What kind of a conference?"

"Well, Brian's had a brainstorm. He thinks that he and I ought to break away from Cutter, Mills as soon as we decently can. Of course we wouldn't leave them in the lurch; but the situation's beginning to ease with lawyers, just as it is all along the line. They wouldn't have too much trouble now filling our places."

Brian rose from the depths of a cavernous wing chair at the farther end of the room and came toward them. "You see what I mean, don't you, Emily? It isn't just that we'd get a lot of satisfaction out of being our own bosses, instead of being shoved around indefinitely by the Ruddy Oarsman and the Artful Dodger. It isn't even that eventually we'd make a lot more money than if they kept on taking most of the gravy. If we had our own firm, we wouldn't just represent an experiment in better understanding between alien groups, the way we have so far. We'd represent an accomplished fact."

"Yes. I do see what you mean. And I think it's a grand idea—from every point of view."

All three went on to the rear of the room, where Simonetta was sitting with a bit of fine sewing in her hands and, for the next half hour, the question of a partnership was discussed, with the shared feeling and expression that, in principle, one had been started already. But it was Brian who made the most significant contribution to the conversation.

"You'd never guess who came into the office this morning and asked to see me—Priscilla's brother, Donald. He said he'd made up his mind to be a lawyer."

"Why, the poor kid hasn't even got through the local high school yet, has he?"

"Yes, he has. More through good luck than through good management, if you don't mind my saying so, Emily. What's more, he's somehow got enough points to get into Harvard."

"He hasn't!"

"I tell you he has. And now his idea is that he might cram a four years' college course into three years and that after that. . . . Well, to make a long story slightly shorter, I told him there'd be a place waiting for him with Collins and De Lucca any time after '52 that he was ready for it. So eventually, we will be having a Forbes in the firm, too."

He was half afraid that she might say, "I don't doubt it, if that's what Donald's made up his mind he wants. After all, he's Priscilla's brother. . . ." But, instead, she merely nodded, rather pensively, and he realized that her thoughts were without rancor and that they had taken her in an entirely different direction from the one he had feared. There would be a Forbes in the new firm, too, and she was glad of it; she would have been sorry not to have her family, or one like it, represented. But she recognized that it was not a Forbes, or anyone like a Forbes, who was to head the firm, to lend it prestige or to assure it sound financial standing. This was to be done by two men named respectively Brian Collins and Pellegrino de Lucca, whose immediate forebears came from groups long misprized and long underestimated. The days of such discrimination were numbered; and though the part she had played in bringing about this change was small, it was not negligible. She was not a failure after all. . . .

As the campaign advanced, Emily formed the habit of going to the De Luccas' house whenever she could slip away from her own, in order to listen with them to the political news as it came over the radio. Pell had suffered no compunctions in telling Brian of this arrangement, and not infrequently the latter eluded his lieutenants and also put in an appearance at the "love nest." Emily had come to recognize the probability of such brief visits, which she neither fostered nor discouraged; but it had not entered her head that Brian would make one on election night, or that she would hear from him directly until the following morning. However, when the returns began to come in, he called her over a private wire, and told her that the contest was "too close to be comfortable." An hour or so later, he telephoned again and said he wanted to see her at once.

"You can't leave headquarters now, can you?" she asked, genuinely puzzled.

"I don't know how anyone's going to stop me, if I just walk out. Nobody's put a ball and chain on me yet."

"But—"

"Stop saying 'But'! As I've told you before, I wish it weren't such a favorite word of yours. I'm coming to Pell's, but you're right, I haven't got much time to spare, and the longer we talk over the telephone, the less time we'll have to talk face to face. Good-by."

Within five minutes, he appeared, in the whirlwind fashion which had always been more or less normal for him, but which had been intensified by his recent violent activities. Pell and Simonetta, simultaneously murmuring something incoherent about another radio upstairs, disappeared after the briefest of greetings. Brian was apparently quite oblivious of them in any case. He went up to Emily and put his hands under her elbows, not roughly, as he had done once before, but nonetheless firmly.

"Listen," he said, "this thing is getting closer and closer. I still think I'm going to win. I meant to ask you, again, to marry me, after I was sure I had. But I changed my mind. I decided I'd rather ask you before I was sure. I decided I'd got to find out whether you had enough faith in me to believe that, even if I lose now, I'll win some other time."

"I've got all kinds of faith in you, Briny."

"Don't you dare add 'but' to that! Have you got enough faith in me to tell me, this minute, that if I lose you'll come and live with me in South Boston until I can take you to a bigger and better place? You know I'd never come and live in your house. You can carry along as many of your trappings as you like, but you've got to let me provide the place for them—and for you. See if Pell wouldn't like to take over your house—of course he'll be the real head of the new firm because he'll stay in Boston all the time and I won't. He'll need a house like yours. Besides, this one won't be big enough for him and Simonetta very long. And they belong on Joy Street. You don't any longer and I never have. I won't pretend to that or anything else. I don't want you to pretend. I know you don't care for me the way you cared for Roger, much less the way you cared for David. *I know you never will.* But you care in another way and it's a good way. Since you've got so much faith in me, you ought to be able to take my word for it that I'm right again. And you know I love you with all my heart and soul. Will you marry me whether I win or lose? Yes or no?"

"*Yes!*" Emily said.

It was two o'clock in the morning when he came back for her. They did not say much to each other in the course of their drive to South Boston. Brian had given his lieutenants the slip again, with great difficulty this time, and he knew he would have to drive fast to get home before they caught up with him. But they still had not done so when he opened the door of his father's house and all the family rushed forward to meet him. He waved his hat with his free hand and shouted a joyous greeting.

"Emily and I are on our way to Washington!" he cried. "But we thought we'd stop in here first to say hello and to let you know we're going *together!*"